The Year of the Red Door

A Fantasy

by

William Timothy Murray

"Whosoever discovers the Name of the King,

so shall he become King."

The Year of the Red Door

Volume 3

A Distant Light

William Timothy Murray

"Whosoever shall discover the Name of the King,

so shall he become King."

A Distant Light
Volume 3 of The Year of the Red Door

Second Edition

ISBN: 978-1-944320-37-9

For permissions, review copies, or other inquiries, write to:
Penflight Books
P.O. Box 857
125 Avery Street
Winterville, Georgia 30683-9998
USA
infodesk@penflightbooks.com

Be sure to visit:

www.TheYearOfTheRedDoor.com

pfbrev180211/1

To
Sara Kahan

Table of Contents

Preface ix
Maps xi

Prologue   How a Name is Given 3

Part I
Chapter 1   The Token 9
Chapter 2   Memories and Dreams 25
Chapter 3   A Close Call 53
Chapter 4   The Ring of Valor 79
Chapter 5   Aremon and Seleesa 93
Chapter 6   Of Madness and Butterflies 103
Chapter 7   The Carrion Bees 128
Chapter 8   The Ring of Fire 142
Chapter 9   A Loaf for a Pen 150
Chapter 10 The Cult of Wokan 160
Chapter 11 The Wickerman 193
Chapter 12 Repast and Reunion 205

Entr'acte   So One Dream Ends 221

Part II
Chapter 13 Valkose the Demon 227
Chapter 14 Forest Islindia 246
Chapter 15 The Feast of Solstice 282
Chapter 16 Across the Haunted Lake 308
Chapter 17 The House of Hemlock 331
Chapter 18 A Kiss to be Remembered 357
Chapter 19 Moon's Henge 374
Chapter 20 Linlally 381
Chapter 21 The Library and the Palace 403
Chapter 22 The Last Book of Nimwill 429
Chapter 23 The Scribblers 448
Chapter 24 Menagerie Macabre 473
Chapter 25 The Shapeshifters 487
Chapter 26 Flight From Danger 498

Afterword 523

Preface

Welcome to *The Year of the Red Door*. For those of you who are curious, I invite you to visit the accompanying web site:

www.TheYearOfTheRedDoor.com

There you will find maps and other materials pertaining to the story and to the world in which the story takes place.

The road to publishing *The Year of the Red Door* has been an adventure, with the usual ups and downs and rough spots that any author may encounter. The bumps and jostles were considerably smoothed by the patient toil of my editors who were, I'm sure, often frustrated by a cantankerous and difficult client. Nonetheless, I have upon occasion made use of their advice, which was sometimes delivered via bold strokes, underlines, exclamation points, and a few rather cutting remarks handwritten across the pristine pages of my manuscripts. Therefore, any errors that you encounter are due entirely to my own negligence or else a puckish disregard of good advice.

For those of you who might be a bit put off by the scope and epic length of this story, I beg your indulgence and can only offer in my defense a paraphrase of Pascal (or Twain, depending on your preference):

I did not have time to write a short story,
so I wrote a long one instead.

The Author

Maps

A Note from the Cartographers

The geography and place names depicted on the following maps are generally accepted to be accurate as of the year of their preparation (869 Second Age). Distances are approximate, given the scales of the maps. However, these are only intended to give a general sense of the scale and relationship of the various regions and features. They are not intended for travel or navigation. Any mishap as a result from the use of these maps for such purposes of travel are the responsibility of the user, not the mapmakers.

For maps more suitable for travel within particular regions of the world, all interested parties are invited to inquire at our establishment.

Brannon & Gray Cartographers
No. 16, Miller's Pond Lane
Duinnor City

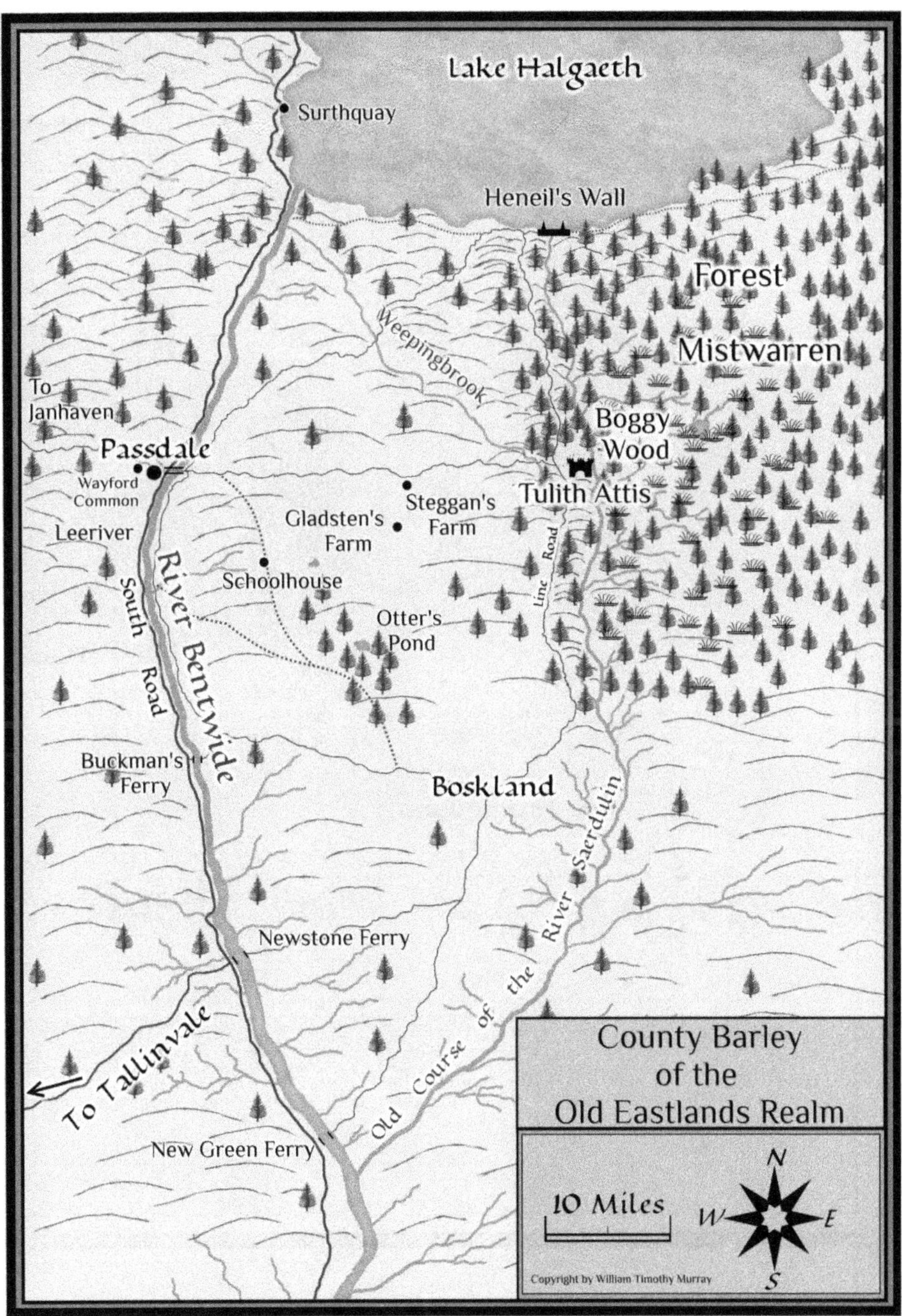

County Barley
Detailed maps can be found at:
www.TheYearOfTheRedDoor.com

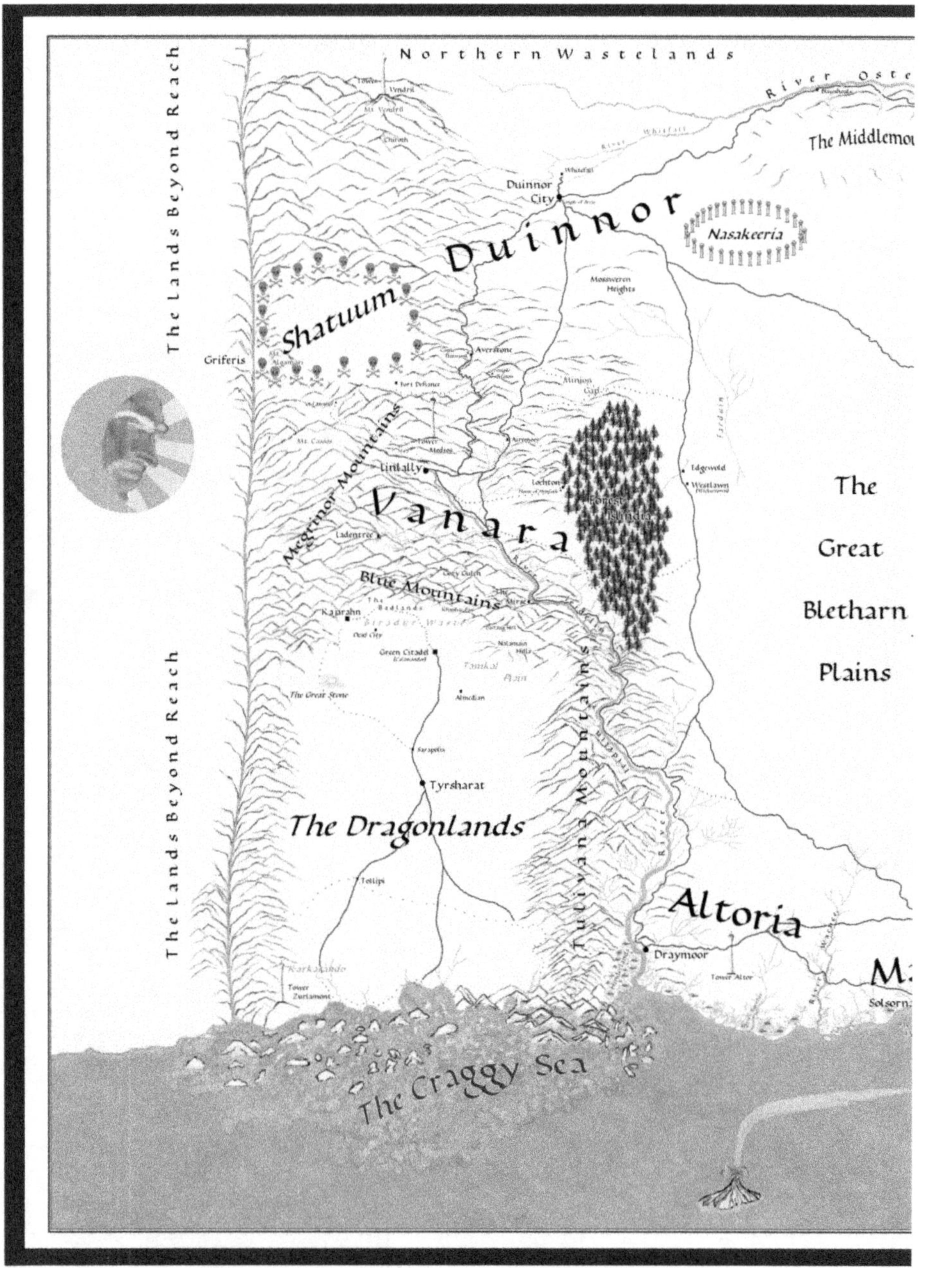

The Western World
Detailed maps can be found at:
www.TheYearOfTheRedDoor.com

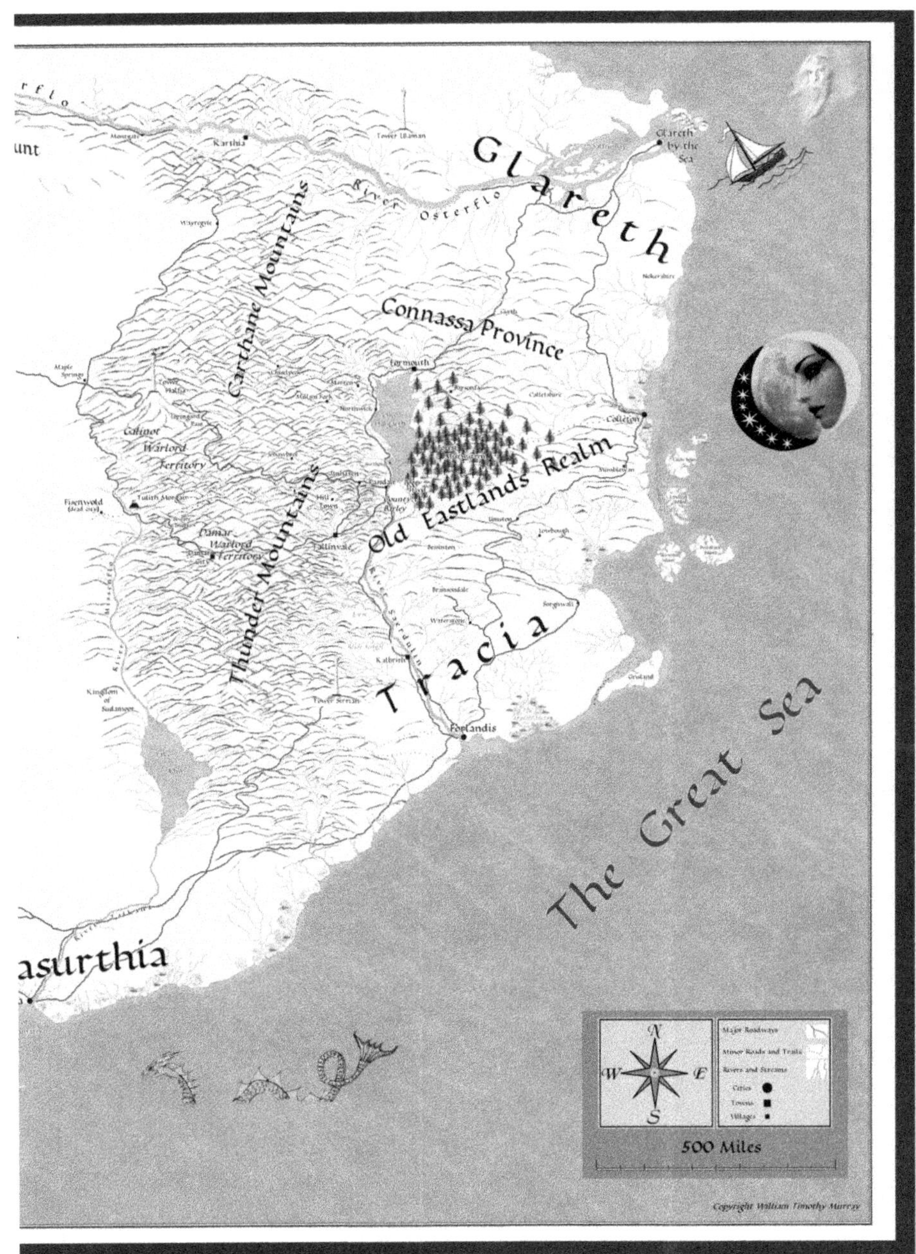

The Eastern World
Detailed maps can be found at:
www.TheYearOfTheRedDoor.com

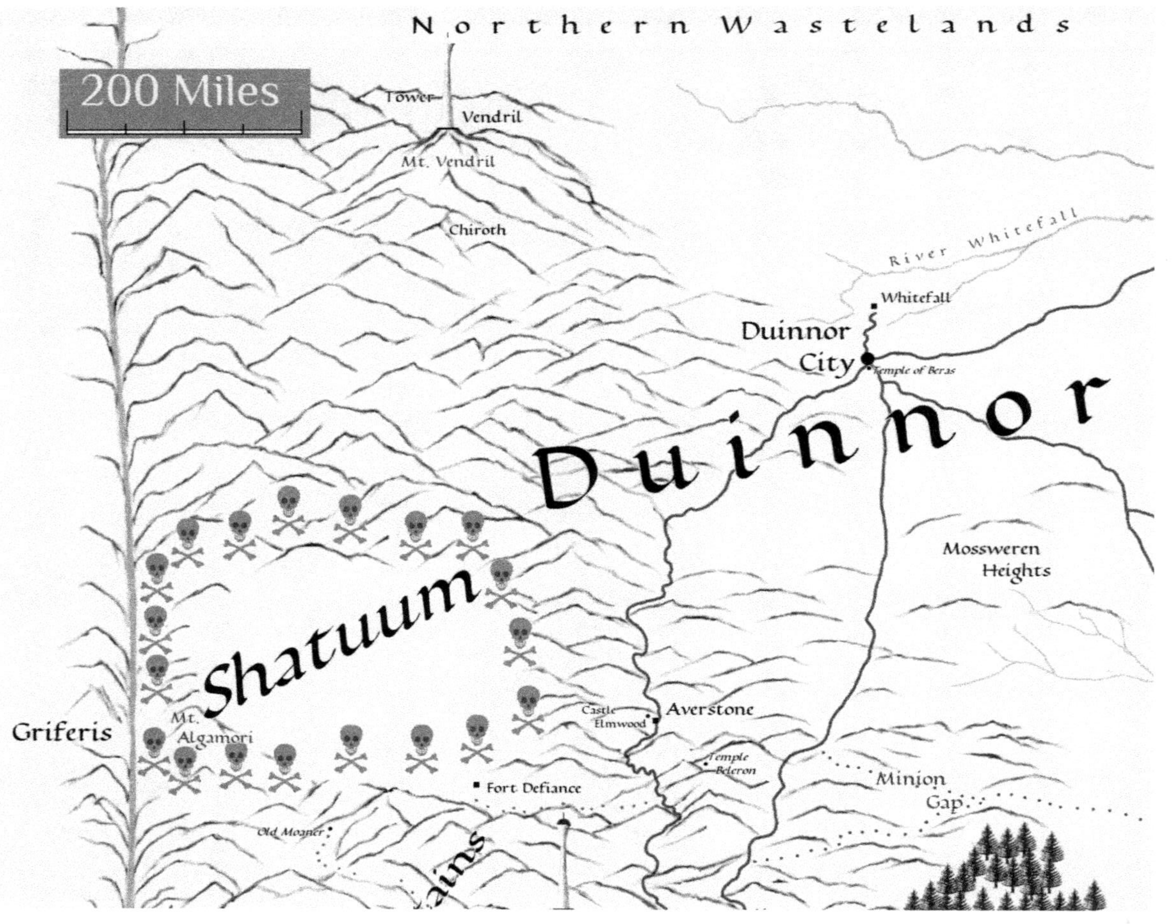

Duinnor & Shatuum
Detailed maps can be found at:
www.TheYearOfTheRedDoor.com

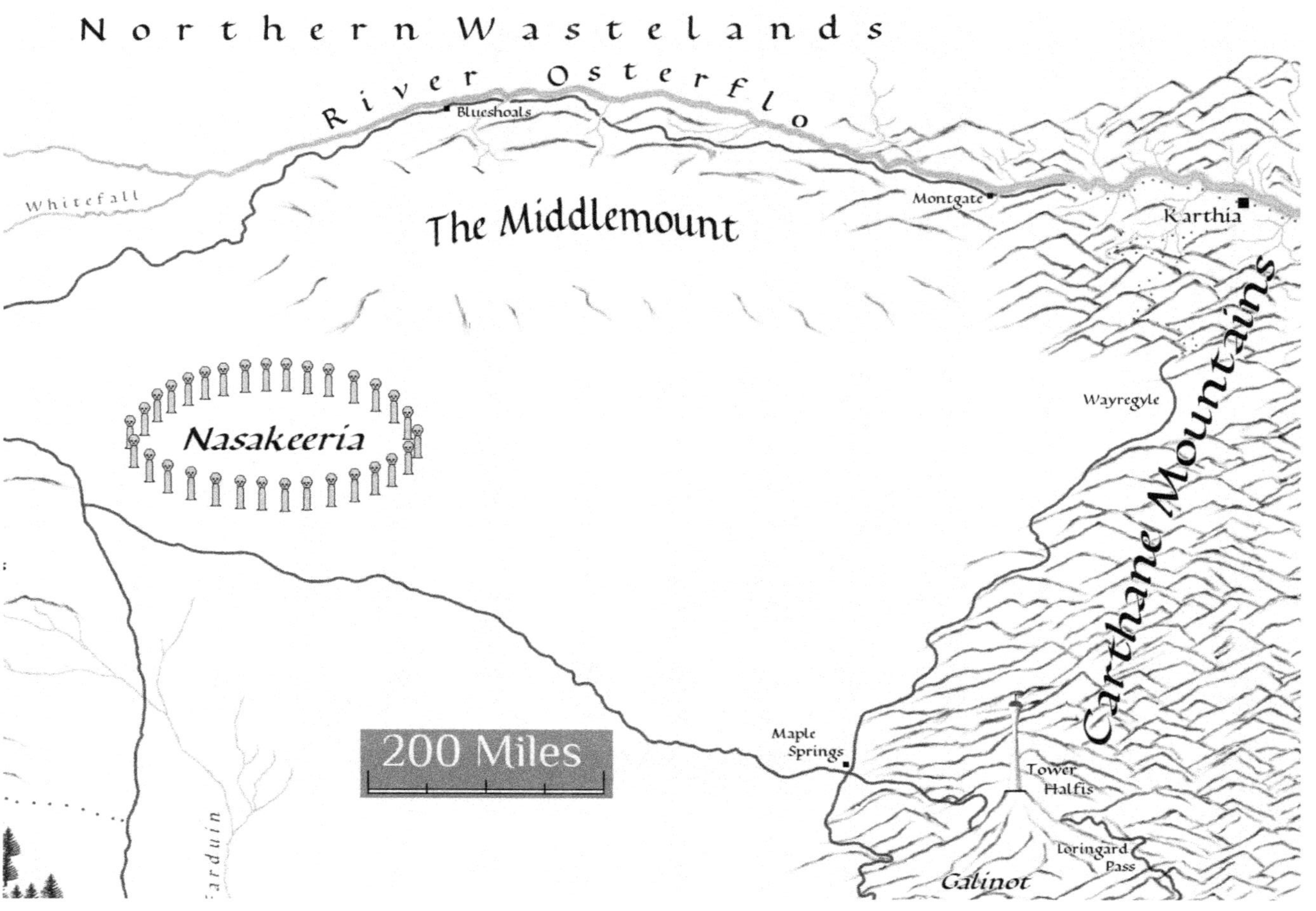

Middlemount & Nasakeeria
Detailed maps can be found at:
www.TheYearOfTheRedDoor.com

Glareth
Detailed maps can be found at:
www.TheYearOfTheRedDoor.com

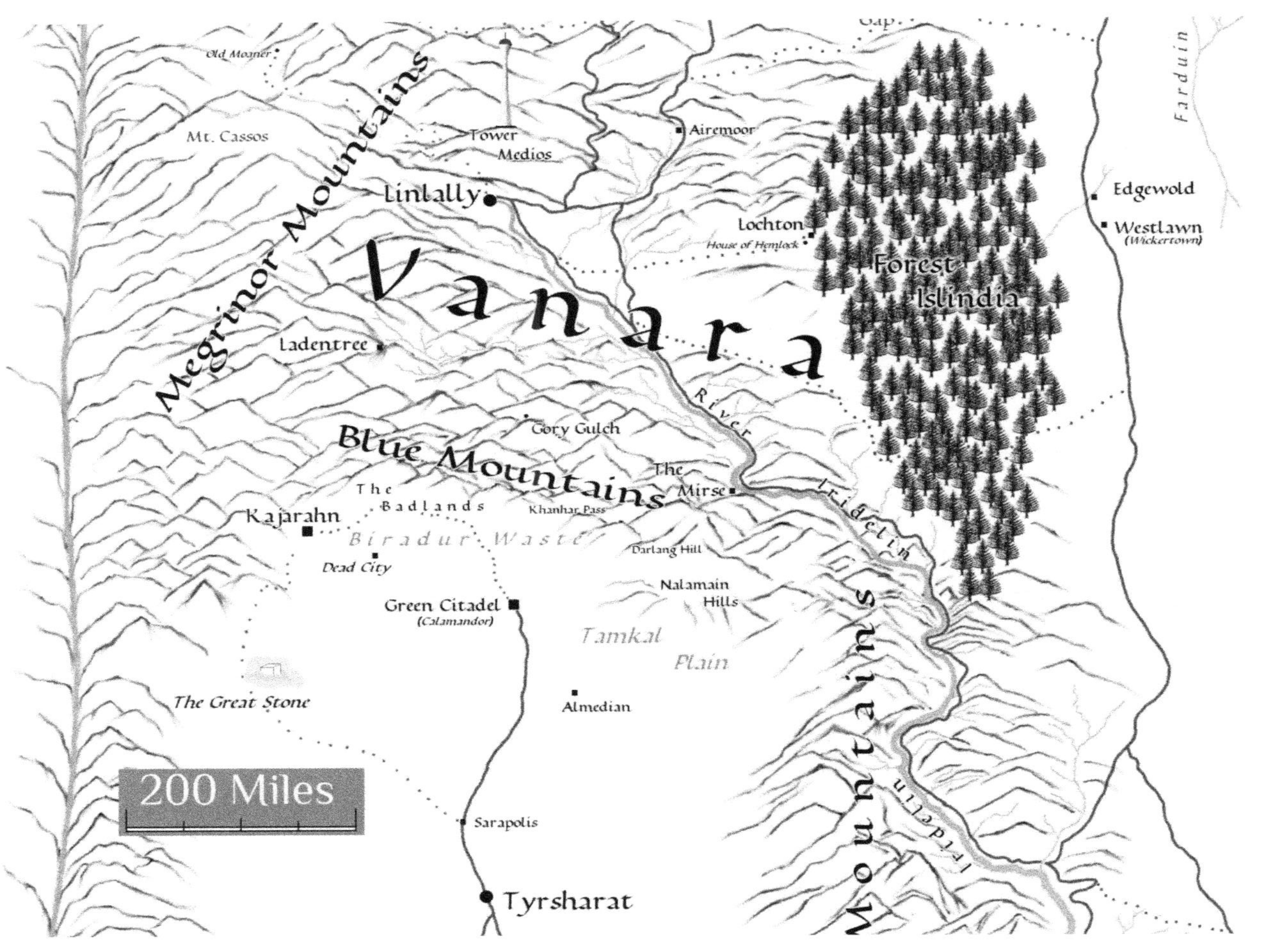

Vanara
Detailed maps can be found at:
www.TheYearOfTheRedDoor.com

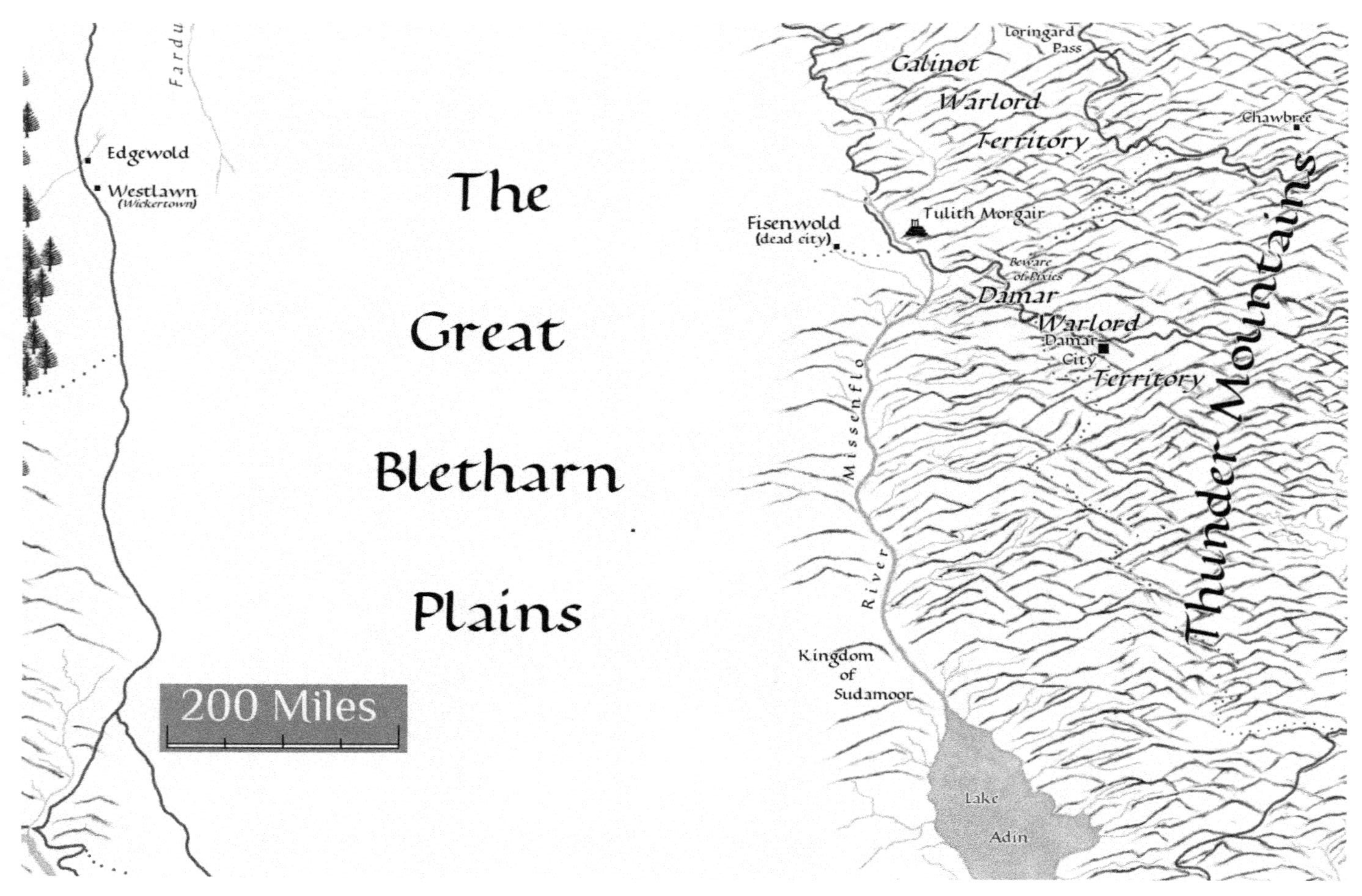

The Great Plains of Bletharn
Detailed maps can be found at:
www.TheYearOfTheRedDoor.com

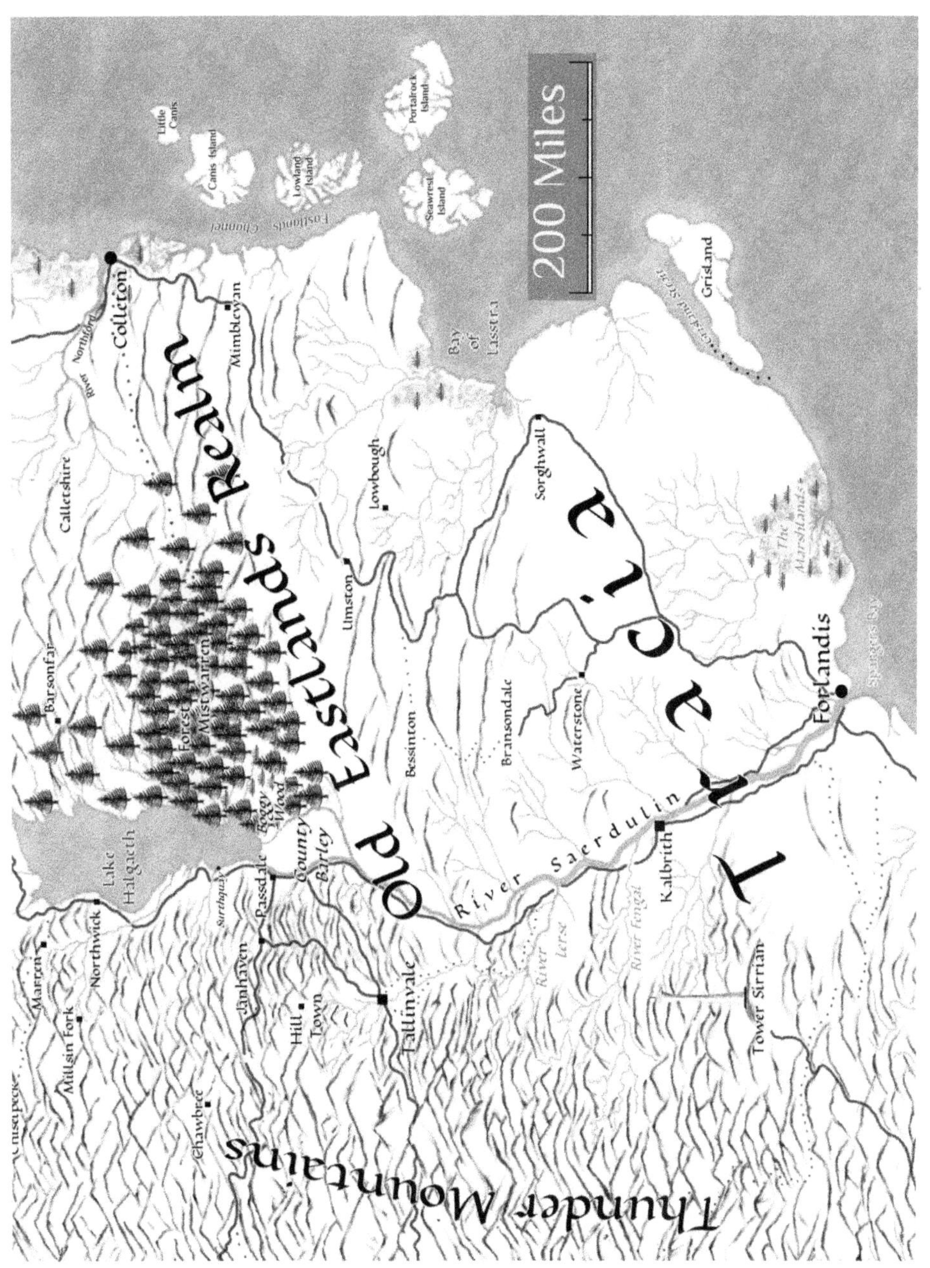

Tracia & the Old Eastlands Realm

Detailed maps can be found at:

www.TheYearOfTheRedDoor.com

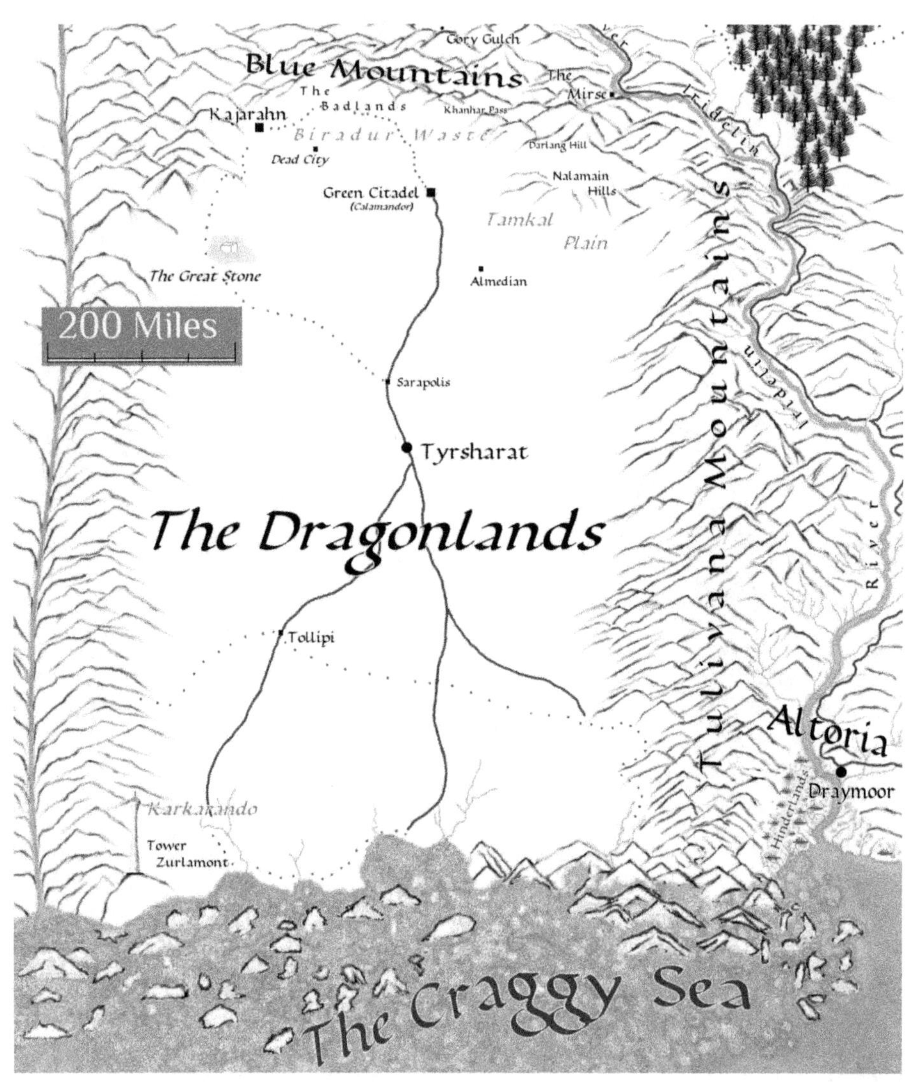

The Dragonlands
Detailed maps can be found at:
www.TheYearOfTheRedDoor.com

Altoria & Masurthia
Detailed maps can be found at:
www.TheYearOfTheRedDoor.com

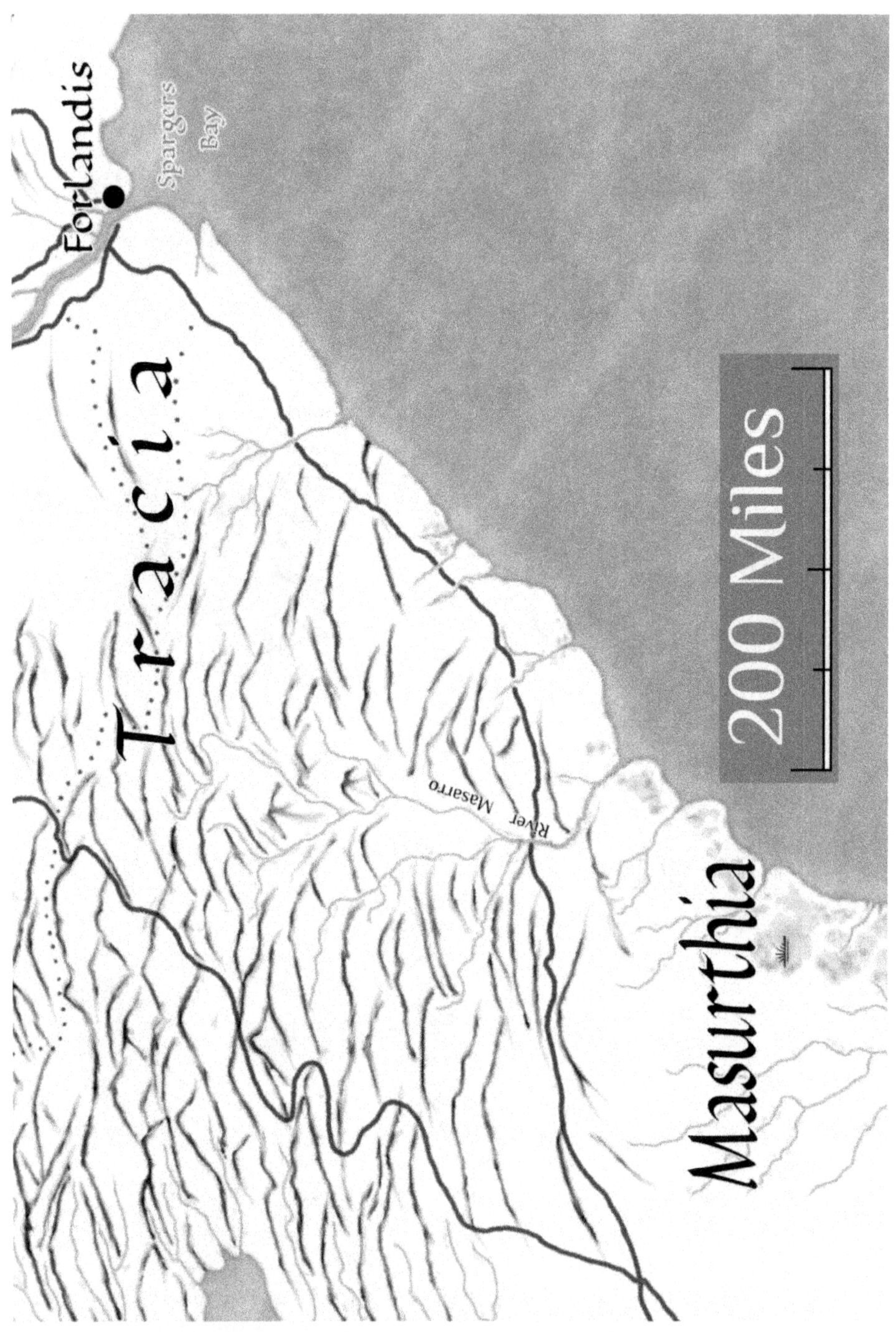

The Frontier between Tracia and Masurthia
Detailed maps can be found at:
www.TheYearOfTheRedDoor.com

A Distant Light

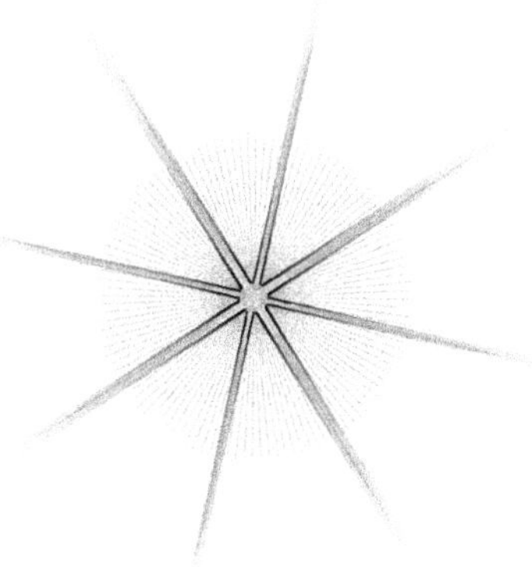

"Whosoever discovers the Name of the King,

so shall he become King."

Prologue

How a Name is Given

"Papa, do ye know what it is we ask of ye?"

The old man nodded, taking the infant into his arms, and leaned back comfortably on his straw-stuffed pillows. His arms were no longer a testament to his barrel-chested life; now they were thin and frail, and his field-reddened skin was but a faded pale rose. Although weak of strength, his sureness was still there as he cradled the child lovingly. His wispy hair still had a strand or two of gray around the ears where the snow-white mane of his last years had not yet taken hold. Infirm with age, broken at last by the hard work of his life, and feeling the weight of all his days upon him, his breath was shallow and labored, and his voice wavering and soft, barely audible over the noise of the storm outside. But his eyes were steady and still had the same wild gleam that had always radiated so mysteriously from such dark, almost black pools. Now, he looked at two sets of eyes with just the same glitter as his own. One pair belonged to his grandson, who was just a fifth his own age, sitting beside his bed on a stool. The other pair, not long in gaining their true color, smiled serenely up at him from his arms.

"Aye," the old man said. "I know what it is ye ask. A practice long fallen away from the humble likes of our house. But now our house is joined by this here babe to a noble one, an' made proud by it, too. It's good, I think, to renew the old ways in this manner. An' it's a comfort to me, be he ever lord or pauper. Aye, it's a mighty thing to coddle new life at the time of me own passin'."

He reached out a hand to grasp his grandson's and said to him, "Yer daddy an' mama would've been so proud of ye, boy! So proud! As I am, an' always have been." His voice cracked, and his eyes filled with mirrors of light. "A fine fam'ly yer raisin'. A fine wife an' son."

The wet wind blew hard and gusty through the night and across the fields. It shook its way through the trees and hummed past the closed shutters of the cottage. There was another sound, too, low and mournful, at first, a sound that caused the young father to shiver with fear. His wife, abiding nearby, paled as her blood ran cold at the sound. Even the little thing in the old man's arms appeared alarmed when he heard it, and its eyes widened for a moment. Then the baby's alarm passed, and he cooed as he grasped the cuff of the old man's nightshirt with his chubby little fingers.

"Aye, aye, thar," the old man nodded, pulling the baby's swaddling around more warmly. "Ye hear, too, don't ye?" he said to the child. "She's sung to me these last two nights, an' I've put her off. Yes, I did. After tonight, though, she'll sing no more at this cottage, thar's a fine little feller!"

The father of the child stood from his bedside stool, and his wife put her arm around him, looking on.

"At first, I feared her, too," the old man said to them. "But then I came to understand her words, an' they soothed me pain to almost nuthin', an' her tune calms me spirit, besides. Listen! Ah, tonight she sings most sweetly!"

The young couple held each other as they stood beside the bed, shuddering at the voice coming out of the stormy night. To their ears the sound passed from moan to shriek in company with the building wind. Large drops of rain then came, pelting the thatch roof with muffled thumps, and clicking away at the windows and walls. With an explosive burst of wet air, the shutters and window became unlatched and banged inward just as the singer outside hit a shrill discordant note. The husband sprang up to refasten the shutters, gripping one in each hand. But when he looked outside, he hesitated. There he saw the banshee standing just five or six feet away, almost near enough to touch, if she had been made of stuff that could be touched, and if he had the long-armed courage to reach out to her. She floated, misty-shaped, in gray-draped shrouds, her lips bursting red, her skin pale and watery-white, and from her sunken eyes gleamed a strange blue fire. A few thick locks of her dripping black hair whipped in the wind while other strands clung heavily against her uplifted face, which was raised, like her arms, to the flash-split blackness above. She lowered her head to look at the man peering at her from the window, and, somewhere distant, far behind the iron and branch-ripping rasp of her voice, he perceived a different voice, a softer tongue, with words almost to be made out. But before her gaze fell full upon him, and before the sweet hidden voice could make itself understood, a shiver swept over him and he quickly closed the window and secured the shutters. He then turned back to those within, saying nothing of what he saw or heard.

"Alrighty," the old man said. "I'm mighty tired. So leave us now, if I'm to do this. Me time grows short, I can tell. An' I must yet consider what name I am to give. Go in yonder, why don't ye? Sit in the next room. An' peace be with ye!"

"Peace be with ye, Papa," said the grandson, kissing his child and then the cheek of his grandfather, the only parent he had ever known.

"Peace be with you, kind sir," said the grandson's wife, kissing her child and the cheek of her dear relation.

"Peace."

The couple reluctantly took their sad leave and retreated to the next room, closing the door softly behind them.

The old man looked down at the baby boy and sighed.

"I never figured it'd all come about this way." He shrugged, then smiled. "But a promise long ago given is now kept, I reckon. An', though I figured I'd never see ye, an' certainly not like this, I never lost faith. An' for it to be up to me! Me oh my! How things have a way of comin' to pass! Now. What name shall I give ye?"

In the adjacent room, the child's parents abided the night without speaking. They sat together near the cooking hearth, their chairs pulled close to one another so that they could lean together and hold hands and put their arms around each other as the tempest blew about the cottage and blasted the windows. All the while, in communion with the windy storm, the strange singing wailed high and low, hissing and moaning through the cracks and crevices in the doors and windows and walls. The young man put his head on his wife's shoulder and cried. She held him and patted his head, tears running down her own face as her heart broke for him. The hours passed reluctantly until dawn when the rain at last abated, and the silence of a fog-blanketed morning was broken only by the drip of soggy eaves. Together, hand in hand, they went back to the deathbed, and when they opened the door and peered in, it seemed that the old man was sleeping peacefully. The child, still cradled in his arms, cooed as he reached with his tiny fingers and touched his great-grandfather's grizzly chin. In the dead man's hand was a note saying, "It is done."

The young father took up his child and the note, and he let out a sob that he tried desperately to stifle. Passing the child and the note to his anxious wife, he then pulled up the little stool next to the bed, took up his grandfather's cold hand, and wept without restraint.

Part I

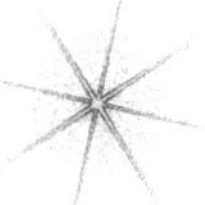

Chapter 1

The Token

Day 101
144 Days Remaining

Robby and his company left Ashlord standing a respectful few feet from the bear not far from the cottage among the overgrown gardens near the well. They had made their goodbyes, Sheila finding it harder to do than the others, though it was not easy for any of them. Ashlord had insisted that he would not need his horse, and that watching after the animal would only hamper him. So they took off its saddle and reharnessed the beast so that they could relieve their remaining packhorse of some of its burden. When this rather somber chore was done, Ullin made another attempt to persuade Ashlord to continue with them. Ullin was fervent, and the others were hopeful for a last-moment change of heart. But the mystic, smiling, was not to be moved, and he looked at his companions sympathetically.

"I must do this thing," was all that he said.

So he watched the group lead their horses away along the narrow path that went back through the woods to the road. Robby and Sheila trailed at the rear of the line, and both turned for a last quick look at Ashlord before disappearing from sight, first Robby, then Sheila. Before the brush obscured their view of each other, she and Ashlord shared a brief glance across the misty clearing. In that briefest of moments, Ashlord perceived Sheila's strained smile, and, to his eye, she indeed had every aspect and appearance of Esildre that had so startled the Nowhereans. Ashlord's mouth dropped open in surprise, then she disappeared into the foggy brush and was gone. In that same splinter of time, a cool breeze blew away the last mists left by the evening's rain. Cracks of blue sky allowed glistening beams of Sir Sun's slanted light to fall on the mystic and the patient bear as one turned to the other. The beast made a plaintive rumble, twisted her hulking body gracefully around, and ambled off into the woods. She paused and looked over her shoulder at Ashlord. He nodded and followed, and Certina fluttered nervously after them.

• • •

Once on the path, and having mounted their horses, Ullin led his charges downward along the wide track, and they soon reached the western foothills where the way took them northward. Occasionally, as they crested the rises, they could see strands of the River Missenflo below and off to their left, a silver ribbon in the morning sun. Beyond, the gray-green Plains of Bletharn stretched to the horizon. By noontime, the air was clear of any clouds, but tufts of mist were still floating up the blue-green slopes and curling away over the mountaintops. The air was fresh and clean after the rains, cool enough for them to keep on their cloaks. They said little, keeping to their own thoughts, until a call from Sheila made them turn in their saddles. Behind them, about a mile away, were over a dozen fast-moving riders in drab Damar garb. As the last of the riders disappeared between the hills, the ones in the lead came over the next one nearer.

"They are closer than we thought," said Robby.

"They must have kept moving all night. We must hurry!" cried Ullin. "Make for the crossing, just there. Spare not the horses!"

He pointed downhill, intending to take them off the road and across the remaining slopes in a race to ford the river.

"But I must go north. To Tulith Morgair!" Robby called back.

"It is out of our way. We must hurry, don't you see? Cross the river, and get to the safety of the plain beyond. The Damar come too fast," Ullin answered as he hurried to Robby.

"Let's go! Let's go!" cried Billy.

"There they are!" pointed Sheila as another rider topped a nearer hill at a gallop. "They've seen us!"

"I must go to Tulith Morgair! The rest of you go on. I'll make my own way, if I can."

"Why? There is nothing but ruins!"

"I cannot tell you now. Afterwards."

"Have ye gone mad?" Billy yelled impatiently.

"I mean to find out!"

Seeing that Robby was fixed and determined, Ullin nodded. He stood in his stirrups, quickly surveying the approaching force. Twisting around, he scanned the lay of the land on ahead, and then glanced westward toward the river.

"North, then! To Tulith Morgair. But fly!" he cried. "Go! Go! Go! Billy, you and Ibin follow Robby and keep close to him. Sheila! Stay with me!"

Robby kicked hard, and his horse sprang forward. Billy and Ibin followed, urging their own mounts and the packhorses to an awkward gallop. Ullin waited until they were at the top of the next hill and passing over.

"Come!" he said to Sheila. Together they rode on up the hilltop and then down the other side a short way before Ullin drew Sheila to a stop and jumped from his saddle. She saw him take his bow and quiver, so she dismounted, doing the same. They ran back up the hill, almost to the top, and took positions across the path from each other behind some brushy rocks. They notched their arrows upon their bowstrings. From their vantage they could peer down the hill and see the Damar riders charging upward in a line.

"Wait," said Ullin. "Wait."

Sheila watched Ullin rather than the Damar riders, trying to steady her breath, forcing her fingers on the bowstring and notched arrow to relax somewhat. Ullin turned away from the Damar, closed his eyes and moved his lips silently. A moment later, he opened his eyes, looked at Sheila, and gave a nod.

Together they stepped into the roadway, the riders barely thirty yards away, and, side by side, their bowstrings sang. The first rider went down and then the second. The next three tried to turn around, but only one did so, the two on either side of him crashing from their mounts. The Damar were now careening back down the hill in disarray and panic, and Sheila let fly another long shot that found its place.

"Let's go!" Ullin pulled on her arm. Already he could see that orders were being given, and the Damar were splitting up to outflank them on either side. Sheila and Ullin got back to their horses and galloped off. They could see their companions two hilltops away, going at an agonizing pace, and that Ibin and Billy were having trouble with the slow pack animals.

"How far is the place?" shouted Sheila over the din of their horses.

"A mile! And a little more, at least."

"We'll never make it!"

As soon as she said that, she realized that Ullin knew it from the onset, and she saw that he was looking for a suitable place to spring another trap. He seemed all business, emotionless, calm, and every move he made was with purpose, every turn of the head to see around a rock or tree, every touch of his hand on the reins, every nudge he gave with his heel to his mount. This was from his long experience at such things, and she gained a bit of confidence when she realized that he was a survivor of battles more fierce than she could imagine. This predicament was probably a small thing to him.

"They won't be so easily fooled again," he called to her as they passed over the next hill.

They raced down through the dale and up and over the next rise. A moment later, the two Damar seeking to outflank them came together in the dale that their prey had just passed through, and they looked around cautiously, their swords drawn. Seeing from the tracks that their quarry had already gone by, they considered the next rise. It was not steep, and they could see in the distance Billy and Ibin tugging at the pack animals, one of which decided to buck so violently that the packs were in danger of coming apart. They smiled at each other as Billy gained control of the animal and then disappeared from sight. The other Damar riders joined the first two, and they elected one of their men to ride up the hill and scout the way. This the unhappy warrior did, but dismounting and crouching low in front of his horse as he came to the top. The other Damar below saw him pause for a moment, stand up straight, and then proceed slowly out of view. It was not long before he reappeared on his horse and beckoned. As they hurried up the slope, the scout ambled on ahead along the way at an easy pace. At the top, they saw him follow the path as it turned sharply to the right, and he waved to them again just before he passed into a copse. They quickly rounded the bend and entered a narrow brush-lined way where they were met by a hail of arrows from either side. Six of them fell before the other six could turn and gallop away.

Sheila stepped out from behind a tree and, on the other side of the path, Ullin emerged, tossing off the cloak and helmet of the dead scout.

"I have one arrow left," he said as they ran to their horses.

"I have two," she called back. "There are more on the pack animals."

• • •

Not very far ahead of Ullin and Sheila, the rest of the company made their way down a hill and onto a broad headland covered by tall scrub and a few pines and thin oaks. As they went north, the land on the right rose sharply into the hills. To the left of their path, the land fell away smoothly toward the river. Ahead, in the middle of the headland, jutted the leg of a mountain, its bare rocky ridge rising sharply at its end where, perched at the edge of its high top, was a small stone structure. As they neared the base of the cliff, they passed through bramble-covered walls, and the path abruptly ended at the foot of a wide stair. Without hesitating, Robby jumped from his saddle and led his horse upward, calling out for the others to follow.

The stairway was wide enough for several horses abreast, the steps were spaced far apart but not high, and they made good progress as it led them upward and along the south face of the cliff. Gradually it became steeper, and as they climbed around the western side, they had a clear view of the river below and of the plains that rolled away. To the north they could see as far as the snow-capped Carthane Mountains. The stairs continued to curve upward, taking them through an arched keep. Now the nature of the rock changed from natural to cut stone, and they realized they were at the base of the fortification itself. Here, in the northeast shadows, the wind was hard and cold and the stairs wet and mossy. Twice Billy slipped, and once one of the pack animals lost its footing momentarily, causing them to proceed with more caution along the brink. The stairs cut suddenly to the right and rose up between two high walls. Above them they saw a gate, its broken portcullis sagging, and overhead the battlement loomed with arrow slits. The confining corridor climbed steeply without stairs, strewn with blocks of stone and chunks of masonry out of which struggled stunted myrtles here and there. Swallows scattered away at their approach, whistling in alarm and startling the group. Entering through the gate, Robby came into a broad open courtyard of sorts, a round area surrounded by low battlements. Against the western side stood the remains of the signal tower.

It had once been a covered structure. Firewood was kept below, and above had been a second level, made entirely of masonry with a tile roof wherein a large signal fire could be lit. The upward parts of the tower were long collapsed, but the columns that had once held it were fairly intact. These six were in the form of statues in various states of decay, each over twice the height of a tall man, all facing inward toward each other. As Billy and Ibin came into the courtyard, Robby let go of his reins and made his way to the tower ruins, picking his way around loose stones and blocks left over from the destruction of the place. Stepping up onto the circular dais around which the statues stood, he climbed over more fallen blocks and looked around.

"What's he about?" Billy wondered aloud as he helped Ibin with the packhorses.

" 'Look for your great-grandfather,' " Robby muttered quietly to himself. "But which one?"

Three of the figures were carved with the aspect and garb of warriors, with helmets and breastplates. One of them held out his hand that rested on the pommel of a great sword, the blade of which was now broken away from the hilt down. The two soldiers on either side of this one were likewise posed, but their arms were broken off and lay shattered among the rubble. One lay just at Robby's foot, its coarse hand still curled around the shaft of some long-vanished weapon. The other three figures were attired in robes, and their foreheads were circled by rusty bands of iron. The one in the middle also wore a carved crown and held in his crossed arms a scepter and a mace. One of the others held a book by his side and a scroll against his breast. The last one stood with his hand outstretched, palm up, as if in a gesture of explanation, and in his other hand he held a plain staff made of iron, topped with a ball of tawny brass.

"Here come Sheila an' Ullin!" Billy called out.

Glancing over, he saw both Billy and Ibin waving from the wall downward. Robby turned back to the statues. They were blackened with soot and grime, the low sun making their beardless faces gaunt and shadowy. It occurred to Robby that these were Elifaen faces, and saw in one the likeness of Serith Ellyn and Thurdun, while another looked akin to Lyrium and her daughters. As the sun drew downward in the sky and the light softened, the visage of the one with the outstretched hand changed. The face gained a tint of gold sunlight and the weatherworn stone countenance was smoothed by the brush of shadow and light around the eyes and nose. Robby saw a clear resemblance to his mother. Moving toward it, he climbed onto an overturned block and stared up at the statue.

"Ibin!" he suddenly called out, "I need your help!"

"Whatisit, Robby?"

"What're ye up to, now?" Billy called, following Ibin through the rubble.

"I need a lift, Ibin. Lend me your shoulders, would you?"

"Alright."

"Stand right here, then. No, here. Yes."

Using the statue's leg to steady himself, Robby tried to climb up onto Ibin without giving the big fellow too many bruises. It was awkward, but Ibin helped as much as he could by bending over and then, once Robby was sitting on his shoulders, offering his hands as supports for Robby's feet as he attempted to stand.

"Steady! Steady!" Billy coached Ibin as Robby teetered awkwardly, though Ibin was as steady as the statues that surrounded them. Still clutching at the statue next to them, Robby managed at last to stand upright. But the fingers of his other hand barely touched his goal, the stone arm outstretched above him. Undoing Swyncraff, he whipped it around the elbow of the statue and hoisted himself up clear of Ibin until he got his free arm around the stone.

"Careful! Careful!" Billy muttered while Ibin watched, holding his arms out, ready to catch Robby if he fell.

Robby swung his legs around, hoping—now that it was too late for caution—that the stone was strong enough to support him, and after a couple of unsuccessful tries, he got himself atop. But when he raised his head, he found himself facing the wrong way, the statue's face curiously blank at Robby's ludicrous position. Sliding himself up the shoulder, he put his arms around the statue's head and carefully stood so that he could turn himself around. As he did so, a reddish glint caught his eye, breaking his attention and causing his foot to slip.

"Whoa!" cried Billy, just as Ullin and Sheila entered the fort and hurried over.

"What's he doing?" asked Sheila, panting from their run up the stairs.

Billy shook his head. "I think he's gone mad."

Ullin opened his mouth but said nothing, staring up at Robby who, by now, had regained his footing and was craning his head, trying to make out the light in the far northern distance. He saw it again, a steady red glint that seemed to hover just over the hazy blue peaks that lined the northeast horizon.

"Robby, what do you see?" called Ullin.

"A light. I think. Northward, over the edge of yonder mountains."

"It is the Tower Halfis," Ullin said.

"Is that what you came for?" asked Sheila. "To look about?"

"No."

Robby eased himself down, straddled the arm, and scooted himself along, his legs dangling on either side. "Halfis," he said to himself as he moved closer to the statue's hand. "I've heard of that place, I think. Oh!"

He saw that, indeed, the palm of the hand held something. It was a ring, and it rested on a blue flower. He moved more quickly now until he was within arm's reach, lying down on the forearm of the statue. Billy and Ullin glanced at each other as Robby picked up the ring and held it out. "This is what I came for! And this!" He held up the blue flower for them to see, then dropped it to Ullin who caught it in his cupped hands.

"Is that a ring?" Billy asked.

"How did you know it was there?" asked Sheila.

Robby did not answer since he was now occupied with backing up. He used Swyncraff to swing himself down, and Ibin moved carefully to help him.

"I'vegot, I'vegotyou!" Ibin said as he grabbed Robby's waist. With a tug, Swyncraff came loose, and Ibin gently lowered him to his feet.

"Thank you, Ibin!"

"You, youare, youareverywelcome, Robby."

The others gathered to look at the objects.

"This ring rested on that flower," Robby said.

Ullin looked carefully, gaping first at the ring, and then at the flower in his hand. His other hand went absently to his breast where, beneath his blouse, his locket dangled. He handed the flower to Sheila and took the ring that Robby held out to him. It was of black metal inlaid with a fine filigree of gold in such a way that it had the appearance of lace.

"This ring was not made in any of the Seven Realms. There is only one land that I know of that produces such designs as these." He handed the ring back to Robby with a look of astonishment on his face. "And only one land where this flower grows. That land is nowhere near here. Not within five hundred leagues."

"Where?" Sheila asked.

Ullin shook himself. "I may tell you when we are safely away, though I would dearly like to hear how Robby knew these were here, and how they came to be here in the first place." He moved over to the south-facing wall. The others followed with him and could see over all of the hills and along the roadway until it entered the forest some miles away. "If I have my count right, two Damar riders broke away and rode back. To summon more men, I think."

"Why do they persist?" Robby asked.

"It's the price on yer head, Robby," Billy put forth, crossing his arms and putting a foot up on the parapet. "Ashlord showed us the papers he found. An' he suspected somethin' 'tween Bailorg an' the red-bearded feller we saw at Tallin Hall."

"I think Billy must be right," Ullin agreed. "They seem a little too persistent. They must hope to share the bounty amongst each other."

"How long will they be?" Sheila asked. "Surely we can be across the river before they return?"

"If they ride hard, they may make the gorge in but a few hours. From there, if they set out right away with more riders, they could be back here before sunrise. But they will be cautious, surely," Ullin considered aloud. "This place overlooks the only ford within ten leagues north or south, so they will certainly come here first. This place is also claimed by the Galinots and all the lands to the north are controlled by the Galinot warlord. If we go north, I do not think the Damar will long follow. But our chances of running into Galinot soldiers would increase, and they are none too friendly with Duinnor or the Eastlands. They have always permitted the King's Post to pass through their lands fairly unmolested, but I cannot say how they may receive us in these times. I'd rather not take the chance."

"Wouldn't it be better just to cross now and put as much distance on the plain while we can?" Robby asked.

"Probably. But with no cover on the plains, the Damar would soon overtake us," Ullin pointed out. "We and our horses will soon need rest. Coming here may have been the best thing after all. It forced a fight that turned them back."

Robby noticed Ullin's near-empty quiver while Sheila rummaged on the pack animals for her extra arrows.

"Ain't thar some way of throwin' 'em off?"

"Well, we can't stay here," Sheila added, finally finding the bundle. "We'd be trapped!"

"And who's to say the Galinots don't have wind of us?" Robby argued. "They may have their own bounties."

"Then let's cross the river now, before the Damar catch up!" Ullin agreed going over and rummaging through the packs while Sheila filled his quiver. "Gather some brush together and let's start a slow-burning fire."

"Why?"

"They'll be sure to send a scout to keep an eye on this place." Ullin moved quickly as he explained. "It will be some while before the scout shows up, maybe just after dark. He'll see smoke and light. I'm hoping he'll think we camp here for the night. If he's a good soldier, he'll come close enough to watch the path that leads away from here, but will wait for the main body of Damar. If he is a very good soldier, he'll check the riverbank for tracks, and our ruse will do no good. But I'm hoping," he said, placing the candle between some cracks in the south parapet," that he'll be a typical Damar and no more."

"So you're thinking that the Damar will storm this keep when they arrive?"

"That is my hope. And they'll be slow and careful about it, wasting their time while we put good distance between us."

They worked quickly, under Ullin's directions, arranging the fuel so that it would not burn too quickly and so that ample smoke would be made when it was lit. Satisfied with their work, Ullin was the last to leave, lighting the fire and the candle. When he was sure they would stay lit and burn according to his plan, he made his way down the winding stairs and led the group away from the looming cliff, through the brush off of the path, and across the rocky stretch of headland to the river.

"We'll go into the river here," he said, "and keep in the shallows until we find a place to ford. Hopefully, they'll not pick up our tracks."

The water was cold and their horses reluctant, but they coaxed them down the sharp bank and into the Missenflo. It was soon up to their elbows, and the rocky bottom made progress slow and tedious. They kept within a few yards of the bank, going back southward for nearly an hour before the river widened and became somewhat more shallow. Ullin directed them to follow him away from the bank, staying in deeper water but still going south with the current. When they were nearly in the center of the flow, Ullin judged it shallow enough to cross, still some distance from the stone pillars that marked the usual fording place. Going across the current was more difficult, and they often slipped, but when Ullin, nearing the far bank, turned north to go back upstream, they had an even harder time of it. By now they were all tired and shivering, and as soon as Ullin found a place along the bank that was not too steep, he led them up and out of the water. This they managed with a great deal of puffing and scrambling and slipping and pulling on reins, and a little cursing, too. No sooner than they were all up and out, panting and dripping, than Ullin ordered them to mount up.

"We must ride hard before dark."

This they did, but the terrain near the river was rough with brush and little streams, tributaries, and a few boggy places down in gullies. These they negotiated as quickly as they could with only minor stumbles and mishaps. By the time the sun was setting, they had just made the far rise of the river basin, and before them stretched the plain. It no longer looked flat as it had from the heights of Tulith Morgair. Now it appeared as a blue-green sea of grass-covered waves, its gentle crests and troughs mysteriously frozen as if in a painting, and the only movement to be seen was the shaking of nearby grass in the breeze.

They moved on, cold and miserable, and would have traveled faster but for the failing light. Lady Moon, her fan covering nearly all of her face, followed quickly into her husband's fading glow, but at least the stars gave their light to the fleeing group. In the open, with hardly a tree in sight, they felt exposed and cautious after so long in the sheltering cover of the forest and mountains. Without encouragement from Ullin, they all urged their horses to move as quickly as they dared. Ullin kept a watchful eye on them, then he slowed his pace so that they came closer together.

"There are few landmarks to be seen at night," he told them. "Stay within sight of me. It is easy to get lost here, even in daylight. If you become separated, give a yell, and we will all come together to look for you."

They managed to stay close together, and, in spite of their sorry and soggy condition, they did not complain at the pace. When they came over a rise and looked back, they saw the last remnants of daylight on the highest of the Thunder Mountains, and they could just make out a thin trail of smoke blowing from the fire Ullin had lit at Tulith Morgair. The light atop the mountains quickly faded as they continued on, and the eastern horizon loomed with murky shadows hunched against the starry sky. Robby thought of Ashlord, and he found himself glancing upward, remembering how Ashlord had pointed out various stars those months ago on Haven Hill.

Ullin picked out their way carefully, trying to avoid needless turns, keeping the North Star in the same position over his right shoulder. His experienced eyes, even in the dark, chose the way he thought would give them the greatest distance and speed that they and their pack animals could muster. Sometimes this meant going straight up a hill, and sometimes skirting gullies too steep for safety. He was pleased at how Robby and the others handled their horses, and how they followed closely without complaint or hesitation. Hour after hour, he kept them moving as the stars wheeled overhead and sank away into the west while new ones came up behind them. When the bright wandering star called Palatar rose in the east, Ullin found a broad dale at the base of which ran a small stream. There he stopped and dismounted.

"We stop here to rest, to change into dry things, and to wait until daylight. Sheila, will you and Billy take the first watch as soon as you are changed? Up there on that rise just yonder would be a good place. We'll see to the horses. Stay low and when Palatar, yonder, is halfway to overhead, one of you come and wake me." As he spoke, he unfastened a blanket. "Blankets only, Ibin," he said as he saw Ibin making as if to remove his horse's burdens. "We keep the horses saddled tonight."

As Sheila and Billy moved off, the other three tied a rope to each horse and fastened it to a sturdy bush. Ullin drew his cloak about him, not bothering to change his clothes, and stretched out on the ground with his rolled up blanket under his head.

"No fire," he said as he closed his eyes.

Ibin looked at Ullin questioningly, then at Robby as if for appeal.

"There's some smoked beef in the sack there," Robby said. "You can have three big chunks. I'll have a couple, and why don't you take some up to Sheila and Billy before settling down?"

"Aright, al, alright, Robby. I'm, I'm, I'mprettyhungry."

• • •

She stood as before, on a high dune in a sea of sand, and the sun, just as before, was sinking low and golden red, spreading its molten light across the powdery waves. Only her eyes showed through the shemagh that wrapped her face and helmet, and her gloved hands held together the long black cloak covering her from shoulder to boot. Robby last remembered changing his clothes and wrapping up in a blanket, too tired and cold to worry about Ashlord or their Damar pursuers. He spoke as soon as he saw her.

"I have the ring."

"Yes, I see."

"Does it have significance?"

"Somewhat. It was once an ordinary ring, given as a memento of friendship, but it became a kind of family heirloom. Our law holds that if no son is heir, all inheritance must go to the crown. My father has no living sons, and he gave it to me, to keep in secret, for it means a great deal to him. I give it to you as a token, from my family to yours, of peace between our two houses. And as a sign of my sincerity."

"Why do you do this? Would not a pact with me, with my kind, put you in danger?"

"I do it out of hope. Yes, I fear discovery. I am closely watched. But I am not the only one of my kind who knows of you and who hopes for an opportunity through you."

"Opportunity?"

"For peace."

"Hatred runs deep," Robby shook his head. "And mistrust deeper, still. On every side Men and Elifaen are divided and make war against each other. Some have joined with your kind, even, and threaten the destruction of the Seven Realms. And I must admit that I have little trust, these days, of anything. Or anyone. Even you. I see little hope for peace."

"Few do, these days, even those who truly long for it. But isn't longing a kind of hope?"

"It is not enough to long and to hope. Action is needed. You know this, elsewise we would not be speaking. There is something you want of me, surely."

"Yes. Why else would I take this risk?"

"You say risk. But I know nothing of your people. I know nothing of the workings of your land or rulers and have no way to see for myself what risk you may be taking. For all I know, this is a ploy. Some plot aimed not for peace, but against Duinnor."

"I cannot in one night show you all the sorry history of what my people have endured," Micerea replied. "I cannot in a lifetime show you. We have been shackled, beaten, murdered, lied to, and betrayed. We are made into hateful beings, our bodies broken by our masters and poisoned by sickness. But we awaken, slowly, and begin to unite. I tell you now, there is a willingness among some of my people to take action, even though most lack the means. We who hope are weak and therefore cautious. We look for signs and directions. Our gods do not answer our prayers in ways that we understand, and each day that passes is worse than the day before. Our land is a land of oppression and injustice at every turn. Those who rule abuse their might and power in order to increase their wealth and influence. They cloak themselves in falsehoods, claiming the rights of the gods to rule. They support false temples and ceremonies to placate our people and to dupe them and to foster obedience. My people, fearing retribution if they do not openly show support for our rulers, willingly stone those who speak against our rulers. And if those who speak out are too popular to be stoned, they are imprisoned or made to disappear. Even powerful houses and great generals must bow and are not safe."

"But why do you look to me? My fate seems tied to Duinnor, not to the Dragonlands."

"All fates are tied together. The wars between my people and yours serve only to support the oppression that grows in all lands, north and south, green and sandy. Duinnor is not inclined toward peace because its power rests too much on preventing Vanara from gaining supremacy among the Realms, as it would if peace were to be long established. Vanara is not inclined to peace because of the long and vengeful temper that these wars have fostered. But if they could be made to want peace, or at least a truce, then the question of land and other matters may be settled by some means other than combat and strife. If Duinnor's courts prosecuted those who murder my people, then vengeance upon your people would no longer have the cloak of justice and duty. The circle of violence might be broken. If that happened, our oppressors might be weakened and other leaders might arise, emboldened to assert themselves."

Robby, though ignorant of many things, saw the sense of this, and he nodded.

"That would be difficult for Duinnor. Without support throughout the Realms, making criminals of heroes would certainly spark revolt. Some sign would be needed that it was in the interest of the Realms to do so."

"Is injustice ever in the interest of any realm of the earth? Is any interest greater than justice? This is what we long for in our own lands and hope for it no less in all other lands of the world."

"My father used to say that no justice may come of beings of this world, and that only the gods, if they care to, may fairly dispense such as that."

"What he said may be so. However, it is not in the achieving but in the attempt that we must make a start. Godly perfection is not to be found in those who are not gods, only some satisfaction that lets life go on without making thievery, revenge, or malice into things of honor or pride."

Robby and Micerea looked earnestly at each other, neither quite knowing how to proceed.

"I am not a king," Robby finally said. "If I were, I would consider your words, but I have no experience to guide me. My education is poor, and I have few allies. I don't even want to become a king."

"Others do."

"What do you mean?"

"You are not the only one to seek Griferis. There have been many others before you who have looked for that place. Even some of my own kind. But Griferis cannot make you a king, if I understand the legends correctly. It can only make you able to be a king once you become a king."

"I don't understand."

"To be a king, one must already have the throne. It is rule that makes a king. What kind of king would you be?"

"I don't know. And, anyway, how do you know about me? How do you know what I seek?"

"I was also told by my father, when he gave me that ring, that if such a king arose, he would come out of the eastern lands of Men. So I have kept watch on that land. That is how I found you. Perhaps I may sometime tell you more of the ring, if you wish."

"How did your father know?"

She suddenly turned her head, looking westward at the last edge of sun.

"My time is short and I must go. Think on what we have said. If you wish, I may guide you in certain things. Teach you. It is not safe for us to continue. I must go!"

"But how do I—"

A hot wind stirred and blew dusty and dry across the dune. Micerea's robes whipped in the sudden gust and the sand obscured her from view.

• • •

"Wake up, Robby."

Billy paused and then bent down and tapped Robby on the shoulder once more.

"Wake up! Time to go!"

Robby stirred, then, just as Billy was about to give him a gentle shake, he opened his eyes to a sky that was growing lighter with the coming dawn.

"Time to go, Robby," Billy repeated, giving Robby a hand up. "Oof! Ain't ye the sleepy head!"

By the time he got his bedroll together, the others were already in their saddles.

"Sorry," he muttered as he got his feet into the stirrups.

Ullin looked at him with some concern, then reined around and led the way westward. When they topped the rise, Robby was surprised to see how little they had actually traveled in the night. The Thunder Mountains were still easily seen in detail even though the sun had not yet cleared them.

• • •

It was a long day of riding, and they went swiftly. Their way became easier after midmorning when the terrain smoothed out onto a vast low plateau. There were very few trees and some brush, but they were clumped together within far-scattered islands. The grass was tall and still mostly green, though dry, and game was often seen, usually scurrying away in the form of rabbits and odd little creatures with the looks of overgrown chipmunks. These darted down holes upon the travelers' approach and, after the riders passed, came back out and stood in groups, high on their back legs, peering after them.

"What's that?" asked Ibin pointing away south where a herd of deer-like animals moved quickly, leaping and running.

"Antelope," Ullin said as they paused to look. The tan animals were so thick in the distant herd that they looked almost like a piece of cloth moving away with the wind, undulating up and down as it blew across the plain.

"Must be hunnerds of 'em!" said Billy.

"Look!" Robby pointed back at the Thunder Mountains.

"What is it?" Ullin reined over next to him.

"Just there, on the far side of that first mountain there."

"I don't see nuth—"

Billy's words were cut off as a tremendous red flash on the other side of the mountain put it in instant shadow and lit the higher mountains behind it with a garish glow. In quick succession several more flashes lit the mountains and the sky above, followed by a glow which intensified and turned from red to orange to yellow and then into the blinding blue-white of lightning. This was accompanied by a great cloud of black smoke, filled with veins of bloody fire, churning up into itself and rolling heavily over the mountains and between them through the passes like an overflowing cup of hot pitch. The brilliant light faded until only the boiling cloud remained, and a low rumble met their ears, akin to the sound of thunder, deep and hard, growing louder and louder, beating upon their ears like mighty kettle drums. At the crescendo, the horses became uneasy and fearful, and the riders struggled to maintain control of them. The sound roared past like a great invisible wheel, rolling away across the empty plain. Moths flew in their bellies as the company watched, each aghast with the same thought, but it was Ibin who spoke it.

"Ashlord!"

A moment longer they watched in silent horror. Behind the distant ridgeline, the edge of the sky brightened as the sun, low and out of sight to them, turned the mountains to shadows against the backdrop of dawn. As they stared, a small black shape appeared, shooting up and over the mountain, moving fast and trailing a line of dirty black vapor. It approached them faster than anything they had ever seen. They could hear its high-pitched shriek as it came at them, growing so loud they could not hear their own cries or the screams of their bucking and rearing horses. It passed overhead in the blinking of an eye as the riders below fought to stay in their saddles and as the pack animals bucked and tore away. In that brief cringing moment, they saw what appeared to be a sheet of shredded black cloth, tumbling over itself, jerking back and forth in a jagged course, as prey may dart this way and that to avoid capture. Its voice wailed out deafening words in a horrible unknown tongue. It streaked away into the west, leaving behind a swirling trail of sooty sulfurous vapor that sank down and settled around them. It was only a moment from coming to going, but it filled each of them with such dread and fear that it was all they could do to keep their hands on the reins of their panicked and twisting mounts. Ibin, even as he tried to regain control of the pack animals, cried out a sob, great tears rolling down his face. As Sheila's horse tore away with her, and she battled to control it, she felt the blackness of that horrible night, months ago, come back to her with every nuance of despair she felt then, and more. Robby, striving to stay on his spinning horse, tasted again the madness of confusion and hopelessness that he felt at Tulith Attis. For his part, Ullin's fear swelled into anger and defiance at the receding object, and an irrational desire nearly overwhelmed him to chase the vile thing and hack at it with body, sword, and soul. It was Billy, though, who first regained control of himself and his mount.

"We should go back for him!" he shouted, pointing at the mountains as he rode over to help Ibin with the pack animals.

Sheila looked anxiously back from a little distance away, coaxing her horse to calm; but she nodded in agreement, her heart still too full of terror to speak.

"We could not help him!" Ullin cried, his anger at the shrieking nightmarish thing making his words harsher than he intended.

Robby was unsure if Ullin meant that Ashlord could not have used their help or that the mystic was now beyond any help. But he did not question Ullin and felt his own pounding heart sink into the hardness of determination.

"Then let us be away from here!" he said sternly. Ullin nodded, reined around and started away. Robby followed, and then, more reluctantly, the others did likewise.

They had only gone a few yards when there came a mighty crack behind them. Turning, they saw a brilliant bolt of lightning shoot up from the mountains and arc toward them. Like the splitting of a towering tree, it cracked overhead and passed, followed by a refreshing breeze in its wake which entirely cleared the air of soot and sulfur left by the first apparition. Blinding as it was, they all instinctively looked with their hands over their eyes as the brilliant bolt streaked by. Robby was briefly filled once more with the terror he had just recovered from, but, as quickly as he looked up, the feeling passed and was replaced by inexplicable hope. For he saw, at the head of the bolt that flashed by, the vague and blurred shape of an arm outstretched, holding a long bright sword.

Chapter 2

Memories and Dreams

Day 102
143 Days Remaining

Robby did not speak about what he saw, or thought he saw. Yet the spirit of the others seemed lifted, too, if lifted they could be. At least the way onward was easy, and the hills were broad and gentle, so they traveled steadily and far. The mountains behind them slowly receded, and they saw no signs of being followed. The place teemed with wildlife, more antelope, rabbits, and more of the creatures they called chunkmunks because of their size and resemblance to chipmunks. There were also hawks and lark and smaller birds wheeling or soaring or darting low through the grass, some tittering as they went. When a bevy of quail took to the air just in front of them, the sudden chorus of wing-drumming and whistling mildly startled horse and rider alike. And once, Sheila saw a snake, long, thick, and black with red and yellow and orange bands, sliding away just beneath her horse.

Ibin made an attempt to let his horse follow Robby's while he strummed his mandolin, but they moved too fast, and his mount was more inclined to veer off toward delicious-looking clumps of grass than to follow the others. So he gave up and put the mandolin back over his shoulder, took up the reins again, and satisfied himself by humming.

They came up a rise, and Ullin paused, allowing Robby to come alongside. Just below and before them was a little line of path that curved from south to northward. Behind them, the mountains of the east were a low blue haze and to the northeast, they could see the higher peaks of the Carthanes, their tops almost invisible under their caps of sky-colored snow. Before them, the plain stretched to the horizon in gentle undulating monotony.

"I will ride back a ways and scout the Damar to see if they still come and how fast," Ullin said. "The rest of you should follow this path northward until it ends where it comes into another way. The place is marked by stones. If you keep to this path, you will not miss them. Turn west on the new path. The way will pass through the ruins of an old city. Just stay on the path. You may reach it before dark. I will rejoin you there. You should be safe enough since no one lives there. These ways are seldom used, but avoid anyone you may see. Once you enter the ruins, the path will take you to a little stream near the other side of the city. There, among the ruins, a low fire can be made in their shelter after dark. Keep it a small fire, and be sure to set watches."

By now the others had come alongside and were listening.

"Remember: keep to the path. It is easy to get lost on the plain. If for some reason you must leave the path, keep the rising sun behind you and the setting sun before you just on your left. West by northwest is your course. I will hurry!"

Ullin made off at a good pace the way they had come, and after watching him for a moment, they continued along as he had directed. The path had few turns and was easy to follow even though it was no more than a line where the grass was thinner than elsewhere. The day grew warm in spite of the insistent breeze, and after a couple of hours they had all stripped to their blouses. Robby, uncomfortable as leader in Ullin's absence, nonetheless set a good pace. By mid-afternoon they came within sight of four stone columns, made of stacked square blocks, each set at the corners of a crossing. Runes were carved into their sides and all had the remains of bird nests atop them. As they made their turn westward, Ibin looked down onto the top of one of the columns and saw in the nest the remnants of small pink shells dotted with blue, and he reached down and deftly picked one up. This he examined as they went along and later passed it to Sheila.

"Whatkind, Sheila, Sheilawhat, whatkindofbirdmadethis?"

"I don't know, Ibin. But it is very pretty."

This westward road was a bit wider, but still much overgrown, and took them along in easy strides. Every so often, they saw stone markers beside the way. Some were tumbled over or leaning half-sunken, and Robby thought they must be mile markers because he recognized a few of the old runes as numbers.

• • •

Ullin rode a good horse, but one that was not as accustomed to Ullin's demands as Anerath. Not so swift or sure-footed and without the stamina of Anerath, but few horses had all those qualities. He missed Anerath's ability to anticipate turns and even sudden gallops. Most of all, he missed Anerath's companionship; no other horse was ever as loyal or as watchful. On the long journey from Duinnor to Passdale, it would often be Anerath who sensed danger long before Ullin's unusually keen ability did so. Or, at times, Anerath would wake Ullin as if to say, "Time to go!" and nudge him as he lay in his blankets, still exhausted from the previous day's ride. Around other horses, Anerath served as an example, and though he rarely challenged the dominant horse, he inspired all to greater strides and longer runs. Between Anerath and Ullin there was a kind of challenge, too. At least Ullin felt so, and it was he, the rider, who often felt guided in an odd way by Anerath's mood and spirit. He felt, too, that Anerath genuinely liked him and sought to please him, not because Ullin was his master, if ever

Anerath could have one, but because Ullin was his friend. And Ullin, for his part, certainly felt the same. Yet he was also humbled by the horse's affection, for who can claim a king or a queen as a true friend? And Anerath was kingly, indeed, in bearing and in might, in gentleness and in his authentic and steadfast loyalty.

The horse Ullin now rode certainly had spirit and determination, and he would go faster and farther than he was capable of sustaining, tiring himself and becoming a little clumsy if Ullin did not check him.

"You're doing fine, boy. Just fine," he said, reaching down to pat his mount's neck. "Just a little farther, and then we'll turn back for the others."

With a series of gallops and fast rides, Ullin kept to the low places as much as possible. At each rise, Ullin dismounted and walked ahead, carefully surveying the next stretch, crouching until he was certain there was no movement, no riders to be seen. It was late in the day when he finally picked up the Damar tracks, well south of where his group had passed. He followed them for a few miles until he saw where they had turned even farther south and then where they had turned eastward, heading back toward the river. He judged them to be around two dozen horses, and he continued to track them until he was confident that they had, indeed, given up the chase. By now, he was once more well within sight of the mountains, lit by the late afternoon sun behind him, and he could even just make out the brushy banks of the Missenflo. Smoke no longer rose from the mountains, but the blue-green color of the forest was darker in the spot where he suspected Ashlord had been. Like Billy, he was tempted to go back there. But he knew his place and turned his horse northwest to catch up with his companions.

• • •

What at first they took to be a wooded copse, they now saw were brambles growing up and around partially standing walls and columns. In the slanting light of the setting sun, long shadows reached out to them as the ancient road took them into the ruins. They passed between what must have once been a gate, but all that remained of it were two pillars on either side, one broken off halfway and the other tumbled entirely onto the ground, a heap of huge blocks half buried in the earth and covered with brush. There were trees, oaks and poplars and elms and even a few dogwoods as well as a profusion of vines, some still in flower. Even though there was still plenty of open ground, the group felt somewhat closed-in after so long in the uninterrupted space of the plain. They continued for another hour, going more slowly and carefully, passing under the stately remains of what must have been glorious temples and meeting places, arenas and theatres and places of government. Ruins of palaces abounded as well as more humble dwellings. Most of these were but rubble, but some still had their fronts standing, and many still had substantial portions of their walls and columns intact, though supporting nothing above. The interiors, long open to the sky, now contained huge trees and thick brush that crowded through the cracks in the structures and reached out through windows and doorways.

The road coursed down gently through the abandoned city, following along a small trickle of a stream that was choked with chunks of block and reeds, until they came to a place where the way crossed through the shallow water. The remains of an old bridge spanned the stream, its roadway long gone. Some of its supporting arches still stood, some were crumbled away, others sagged precariously. And the travelers tried to imagine why such a bridge would be needed for such a small and shallow brook. Robby led them along its bank and soon found a good place away from the path, sheltered by a high wall, and that was where he decided they should camp.

"This place has a strange feeling to it," commented Robby as he and Billy loosened their saddles.

"Gives me the willies," Billy replied in a near-whisper. "I wonder what happened? Why ever'body left, an' all."

"I just hope it is truly abandoned," said Sheila putting her saddle down. They paused and began looking around with added caution. The place was quiet, though some birds tittered in the trees and several late-season cicadas buzzed.

"Ullinsaid, Ullinsaiditwassafe," offered Ibin with cautious optimism.

"I'd feel better if he was here," said Sheila.

"Yeah, an' ol' Ashlord, too," added Billy. "What was that, what we saw this mornin'? D'ye think he came on some other witches?"

"I shudder to think. Something worse is what I fear," answered Robby as he led his horse to the stream.

"Worse 'an witches?"

"I think we ought to set watches right away. Maybe up on that wall. Looks easy enough to climb."

"How 'bout a far an' somethin' to eat?" Billy asked, and not only for Ibin.

"A sheltered fire. Maybe after dark. So the smoke won't be seen. Let's see to the horses, first. Sheila, will you be our lookout for a bit?"

"Certainly."

By the time the first stars were beginning to light their tiny lamps, the travelers had gathered wood, taken care of the horses, laid out their blankets, and done all that was needed to light the fire and cook. Above them, at the highest point of the wall, Sheila kept an eye on things. She could see just under the thickest limbs for at least forty yards in nearly every direction before other ruins or growth blocked her view. She sat with her legs crossed, as still as one of the old statues that sagged nearby, knowing from her experience as a huntress that in dim light or bright she would probably not be seen if she did not move too much or too suddenly. Her bow rested across her knees, an arrow on the string and her quiver over her shoulder. But she saw nothing other than a few squirrels squabbling in the trees and a chipmunk that wandered close by before it saw her and bounded away with a loud chirp, its tail up in alarm. The katydids with their rhythmic buzzing were very loud compared to the open quiet of the plain, and she found it uncanny how they lulled her. She could see and hear the boys below going about their work, and her stomach growled when she saw Robby cutting carrots into a pot. A little distance away, the horses were tethered by the stream, one lapping the cool water while the others munched on grass. She knew that their senses stretched beyond her own, and so she kept an eye on them, too, for any sign of anxiety.

As she kept watch, and night overtook day, she let her mind turn over the events of the past few years. She had known the three boys just about all her life, at least in passing. But she remembered, or cared to remember, very little of her earliest years.

She grimaced at the ever-present memories of her uncle's behavior, his drunkenness, the beatings she had received for any minor mistake she made with her chores, or just because he was drunk. She had learned early to encourage his drinking, in hopes that he would quickly become too inebriated to catch her and would pass out. After she was sure of his stuporous snore, she would sneak away to play in the fields and woods, coming back before he woke up so that she could make him breakfast. After he arose, and while he ate in miserable hangover, she would begin her yard chores, catching sleep when and where she could throughout the day. To further placate Steggan, she brought fish she had caught, or game she had learned to snare and hunt. By the time she was eight or nine (she did not know her true age), she had learned enough tricks to come and go as she pleased, doing less and less on the farm and more and more wandering in ever-widening circles until she knew all of Barley from the Bentwide to the Line Road and from Farbarley to Boskland. After each of these forays, and upon her return to the slovenly farm that was nonetheless her home, she had to endure the beatings he gave her. But they were not too bad as long as she waited long enough for the drink to have its way with him.

She remembered Ullin and his gifts to her, and how, that night, she carefully hid all those things, intentionally smudging up her face so that Steggan would suspect nothing. For years, those objects, the only things she felt she owned, were her secret treasures. She often stole away, going to the place where she had hidden them, to take them out and admire them in moonlight or by day, gaining some temporary comfort from them.

She recalled strangers coming to the farm from time to time, Mr. Broadweed among them, and discussions about her and her well-being. Almost always, she remained outside during those visits. Listening at the window, she understood little of what they discussed with Steggan. She feared those people. She feared they wanted to take her away, very likely to some worse place. But always afterwards, sometimes for as long as a day or two, Steggan treated her better. Maybe he feared they would take her away, too, to someplace where other children lived, someplace where the children did not have to cook or wash or weed or help with planting or harvest quite so much. But Sheila hated other children almost as much as she hated Steggan. Teased and taunted by them, she became the worse one for doing so to others, playing whatever mean tricks she could and in a spirit of meanness, too, taking revenge on the other children for her own condition. Otherwise, she avoided them all, taking more pleasure from fishing.

It was an old man—she never knew his name—who taught her how to fish, which ones to throw back, and how to clean and cook the others. Sitting alongside him on the banks of a woodland pond, hardly speaking a word for hours, she learned from his profound demand for silence that not all men were like her uncle, and this was a deep mystery to her, although it was a lesson she would soon forget. At first, she would prattle away, and he rarely said a word unless it had something to do with the hook, line, or bait. After a few days of visiting his camp, she settled into a similar silence. Nearly every day for an entire summer she saw the old man. Saying only what was necessary, he showed her how to bait her hook, and how to wait for a nibble to become a bite. She brought eggs to him, but she would not say where she got them from, and he shared his meals with her. He never asked her name, and she never asked his. But, while she was with him, she felt safe. Then, one day, after a couple of hours of fishing beside Sheila, he dropped a line in his usual manner, handed her the pole, stood and pulled up his pack, and said, "Well, I must move on. It has been a pleasant summer for me, and I have enjoyed your company. Perhaps I will come back this way someday." He nodded, gave his little camp beside the pond a last look and, without so much as a goodbye, marched off eastward. She never saw him again, and she never told anyone about him. But she looked for him every summer. It was the very next day that she first met Robby, in a manner of speaking.

Needing to do some trade in town, and wanting to make a show of his good nature and domestic tranquility, Steggan decided to take Sheila with him.

"An' we'll be crossin' over the big bridge. That'll be fun, won't it?" he said in an effort to make her cooperate.

It did not work. She rebelled against the bath he made her take, the scratchy clothes he made her put on, and against riding in the cart. So often did he have to grab her and pull her back into the cart that he finally tied her by her ankle to the seat. She screamed and wailed, cursing him and enduring his slaps until finally he stopped the cart within sight of the bridge.

"Listen to me, girl, an' mark well what I say. I want ye to take a good look when we cross the bridge. Pay special care how high it is, an' think on how deep the river must be as we cross over."

Steggan looked at her with such a terrible expression of seriousness that she stopped her struggle and stared at him in frightened surprise.

"If ye don't behave like the perfect lady, if ye cry or squawk or cause any kind of noise or trouble, I'll be rid of ye on the way back by tossin' ye off the side. Do ye understand me, dearie?"

Such was his tone, his very careful way of speaking, that she believed him.

Sniffling, puffy-eyed, and pouting, she sat in the cart outside of the Ribbons' store while he did his business inside. A boy was sent out now and then to load some things into the back of the cart. The boy, about the same age as herself, was a bit shorter than she, with a thick mop of curly black hair. He was somewhat pudgy, well-fed and pasty-looking as many townspeople were. She despised them for their health and wealth and cleanliness, and for their noses that were, more likely than not, upturned at her.

The boy eyed her cautiously each time he came out, and she paused in her struggle to free her ankle only long enough to glare at him. He said nothing, did not frown or smile, but only put the sacks into the cart and went back inside, looking at her all the while with his round black eyes. She resumed her struggle with the knots and did not notice him re-emerge from the shop until he was standing on the cart step beside her, reaching into where she sat. She flinched away out of surprise and was astounded at how, with only the touch of one hand, he was able to deftly loosen the knots. She gaped at him, full of surprise and some dismay that he could so easily do in a moment what she could not do after a long struggle at the rope. But before she could speak, the boy did.

"Here. Daddy told me to give you this," he said.

He held out a bright red apple, bigger than her fist. She hesitated, reached out, and hesitated again. Eyeing him suspiciously, she snatched it away and held it close so he could not take it back. She saw a little smile on his lips before he climbed down from the cart and turned to go back inside. Then, shaking herself out of her confused state, she leapt off the cart and ran down the road and across the bridge away from town as fast as she could go, not stopping until she reached the first hill. There, after catching her breath, she ate the apple, looking down on Passdale and laughing at her escape. She paid for it later when Steggan came home.

Things continued on for another year, marked only by a failed attempt to go to school. Failed, because Sheila would not abide the taunts of the other children, even the good-natured joking, and because her uncle was not all that keen to do without his servant, "lazy, mean, disobedient, ungrateful, an' wild though she is," as he said. That year, too, he once gave her such a beating for dropping his breakfast bacon that she spat blood for a day afterwards. When she recovered, she ran away, only to be caught three days later stealing eggs from a neighboring farm, and she was hauled back by an outraged and much bruised neighbor. The Sheriff of Barley came out and insisted that Steggan pay for the eggs Sheila had broken in her effort to escape capture, using them as she did for missiles against her pursuers. As a result of this fine, Steggan gave her another beating.

A few days later, the Sheriff came back to collect for the neighboring farmer, and, seeing Sheila's state, he asked her how she came by the bruises and cuts. When she told him it was from tussling with some other children and from falling down a ladder in the barn, he looked at her suspiciously, and, seeing the fear in her eyes, he pressed her no further. But the Sheriff told her uncle that he should be ashamed for not watching out for the girl any better than he did. Steggan told the Sheriff to mind his own business. To that, the Sheriff replied that he took his oath seriously and that if any harm came to Sheila he would do his duty and hold Steggan to account.

The next day, he came back with two of his men and his wife. That was how Sheila first met Frizella, who was round, earthy, kind, and as tough as leather when it came to having a look at Sheila's cuts and bruises. Sheila resented the whole thing and shied away. The men left the two inside together and Frizella set about catching Sheila. Outside, the men must have been amused as they listened at the noise from within—pots and pans crashing, thumps and bangs, and Sheila screaming curses while being chased around by Frizella. Sheila put up a good effort, but Frizella was too wily and quick, and soon had her in a vise-like grip and was forcing her clothes off. After squirming and trying a few kicks, Sheila gave up. Soon she was naked, sitting on a chair as Frizella fetched water and cloth.

"Yer uncle's a shameful one for keepin' ye this way!" she said in disgust, looking about the place as she washed Sheila's cuts. "Hold still an' stop yer wincin'. I know for a fact it don't hurt that much!"

Sheila said not another word the whole time and finally gave in, enjoying, in spite of herself, the woman's soothing touch with washrag and towel. Afterwards, when Sheila was once again dressed, she looked at Mrs. Bosk with such pitiful intensity that the woman burst into tears and gave her the first hug she ever remembered having.

"Thar, thar," Frizella cooed. "Thar, now. Do ye know the big ol' brick house way on the other side of Barley? I think I've seen ye roamin' the woods thereabouts."

Sheila nodded.

"That's me own house, now. An' the Sheriff'll be master of that hall, too. If ever ye have a need, or just care to visit, come knock on that door, d'ye hear me?"

Sheila nodded again.

"I'm Frizella. Knock on that door, an' ask to see me, an' we'll have ourselves a nice visit. Whenever ye please!"

Then Frizella Bosk stood up and let the men in. She gave Steggan such a tongue-lashing over the state of the cottage that Sheila feared Steggan might strike the woman.

"It's easy for the likes of ye!" he said. "What with all yer silver an' gold an' fine houses an' great lands. Us poor folk scratch out the best we can!"

"Don't talk to me 'bout bein' poor, mister!" she shot back. "How dare ye forget yerself! An' ye don't know me nor me folk none at all, if that's yer notion. An' thar ain't no poverty worse than a lackin' in common manners, especially to yer own kin! It's a wonder folk 'round here even trade with the sorry likes of ye, so rude are ye! An' if ye think ye got it bad now, just forget yer duty to this young'un an' I swear by Beras I an' all me kin'll make ye wish an' long for these prosperous days to come back to ye!"

She stormed away from him in an indignant huff, saying to Sheila, "Don't forget what I told ye!"

The Sheriff followed, but turned and said, "It's bad enough for ye to offend yer own kin, Steggan. But I'll not have ye offendin' me wife er the law either one, er ye'll end up like yer other kinfolk."

"Do I hear ye make a threat?"

"Ye certainly do."

Sheila cringed the whole while, nearly beside herself in fear. Yet, when Steggan slammed the door and turned back to her, he cursed and, thankfully, reached for the jug of whiskey on the shelf instead of her.

"See to the chickens!" he bellowed, and Sheila fled from the house to do her chores.

• • •

By now it was dark, and the firelight from below her perch flickered in the lower branches and threw out a golden glow around the camp. Sheila tried not to look at the fire so as not to spoil her vision, but her gaze kept roaming back to the boys. Behind her and all around was in shadow. She could see a few stars through the limbs, but she mapped in her head, from the experience of many nights spent outside, where the trees were, the path, and the ruins, what dark blot was actually a mass of tangled vines and which was a pile of stones. The horses were at the edge of the fire-glow, but they remained calm. The aroma of food wafted up to her and sent her stomach into a frenzy of growls, and she was thankful when Robby climbed the wall with a couple of bowls. She was amazed, too, at how easily he did so in the dark and with both hands full. Though high, perhaps nearly thirty feet, it was a thick wall, and once he picked his way up through the tumbled stairs and came onto the top, he made his way quickly to her. Putting aside her bow, she took the food he offered. He undid a strap over his shoulder and put a water flask between them as he sat.

"Thank you."

"It isn't much. Just some carrots and broth and some chunks of hard bread. There's a little salted ham in it. A few spices. I'm afraid the carrots are a bit dry."

"It's good. Oo, I'm so hungry!"

"Oh, yeah. Almost forgot!"

Robby reached into his pocket and pulled out a dark something and gave it to her.

"Here you go."

"It's an apple!"

"Millithorpe packed a sack of them for us. I already ate mine."

They supped, and though they could not see Ibin directly below them where he sat leaning against the wall, they heard the soft plinking of his mandolin. Sheila quickly finished the soup, noisily slurping down the last of it in a very unlady-like fashion.

"Sorry," she said, wiping her mouth.

Then she bit into the apple. After savoring it, closing her eyes to its sweetness, she spoke.

"I was just thinking of apples a few moments ago."

"Oh?"

"Well, one in particular. The first one you gave me."

"Huh?" Robby thought a moment. "Ah, you mean at the store. When we were kids. I remember. Just barely."

She munched, contemplatively, then said, "I never thanked you for it. Or for untying me."

"None needed."

"What made you do that?"

"My dad told me to."

"He did?"

"Sort of."

"What do you mean, 'sort of?' "

"Well, I thought your uncle was your dad, and I asked him if we could play."

"You did?"

"Yes, and Daddy gave me an apple to give to you."

"What did my uncle say to that?"

"I think he tried to put it on his account or something. I don't remember. When I got to the door, I saw you tangled up in that rope."

"You mean you didn't know that my uncle tied me up that way?"

Robby shrugged and shook his head. "How was I to know? At least, that's what I said when I owned up to it."

"Oh, I can only imagine how angry Steggan must have been with you!"

"Up to that point, I had never been so frightened of anything in my life. I even cried, and Daddy pulled me under his arm in a protective kind of way. But your uncle stormed on out, and my dad told me I didn't do anything all that wrong, but maybe I should mind my own business."

"Mmm, delicious," Sheila said. "That was a long time ago."

"Seems like it. But I don't count that as when we met. Nor the times you ventured to the school. Nor the times I saw you out at the Bosk place."

"You must mean at the pond."

"Yeah."

"Me, too. I mean, that's where I mark our first real meeting. I suppose I was fairly immodest."

"I didn't mind."

"I'm sure you didn't!" She giggled.

She did not mention how she had just been thinking of that same place, and of the man who had taught her how to fish one long ago summer. As she ate her apple, with Robby sitting quietly beside her, they both thought back to their first real meeting.

• • •

Robby's father believed that work was important and that earning a living for his family was the most important thing a man could do. He raised his son in that belief, too, having him help out in the store whenever possible almost as soon as the boy could walk. But Mr. Ribbon also believed that the store was only the means, and that making a living was so that life could be lived.

"Thar are more important things than gold er silver, me boy," he would say. "An' though they have thar place an' time when nuthin' else'll do, so do other things. So do other things."

And so Robby was given time to go to school, to practice his lessons at home, and to play and be with other children. As he became older, stronger, and smarter, Robby was taught more about running the store. With a growing sense of his responsibility, he spent more and more time minding it or running errands all over Passdale and Barley on the store's business, which he came to think of as his own business, too. Running errands was his favorite thing to do since it gave him a chance to get out and about, to ride horses or drive wagons. His father appreciated these aspects of his son, especially because Robby did all these things so well. So, when sending him out on a lengthy errand, Mr. Ribbon would often tell Robby to take his time, maybe drop in on so-and-so, or go see if Mr. Broadweed had any new books to read. And at least once every week, and sometimes more often, Mr. Ribbon would tell Robby that he would not be needed at all at the store, and that if things got too busy, Mirabella would help. Sometimes his father would give Robby a portion of his earnings to take a horse from the livery down the road, or to have Mrs. Painmoor make a new shirt or coat for him.

It was on one of those occasions that Robby obtained a horse early on a late-summer morning when there was no school to attend. He packed a bag of food, a few books, and his writing things, and he rode out along the Bentwide, crossing the bridge and keeping on the path that ran on the east bank going south. At first he thought to go out to Boskland to see Billy, and he took the way that led southeastward when he came upon it. But when he got to a fork in the path, he suddenly decided to strike off north through the middle of Barley instead of turning toward his friend's home. This was a patchwork of small farms and fields, woods and streams, and the path he leisurely followed took him past cottages and between fields and along the edges of ponds and through thick woods full of heavy ancient trees, drooping with leaves, cool and shady. In one such copse, he came along a large pond, the far side of which lapped against a cornfield rising up over a hill. He stopped and walked his horse through the trees until he found a mossy clearing on a shady bank. Soon he was sitting next to the water, his boots off, leaning against a tree and letting his feet soak.

It was a charming scene that surrounded him as he took out his lesson book and read, and he felt its peacefulness. He looked up every once in a while for long pondering moments, gazing over the silvery-blue pond, sometimes smooth and glassy, and at other moments rippling with an otherwise imperceptible breeze, or with silent spreading rings where a fish touched the surface. A turtle basked on a tree stump that was partially submerged and leaning at an angle. It with its joined reflection gave the appearance of an arrowhead. He took out his pen and ink and a bit of paper and began copying with careful hand a passage of verse.

"So are ye goin' to stay here all day, then?"

Startled, Robby looked around but saw no one. He had almost convinced himself that he had imagined the voice when he heard it again, coming from his right.

"I said, are ye goin' to take all day to read ye book an' do ye writin', then?"

Then Robby saw the source, a brown face a few yards off, peering through a bush that grew from the bank and overhung into the water. The face hovered over the water, and Robby could just make out through the bush a person crouching low with one hand holding aside a branch and the other crossed over her breasts just below the surface.

"Oh!" Robby nearly upset his ink bottle. "Pardon me! I mean, where did you come from?"

He scrambled to gather his book and papers as she answered.

"This is whar I've been all along, ain't it? Was just takin' me bath, now wasn't I? 'Til ye come chargin' through the trees an' then took up sittin' thar."

"Oh!"

"Didn't ye see me things?"

Robby looked about and only now saw a bundle of clothes at the edge of the clearing beside a bow and quiver and what looked to be a fishing pole.

"No, I'm sorry. I guess I missed them. I'm awful sorry. Shouldn't you be more careful about where you bathe?"

"I always take a dip here, don't I?"

"I wouldn't know. I mean, anyone might happen along, mightn't they? I could've been some rogue or brigand, without qualm nor care."

"Ha! That'll be the day! Yer no rogue, Robby Ribbon!"

"I think I know you, too. Sheila, isn't it? I've seen you in Mrs. Bosk's kitchen a time or two."

"Aye, an' yer the friend of that no good Billy Bosk an' his sidekick, Ibin."

Robby, who had at last gotten his boots back on and was now stuffing his things into his bag, felt his face turn red, though for the life of him he did not know why he should be embarrassed.

"Ye don't need to go," she said. "Only turn away, likes, so I can get me clothes on, an' then I'll sit with ye awhile."

Robby faced the other way, standing awkwardly and hearing the dribbling of water as she climbed out. He put his lips together to blow a silent whistle and rolled his eyes around as far as they would go, but dared not move his head.

"Ye can turn 'round, now," she said, sooner than Robby expected. She had pulled on her buckskin breeches and was just putting on her blouse. Seeing what he should not have seen, he jerked his head away for an additional moment until she got her blouse down and began lacing it up. Her long brown hair was dripping over her shoulders and the blouse stuck to her wet skin. And in a most attractive way, too, he thought before he realized what he was thinking. She slipped on a bodice and began lacing it up. Seeing his discomfort, she said, "Have ye never seen a girl, Robby Ribbon?"

"Yes," he said defensively and rather weakly.

"Not much to see, I don't think. Don't know why folk make such a fuss."

"That's a matter of opinion," Robby replied. "I mean, on a case by case basis, of course. Some folk you'd rather not see naked, of course, while others, I mean—"

"I'd just as soon do without clothes," she said casually, " 'cept in the wintertime, of course."

Robby jutted out his bottom lip and raised his eyebrows in thought, nodding in agreement as she finished her bodice.

"Uh huh," was all he could manage. She slipped a knife in her belt and picked up her fishing pole.

"May as well take ye place, like before."

"Well. I think I had best be moving along and leave you to your fishing."

"Don't be silly. I'll not make a sound to disturb ye, an' I reckon the scratchin' of yer pen won't upset the fish."

"Very well, then. If you are sure."

He took up his place again, and she sat on the bank a few feet away and dropped her line. Robby did not know much about fishing but he knew enough to keep quiet, so he took out his things and resumed his copying. They sat for a long time, not speaking, with Robby glancing at her fishing line as often as she glanced at his pen. When he reached the end of a sheet and turned it over, she lifted her pole and baited her hook with another lure and tossed it back out.

"So what is it yer so busy writin'?" she asked.

"I'm just copying. Some old verse from one of Mr. Broadweed's books."

"Hm."

For a long moment, Sheila looked at her line where it met the water.

"So ye can read as well as do the writin'?"

"Why, yes. They sort of go together, you know."

"An' yer a fair reader an' a fair writer, too?"

"I would say fair. But I like reading better than writing. My writing is not as neat and pretty as I wish it could be."

"An' ye learned it all at Mr. Broadweed's schoolhouse?"

"A good bit of it, yes. My parents gave me lessons, too, though."

"Hm."

She watched her line, studying the rings that fanned out from it.

"It must be purty hard," she then said. "An' take years an' years to learn it all."

"Oh, well, it's not that hard, else they wouldn't teach children, I suppose. It takes a little work and some practice. Like anything else. But once you get started, you sort of start learning on your own."

"An' can ye do the numbers, too?"

"Yes. I have lots of calling for that since I help out at the store."

"Hm. I suppose so."

"I think you have a bite, there."

"No, just nibblin'. I think he's playin' with me."

"Oh. You know better than I do. I wouldn't know a nibble from a knot."

"So ye don't fish?"

"Not so much don't as can't. I don't know how."

"Get away! Don't know how to fish?"

"Never been taught."

"Oh."

Sheila looked back out across the pond. After a moment, Robby resumed his copying, glancing every few moments at Sheila who seemed deep in her own thoughts.

"Can ye show me? What it is, I mean, that ye write?"

"If you'd like."

She moved over with her pole and sat next to him.

"I'll just watch."

"Tell you what. I'll start over with something new."

Robby put away the book and took out a fresh sheet of paper and put it on his writing board. He put away the ink and pen and took out a pencil.

"I've seen one of them before," she said. "It marks without usin' ink."

"Yes."

As she watched, Robby slowly wrote a short sentence.

"That's me name, it is," she said, grinning and putting her finger on the first word. "An' that word is 'the.' "

"So you can read some."

"Just a little. Sometimes, when no one's lookin', I watch the lessons from outside the school winder. An' I scratch the dirt with a stick to make letters."

"You do? Why don't you ever come in to school?"

"Oh, no! I tried that! Ye pro'bly don't recall. I just can't stand bein' inside cooped up w'all them folks sittin' in thar. An' that ol' Broad-weed!"

"He's not so bad."

Robby suspected it was the other children that had caused problems for Sheila. He did remember seeing her a few times at the edge of the schoolyard and once in a tree just beyond. He hoped he had never teased her, but, to his embarrassment, he could not swear that he never had a part in any schoolyard taunts that may have been directed at Sheila. "Well, I'm sorry. Do you know this word?"

She strained but shook her head.

"Do you know the letters in it?"

Again, she shook her head.

"The word is 'pond.' "

" 'Sheila, the pond. Sheila, an', ro, rob, oh, Robby! That's yer name. Sheila an' Robby s, ss--' Oh, tell me what it says!"

" 'Sheila and Robby sit beside the pond.' "

• • •

"Sheila and Robby sit beside the pond," Sheila said. "I miss those days. I was so excited. In more ways than one, as it turned out."

"That was a good day," Robby nodded, "and led to many more good days."

"So much has happened since then. So many changes."

"Yes. Much. Sheila, with all that's been happening, I just want you to know that I am still very sorry about the baby. And for what happened to you. I should have been there for you."

"I don't know how you could have been. It is my fault. Losing the baby, that is. I should have run away sooner. Or maybe I shouldn't have kept it a secret from you. But I was so afraid."

"Of me?"

"Of everything. But now," Sheila shrugged, "well, I suppose I didn't look after that little life very well. And now I wonder what would have become of us, the baby and me, that is. If I was now a mother on the run with a tiny baby, like some of our people...."

Her words trailed off. Robby, too, had often thought about the baby, before and since the Redvests came. And, as much as he appreciated Sheila's presence in their company, he felt guilty for it, too, knowing that if the baby had lived, she most certainly would have remained in Janhaven with Frizella and his mother. That is, if Sheila and the baby had made it out of Barley during the attack. And, in his heart of hearts, he could not be certain whether he would have set out on this journey without her, which made him feel doubly wretched.

"And things keep changing," she said, looking at him. He returned her glance, but could not see her expression since her face was oddly shadowed and hued by the flickering light of the campfire below. "As quick as things are one way," she continued, "and as soon as I've almost got my mind around how things are and what I should do, everything gets thrown off by something new."

"I know. I feel the same way," Robby replied.

They sat for a while.

"You haven't been talking to me much lately," Sheila said. "I guess we haven't had much of a chance, though."

"Yeah, I know."

"This business about finding the ring is very strange, on top of everything else," she went on. "A part of me is hardly surprised anymore at anything, what with all that has happened. *Is* happening. Yet, everything is so unsure. The very ground underneath me seems shifting. It's as if even I am changing, and in ways that are frightening. It sometimes feels like I'm someone else altogether, and the real me is just looking on."

"I've had that feeling, too."

"I wonder if we all have?"

"Maybe it's just natural, given what we're going through. Everything all upside down."

Sheila shook her head, giving Robby the impression that she was driving at something else.

"Too natural," she said. "Like I'm sliding into something and—here's the thing—I don't care. But I know I should care. That's what worries me."

"I don't think I understand. Maybe you're still upset over Ashlord. Or over the horse back at the bridge."

"No. I mean, of course I am. I'm upset at everything! But this began before the bridge. Before we left Passdale. Only it grows stranger."

"What is? What's growing stranger?"

"Me. This way I am. I can't help it."

"Sheila. I don't understand what you are trying to tell me."

Robby sensed a stiffening in her as she looked away.

"I think I should have stayed behind in Janhaven. I don't think I should be here."

"I'm glad you are. I mean, I'm sorry you are, in a way. Just as I'm sorry we're not all still in Janhaven. I'm sorry because I know it's on my account that you feel the way you do. But I get strength from your presence. And we are all glad you're with us. I don't think any of us would be alive if you had stayed behind."

He reached out and put his arm around her, and though she yielded a little, he felt the tension in her body.

"Why don't you leave the watch to me for a while," he suggested. "I'll wake Billy to take over if I get too tired."

To this she agreed, and she gave Robby a kiss.

"I love you, Robby."

"I love you, my dearest Sheila."

She placed her bow on his lap, picked up the bowls, and made her way down the wall to the camp. Robby watched her prepare her bedroll and stretch out. After a while, the fire died down somewhat, Ibin's strumming stopped, and Robby was the only one awake, feeling very much alone as he fingered the ring in his pocket.

The night wore on and a chill descended, muting the katydids and crickets. Robby pulled his cloak about him and over his head. He tried to remain alert. But, between his own thoughts and his desire for sleep, it was difficult. Every few moments, he jarred himself to attention, thinking he saw a movement or heard an out of place sound. It was always nothing, and his alarm passed slowly, as did the hours. Finally, when he could not stop yawning, he climbed down from the wall and woke Billy, handing him the bow and arrows.

"Not sure ye ought to trust me with this contraption," Billy joked.

"Take it anyway," Robby said. "Just make sure you watch for Ullin. I'm worried that he's not back already. The wall, up there, is a good place, but you'll want your long cloak. It's getting cool."

"Right."

Robby settled down beside Sheila, and Billy picked his way up along the wall and began his watch. By now the fire was just low flames over embers, giving little light to see by. But Billy was keen-sighted, and he was soon able to pick out the shadows of brush from the path. The breeze was so gentle that it hardly swayed the tops of the trees against the stars. Below, he could make out the large obscure shape that was Ibin, but, even though he knew where to look for Sheila and Robby, he could not see their forms clearly. There was a night bird that began to chirp some distance away, and the drone of the few insects induced a still, meditative state in Billy, rare to him. Like Sheila and Robby before him, his thoughts turned to the past few days and weeks. He pondered all he had seen, and he realized that he was coming to understand something more of the wide world about which Robby had so often expressed a yearning to see. Old talk about leaving Barley to find adventure now seemed childish. There was regret, too, in his heart, for having done so little to take on the responsibilities of his father, of not being at his father's side when the Redvests came, and of doing so little to fulfill the hopes his father had likely placed in him. He felt poorly prepared, poorly educated, and even poorly able to grasp the scope of his small role in things. Perhaps leaving Janhaven was a bad idea. Maybe he should have stayed and, as the new Master of Boskland, sent someone else with Robby. If Ashlord was right when he told them that little help would come from Duinnor under the present King, and if Robby was to become the new king, what could a Boskman do one way or the other, anyway?

"Unless Duinnor wakes up or gets a new king," he mused, "Redvests an' Dragonkind will have Barley, for sure. An' them that mean to stop ol' Robby, well, they'll have a scrap on thar hands is all I gotta say."

This thought, and the renewed determination that it brought to him, calmed Billy. In the dark, his face took on that wry smile and his eyes glittered with the same expression that always came over him when a fight was stirring. In spite of his efforts to reform, there was really little else he enjoyed better than a good scrap.

At that moment, a large shadow detached itself from a tree near the path only a few yards away and moved toward the camp. Billy raised the bow, but before he could get the arrow properly notched, he heard a voice.

"You make a poor watch, Billy Bosk."

"Ullin! Whar've ye been?"

"Watching you, for the past half-hour or so. And scouting around your camp. You can come down from there. All is safe for at least two leagues around. You picked a good spot. The fire can't be seen until one is right upon the camp, and well off the main way. Good water."

Billy picked his way down, saying, "Robby found this place, not me. Thar's some soup yonder. I'll stoke up the far."

Ullin took care of his horse while Billy got the fire going again and soon enough Ullin was devouring the soup. The others were roused by the commotion and greeted Ullin with gladness that he was back.

"So no Damar?" Billy asked.

Ullin shook his head, swallowing. "They turned back. Never even picked up our trail."

"That's good news, at least," said Sheila.

"Any signs of Ashlord?" Robby asked.

Ullin shook his head. They let him eat, and after he was finished, he pulled out his pipe and leaned against his saddle in his easy way of long practice. After a few puffs, he said, "Robby, I think we would welcome some explanation for going to Tulith Morgair. Though we got away safely, it could have easily been otherwise."

"Yes," Robby nodded. "I'm sorry. But it was important. I'm not sure how much I can tell you. Or even how much you might believe. I should dearly like to talk to Ashlord about it."

His companions' firelit faces told him that this had been on their minds, but they had the patience to wait for Ullin's return.

"I think the first thing I should tell you is that I met someone a while back. I won't tell you when or how it came about because I was asked not to say. But a person came to see me. You'll have to trust me on that, too. Anyway, the person that I met is in danger in no small way because of coming to me. If the person is discovered, it would go badly. Very badly. For now, I can say little about the person. Only that we might have an ally, of sorts. As a sign of sincerity, I was told to go to Tulith Morgair and to look for my great grandfather, and there I would find this ring."

He turned it over as he spoke and held it up briefly.

"I was not sure it would be there," he went on. "Partly because I did not trust that the person was actually a real person. I know, it sounds silly. Please don't ask me to explain. Anyway, I certainly did not expect a fresh flower, too."

Ullin had the flower in his hand, having been passed from Robby. It had lost much of the blue color of its petals, turning to white, and Ullin saw that it was beginning to decay.

"I hope ye'll not put the ring on," said Billy.

"It hadn't occurred to me. Why?"

"Why? 'Cause thar ain't no tellin' what kind of ring it is! Might be some kinda trick. Might put some sorta spell er hex on ye!"

"I truly doubt it," chuckled Robby. "I don't think the person it came from trusts me all that much, and yet, now, I think I'm beginning to trust her."

"Her?" Sheila responded to his slip.

"Well, yes. Her," Robby said, embarrassed at his gaffe. "Oh, good grief! That was my mistake for saying so. But until I learn more, I can't tell you all that much about her. I know this is asking a lot of you, that you deserve a better explanation. I just don't think I should tell you more. For one thing, I actually don't know all that much about her myself, really. For another, I want to gain her trust, in case she may be able to help us. I want to be able to honestly say to her, if we are ever in touch again, that I've kept the secret of who she is safe, that I have not told anyone. Although I was suspicious of her when we met, I more or less gave my word not to tell anyone, and I need to keep it."

"How is it that ye get messages back an' forth?"

"It's part of her secret, and I promised not to tell. If the way is made known, her enemies—who are perhaps our enemies, too—might discover her."

Ullin withdrew his pipe, saying, "I think we should not question Robby too much on this. I pray you will be cautious, though. As far as the ring goes, there is nothing to fear of it. It is quite harmless."

Robby had the sense, and perhaps the others did, too, that Ullin understood more than he would say. Billy and Sheila glanced at each other, but Robby was thankful for Ullin's stance.

"Ullin, areyou, areyou, Ullinareyougoingtoeattherestofthesoup?"

"No, Ibin. You have it."

"Tell us about Tower Halfis," Robby asked. "I think I have heard of it."

"It was built in the First Age and is one of seven such towers. Halfis sits atop the mountain of the same name and is nearly a thousand feet high from its base to its top. It is made of smooth white marble and is topped with a ruby-red dome that glints like glass. A few miles away is Loringard Pass. I have often gazed at the tower when taking that route to and from Duinnor. The tower has no doors or windows, and there is no stair or means to climb up the smooth stone that it is made of. I have heard it said that travelers have seen a figure standing at the top of it, where the dome is. But I have never witnessed that. Others say that it is inhabited by spirits and wraiths and shades."

"What's it for?" asked Billy.

"No one knows, nor do they know what the other six are for, why they were built or even who built them. And no one understands the manner of their construction."

"Now I remember," said Robby. "Mr. Broadweed had a book on travels and marvels. It said that the towers are all just alike except that each has glass of a different color at the top, shaped like an upside-down bowl."

"That is true. Halfis has red glass, and the one in Vanara is light blue in color. Duinnor's color is white or clear, I think."

"Built in the First Age, eh? An' they've been standin' all this time!"

"Ashlord once told me that in the First Age the Faerekind, or the Elifaen, built many marvelous things," Sheila said. "Heneil was one of the great master builders, but there were others, too, he said. Many of the things they made were mysterious in design, the way of their making lost, along with the reasons for making them. Other things, he said, were of a dark purpose and best avoided. And he said there are lots of places that remain from past ages, places where no one goes anymore."

"That is so," agreed Ullin. "This very place where we camp was once a large city, called Fisenwold. It was in decline when my father was young. Mirabella told me that my grandfather brought her brothers here once. While Lord Tallin conducted his business, the children attended a great festival and rode on large wingless birds for amusement and saw many other wonders.

"The city was already in decline. Ever since the Great Dragonkind Invasion. At last trade failed, wars took the men away, and drought came, an earthquake, then the fever. The city people quickly dwindled until none were left. The stream that passes through here was once deep enough for the barges of the wealthy and for irrigation. Now it is but a trickle."

"Kinda like the Bentwide," commented Billy.

"Except the Bentwide, like the Saerdulin, has gone back to the way it once was. This stream grows smaller every year. Soon it will be but a dusty track. And so now this place is abandoned, full of ruins, full of forgotten memories."

Ullin tried to stifle a yawn.

"You need sleep," Sheila said.

"Yes, I do."

"I'll keep watch," Billy said, rising. "Go on to sleep."

"Very well. We'll leave when the sun is full up. Let's be sure to fill the water bags and flasks. Crossing the plains will take a fortnight at least, and there are only a few places for us or the horses to drink from," Ullin said, now yawning without reservation.

"We'll wake you when all is ready," Robby said.

"Very well."

Billy moved on to take up his post atop the wall as Ullin settled down under his blanket. Robby and Ibin went to their bedrolls, but Sheila remained sitting and stared at the fire for a long while. Robby, lying on his side, watched her, wondering what it was that she had tried to tell him, until his eyes grew too heavy.

• • •

In his sleep, he dreamed of a frosty morning in Passdale, icicles hanging from the porch roof. He stood inside the store, looking through the glass in the front door, and, incongruously, holding the reins of Anerath who stood patiently behind him, impossibly squeezed between the tables and shelves. His father quietly scratched a quill against a ledger page at the desk off to the side. Sir Sun, smiling, came walking over the eastern Barley hills, and his golden morning gaze landed on one of the icicles, filling it with a sparkling brilliance that was blinding. Yet the light was hot, and all faded from view until only this twinkling jewel remained, transfixing Robby's attention with some mysterious importance as it turned from gold to red to green and at last faded to an intense point of blue-violet. The point of light seemed to touch him through and through, and he felt himself drawn into it. Suddenly, it was no longer a point of light that he saw, but an entire sky, the color of dusk without a wisp or hint of pink cloud. Underneath this sky, not three feet from him, stood Micerea. Somehow, this did not surprise Robby at all.

"How is it that we may speak and understand each other, though we speak in different tongues?" he asked.

"It is a mystery of the dream world," she replied. "My teacher said that when we dream, the ears hear the Dream Tongue, regardless of the language spoken with the mouth. If I understand a word and speak it, you will understand it, too, if you know the word in your own language. If you do not know the thing that the word is for, you will not hear it in the Dream Tongue, but in the tongue in which it is spoken. It is something like the First Tongue, I suppose, that the Faerekind once spoke."

"I see. I have been told," Robby said, "that I have spoken the First Tongue, although, when I am doing so, I don't think I hear my words in the way others hear them."

"If that is so," Micerea looked at Robby with wonder, "and you know and speak the First Tongue, then it means that you have great power."

"I don't think so. I think it is just a strange gift. And not one that I can control. When I speak it, it is without effort and without trying. Later, when I try to say it again in my common way of talking, I cannot."

"Then it means you still have much to learn."

"Obviously. I want you to tell me about the ring, if you will. By virtue of its presence at Tulith Morgair, and the flower, too, I now believe that this is no mere dream that I am having. Yet I am full of wonder. And, I must say, I have misgivings about our meeting and our way of meeting."

"I understand," Micerea said. "And I will try to explain. I do not have the means to act in the world as many do. I have no influence and no power of any consequence in my own lands. Yet I am not without eyes. And, unlike many other children of my lands, I was raised by my parent to keep my eyes open to the world. So I am blessed to have the ability to meet you in this way. Otherwise, I would have no power at all to shape things, to make things better for my people. I will tell you frankly: I seek nothing less than my people's freedom from oppression. Though most of my kind accept the way things are, there are some of us, a few, who are willing to do what we can to change the world."

"What oppression do you speak of?"

"Age upon heavy age of it. Did you know there have been times when Men and Elf and Dragonkind freely met and traveled in each other's lands? Few times, it is true, but it has happened, and those times show that it is possible to have some peace between our peoples. But truces fail. To weakness. To the lust for revenge. To greed."

"I have heard of something of the sort. One of your people once was a guest in the home of my family, I am told, in Tallinvale."

"Gurasa."

"Yes, that was his name. You know of him?"

"I am his daughter."

Robby suddenly felt an odd sensation in the pit of his stomach. He remembered with exact clarity the room he stayed in at Tallin Hall. The apparition that appeared just before his meeting with Lyrium. The figure who sat in the darkness, writing at the little desk. The sensation of a person who, when Robby spoke, was as surprised at Robby's presence as Robby was at his. The face that turned toward him.

"I think I actually dreamed about him," Robby said. Then he gave a mild laugh, "Silly."

"Then you have some knowledge of him," she said. "Does that not explain something of the position I am in? The daughter of a great and mighty general of my people, a leader respected and venerated. The ring I gave to you, my father had specially made for one of your household. He had it sent by various means from the far land where it was made, through the deserts, and to the greenlands. The voyage of that ring through our lands and how it passed into the greenlands of the north is a tale of itself. But it was a gift he intended for a friend. It was a parting gift. Shall I tell you of it?"

"Please do."

"Fifty-eight years ago, by your reckoning, my father returned from the greenlands, as we call your realms. He was a young man, and while on his journeys he made friends and acquaintances with many Elifaen and many Men. Even the one called Collandoth was known to him. His dearest friend, however, was Dalvenpar, your mother's eldest brother. When my father visited and returned, it was during a brief time of truce between our lands and yours. And when my father returned to his desert home, he had the ring made and had it sent to Dalvenpar. That was also a time when our royal family was struggling within its ranks. When King Basadurmandis died, his son, Salzadur, threw off the new ways that his father had encouraged and began ousting all those who opposed or criticized his rule. And he, too has since died, making his son Belsalza king. He is even more cruel, and he has sworn to resurrect Kalzar's glory, and to move the Great Stone to its place in the city of Tyrsharat and claim from the Elifaen their promise."

"The Great Stone?"

"Do you not know of the Great Stone?"

"I have only recently heard of it."

"It was that which began all the miseries of my people."

"Your miseries?" Robby remembered the story that Ashlord had told them, but it had nothing in it about the plight of the Dragonkind, only that of the Faere. "Please, let me hear your way of telling it."

"Very well. It was before even the First Age, before the Fall of the Elifaen and the Sundering of the Faerekind, but it led up to it. It was told to our first King, whose name was Kalzar, that if a rock of marble twenty times his own height in breadth and width, that is, eighty cubits tall and wide, was cut and placed in the city Tyrsharat, that Alonair, the brilliant Faerekind sculptor, would carve of it a wondrous statue that would be the envy and wonder of all the world. This Kalzar strove to do. The rock selected was pale white marble, and it took many years to cut it and free it of the mountain quarry. Roads were built and tools fashioned for moving the Great Stone, but all seemed against its progress. Tributes were increased for the feeding of the thousands that worked the stone, free men of our kind were made slaves, and captives who were taken in battle, too, to pull at it and to push against it. Horses and oxen were also used, but moving the Stone was a task too great even for the mighty Kalzar. His armies were weakened by the diversion of resources, and they suffered defeat after defeat. There were uprisings against him, and against the Stone, and these were cruelly quelled. Meanwhile, the desert sent wind and sand to cover the way and to bury the roads. Disease and weakness plagued the workers. So, after twenty years, the Great Stone was not even twenty leagues from where it was cut from the mountain.

"Kalzar was infuriated. He grew convinced that it was a task of spite set for him by the Faerekind. Perhaps he was correct. He gave up the task, and he began using the resources of our lands to rebuild his army and to increase his might. At last, he sent his army to attack the greenlands of the north where the Faerekind lived. Kalzar's army was defeated, and the Faerekind retaliated. The Faerekind attacked and massacred all they found in the Dragonlands, sparing only those they could not reach before Aperion, the Faere King, stopped his people by some magic and recalled them. It was then that the Sundering took place, when some Faerekind lost their wings and others departed the world.

"Since then, in the ages after Kalzar, other rulers have attempted to fulfill the challenge, but all have failed. Our present ruler, King Belsalza, has not even begun the task that he proclaimed he would accomplish. And so the Great Stone rests where it has for thousands of years, partially buried in the desert sand. I am sure that tales of these things are recorded in your books and scrolls."

"I have heard something of the story that you just told. But I never have had a book to read it from. I learned of the Great Stone from a story that Ashlord told not very long ago."

"Then you have had a poor education for one who is to be King. You are at least fortunate to have been told by Ashlord. Many have forgotten the tales of our history."

"Why do you say I am to be King?"

"It is written, and it shall be done, that from the greenlands of the east shall come the Knower of the Name, and he shall bring forth defeat to the Dragon and shall break the age and restore the Elifaen. In our books, it is warned that this New King of Men and Elifaen would arise when the great sword of Chaldron was lifted to the heavens, and he would be the downfall of the House of Kalzar. Chaldron is a heavenly apparition that rarely shows itself, but some of those of our kind who watch the heavens say it will soon come again. And the House of Kalzar was restored to power fifty years ago by our former king, Salzadur, after all these ages. Salzadur's son, Belsalza, now rules the Dragonlands, and he makes much of being descended from Kalzar. So, it seems that the time is nigh at hand for a new king to come."

"Hm. Maybe. But I am ignorant of much, and, besides, I doubt if I will ever be King."

"Lesser men than you have been kings. We will speak of this again, for it is why you and I meet. But I was telling you of my father and the ring. My father gave that ring to Dalvenpar, your uncle, as a token of their friendship. But not long after he returned to the Dragonlands, my father was called away to serve our king, as were all of the males of our people. Obedient to his king, my father was sent to the ranks of the army to be trained as a soldier. This he did, with all honor, but little relish. He had no choice. He had many brothers and sisters and his parents and both grandparents were still alive, as well as cousins and nieces and nephews. If he disobeyed, he knew that they would be put to the block or sent away to the mines. Then, just as now, spies were everywhere, and my father had little hope of escaping service. But he was a bright and able soldier and rose through the ranks quickly and became a powerful general, young and vigorous. He led his men to victory after victory, and his name became famous among our people. He was rewarded for his service by our king, and all the great houses of my kind honored him.

"Then came the great invasion, when a vast army of Men and Elifaen came south and laid siege to Calamandor, the chief city of our northern province, which is called the Green Citadel by northerners. You see, the nephew of our king ruled Calamandor. He was brash and hotheaded. He sent forth his armies to harry and attack the greenlands, at last provoking battles, which he lost one after another, until the allies of the north were at the walls of the city itself. My father was sent with his army to break the siege. It was my father's plan to outflank the intruding forces, then to cut them off from their retreat. He intended to then sue for truce, forcing the surrounded army of Men and Elifaen to surrender and to give a promise never to return to these lands. My father nearly succeeded. The northern army was surrounded and cut off from retreat or aid. But when King Belsalza heard of my father's plan, he was enraged and ordered my father's return to his court, relinquishing command of the Dragon armies to another general sent to replace him. This angered the army, loyal to my father, and they threatened to revolt. But my father spoke to his soldiers, going amongst them, telling them to be mindful of their families, just as he must be mindful of his own, and for his faithful soldiers to abide by their oaths, to do their duty to their homeland and sovereign, and to follow the orders of the new general. In this manner, by demanding that he and the new general be received by his many field captains and lieutenants, he delayed any action of the army. During this ploy, my father secretly sent a messenger to the Northmen, telling them to flee, explaining that his word of truce was broken by the Dragon King, and he could no longer vouch for their safety. He swore in his message that he would not take part in any attack upon them, but that he could no longer prevent one. No one knew he did this except the messenger, a Northman who had been captured, and a few trusted guards and escorts. When word reached the Dragon camp that the invaders were escaping northward,

Gurasa began his journey home, taking with him the Al Sairs, his household army that had kept the northern flanks closed to the Northmen.

"The story is then told that the men of the north, instead of retreating as they had promised to do, regrouped and wheeled about to mount a futile counterattack. When my father heard about this, he was enraged and insulted that his gesture was thrown away and wasted. He and a number of his guard rode back, too late to stop the slaughter. The Northmen were quickly routed and not one of ten made it home across the mountains. Our people call it the Great Victory. In the north, it is remembered as the Road of Dry Blood. My father was horrified at the waste and slaughter that he saw, of Men and Dragon and Elf alike, and he tried to stop it. Riding over a hill, he came upon the scene of an ambush, looking down from a hill just as a group of stragglers were being attacked. The Northmen had little resistance to offer, so hungry and thirsty and weary they were. Yet there were two who fought back against back with great skill and valor against the Dragonkind pursuers. But they were no match for the arrows that struck them, and one of the Northmen shielded his comrade from the missiles, taking them into his own body. When my father saw all this, and saw the sacrifice made, he ordered the attack to cease, and he charged downward, for he had recognized the fallen one as his long-missed friend, Dalvenpar. The other one, seeing only the charging horses, picked up Dalvenpar's sword and, beating back the nearest of the attackers, fled before my father arrived.

"All this was told to me by my father's aide, a faithful lieutenant who was there. He described to me how my father cradled the stricken Northman in his arms, clutching hands and speaking in the language of the north until the man died. And then, I was told, my father wept most bitterly and long, to the shock and amazement of the soldiers around him. This ring he then took from your dead uncle's finger and put it on his own. From that day forward, my father was a sick man, unfit for service or duty. He said not a single word, not during his trial, nor when he was vindicated by his loyal friends and comrades. For seven years he spoke very little, nor did he even leave his house. But he wept again when my mother died, and from that day I was the only comfort he had in the world."

As she spoke, Robby saw visions of the things she described, unfolding out of a brown sandy mist to her right, or fading away from the gray clouds in the distance over her shoulder. It was as if he only had to think on a thing and some representation of it would appear. He realized that he had no imaginings of what a Dragon warrior would look like, or how a mighty general might be dressed, or the shape and size of a destroyed city. He knew not the colors of one regiment's banners from the next, but there they were. This was when he understood that, as Micerea spoke, her knowledge of what she spoke joined his own ability to dream and to envision the events she related.

"Now you know that we are joined, in a way," she went on, "at least by the mark that grief has put upon our two Houses. And there are other things that link our Houses, things that I will not speak of. Do you believe me? Do you believe what I have told you?"

"Yes. I do believe you," he nodded. Her eyes showed that she was relieved. "But I believe because of the ring and the flower, for one, and more for your tale. And I have my own reasons for believing you, too. But dreaming like this is very strange to me. Tell me, do I guide this dream, or do you?"

"I guide this dream, though you might find it within your ability to do so. This is a place, like any other place, and it has its own landscape, its own rules. We may look upon the dreams of others who do not walk this realm, and even play a part, but that is very dangerous. If those who do not have this ability discover that we possess it, they may do terrible things in fear of us. Here, as elsewhere, you cannot always know friend from foe. There have been those who walk this space with powers much beyond what I possess. And there are others, somewhat like you, who stumble around, not knowing what they do."

"I think I can come here on my own," Robby said. "I mean, without your help or prodding."

"Yes, you can. You just don't have much practice at it, yet. Soon, though, you'll learn enough to go where you wish and to see what you desire to look upon. It is a great power. But be warned: there are many dangers. You cannot be everywhere at once. And when you are here, your body gains nothing from sleep and wastes slowly away. If you stay too long, your body will not permit you to return to it. It will resist you."

"How long?"

"Time here does not move with the stars. You must be sensible that, here, a few moments may cost your body several hours. Or, what may seem a lifetime in this realm may only be a yawn of time for your body. We must be careful. It is not wise to stay away very long, or lose sight of your place of slumber."

"What is this place called? This dream-world?"

"I was told it is called the *comaria*, but others call it *nillumenum* which means, 'faraway lamp,' or 'distant light,' though I don't know why."

"Well, how do you find me?"

"I know where to look."

"What does that mean?"

"I mean that I know how to find my way through this landscape. From practice, I know where the place is that your spirit will be."

"But what if I'm off somewhere? I mean, what if I wander off, say, to drop in on somebody dreaming in Duinnor, or some place far away?"

"It doesn't matter. If I know where your body slumbers, I can follow you from there. Or, if I know that you go to Duinnor, I can meet you there. If I know neither, I can still find you by looking for your spirit in other ways. That would be more dangerous because I might stumble into someone else, someone that I do not wish to reveal myself to. And I cannot stay long with you, for I am being watched. I mean to say, there are others who might suspect my abilities and might send their own agents into this realm to spy on me. To spy on us."

"Would you know? Would you know that you're being watched?"

"Did you know that you were being watched? I have to go, now. And you should sleep."

"Wait! What about the spies?"

"Sleep now!"

She faded from view, and Robby had the vague sensation of being adrift in a fog, with images of the plains, of Tallinvale, and of Nowhere mixed together. He shivered, standing again in the store in Passdale, looking at the icicles dripping in the sun.

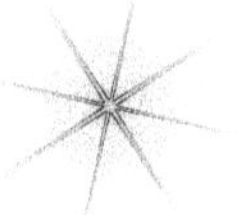

Chapter 3

A Close Call

Day 103
142 Days Remaining

The next morning came soon enough, cool and brisk with a northwestern breeze. Ibin woke first, and, knowing his duty to belly and brethren, he stirred up the fire and cooked breakfast consisting of hominy, sausage, fried apple chunks, slices of tomatoes, and even a pot of coffee. His companions were all amazed at his cooking ability, but they had to admit that if he knew half so much about cooking as he did about eating then he must be a prodigious good cook, after all. Even Billy was surprised and wondered how he did so much with so few pots.

"I reckon durin' all the time he spent in me mum's kitchen, he must've picked up a thing er two."

Robby was sluggish. He finished his meal without saying much—being too preoccupied with his own thoughts—and he began preparing the horses. As he did so, Sheila woke Ullin and served him a plate and cup.

"Thank you," he said as he took the plate from her. He took a sip of coffee and then, more loudly so that the others could hear, "There will be little water for many days, perhaps a week. So, fill the bags and flasks as full as you can."

Sheila then went to help Robby with the horses, while Billy cleaned up the pots, and Ibin fetched water.

"You slept heavily," Sheila said to Robby as she tightened a saddle cinch.

"How would you know?"

It sounded rather harsher than he meant, so he added, "Did you sleep at all?"

"Yes," she said defensively. She threw one of the packs up onto a horse and began strapping it down. "A little. Until I spelled Billy."

"I'm sorry," Robby said. "I'm not yet awake, I guess. Don't know why I'm so grumpy."

"My sleep grows lighter and lighter with each passing night, and yours heavier and heavier," she said. "We seem to be going in opposite ways."

She looked at him, as if expecting a response. He understood that, but tried to cast it off with humor, saying, "I think we'll both go west, today."

• • •

They crossed the stream with little trouble as it was only inches deep, and passed between the remains of high arches of the bridge ruins that rose up around them, now cracked and holding up no roadway, a silent testament to the height that the stream once reached. They made their way through the overgrown ruins of Fisenwold, following what must have been streets once busy with commerce and commotion. Now it was a forlorn place, but not without some beauty still left in it, from the pale white frescos on the remaining buildings, to clusters of columns still standing as proudly as they ever had, even though they now served as supports to the thick vines that clambered up their sides. Some of these vines supported moonflowers that were already folding to sleep, while others held morning glories that would soon be waking up with the coming day. Bits and pieces of statues lay scattered amid other fallen chunks of ruin, and in every nook and cranny sprang tenacious and unflinching life, oblivious to the presence or absence of human dwellers. There were thick clusters of asters, bushes of rosemary that released their pleasant aroma as the group brushed through, red and purple sage, tall bushes full of over-ripened blueberries, and long runners of wisteria. In and among all the brush and flowers flittered busy wrens and nervous finches and noisy titmice, going about their song-filled morning chores with great enthusiasm and purpose. Thus, by the time the company reached the edge of the city, and the plain stretched out before them, they all felt the city not so forlorn after all, though it seemed sadly forgotten.

By noontime, the city was out of sight behind them, and in every direction the plain spread out and even the mountains of the east were lost to view. They traveled all day and made good progress, though they followed no road or path, for the rises and falls were so gentle that by nightfall Ullin judged they had made ten or twelve leagues at the very least. They camped just as the last of the western day disappeared, and the eastern stars were beginning to shine. There was very little fuel to be had for a fire except grass and a few clumps of bushes that yielded a few dried twigs. So they ate a cold meal that evening and, after agreeing upon the order of watches, they settled into their bedrolls to sleep. Morning came soon enough, and they used the last of their fuel to make coffee, which Robby seemed to relish more than the others. The next day was much the same, and the day after that, constantly, steadily going west by northwest.

• • •

Ullin kept them moving at a steady pace, keeping his bearings and guiding their course by the sun and moon and stars. They took only a few brief breaks from their saddles, to walk away any stiffness, and they ate their midday meals quickly, though with enthusiasm. At each nightfall, or soon after, they camped. They had a fire if there was fuel, but often there was none to be had in the grassy expanse. Whether with hot meals or cold, Ullin sat with them, listening to their banter and talk, sometimes answering questions, and always assigning watches before turning in. He seemed pleased that they could tell time by the stars, unlike so many he had encountered who ordered their lives by other means, by city bells and the cry of night watchmen, or by the clocks that some people owned. And he always turned in first, though it was not unusual for him to rouse himself to make sure that whoever was standing watch was not asleep, or remaining on watch beyond the hour of relief. He took the last watch before sunrise, waking the others before the new dawn to eat, and instructing them in the preparation of the horses for that day's leg of the journey. At each dawn, he led them away from the rising sun.

Few noticed the growing urgency with which he drew them onward, or gave much thought to his increasing preference to ride hundreds of yards ahead, stopping each hour or so to let the rest catch up, to check on their condition, and to regroup them before he outpaced them once more, never going so far ahead to be out of sight for more than a moment. Perhaps they thought his behavior was only natural, in keeping with his training, or maybe they assumed that he truly mirrored their own reasons for haste and care. And they would have been correct, as far as those assumptions went.

But neither did they take much notice at the odd way he sometimes answered them, or how he sometimes looked, almost stared, at Sheila. These moments passed quickly, and if anything disturbed Ullin's thoughts, he spoke nothing of it.

• • •

At night, Robby dreamed. And Micerea came to him. One night, they stood together on a high dune overlooking a sea of lesser ones that stretched to every horizon.

"As I said before, I am being watched," she said. "Though my father is old and frail, he is not trusted by our King. Only recently has my father confided to me that he longs for change and has used his cunning, over the years, to establish communication with Vanara. He desires peace between our people and the north. He has gathered others who are like-minded. But they are very few and have little power or influence. With the greatest of caution, he is ever working to maintain the safety of his group and to promote his cause. His health is now failing, and he can no longer do the things he once did. Thus he came to me and confided in me so that I may be his helper.

"In the western province, there is a Free City, called Kajarahn, ruled by a prince and a council of rich traders. It is a place where every marauder, every pirate, thief, and criminal may go. But it is also a place where cunning merchants may trade their goods from all over the world. Vanara sends goods from the east and north, and that realm controls the only trade routes from the north to the Free City, though Duinnor, it is said, strives to wrest it from Vanara. At any rate, some of our league use the routes to pass messages back and forth, though it is very dangerous. And my father has even enlisted me to carry messages for him."

"I don't understand about the city. Does your king rule it?"

"Indirectly, the city's rulers pay our king his tribute. King Belsalza permits the city its autonomy so that he may profit as well as any from its status, both in gold and in intelligence. All find the arrangement convenient. But the rulers of Kajarahn are wary of every side, not wishing to provoke any against the place, for their army is small. I believe that some who hold power in that place are against any truce between the Dragonlands and the north, for it would spoil their monopoly on the trade by opening new and more direct routes. So, it is a hotbed of intrigue. Renegades of every race take refuge there. Murders and kidnappings are common, and all manner of vice is, too. It is said that whatever a person may wish, they may obtain it in Kajarahn, for the right price."

"It sounds like a very dangerous place," Robby commented. "But one that could be useful. If we ever needed to throw our lot together with your fellow conspirators."

"Perhaps. But few in our league know who else might also be a part, for only in secrecy may we find some bit of safety. I know only a few of them. And my father wishes for me to maintain, even with them, my reputation of sloth, and he has directed me to always act spoiled, and delicate, and shallow-minded. But, in private, he has seen to my training with sword and dagger, and I can ride as well and as swift as any. From a small child, he has trained me in these things, making games of the work of learning. Now I see that it was never a game to him. He provided me with every ostentatious luxury to flaunt, and takes every opportunity to publicly bemoan my extravagant lifestyle. Privately, we laugh. I think I've always known I was to play some role in his affairs."

She looked away over her shoulder.

"Our time is up. You must return. We will speak again tomorrow."

And Robby did return, waking briefly to cold evening air and wheeling stars before drifting off into his own mundane dreams.

• • •

Micerea kept their nightly meetings short, saying that Robby needed his sleep to have some strength for the morrow's travel. But Robby, excited by this new existence, was thrilled at the possibilities, and he could hardly wait until nightfall when his party would make camp once again. He often hurried through his chores and meal, and was usually the first to his bedroll, too, so anxious he was to return to Micerea.

"How did you take the ring and the flower to Tulith Morgair?" he asked her. "It seems to me that we are but air, or less than that. Even air may touch and move things. Yet I do feel, I touch things differently here. As if I am too weak to make my touch felt. You must be very strong in order to have taken those things so far."

Micerea shook her head with a laugh.

"Oh, no. It is not possible, I think, for us to have any influence upon objects that are not in our dreamworld, though we may see all the things there are to see of the waking world. You will come to understand our limits, just as you come to be more practiced in the art of dreamwalking."

"Then how did you take the ring and the flower all the way to Tulith Morgair?" Robby asked Micerea.

"I know a Familiar, and from time to time he aides me. He is like Ashlord's companion, Certina, except he no longer has a companion. I do not know his history, not altogether. I think his companion died. Nonetheless, this Familiar is an important member of our cause, though he be not Dragonkind, nor Faerekind, nor Mankind."

"A bird, then?"

"Yes. That is his form. But he chafes more in his form than Certina does in hers, and he yearns to be free of it. His only joy is in flight, which he does with little effort and with much grace."

"Does he have a name? And why don't I ever see him with you?"

"He is not bonded to any, as I said, and is very reclusive. He abides with no creature, nor will he fly with any or dine except alone. His name is Fallendine. He is a vulture."

"A vulture?"

"Yes. A much maligned creature. Somewhat like my people are in the eyes of yours."

"Hm. How did you find him?"

"He found me. I do not know how. By his strange power, Fallendine made it known to me that he would give his services to me when he could, though he flies far and wide, and I seldom see him. At first, I was afraid of him. Even repulsed. My people regard vultures as loathsome creatures, dirty and foul. And, because they eat the dead, they fill us with horror."

"Our people, yours and mine, are the same as far as that goes," Robby admitted. "Your league. You said before you did not know how many serve your cause."

"That is so. I think there are only a few. I do not even know if we have a leader. But my father tells me that if we succeed in our work there will be many others who will join us. Some, even, in the ranks of our armies. But no one except my father knows what I do, that I am a dreamwalker. It was he who helped me discover my talent, and guarded me against discovery by others as I grew up. And he found a tutor to help me bring discipline to my gift. Since my tutor was lost to me some years ago, I have had to continue learning on my own. I do not like to dreamwalk. It frightens me. But my father set me the task of watching the House of Tallin. And now, it is my task to guide you, if I can, and to help you become King of Duinnor. To show you the ways of my people, if I may, so that, as King, you might bring about change."

"Is that how the others think? The others of your league? That to help me is to help their cause?"

"Only my father knows of you. You are a secret between my father and me."

"You seem to have a lot of secrets."

"Yes. I must have them."

"Because you are watched. And if caught, you will be killed."

"Yes. Our enemies do not rest. They are ever-wary, nervous, and see conspiracy everywhere, even where there is none. Look there. See the chambermaid who goes along the hallway? She has been employed by my household all her life. But she is also paid by the agents of Belsalza's court. And there are others in our household, too, who receive bribes. My father, in his earlier years, was too outspoken. Belsalza was not pleased, but my father's fame and reputation protected him. Pressure was brought against my father's house, and he learned to guard his tongue. Now he feigns dotage and by all appearances leads a quiet, retiring life. He reads, collects desert insects, writes verse, and manages some of the affairs of our town. Until recently, I have not been as carefully watched as he, so I was able to become a helpmate and messenger for my father. I traveled far and wide on his business. That his how I met—that is to say, how I *have* met many interesting people."

Robby did not miss how she caught herself almost divulging a name. Probably one of her fellow conspirators, he thought. It reinforced for him how tentative she seemed in some ways. She was apparently as nervous as he was, though she hid it fairly well.

"My reputation as a lazy, silly, and rich pleasure-seeker helps me go undetected," she went on. "The spies continually report my ways and how my father indulges my craving for luxury while his estate's fortunes wither at my spendthrift habits. So I am considered a punishment to him, and a deserved one, according to those who have our King's ear."

"If members of your league do not know of me," Robby asked, "what do they seek to accomplish?"

"They are a diverse group, so my father says. Only he knows the extent of their power or numbers. But he says that some seek only eventual peace and trade with the north, to increase the prosperity of their tribes and towns. Others want more, and some have dared to speak to my father about gaining independence for their regions. Hotheads, my father calls them. And he fears they might someday act rashly and threaten us all. There are others, too, more timid. All are not good-hearted people, my father says, and I think he means that some may even be criminals or power-seekers. But they all share a yearning for freedom. And they are wise enough to know that the change they long for cannot come through war, though most others of my people believe that to crush the northern realms is the only way to gain peace."

"So you oppose the alliance between your people and the Redvests of Tracia?"

"I do not know of any such alliance, as I have told you. It is difficult for me to believe that King Belsalza would make such a pact with the sworn enemies of our people."

"Would your people, that is, your league, support it?"

"I don't think any of my kind would be comfortable allying with Men or Elifaen. Certainly not openly. You say that our armies are poised to attack in the south and east, across the Tulivana Mountains?"

"That is what we think."

"I do not see how it could be done. Those mountains are a strong barrier. And on the other side of them, to the east within Altoria, is a vast marshland, uncrossable by any traveler, much less a great army."

"Perhaps they will be brought by sea?"

"Our coast is rocky and treacherous, and what little wood we have is too precious to build ships enough to carry armies."

"Well, they must have found some way through or around the mountains and marshlands!"

"We may speculate later. Now you must go to your sleep!"

The Dragonkind woman accompanied him back to his camp and departed her own way. But Robby was not yet ready to leave the dreamworld. Still dreamwalking, Robby saw Sheila keeping watch while the rest of his companions tossed and turned, snored, or lay still and quiet in their sleep.

• • •

If Robby had been forced to describe those things that he perceived within the dreamworld that he walked, he would have only been able to give a faint and muddled depiction. He quickly sensed that, in dreams, everything seemed imbued with meaning upon meaning. The slightest thing that would be ignored if encountered while awake might in dreams take on a significance beyond the reason of words. Such things and their meanings filled the dreamer with their importance, touching upon all the senses of the heart. Yet, when aroused from sleep, most of that sense of importance faded so quickly that, when remembered, if at all, those dream-things seemed weak and difficult to grasp.

Robby was beginning to learn, though, that the fading significance of things dreamed is only a trick of the mind. The waking world has its own demands, and in that world a person must use those senses suited for it. During waking hours the ethereal body that goes into dreams must rest. So that when wakefulness comes to one part, another part goes to sleep. And as one world drifts away, so, too, do many of those things that are perceived within it. Robby wondered if there was any such thing as true sleep, except perhaps in death. And maybe not even then. It was dawning on him that never having ultimate and complete rest was simply a face, a burden, of our existence.

Robby also grasped that dreamwalking had obvious advantages. The ability to look at the world, and more of it, while still asleep. The ability to eavesdrop on even those most private of acts, even upon the dreams of others. Dreamwalking was a powerful gift, indeed, and would be the envy of any ruler. But it was not always easy to tell what was real and what was the product of imagination or fantasy. Although distances weakened the dream projections of others, or so it seemed, Robby's own projections were always with him. When he was with Micerea, it was easier to let her dream "outshine" his own. When he was alone, it took some effort, at first, for him to know that he was dreaming.

Soon enough, though, Robby was able to be aware of his own tendency to dream, and, each night as he gained practice, he gained more control over his dreams until, at last, he could dismiss them altogether. That was when the true landscape of the dreamworld revealed itself to him, and new temptations, too.

• • •

The urge to enter the dreams of others was tremendous. Robby found that he could easily see what a person was dreaming, as their visions shifted and moved against the inner film of a bubble that surrounded their sleeping form. But he learned that if he just walked in through the film, the bubble would burst and the dreamer would wake, at least momentarily. He had better luck by gently pushing against the bubble, letting it coat him with its ethereal substance and reforming behind him once he was inside the bubble. This took a great deal of practice—and he caused many interruptions to his companions' dreams, and their sleep—until he became expert enough to quickly, but gently, slip into their dreams. To Robby's credit, this process of learning was stressful because he was loath to disturb his friends' much-needed rest. And there was something else that he discovered: Dreams were filled with powerful emotions. So powerful that his own heart tended to take up those emotions sympathetically. On more than one occasion, the strain woke him up, full of profound sadness or fear. But sometimes he awoke filled with the lingering joy of the dream he had just visited.

So it was that he came to know his companions like no one else could. The capacity of their hearts was stunning. The varieties of dreams they had and the palette of their emotions filled him with awe and wonder and with such a deep love of them that at times he felt that his own heart might burst.

But Robby, ever a fast learner, found out that by watching from outside a dream he could sense what emotions were within it, or how powerful they might be. By placing his hand softly on the outside surface of the dreamer's bubble, and by paying close attention to the sensations he felt, he could easily foretell what joy or terror filled the interior, emotions that he could not always discern from the images projected onto the interior surface of the dream-bubble. So he learned to judge whether to enter, sometimes too somber of mind to enjoy the hilarious antics of Billy, for example, and sometimes too weak to endure Sheila's bouts of fathomless sadness.

Between the bubbles of dreams, the ether was not perfectly clear. As Robby looked across their campsite, he saw both the landscape of the wakeful and that of the dreamworld, overlaid upon each other. He could see shapes moving, some very small, flying about like tiny moths or other insects. When he listened very carefully, he thought he heard the fluttering and buzz and hum of wings. Most were mere specks to his vision, colorless shadows, but some glowed with a dim bluish light. These were like fireflies, but their light did not wink, and when they alit on a bubble, they brightened noticeably. Further time and observation made him understand that some of the little creatures (for he was convinced they were living creatures) were attracted to only certain kinds of dreams, each type having its preference. The ones that glowed blue, he noted, liked dreams that were joyful or full of warm feelings. Others seemed to prefer dreams that were mildly anxious, and these creatures glowed with greenish-yellow light. Still others of these tiny creatures buzzed harshly toward dreams of nightmare, glowing blood-red as they came to light upon the outside of the filmy bubbles, and they pushed their needle-like noses in through the dreamer's bubble while their wasp-like tails tapped against the bubble. As the dreamer's dream went from emotion to emotion, these creatures came and went, as if drawing sustenance from the emotions.

Robby was fascinated with these creatures, as with everything he experienced, and he eventually saw that a group of the blue creatures would flutter and swoop around a red one as if to shoo it away. Sometimes it worked and sometimes it did not, and sometimes the red ones would mass against those that were blue, driving them away from a dream. Robby realized that they were feeding, indeed, on the dream, and they were jealous of their meal. But, more than that, by their touch, they stimulated the dreamer to produce more of their favored emotion. Interestingly, when he realized this, Robby tried waving away the red creatures from his companions' dreams, and he had some success, although they quickly returned. Once, when swiping at a large red one on Ullin's dream, he actually swatted the insect. Instantly, a sharp pain of intense fear shot through him like a bee sting, and, more surprised than hurt, he immediately awoke and sat up on his bedroll.

"Hm," Sheila heard him say as he waved his hand, "I must be careful when I do that."

Before she could respond, he slumped back down and went instantly back to sleep.

• • •

Night after night, he continued his explorations. But the longer he dreamwalked during a night's slumber, the sleepier he became. It was another realization, as if his body was recalling him, urging him not to wake, but to rest, to let go his control and simply sleep and dream as his companions did. There were many subtle aspects of this exertion, certain efforts that were more tiring than others. He could stand outside of dreams for hours, nearly as lively and alert at the end as when he began. However, as soon as he touched the film of anyone's dream, he felt his vitality ebbing away. It was as if he had not yet acquired the strength that he needed for such exertions. So Robby spent much of his time remaining outside of the dreams of others, as tempting as it may have been to join them, but he looked in on his companions, nonetheless.

Robby was changing. His abilities forced upon him a new and disturbing perspective of the nature of things. His power to dreamwalk revealed forces at work beyond his prior comprehension, forces that followed rules that were different but strangely parallel to the rules of the wakeful world. It was, he soon grasped, just another aspect of existence, one that perhaps had been occupied by the Faerekind in their early days. He wondered if this dreamworld was where the First Tongue originated, where the connections were made that the Faerekind once shared with each other and with all of the things of the world. When they lost their wings, Robby mused, perhaps they lost much, much more as well.

• • •

So, on the whole, the days of travel were not unpleasant for Robby and his companions. They made steady progress, having long ago left behind the hazy blue of the Thunder Mountains in the distance. Now only the same light-green sea of grass was behind as in front and on either side of their course. They talked a great deal, and Billy did so, especially, chattering away at Ullin so steadily for nearly half of an entire day that Ullin finally asked him to go back and see how Ibin was getting along with the pack animals. Billy did so without the least sense of why the request was made. He soon took up an entirely new line of discussion with Ibin—very one-sided, as was usually the case with the two—on the merits of the wide open plain insofar as seeing any approaching threat as compared to the advantages of having some tree or rock to hide behind if something unwelcome did come along.

That same evening, after Ullin relieved him from watch, Robby eagerly took to his bedroll beside Sheila. He almost immediately fell into sleep, and he just as quickly began to dreamwalk. He looked around the camp: Ullin, with a blanket over his shoulders, was checking the horses while Sheila rested peacefully and Ibin snored fitfully. A falling star shot across the sky, drawing Robby's attention, and he watched its trail fade for several moments. As Robby turned away, he noticed a disturbance nearby and saw Billy tossing and turning. The ether about him glowed a pale orange, flickering as red insects swarmed onto the wavering bubble of Billy's dream. Robby waved away the gnats and stepped through, into Billy's dream, and hot smoky flames shot up around him. There was yelling and commotion and Robby realized he was atop the burning roof of Bosk Hall. At the edge of the roof were a group of Boskmen, Billy and his father among them, choking and coughing in the dense smoke as they shot arrow after arrow down at the surrounding Redvests in the yard. Billy's fear and desperation charged the atmosphere, and the entire scene throbbed with his pounding heart. Robby knew this dream was only a construct of Billy's imagination—that Billy had been miles away, captured by Bailorg. Yet, like all dreams, it seemed acutely real, and the power of Billy's anxiety infected Robby, setting his heart pounding and his lungs pumping.

Robby grabbed Billy's arm, "Wake up!"

"Robby! Grab that bow an' let'em have it!"

"Wake up!" Robby shouted.

The roof suddenly lurched and shifted downward a foot, throwing all to their hands and knees as a roaring inferno broke through a large crack. Hot roof-tiles and churning embers flew everywhere. Billy cried out and reached to grab onto his father to stop him from sliding into the flaming void. It was as if time stood still, Mr. Bosk falling, his terrified eyes looking up at Billy, and Billy's voice moaning out a wail as if it would never end.

"Wake up! Billy! Wake up!"

Something was holding Billy in the dream, and it was taking delight in his torment. Robby sensed it just before he saw the thing. It had a head like a snarling dog, with teeth and fangs dripping with red foam, but with a terrifying human aspect. The creature's snout protruded into the scene, eating the burning timbers, shaking its head to rip pieces of the dream away, and devouring the shreds with snarls and snaps.

"Great stars!" Robby reflexively backed out of the dream, where he saw the creature more clearly, a shaggy shadow, like a cross between a man and a dog, clawing from outside of the nightmare, with fiery insects swarming around its hunched shoulders. It was feeding on Billy's nightmare, and with every bite it stoked Billy's terror even more, as if locking him within the experience.

Robby instinctively recoiled and entered a black dreamscape devoid of any recognizable image, like a sea of undulating liquid-light. He had no time to take in the strangeness of the place or to ponder the nature of the rippling scene. Right in front of him was the creature, its head was shoved down through the layers of ether that was Billy's dream, and it twisted its body and shoulders as it mauled, shaking its head as it continued to tear away chunks of the dream, and raising up to better snap at the flying bits with its awful teeth. In this violent manner, burning timbers were flung about, bits of Billy's father, chunks of roof or brick, and parts of the Redvest attackers. Even shreds of the starry sky were viciously gobbled, and the sound of crackling fire, the yelling, and the crashing timbers all eerily echoed with every snap and snarl and grunt of the beast. Terrified,

Robby took all this in during the briefest of moments as the beast sensed his presence, turning its red eyes toward him. Immediately, he was engulfed by hundreds of the red insects. They stung his hands as he swatted at them, and horribly unpleasant images swarmed before his eyes. The doglike creature gnawed and swallowed a large chunk of billowing smoke, all the while keeping its gaze intent upon Robby. Then it rose up onto its hind legs, twisting its head, sniffing. Robby saw more in the creature's eyes than mere curiosity. There was also...*desire*.

"Begone!" Robby cried, reaching for Swyncraff at his waist. But his hand passed right through his own body. The creature dropped to all fours, emitting a low snarl, and moved toward him. Robby felt something seize his chest, a panic that stopped his breathing, that prevented him from uttering a sound, not even a moan, as the creature approached.

Suddenly, he heard a cry and somehow awoke. Tossing off his bedroll in a panic, and sitting bolt upright, he blinked, looking around at the campsite. Nearby, Ibin, too, was roused by the noise and looked toward Billy. Robby rolled over and up onto his knees just as Ullin passed quickly by in long strides and bent over Billy.

"Billy!" Ullin gave the Boskman a gentle but firm shake. "Billy, wake up!"

"What? What?" Billy opened his eyes. "Oh me gosh!"

"You were having a bad dream. You cried out very loudly."

"Oh." Billy, disoriented, looked at Ullin, then at his companions. "Sorry. Gosh! I'm very sorry!"

"Are you alright?" Sheila asked, arriving behind Ullin.

"Yeah. I reckon so. Lo! I dreamt I was atop the hall, Bosk Manor, that is. It was burnin', an' then me ol' man...I mean...the roof fell into the far, an' he got swallered up, an' I couldn't do nuthin'..."

"Itwasjustabaddream, Billy," Ibin told him.

"Yeah. Right. Oh me gosh!"

Billy nodded, still very shaken, his eyes glistening, and he gave Robby an odd glare. Robby almost said something, but managed instead a smile that he hoped was sympathetic.

"Well, dawn is breaking, anyway," said Ullin. "We should probably go ahead and get a move on."

• • •

Hours later, after the morning mists had evaporated from the dewy grasslands, Billy was silently turning some great matter over in his head as he rode alongside Ibin. While making various facial contortions that included pursing his lips, cocking his brow, tilting and shaking his head, and then nodding, he counted off using his fingers while trying to keep a grip on his reins. He did this for a long while, and started over many times, before he finally came to his conclusion.

"I figure it's been twenty-eight days, tharabouts," he said to Ibin, "since we left Janhaven."

"Hasit, hasit, hasitbeenthatlong?"

"Yep. An' so, given that, an' given we'll likely go faster now out here in the open, I figure we'll make Duinnor in another week," he said. Ahead, Ullin chuckled.

"We have farther to go than you think, Billy." Ullin twisted in his saddle to call back to Billy. "It will be closer to six more weeks, at the very best."

"What? Naw! That long?"

"I think so." Ullin turned back around, facing the way he led them. "At the least."

Billy was silent for a long while after that, busy doing another set of sums until he at last shrugged.

"Dang!"

● ● ●

At the rear of their line, Robby and Sheila rode next to each other, and, though they did not talk much, they enjoyed seeing all the animals and plants, and pointed at herds of antelope and bison that grazed in the distance. Once, they discerned a low, large movement only about fifty yards away. They saw the tall grass swaying as the creature moved, and then they glimpsed the swish of a long fur-tipped tail. Ullin saw it, too, and halted, standing in his stirrups and craning his head. Settling back into his saddle, he twisted around and said, "Lions. Three of them."

He smiled when a look of terror crossed his companions' faces, and Sheila reached for her bow.

"They won't bother us," Ullin assured them. "They prefer meatier game." He nodded at a herd of antelope. "Upwind, there."

They continued on, following Ullin a little closer than before, until their nerves eased.

Later, Robby, glancing at Billy, could see by the way the Boskman's lips were pursed and his brow furrowed that he was deeply meditating on something new that, Robby was sure, they would all soon hear about.

"Well, here's a question," Billy pronounced. "That is, how come we don't talk about our dreams more than we do?"

Sheila turned in her saddle and looked at Billy, while Ibin shrugged and said, "Idon't, Idon't, BillyIdon'tknow."

"The thing is," Billy went on, satisfied that he had Ibin's attention at least, "we spend a lot of time dreamin', it seems to me. Now, as to everyday matters, we jabber on an' on about 'em. When we meet up with someone, we tell all the news about what we've been at, all the doin's, an' comin's, an' goin's. An' we talk on an' on 'bout the weather, an' crops, an' every manner of thing we spend any kinda time or effort upon."

"That'srightwedo, wedo, wedotalkaboutalotofthings."

"We do, indeed. But how often do ye hear someone ask, 'How whar yer dreams last night, friend?' Or, 'What have ye been up to in yer sleep?'

It's very much like a big part of our lives is just ignored. An' we rarely bring it up at all unless we dreamed somethin' scary or weird."

"Well, why do you think that is, Billy?" asked Sheila.

"I don't rightly know," Billy shook his head. " 'Cept that a bunch might be kinda private, an' embarrassin'. Like one time I dreamed I forgot to put on me britches when I went off to school one mornin'."

"Yeah," Sheila giggled. "Who wants to hear about that?"

"That's me point, 'xactly. But what about all the rest?"

"Maybe it isn't something folks think is very important."

"Maybe, Sheila. Maybe. But, only, well, I'm not so sure. I heard tell that dreams can sometimes tell ye things. Maybe they can, or maybe they can't, but it don't seem like somethin' we oughta pay no mind to."

"Hm." Sheila turned back around, and saw Robby smiling privately to himself. "What do you think?"

"Who me?" Robby looked up from his reins. "Well, I'm with Billy. Dreams are too important to ignore."

"You think so?"

"Yes. I do."

"Billy," Sheila turned back around in her saddle, "is all this about the bad dream you had last night?"

"Naw, not so much. I been ponderin' on it for quite a spell."

"I see."

She settled back into her saddle and looked at Robby, who nodded back at her seriously. She snorted, trying to stifle a laugh.

• • •

So they continued on across the plains. Besides the Boskman in their company, the antics of the chunkmunks provided entertainment, too. The creatures scampered about, sometimes bumbling into each other in their frenzy to hide from the passers-by, piling down into their burrows. Almost immediately afterwards, a head would pop up, gazing at them. Quite often, this lookout would be bumped aside as another head came up to have a look, too, and sometimes four or five all stretched and craned out of the same hole together, standing tall on their hind legs with their little black noses high into the air, their small round ears twitching, and their large eyes full of curiosity.

Laughing at them, Sheila nudged her mount up alongside Ullin's and said, "I never thanked you."

"For what?"

"For the soap. The looking-glass. The dunk in the river."

"Oh. You are most welcome. It was a little thing. As were you, at the time. I daresay, I'd think twice about it now!"

"As well you should," she said, "as it might well be you who would get the dunking, instead!"

He glanced at her, and, for just a moment, he saw Esildre riding alongside of him. His smile vanished, and goose bumps spread across his arm and down the back of his neck. He tried to blink the vision away as Sheila talked on.

"I find myself finally able to say thanks, these days, for old kindnesses," she said, smiling. When she turned and glanced at Robby behind them, Ullin saw Sheila's own face return before him.

"Is that why you love him? Because of his kindness to you?" he asked before he could stop himself. She was surprised at the question. And there was an odd strain in his tone that caught her off balance, too.

"I suppose that may be part of it," she said, suddenly feeling defensive. "When it comes to falling in love, kindness doesn't hurt matters, you know. The rest of it, well, I can't explain. Haven't you ever been in love?"

Ullin faced ahead with a stony expression.

"No. I never have," he stated.

Again, Sheila wondered at his odd tone of voice. Looking ahead, too, she thought about his edgy mood.

"I don't believe you," she said.

Ullin shot her a look of such pleading that she was taken aback, and she was about to apologize.

"You are right. But it doesn't matter anymore," he said before she could speak. "I'll ride ahead for a bit. Gettup!"

He nudged his horse into a trot and moved on over the rise before them and then out of sight.

"I must shake myself out of this!" Ullin said to himself as he dismounted and led his horse along. "What manner of strange weakness has possessed my mind! That I cannot know who is who? Nor even what I feel, whether it be lust or some more honorable kindling of feeling? Who has done this to me? Was some dark enchantment laid upon me by Esildre, muddling my eyes with false visions of Sheila? Or is it Sheila, taunting me with some girlish spell to addle my thoughts and to distract me from the dangers we face? How pathetic I am! Am I not a man, with a man's will? Does it matter who or what may be the cause of my bewilderment? Am I such a lamb that I cannot resist, regardless of the source of this evil distraction?"

Shaking his head and muttering thoughts aloud, he walked on, leading his horse by the reins down into a slight depression. In spite of his distractions, he instinctively looked for the easiest way up the far rim for the others to follow. His long practice of wariness had its own habits, separate from his deliberations and, even though his thoughts were far from what he saw, his eyes still surveyed the outstretched landscape as he made his way up the slope on the far side of the little basin.

"That ring! How did he come by it? How can it be that she lost it? The very ring! Or did she freely give it up? Oh, that I had never left you!" he cried out. "What a fool was I not to have taken you and fled to some far-off land! A place to live out our days without anguish over the grim yokes of the world. What a fool! What a fool I am!"

A hint of movement caught his attention, and he momentarily passed it off as only an antelope. He flinched as his mind's eye opened, and he froze into a half-crouch, like a wild animal at the scent of a predator. He gazed intensely westward, his eyes wide, until he was sure of what he saw. Still crouching, he turned and hurried back down the slope, urging his horse backwards, glancing eastward at his party already coming over the rise and descending into the depression.

"What's 'at about?" Billy asked, seeing Ullin hurrying back to them.

"Get down!" Ullin told them, not too loudly but with command in his voice and waving his free hand at them. "Get off your horses! Lead them quickly down into this depression. Quickly! Quickly! And keep very quiet!"

They immediately did as he said and followed him until they reached the bottom.

"Billy, come with me. The rest of you take care of the horses. Keep them quiet for goodness sakes! And be ready to flee or fight. Keep low. There are others on the plain we may not wish to meet."

Crouching as Ullin did, Billy followed, and they ran up the rise and then crawled up the last few yards. Careful to keep their heads low, they scanned the open grasslands ahead.

There were about forty of them, dressed in light robes, blending so well with the plain that, at this distance, they were difficult to distinguish. They moved about in a tight group, busy with some task. One of their number stood aside from the others at a tripod, sometimes stepping around it, apparently making some adjustment to it.

"What're they doin'?" Billy asked in a hushed tone.

"I cannot say. Keep watch. I'll be right back." Ullin slipped down the bank and trotted to his horse.

"What is it?" asked Robby.

"I don't yet know. Stay here!"

After a moment, he was back with Billy and was holding a leather-covered brass tube to his eye.

"A spyglass! Whar did ye get it?"

Ullin twisted the tube carefully.

"From one of Captain Makeig's men, Winterford. I traded for it. He may have gotten the better part of the bargain. Oh!"

Ullin went stiff, riveted to the spyglass. Suddenly he turned over on his back and slid down the bank with a look of intense concern.

"What is it?"

"Come along." He tugged Billy's pant-leg. They scrambled down and then ran to the others.

"There is a party of Dragonkind soldiers just over this rise, about three hundred yards west of us," he told the group. "I made out forty-three of them."

"Dragonkind! What are they doing here?"

"I don't know, but it stands to reason that they'll have scouts roaming about. It's a wonder we haven't been seen already. These grasslands must be throwing off their senses."

"Can we go around them?"

"Not without backtracking quite a long distance. Thank heavens the wind is out of the west or they may have scented us."

"So what do we do?"

"Wait for them to pass by and hope they do not come this way. Be ready to move quickly, in case they do! Ibin, keep the horses calm. Soothe them the best way you can. They sense the Dragonkind and are uneasy. Billy, Sheila. Do you know the call of the wood shrike?"

"Ye mean its whistle?" asked Billy.

"Yes."

"Something like this?" Sheila blew three soft whistles followed by two of a higher note. "Except much louder," she added.

"Yes, that's it. Billy?"

"Yeah, I got it."

"Good. Take your weapons. Billy, go up on that rise just there and stay low. Find a comfortable place down in the grass. Take a blanket. Lie down and keep an eye out. Make the call three times as a warning that you see something. Making the call one time only is your way of saying that you are still there, and all is well. When you hear my whistle, return with one call of your own. Got it?"

"Aye. One, all is well. Three's a warnin'."

"Take a water flask. Sheila, the same for you but opposite Billy, say, over there on the south of the rim. Robby, come with me. Keep the horses calm, Ibin. Let out a yell if you see any Dragonkind!"

"IwillIwill!"

Robby followed Ullin back up the bank, crawling until the plain was in view. Ullin took a look with the spyglass, then handed it to Robby.

"Just look through it until you see them. Turn this part to make the vision clear."

Robby took the apparatus and mimicked how Ullin had held it, twisting the eyepiece as he looked through it. After several moments of trying, the blurry scene flashed into sharp detail.

"Oh, my!" he said, at the wonder of the device, then, "Oh!" at what he saw.

"The one near the tripod is writing, I think," he told Ullin.

"My guess is that he is making a map."

"But what are all of the others doing? They seem like they're just wandering around and around in circles. All bent over. Doing something to the ground. Or maybe looking for something. What are they up to?"

"I cannot guess."

• • •

The day wore on as the two took turns watching the Dragonkind continue their odd activity. Ibin kept the horses settled by tirelessly going from one to another, stroking them and giving them soft words of confidence. Though he smiled when he faced them, his heart was full of anxiety. As he soothed the horses, he often looked toward his companions who kept watch around him. From the bottom of the bowl-like depression, he could not see them clearly as they were all lying in the tall grass and facing away. He was reassured by his companions' soft whistles, for they not only told him that his friends saw no danger, but the calls also reminded him of home and the birdsong-filled woods and fields of Barley.

Ullin finished his call and listened for the reply. From his right came Sheila's perfect imitation of the bird, foreign to these lands. From the opposite direction came Billy's response, a less confident and definitely flatter rendition. Ullin grimaced and turned back over onto his belly as Robby handed him the glass. Just as Ullin raised it, the wind gusted and turned, shifting around from the west to the south, and it then died away. The sun's heat intensified in the lull, and the day became very warm in only a few moments.

"I still can't tell what they are doing," commented Robby.

"Me, neither," Ullin kept his eye to the glass. "It looks as though they are spreading something on the ground."

He shifted to gaze around the area, refocusing the device, and his eye caught something much closer. Trying to find it again in the glass, he slowly swept back and forth until he had it, and he quickly focused on a Dragonkind, less than a hundred yards away. He was nearly invisible in his cloak, and he was crouching with one hand on the ground and his head up, somewhat like a dog, sniffing. The figure rose up into a half-crouch and turned his head to his party behind him. Ullin heard no sound, but immediately the rest of the Dragonkind in the distance stood upright and faced their way. They scurried about quickly, the one with the tripod knocked it over, and the entire group fell to the ground, disappearing into the grass.

"Uh-oh. We may have been smoked."

"Where did they go?"

"They're still there, lying low. But there's one close by who looks like he may move this way. No. Wait. He's moving back to rejoin the others."

The lone figure retreated, sometimes only a vague movement in the grass, sometimes just a head and part of a shoulder, until Robby could see him no more. Shortly afterwards, they saw the party rise, sling packs across their shoulders, and form into a line. As they began a quick march northward, five of them detached from the group and trotted ahead, fanning out eastward and westward of the main way. In only a few minutes they were all out of sight.

"They're gone," Robby said.

"Not quite," Ullin passed the glass to Robby. "Look there, a little south of where they were."

Robby scanned the plain but saw nothing at first. A movement caught his eye, and he made out four figures, small as dots, spread very wide apart from each other, moving north and trailing the main group.

"Their rearguard," Ullin explained. "I counted fifty-two, altogether. That's nearly half a company. No armor, lightly equipped, no mounts, but moving fast. More than a thousand miles from their nearest stronghold!"

"Where are they going?"

"I haven't the foggiest. But if they continue that way, they won't go far. Nasakeeria is but three weeks fast march north of here."

Ullin took the glass from Robby and watched the trailing Dragonkind soldiers until they disappeared. For a long while afterwards, he continued to examine the plain for any other sign of movement.

"The day gets late," he said, putting away the glass and slinging the case by its strap over his shoulder. "I'll go on ahead. Gather the others and follow at an easy pace, keeping me in sight until you catch up."

They trotted down to the horses, and Robby called to Billy and Sheila as Ullin rode off, disappearing for a moment over the rise until they mounted and could then see over the top. Ullin was already far ahead, and they followed cautiously, their eyes raking the grass from horizon to horizon, alert to any movement or sign of danger.

Ullin's arm shot up.

"Hold up!" Robby cried, reining to a halt and raising his arm as Ullin had. Sheila came alongside, watching Ullin dismount and lead his horse back and forth, examining the ground.

"I can't say I like being out in the open like this," she said, looking northward.

"Me, neither."

At Ullin's signal, they resumed their advance and soon caught up with him. He was still looking at the ground. It showed little sign of disturbance where the Dragonkind had been and even the grass was not as trampled as one might have thought. They pulled up around Ullin but did not dismount.

"They took great care to cover their signs," he told them. "Very odd. The ground is very soft. And, look, it is turned up in places."

He grasped some long stalks of grass and lifted a large clump freely from the ground. Underneath was fresh soil.

"It's as if they pulled up all of the grass, spread dirt everywhere and carefully replaced the grass on top. See how the whole area has a little bulge to it?"

They would not have noticed if he had not pointed it out, but a wide circle of about thirty yards was built-up ever-so-slightly. Ullin drew his sword and began walking around, thrusting it into the ground every few feet.

"Where did the dirt come from?" asked Sheila. "Why would they make a little hill like this?"

"D'ye think they buried somethin'?" Billy asked.

"What would be so big to pull up so much dirt?" Robby asked.

"I don't know," Ullin shook his head, continuing to probe the ground. In most places, the sword went down only a foot or so, sometimes less, but other than a few rocks, he turned up nothing strange or unexpected. Finally, he stopped, put away his sword, and looked around, his hands on his hips, looking first at the eastward horizon, then toward the west. Drawing forth his spyglass, he did the same again, peering through it intently in each direction for a long while.

"The mountains of the east are out of sight," he said with finality, putting the glass away. "And those of the west still too far off to see. There are no landmarks, no points of reference as far as I can tell. Yet they must have mapped this location, so as to find it again. How they did so, I can't work out, unless…"

"Unless what?" Billy asked.

"Unless they worked out a way to measure the stars during daylight and they have northmetal."

"Northmetal? What's 'at?"

"It is a rare metal, like iron. But if you hammer it thin and make a tiny blade of it, and then if you balance it on a pin, the northmetal will turn and point north. I've seen the like used in Glareth by sea captains. By its use, you can stay on a course, even when clouds obscure the sun and stars."

"Humph!" said Billy. "Never heard of such!"

"But why all the fuss with the ground?" Robby asked. "What's so special about this spot on all the plains?"

Ullin got back onto his horse and reined around.

"I cannot say, and we can't stay all day trying to make sense of it," he said. "Let's move on."

"This is all very strange," said Sheila, nudging her horse to follow behind Robby.

"I agree," Robby nodded. He was about to say more when his horse heaved sideways, its front right leg sinking rapidly into the soft ground. The frightened beast, in an effort to keep from stumbling, threw Robby over its shoulder. He hit the ground hard, losing hold of the panicked horse's reins, and as he tried to stand he felt himself sinking. There was a cracking sound underneath him and a couple of downward lurches, then the ground fell away beneath him.

"Robby!" Sheila screamed, trying to get off her spooked horse. Horrified, his friends saw him scratching and clawing at the edge of a hole that was opening underneath. Then he disappeared, and they heard his cry cut off by a muffled splash.

It was cold and black, and Robby felt no bottom. Swallowing foul-tasting water through his nose and mouth, he flailed about until his hands touched the clammy sides of the pit. He came up for an instant, coughing and choking violently, and went down again, still struggling to control his panic, the weight of his wet clothes pulling him under. He felt another kind of blackness overcoming him and he became disoriented, unable to tell which way was up. Somehow, he managed to dig his hands into the slippery walls and lift his head above water, holding himself and coughing uncontrollably, gasping for air. From somewhere above, he heard muffled shouts calling to him, but his coughing and wheezing was so violent that he could not muster a response, and he felt his grip slipping. He realized he could not hold on, even with frog-like treading against the wall. Keeping one hand on the wall, he took a short breath and let himself slide downward while with the other hand he quickly reached for the dagger that he hoped was still on his belt. It was. He drew it and plunged it into the wall and pulled himself up. It came loose, along with a cascade of dirt and mud, but after two more tries, more swallowed water, and much grunting and coughing, he managed to set it firmly. Holding the dagger with both hands, he hoisted himself just out of the water and forced himself to be still lest the blade come loose again. Some of the water drained from his ears, and he tried to calm himself before he answered his friends' desperate calls.

"I'm here!" he said hoarsely, and then, after more coughs, "I'm alright!"

"Hang on, Robby!" Billy called down. "Hang on! We're gettin' a rope down to ye!"

Robby glanced up, trying to blink away the water and mud that ran out of his hair. He saw, about twenty feet up, silhouettes of heads protruding from the edge of a bright blue circle.

"Grab hold!" Sheila told him as a rope uncoiled downward.

"Try puttin' yer arm through the loop!"

"Got it, got it! Alright! Can you pull out some of the slack? I'm starting to slip!"

"How's that? Ye can put yer weight on it. We've got this end fast."

After a bit of a struggle, Robby had the rope running around him and up under his armpits.

"Can we pull you up? Are you all set?"

"I think so. Yes!" Then, more to himself, he said, "Please get me out of here!"

Robby grabbed his knife, and, as he was carefully hoisted upward, he used it as a pick, driving it into the wall with both hands to help lift himself. Growing more confident as he neared the surface, he sheathed the knife. At last, with many hands reaching for him, he was quickly pulled out of the hole where he collapsed with a fit of coughing and shivering.

Sheila and Billy knelt beside him, pulling off his coat.

"Gar! These clothes alone must weigh a stone!" Billy exclaimed, tossing the heavy vest aside.

"We need to get you out of these wet things," Sheila told Robby as he shivered and coldbumps ran across his arms. Ullin handed him a flask, and he took a couple of swallows of Fetch, sending its warming glow down deep. In no time, they had him stripped with blankets draped around him, and Sheila was rubbing his shoulders and arms briskly. The others sat close beside him, watching with concern.

"WellIguess, wellIguesswe, Iguessweknowwhereallthedirtcamefrom!" Ibin blurted out.

"Right," nodded Billy.

"The que-que-question is, w-w-why?" Robby agreed through an intense shiver. "Why dig a w-well out in the middle of n-n-nowhere. Brrrrr! And then cover it up and hide it?"

"They prepare for war. Invasion," Ullin stated, putting another blanket around Robby and pulling it up over his head. "They must be planning to send an army this way. My guess is they mean to move swiftly, bypassing the towns and villages along the eastern and western edges of the plains where most of the streams and rivers are. Instead, they must intend to cut straight up the middle of this plain. Few people travel this way, and they must figure that the snows this winter will cover the signs of their digging until spring when new grass will grow, making the well harder for their enemies to find. I'll wager this is one of a line of wells from here southward all the way to Altoria. And I'd wager, too, they aren't the only party of Dragonkind digging on this plain."

"A lot of good this water will do them," Robby chuckled. "It's about as foul and salty as it can be! Can't you smell it on me? On my clothes?"

"Yeah," Billy said. "I do. Smells like sulfur, er some such."

"It's been salted," Ullin said.

"What?"

"We call it salted," Ullin explained. "But it is made to taste like water from their own lands. They've added some kind of minerals to it. It may smell foul to our nose and even make us a little sick, but it is not harmful. It isn't like seawater."

"That's peculiar," Sheila said. "Why go to all that unnecessary trouble? Why not just enjoy fresh, clean water?"

"It is hard to explain," Ullin shrugged. "I'm not sure I understand it myself. But it has to do with their rituals about water, which is precious in their lands. To them, adding these unctions to the water purifies it, or so they think. But I've heard it said that some Dragonkind fear to drink the same water that we of the northlands do."

"Piffle!" Billy said, indignantly.

Ullin cocked a brow at Billy but did not respond.

They sat around silently for a few minutes as Robby warmed and dried.

"So they mean to send an army through here next spring er summer, let's say," Billy put forward.

"That's my guess," answered Ullin.

"An' they got these here various parties out preparin' the way. An' ye reckoned 'round forty er fifty er so in the bunch that did this?"

"More than that."

"Do ye reckon them other parties are all movin' north'ard, too?"

Ullin hesitated and nodded, slowly.

"So, let's say they all get up north," Billy continued. "What then? A hunnerd, mebbe two hunnerd Dragonkind? Somewhar up 'round them forbidden lands of Nasakeeria. What then? What'll they do, d'ye reckon?"

"Assuming they are not foolish enough to enter that place," Ullin thoughtfully said. "If I had an army, even a very small one, deep in enemy territory, cut off from support, I would try to get my soldiers safely home. But these are Dragonkind. My guess is that they are elite fighters, battle-hardened soldiers each one, devoted to their cause with fanatical zeal. Safety would only be a concern where stealth was required to carry out their mission."

"If the mission is to dig wells, and make ready for a vast army to come," said Robby, getting up and checking his horse's leg with one hand while holding the blanket with the other, "what would such a force be able to do afterwards?"

"Well, they would have to turn east or west, around Nasakeeria. They'd probably seek to return to their own forces, to act as scouts and guides for the main army and to deliver their maps. If I were a Dragonkind general, what would I do?" Ullin rubbed his elbow. "I'd split my force. The maps must be delivered. I'd send a fast-moving group carrying the maps back southward through the center of the plains. Maybe one small group, fifteen or twenty runners at most. I'm just guessing. But I would take the rest of the force somewhere to hide and wait out the winter. When spring came, or when I received word, or at some prearranged time, I would lead out my force. But where would I strike?"

Ullin thought for a few moments as Robby rummaged for dry clothes and got dressed.

"I don't know," Ullin said, standing. "But I do know that we need to keep moving. Are you recovered enough to keep going?"

"I think I'll be fine, and I'd just as soon not hang around here. My horse seems well enough in spite of his stumble. Aren't you, old boy? Yeah, not fair putting hidden holes in the ground, eh?"

Robby gave him a friendly rub on the neck before climbing back into the saddle.

"Areyousure, areyousure, areyousureyouareallright, Robby?" Ibin asked coming along beside him and putting his arm around him with a squeeze. "Thatwasvery, thatwas, thatwasveryscary."

Robby returned the hug with his free arm and reassured him, "I'm fine. Much better up here than down there!"

He adjusted his wet clothes over his saddle in front of him.

"Let's be off!" he said enthusiastically.

• • •

The rest of the day was uneventful, and they managed to put a great distance between the well and sunset. They had no fire that night and slept between their watches as best as they could on cold food and chilly ground. Robby, who had the first watch, woke Sheila to take the next, and they chatted for a few moments about his uneventful watch, before he slipped into the warm spot between the blankets that she gave up. As he fell asleep, he was thinking about her, realizing that she was right: they were growing apart. Their chats were light and brief, and though they were spending more time together than they ever had, it seemed only to make their growing distance more apparent.

He knew that it was partly because he kept secrets from her, that she needed to be part of the concerns of his heart. Yet, he could not find the private time to express those concerns to her properly, without breaking his word to Micerea. Even if he could explain the dreamwalking and the Dragonkind woman, how would Sheila react? Just now, after waking her, they had only chatted about the bright stars and how quiet the night was. Yet, he thought as he huddled under the blankets, "She is right there, not forty feet away. All I have to do is get up and go to her."

But weariness and sleep tugged him under. Before he knew it, he was dreaming of his mother who, inexplicably, was sitting beside Sheila in the darkness and talking about how she missed Robigor so much that her heart ached.

"I miss Robby, too," Sheila said, and Robby knew they were talking about two different people.

"If only he would come back," Mirabella went on, as if not hearing Sheila's words.

"If only he would come back," Sheila echoed. "I'd kiss him all over and never let him go again!"

"I'd kiss him all over and never let him go again!"

Their words merged, it seemed, and became muddled as he drifted out of the dream and deeper into slumber. Then he heard more.

Robby's dreaming eyes were blurred with grainy sleep, and it was dark, yet he could still make out two figures chatting. But now Mirabella was gone, and the two looked very much like Esildre. Robby blinked, trying to keep his eyes open as one of the two wavered, shadow-like, in and out of view, sometimes there, sometimes not.

"I'm not sure I can have a child, anymore," said the other.

"But it is worth a try, is it not? After all, between us, one of us is sure to succeed! And two of the House of Tallin, right here!"

"But one grows less interested in me, and the other, though he fascinates me, looks at me lately only with sadness and pain. Sometimes with anger in his eyes and even, I think, with fear."

"It does not matter. And therefore he sees me in her form. Since her curse did not ruin him, I came along with you to complete the work of it. You know I am not her, and you give me reluctant ears. But he hears me when I speak, even if you do not."

"I wonder how long he will treat me so."

"As long as I have influence over him."

Robby could not follow the meaning and had a sense that there were some numbers that he had to add up, and that somehow this talk was only to distract him from putting the crowded shelves in order. In the dark, it was hard to see the contents of the jars or read the labels, and a night breeze kept shifting the page of his ledger book. He saw a light inside one of the clear jars. Looking closer, it appeared as if a window was suspended within the jar. And, through it, he could see far across the plain, unto the far western mountains and down into the south. There was a faint light, like a single steady golden flame from a lamp. It did not move or waver, yet Robby could make out nothing else. As a star, it hovered before him, hopelessly out of reach, yet a beacon, a warning, a guide, a fearful hope.

He woke up and blinked, having the nonsensical notion that Lady Moon was grinning rather mischievously at him from above, her fan far enough from her face for her expression to be clear. It was a queer feeling, and he shrugged it off, shifting over onto his other side, and saw Sheila sitting alone on a little rise a few feet away. She was facing away, gazing upward. Rolling back over, he thought perhaps the Lady grinned at Sheila instead, and then he closed his eyes again to let sleep retake him. At first it was deep, quenching in its darkness all his worries, his fatigue, and all his thoughts.

• • •

After what might have been but a moment, but felt much longer, Robby saw the light again. He was mesmerized by it, having no sense of whether it was above or below him, or whether it was at his nose or a thousand leagues away. He watched the light, but it did not change until he stepped closer. Then it expanded and engulfed him in blinding brilliance. Blinking at the brightness, he found himself standing in the dusty street of a desert city, a place like he had never before imagined, crowded with burning sunlight and noisy merchants, clanking soldiers, and sweaty workmen. They seemed not to mind that he was there, even though he was of another race, an adversary. He was filled with wonder at the dusty beauty of the place, the vibrant colors of the curtains and pavilions that fluttered in the breeze, the sensuous music that wafted over walls from hidden courtyards, along with the fragrances of exotic perfumes and blossoms. He wandered without care, looking at and listening to the city, stopping for a long while in a market to look at the goods and to listen to the haggling of buyers and sellers. He stopped to watch an opulent sedan pass by, held high by four nearly naked Dragonkind, muscles bulging and glossy with sweat and oil. Upon the sedan, underneath the shade of a square parasol, reclined a young woman of the loveliest proportions, with long jet-black hair, and with a circlet of gold about her head from which dangled long chains of precious and glimmering gems. Her eyes, dark and lined with shadow and blue paint daubed with flecks of mica, were closed. She rested her head on a pillow, lying on her side, exposing her curves and much of the soft brown flesh of her body through the cool fabric of the sheerest gauze. As they passed, her servants went before the sedan clearing the way with whips and swords. As one of the whips lashed out at a group of beggars too weak to quickly move, the tip of it passed right through Robby, yet he felt nothing. Her eyes opened sleepily, and she looked straight at him. She flinched and sat up. Looking again in his direction, she had obviously lost sight of him, but she earnestly kept looking as the party receded. Smiling, he leisurely followed the procession as it moved through the city and on toward a palace atop a hill.

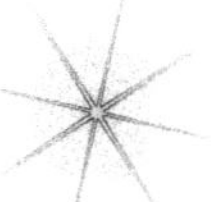

Chapter 4

The Ring of Valor

Surely these were days of unrest, for nowhere, it seemed, could things remain the same as before. As Robby and his company traveled westward, overcoming obstacles and threats as they went, the people they left behind also went forth into each day to toil toward an end just as uncertain.

In Tallinvale, the countryside was being emptied of its inhabitants. From the day Robby's company left Lord Tallin's domain, messengers had been spreading word of a vast army soon to march into their lands. These warnings, and Lord Tallin's offer of lease and refuge, did not go unheeded. Most of the people of Tallinvale expected such news and readily agreed to Tallin's offer, though a few stubbornly remained on their farms. Others took their families and sought to escape north or westward, away from the lands that would soon be filled with war. Some fled to the Galinot warlord's domain, northwest of Janhaven, taking the easy way west through the Thunder Mountains and Damar territory. Others, fearing the warlords, tried making their own way to Duinnor, passing through Janhaven, and taking the summer roads through the peaks of the Carthanes, attempting the high Loringard Pass. But none who fled made it far. Most fell into the hands of the Damar, who ruthlessly cut them down. As for those who gambled upon Loringard Pass, the summer was long gone, and their bodies might be found by future travelers, revealed when the ice and snow that trapped them melted away.

The scouts of the Thunder Mountain Band soon observed these activities along the border of their territory, and even received one of the Tallinvale couriers in their town. Hearing the courier's news, Makeig accompanied him on to Janhaven to speak with the people there. Lord Tallin's plan to make a stand was received with much concern. The people of Janhaven, and the refugees among them, debated hotly whether to flee south to the protection of Tallin City or to stay and make their own defense. It was obvious to Mirabella, and the others, that they would soon have two fronts to defend against: one to the east, against the occupation force in Barley, and another to the south as the Redvest armies spread around Tallin City, driving a wedge between Janhaven and Tallinvale. And the invaders were apt to send forays northward against Janhaven.

"When does Lord Tallin expect the enemy's arrival?" Mirabella asked the courier.

"We have not been told," he replied. "But surely they come quickly, else why the haste to spread the news?"

Mirabella, in the three weeks since Barley had fallen, had not been idle. Nor had the other refugees in Janhaven. They had quickly agreed to consolidate their efforts with the people of Janhaven led now by Furaman, those of Barley led by Mrs. Bosk, and the Hill Town folk under Captain Makeig's leadership. Together they worked to secure the east road and to fortify the Narrows against any further attack from Passdale. They settled on a way to ration food that seemed to have some chance of getting them through winter. Mirabella and Makeig established training exercises, too, teaching the use of sword and bow, how to sneak around in the woods, and how to make use of cover in a fight. It was an irony that the inhabitants of Janhaven, who were as inconvenienced as any by the arrival of the refugees, were also grateful for the spirit of the newcomers, for their willingness to work and fight in the defense of Janhaven, and for their desire to throw out the Redvests and take back their lands. Indeed, to take back their homes was a dream the refugees incessantly talked about, in spite of how hopeless such an effort seemed. Many had relatives still in the hands of the Redvests, captured sons and daughters, and were eager to rescue them, or at least have word as to their condition. The presence among them of the proud Bosk folk, especially Frizella Bosk, and the tough, if not rowdy, Hill Town fighters, all of whom conducted themselves with admirable good manners, was a comfort to the Janhaven people as well as the Barleyfolk. They took comfort from one another, wherever they were from, and there was rarely any serious strife or discord between them. The overriding fact that invaders were in the land, and more were coming, served to push them past slight misunderstandings and to resolve the difficult issues that weighed upon their survival.

But, if you asked any of them who their real leader was, they would be sure to say it was Mirabella Ribbon. It was she who took on the role of their united leader, who filled the void of military discipline left by her nephew, the Kingsman, and who seemed to be every place where leadership, example, or help was needed. She was as likely to be found standing a night watch over the roadblock at the Narrows as she was hefting a newly forged sword at the blacksmith's, to judge its metal and his skill. Or one might find her meeting with the scouts she had organized, discussing the news they brought back from their sorties, news of any Redvest movements in Barley, their activities in Passdale, their numbers and their watchposts. On Anerath, she rode hither and yon, meeting, gathering herbs for Frizella's infirmary, rushing to give her instructions to the reformed militia, or to train their new recruits. And, every once in a while, someone might come upon her on the road sitting as still as a statue in her saddle, or standing alone before a fire, or sitting in the corner of the infirmary or some meeting room, completely silent, her head tilted, her eyes down in deep meditation.

It was another week after the courier's news, and only after much debate both in Hill Town and in Janhaven, that their decisions were made. So, on the very same day that Ullin spotted the Dragonkind out on the plains—the same day that Robby fell into the hidden well—Captain Makeig, Mr. Furaman, and Mirabella set out for Tallinvale. They rode swiftly, stopping for neither rest nor water, until they came to the village of Bluepine, where they were amazed by what they saw. All of the cottages and buildings had been knocked down, and wagons were being loaded with as much of the building materials as the people could strap on. Here and there, fires burned the things they could not move or were deemed unsalvageable, and the air was thick with smoke. Slowing to a somber gait, they spotted Mr. Deedle, sitting in a chair in front of the pile of rubble that was once his tavern, his apron stained with dust and soil. But he smiled happily and got up to greet them.

"Welcome, noble travelers!" he cried cheerfully and bowed. "How's Miss, er, Lady Mira this fine day? Hullo, Captain, Mr. Furaman!"

"Mr. Deedle!" Mirabella dismounted and gave the old man a hug. "How sweet of you to remember me! But, oh my, your lovely tavern! All of your houses!"

"Ah, well. But we'll get 'em back, I daresay! An' better 'an before, too, I'll warrant! Once these troubles are passed by, that is. Lord Tallin's as good as his word, as all well know, an' his word's better 'an gold. Yep. I reckon we'll be finished with all this takin' apart by this time tomorrow, leavin' nuthin' but ashes an' stone for them Redvests comin' this way. It grieves me that I've not a drop to offer ye! All me stock—lock, kettle, an' keg—rolled away this mornin' to Tallin Town. Which is whar yer all headin', I reckon?"

"That is so."

"Well, then. Mebbe we'll get to raise a pint in them parts after awhile?"

"We only go on brief business, then back to our own people."

"So ye ain't 'vacuatin' those parts?"

"No. We mean to stay out the winter."

"O-o-o! I hope that's not folly, what with them Redvests already in Barley, an' more comin'."

"That is also our hope. But we must move on. Best of luck to you, Mr. Deedle, and to your family!"

"Aye, thank ye, Miss. An' to yer own!"

The trio rode on, guiding their mounts off the roadway many times to make room for the wagons and carts going full and returning empty from the south. It was gloomy traffic, too, and most of those they passed by were clearly worried, anxious, and tired. As the byways and paths of the countryside converged onto the road, the riders from Janhaven more often had to make way for the crowds until, by the time they reached the last hill overlooking the valley, the road was completely clogged with carts and wagons and great numbers of people carrying bundles and baskets and bags filled with their belongings. Here, they encountered the first soldiers of Tallinvale, smartly dressed in their green and gold tunics and surcoats, making an attempt to redirect some of the carts to the western side road to enter that way into the city. By the use of colored flags on long poles, they signaled down to other soldiers who manned the canal bridges and, by likewise signals from them, to the city gates. By these signals, they managed things so that traffic flowed first toward the city, then, after a pause, flowed the other way, the carts and wagons of the outward flow emptied so they could return for more burdens.

"Ye sure them Redvests ain't comin' today?" Mirabella heard one wagoneer say to another.

"It'd be a fine mess if they did, eh?" was the reply.

After a short wait, Mirabella led her companions along the banks of the road to get around the jam until they could pick their way down hill to the next checkpoint. She conferred with the sentries until the all clear came from farther along, and they rode quickly to catch up with the last of the train now entering the city through the North Gate. There, they saw Weylan directing soldiers at the gate, all heavily armed. He waved the travelers through the portcullis in a very serious fashion, having recognized Mirabella, but not having the time to make a proper greeting.

Mirabella had never seen the city so crowded or so filled with activity. On the parade grounds just inside, war preparations were under way. Large trebuchets were being built, thick timbers were leaned into place against walls of nearby buildings to shield against arrows and missiles, stones and other projectiles were neatly stacked, and baskets bristling with new arrows were being distributed. Seeing an officer talking with a group of soldiers, all looking at a large unrolled parchment, Mirabella dismounted and led her companions to the group.

"No," the officer was saying to the other soldiers, pointing at a building some few yards away. "It is too close. Those shops will have to be pulled down, or else we won't have room to shoot. I know it's a shame, but there's nothing for it. Do you want a trebuchet that we can't even use? We can't put it closer to the ramparts or we'll only be able to turn it slightly to the left and right."

Nearby was the almost completed structure of a large trebuchet, and, as Mirabella approached the officer, she saw that they were studying a chart depicting this portion of the fortifications and outer fields, with lines of trajectory shown fanning out from the place where the war machine was being assembled.

"So get that wall down! Training is to begin in the morning, and we'll work all night if we must. We still have to complete Battery Eight and Twelve, too!"

"Excuse me," Mirabella interrupted him as he rolled up the plan. "Is Lord Tallin about? Do you know where we may find him?"

The officer glanced at her, saying, "Most anywhere, I imagine. I've only seen him fifty times in fifty different places today. Oh, pardon me! Lady Mirabella! Please forgive my curt answer!"

"That's all right, Hemmings. We are all a little pressed these days."

"Yes, so we are. The Redvests will be on the move any day, now, and we have much to do in way of preparing a reception. Your father, I imagine, is busiest of all. He could be anywhere, or could appear here at any moment. No! No, no! Not that way, you fool!" Hemmings suddenly broke away, pointing and shouting. "You've got it backwards, unless you mean for us to bombard our own people! Turn it the other way 'round! My apologies, Lady Mirabella. They mean well, but half our countryfolk don't know a hilt from a halberd. I reckon they'll be learning soon enough. Maybe! I think you might find your father at the East Armoury. It's the next closest command post, and they'll have runners there that should know where he is. Please excuse me. Look! Look! Lower it back down! All the way, so we can turn it the other way, don't you see?"

The exasperated Hemmings strode off, pointing and cursing at his workers. Mirabella turned and motioned for her companions to follow her.

"This way."

"I'd forgotten how big the city was," said Furaman to Makeig.

"Don't look big enough, if ye ask me," Makeig replied as they tried to make their way along, for it seemed there was not an inch of peace anywhere within the walls, nor was there much in the way of space for it.

"Where they'll put all these people an' livestock, I'll never guess!" continued Makeig over the noise as they pushed their way through the throngs. There was no longer any direction of flow, and every lane and plaza was choked with people and animals, carts and wagons, and squads of soldiers, all pushing and easing their own way. Yet everyone seemed to know where they were going, or, as groups consulted with each other amid stream, they soon learned as a result of shouting and pointing and other gestures. Makeig and Furaman, eager to keep up with Mirabella, were thankful for her red hair and tall stature, but their horses were not so calm as hers and they constantly needed soothing and coaxing. At last they reached the eastern side of the city and the crowds thinned, somewhat, before a guarded barricade blocked their way.

"No admittance. You must go around," said one of the sentries.

"We were told we might find Lord Tallin at the East Armoury," Mirabella told them as she dismounted, then added, "I am his daughter."

The two sentries eyed her and her companions and exchanged a look of uncertainty.

"She is who she says she is," came a voice from just behind her. It was Dargul, and, after he bowed to her, she gave him a hug.

"It has been too many years," he said.

"Yes. It has. I am sorry."

"You are not entirely to blame for your long absence," he said. "As we all know. Besides, you have your own family and your own life apart from this place and its shadows."

"Actually, I used to rather enjoy its shadows."

"Did you? Hm. Did you know that I recently had the pleasure of meeting your son? A fine young man, indeed. Pray, tell me: have you had word of your husband?"

"No. I only hope that he is safe. At best, he is still far from Glareth. Yes. I know of my son's visit."

"And what of the other people of Barley? How do they fare?"

"Well enough, considering."

Dargul waved aside the sentries and gestured for Mirabella and her companions to follow, leading them out of the lane and into another parade ground where workmen were putting the finishing touches on two more trebuchets.

"I expect you know Mr. Furaman?"

"Oh, yes," Dargul shook the trader's hand. "We go way back. How have you been?"

"Good, good. Considerin' all, better than most, I expect. And you?"

"Fine. Just fine."

"And this is Martin Makeig, of Hill Town."

"Ah, Captain Makeig! A pleasure to make your acquaintance, sir."

"Likewise, sir. Likewise. Ye know me rank?"

"Of course. Your exploits are well known to many here in the city. You are quite a bother to the Damar, which is much appreciated, I must say. I hope you come to enlist with us against those who deposed your Ruling Prince?"

"Ah, well, sir. That remains to be determined, somewhat, after a bit of parley with yer Lord Tallin."

Dargul stopped a short distance from the nearest trebuchet where several shirtless men on ladders were grappling with an iron pin while another, perched on a crossmember, pounded away at it with a large hammer, driving it through a bore on the war machine's frame. Dargul gave Mirabella a concerned look.

"I see," he said, looking from Makeig to Furaman, then back to Mirabella. "So you do not bring your people here?" He had to fairly shout over the ringing hammer and the din of other work surrounding them.

"No. We've come to discuss our plans with Father. If he'll see us."

Dargul nodded, absently looking at the workmen as he took off his hat and scratched his head. "Oh, he'll be thrilled to see you. Indeed, I believe he already has seen you."

Mirabella followed Dargul's gaze up toward the workman with the hammer who handed it off to another man, then scrambled down, his long white hair flying as he jogged over to them.

"Father?"

"Mira! Mira! You've come at last!"

Father and daughter met in a long embrace then released each other with Tallin holding his daughter's hands, squeezing them gently.

"I am so sorry, my dear," Tallin said. "So sorry. Can you ever forgive me for being such a fool?"

In a way that a thousand stories could not explain, they looked at one another, still clutching hands in silence, and let their eyes tell everything that needed telling, and much besides. In that moment, all the pain and hurt that had been between them for so long vanished and became meaningless. Lord Tallin saw much else, too, in his memory's blast of visions, his wife's face, his eldest son's smile, his youngest son's fierce determination, and his own daughter's strength of love. And she, at the same time, saw and felt the unquenchable fire of her father's passions, his unbearable memories, the fortitude to withstand them, and his desire to be her protector and her comforter.

Of the two travel companions with her, Furaman knew something of the pair's estrangement. Through his many dealings over the years with Tallinvale and with Mirabella's husband, Furaman had picked up enough to understand this moment. Makeig knew much less, though he was not blind to the obvious relief of those around him. Dargul watched with a smile of pleasure and shook his head at this display, an aspect of tenderness he had never in all his years witnessed in Lord Tallin.

One of the other workmen brought Lord Tallin's blouse and tunic and he put them on as he spoke.

"Have you had word or news of your husband?"

"No, Father. It is too soon to hear, if all is well with his journey."

"Of course it is. I recently had the pleasure of becoming acquainted with your son. He is more than a fine young man."

"He is a credit to his father, my lord. And to his grandfather, if I may say so."

"More to you, most likely! Perhaps we'll have a chance to speak more of him later. Mr. Furaman, I believe?"

"Yes, Lord."

"And this can be none other than the famous Captain Martin Makeig."

"Aye, sir. Though infamous might be more to the way most folk think. As for any misdeeds, I must plead the exaggeration of tellers of tales."

"Come, come! Your exploits at sea, particularly at the battle of Grisland Strait, can hardly be an exaggeration."

"Ah, well, yer Lordship, that was a long time ago. An' we lost. I thought ye might be more mindful to me recent activities. Somewhat shady, one might say."

"Lost the battle? Nonsense. Your maneuvers, one ship against six, allowed Prince Lantos to escape. You ran two into rocks, set fire to three, and rammed the last! And you still managed to save many of your crew. As for the other activities, well, perhaps we all have certain unpleasant necessities and regrets."

"Aye, sir. But, if I may say so, sometimes a foul wind's better than the doldrums for gettin' ye back on course, so to speak."

Tallin nodded. "And there you have it. Well! Oh, daughter! How your face gives me hope!" He gave her another one-armed hug as he took his sword belt from another worker. "Dargul! A quick word on the valley?"

"Another day should see all of the material brought in that can be mustered. All is moving to your plan with few delays."

"Good. Very good. Mirabella, do you mean to bring in the people of Barley and Janhaven?"

"No, Father. That is what we've come to discuss with you."

"Oh. Do you understand the position they will be in if they remain where they are?"

"I believe so."

"I see. Will you yourself stay here?"

"No. We all must be on our way back as soon as we can. Before sunset, if at all possible."

"Lord Tallin," Furaman said, "we come to speak to you about our situation. To seek your counsel and, perhaps, obtain your aid."

"I see." Lord Tallin's look became grave. "Let us go into the armoury here and speak more privately. Just this way. Janston!"

"Yes, sir!" A young soldier came running up.

"See to these horses. Have them fed and watered and give them a break from their saddles. Trust Starmink to the task, and tell him I'll need my mount readied for later this day."

"Yes, Lord."

"This lad will take care of your horses," Tallin said to Mirabella. "And that's a particularly fine looking fellow, there!"

"His name is Anerath, a Duinnor race," Mirabella told him as she passed along her reins. "On loan from Ullin."

Tallin nodded as he took them to a guarded doorway into a low stone building. The sentries opened the doors for them and they strode inside, going down a flight of steps into a broad room.

"Will you have a chance to come up to the house, Mira?" Tallin asked as he led the way. "Windard and the others would be very happy to see you. And there is a little box of things that I've been meaning to send to you."

"No, Father. I would dearly love to see Windard, but we have little time. What little box do you mean?"

"Oh, just some trinkets, bits and pieces. They may be better off remaining where they are, though. This way, if you please, gentlemen."

It was just as busy and noisy inside as it was outside. A familiar place to Mirabella, the large front hall was full of orderly rows of racks and shelves and stands holding shields, armor, swords, and other weapons. In the back was a separate shop where the noise of ringing anvils and the whirring grizzle of blades against sharpening wheels merged with the stamp and stacking din of men bringing more arms to be stowed at the ready. Tallin led them to the side of the hall and into a small room. It was almost entirely taken up by a large table covered with a broad cloth map of Tallin Valley, showing the defenses of the city in detail, its walls, its canals, and the surrounding lands. It was also strewn with rolls of other maps and charts, a stack of blank paper and various bottles of ink, quills, dividers, and rulers.

To the side of the large map, in a special tray, were hundreds of small red tiles sorted and stacked, some with little wooden pennants stuck into them, and others with figures of war machines or shields painted onto them. A similar tray held like tiles, but of green hue.

"It's been a great while since I've looked upon a battle map," Makeig commented with interest. "I hope ye won't be needin' all them red tiles."

"My hope is that we will need more," Tallin stated bluntly. "Our aim is to draw off as much of the enemy's southern force as possible. To bring them here in great numbers, and to make them as miserable as we may, for as long as we can, and to cut them down so that their leaders must send more and more."

Tallin pulled a chart from a nearby case and unfurled it over the great map on the table. It showed the old Eastlands Realm and part of Glareth Realm, the Thunder Mountains and southward well beyond Tallinvale to the borders of Tracia.

"Already there have been sorties along the River Road here, south of Barley and along the valley, here, here, and here. To the west, the Damar are advancing, village by village, emptying them of men and boys for conscripts, creeping nearer to the western heights overlooking our valley. We watch, but do not interfere too much, to make all seem very easy. Their parties have numbered less than forty or so each; when they come in strength, our opposition will begin, to coax them to commit greater numbers. My guess is that the first skirmishes with the Damar may happen next week, perhaps a little before. As for the Redvests, we intend to make our first stand here, along this line of terraces, about twenty miles south of here. But our intention there is to engage the frontal forces and cause them to commit heavier forces to make flanking actions to our east. At that time, or fairly soon after, I expect the enemy to swing around to the north, between the city and the far high hills. Hill Town and Janhaven will then be cut off from us. Passdale and Barley, now occupied, may receive further attention, perhaps replacements. Since we intend to make them lay siege, they would almost certainly make forays toward Janhaven."

Tallin looked at them seriously, "Your supplies will be a plum for their picking."

He watched the three nod, then added, "The Damar will likely push through from the west, as well. There will be little Tallinvale can do to stop them."

"All of what you tell us," Furaman answered, "is just how we figured. And, we admit, it's a precarious thing. Miss Mira, er, Lady Mirabella has a plan, along with the Captain, here."

Tallin lifted an eyebrow. "As I should have guessed."

"But we will need help, if we are to carry it out proper-like," Makeig said.

"We have enough fighters," explained Mirabella, "but not enough arms. Our blacksmiths are working day and night, and so are our woodworkers. We need more and better than they can make, and sooner. Bows, long and short, mostly short, and arrows. Swords and fighting knives, too. Plus cloth and leather."

Tallin crossed his arms and put his chin down. Mirabella could tell that he was already making calculations.

"And your plan?"

"We mean to take back Barley. Or at least make an attempt to free as many of our people as we can."

Tallin looked up with mild surprise that seemed exaggerated on a face that was rarely astonished. He held his hand up for her to pause as he went to the door where Commander Brennig was standing with a few papers in his hand. As he and Tallin had private nods and words, the commander eyed Mirabella and her companions. She recognized him, though he was only a teenager the last time she had seen him. He was now tall, strong, in his late thirties, worn by years of responsibility, his shoulder-length brown hair streaked with gray. Though he listened to Lord Tallin, he was looking at her. Something in his long glance, steady and fadeless blue—or perhaps it was only the memory it ignited—gave her heart an uncontrolled flutter, and she knew that her father was not the only man in Tallinvale who wished she had never left. She turned quickly to study the map and to hide her blush.

"Pardon the interruption," Tallin said as he came back in, closing the door. "Take back Barley, you said?"

"Aye, sir," confirmed Makeig.

"And if you succeed, do you think you can hold it? When the siege is laid against this city, the Redvests, backed by the Damar, will hardly tolerate a strike so near to their main body. Perhaps you do not understand that my aim is to draw as large a force from the south as possible. It is the only way to buy our Realms time. A larger war, the likes the earth has never seen, is in the making, and it appears that Tracia gathers all her strength for an assault on the west in the spring. I mean to weaken that assault, since I cannot hope to stop it. I expect them to send at least twenty-five thousand Redvests against me, but I'm hoping for five times that number. They could easily spare a few thousand to send to

Barley. And when they get cold and hungry, they will look to Janhaven for its stores."

"If they come in force," Furaman shrugged, "there's not much we can do, anyway."

"But we hold the passes on the roads north of here, an' along the west of the middle ridge," said Makeig. "As well as the pass on the road from Janhaven to Passdale. They're bein' strengthened every day. An' there's no room for a great army to maneuver in them hills. Between stone an' tree, we'd cut them to pieces long afore they got within ten miles of Janhaven."

"So the only way for them to come," took up Mirabella, "is by way of the old road along the Bentwide, or the long way around, through Boskland or farther, up past Tulith Attis, and at us from the east and north. Either way, we know the land, and we think we can hold them back. At least for a time."

"For a time," Lord Tallin repeated, giving her a nod. From the way he looked at her, she saw that he knew about Robby's quest. "That is the nub of it, isn't it? Time."

While Tallin and Mirabella held each other's gaze, Furaman speculated aloud how Glareth might respond to the invasion news. Mirabella saw that her father held his hands together and, in a manner that seemed not worth noticing to the others, she saw that he tapped with his left index finger a ring on his right middle finger. It was a Ring of Valor, awarded only to those Kingsmen who showed extraordinary bravery in battle, and given by the King himself. She remembered, as a small girl, finding it buried in her father's dressing bureau and her mother explaining to her what it was and the honor of owning such a ring. Her father came in unexpectedly, and she asked why he did not wear it.

"I'll wear it again when there's a king worthy of wearing it for!" he answered flatly. Now, so many years later, he tapped it to get her attention, to spark that memory. And he acknowledged it with a slight nod and a mischievous narrowing of the eyes. Mirabella took his meaning and smiled, looking away.

"…and we think some relief may arrive from Glareth, maybe before Midwinter," Furaman concluded.

"Perhaps," said Tallin. "Let us hope so. I, too, sent word to Glareth, but the long way around. Hopefully, my son-in-law will arrive first and Glareth will be fairly stirred up with his news by the time my agents arrive with my own report. Tell me, Makeig, how do your people stand?"

"Lord Tallin, though we be mostly Tracians ourselves, I figured ye'd already be clear on where we stand. I'll lay it out, plain as I can, to be open about it. True, me folk are almost all Tracians, displaced by the enemy of the rightful throne. For years, even afore I came along to the hills, they struggled to make a new home. An' for years, the Redvests have sent their assassins an' their spies an' their troublemakers against us. There're many among us who still long to return to their land an' kin, to their callin's, professions an' former livelihoods. An' many have scores an' accounts to settle. Others call Hill Town home, an' have no desire for any other, particularly in a country that so abused 'em an' ran 'em out. Even they hold grudges an' would spitefully defend their present home against all comers. We know we may be fightin' against our own kin an' kith, an' so all this business may indeed be grim an' sad. But ye'll find none but stalwart hearts an' able hands amongst us, sir."

"Hm," Tallin pursed his lips. "I am glad to hear so. Perhaps it would interest you to know that three days ago two agents of Tracia were captured not far from here and are now guests of my dungeon. They freely admitted they were envoys sent to parley with Hill Town, to come to some accord and arrangement with your people, just as, they said, they were in accord with the people of Tallinvale, by treaty. I took the liberty of removing from them all of their papers and belongings, accused them of being spies, and put much fear into them for their lives while they await their fate. They carried deeds and seals, guaranteeing the return of lands in Tracia, settlements of damage, reinstatements of titles, and, for many of you, generous commissions as officers of their armies and navies."

"Ye don't say!" Makeig was clearly flabbergasted. "Well, ain't that rich! Their gall's as boundless as their treachery!"

"You, in particular," Tallin went on, "are to be offered, in addition to the return of your estates and a prince's ransom in silver, a squadron of ships to be placed under your command."

"Why, I, I...!" Makeig, red-faced, was stunned by this news, but then laughed. "Ha! Ye gotta hand it to 'em. They know just where to stick at a man's longin'. Sure, I'd give me right eye to feel a swellin' deck under me feet once more. But I'd never collect on such a fool's bargain. They'd put me head on the topmast quicker than spit! An' all me men'd be hanged on the yardarms side by side, too."

"No doubt you are right," Tallin gave a wry smile. "And I am sure that the envoys they sent sincerely believe they are honest brokers of a legitimate offer."

"What're they tryin' to pull, is what I'm wonderin'," said Makeig, putting a thumb under his belt while scratching his ear.

"They are mere agents. But those who sent them want to test you and your people, perhaps gaining by bribery some additional security in a soon-to-be hostile land. And it is easier to send two men with lies than two thousand with steel."

"They prepare the way," Mirabella put in. "They want you to guard their northern flanks when they move against Tallinvale."

"That's the gist of it," Tallin agreed. "According to their papers, the envoys would require you to remain where you are for a period of one year, putting yourself at the disposal and under the direction of Redvest generals until released to return to Tracia to claim your rewards."

"Ha!" cried Makeig.

"I think you should release them, Father," said Mirabella. Everyone looked at her in surprise.

"What do you mean?" blurted Furaman. Makeig stared at her, squinting with suspicion.

• • •

While they discussed Mirabella's idea and made plans, they could hear the continuous din of work in the armoury shops and workrooms all around their chamber. Once there came a tap on the door and Dargul entered quietly, placed a small scroll of paper on the table, nodded to Tallin and said, "The report from Six Company." He retreated back through the door. Mirabella caught a glimpse of him, just before he closed the door behind him, as he waved a hand to stop others from entering.

"So," Tallin summed up, "the weapons you need will depart tonight, regardless. If we can find the cloth you need, it will come, too. If we must dye some up, it may take a few days to reach you. The men bringing the weapons will report on that and anything else that may arise. I would feel better, however, if each of you took as many bows and full quivers as you can manage."

He stepped to the door and opened it to a half-dozen expectant faces, all men and soldiers waiting to report or deliver messages or to ask for orders. He looked past them and shouted, "Belstag!" and gestured to summon someone. A moment later, a burly leather-aproned man approached, taking off a pair of gloves.

"Yes, Lord Tallin?"

"In here, if you please. I'll be with the rest of you shortly."

Tallin closed the door behind Belstag, saying, "This is the East Armormaster, and none knows his trade better. Belstag, we must give up a good supply of arms."

"Sir?"

"I know. What do you need to make up the difference in five hundred long-shaft arrows, two thousand short-shaft, fifty longbows and a hundred and fifty combat bows? Plus a hundred and fifty yeoman's swords with scabbards and belts?"

"Sir? Let me see…two thousand…five hundred…um…. I think we'd be fine on the bows and arrows. But, my lord, that's a week's worth of swords, with every man slingin' and poundin' iron! Another week or ten days for—"

"We can recruit more men."

"Well, we're fairly trippin' over each other as it is. No. What we need is to get old Furnace Number Three fired up, more wood and coke, and more good iron."

While Belstag spoke, scratching his gray-stubbled face, Tallin hurriedly wrote and pressed an ink seal on to various slips of parchment.

"Very well. Take this for the shipment orders, and have it made ready and loaded to move by nightfall. Here, take this one, too. It is your order to requisition what you need to run Number Three, and here, give this one to your captain, Kellins, isn't it? He'll obtain what you need."

"As you wish, sir." Belstag took the papers and frowned at the visitors.

"Right away, Belstag. Don't lose a moment!"

"Yes, Lord Tallin!"

"And send Dargul back this way if you see him!"

The door shut again and Tallin turned back to the group.

"Surely I try the patience of my people as never before!" he said to them, picking up the report that Dargul had left earlier and taking a moment to unroll and glance at it. "But soon we will all be tried of more than mere patience." He tapped the note with the back of his free hand. "Nine thousand footmen and three thousand heavy infantry crossed the River Lerse to the southeast day before yesterday. Ahead of them ride five hundred horsemen."

Tallin pointed to a place at the bottom of the map. "I expect part of each of these forces will turn inward, seeking to cut off and secure our southern line of keeps and outposts. But they will find them abandoned. The enemy will then resume their march northward into our valley, but meet little resistance, save for harassing strikes, until they reach these dales, along here. That is where we prepare to do them fair damage in quick assaults. After that, we will offer little resistance until they come before our walls. So," he looked at the group, "unless they make a mistake, at the latest, they will be here in three days."

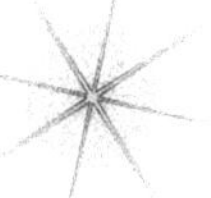

Chapter 5

Aremon and Seleesa

The forbidden land of Nasakeeria, somewhat in the shape of an oval, was about 200 miles wide from east to west, and 100 miles from north to south. If the bones that surround its border are not enough to turn back lost and hapless travelers, its entire circumference is also marked by stone pillars placed roughly every 500 yards. Each pillar stands some eight feet high and is topped with a carving in the likeness of a human skull, and upon each pillar is inscribed a warning which forbids any to go beyond that point. The making and placement of these markers, over 3,500 in all, was a great undertaking, ordered by the Sixth Unknown King in the Year 493 of the Second Age. Duinnor workers began the task of installing the markers to the west of Nasakeeria, progressing slowly north and eastward around the rim of that land. Had they chosen to go around the southern side first, it is likely their work would have warned off the Dragonkind armies that swept northward in the Year 506. Luckily for Duinnor, the Dragonkind ignored the encircling piles of bones and marched on into Nasakeeria, just as Duinnor's own army did nearly two centuries earlier, and they met with the same fate.

Often interrupted, sometimes for many years, the great project of erecting the warning markers was completed nearly sixty years after it had begun. Even before its completion, Duinnor regularly sent Kingsmen, often while on training maneuvers with their young recruits, to reconnoiter the entire circumference of Nasakeeria, to inspect the many warning pillars, and to make reports about anything unusual or out of the ordinary they might see. So it was in the year 868 S.A., that the Kingsmen first saw towers rising up within Nasakeeria. With their spyglasses, the men of Duinnor studied the structures from afar, making sketches and estimating their heights. They were of stone and wood, and seemed to be no more than a hundred feet tall, but no builders or occupants were ever seen. As the years passed, more of these structures appeared. And it was apparent that the builders did their work at night, refusing to show themselves to any outsiders who watched. When these watchtowers went up, for that is what they were, Duinnor realized that Nasakeeria was not a place of evil spirits and ghosts, but the abode of people, of some kind or other, who knew how to build and how to watch. And, as time continued to pass, and as more Kingsmen studied the place, some reported that they saw brief flashes of light from those towers, similar to that which might be seen when the sun glints from the lens of a spyglass. The Kingsmen who watched were themselves being watched and studied.

• • •

So, on the day that Mirabella went to Tallinvale and saw her father for the first time in years, and on the very same day that Robby fell down the well dug by the Dragonkind soldiers, Prince Nightar of Nasakeeria stood watch upon one of those towers and gazed northwest across the border. Although the land was dusted with snow, it was a clear, bright day and made for easy watching. Seeing nothing more out of place than a herd of deer moving across the distant hills, Nightar put down his spyglass, a device of glass and metal that was thrown across the border many years before as an intruder was consumed by the Ring of Fire. It was collected long before Nightar was born, and handed down to Nightar by his father as an item of special power. Nightar carefully wrapped the precious device in a cloth and put it into his shoulder bag, wishing that there were more such things in his lands. And, as he climbed down from the tower, he also wished that he had more people to man each of the sixty towers around Nasakeeria, so that all of the border could be watched all of the time. It had been difficult enough to build the watchtowers, and the effort taxed his people's labor and resources to the limit, taking many years to complete the few that now stood. Yet it was not enough, to his way of thinking, for there were wide gaps between them where towers had not yet been built.

The human occupants of Nasakeeria were few in number, and were growing fewer. They barely managed to maintain their society's ancient traditions, ways that went back in time to their long migration from their homeland over two thousand years earlier. Their numbers swelled from the original sixty thousand who settled Nasakeeria to nearly two hundred thousand but a few generations ago. Then came drought, famine, and plague. Many villages were abandoned, their chief town of Eldadoor fell into ruination, and unrest threatened to plummet Nasakeeria into chaos. But for the wise and stern leadership of Prince Nightar's great-grandfather, all might have been lost. Only within the past few years of Nightar's own reign did things begin to improve. His people were hardworking and resourceful, and, as a result of their cooperation and determination, their farms produced food that, if not abundant, was more than adequate. His people were living longer, and their children were healthy. Still, the years of hardship and strife served as a stern reminder that his people would not soon forget: these were not their lands. The fact of their long presence here was rooted in ancient history. Moreover, the bordering Ring of Fire which mysteriously sprang up from the ground and devoured the flesh of all who walked on two legs not only protected his people but also trapped them within its borders. Aperion's ancient gift to their ancestors who fled the Dragonlands was also their prison. But for a few gifted ones, like the old Traveshia and her young pupil, Seleesa, none could pass out from Nasakeeria unless they suffered the same fate as those who tried to enter.

Nightar's people yearned to be free. Each generation dreamed of returning to the desert city that their ancestors had abandoned during the time of Kalzar, whom they called The Despised. Each generation heard and repeated the tales of their beautiful city with its clean fresh water that coursed up from a lake in the middle of the city and flowed out from it to feed the surrounding fields and vineyards. At every celebration and ceremony, they repeated the tale of their departure and the long trek northward to flee Kalzar's despotism. And, at every burial, and on other somber occasions, they offered not only prayers of thanks for their deliverance from Kalzar, but also of the promised hope of someday returning to those lands and to their abandoned city.

As Prince Nightar took up the reins of his horse and led the animal away from the tower, all these things weighed, as they ever did, upon his mind.

"Let thy mercy be upon my heart," he recited an ancient prayer to himself, "and thy solace rest upon my soul. Oh, Beras, give me the strength of thy wisdom, and let the light of it be my guide for my people's sake. I pray that the day of our returning be at hand, and if the day of our returning is beyond the days of my life, let it be according to thy will."

As he said the prayer, Nightar's mind was upon new worries. He touched his bowed forehead with his hand, then put it over his heart, just as a runner approached.

"Prince," said the runner, nearly out of breath, "Traveshia says that Seleesa has awakened."

"Ah! At last!" Nightar replied, springing up into his saddle. "Thanks be to Beras," he touched his head and his heart again, "and thank you, Shazarra, for bringing word!"

• • •

When Nightar came over the hill, he could see Aremon the Hunter pacing back and forth before the door of his cottage. Seeing him, Aremon trotted out to take the bridle.

"I am told she has awakened," the Prince said, jumping down from the saddle.

"Yes, Prince."

"And so she has truly survived her ordeal. Has she spoken of what, if anything, she has learned?"

"No, my lord. She remains weak from her long delirium, and is still in bed. I obeyed your command, and sent word to you right away. But, Prince, I beg your indulgence before we enter."

Aremon bowed low.

"What is it?"

"You know how the little owl left her, and that Seleesa has for these weeks been in a terrible condition, hovering between death and madness."

"Yes."

"And you know, my Prince, that I have refused to have her removed, begging that her teacher, the enchantress Traveshia, make her potions and her remedies here instead of removing Seleesa."

"I am very well aware of that," nodded Prince Nightar impatiently. "And I am aware of your attachment to the girl. What has this to do with the business at hand?"

"I only beg that care be taken not to press Seleesa overly much," Aremon said. "As I said, she is still very weak."

Nightar squinted. "She has said something, hasn't she?"

"No, my lord, I mean, yes. Not of what she has learned, though."

"Then what of?"

"She mumbles that she must depart from us."

"Oh?"

"Yes, my lord. We all know what that would mean. That she would have to assume the form of her totem animal."

"That is yet to be decided. Let me enter and hear her myself."

"Of course, Prince. Forgive me. This way, and please be welcome."

The Prince was amazed at how clean Aremon had made the place. When he first met with Seleesa, after the owl was brought here, the cottage was a wreck of pelts, hunting bows and arrows, cups, dishes, half-eaten meals, dirty clothing, and broken stools. Now all the stools had been mended, the cups and dishes were neatly stacked on a shelf, the clothes put away, the floor swept, and the pelts gone. The workbench, where Aremon made his hunting tools, still showed signs of activity, but of a very orderly nature. The window shutters were open, allowing ample sunlight in, and fresh air wafted gently through the one-room place. He noticed, too, to one side on the floor, a blanket where Aremon had apparently been sleeping. Against the opposite wall was a cot, and Seleesa was sitting up, sipping from a cup as they entered.

Aremon brought over a stool and placed it beside the cot and gestured to Prince Nightar to be seated.

"Prince." Seleesa bowed her head.

"Seleesa. I hope you do not mind this visit."

"Not at all, my lord. I am deeply sorry that you had to wait all this time to hear from me."

"We feared we might not hear from you at all," said the Prince with a smile. "Indeed, we nearly gave up, thinking your undertaking with the little owl was ultimately too much for you. Has Aremon told you how long you have been ill?"

"He told me that it has been nearly three weeks."

"Yes. Three weeks full of delirium," Nightar nodded. "Traveshia wanted to move you to her hut, but when she saw the destruction you wreaked upon Aremon's place during your delirium, and how it took his entire strength to restrain you, she thought better. She tried several potions and elixirs on you, but none seemed to help much. Although, given Traveshia's growing distraction, not to mention age, I wonder if she mixes her potions correctly."

"I understand your concern, Prince Nightar," Seleesa replied. "She does seem to grow more distracted with each passing year. I am thankful, nonetheless, for her attempts to help me."

"Well. Aremon has done wonders with this place, I must admit," Nightar said, looking around once more and nodding to Aremon, who appeared somewhat embarrassed. "But I must say that I had nearly given up hope that you would recover. I feared your ordeal would be the end of you."

"Yes, it nearly was. The visions of the Familiars are not intended for those they do not wish to share them with. I am afraid I became lost in the creature's visions and memories."

"But you have survived. And we are all gladdened that you are now recovering, praise be to Beras." Nightar glanced at Aremon as they all touched their foreheads and hearts. "Some perhaps even more than others."

"Aremon, as Traveshia told me, has been a fine nurse and caretaker, my lord." She smiled at Aremon. "I am very grateful for his devotion during my illness."

"As are we all. And do you feel well enough to say what, if anything, that you learned from the little bird?"

"Yes, I am happy to do so, my lord. But I would like to try again with the creature so that I may resolve a number of questions that I still have."

Nightar frowned, looking at Aremon. "Then you do not know…"

Seleesa looked at Aremon questioningly.

"I couldn't help it!" Aremon blurted out. "After you fell into your illness, I was angry at it. I took it immediately out to kill it."

"Aremon!" Seleesa was aghast. "You didn't!"

"Er, no, of course not! I, I mean, I—"

"Traveshia also wanted to try her charms with the animal, once you had succumbed to it," Prince Nightar broke in. "But it seems that our mighty hunter lost his nerve."

"My lord?" Seleesa looked back and forth from Aremon to the Prince.

"I had to!" Aremon stammered. "I was hexed by it, yes, that's it! The owl put a terrible hex on me!"

"Enough of your tales!" Nightar commanded, holding up his hand. Turning back to Seleesa, he gave her a look of exasperation. "He let the creature go."

"He what?"

"He released it to fly away."

Seleesa stared at Aremon, who shrugged, then she smiled, shaking her head.

"We will have words, Aremon," she said.

"Yes, my lady."

"We have already settled the matter," Nightar said, "although I have a feeling that the sting of your rebuke will be greater than that of his Prince."

Aremon started to protest, but Nightar's upheld hand once again silenced him. To Seleesa, he said, "Let us proceed. It was apparent that the owl sought to escape the black eagle. Do you think the little one realizes who we are?"

"I was very careful. No. I do not think she knows. Of course, she recognized us as Dragon People, but our kind she had never before seen. She will certainly relate that to her companion."

"So the owl did not learn where we are from?"

"I do not think so, my lord. I made every effort to be the cup to receive her visions, rather than to spill mine into hers. My Prince, I must cut to the quick of the matter. I believe she is in league with our Liberator."

The Prince looked at her blankly.

"What do you mean?"

"I mean to say that, through the owl's eyes, through the visions of her memories, I have seen the Hidden One who is prophesied to bring about our people's return to our homeland. I believe she has been in his company, that her business in Duinnor has to do with him, and that she was returning to him when she flew into our lands."

"Her companion? Our Liberator is a Melnari?"

"No, my lord. The Familiar's companion is not the one foretold, but one who is much in the concerns of her Melnari. I believe her Melnari and our Liberator are in league."

"Our Liberator. With a Familiar, then, and a Melnari."

"Yes. One she called Collandoth."

"Tell me why you think the owl has anything to do with the Liberator that was foretold to us?"

"First, there is the black eagle. It had no other coloring, and even its beak and talons were black. We have learned from Traveshia that such black eagles serve Secundur. It is as Traveshia has told us, and Balamine before her, that they roost in Duinnor, now. It is clear to me that the little owl came from Duinnor, and the black eagle was dispatched to stop her from reaching her destination. This tells us where her loyalties are, and also that Secundur keeps watch upon Duinnor and keeps servants there."

"Yes. Yes, that much seems apparent."

"I carefully coaxed her memories from her. Many, anyway. It was difficult, for she is a stubborn creature, petulant of character, and strong-willed. And there is much within her that does not pertain to us."

"What did her memories show you?"

"I saw a young boy, attacked by wolves. He was at first saved by soldiers who had been conjured into stone, those placed as guards within

Tulith Attis, the old fortress that the forebears of our Order have told us about. They were about to slay the boy when the owl's Melnari and a young girl rescued him from those soldiers. Now, in the company of the two who rescued him, and with three others, the boy travels west from those parts."

"If Heneil's stony guard have been aroused, then the Bell must have been rung. Could that have been what we heard some months ago, that shook the ground and made our metalwares jingle and our cymbals crash?"

"It must have been. I am convinced so."

"But why do you suppose that the Liberator and the Bellringer are the same person?"

"Because of the little owl's message. She went to one called Raynor, in Duinnor. He is also a Melnari. It was part of Balamine's tale that a Melnari called Raynor was an important person in Duinnor. The owl related to him the events at Tulith Attis. And she was instructed to say to Raynor, in her way, that the Hidden One goes to seek a place called Griferis."

The Prince stood and went to the window to gaze out. Seleesa and Aremon looked at each other, then at the Prince.

"After all this time. Can it be true? That we may leave this accursed place and return to our ancient home, that the waters of our homeland will be restored, and those lands will be made fertile once again?" Prince Nightar turned back and faced them. "To Griferis he goes?"

"Yes, my lord. But what is this place, Griferis?" Seleesa asked.

"It is a place of reckoning," Nightar said. He glanced over his shoulder at Aremon. "There are many things that are kept secret from those not of our Order, Seleesa."

"Perhaps I should leave you two alone," said Aremon, bowing and going to the door.

"Stay," said Nightar. "As head of the Order, it is I who decides what is told and what is not told when our members return to us. Unless any are cast into our lands by Aperion's Fire, no books or scrolls may be brought to us from the outside world. So only by sending forth a member of the Order may we learn the happenings outside our lands. Neither of you are old enough to remember Traveshia's last Returning. But everyone knows Traveshia must relate what she has learned to all, just as previous members of the Order have done. What neither of you know is that a member of our Order, upon returning to us from the outside world, must first relate all she has seen and learned to the Head of the Order and to his scribe in private. It was decided by my ancient forebears not to reveal any knowledge of Griferis to others except that they be the Ruling Head of the Order or one sent forth into the world. When my father died, and I became Prince, I read all of the scrolls, all of the things as told in secret to my forebears. The scrolls say that the old King of Vanara, Parthais, greatly feared Griferis, and so he made a pact with Secundur, giving to him lands all about Griferis so that no one would dare go there. Those are the lands now called Shatuum."

"What did he have to fear of the place?"

"It is said that anyone who enters Griferis and survives its torments will be fit to rule," Nightar explained. "Parthais feared that his throne would be taken from him. If the Hidden One, our Liberator, has now come into the world, and goes to Griferis, it means that he aims to become a ruler."

Seleesa nodded. "I learned more, and I can only conclude that others also know of his quest. A great war is in the making. Men of the East, in a land called Tracia, are now joined with the king of the desert lands, who claims to be a descendant of Kalzar the Despised. They aim to join together in conquest of their neighbors. The land from which the Liberator comes has already been taken, but he escaped capture. The owl took these tidings with her to the Melnari of Duinnor, to the one called Raynor."

"If this is true, and Kalzar's blood rises against the Liberator, well, then his enemies are our enemies. And whether the enemy knows or does not know of his quest," the Prince suggested, "war can only threaten to stop him. Surely the accursed Secundur must have a hand in bringing this to pass. Tell me, does the Liberator know that Shatuum surrounds Griferis?"

"I have no way of telling what he knows. But if that is known outside our lands, then surely the Liberator must also know."

"Then, if the black eagles watch, Secundur must know that he comes."

"But the message to Raynor was that they go to Duinnor."

"A ploy. Or perhaps there was more to the message than you have conjured."

"Prince," Aremon spoke at last, "if the Liberator comes, and if the black eagles fly from Duinnor in search of him, would not that mean that the Unknown King of Duinnor also knows something of all this? And that he and Shatuum are in league?"

Prince Nightar and Seleesa looked at each other.

"It is possible," Seleesa said.

"And so it is possible that it is the throne of Duinnor, not that of Vanara, that the boy seeks. So," Aremon continued, "even if Secundur is reluctant to break out from Shatuum, why should Duinnor hesitate to send forth its might to stop the boy?"

"I can think of no reason why it would not."

"But that is where the owl went," Aremon went on. "So perhaps not all in Duinnor are arrayed against a New King. We have been cut off from the world. How may we divine this or that? It has been many years since Traveshia last took on the form of her totem and sojourned for news of the world. If the Liberator now strives to replace the King of Duinnor, and all are lined against him, what hope may he have?"

"Aremon makes my next argument for me, my lord," Seleesa stated, "though he does not intend to do so. Traveshia is too old, now, to go forth as she once did, and I have been put off too long by her. I should do what I am trained by Traveshia to do."

"You wish to leave Nasakeeria."

"Yes, lord. None but I may now leave."

"You forget, there is one other," Prince Nightar stated.

"Sire, you are needed here, surely," Seleesa replied. "And it is my duty, since I was ordained to go in quest of news, just as Traveshia has done, as Balamine did before her, and as one of each generation of our Order is chosen to do. I am the last pupil of the Order. No one else has endured the tests. If I am the only aid we may send, then should I not go?"

"What may you hope to accomplish?" Nightar asked. "Will you seek out the Hidden One in Griferis? Or would you go to Duinnor and learn how things stand in that place?"

"That is for you to decide, my lord," answered Seleesa. "Wherever I am sent, I will strive to learn what I may, and do whatever it is that may help our Liberator and our people."

"My lord!" Aremon protested. "Seleesa is still weak, and who knows if she would help or hinder? Seleesa should remain here, using her powers to help us be watchful as she regains her strength. Besides, aside from Traveshia, only you and she remain of the ancient Order, and only a female of the Order may restore the waters of our ancient home. If the day approaches when we are to leave in search of our ancient lands, and should something happen to Seleesa, our hope would be lost!"

Prince Nightar went to the door.

"It is two days before the full moon, and too soon for you to be ready or strong enough," he said to Seleesa. "So it will be another month, and after Midwinter's Day, before you may transform into your totem. Use these next few weeks to gain back your strength and to make yourself ready. Meanwhile, I shall decide upon your destination."

He stepped out, hesitated, and then called back to her, "You will be taking Aremon with you."

"My lord! No! It is too dangerous, he is not trained, and I haven't the power to transform another!"

"You forget, again, Seleesa," Nightar said, turning to face her through the door. "As your Prince, I am head of our Order and have the power to leave in the form of my totem. If what we have discussed is true, then our Order comes to an end anyway. I will, therefore, give up my place, and relinquish my totem to Aremon. I shall charge him with your protection. So you may as well strive to prepare him, too. Once you two are safely departed from here, I shall seek to prepare our people for our long trek. Prepare yourselves!"

"Yes, my lord."

"As you wish, Prince." Aremon smiled. He watched Prince Nightar mount his horse and ride away. Grinning, Aremon turned back to the frowning Seleesa.

"And you thought you'd have all the fun to yourself!" he said.

"Don't be a fool, Aremon!"

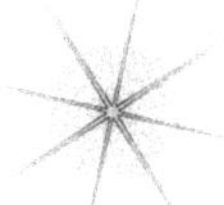

Chapter 6

Of Madness and Butterflies

"So, you have managed to find me," Micerea said to Robby, rising from her body on the pillow-laden bed and standing before him. Clothes flew through the air and placed themselves on her, straps tied and tightened themselves, armor layered on, shemagh wound, sword slipped into place, and cloak draped over her. In less than the twinkling of an eye, she became a fierce warrioress. Robby felt that perhaps he had erred. He stood up from where he had been sitting crosslegged for many hours, if hours had any meaning here, waiting for Micerea to dreamwalk. This was after he had followed her back to her small palace, attended her meal with her, and her bath, and her toilette prior to bedtime. All while dreamwalking, of course, and completely invisible to Micerea and all those who waited upon her. Robby learned much about the opulence of her existence, attended at every turn by servants and maids, her hands touching nothing but that it was handed to her, and every utensil she used, from brush to fork to mirror, all made of ivory or jade or gold or other precious material. He was amazed that he could actually smell the incense burning in the halls and the spice perfumes of her bath. There was, too, a sense of shame that he watched, followed, listened in on conversations, and only averted his eyes from her when the mesmerizing effect of all he saw was suddenly broken by his own realization of embarrassment. When the sun sank, it sank fast. But she was restless, and it was longer than Robby expected before she was asleep, and longer, still, before she emerged.

"It was actually fairly easy. I apologize for the intrusion," he said to her, attempting a bow. "Is it wrong that I sought you out? "

"No, not wrong. But dangerous. And I am surprised that you could do so. You learn very quickly. And I certainly did not mean for you to find me in such an impertinent way."

"Forgive me," he bowed again. "But I am new to this land, new to this way of dreamwalking. I saw the light and followed it, and it led me to this city. I saw you pass through the market, and I followed. I did not know for sure that it was you. And I must say, it is true what my people have said, that Dragonkind women are among the most beautiful in the world. You are remarkably different in appearance than the Dragonkind I have seen."

"There are more than one Dragon People. And if you mean to compare me to the servants or those you see in this city, then you are not only comparing one tribe to another, but also one of the Alziekfria to those who are not."

"Alziekfria?"

"Such are the ruling families called because they partake of darakal, a rare and expensive herb from which an elixir is made for the wealthy or favored of our people. Because of the elixir, we Alziekfria do not grow the scale-like skin, nor the thin silver hair. We do not lose our noses, our lips do not thin, and our tongues do not wither."

"Only certain families have this herb or elixir?"

"As I said, it is expensive. Also, it is given only at service-rites, as a part of our religion, once every month. Only those of us who are favored may partake in that rite and receive the boon of darakal. It is a way of ensuring that the ruling families remain the ruling families. And, of course, the rites are controlled by our King and his priests, and each family must pay a tribute to honor the Dragon-Gods in order to receive the boon."

"What happens when a family does not pay, or when someone no longer receives the elixir?"

"If it is because they oppose the King, they are soon eliminated. If they simply cannot afford the tribute, and no one will pay for them, then they wither and become like the Drago, what we call the ordinary people. Those who have that fate are often made outcasts, finding no place among the Alziekfria nor among the Drago. They often die because their bodies cannot endure the change and suffering that the sickness brings."

"A sickness from just living in the Dragonlands?"

"Yes. There have been many attempts to find the cause and the remedy. But many among us think that our rulers now prevent any further attempts to find a remedy so that they can use the herb to control their subjects and to retain their power."

"So the herb, or the elixir, is not a cure?" Robby asked. "I mean, the healing that it brings does not last?"

"The elixir is made from the herb. No. If one is already stricken, one portion of the elixir will begin to work within days. But within a few weeks the sickness returns. One portion is enough to strengthen one, but not to rid one of the scales or to thicken the hair. If one is healthy, though, and has taken the herb all one's life, only four portions are usually needed each year. Some tribes seem better off than others, and some think it is because of where they live. It is said that those who live in the Free City, Kajarahn, need darakal less than others do. Possession of the herb is strictly controlled, though there are ways to obtain it illegally. Those who are caught with the herb or its elixir, and who are not authorized to have it, are summarily executed."

"Alziekfria. Drago. Do the people much resent all this?"

"Some. Some very much. Some call my kind Worms, or Grubs, because of our fairer skins and lighter complexions make us appear more akin to the Northmen than others. But most Drago are too busy and concerned with their own lives. Life here is harsh. Most often, it is short. That is why the Drago have so many children, for they are the weakest among us and only one in three may live to have his own family. Look here."

Micerea motioned Robby to a window overlooking the city. They passed through it onto a high balcony, and she pointed to the east at a fire burning some miles away outside the city.

"That is this city's pyre. It burns only with the fuel of our dead. It is there that the bodies of the dead are taken, and placed into the flames. When a day passes that no one dies, it will extinguish itself. "

Robby stood and watched the far flames and the long lines of torches that moved toward it. It was hard for him to comprehend what he was seeing. The lines seemed to inch along, advancing upward back and forth along the side of a broad ridge, going up to where the great pyre burned.

As they looked, she took Robby to the place.

The procession was long, and no one could remember what year the line began nor could guess when it might end. Its length was a mile from end to end, and it was in constant motion. Newcomers steadily replenished its rear, as those that reached its end wandered away, having sadly delivered their burdens. It snaked back and forth upward along the sharp ridge to the Spirit Fires. Here, atop the ridge, the priests accepted the carefully swaddled burdens from the people as they came, and, with the practiced care of centuries of recitation, they spoke gentle words of comfort to the bereaved as they dolefully went away. The carefully wrapped bundles were placed reverently upon the pyres.

All along the rising path, from the base of the ridge to the top, stood acolytes, spaced many yards apart from each other, waving censers so that the scent of the incense wafted all around the pallbearers and mourners as they passed. The acolytes also spoke to the bereaved saying, in the language of those parts, "Grieve not for the end of suffering, nor for the light that shone," or "May peace be upon your heart and solace upon your brow," or "As the morning dew is sweet and vanishes before the rising sun, so is the life which is bestowed and which is taken back unto the Giver of All Life."

Robby and Micerea returned to the balcony, and she spoke more about the plight of her people.

"The wind ever blows from the west, carrying the smoke away from the city," she commented over his shoulder. "To the place of rebirth, it is said, where the sun rises each new day."

After looking for a while longer, Robby turned to her.

"But what of the soldiers? They do not appear weak."

"They are not, for the most part. Those with skills, such as warcraft, are usually rewarded with patronage by one of the great Houses, and given the darakal elixir once or even twice a year, always in a ceremony in honor of the King. Only the great Houses may afford it, for there are millions who seek it. When a great House falls, which happens every once in a while, its armies and craftspeople suffer. Still, many, many people do not take darakal at all. Those who are poor and without a sponsor, unattached to any great House. The armies swell with those, too, seeking to distinguish themselves so that they and their families may partake."

"And your rulers prevent your physicians from seeking a cure."

"Yes. It is considered acting against the wishes of Beras and the Dragon Fathers who made us."

"Beras? So you worship Beras, too?"

"Why not? Does he not oversee all, in this world and the next? Why does that surprise you?"

"I don't know. I just never thought of it, I guess. Where I come from we aren't very religious, I'm afraid. I mean, we just go about our lives and live the best we can, and we don't much delve into spiritual matters. But I know others of our lands do, especially some of the Faerekind, that is, the Elifaen."

"It is true that we are sworn to hold our King, Belsalza, in reverence, he being the voice of the Dragon Fathers of our race and their most direct descendant, through the Mighty Kalzar. But even he acknowledges that those dragons that brought us into being were in turn made by the children of Beras. And so Beras is an important figure in our religion. Overseeing, as I said, all things."

"There is so much I do not know. I'm glad that you tell me these things."

"It is my honor, if not duty, to do so. I hoped that you would be open to such learning, and that is why I have traveled here to this city and to this palace. I have been on my way to this place since we first spoke, before you found the ring. If you do not know, we are in the city of Sarapolis, and within this palace is one of the finest libraries in all the Dragonlands, vast in lore and knowledge. Sarapolis lies between Tyrsharat and Calamandor, the Green Citadel. It also rests on the caravan route southward from the Free City of Kajarahn. Many of the library's works come by way of the Free City, and many of the writings are in the Common Speech of the northern lands. Some are in the Ancient Tongue, not unlike the language that my people speak. I seek to arrange for one of my servants, a scribe, to read to me from these books as I sleep, during your dreamwalking visits with me here. He does not understand why I make the request, and he need not know. He is fluent in the language of the north and east. I thought that this may be a way for you to learn during your travels, while your body sleeps. It will be difficult and tiring. If you agree, I will complete the arrangements."

Robby shrugged. "Sounds like a wonderful idea to me. Are you sure it is safe? Won't someone suspect why you do it?"

"I think I will be safe." She smiled. "This palace is that of a friend of my father's who has three daughters of his own, whom I enjoy visiting from time to time. I am safe, here."

"Very well, then. When do we begin?"

"If you wish, tomorrow night."

"When I began to dream, it was well after dark," Robby said. "But when I arrived here, it was still daylight. Why is that?"

"The distance between us is great. It took me a long time to understand it. But I have consulted with wise men of my land, and I have looked at books. It seems that the world is large, and day and night are different in different places. They say that the sun and moon and stars tread a long path over the world and that when they have gone out of sight from one place, they come into view somewhere else. So when morning comes in the east, it is still night here. And when morning comes here, the day has been bright for many hours in the east."

"That could make it awkward for us to meet. I have no way to tell what each day or night may hold for me. But I will strive to attend as best as I can."

Micerea began to fade, and the structure of the palace became muddled and transparent.

"You begin to wake."

"So, how do I find my way back? I was only lucky this time."

"The same way as you found me before. You recognize me, now, by my dream aura. Everyone has a different one. It is how I find you, going from dreamer to dreamer, like stepping stones, following your aura. As you have discovered, distance has little meaning here, and the aura can be seen from wherever you look. You will see it again if you look for it. It will appear to you as a distant light. Those who do not have the ability to dreamwalk appear differently, more fuzzy."

"Yes, I have noticed that. But your dream aura—is that what you called it?—your aura does not waver."

"Nor does yours. It is how I realized you had the ability. It is what drew me away from Ullin to watch you instead."

• • •

Over the next days, as Robby's company continued their way westward, little changed in the landscape. The same rolling plain stretched and stretched, and one night's camp seemed very much like the one before. Robby quickly gained a reputation as a hard sleeper, difficult to wake. There was growing concern among his companions because he seemed plagued by strange fatigue. He yawned nearly all the time and grew less talkative than ever. By week's end, he had the look of someone who had not slept at all, even though Ullin made a point to stop early in the evenings and leave late in the mornings to allow as much sleep as he felt they could afford. Yet he clearly saw that Robby did sleep, and he seemed to sleep soundly. He saw also that Robby seemed to have retained his appetite, eating as much as the others, even as much as Ibin, whenever they could have a meal. But his clothes began to look loose upon him and his face drawn. Ullin worried that Robby was growing ill.

One evening just after sunset when the sky was still light, Sheila came to relieve Ullin from watch, and he asked, "I wonder if you have noticed whether Robby seems hotter than normal upon his skin or brow?"

"What care you if he is hot or cold?" Esildre suddenly shot back at him with a smile. "Surely he is only a boy, with the up-and-down heavings of a boy's heart."

Ullin, shocked at the assault, felt a shadow sweep across his brow. "Get away from me! You have no place here!"

"Pardon me?" Sheila looked at him in bewilderment, obviously hurt by his words. "Why do you say such things?"

"Why do you say the things that you do?"

"I was only trying to answer your question! Do you want me to take the watch or not?"

Ullin, embarrassed and ashamed, put up his hands as in surrender, shaking his head. "I am sorry. I am sorry! I am ill-humored, of late, and I misunderstood what you said."

"Ullin. What is wrong? Why do you treat me so coldly? What have I done to offend you? Please tell me. For the sake of our friendship."

She came close to him and reached out and put her hand on his arm, looking up into his face and earnestly searching in the dimming light. She felt him stiffen, and he closed his eyes.

"I cannot say what is in my heart. I am muddled. You have done nothing, I swear, to deserve my ill-treatment of you. Please, for your own sake, keep your guard around me. I fear many things. Too many things. I beg your pardon. Do not judge me too harshly, but be wary of me, I beg you."

He opened his eyes and saw her face close to his.

"You should not be caught up in all this," he said. "And yet your heart may be the strongest of all here. Perhaps it comes of your trials, this strength that you have. Your beauty, too."

"I do not feel strong around you, Ullin," she said. "And I do not feel beautiful. Except that you make me feel so. You no longer look upon me as a child. When I was a girl, and I combed my hair with the brush you gave me, and looked upon myself with the looking-glass you gave me, when I held the remains of the soap to my nose and breathed in its sweet spring smell, I thought of you."

"Do not say such things!"

"Sometimes I dreamed of you, longing for you to return and take me away. As I grew older and grew into womanhood, I did not put away those girlish dreams. I bathed away the soap you gave me long ago, but never the memory of the warm kindness of that gift. And though I knew nothing about you, not even your name, I secretly still hoped you would return. Sometimes I dreamed that we might be kin and that you might come back for me. Sometimes, I longed only for company with you, as only a man and a woman might have company. This was all before I met Robby. Mostly before. Do you think I came on this journey only for Robby's sake?"

Ullin looked at her without speaking. Now he was truly torn, yet his regained composure revealed nothing to her, only concern at her words.

"I am sorry," he finally managed to say. "You asked me the other day if I had ever been in love. Yes. I have been. And I still am. I have given myself to another, though she be far away. I doubt if she feels the same for me, if she ever did. Someday I would like to find out. Regardless, even though my heart is imperfect, it is the only one I have, and it is hers. I am sorry."

"There is nothing for you to be sorry about," Sheila answered. "Perhaps your coolness toward me is because you sense my feelings, and so you are rightly honorable in retreating from them. I would expect no less of you."

Better for her to think that, Ullin thought, than to have her know the truth of why she made him nervous and jumpy.

"Perhaps," he said. "Well. It is a quiet night. Thank you for taking the watch. I should get some sleep."

"Sleep well, then."

Ullin moved away, then stopped. Over his shoulder, he asked, "Could you say again your answer to my question?"

"I said, he is no cooler nor warmer than seems fitting."

Ullin nodded and walked away.

• • •

Warm or cool, Robby was not keeping company with his traveling companions during many hours of the night. He soon mastered, in his sleep, how to find Micerea's peculiar light, and by following it, he was able to find her. He also began to learn how to control other aspects of the experience, his attire, mainly. But, sometimes he failed to get it right, and he was rather embarrassed when, after meeting Micerea and talking excitedly to her for a long while, she finally managed to indicate to him that, although his boots and vest were perhaps the finest she had ever seen, he seemed to be lacking those articles of clothing worn between the two. She was kind about it, at least, and did not laugh at him that time. But she did fall into giggling hysterics the next night when he appeared with a broad, bushy beard.

Micerea had, indeed, made the arrangements as promised. In order to divert any suspicion that she could be involved in serious pursuits, she, with the help of her father, had developed all of the outward signs of decadence and frivolity. Years in the making, this front enabled her to be outside of suspicion, giving her the freedom of movement that her father did not have. And, now, she made use of it again, for Micerea was known among the servants and all her acquaintances as a spoiled, demanding, and rather shallow-minded girl, accustomed to having her own way.

So her directive that a scribe was to come and read to her whilst she slept, so that she could, as she put it, "learn without the tedium of study," was met with glad obedience, for who can gainsay the rich and powerful their fads and follies? Micerea knew, however, that the servants complained among themselves even though they were never surprised at whatever whim she might have. One day, while being attended by visiting female acquaintances from another high-placed family, she explained her nocturnal request.

"I heard that a wealthy wise man, one who lived near the city of Tollipi, was not always so wise," she told the gaggle of attentive girls. "But he was always wealthy. He paid scribes to come to him at night while he slept and read to him during those hours when he could not manage his business. In this manner, it is told, he learned all that there was to know and became wise, yes, and by his wisdom became wealthier still."

"I never heard of such a tale!" declared one young lady.

"Oh, yes. It is so," Micerea insisted. "He became so wise and so wealthy that the King himself feared his power. And so, one night while astrological books were being read to him, the King sent his assassins to do away with him."

"Well! He wasn't so wise after all, was he?"

"As it turns out, it is told that the wealthy and wise merchant was not killed. He had an overseer who had been secretly stealing from the caravans. The wise man discovered this, so, telling his overseer of his method of becoming wise and wealthy, he offered his own bed so that the overseer could see for himself. The assassins, who must answer to the King, of course claimed they had dispatched the correct man. But on the night of the murder, the wise merchant and all his wealth disappeared from the city, and no one knows to this very day where he went."

"Oh, what a tale! Wherever did you hear of such a thing?"

"It is a famous story. I'm surprised at you for not knowing it. Anyway, I'm thinking of trying it. In fact, I think I shall. This very night!"

"Whatever for? You are wealthy enough," a giggling companion said, then aside to another in a whisper, "and she'll never be wise!"

And so, to the surprise of none, Micerea set her wishes into motion that very night, making a great show of it, arranging for the scribe to be ready to come to her bed chambers. A place was made behind a veil, and the scribe was supplied with books and lamps and a chaperon, of course, and was commanded to read aloud while Micerea slumbered.

Her plan worked well as long as the books were read in the Common Speech of the Northern Lands. But when, after many sessions with Robby, she decided he should learn the Ancient Tongue, which the Dragon People spoke in various dialects, she made a new request of the scribe.

"To better my command of our own tongue," she explained, "you will place your finger under each word, reading very slowly, pointing to each word."

And the scribe did that, at least for an hour until, exasperated at the silliness of the whole thing, he rolled his eyes. Glancing at the chaperon, an old lady who had nodded off in her chair nearby, he closed the book abruptly and began nibbling on some dainties left for him. This infuriated Micerea, and she apologized to Robby for the interruption.

"I will correct this lapse before tomorrow night," she told him.

The next day, while Robby and his company traveled along the wide grassy plain, Micerea summoned the scribe.

"I expect all those in my service to follow my instructions," she told him. "And yet, when I awoke this morning, I did not feel complete. I believe that your readings are helping me, but I simply do not feel that last night was very good for me. Tell me, was there some disturbance that interrupted you? I asked my chambermaid, who was chaperon last night, but I think she may have dozed."

"My lady," the scribe answered, obviously agitated, "in truth, I grew weary. I am old and my stamina is not as it once was, and the darakal spice does not rejuvenate me as it did in my younger days. I beg your forgiveness, but last night I grew weary and weak so that I could not continue."

"Hm. I see. Well, I am not without a heart, but I insist that you adhere to our agreement or else I must find some other scribe to accept my generous silver. I put it to you this way. From now on, you must abide in the outer chambers after you complete your readings. When I awake, I shall pay you, or I shall have you taken away to be expelled from our service, depending on how pleased I am with the night's reading."

"Yes, my lady."

"I suggest that you see to it, then, that you are well rested before you arrive."

"Yes. I shall, my lady."

And that was how Micerea resolved the problem with the scribe, once and for all, and that was how, night by night, Robby's knowledge steadily increased. When he was awake, he and his company moved westward. And when he slept, Robby traveled south and became more sophisticated in his understanding of the world, the history of the Three Races, and the circumstances of his own time.

Before beginning each selection, the old Alziekfria scribe would explain something of what was known about the work, the author, or the age during which it was written. This he did extemporaneously, it seemed, as one who was accustomed to sharing knowledge and lore. Each night new tales were read or recited, sometimes they were quite fanciful and even touching, other times full of violent adventure, and sometimes so dry and boring they made Mr. Broadweed's sleepy lectures seem livelier than a carnival act. Yet Robby learned. Much that was read was written by Men or Elifaen. Robby wondered how such works came to be here, so far from the lands of their authors. Sometimes he recognized bits of stories or even a familiar passage of verse.

Robby felt no fatigue while listening, most of the time standing nearby to look over the scribe's shoulder. Sometimes he sat on the window ledge overlooking the city. Micerea remained close by to answer any questions that he had. And he had many. At first he was reluctant to speak, as if those awake in the room might see or hear him. But after a few nights, he grew accustomed to being invisible and soundless to them and spoke more freely and asked more questions. Sometimes his questions were about the people in the stories and sometimes about the places mentioned that he had never heard of. Micerea could not answer all of them, but often, on the next night or the night after, the reading would be arranged so that something was repeated from earlier, or some explanation came by way of the next scroll or volume, or the very question Robby had asked was expounded upon in a lecture by the old one.

At first, when the readings were in the tongue of the Dragonkind, Micerea translated as the old one read. But by week's end, Robby, to his own great surprise, easily understood most of what was said, and even found himself conversing with Micerea in her own tongue almost as naturally as his own native language.

"I wish he would continue a little longer," Robby said to her one night as the old one bowed to the sleeping lady and made to leave. "It was just getting interesting."

"His task is done for the night," Micerea stated. "But look at yon open book, on the stand, just there."

Her rooms were extravagant. Lit by marvelously blown glass lamps, there were multicolored tiles laid in floral patterns on the ceilings, and fine tapestries hung on the walls. There were porcelain basins of water on enameled stands, gold-crusted fans, and dressing cases of fine old woods. Her bed was as lavish as any he could imagine. There, her sleeping figure was peacefully relaxed among many silken sheets and finely embroidered pillows, her attractive form barely obscured by a tent of fine gauze that draped over her. Her dream-figure, though, was no less attractive. Gone were all her manly accoutrements, her weapons and armor, and her only attire was a thin, sheer robe over a simple, loose halter. She pointed again from the divan where she reclined and he moved over to look at the book. It was a large volume, opened to an illustration.

"I left it like that so that you could see it," she said.

It was a depiction of a desert scene, a broad expanse of sand fading away toward a low line of far-off mountains. In the foreground were two Dragonkind on horseback wearing sun-protecting robes and head gear. One of them pointed at an object some distance from them, a huge cube of stone, partially sunken in the sand at a sharp angle, its shadow long and black away from the setting sun, stretching back toward the two observers.

"It is a book of sights to see," Micerea explained. "It belongs to my father who, in his youth, traveled wide and far. He did the artwork and the writing and had it bound and copied."

"Your father painted this?"

"Yes."

"It is very nice. Very well done," Robby bent to look even closer at the detail, seeing how the robes of the men whipped in the wind, and how a little cloud of sand swept around the block of stone to pile up on the other side where a group of tiny figures stood gaping up at it. "If these proportions are right, it is a massive stone. How far is it from its quarry?"

"Less than twenty leagues. The mountain in the background is where it was cut. But it remains where my father saw it, abandoned nearly a hundred leagues from the city it was intended for."

"Hm. Are there any stories about how it was moved?"

"Yes. But they are not pleasant ones. Those stories are repeated to our youth and on many occasions. There was much suffering by our people because of it. Kalzar's obsession is never spoken of, but the task was beyond him. Beyond the ability of our people. Many died and were maimed when it was cut from the mountain. Even more in the moving of it. Countless numbers suffered under the whip, and the effort drained the land of food and resources. Many starved so that those workers could eat. Sickness brought many to death. And Kalzar's army turned on its own people to quell revolt. It has since become a kind of shrine to our sufferings and a reminder to us of our enemies."

They remained silent for a long while, Micerea sitting comfortably on her divan while Robby continued to look at the illustration. Her mood was more somber than usual, and her mind wandered to other things. She noticed Robby fingering the edge of the page.

"What are you doing?" she asked, smiling.

"What? Oh, I was trying to turn the page, I suppose."

She chuckled. "Keep trying, if you wish. But you'll never do it."

"The thing is, I can feel it. Feel the page. But it's like water. No. More like thick layers of air. I can feel, and I recognize the texture as paper, but…"

He concentrated his effort, but to no avail.

"I don't understand. Not any of this. How can I feel this, when my fingers are miles and miles away? How can I hear? How can I see when my eyes are closed in sleep?"

"We are like children." Micerea got up and came to Robby and put her hand on the book for a moment, then passed it through the book and through the stand that it rested on, and then she looked at her palm. "When you awake, do you understand how it is that your eyes see? And, in your mind, do you reside within your eyes? In darkness, or when you close your eyes, do you not still have other senses? And, though in darkness, do you not still see the image of things, people, even, though you are far away in leagues and in time? The faces of your friends and family? The fields and rivers of your home?"

"I suppose I do. In a way."

"I do not understand, either, how the world works. Or how we do what we do. Perhaps someone will someday discover the secrets of these things. Maybe, in the future, people will know all about them and not be as ignorant as we. How the eyes work. How it is that we can conjure up the faces of our friends, even when our eyes are closed. Some say these things are the craft of the gods, and that their work is beyond our ability to understand."

"Hm." Robby frowned. "I think that perhaps, indeed, some things are beyond our ability to understand, whether or not those things are the work of gods. But if we are like children, might not our abilities grow, over time, as do those of children? With practice and with instruction and with curiosity? So that what we don't understand today, we may come to understand tomorrow? Or maybe, as you say, our children may come to understand things that we do not."

"Yes. Perhaps."

"Well, I, for one, am feeling particularly childlike, these days. The more you show me, the more I dreamwalk, and the more I see and dream of the world, the more ignorant I feel!"

"I know how you feel. It is humbling, is it not? But I'm sure you would rather be doing other things, having brighter adventures. I would, too."

"Yes. And I'm sure you would rather not be taking all the chances that you do, holding my hand, so to speak."

"Soon, I think, you will be instructing me."

"Oh?"

"Yes. I saw from the very beginning that you dreamwalk with little or no effort. That is a mystery to me, for to do this, to be here, is very taxing upon me. It is as if I'm walking sideways all the time, or being pulled sideways."

"Well, yes. I sense that, too. But after a few dreamwalks, I hardly notice it at all, now."

"That's what I mean. You are so easy here. You even seem comfortable."

"Why, I am, in fact."

"I'm not sure that is a good thing. You may take chances that you should not. And you wear yourself out with fatigue. You need sleep, Robby," she said. "These nights have been good, but there is a price and your body shows the signs. You grow thin."

Robby looked at himself, patting his belly.

"That is not what I mean. I mean you grow dim. Soon, I'm afraid, you will be as pale as glass. It takes strength to be here, to do this, and strength to return. Such strength is taken from your waking time. It is not true sleep nor true dreaming while you are with me. Those are things we both still need."

Robby realized that Micerea was tired, too, and he decided not to argue. Soon he was back in his own slumbers, then another tiring day in the saddle. Truly, he was as Micerea warned, so tired and so lost in his own thoughts that he hardly noticed when the day was done. But many leagues more were behind him, and it was time once again to rejoin his tutor.

· · ·

"You are doing well with our speech," Micerea told Robby. "But you still have far to go."

Robby hovered horizontally over the shoulder of the reader as she spoke.

"I wish you wouldn't do that. Standing on your feet is no more tiring and far less disconcerting."

"Sorry," Robby shrugged, turning himself right-side-up and easing down to the floor.

"There is more to be learned than can ever be known by any one person," Micerea observed. "And I am a poor teacher. Naturally, I want you to understand my people, but you must also understand your own. However, we have so little time, and you need your strength."

"You are not a poor teacher," Robby said. "But I have so many questions. Not only about the world, but also about dreamwalking. For instance, why can I not travel wherever I wish to go? I long to see my mother and to know how my people fare. And to look for my father, if that is possible."

"You will gain that ability someday, I am sure. Not only is it difficult, but it is also dangerous."

"How? What do you mean, dangerous?"

"Difficult because, as far as I know, the way is lit only by dreams. The farther you travel from your body, the less your own dreamlight suffices, and the more you must depend on the dreams of others. At least, that is how it seems to me. It is like jumping from stone to stone, and if one gives way as you travel, you are pulled back to where you began. It is very frustrating. And it can be a fearful and troubling thing to see the dreams of others. It was very difficult for me to find you and to draw you forth into my dream. But it becomes easier and easier, since you are now more practiced, and because you now know how to look for me."

"Why is this dangerous?"

"We are not alone, not the only dreamwalkers. Others also travel in this realm, or so I was taught by my teacher. What if one of them found out about us? Our liaison would be hard to explain. And, besides them, there are creatures we would not care to encounter."

"I think I have seen some of those creatures," Robby said. "I intended to ask you about them, but I kept forgetting to do so."

So Robby told her about Billy's dream, explaining somewhat, too, about how the Redvests attacked Billy's home, and how it was defended by the Boskmen who were not at the festival with Billy. When he described the insect-like pests that swarmed around Billy during his dream, Micerea nodded with a concerned look.

"What you describe are what my teacher called 'cindergnats.' I have seen them, too. Such a cloud of them hovered over and pestered you when you were wounded by the wolves at Tulith Attis. So many that even I was frightened. I believe there would have been many more but for the powers of the Melnari, Ashlord, and his herbs and potions. They almost entirely fled from you when the girl, Sheila, tended you. I do not know how such things work. But that was the first time I ever truly saw you. Those little reddish creatures delight upon bad dreams. And the discomfort of the sick and feverish, as you were, attract them as flies to honey. But they do not much bother those who dreamwalk. They cannot abide the aura for very long."

"But what harm do they do? These cindergnats?"

"None, except they rob sleepers of peaceful rest. They are a nuisance, but they may attract the attention of others, not so harmless, that roam the dreamscape."

"Yes, as I have seen, and as you have warned me, before. A beast, like a dog that stands upright, or a bear, perhaps, but lean and dark and foul."

Micerea was clearly agitated, and paced quickly back and forth, before answering.

"I have warned you not to venture about without me! You must be wary of your actions! You must stay within dreams, and never venture outside of them. The realm between dreams is dangerous, filled with terrible and inscrutable creatures. The line we follow, from your dream to mine, skirts that place, and we move quickly to avoid detection. Only once before have I gone to the place between. It was with a companion, a fellow student under the same tutelage as I. But only I returned. I think she was taken by those creatures. And my mentor, my tutor, was also taken by them, I believe."

"What are they?"

"They have no name, as far as I know. My tutor warned me about them. He said they have no allegiance, but sometimes do the bidding of the Dark Lord of Shatuum. They are hard to describe and harder to escape from. They have what I can only describe as teeth and claws. Perhaps some are witches, casting forth their spirits into the night. Maybe they are shades of the dead, still roaming the earth in search of revenge or release. Or maybe they are those who are not dead and are not welcome in the Next Place, having never been among the living. I do not know what they are. In the waking world, they would appear as shadows, just as the Dark Lord himself is said to."

The rest of the evening was uncomfortable. Micerea remained upset. At first, Robby was sure his actions had somehow angered her, and he regretted telling her about his explorations without her. It eventually occurred to him that she was actually frightened. That she ventured into the dreamworld at all, overcoming her fears, was a testament to her bravery. But she held back, playing it safe, too safe for Robby's liking. There was too much to do, too much to learn. He realized that he would have to risk going against her advice if he hoped to gain any real ability.

• • •

Robby grew more miserable in the saddle with each progressing day. Not only did he feel tired, yawning constantly, but his mind, too, was dulled by his exhaustion. While Billy chattered away about this and that, Robby was more distracted than ever and completely missed the point of several jokes and puns. He also failed to notice the concerned looks his friends gave him. Yet, as distracted as he was by the night-time tales that cluttered his head, he was not so oblivious as to miss the tension that seemed to grow among the members of his company. Everyone seemed rather separated. Ullin kept ahead, Sheila some distance behind him, and they all lined out in a long string so that Robby, keeping to the rear, sometimes could not even see the Kingsman. Billy all but gave up trying to converse with anyone, and Ibin, normally so cheerful and steadfast, did not have the heart to even hum. It occurred to Robby that their pace had slowed over the past days. Ullin did not press them as hard as before. And he realized they had been stopping more often than before. "To rest the horses," Ullin sometimes said. "To get my bearings," he explained at other times. Whatever the reason Ullin gave, they were long rests, and Robby usually fell asleep as soon as he had walked the stiffness from his legs and had stretched out on the grass. The week passed, and part of the next, and this continued. It was on a noonday stop that Robby mentioned his suspicions to Sheila.

"Ullin stops for me, does he not?"

"We fear you are sick, Robby," she told him as she sat down beside him. "You sleep hard at night, yet seem to gain no rest from it. You eat well, but seem to gain no nourishment. You look pale and drawn, and you have lost a stone in weight. Even Ibin has not lost such a proportion of his weight since we left Janhaven as you have these past many days. We worry."

"I am tired," Robby said, lying down in the grass and putting his arm over his eyes. "I will be fine, though. *Sarkul al denar barath, as they say in the south, er barath nay telor.* Forward the stone inches, or inches not at all."

"What do you mean? What stone? What is that supposed to mean?"

"It doesn't matter. I will be fine. Perhaps tonight I'll sleep better."

He did not hear her reply, for he was already drifting away, only to be awakened by Billy with the usual and unwelcome, "Time to go!"

"Already?"

"Already, two hours later than when we stopped!"

"Oh."

They continued on, Robby a bit more refreshed and, after becoming fully awake once again, in better spirits than before. After another hour of silence, Sheila nudged her mount up next to Ullin.

"It is sleep Robby needs," Ullin said to her before she could speak. "I don't understand why he needs so much these days. Yet see how much better he does now?"

"Yes. It seems so. But he sleeps at night as we all do, as much or more than at the beginning of our journey."

"It is a mystery."

"Here's another: Have you ever heard the saying, 'Forward the stone inches?' "

"Yes. It's a saying common among the Dragonkind. Why do you ask?"

"What does it mean?"

"It just means that things are going as well as they can go when things are hopeless. It is used in the same manner as when you are greeted and asked how it fares, and you say, 'Oh, I can't complain.' It's just a thing to say."

"Do others besides the Dragonkind use that saying? About the stone?"

"I don't think so. I don't know. *'Sarkul al denar barath'* is how it is said. It doesn't make a lot of sense when translated. No others have the stone that they do. It refers to the Great Stone of Kalzar, the first Dragon King, and the difficulty of moving it."

"You mean the stone that Ashlord told us about? When he told us the story of how the Elifaen lost their wings?"

"Yes, that is it. It is sometimes blamed for the Scathing of the Elifaen, even to this day."

"Could it be that is what Robby is going through? The Scathing?"

"I don't think so. Maybe. Did he use that phrase, *sarkul al denar barath*?"

Sheila said nothing, afraid of the implication.

"He did, didn't he?"

"Yes."

Ullin shook his head. "How did he come to know it? A boy from the Eastlands. And to know other things, besides?"

"I cannot say. Perhaps none of us are who we seem to be. Or who we wish to be with."

It was Esildre who now rode alongside him, and Ullin looked at her sternly.

"Why are you surprised that I am here?"

"Who is it that I talk to? Why do you take this form?"

"This likeness I wear only to please you. And I am now accustomed to it. You do find me pleasing, don't you? Just as you found her pleasing, too?"

"It does not please me for you to use my friends in such a manner."

"Use? Or help? You fool yourself! Who was it that you took back in the land of the little ones? Was it your lover? Or was it Esildre? Or was it me?"

"Do not ply me with riddles, witch!"

"I only come along for the ride, dear Kingsman."

"Begone! Or do your worst work and be done with it!"

As his hand went to his sword hilt, Esildre's face evaporated and only Sheila was there, her own face red and aghast, tracks of hot tears crossing down her cheeks, and her eyes stinging with confusion and disappointment. She halted, as if the wind had been knocked from her, hardly able to breathe, so shocked by Ullin's outburst she was, and she let the company move past her as she tried to regain her composure. Ullin, fuming at himself, kicked his horse into a gallop and raced far ahead. Robby, who had seen enough to sense that something was terribly amiss, immediately rode up to Sheila.

"What happened?" he demanded. She shook her head, speechless. He reined over, dug his heels into his horse, and charged after Ullin. It was a full minute of hard, fast riding before he caught up. Coming over a rise, he saw Ullin halt below and jump from his saddle, letting his horse ramble away as he clutched his head with both hands, staggering as a drunk or wounded man may do. He fell to his knees and gave an animal-like cry of anguish just as Robby raced up and flung himself down from the saddle. Running in long strides, Robby pulled out Swyncraff as the Kingsman drew his dagger and raised it to his throat. Just before the mortal stroke was made, Swyncraff curled around Ullin's wrist and the blade was jerked away, flashing as it flew off into the grass.

"You would cut my throat along with your own?" Robby screamed angrily. "What chance do you think we have without you? Why this?"

"Madness! Madness has overtaken me! You cannot trust me! Nor can I trust what I see or hear. I know not my heart or my mind! Day and night, apparitions come to taunt me and tempt me to anger. I know not what is real and what is delusion. Leave me!"

Ullin scrambled away on his hands and knees, searching for his dagger.

"Leave me!" he shouted. "It is fitting that I die here and now, while I have some dignity left to me, some power to act. Before I become despised by my friends and a pathetic, blithersome idiot!"

Robby dove onto his knees before Ullin, blocking him from the dagger, and giving the Kingsman a hard shove back.

"What is it? Tell me! What plagues you?"

Ullin clutched Robby by his collars and drew him close. "She will not leave my head! I cannot berid my thoughts of her. She whispers to me and she taunts me, knowing I cannot resist her. I have been bewitched! You can't understand. I can't make you understand because it is madness. My madness!"

"Sheila?"

"Yes! No! It is Esildre, speaking in Sheila's place. Words that Sheila does not say!"

"What?"

"I cannot explain. I am bewitched!"

Robby stomach twisted with new fears, new confusions, but as he pulled Ullin's hands off his collar, he was determined about one thing at least.

"You swore to serve me as your king, Ullin Saheed! Do you resign yourself from me? Do you turn away from me?"

"It is for the best!"

"No! I do not permit it. You must see this through! You must promise to hold yourself together, man! Lives are at stake! If you fall to this shadow, we all may fall. Promise me you will do no harm to yourself. Swear to me! Swear to me now, Ullin Saheed, that you will not do harm to yourself, ever!"

Ullin nodded through his tears, clutching Robby's hands to his forehead and sobbing like a child.

"Forgive me, but I do not think I can."

"Damn you! I'll have your oath! Swear it to me! Swear it! Upon the blood of your mother, swear it!"

"I swear it! Oh, I swear it by the blood of my birth! Let my name forever be cursed if this oath I break, and let shame be upon my House. I will do as you say, I swear. Oh, misery! Oh, folly, this is folly!"

"Good! It is done!" Robby, with anger still coursing through his face, his chest pounding, stood and pulled Ullin up. "Now, stand up and tell me what it is that Sheila has done."

"Sheila has done nothing. It is not Sheila, but Esildre that I fear. Only it is Sheila's likeness through which Esildre has worked her charm upon me, so that I can never escape her as long as we travel together. I must beg Sheila's forgiveness. She has done nothing. But how can I face her? I fear to face her. I am ashamed to face her!"

"Tell me, does Esildre come to you only when you are awake?"

"Yes."

"And does she come to you only when Sheila is before you?"

"Yes, that is the way of it."

"What is it that she wants of you?"

"I do not know. But something foul, I'll warrant. She talks against our company. She says things that are…poisonous."

"In that case, do nothing in response to Esildre. Do not answer her. Do not look upon her face or acknowledge her presence before you. Do not heed her taunts. When she appears to you, come to me immediately, excusing yourself aloud. Turn to me and tell me when she is present, even if I am asleep. Listen to me! Ullin! Listen! Esildre cannot harm you. It is Sheila who rides with us, not Esildre. Sheila would do nothing to pain you or to bring harm to any of us. Don't you understand that? Ignore Esildre's voice. Do not acknowledge to her that you even hear her."

By now, the others were catching up, and Robby glanced their way.

"Do you know how this came to be?" he asked the Kingsman, who was rubbing his brow.

"No! No! I mean...I'm not sure! She appeared before me, back in Nowhere. Near the pool not far from the cave. I could not resist her...I don't know what came over me. She took," Ullin put his hand on his shirt, over the locket that hung there, "she took the form of someone I was longing for. I thought it was her, though she is leagues and leagues away. We...that is to say, I thought it was a dream. Until I felt the wounds she gave me."

"Enough for now," Robby said, gesturing at the rest of their companions, now nearing earshot. "Perhaps I will ask you about it again, when the time is right. For now, do not forget your oath. Do as I have instructed. Try to ignore the visions of Esildre! Do not look at her or answer her. Let me know when she comes to you, if you can."

Sheila and Billy saw Ullin nod to Robby as they gathered their reins and awaited them. Ullin led his horse to Sheila.

"Forgive me, I beg of you," he said. "I fear I am preoccupied and muddled. Please bear with me, if you can. My treatment of you is not warranted by anything you have done, and I am truly sorry for my outburst. For anything hurtful I have said or done."

Sheila looked at him with confusion, straining against her desire to ply him with questions, but something in his manner, and in Robby's angry face, told her to forebear. She only nodded. He sheepishly got back on his horse as Robby came up and handed Ullin his dagger.

"Here," he said. "It is not like a Kingsman to drop his dagger."

"Not like a Kingsman, at all," Ullin said, taking it and slipping it into its sheath. He reined around to ride ahead as was his custom.

"What's with Ullin?" Billy asked.

"Just a misunderstanding," Robby said, then looking at Sheila, added, "Don't judge him too quickly if he says odd things. Let us be on our way."

"Good grief!" Billy muttered, tugging on the tether to the packhorses and nudging his own mount to follow Ullin. "Misunderstandin'! That's all we need!"

Ibin followed Billy, smiling nervously at Robby and Sheila.

Robby got into his saddle and trotted up beside Sheila.

"Sheila."

"Yes?"

"I would like for you to keep your distance from Ullin for a while."

"You would?" she responded. "You have nothing to fear, Robby. I do not desire Ullin's company right now."

"I know better, my love," he said, trying very hard to be gentle. "It is not you that I worry about."

"Well, maybe you should," she said. "Just a little, anyway!"

"That is not what I mean. I do worry about you!"

"You do not know my heart!" she said, unable to stop herself. "I hardly know it myself, these days. I tried to tell you. Back at Fisenwold, up on the wall. Things are changing, Robby."

"Sheila, I'm not jealous. I just don't want you to be hurt. Ullin is not himself, these days, and I just think he needs a little distance from you."

"Not himself! Himself? How can you say such a thing? You! Can you not see the changes in your own self? It is *you* we worry about. *You* are why we are here. All of our hope is in *your* quest, which has become ours. But look at yourself! You can hardly stay upright in the saddle, so starved for rest you are! Your clothes hang loose on you. In another week, will you be able to even stand? And you say things that none of us understand, things of the desert lands where you've never been and have no knowledge of. You even speak in some other language. Not the First Tongue, we all understand that when it is heard. Some other speech. I hear you mutter it in your sleep. Yet you say *Ullin* is not himself? You tell me to stay away from *him*? You say you are worried about him? About me? Perhaps it is *you* that I should stay away from!"

She let that have its effect upon Robby, then added, "I keep the company that I choose to keep. As I always have."

She kicked her mount ahead, leaving Robby frustrated, annoyed, and somewhat angry. There was little he could do but follow along, pondering all that had just happened. But he could make no sense of it.

• • •

For the rest of the day, they rode in uneasy silence. When night came, and they made camp, there was still an uncomfortable feeling among them. They took care of their horses, ate, set watch, and did all the usual things. Ibin and Ullin swapped the mandolin back and forth, but even that seemed a joyless effort. The next morning they started out early and were as silent as the lifting mists throughout the morning. Billy made some attempts at joking during the midday, but there was little inspiration in his wit. The animals were a welcome relief, the never-ending wonders of the antelope and of the distant buffalo. The ceaseless tittering of field wrens and the sudden starting of quail filled their passage through the sea of grass with moments of distraction from their worries.

Ullin kept ahead of them, easing his pace somewhat to let them enjoy the antics of the chunkmunks. He paused at the top of a rise to wait for them and, as they caught up, he said, "Here is something that will surely give our hearts a lift."

"What is it?" asked Sheila.

"See for yourself," he motioned her onward to the top. Robby saw her pull up her horse and stare, mouth open, but he could not yet see what she saw. She dismounted and led her horse down the far side and out of sight. When he caught up with Ullin, he looked at him curiously and the Kingsman grinned, motioning him on. When Robby topped the rise, he, too, paused for a moment in wonder.

On the plains below, were thousands of flowers, yellow and blue, still blooming and buzzing with bees and hummingbirds and, yet, something else. The whole scene, as far as the eye could see, was ablaze with yellow and orange. And Sheila, passing through the knee-high flowers, the nearest of which were some fifty yards down slope, set these petals stirring up into the air all around her. It was then that Robby realized the orange-colored petals were butterflies, countless thousands of butterflies, swarming all over the flowers. Sheila turned around, facing back toward her companions, and laughed with delight at the delicate creatures landing in her hair and on her arms and shoulders.

"I've never seen the like!" she cried to them. "It's like a dream!"

Robby passed on down to catch up with her, wordless at the incredible sight stretching as far as he could see.

"What is this place?" Billy asked Ullin as he and Ibin followed him into the field.

"It is called Laeleth's Stream," Ullin replied. "And it runs for nearly forty leagues north to south. Yet it is only a few furlongs wide."

"It's amazin'!"

Ullin nodded. "Legends tell that it follows the course that Laeleth and her lover, Celefar, walked when they were reunited. They became so enraptured with each other's company that they gave no thought to time or place, as they strolled arm in arm for days without need of rest or food or water, and with no notice of daylight or moonlight, all their wants fulfilled by the love they held for one another and the joy of their reunion. You should see this place in the first weeks of spring!"

• • •

Long after they had passed through and left it far behind, the joy of Laeleth's Stream lingered with them. Yet Robby felt a sweet twinge of melancholy, yearning for Passdale and its own sunlit fields. After a while, he and Billy fell into a conversation about the folks they left behind in Janhaven. Not heeding Robby's warning, and in spite of the unpredictable treatment she might receive from Ullin, Sheila rode ahead alongside the Kingsman.

"Why should he be King?"

Ullin tensed at the voice, but kept his eyes forward and did not look at the rider who came alongside. He did not want to see Esildre's face anymore, much less where it did not belong. But his will came back to him, and he turned sternly to her, only to see Sheila looking blankly at him.

"What did you say?" he asked, feeling a private embarrassment redden his cheeks.

"I am afraid of the ring," she repeated. "The ring Robby found back at Tulith Morgair. You seem to know something about it. I wish you would tell me."

"It is just a ring."

"No, not just any ring. There is something to it. It may not be a magic ring, but it is special in some way. And the manner of Robby finding it, the mystery, well, it troubles me. Perhaps there is magic in that?"

"I cannot say. It is a mystery to me as well."

"But you recognized the ring. I saw it in your face when he first showed it to you. And you were familiar with the sort of flower that was with it."

Ullin did not reply.

"I feel a terrible dread about it," she insisted.

"If I told you where I think the flower came from, and the ring, too, your dread would but increase. Yet, I think there is nothing to fear of them, nor of the giver. That part I cannot explain to you without breaking faith with Robby, for he wishes to protect the identity of the giver. I have not spoken with him about my knowledge, or how I know who must have given it; I will let Robby be the one to speak it, if it is to be told at all. Robby is full of mystery, and the mystery that surrounds him deepens. I do not understand how Robby knew the ring was at Tulith Morgair. And I do not understand how it could have been placed there for him to find. It seems entirely impossible. But he has the ring, and he found the impossible flower. It is a puzzle. All I can say is that we must trust our faith in each other, Sheila. Even when it is severely tried," he said, daring a glance at her. "For each of us, different things, different faiths, and in different ways. If Robby becomes King, it will surely be by some means beyond the reckoning of the rest of us. We must do our duty to him. We have already started, and must continue."

Sheila said nothing for several moments, riding along in silence. At last, she turned back to Ullin.

"What you say does somehow reassure me: That a thing may seem fearful and disturbing on the surface, but really be safe when seen another way. Like the old dog my uncle once kept, appearing vicious and always snarling and growling. All he wanted was kind attention, which he never got from Uncle Steggan, but the poor creature was always as a puppy with me. The ring and the flower may be like that, after a manner. Safe."

"For us, anyway. At least I believe so."

"That helps. And I thank you for saying so. Can you not tell me something of the flower?"

Ullin looked at her and nodded.

"It grows only in a land very far away. In another tongue, it is called a *Cronosis*. To those in Vanara, it is known as the *semiluna*, the Fortnight Flower. On the day it blooms, it is a dark brown color. When it is picked, it begins to change color. Within a day, it fades to a dark red. By week's end, it is a green color, and on the last days fades to blue. Finally, on the fourteenth day, it turns white and quickly decays to nothing."

"Wait. That means it was picked no more than two weeks before Robby found it," Sheila realized. "So how, in that time, did it get from its faraway land to Tulith Morgair?"

"The same way the ring did. And that is the mystery of it."

They rode in silence for a mile or two, then Sheila dropped back a little and listened to Robby and Billy who rode behind her and were chatting about the Nowhereans. They were discussing whether the little folk could, indeed, build a platform in the treetops for the swine, and, if they did, whether it might truly break Bailorg's curse.

"An' that Esildre," Billy went on, "she's a mystery, ain't she?"

"How do you mean?" Robby asked.

"Well, showin' up like 'at," Billy explained. "I mean, when she did. Like it was all planned out, like."

"Yes, that was strange."

"An' her bein' the one who give 'em thar way of poppin' all 'round, like they do. An' I don't think Ashlord much trusted her, neither."

"Hm. I wish he had said more about her."

"An' now she goes off eastward, to Janhaven, er Tallinvale, one er the other."

"Yes. The Elifaen do seem to have strange abilities, uncanny powers," Robby nodded. "Like Lyrium, too, and the manner of her coming and going from Tallinvale. Her coming to see us, knowing we'd be in that region."

"Aye. It's as if we're bein' watched. Gives me the chills. I think too many folk know 'bout us, Robby."

"Believe me, I've had the same feeling, Billy," Robby said as he thought of Swyncraff about his waist and about Serith Ellyn and Thurdun. "And those who know about me seem to know more than I do!"

"Mebbe. An' I think Esildre suspects what we're about. An' even though I can't help bein' glad she goes elsewhar other 'an our own way, I'm uncomfortable at the idear of her goin' east."

"Why's that?"

Billy shrugged. "Can't say, 'xactly. It's just…I dunno, Robby. I guess I can't decide rightly which side she's on."

Robby nodded. "Yes. A mystery, she is."

Of all the Elifaen he'd met in recent months, she was the only one not clearly for or against them. There was nothing subtle about Bailorg, being decidedly pitted against Robby's company, but neither was there anything too subtle about Serith Ellyn and Thurdun or Lyrium when it came to their support, as mysterious as they were.

"Maybe she's not on either side, Billy. I mean, maybe she has her own concerns. Or maybe she doesn't realize there are sides at all."

"That's what makes me wonder more about what Ashlord might say. She'd be against the Redvests an' the Dragonfolk, surely, as we are. Only, in a way, we've set ourselves again' Duinnor, even though we go thar for help. If she'd any inklin' of what we're *truly* up for, I mean with the king stuff an' all, I wonder if she'd stand with us?"

"She'd have to be crazy," Robby blurted out.

Billy shot a look of concern at Robby, but saw him smiling back. "Ah," Billy chuckled, "so we're all daft. Is that it?"

It was the first hint of a joke from Robby in ages, and the relief of it made Billy chuckle again. Just ahead, Sheila smiled, too. The bit of relief that the humor gave passed too soon, and Robby retreated again into his own thoughts. His mood might have spread over all of them but for Billy's compulsion to chatter on, which, as ever, proved too distracting for deep or gloomy thoughts.

Billy always did most of the talking among the group, though much of it was of no importance to anyone but Billy himself, and Ibin, from practiced courtesy. Unlike most who became quickly impatient with him, Robby did not mind. He had concluded years earlier that it was Billy's way of thinking things through. Billy would talk to anyone who would pretend to listen, and Robby suspected that his chat did not cease merely because no one was present to hear. Lately, Billy seemed fixed on how a common fellow, "like, say, Robby," might conceivably become King. After trailing along beside Sheila at the rear of the group, regaling her with his amazement at such a "propersishun," and restating for the umpteenth time the "purposteriorness" of it, he took a deep breath.

"Right, then," Billy concluded. "So what if the King is like ol' Robby here. I mean, what if he got his name on the deathbed of another feller an' don't know his own name, neither? Then, if Robby is to know it, he must find this dead feller what gave the King his name, an' have him tell Robby what it is. Don't that make sense? 'Cept, of course, to get to the dead feller what named the King, in the Place of the Dead, ol' Robby'd have to be dead hisself!"

"Seems the way of it, now that you put it out like that," nodded Sheila.

"An' that don't seem right by any stretch. I mean, it seems fairly hopeless, don't it?"

"Yes. It does."

• • •

Billy said nothing that Robby had not already pondered a thousand times. And he wondered that it took Billy so long to finally reach the obvious paradox that seemed plain enough from the start. To him, there were three distinct problems about it. First, he would have to die in order to go to wherever it is that dead folk go. Secondly, he would have to know who to look for in order to ask for the name. But, assuming everything else could work out, how on earth could he learn who that might be unless he knew who the King was in the first place, to whom he might have been born to, and who might have named him? It could take years to work that one out. And there was another minor problem: How not to be dead any longer? One does not just visit the Place of the Dead and then say good day and adieu. At least nobody he ever heard of had done that.

The more he thought about it the less he liked thinking about it. After all, it *was* the most preposterous thing imaginable, if you put a sober mind to it.

"You'd have to be mad to give it any cred—"

He stopped in mid-thought, instinctively jerking back on his reins.

"What's the matter, Robby?" Ullin called to him.

Robby shook himself and nudged his mount onward. "Nothing, nothing," he replied. "Just got lost in my thoughts."

"Robby?" Sheila pulled up next to him on one side while Billy came up on the other. "Are you ill?"

"No, no. I'm fine. I think I'll ride up ahead a bit."

He nudged his mount harder and trotted off ahead, leaving Billy and Sheila looking after him and then at each other.

"Lo!" said Billy. "He turned white as a sheet!"

"Like he'd seen a ghost," Sheila answered back. "Maybe he heard what we were talking about."

Since nothing they said could have been anything new to his thoughts, it did not matter if Robby had heard their morbid chat. What was new was a plan, which instantly took shape in his mind, a realization about what Lyrium had meant as to not being stuck in the paradox he thought it was, but being stuck in another one altogether. Yes, he would find a way to the Land of the Dead. And he would find a way out, too. Those two pieces of the puzzle now were as clear to him as was the middle piece: He now knew precisely whom to seek out in that place, for it came to him as if out of the clear blue sky. Robby realized who it was that had the Name he needed. And it was not actually about the Name at all. It was about the getting of the Name.

"Ashlord was right," Robby nodded to himself. "Back there in Janhaven that night. He said the answer would come to me. It all fits, now. I just wish there was some other way to do it!"

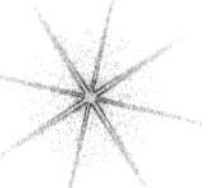

Chapter 7

The Carrion Bees

The sameness of the rolling plain was like that of the ocean, varying with light and texture mile after mile, never the same in particulars but ever alike in the vast theme. It made the company feel puny and yet grand for the witnessing of it as they moved steadily onward. The days grew cooler, one after the other, and Sir Sun went sooner and sooner to his rest after each slanted run across the broad sky. Nights were chilly, but not too uncomfortable, and the travelers spoke of how warm the weather was for the season and how the plains hardly knew that summer was over. They took great pleasure in their evening meals under the winding stars, the view of which, from horizon to horizon, never ceased to fill them with awe. It was not a bad time for the travelers, though Ullin and Robby seemed to grow more distant from the others with every mile, each for his own reasons. But everyone took measures to be especially respectful of each other, of Ullin's moodiness, of Robby's growing fatigue and the shortness of patience he frequently displayed, particularly when roused from sleep. So they ventured onward at an easy pace, but one that put many miles behind them each day.

Ibin often asked Ullin, "Howfar, howfar, howfarhavewecome, today?" Ullin would look at the sky in thought, then say, "Oh, maybe ten leagues," or "Around fifteen leagues, I imagine," or some such measure that might satisfy the big one. Ibin, after some consideration, would then pose, "And, and, andhowfarisityettogo?" To which Ullin would usually shrug and say, "Not so far as yesterday, Ibin."

With every passing day, Robby grew more aloof from his companions. Billy and Sheila could not but notice that Ullin, who knew Robby least well among them, seemed to treat him with a kind of deference, almost reverence. And although they did not share their observations with each other, they wondered if Ullin knew something they did not. Or whether the Kingsman was now looking to a new King. The recipient of Ullin's treatment showed every sign of worry, except perhaps with his appetite which, like the others, was a constant presence since they carefully rationed their provisions. Robby rarely smiled, even at Billy's most witty remarks, and he seemed to be growing gaunt about the cheeks and eyes. When he did smile, it was without his normal exuberance: always with a kind of half-turn at the corner of his mouth, as if, in spite of the joke just made, he saw some deep, not-to-be-shared irony. Sensing Ullin's coolness, Sheila hung back with Billy more often. And as the company made their way across the wide plain, Billy and Sheila more often spoke of their concerns to each other.

"He just don't seem hisself," Billy commented one day, quite out of the blue.

"He who?" Sheila asked looking ahead past Ibin and the pack animals at Robby and Ullin who were riding side by side in the lead.

"Why, Robby, I mean. Though Ullin's a bit off his mood these days."

"They've both got a lot on their minds."

"Yeah. Sure. I reckon so."

Little could they guess that Robby's toil was greatest while they slept. Each night he went to see Micerea. On the nights when she turned him away, saying that he needed to sleep—and often she did—he would instead wander inside the strange dreamworld rather than returning to his bedroll. It was a peculiar condition, he knew. A part of him constantly warned against dreamwalking, and during the tedious daytime rides, as alone in his thoughts as he was in his saddle, Robby would often promise himself that, this night, he would truly sleep. Just sleep. But when his eyes closed, he was fitful and full of anxious dreams, like clouds around his mind. Swirling scenes of violence, such as he had seen at the bridge crossing the gorge, mixed with visions of the mountain witch, and unaccountable fears that he should be minding the store back in Passdale, all churned themselves into nonsensical settings. Once the little Millithorpe was seen clapping his hands gleefully as he entered the store, shaking his father's hands vigorously and introducing Esildre to Robby's mother. This dream blended into a bizarre battle between the Janhaven folks and weird shadowy people who came down out of the mountains and ate away the trees like great beavers. As this happened, the Barleyfolk, including Mrs. Bosk, only shrugged. Eventually, part of Robby's mind would awaken, and he would see a way out. Exhausted by the nightmares, he slipped away from them, and passed from sleep into the sleep-that-is-not-sleep, looking for the crack or splinter or glitter of light through which he might pass on to somewhere else.

Night after night this went on. Sometimes Robby found himself not in a dream of his own making, but someone else's. At first he could not tell who the dreamer was. He would surmise that it was Ullin's dream he was in, or Billy's or Sheila's. Sometimes their dreams were as disturbing as his own, and he watched, fascinated by the mysterious inner workings of his companions. But often his presence in their dreams was an embarrassment to him since he saw private things that he thought no one should see in another. Sometimes, he saw himself, too, not as he thought himself to be but as he was perceived by the dreamer or the dream; it was not always flattering, but it was not always insulting, either. Nonetheless, he strove to understand them and to pay attention, often seeing meaning where there was none, and yet sometimes failing to see what should have been plain as day.

Sometimes his companions' memories warped into the fabric of a fantastical story. Other times—most times, in fact—their dreams were jumbled, or filled with such anxieties or desires, or deep melancholic feelings about things which escaped Robby, leaving him confused and infected by the deep moods these visions cast over his own heart.

Robby said nothing about these things to Micerea, fearing that she would scold him for his impertinent intrusions, and he knew she would be right in doing so. But he could not help himself. A craving to witness his companions' dreams filled him with unbearable urgency so that, sometimes, his mind wandered to them instead of staying on the lesson that Micerea was trying to impart. Yet, when she asked after his well-being, Robby always answered carefully, suspicious that she might be aware of his ventures into the dreams of others.

• • •

One night, he wandered into Ullin's dreamworld, and he was a bit shocked to find the Kingsman and a young woman lying naked on a bed of flowers. They had just made love, he surmised as he watched from the shadows of a wall. Her back, curved and lovely, was to Robby, and her black hair draped over Ullin's shoulder as she bent over him and kissed his chest. Incongruously, a small animal stirred at Robby's feet. It was a rabbit. The girl turned to face Robby, and at once he saw that it was Micerea.

"You do not belong here!" she said.

"What was that?" asked Ullin, roused from his bliss.

"I speak to your companion."

Robby quickly hid behind a column as Ullin looked his way.

"True enough," Ullin said, "but we are lucky that he led us here."

The rabbit suddenly hopped past Robby, startling him. As he watched it go to Ullin and Micerea, Robby felt trapped. Even though he thought the dream was of his own making and of no consequence, he felt a deep pang of jealousy. Shaken, he struggled to find a way out, as if by waking up he could shatter the vision and the woeful sentiment he felt. To his relief, he felt the urging of his own body, and, without even thinking, he found himself sitting upright from his blanket.

"Perhaps I am becoming my own worst enemy," he muttered.

Low mists rose through surrounding grass, illuminated by Lady Moon's shy face. Beside him lay Sheila, and he could barely make out the dark shape of Ibin standing watch several yards away. Ullin and Billy lay sleeping nearby. He reclined, his eyes open for a good while before sleep took him again.

The next night, Robby was with Micerea again.

"You seem distracted, Robby."

Robby nodded.

"I am worried about my companions," he said. "You never ask about them."

"I have little to ask about. They appear loyal to you and have taken the fulfillment of your quest as their own mission."

"Does not even Ullin interest you?"

"All of your friends interest me. Ullin especially interested me for a long while, for it was he that I found first when I came to look for you. He is of the same House as you, and, for a time, I thought it was he who might become the new King. That was before I knew that his mother was mortal, and before I knew about you. I kept an eye on him, so to speak. Eventually I learned that he had an aunt, but in my dream sojourns into Tallinvale I could find no sign of her."

Micerea spoke very carefully, choosing her words with much deliberation, not removing her gaze from him.

"Then I thought to look in Passdale, where Ullin ventured. It was there, on the day he charged you to go to Tulith Attis, that I found you. Indeed, you were the Hidden One. So complete was your mother's departure from Tallin Hall, that I never heard her name spoken there, or knew what became of her. For a time, I did not even know Lord Tallin had a daughter, or that Dalvenpar had a sister. I am sorry if this is disturbing to you, that I was spying upon your family. That was what I had to do. I would not have found you otherwise."

Robby was sure that what she said was true, but also that she left much out of her explanation.

"How long? How long did you look before you found me?"

"Ever since I learned to walk in dreams. It was three years ago that I began my quest to find you."

"Ullin knows a great deal about your lands, your people," Robby prodded. "Perhaps you know something of how he came by his knowledge."

"Surely you know that he fought in our lands, that his duty as a Kingsman brought him south and into the desert to fight against my people. Other than that, he has also studied a great deal and learned much from his family as well as from Collandoth."

"Am I the only one...," Robby began but faltered, hearing a certain tone in his own voice that disturbed him. He tried again, "Have you had other pupils?"

"No. You are the first and only one I have revealed myself to in this way. It is dangerous for me, Robby."

"There is something you have not taught me, to go where I wish beyond the bounds of my vision, except when I perceive the distant light. But you ventured all the way to the Eastlands, and without there being another to open the way to you by their dreams."

"There are always dreams, Robby, day and night," she smiled. "As I said before, like following stepping stones, one to the next, one may travel far while dreamwalking. So far, you have seen very little. But shall we continue our lesson? Tonight we will listen to the singing of some traditional songs of my people. Come."

• • •

The conversation with Micerea did not satisfy Robby. He felt certain that she held something back. He lacked the will to press her on it, though. He was still unsatisfied later on when, after he was dismissed by Micerea, he visited the dreams of his companions. Sheila dreamed sweetly of her stay in Passdale, and Billy tossed and turned in a flight of fancy during which he went knuckle to knuckle with Bailorg. Ullin's dreams were muddled, snippets of a sandy desert storm, snatches of riding Anerath through an icy mountain pass, both horse and rider with their heads bent low against the driving snow, and flashes of boisterous parties where Kingsmen danced on their shields.

• • •

Strangely, only Ibin's dreams seem comforting to Robby. True to nature, Ibin often dreamed of food in plentiful supply, and Robby thought nothing of pulling up a chair beside the big one at whatever table was set. Once, he helped Ibin fill huge baskets with sweet pies and little kegs of ale that they picked from the sagging branches of a tree. But there were other things in Ibin's dreams, too. They walked down the road on a summer day in one dream, with Ibin waving and chatting in a friendly manner to all they passed. Just an ordinary dream about an ordinary thing. In a different dream, Ibin rode along on Buckie, the stalwart pony who tolerated only Ibin and in the most gleeful way. Robby floated beside them on long light strides as Ibin held forth to Buckie much like Billy might go on to Ibin. Yet Ibin stuttered and stammered not once, nor did he ever in his own dreams.

On another night, Ibin dreamed of teaching a young child how to play his mandolin, while Robby sat on a stool and watched from the corner of a modest but comfortable cottage. Though snow fell outside, a nearby hearth kept the place warm and cozy. Ibin sat on a low stool himself, the child before him high up on a tall chair, his little arms barely reaching round the instrument to the strings. Ibin carefully and patiently pointed out where the child should hold each finger. A golden-locked young lady entered from another room, her curls draped over her shoulders as she undid an apron and hung it on a peg. She knelt behind Ibin and put her arms around his thick neck and kissed him on his cheek. It was then that Robby saw the resemblance of the little boy to the couple who now beamed proudly as he picked out a simple tune. It was so sweet that Robby's vision blurred with tears. A subtle thing, perhaps, but Robby never looked at Ibin the same way again, nor thought long about Ibin without thinking of the fellow's unspoken longing for hearth and home, and a family of his own.

To Ibin, then, was where Robby went when he could not find his sleep, or when he could not bear his own dreams. And it was only with Ibin that Robby found any ordinary peace of being, such as he remembered from Passdale. The kind that seems so trivial until one realizes that it has been lost.

• • •

Billy, for his part, wondered why, all of a sudden, he seemed to be having so many dreams with Robby in them. "Even though," he thought, "it ain't all that unnatural for a friend to dream of a friend, I reckon."

It was not an uncommon thought in the minds of all the company, but none spoke of it. Uncanny, they felt, how he seemed to just hang around, not doing much, not often participating unless it was to be helpful with some little something, just observing, mostly, usually smiling (which was a relief to see him do, actually).

"I suppose, too," Billy went on with his thoughts, "that ol' Robby's always been a odd sort of bird. Why ought he be any diff'rent in me dreams?"

• • •

But there were many distractions, however wound up in their own thoughts the members of the company became. Once they saw a bright red fox, slinking through the grass, throwing a mischievous grin at them. A few days later, they saw a flock of white egrets take to the air some half-mile away, wheeling around broadly through the sky like a silver cloud until they gracefully settled back down, disappearing behind the tall distant grass at about the same place from where they had emerged. That night, while they camped below an easy bluff and before they posted their watch, they were startled to look up and see the tall silhouettes of antelope passing by in a long silent line.

• • •

It was not long past noon on the following day when they spotted a cloud of dust far off on the leftward horizon. Ullin stopped to study it.

"Is it a storm?" Robby asked.

Ullin said nothing, but suddenly he stood in his stirrups, looking quickly around in all directions.

"What is it?" asked Sheila anxiously.

"Dragonkind?" called out Billy from the end of their line.

"A stampede of bison!" Ullin answered as he twisted in his saddle and pointed to their right. "That way! We must make for that little rise! Hurry!"

He reined around and led them away to the northeast, somewhat back the way they had come, urging the others to gallop as fast as the pack animals would go. At first, they could not see where Ullin directed them, but after a few moments of hard riding, Sheila could make out a small broad hill, no more than seven or eight feet high at its utmost. Glancing over her shoulder, she saw the dirty cloud rapidly approaching. Before it, flocks of birds were flying up and out of the way. Some of the birds flew right past them so close that she could hear their wings beating and the whistling of their breath as they pumped themselves desperately through the air. Ullin was first to reach the rise, and he immediately jumped from his saddle, helping Ibin up with the pack animals. Grabbing a coil of rope, he began tying it through the bridles of all their horses as the rest came up.

"Grab hold!" he cried as rumbling thunder reached their ears. By now the brownish cloud blotted the sun. "Hold fast to the rope. Hold tight and close your eyes! Keep them together so that they cannot buck!"

Now the rumble of thousands of hooves and the dark line that spread across the plain made it clear that they would soon be in the midst of a vast torrent of flesh. It was as if a brown panicked sea churned toward them, from ground to sky, shaking the earth with its flood. Ullin drew the horses together, winding the line around Billy, Robby, and Ibin's hands and wrists.

"Do not let go!"

Around the little rise, small animals of every kind darted through the grass in panic, several rabbits tore over the hill and shot right between the horses' legs, upsetting the nervous creatures even more. Sheila took hold of the rope to help steady them, but Ullin pulled her away.

"What?"

"Get your bow!"

The growing noise was so great that they were already shouting, and with no little terror in their hearts, the boys held fast the horses. Ullin grabbed his bow and quiver then led Sheila a few yards toward the approaching herd, directing her to stand with him to face the coming frenzy.

"Stand close to me!"

"What are we doing?" cried Sheila.

"We must make a parting! This hill alone will not save us. Aim for those that come straight at us. Bring down as many as you can. But we must let them get very close. Understand?"

Sheila nodded, but she was obviously unhappy with Ullin's instructions.

"We must do this," Ullin cried, cinching down his quiver and notching an arrow. "It is our only chance!"

Sheila nodded again and took aim, pulling back the string with practiced calm that was not in accord with the terror of her heart. She swallowed hard. So dense was the herd, and so crazed did they seem, that they could not turn right nor left in their charge, and their cries and grunts and hard panting filled the air in counterpoint to the steady rumble of their advance. Ullin and Sheila stood, bows straining, arrows pointing, watching the crushing wall speed closer and closer.

"Fly true!" Ullin cried as he loosed his first arrow. It struck a lead bull not thirty yards away and the beast went down kicking and tumbling. Another just behind the first did the same as Sheila's arrow struck home, and, suddenly, an avalanche of stumbling screaming flesh and fur was created as the press behind crashed into those that had fallen. Horns and hooves and great clods of dirt and grass shot into the air in every contorted direction, many of the animals leaping into the air in a last attempt to avoid the pile-ups, the first to be trampled now invisibly squealing underneath the latter. Arrow after arrow flew. Some victims rolled end over screaming end right up against the bank before the two grim archers. To either side, a raging river of sweat-drenched hide, flying clods of earth, and nostril-choking dust flooded around them like an avalanche of living boulders, rumbling so loudly that the company could not hear their own coughing cries. The three boys pulled on the tethers with all their might as the poor horses, wide-eyed and screaming themselves with fear and panic, strove to buck and pull away with such force that the three who clung to the ropes were half-dragged and jerked this way and that. Fortunately for them, the horses were so tightly grouped that one could not move much without first the others moving in like manner; and so the boys barely maintained their hold. Indeed, if it had not been for Ibin's hulking mass, it would have been hopeless.

By now, a pile of carcasses walled up before the onslaught, and yet several bulls still managed to fling themselves over it and onto the rise, one kicking right between Sheila and Ullin, grazing him with a swipe of his horns before dodging around the horses and back down and off the rise. Ullin and Sheila continued to shoot, backing up step by step until they bumped into the boys who struggled with the horses. The two archers now aimed only at those that might make it over or through the barrier, or those that suddenly came inward from one side or the other. At the height of their fear, and almost out of arrows, the herd abruptly thinned and the flood abated, moving rapidly away as fast as it had come. As the dust continued to billow restlessly around them, Ullin and Sheila moved quickly to help calm and settle the horses while strays and stragglers of the herd continued to trot by.

It was only then that the company noticed how crowded the little hill had become. Several rabbits huddled together, crouching long and low with their ears back and hind legs cocked and ready to sprint, wide-eyed and edgy. One of these sat up, ears erect, and looked around. It gave a single emphatic stamp of aggravation before darting off. Billy caught a glimpse of some kind of cat slinking away into the dust, and Ibin's foot bumped into what turned out to be a tortoise, its head just now peeking out from its shell. Ibin, always the quickest to recover when danger was obviously gone, had little wonder at all of the animals that had found brief refuge with them, for to him it only seemed natural that they should do so. He was instead rather fascinated by the beautiful gold and red patterns on the tortoise's shell, and he bent over to look more closely. A tug by the still-jittery horses brought him back to the task at hand as the tortoise and all of the other animals cautiously made away. The company petted and cooed and rubbed the horses, softly reassuring them, and it was some while before they were calm enough to have the rope removed from their bridles. By then most of the dust had settled, and the sound of the stampede was far away to the north.

"What started all that, ye reckon?" asked Billy, looking at the vultures already beginning to alight nearby.

"Could have been anything," Ullin shrugged bending to pluck an unbroken arrow from a bull that had fallen dead at their feet, though it had been pierced forty yards away.

"Whatever it was," said Sheila, going about the carcasses looking for arrows that could be retrieved, "this is a terrible waste."

Ullin nodded, looking around at the pitiful carnage as he walked farther out to find more arrows. Hundreds of bison littered the plain, many still in their death throes, some struggling to regain their shattered legs. Robby, still clutching the rope, gazed southward, studying the wide path left by the stampede, the grass trampled into a dark brown sea of clods, almost as if the earth had been plowed from south to north.

"Whatever it was," he said, still gazing south, "I'm afraid we will soon know."

The others looked at him, then followed his eyes to the horizon past Ullin where there was some low movement. They saw three small black shapes, barely in view, separated by hundreds of feet from each other, moving back and forth in a seemingly random manner. Several times as they stared, some small distant shape seemed to fly up into the air, and small clouds of dust would fly up after it, too.

"Carrion bees!" Ullin suddenly cried out, dropping the arrow-shards and running back to them. "We must flee!"

"What?"

"Bees?"

Already Ullin was pushing Sheila back to her horse and taking the reins of his own.

"They are ghouls! Let's go! They feast upon the dead, and their sting is lethal. Go! Let's go!"

With renewed panic, they quickly sorted out their mounts, got the pack animals lined, and rode away westward, careful to avoid the few bewildered cows that still roamed and stumbled lost and dazed. Impeded by the churned-up ground, they could only manage a slow trot, though the horses were as eager as the riders to be away. As they urged their animals along, they kept watch on the new threat, growing closer, and could now see that the shapes were densely packed swarms. Out from one of these, a tiny dot sometimes shot, usually looping around and back.

"Get on, boy!" Billy nudged his horse with his heels as he watched and tugged the line to one of the pack animals.

From carcass to carcass each of the swarms went, quickly shredding flesh from bone with such violence and fury that entire beasts were lifted into the air and tossed about by the force of the ravenous attacks. As each meal was instantly reduced to a scattering of bones, members of the swarm darted out and up and down, back and forth, to find the next feast. One of these, the size of a man's fist, came at the travelers with a ripping buzz. Ullin turned into it and, with one motion drew his sword and snapped the insect in half. By now, the horses were all at a gallop, and the buzz and drone of the swarms was growing louder, and there was a sickening frenzy of crunching, ripping, and tearing as the bees devoured the hapless bison. The horses, hardly calm after the frightful stampede, were now in full panic of the new danger and needed no urging to flee, only guidance from those at the reins.

Several more bees came toward them, and as Sheila looked over her shoulder, she saw the one in front of the others dart down onto a struggling calf. The other bees quickly followed the first and then came a stream, like a line of black smoke trailing from their last victim to gather at the next. Sheila turned her head away and tried to ignore the horrible sound as she clung low to her horse's neck and kicked with her heels. Thus the swarms moved, sending out fingers to find the next meal even before the last was finished. It was only because of the great supply of dying cattle that the company was able to get away, putting a good mile between themselves and the horror behind before they dared to slow their pace. Still, they kept on, pushing up and over low hills, looking fearfully back from the tops, but never lingering.

* * *

"The horses need rest!" Sheila called out late in the afternoon.

"An' water!" Billy added.

Ullin turned in his saddle and replied, "Just a little longer. I think there's a stream ahead, yon."

"A stream?"

Straining, Robby could just make out a line to their right, extending before them. After riding a bit farther, albeit at a reduced pace than before, he could see low brush, punctuated here and there with small trees. It was soon apparent that the trees kept to the banks of some source of water, but it was another hour before they reached the place. It turned out to be the merest of creeks, only a few inches deep and some two or three yards wide at most, bordered on its low sides by marshy grass and reeds, and a willow here and there.

"We are fortunate," Ullin told them as they dismounted and led the horses into the water. "This, I believe, is the final course of the River Farduin, before the plain drinks it dry. Let the horses cool before drinking. Yes, this stream receives its waters from snows far north of here and only runs until late in the year if the season is unusually warm. I've never been along this way, so I'm only guessing. But I'm pretty sure that it's the Farduin. If so, it marks the end of the Bletharn and the beginning of the west country. The plains give way to more hilly lands where there are towns and villages, farms and such."

"Maybe we can warsh up a bit, too," Billy said, pulling packs from the animals. "Just to get the stench of them dusty steers out of me nose."

• • •

The day's excitements eventually wore off, and the monotony of their travels bore upon them soon enough as they rested and let their horses be idle. They decided to camp there for the night, up on the far banks where it was dry, and for the first time in many nights they had a roaring fire with the plentiful wood that could be gathered along the stream. It was just as well, for the night air turned chilly, and had it not been for their blankets and the fire, they would have been cold, indeed. They cooked a hearty meal of the last of their sausage and potatoes and carrots, and, later on, they passed around the flask of Fetch.

"What sorts live in the parts we come to?" asked Billy.

"Men, mostly. Mostly of Duinnor stock, but some of the south realms from long ago. There is a roadway that leads from Duinnor southward, and it is along its path that the towns are, doing trade with north and south. They are suspicious of those traveling to or from Vanara and some prevent any of the Elifaen from entering their lands."

"Do they stand with Duinnor?" Robby asked.

"For the most part," Ullin nodded. "Their trade relies on Duinnor so I'm sure they are reluctant to withhold their taxes and tribute. Duinnor also tends to look the other way where some things are concerned, and there is little enforcement of the King's Law. We turn northwestward tomorrow and try to pick up the track toward one of the settlements along the way," he said. "We run low on food, as you can tell, and need to reprovision."

"We can always hunt, if need be," suggested Sheila, putting another clump of twigs on the fire. "It's too bad we didn't have a chance to get some of the beef we slaughtered."

"That would have been a mistake. We dare not eat food from the plain. Have I not told you? The animals of the plains cannot be eaten except by those born upon the plain."

"What? No, I never heard that!"

"It is true," Ullin insisted. "Sickness comes to any who eat meat from elsewhere and then eat flesh taken from the plains. No one knows why. Have you not wondered why we have seen no other people? None can establish farms here unless they bring enough cattle and livestock to last a generation. If an animal is born here of those brought by settlers, it carries the sickness that all animals raised here give. Few die of the sickness, but the meat cannot be consumed without terrible pains of the belly and a revulsion for all food which lasts for days."

Ullin's companions all wore skeptical expressions, all except Ibin, whose expression was more of fearful disappointment.

"It is said that these plains were the place where Aperion brought all of the Faerekind to meet, when he summoned them away from their first war with the Dragonkind," Ullin said as Robby passed the flask of Fetch to him.

"Oh? You mean where they were Scathed?" Sheila asked.

"Yes," Ullin nodded. "Some of the legends that I've heard say that it was over this plain that he called them to come and that he made them all to stand on their feet and feel the weight of the earth's draw upon them as they had never done before. And the draw of the earth was strong on the weapons that some of them held, so that their swords and maces, their bows and arrows and their spears all fell heavily from their hands upon the ground at their feet. That was so that the Faerekind could know how all creatures felt the weight of their existence, how the weight of all things was part of their being, whether rock or tree or the things made by their hands, like their weapons."

"Ashlord didn't say nuthin' 'bout that when he told us how the Faerekind lost thar wings," said Billy.

"I know. There are so many tales and legends about the Fall of the Faere, he couldn't tell them all."

"So everyone came here?" Robby asked.

"Yes. Spread out, I imagine, for these grasslands are vast. It is said that when Aperion flew above them, all could see him and hear his voice, and he outshone Sir Sun. And when he opened the way to his heavenly kingdom and invited them to go with him, many refused, as you know. But one legend says that many of those who warred against the Dragonkind with Cupeldain regretted their deeds and went with Aperion. After Aperion departed with his host, some who remained, like Cupeldain, picked up their weapons and flew away, intent to resume their fighting. Those that had nothing to do with the fighting but wished to stay in the world flew back to their homelands. They all soon lost their wings, though, as Ashlord said. Anyway, the plain is littered with ancient weapons, forged during the Time Before Time, and left behind by some of those who departed with Aperion. Other things have been found, too. Of course, when the Faerekind who remained lost their wings, becoming Elifaen, they fell to the earth, and their weapons, too, fell with them and were lost."

"But what does that have to do with how the animals of the plains may make you sick if you eat them?" Sheila asked.

"Well," Ullin said, shrugging, "many of the weapons were dripping with blood. Tales have it that the blood, which was drawn in hatred and spite and anger, stained the grassy ground. Animals that lived here ate the grass and were poisoned, and the animals that hunted, like the lion, were also poisoned by the flesh they ate. And, slowly, all creatures living here take the poison into them. Only the water in this place remains clean."

"Oh."

Sheila tilted her head in thought, wondering if it could be true. Billy shook his head, rolling his eyes.

"If you do not believe it, Billy," Ullin said, "go and hunt. But I will not partake of the meat you bring back. I did not believe the tales either. I made the mistake of eating the meat of a bison that my party hunted on my first trip to Duinnor. We were all sick for days and days afterwards, hardly able to stay in our saddles or even walk. Oh, we were warned, but we paid no heed, being young and foolish and thinking ourselves wiser than lore."

"So no one lives out here at all?" asked Robby.

"Seems a waste of mighty good farmland," added Billy.

"No, there are some people who live upon the plains. They are small clans, mostly, in the south parts. Wild and free of outside rule, skilled horsemen and fierce warriors. They consider themselves to be owners of the plain, guardians of the beasts and rightful partakers of the fruits of the plains."

"Are they Men or are they Elifaen?" Robby asked.

"I don't know. I've never met one, only heard of them. It is said they will not be seen unless they wish to be seen, so stealthy are their movements. Yet the whole plain, from Altoria to Nasakeeria is open to their roaming."

"Well, if we don't find more provisions soon..." Sheila said, not quite believing Ullin.

"I know," he nodded. "As I was saying, we'll make for whatever settlement we come upon and see what we may obtain. This stream marks the borderland between the plains and the west country. The game we will encounter from here on will be safe to eat, if it comes to that."

"You said northwestward?" Robby asked.

"Yes."

"So Vanara is north of us, then?"

"No, it is rather west and south, but there are obstacles between here and there that we cannot cross. A dense and dangerous forest, mainly, and we'll have to go north to get around it."

"Oh. All because we went to Tulith Morgair, I guess."

"No, not just that. Originally we planned to leave from Hill Town, meaning to head west by northwest from there. That would have put us some thirty or forty leagues north and west of where we are now, I believe. Maybe even farther north. But we started from Tallinvale. And pushing through Damar territory kept us somewhat farther south before reaching the plain."

"Oh."

"I've tried to keep us on a westward course, to get us off the plain sooner. Had we gone northwest, we would be another week or two out, with no provisions, and no towns to get any from."

"I see." Robby shook his head at the trouble they had all gone to, were going to, for him.

"Don't fret over it," Ullin stated. "The visit to Tallinvale was uncanny and, perhaps, fortuitous. I wonder if Lyrium knew that our presence there would spark some movement by our grandfather. I wonder if that is not why she arranged our meeting, besides her own purpose. And think of the little ones in Nowhere. Whatever is ahead of us, we leave behind us new friends and allies."

"I suppose so."

" 'At's right, Robby ol' boy," Billy said, nudging him to accept the flask that he held out. "An', besides," he nodded at Ibin sitting across the fire next to Sheila where he was softly plucking the mandolin, "the visit's given ol' Ibin thar, thanks to Ullin, something he ain't never had. Who'd have guessed Ibin would be so good at it!"

Robby looked across the tongues of flame at Ibin, his face almost as angelic as Sheila's in the golden light.

"I think I might have guessed," he said.

Chapter 8

The Ring of Fire

Almost two weeks before the day that Robby and his friends narrowly escaped the stampede and the carrion bees, a party of twelve Kingsmen cadets and two Kingsmen officers departed Duinnor City and rode eastward. Every day that they spent in the saddle and every night that they camped was cold, as persistent misty rain mixed with flecks of snow seemed to follow them mile after mile, day after day. At the end of their tenth day out, they came to the western edge of Nasakeeria, where they made their final bivouac before truly beginning their assignment.

It was to be a routine training exercise, which was frequently performed by small groups such as this one. The campsite, therefore, was one that had been used by similar groups of students for two hundred years, as evidenced by the many old fire rings around the site. Like the countless cadets before them, these youngsters eyed the nearby warning pillar, which was Number 1, as they pitched their tents and had their supper. It was the oldest marker, as it had been the first of all of such markers constructed, as ordered by the King centuries before. With years of gray grime and green moss, the old marker loomed just outside of their camp. In the light of their fires, its large stone skull glowered at the cadets all night long. And the stone likeness was made all the more sinister in appearance by the mist and fog which obscured the tall pillar upon which it rested. In spite of the orders of the two officers in charge of them, the cadets in their tents whispered and talked far into the night, when they should have been sleeping, telling each other all manner of frightful tales pertaining to Nasakeeria. Most of the tales were complete yarns, but some of what was told was true, or at least, in the dark, had the awful ring of truth.

In the morning, which was as dreary as the previous days, they broke camp and saddled their horses, and then they drew lots to split into two squads of six cadets each. Everyone assembled a few yards away from Pillar Number 1, and under its baleful gaze the two Kingsmen veterans reviewed their orders aloud. Each squad was to ride east, one going around the northern border of Nasakeeria while the other went along its southern rim. As they went, the cadets were to mark off on their maps each of the numbered warning pillars that they passed, and they were to note the condition of each one, too. Ahead of time, well before the cadets' arrival here, several markers had been purposefully chalked with words and symbols. Only by examination of each stone pillar would the cadets find these messages, which were to be accurately copied, then rubbed out. The assignment was to be done as quickly as possible, with the fewest number of mistakes, and once a pillar had been ticked off on the maps, there would be no going back to check for any missed messages. An officer would accompany each squad to observe, but neither had any knowledge of which markers held the messages, and could offer no assistance or advice; they accompanied the cadets merely to observe and to enforce the rules of the game. Only when the two squads met up once again on the far side of Nasakeeria would the officers break open their sealed documents which listed the proper messages and markers, and thus judge the two squads against one another.

Finally, the cadets were reminded of an old tradition for this particular training exercise. Whichever squad reached the easternmost marker first, Number 3523, and had found and correctly copied all of the messages, that squad would then enjoy an evening of drinks and dinner at the venue of their choice and at the expense of the losing squad. And, by tradition, if neither squad succeeded in copying all messages accurately, both squads would be expected to serve the Kingsman Stables for two weeks.

So the contest began, and, owing to the fog, each squad was soon out of sight of the other. It would be a grueling and tedious fortnight or longer of hard riding and careful record-keeping. Each squad quickly realized that they could split into relays so that while one cadet stopped to examine a marker, the others could race ahead to the next ones. And so they both progressed, pushing their mounts to their limits with short gallops, taking brief rests while making their notes and checking their maps, then galloping off again. The first day remained misty throughout, with intermittent rain mixed with snow. Yet, by nightfall, each squad had gone twenty miles along their more than two hundred mile course. The second day was without rain or snow, but overcast and colder. Yet the two squads, now some seventy miles apart as the crow flies, continued their hectic pace throughout the day, not stopping until their officers insisted that they do so as daylight failed and a thick fog once more enveloped the plain.

That night, the southern squad decided to light no fires and to eat only jawrock for supper and breakfast, to tend their horses as needed, and depart at the very first sign of dawn to resume their effort. The officer with them did not oppose this plan, but insisted that they set watches according to standing field orders, each watch to be relieved every two hours so that all could get some modicum of rest. Such orders were only prudent and were intended to form and enforce habits in the cadets that ought to be followed whether in time of training or of war. But, this foggy night, those orders would prove deadly.

Five miles directly south of their camp, a party of Dragonkind soldiers jogged northward. These were the same Dragonkind that Robby and his friends saw nineteen days earlier, and this day they had completed the last of their wells. It had been difficult work, and each of the last four wells took two days, so deep they had to dig and so rocky was the ground. To make their task all the harder, twenty of their comrades had been killed by a stampede, and eighteen others by carrion bees, leaving only a dozen to do all of the work of digging. And since their commander was one of those killed, and he had been their navigator through these strange and perilous northern lands, the Dragonkind were off course by over a hundred miles. Thinking themselves well to the east of Nasakeeria, they hurried as best as they could both day and night to reach their secret rendezvous at the foot of the Middlemount plateau, which was actually some hundred leagues to the north and east. There, they intended to meet with others of their kind who stealthily traversed the length of the Bletharn Plains and, by now, had secured food and provisions for the fast approaching winter. But this night, starved, cold, and weak, they stubbornly jogged without rest, sustained by the hope of food and shelter ahead.

So the cadets slept as the solitary watch paced back and forth at the edge of their camp. He pulled his heavy cloak over his head against the wet fog and went to calm the horses that seemed to grow more restless as the hours of his watch crawled by. If it had not been an overcast and moonless night, or the fog not so dense, he might have seen the coming threat. If the light breeze had blown more strongly the other way, the horses might have scented danger and given warning. And if the cadet had not pulled his cloak over his ears, he may have heard something approaching in time to raise the alarm.

When he did at last hear the sound of footfalls, and turned to stare into the dark toward it, the hair of his neck stood on end, and his hand went hesitantly to his hilt. But the first of the Dragonkind did not see him, either, and ran right into the young cadet, colliding hard and knocking him down. In the next few moments, amid yells and confusion, their quick-thinking officer leapt from his bedroll and struck a flare, but it only served to blind and stun nearly everyone.

"Bandits!" the Kingsman cried. "To arms!"

Some of the cadets might have been inclined to think it all a prank, except that the officer who gave the cry and held aloft the flare was suddenly swinging his sword at an intruder before he was himself run through from behind by another. The flare dropped and fizzled out, the horses whinnied and bucked, and cadets shouted as they fumbled for their flares and swords.

"They're taking the horses!" someone cried.

Another flare lit up the scene, and they saw their horses being mounted by the sword-brandishing intruders. Before any of the yelling cadets could make a move to stop them, the Dragonkind galloped away northward. Right past the nearest pillar they rode, then up and over the boney mounds. Suddenly there was a loud hiss, like water thrown onto hot coals, and blue-white flames shot skyward from the ground over which the Dragonkind rode. Stumbling backwards from the intense heat, the cadets watched the flames spread east and west with unbelievable speed, making a wall of fire all the way around Nasakeeria in only a matter of moments. While the swords and belts and other accoutrements of the Dragonkind flew inward toward the forbidden land, their bones, and the bones of the horses they rode, flew outward, flayed of every bit of flesh, to land in a rattling cascade upon the mounds between the wall of fire and the warning markers.

• • •

Within the interior of Nasakeeria, the one called Shazarra was watching from a hill a half-mile from the border. He did not know about the Kingsmen or the Dragonkind, and he was not expecting to see anything unusual. He only kept watch because it was his duty this night to do so. He was trying his best to stay awake and to keep warm as he sat in the open atop his hill, and when the flames lit up the sky and shot east and west around the border, he was stunned, and slowly stood, gaping. Even at this distance, he heard the hiss and whoosh of the flames. A moment later, he felt a hot breeze blow past. He had never seen it happen, not in all his years of keeping watch, and it filled him with fear. He was still trembling, even after the flames had disappeared and all was once again dark. It was several moments before he managed to react. Scrambling to his things, he rummaged desperately through his pack and pulled out a ram's horn. His hands shaking, he put it to his lips and tried to blow, but he was so unnerved that he could not work up the breath. At last, he managed to calm himself, and he blew a long, loud note, and he blew again and again.

• • •

The cadets, still in shock, heard the sound, and they heard when it was answered by a signal drum, and then, more distant, another and another. For the rest of the night, they huddled back to back with their swords drawn, listening to the moan of the horn and to the answer and call of the drums, too afraid to even light a flare to find their missing comrades. As the night progressed, the drums ceased, one by one, until only a few kept beating, answering the horn that continued to blow. When dawn came at last, they found their officer and two of their classmates lying in the wet grass nearby, all dead of grievous wounds. After a brief but heated debate, they decided to first bury their dead. When that was done, they drew lots to choose who would hike westward on foot, making for Duinnor, whilst the rest of the diminished squad carried on eastward to continue their mission. They knew that they had no chance to complete their assignment, much less win the contest, but they were determined by young pride and their zeal for duty and honor to keep on. The morning mists were beginning to clear when they set out, and as they hurried away to resume their work of surveying the markers, they continued hearing the horn and the drums, fading slowly away as the cadets jogged eastward.

Meanwhile, the competing squad had witnessed the bright hot fire that swept past their camp, and were rightly terrified by it. The officer in charge of them first made certain that all of his cadets were present, in case someone had wandered off in the night and had inadvertently crossed the border. Without waiting for dawn, the Kingsman ordered that they break camp and ride together as swiftly as they could back the way they had come and around to the southern border of Nasakeeria to ascertain if any of their comrades were in trouble.

• • •

While all these things were happening outside of Nasakeeria, the interior of that land was throbbing with activity. Not long after Shazarra blew his first notes, his Prince Nightar, who was far off to the northeast in the land's principal town of Nuvodarini, was awakened by the sudden beating of the signal drums nearby to his house. He and his wife sat up in their bed, listening carefully. When there was a pause, they could barely hear a more distant drum before the nearby one resumed.

"The drumtalk says that your cousin signals with his horn," Nightar stated. His tone was calm, but he quickly rose from the bed and began to dress, pausing from moment to moment to listen.

"Is not Shazarra away in the southwest?" asked his wife in a whisper, as she, too, rose and began to dress.

"Yes, Rina," answered Nightar. He paused as he tied his leggings, his head bent to the sound outside. "The drums say Aperion's Fire was seen by many, and it lit up the sky. But Shazarra blew his horn first, before all others who watch our borders. He must have seen its beginning."

Nightar hurried outside, with Rina not far behind him, and already his horse was being brought to him. He was handed his sword belt, and as he strapped it on and strode to his mount, he looked around at others who were coming out from their houses and going to their own horses as they listened to the drumtalk. Walking quickly to the open-sided gazebo where the drumtalker beat out his words of acknowledgement from the great hanging drum, Nightar put up his hand and the drummer ceased.

"Say all are to cease their drumtalk save those who have talk from Shazarra's horn. Tell Shazarra that I come."

"Yes, Prince."

Nightar then went back to his horse where his chief men waited on their mounts. He nodded to them as he mounted and together they galloped away. It was far to Shazarra's watching place, and Nightar and his riders rode hard and swiftly along paths that they knew well both day and night. As they passed through each village along the way, the chief man of the village joined on his horse with them. The village's drumtalker beat a message saying that the Prince was coming, and then he put down his mallets. And so through the night they rode, and through the gray dawn when it came. One by one as they passed through villages, more men joined Prince Nightar's party. And, one by one, the village drumtalkers went silent. Nightar and his retinue rested their horses only once and took water with them at a cold stream, then they continued on. It was noon the next day, with riders and mounts nigh upon exhaustion, when Shazarra saw them coming and took his horn from his lips. Nightar dismounted at the base of the hill, and trudged up the steep slope, bringing with him a waterskin while the others with him, which numbered over two dozen by now, followed afterwards.

"Where?" he asked as he handed the waterskin to Shazarra.

"There, my lord," Shazarra pointed.

"Drink," Nightar commanded as he put his spyglass to his eye.

"Thank you, my lord."

While Shazarra gratefully drank his fill, and the chiefs gathered around, Nightar studied the terrain where Shazarra had pointed.

"What did you see?" he asked, still gazing through the glass.

"It was foggy, my lord. But I saw a bright glow of white light," Shazarra related. "A firestick, I think. It went out, but two more such lights appeared in the same place. At that moment, I saw a tower of blue-white flame rise up, as high as where we stand, or higher. It spread quickly to the right and to the left, faster than I can say this. It was as a blinding wall of light. It burned hot, my Prince, and I felt its heat from where we now stand, and heard a sound like wind. As suddenly as it came, it disappeared."

Everyone listened to the account, waiting for Nightar to speak. The clouds of the day before had parted, but in the clear daylight Nightar could see no sign of anyone across the border or beyond. His glass showed him, though, a narrow band of dry ground, scorched clean of grass, just on this side of the low mounds that were the grass-covered bones which surrounded these lands.

"Elgasi, Galapar, and Sharif, come with me," he said to three of his men as he put away his glass. To the others he said, "We go to take a closer look. Wait here, and let Shazarra have some rest. Bring some victuals to him, if you have any."

Nightar and his men rode down through the stream at the base of the hill and across the sparsely treed flatland toward the border while those on top of the hill watched. When they were within a hundred yards of the ring of scorched earth, Nightar slowed and then halted, taking out his spyglass to look once more. He was now close enough to see the new white bones that littered the mounds, and he was even able to count at least three skulls of men and three of horses. He thought, however, that there were more bones than three men and horses would account for.

"My lord."

The rider next to him pointed nearby where a bit of cloth fluttered in the brush. Nightar dismounted and walked over to it. It was an old shirt of linen—he had never seen such weaving—and there was a belt also dangling from the bush.

"Come!" he called to his men. "Let us search for more such things as these."

Almost immediately, a man called back to him, holding aloft a sword, still in its leather scabbard. Nightar hurried over to look at it while the other men also began finding swords, shoes, clothing, and other articles.

Nightar looked at the sword, a lightweight weapon, thin-bladed and less than a yard long with a slight curve to it and a leather-wrapped grip. Pulling it out from the scabbard, he examined the dull, discolored blade, noting that it appeared intentionally darkened. But its edge was keen, and its point sharp. He was about to put it away when he saw, near the tang, a mark stamped into it. Suddenly he snapped the blade back into the scabbard and called to the men.

"Bring all that you find to me here."

After another hour of searching, Nightar was carefully examining a considerable collection of things including, besides clothing and weapons, the contents of several shoulder bags. There were items such as flint and steel, some cord tied with knots at regular intervals, rope, four short-handled spades, and two mattocks. But what interested Nightar the most were several unusual devices, some made wholly of metal, and an odd tripod, made of wood and brass, with metal hinges to fold away. One of the metal things was made entirely of brass, and had a tube made onto it in a manner that allowed it to slide along a crescent frame. These items seemed somehow familiar to him, but he could not think of why. There was also a leather case filled with writing tools, including a bottle of ink, numerous short quills, and a little book filled with writing in a script that, like the other things, he almost recognized.

Sitting on the ground with many of these things in his lap, he decided that he would need to examine them at length later on, and he was putting the things back into the case when a small box slipped out. It was made of oiled leather, no bigger than his hand, and when he opened it, there was another small wooden box within. When he lifted the lid of that one, he was fascinated to see a thin bit of flat metal, shaped like an arrow, balanced on a pin within the box. It seemed loose, and when he turned to put it out of his own shadow to see it better, he was surprised to see that although the box turned, the little arrow within it remained in the same position. Indeed, no matter which way he turned the box, the arrow always pointed the same way. Looking up in that direction, he suddenly realized that it was pointing northward. Fascinated, he stood and walked around, staring at the device; no matter which way he turned, as long as he held it steady and level, the arrow always pointed north. Suddenly he looked at the other contents of the case, the brass device, the little book of scribblings, and at the nearby folding tripod.

"Everything is to be taken to the Great House," he called out to his men as he put away the compass. "They are to be laid out in the council room, and no one is to be admitted inside. No one is to see any of these things, nor are you to say a word about what we have found."

"Yes, Prince."

"Carefully bundle everything up in your bedrolls and go quickly. I will go back up the hill and talk to our chief men. I will follow you very soon back to Nuvodarini and come directly to the Great House. Remember, no one is to look upon these things, and you are not to speak of them."

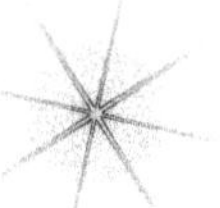

Chapter 9

A Loaf for a Pen

By the end of the next day, just as Ullin had predicted, the land became more varied and hilly. This was a relief, in an odd kind of way, though it made the going more difficult. But it was good to see trees in greater abundance, and often they rode through small woods nestled between low ridges, the tops of which remained grassy though somewhat rocky, with great gray stones jutting out in places.

"Look there," Ullin pointed to their left as they rode over one of these rises. Below, in an open flat plain, were dozens of squarish stones, some nearly twice the height of a man. Most stood upright, in a wide circular arrangement, but some leaned over, pointing sunward.

"What is it?" Sheila asked.

"Some kind of ancient temple, perhaps," Ullin shrugged. "I've seen standing stones something like that in Vanara and even in the Eastlands. Ashlord told me that they are from before the First Age, but he did not know their purpose."

They continued up the ridge and could see a great distance from its heights. To the north and west were the clear patterns of farmlands with their patchwork appearance. Behind them rolled out the plains like a vast carpet. But Ullin's eyes were upon something to the southwest, far away on the horizon, and he shielded his eyes from the sun to look harder.

"What do you see?"

"I don't know. That dark shape covering the farthest horizon, just there. See it?"

They all rode up and together studied the dark-colored horizon.

"A forest, mebbe?" Billy offered.

"Maybe," Ullin answered, taking out his spyglass and giving a long look.

"I don't think so," he said at last. "I can't tell. It is in the southwest. If it is the forest, we are much farther north than I would have figured. No, I don't think so. We haven't even crossed the Long Road that leads from Duinnor to Altoria. And we just now see farmlands. I don't know what it is, but I don't think it is forest. Whatever it is, we do not go that way. The sun sinks quickly. Let us make a few more miles before camping. Tomorrow or the next day, we may find provisions."

• • •

The night was uneventful, and not as cool as previous nights as a thick blanket of clouds moved over them. Ullin woke them early, and they went through the usual routine of eating a modest breakfast, putting away their things, and getting the horses ready. While tying their shoulder bags to their saddles, Robby looked across the dimly lit landscape, gray and cold and barren, and then over his shoulder at Billy, who was rechecking his cinches.

"I never thought I'd say this," Robby said, "but I think I actually miss the store."

"I thought ye always said it was borin'."

"That's what I miss!"

"Well, I don't reckon I blame ye. This ain't much like the sort of 'ventures we used to dream on."

"No, it isn't. But there's another thing. At the store, I mean. I was beginning to get good at it, you know. Handling things, trades and sales. Inventories and such."

"I reckon so, since ye spent more time thar than most anywhar else all yer whole life. An' ye proved yer skill back yonder at Nowhar."

"But now I'm a fish out of water," Robby went on, "and I hardly know a thing, it seems, compared to what I need to know. About what's ahead, coming up. You know what I'm trying to say."

"Well, thar ain't no denyin' it's a lot on yer plate. An' the idear of bein' a king," Billy dropped to a whisper, as if saying such a thing was wrong or dangerous, "why it's enough to put anyone off a meal. But mebbe when we find Griferis ye'll feel different. Ashlord told me it's like some kinda school. An' ye always did fine in school, didn't ye? Which reminds me. I dreamt the oddest dream last night. We was at Broadweed's school, us two, an' we...."

Robby smiled and feigned interest, letting Billy relate the dream, though he was already quite familiar with it, having been there.

• • •

By dawn, when they were miles farther along their way, a gentle rain was falling, and it kept up steadily all morning. By the time they reckoned it was noonish, they could see fields and pastures here and there, and they came upon a narrow farming path, obviously cut by the wear of carts and cattle, and since it went their way, they followed it. Now and then, they lifted their hoods for a better look around, thinking they smelled smoke, but they saw no source of the odor. Later that afternoon, the rain came heavier on sudden gusts of wind. Though it was not very cold, the company was fairly miserable, and they wondered if a dry place could be found for the night. When they came around a bend in the path and upon a cleared field, Ullin drew them to a halt.

Ahead and across the field was a farmhouse that was tumbled into a pile of charred ruins. There was an outbuilding, too, made of stone, but its thatch roof was gone and only a couple of timbers of the rafters remained, black and broken. There were no cattle or livestock, nor presence of any living thing.

"Let's be careful," Ullin instructed pulling his cloak away from the hilt of his saddle sword. As they neared, they saw that this was not recent work, though the timbers still reeked of the fire.

"What's 'at?" Billy pointed to an object standing some few yards away from the ruins. It was a kind of effigy, erected of sticks and wrapped round with lengths of wicker vines into the shape of a man. It stood facing the house, arms down along its sides, its face a featureless wrapping of vines, some with broad withered leaves still attached.

"Wait here," Ullin told them as he got down from his saddle. He handed his reins to Robby and approached the place, looking carefully at the odd effigy as he neared the house ruins. He picked through some of the timbers, gingerly lifting a few aside to look underneath. Finding nothing, he went to the outbuilding and looked around there and then he went back to the main ruins. He crouched down at several places, looking at the ground, picking up a few twigs, and finally came back.

"This happened a few days ago. I found no bodies, but there is much trampling about."

"Was it an accident, maybe?"

"No. If your house catches afire, why would you trample your gardens that are nowhere nearby? Everything is still inside. No one has come to remove the tools and metal things that could be salvaged. There are signs of struggle, mostly covered by the rain, but enough to tell that a large group of people were here, fifty or so."

"So what's that thing in the yard?" Sheila asked, pointing at the wicker effigy.

Ullin shook his head. "I don't know. Maybe those who attacked this place left it behind?" He got back into his saddle. "But I don't like the looks of it."

"Meneither," agreed Ibin. "Whereare, wherearethepeople,now?"

"No bodies, so I guess they went away."

"Whar to?" Billy asked.

"That way," Ullin pointed southward by west. He nudged his mount forward. "Let's go."

"Do you think war has reached here?" Robby asked as he rode up alongside Ullin.

"I don't know."

They kept on, very cautiously, all with their hoods back, in spite of the rain, to keep an unrestrained watch on their surroundings. It soon tapered to a misty drizzle as the day began to darken into evening. They hoped to find shelter, a barn, perhaps, or some natural cover. But the land was open and sparse of trees, and they had little hope of seeing any shelter in the starless night, anyway.

"We may as well move off the path and find rest the best way we can on the wet ground," Ullin said at last. "We can use the tarpaulins on the pack animals for a bit of ground cover. Not much hope of a fire tonight, I'm afraid."

"Might not be safe, anyway," Sheila said, "given what we saw earlier."

"True enough."

• • •

It was not a comfortable night. They decided upon their watches, Robby taking the first one while the others tried to settle under their blankets. They munched on dried jerky and ate the last of the nuts given to them by the Nowhereans, and they struggled into a wretched sleep. By himself, Robby stayed on his feet, there being nowhere dry to sit, and he wrapped a blanket around his shoulders for extra warmth. He walked around and around the camp, careful of where he went so as not to wander far from his companions, nor too close so that he might step on them in the darkness, sometimes stopping to pet the horses. He struggled to see anything, but the night was black and overcast. The air was heavy and dead silent, not a cricket whirred, nor did any night bird sing, and Robby's squishy steps seemed loud to his ears. At last he heard a stirring from the others, then Sheila's voice saying that she would take the next watch.

"Ugh!" she quietly said to Robby. "I made a nice puddle where I sank into the ground as I slept. Now my entire side is soaked."

"Sorry."

"If you can wait a little longer, I think I have some dry things in my pack."

"No problem," Robby yawned. "Take your time."

She was soon back and throwing her cape around her head. A few stars managed to peek through the rolling clouds, but their light was strong enough only to illuminate vague, shadowy mists.

"Can't see a thing tonight!" she said.

"No, but you can hear the slightest sound," Robby replied. As tired as he was, he was in no particular hurry to go to sleep.

"Are you not sleepy?" Sheila asked, putting her hand on his elbow.

He took it and brought it around so that they stood arm in arm.

"Yes, I am. I am more weary than I've a right to be."

"What is on your mind that keeps you up?"

Robby sighed softly and shook his head.

"What isn't? Everything. This whole journey. You. Ullin. Everything just seems bleak and hard, sometimes. Like trying to drive a cart when the wheels don't turn properly and the horse pulls whichever way it wants."

"Oh, Robby!"

"Remember what you told me back at the ruined city? About feeling some changes happening to you?"

"Yes."

"You were right. You have changed. You are changing. We all are. You seem to have some power over Ullin, some kind of hold on him. He is wary of you."

"Why? What have I done?"

"You have done nothing. At least, I don't think you have. He says you haven't, anyway. But since we left the Thunder Mountains, he has been uneasy around you. At first I thought...." Robby trailed off, and shook his head.

"You thought what?"

"I thought that maybe—"

"What?"

"That maybe, while I wasn't paying attention, that you and Ullin—"

"That's ridiculous! I don't believe you!"

"I know. I know! Let's keep it down shall we? This is embarrassing enough, and I don't want the others to hear."

"But Robby!"

"The thing is, Sheila, somehow Esildre is mixed up in it. I think maybe she laid some kind of spell on him."

"I have only my own charm."

Robby flinched at the voice and glanced quickly at Sheila, but it was Esildre on his arm, smiling demurely back at him in the dim light.

"What?"

The vision evaporated, and Sheila looked blankly at him.

"I said let go of my arm!"

"Oh, I'm sorry!"

"Gosh, your grip was like iron! Whatever has gotten into everybody? What is all this about Esildre?"

Robby, still reeling from the brief vision, found that his mouth was suddenly dry.

"I..., I'm so sorry. I didn't mean to hurt you!" he stammered. "Sheila, maybe I'm just imagining things, seeing threats where there are none."

"I wish you would just speak plainly. You seem to forget that we are all here on account of you. The least you could do is be honest and straightforward with us. And with me of all people!"

"I am being as honest and straight with you as I know how!" he said, frustrated with new concerns about his fears. Again, as it had for several days, now, Ashlord's warning about Esildre came back to him. Now his own incompetence threatened to push away the one who cared most for him, and he quickly tried to think of a way of making peace with Sheila, of restoring her trust in him, and, perhaps also to vindicate her love for him. "There is one way I can show you," he said, though his stomach fluttered at what he was about to suggest.

"Show me what?"

"Show you that I am trying. Show you how difficult it is to explain. You'll have to see for yourself."

"See what?"

"Listen. Tonight, if you chance to dream of Barley, go to the pond."

"What? Dream of Barley?"

"Yes. If you dream of Barley, go to the pond where we used to meet. Sit by the old tree at the water's edge."

"Is this some joke?"

"No. Do this for me. For us!"

"How can I know what I will dream about? I may as well dream about Tallinvale, or Nowhere, or even some rabbit hole for all I know. What has it to do with anything?"

"Please, Sheila. Just remember. Go to the pond. Sit by the tree like we used to do. Will you promise me that?"

Sheila shook her head.

"I worry about you, Robby."

"Then help me. Do this for me. Promise!"

"Alright, I promise! I promise. To the pond."

"Good. Thank you. You'll see."

Sheila shook her head again and pulled her cloak more tightly about her.

"You need sleep," she said to Robby angrily.

Robby nodded through the sting of her tone and smiled.

"You are right. Good night, then."

Robby made his way back to the circle where the others slept, trying not to step on anyone until he found the tarpaulin that Sheila had recently used. He gently folded it, trying not to make too much noise, in an effort to make a dry spot. He finally got it situated and crawled between the flaps of it and wrapped himself in a blanket underneath. He was tired and his head hurt. The ground was cold and soggy, and he was worried that he had gambled too much by making his request of Sheila. Now, if only he could do his part, perhaps she would gain more trust in him. On the other hand, even if his idea worked, she might wind up trusting him less than ever. But he had to try something.

• • •

It was not much later, according to how Robby reckoned time in his slumber, that Sheila was beside him, in more ways than one. Together they huddled under their blankets, and they were also at the familiar old pond. He had a book in his hand. She put her bow down and sat beside him.

"Something told me ye'd be here," she said, speaking in her old way and smiling with the old gleam in her eyes that told him that she was truly thrilled to be with him.

"And why not?" he said, careful to play his part. "Is this not where we always meet for our lessons?"

"Truly. But it seems an odd thing to have a readin' lesson out of a book that ain't got no writin' on its pages."

Surprised, Robby looked at the book in his hands. Just as she had observed, the pages were completely blank. Well, he thought, this was her dream after all. "Then we will have a writing lesson, instead. Here, take the book upon your lap. Now take this pen and write down some sentence. Any sentence at all."

"But that is an odd pen," she said, remarking at the loaf of bread that he handed her.

"Truly an odd one," he said, a bit flustered. "But for our purposes it will write just as well as any."

"An' what am I suppose to use for ink?"

"Why, right there is a whole pond of ink."

"Indeed."

She bent over and dipped the end of the loaf into the blue-green water and then touched the dripping end to the page. Immediately, words appeared where she touched.

All the while, as Robby observed the odd writing, he was aware of another presence, lurking in the nearby wood. He turned to brush back some of Sheila's long hair and glanced into the trees. Standing among the trunks was a shadowy figure. It had the form of a person, but had no features that he could distinguish other than the strange wavering wings that floated from its back. Robby's shoulders tightened, and his stomach clenched at the sight, but he forced himself to turn his attention back to Sheila's writing. She was filling the page with word after word, sentence after sentence, and he was aghast at what he saw.

"I hate you. I hate you. I hate you. I hate you. I hate you. Leave me alone!"

"Sheila," Robby asked, his voice shaking, "do you know what it is that you write?"

She looked at him quizzically and laughed.

"Don't be silly! I'm writin' it, ain't I?"

Then she looked back down at the pages and burst into tears.

"No! Oh, Robby, no! This ain't what I wrote! It ain't what I meant to write!"

Robby's plan was going horribly wrong. The dream filled with terrible anxiety, and Robby felt it coming from the shadow-figure like stones, landing in heaps upon Sheila who was trying to rub off the writing from the page as she wailed.

"No, no, that's alright, Sheila! I know!" Robby desperately tried to calm her. "Someone else put that writing there."

He glanced over his shoulder. The shadow-figure was closer than before, a looming terror, incongruous and stark as it stood in the beautiful moss-floored clearing the two lovers knew so well. He looked back at Sheila, but she was no longer there. It was Esildre, and the sound of Sheila's sobs had turned to a low, meanspirited laugh.

"This is not right!" he shouted, jumping to his feet. Esildre disappeared, and there was Sheila again, staring up at him.

"Whar're ye goin'? I didn't mean to write it! I promise I didn't! Robby, don't go!"

It was dawning on him that this was not Sheila's dream he had entered, at all, that it was his own nightmare. He looked around, panic clawing at his chest, and he tried to see out of it, he tried to look for the light, the thread that would lead him back. Something else began to gain his awareness, the light faded, a voice called to him from a far distance. He felt himself sinking. Sheila stood, dropping the book and clutching Robby's arm as the glitter of a sunlit tear ran down her cheek just as if the amber of her eyes was melting and draining away.

Robby awoke with a start and sat up blinking, his stomach in knots of foreboding. Thick fog surrounded the camp, diffusing the predawn light, and muffling all sound. The fog came and went like the silent footsteps of giants, falling and lifting, obscuring even the nearby shapes of Ullin and Ibin as they prepared the horses. Sheila shifted in her blanket beside Robby and sat up, too.

"What is it?" she asked in a whisper, seeing the intense way in which he tried to penetrate the mist.

"I don't know. Just a queer feeling," he said, turning again to look at Ullin. The Kingsman was cinching a saddle and then stood straight and passed a hand down his arm, turning his head to peer into the gray with intense attention.

"Get ready to go!" Robby told Sheila as he scrambled over to Billy. "Billy! Get up! Wake up!"

"What?"

"Get ready to go! Hurry!"

Robby grabbed up his blanket and trotted to the horses.

"Ullin, what do you sense?"

"Nothing that I can explain," Ullin said, glancing at Billy and Sheila as they went about hastily breaking camp. "But the hairs of my arms know something, and so does the back of my neck. What about you?"

"A feeling. Like we aren't alone."

"Blasted fog!" Ullin nodded. "I don't relish blundering into whatever is out there."

"What's that? I smell smoke," Robby said as he hurriedly lashed his blanket to his saddle.

"Uhhuh,Ismellittoo," said Ibin. "Itsmells, itsmellslikepitchpots."

"It does."

Ullin closed his eyes and turned his head this way then the other, trying to sense the way the air moved. "It's useless. I cannot tell which way it comes from. Hurry! Make ready to go. Be quick and quiet about it. I fear some enemy is nearby."

Robby quickly rolled up his ground cloth and tied it hastily onto the saddle, then hung his bag, too. The others worked just as quickly, and said nothing. They all felt it, like the fog, pressing in on every side. Except when absolutely needed to tie off a cord, or cinch a strap, all their eyes strained in every direction.

"Maybe we should sit tight until—did you hear that?"

Ullin nodded and slowly drew his sword. The rest did likewise as they huddled together with their horses and listened. The dense fog swirled around them. They strained, hands on hilts, trying to see or to hear some clue of what was hidden in the mist. Muffled voices and a few shouts, distorted through the gray air. As soon as the company faced the direction of the sounds, other noises came from different directions.

"It's all 'round us," Billy whispered.

As the noise grew closer, it also became more distinct, and Robby thought it sounded like many people softly and randomly clapping gloved hands. Other noises mixed in, thuds and metallic clinks. The noise grew louder, and suddenly dozens of figures came bounding through and all around their camp. Chaos ensued so quickly that it was hard to understand what was happening. One figure, wearing tightly woven wicker armor, was pulling a line of rope tied from hand to hand to six or seven men. This group was surrounded by several other men in similar wicker-wear, and one was pushing the captives along as another shouted, "Run or die!"

As they skirted one side of the camp, moving like shadows through the fog, another group likewise with prisoners appeared passing through the mists on the other side. Several more soldiers appeared, hesitating when they encountered the travelers while others of their kind came up from behind.

"Take them!" someone shouted.

One grabbed Sheila by the arm and tried to pull her away while another made for Billy. Sheila's assailant struck away her sword as another clutched her arm, but, letting go of her reins, she quickly brought out her daggers, slashing and jabbing until one stumbled away into the mists and the other fell dead at her feet. By this time, Ullin had dispatched Billy's attackers and was turning into others who were coming at them, now with their own swords drawn. Ibin tossed one of the strangely armored men against another to knock them both down, and turned to two others who were making a try for Billy's horse when he saw Robby being pummeled by three attackers.

"Watch out, Ibin!" Billy shouted just as a sword was swung at the big man. Sheila reached over and deflected it just in time, then Ibin gave his attacker a crushing blow to the face with his massive fist. Swinging back around, he saw only enclosing the fog.

"Robby! Robby!" He sidestepped a fleeing assailant and tripped over a dead attacker as he tried to move to the now empty spot where Robby had just been.

"Here! Here I—" came the distinct answer, cut off by a cracking sound. Ibin charged into the fog, but after only a short dash found himself alone and out of sight of everyone.

"Robby!"

"Robby!" Ullin's voice came from somewhere behind him. "Ibin!" Ibin took a few more steps, desperately trying to figure which way Robby went.

"Robby!"

"Ibin! Robby! This way!" Ullin shouted. Billy and Sheila, gripping the reins of the horses, added their voices to Ullin's. After a few long moments, Ibin's form took shape and emerged from the mist as he came jogging back to them. He glanced wildly around the camp, and then tears sprang from his eyes as he realized Robby was not there.

"Ilosthim. Ilosthim. IlostRobby!"

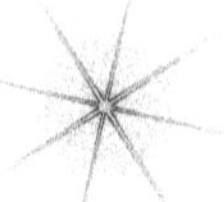

Chapter 10

The Cult of Wokan

Day 131
114 Days Remaining

Ullin and Sheila led the way on foot, as fast as they could follow the tracks through the wet grass. Billy and Ibin hurried behind, tugging the reins of the horses. It was not long before all sounds of the raiding parties had outpaced them, and it was clear from the muddy tracks that, even if they caught up with Robby and his captors, they would be seriously outnumbered in a fight.

"Look here, Sheila," Ullin said. "More tracks merge. It is a great number."

To Ullin's trained eye, more accustomed to tracking two-footed quarry than Sheila's, it was plain that a large group of captives were being moved along by others. Off to either side of the main crush of grass where the captives had passed were two other small lines of tracks. These were likely made by more guards and soldiers, and, studying the ground as he went, he counted at least forty sets of footprints. From Ullin's intense concern, and from her own guesses at the tracks they saw, Sheila felt a growing sense of hopelessness the farther they went. Still, they pressed on. Then, as if the fog was not enough of a problem, there came a downpour, heavy and sudden.

"It is no use!" cried Sheila over the noise of the hard rain. "We'll never regain the trail!"

The group halted, letting the cloudburst drench them, the sound of it filling their ears and shushing all else. Somewhere distant lightning weakly flashed, and a halfhearted rumble slowly passed. Ullin shook his head to Ibin's questioning look, and Billy wiped his face of the streams that ran through his eyes. As abruptly as it had come, the rain halted, and the fog quickly reformed, as thick as before, pressing in like soft but stubborn walls.

"We must keep on as best as we can," Ullin said, his eyes on the ground. "The grass is still crushed at their passing, and the rain has not washed all signs away. This way!"

On they went, for what seemed miles at an agonizing pace. Just when Ullin was about to suggest they simply mount and ride hard in the direction that the tracks seemed to be going, they heard the sound of approaching horses. Immediately, they all armed themselves, and by the time they turned to face the threat, it was coming hard and fast from behind them. Suddenly, a company of riders burst through a wall of mist and bore down on them with lances leveled and swords drawn.

"Brace yerselves!" cried Billy, gripping his sword with both hands.

Sheila's bow creaked, but Ullin stepped into her, pushing it down.

"Kingsmen!" he cried, holding his sword-hilt high. "How fare you?"

The riders, wearing dark green surcoats trimmed in gold, saw Ullin's sword, and they lifted their lances, but came on fast nonetheless.

"What name carries the King's sword?" challenged one of the soldiers.

"Ullin Saheed, House of Tallin and Fairoak, Captain of the King's Ranks, First Kingsman, First Army, Third Engineer Battalion, detached to the King's Post as Special Courier, lately of the Eastlands Realm," Ullin smartly answered. "And what Kingsman asks?"

As the horsemen surrounded the group, their leader dismounted and quickly strode up to Ullin for a close look. "Bartow, Captain of the King's Ranks, Fourth Army, Fourth Assault Battalion, lately of Duinnor, that's who. And what is your sign and word?"

"My sign is this," Ullin held up his hand so that his index finger pointed upward with his thumb sticking out at a right angle, "and my word is library."

"Aye, then," the captain said, "and my answer is this," he held up his hand as Ullin had, curved the two fingers as Ullin had, then twisted his hand so that all his fingers were straight and outstretched, palm down, "and book dust is my answer to your word."

The two nodded, sheathed their swords, and shook hands.

"What brings a First Kingsman out here, far from Vanara?"

"We travel west, but we were attacked this morning by a band of raiders who took one of our party," Ullin explained. "And now we track them."

"Well, you must leave him to his fate, I'm afraid," Bartow said. "We have orders to bring anyone we find to our general."

"But we cannot leave Robby," Sheila protested.

"We must continue on," Ullin pleaded. "We travel on urgent business, and our companion is essential to our mission. Besides, he is our kith and kin, and so we cannot give up."

"My orders are strict and without exception. I am to bring all and any I find back to town. Man, woman, child, friend, enemy, or stranger. No living person may remain, if you take the meaning of my orders." Bartow tapped the sword hilt at his waist. "And all horses are to be confiscated, anyway."

"But we gotta keep goin'!"

"Billy," Ullin said, "he cannot disobey his orders. He is a Kingsman." Then, with a dip of his head to Captain Bartow, "To your general, then. Let us make haste to gain his leave to continue our pursuit."

"I doubt if that will be likely," Bartow said, regaining his saddle. He waved at the other twenty or so riders as Ullin and the others got to their horses. "To Edgewold! Quick pace and lively!"

• • •

Robby felt the knots around his hands loosen at his will, but he held them together so that his captors would have no inkling of his skill. But they were too near, with their swords drawn, and too many to outrun, so he waited and watched for an opportune moment to slip away. Meanwhile, he paid attention to the soggy ground being negotiated. His bound hands were tied with a tether to the neck of the captive in front of him, and the captive behind Robby was likewise tied and tethered to Robby's neck. Already, after two hours into the fast march through the fog, both the one in front and the one behind Robby had tripped and fallen, nearly choking him unconscious each time. Robby was determined not to stumble and inflict such pain on them as he had endured, and, so far, he had slipped only once, but kept to his feet by some miraculous balancing act.

Around him were at least a hundred such prisoners as himself, tied in like manner in groups, being pulled and pushed and shoved by the soldiers. As far as he could guess, his fellow captives were mostly farmers and field laborers, along with several women and children, and there were a few others that he supposed must be from a nearby town by the clerkish looks of their attire. All were being herded by ill-mannered and coarse soldiers, dressed in brown and gray cloaks and wearing tightly woven wicker coverings that were shaped and worn like armor around their chests and backs and covering portions of their arms and legs, too. They were armed with swords and pikes and did not hesitate to use them to prod stragglers or quell the little resistance given by the tired and demoralized prisoners. Robby had obviously been mistaken for one of the local folk, his travel-stained cloak and clothes making him appear not much different from those in the miserable crowd around him. His efforts to explain that he was just a traveler only got him a sharp elbow to the mouth. His lip still bled, but the pain was not too bad. It was the shock of the uncalled-for jab that hurt the most. He had only to look around at the beaten and bloodied faces of his new fellows to understand he had gotten off lightly for speaking.

But there was one among the captives who stood out remarkably from all the rest. He was tall, about Ullin's height, thin but well-built, with mid-length blond hair and defiant blue eyes. Robby saw that blood trickled down the man's chin from the edge of his mouth, and blood was caked on his soiled brown blouse. Another dried stream etched a dark line around his eyebrow and down his cheek. He wore leather breeches, tucked into laced boots better suited for riding or stalking than for marching, and he had the wristbands of a fighter. Indeed, an empty sheath was in his belt, and there was clear evidence of a recent struggle from the cuts and tears in his clothing. He was tied in a separate line of prisoners marching roughly parallel with Robby. And now and then he looked toward Robby observantly.

Robby nodded to him once but was jerked by the stumble of the bumpkin in front of him and did not notice any acknowledgement. After a long while of paying attention only to his own footfalls, Robby saw that the man had somehow maneuvered his line closer to Robby's, and for a while they marched not ten feet apart from one another.

It was late in the afternoon, the fog long gone and the ground was fairly dry when the leader of the captors called everyone to a halt.

"Rest!" he bellowed, and nearly all of the prisoners fell at once to the ground to ease their legs. Robby knelt as best as he could and reached to loosen somewhat the rope around his neck.

"You're not from around these parts, are you?"

Robby turned and saw the stranger lying easily on his side. But for the ropes and knots binding him, he may as well have been lounging on a comfortable couch on the veranda of some fine mansion overlooking sweet gardens. Robby shook his head, his mouth too dry and his breath too short to speak just yet.

"Me, neither. Just got sorta caught up in this mess."

"If ye'd done yer job right, none of us'd be here," growled a man nearby.

"Aw, shut-up! If you had any sense, you would've listened to me and be far away by now. 'Sides, I still ain't been paid." Turning back to Robby, the blond-haired one said, "These fools hired me and a few of my mates to guard their farms. But six against forty ain't good odds, and, as I'm the only one left, that's the proof of it. And not a grain of gold. I'm startin' to think there wasn't any gold, anyways. Which makes you bunch of cowards also a bunch of cheaters! You oughta be ashamed! Ever' last one of you!"

Then, turning back to Robby again, he said, "My name's Tyrin."

"Robby."

"Good to meet you. You got the looks of an Eastlander. How on earth did you wind up here?"

"Bad luck, I guess."

"Tell me 'bout it! This whole land's nothing but bad luck, if you ask me."

"Where are they taking us?"

"To their town, I reckon," he replied. Then with sharp unhidden sarcasm, and a bit louder, "Who knows? We may even meet the grand Pooh-bah himself!"

"Shh!" hissed one of the nearby prisoners.

"Watch yore tongue!" bellowed one of the nearby guards, stomping over from behind Tyrin to give him a hard kick in the ribs.

"Whatcha gonna do? Kill me?" Tyrin hissed back contemptuously, though in obvious pain. "I know your orders are to bring back a hundred, and you're shy by eight already. Or maybe you like the idea of joining us?"

"Maybe you'd like to keep yore tongue in yore head. Or would'ya rather it be on me pike?"

"Do us a favor," muttered one of the villagers with a contemptuous glance at Tyrin.

"Get up! Move out!" barked the leader some distance ahead. As Tyrin got to his feet, the guard gave him another kick behind the knee, sending him sprawling back down, pulling three others with him in a chain of painful crunches.

"Ye'll be the death of us," said one of them, cursing Tyrin.

"Oh, quit your whining!" Tyrin replied.

After not more than a mile, while everyone else grew steadily more depressed and glum, Tyrin seemed to regain his strength, and Robby actually heard him humming a jaunty ditty. In spite of his own pain and worry, Robby smiled at the man's pluck. He was reminded very much of Billy in the hands of Bailorg. With a sudden pang, he missed his friends very much.

"What're ye so chipper about?" growled the man tethered behind Tyrin.

"What's there not to be chipper about? It's a fine day, the air is fresh and cool, the sun's come out, and it's light is warm. Just right for a stroll in the country. May as well enjoy it. Might be the last. Live for the moment, enjoy life, make the best of what you've got, is what I say!"

"Live for the moment! I live for the moment I get me hands around yer throat!"

"Well, ain't you the gloomy Gus!" Tyrin then looked Robby's way with the same terrible twinkle in his eyes and half-grin on his face that he had so often seen in Billy just before some risky sport. By now, Robby had given up making any quick escape—the guards were just too close. As well, any hope of a quick rescue seemed less likely with every step. So as he stumbled on with the rest of them, he took some comfort from Tyrin's presence, strangers though the two were.

The terrain they passed through became hilly, and grass gave way to thick vines with broad, coarse leaves. In some places, large swaths of the stuff had been cleared, and in other places it had been woven into living archways, long and dark, where the heavy air moved little, though it was breezy above.

"Kudzu!" Robby heard the man behind him say.

"The bane of our farms and fields!" muttered another nearby.

They came out and up a hill from where there was nothing but the dark green leaves as far as the eye could see. Here and there, the vines had overgrown stands of trees, pulling some down and fully covering others, making of them weird and grotesque shapes and ominous humps and bulges which, in the slanting sunlight, cast furtive black shadows.

"I guess we know where they get their devilish armor," said Tyrin as they crowded through an opening in the leafy sea. The pathway was rough with crisscrossing vines, leafless from being trod upon, and Tyrin tripped over one and stumbled into Robby, bumping shoulders with him.

"Sorry 'bout that, buddy."

"Watch yer feet!" screamed a guard at all of the prisoners, since Tyrin was not the only one having trouble on the vine-strewn path.

"Do that again when I stumble," whispered Robby.

"Right."

Robby watched for a likely place, as the way narrowed, pushing them closely together. He also watched the guards, judging their distance and the crowd of prisoners between them. Sooner than he thought, he found his chance and tripped. Tyrin immediately stumbled, too, and they both fell next to each other, pulling down many others as they went in a confusion of yells, curses, and groans. Robby quickly grabbed Tyrin's hands and loosened his knots effortlessly.

"How did you do that?" Tyrin whispered in amazement, reaching for Robby's wrists to undo his knots.

"Never mind. Get up!" Robby hissed, loosely wrapping the cord back around Tyrin's wrists so that he could hold it there. "And be ready!"

It was fortunate for them that the others around did not notice, nor did the guards when they came pushing and shoving and pulling people back up to their feet, generously applying encouraging punches and kicks. What was not so fortunate was that after they resumed their march, one of the guards remained just behind Robby, and another took up his position a few feet in front of Tyrin.

The trail they followed grew darker as the kudzu around them thickened and grew tall and tangled overhead. Robby saw little opportunity to make a run, though he had loosened his hand tether and could make easy work of the one about his neck.

"There's but two of 'em," Tyrin said at a narrow pass when the two were forced together. "I say let's make our move, NOW!"

Before Robby could react, Tyrin pulled the rope from around his neck, just as a guard turned around and saw him. Tyrin snapped the freed line around the guard's neck, jerked the line hard, gagging the surprised man, and shoved him into the crowd behind. Turning, he saw the second guard raising his sword to swing when Robby pushed through and parried the blow with Swyncraff, following with a hard left into the man's face that cracked every knuckle on Robby's fist.

"What the—!" cried Tyrin.

"Let's go!"

Together they crashed into the vines, tearing their way through the tangle as fast as they could go. Behind them was the noise of riotous confusion as other captives tried to make their own escape, but they were being cruelly put down by the enraged guards. By the time their pursuers were well into the vines, Tyrin and Robby were forty yards ahead of them. It was rough going, no easier for prey than for predator, ducking through thin spindly trunks, slipping on the debris below, tripping on the grasping runners that seemed to grow everywhere they stepped.

"Wait!" Tyrin cried, grabbing Robby by the shoulder. They crouched, listening, unable to see more than ten yards in any direction. The sound of movement could clearly be heard. "This way!"

Tyrin pulled Robby to the left and shoved him under a rotten log where the canopy above dipped down thick with leaves, then he crawled up next to him. On their bellies, they waited and listened as the noise of the guards drew near. A pair of legs appeared just in front of their hiding place. They stopped, and their owner cursed.

"Leave them!" a not-too-distant voice shouted. "We'll not find them. Let the finger of Wokan have them!"

"Aye. With pleasure," came the response of the one close by, and the legs retreated. Still holding their breath, Tyrin and Robby waited. Soon the sound of the train of captives became muffled and distant until a thick silence was all they heard. Tyrin and Robby waited even longer until at last they breathed easier.

"Where did you get that stick?" Tyrin asked, turning over onto his side and nodding at Swyncraff, still clutched by Robby.

"It is my belt, actually."

"Belt? Well, a mighty odd belt, it is! But I'm grateful to it, and to you! Ha! Ha! We sure gave 'em the slip, didn't we?"

"Next time, give me a little more warning."

"Sure, sure."

Their voices sounded uncanny loud and hollow in the closeness of the silent tangle, and, as a nervous reaction to the sound of their own words, they listened a little longer just to be sure.

"I wonder what all that 'finger of Wokan' stuff was about?" Tyrin asked, in a more subdued tone of voice.

"I think that's what it was all about," replied Robby, turning over and pointing to their legs. Several runners had somehow managed to wrap themselves around their shins. As they watched, another slithered around Tyrin's ankle.

"Whoa!" Tyrin yelled, sitting up and kicking himself free until he could stand, pulling Robby up along with him as he stamped on the offending vines. "That's not even funny!"

"Not the kind of place to take a nap in," Robby agreed, pulling a vine off his shoulder.

"Ain't that the truth!"

"So. Which way is which?"

"Hard to say. But from the sunbeams over there, that way must be west. I'm all for getting as far away from here as I can."

"Probably too risky to go back to the path we came in on."

"And our crashing around in here's liable to be heard for miles."

"I doubt it. Everything is pretty well muffled by the thickness of this stuff."

"Well, maybe. And I reckon who's listening anyway? But night's coming, so let's be off!"

"West, then."

As they picked their way through the great curled vines that coiled in every imaginable way, Tyrin asked, "How much do you know about these parts?"

"Nothing at all. I'm just passing through, going west to Vanara."

"Vanara, eh? From whereabouts in the east?"

"Passdale."

"Passdale. Passdale. Yeah, I think I've been through there. Near Lake Halgaeth, right?"

"Not too far south of it."

"I know the region, being originally from Glareth, myself. A long way from home. And this ain't a land to hesitate in, if you take my meaning. Here's the short version, as much as I've pieced together, anyway. There're these two towns nearby, one's called Edgewold, on the north side. The other's called Westlawn, off aways to the south. Well, these two towns have been feuding for a long time. I don't know why and don't care. Anyway, about three or ten or fifteen years ago, there come up this bunch of folk from somewhere else—I don't know where from—and they start spreading this new religion of theirs. At first, so I've been told, they were pretty well put down. But then the cult started taking hold, in both towns, until Edgewold kicked 'em out for all the trouble the folk were making over it. So the cult-people all went down to Westlawn, and with their brethren already there, they pretty quickly took over. They have this one guy they more or less worship. Some kind of grand wizard or something, fancy weird powers an' all. He pretty much runs things.

"And they got these pernicious weedy vines going that they brung in from somewhere, and they pretty much worship it, too, in the name of their god, called Wokan. Well, so then the Westlawn folk started getting rid of those that didn't hold with their cult, so I was told, taking over farms and driving people out of their stores and homes. They killed a good many, cowed the rest, or made slaves of them, or infested their fields with this stuff so as to make farming dang near impossible. They had a lot more sway in the southparts where there wasn't much in the way of other towns and such. I've been told that south of Westlawn there's nothing but this viny mess."

"So," Robby put in, "how did you get involved? Are you a soldier?"

"Aw, heck no! I'm more what you might call hired help. A couple of years ago, the Wokan cult started raiding farms up north around Edgewold. There were reprisals and so forth until a kind of war started up a few months ago. Me and my mates were up in Duinnor, and we heard about the troubles and figured we might help out some. So we came down and were hired on the spot by a group of farmers. Most folks got off their farms and took up in the town, but a few stayed on their land. Our job, even though it was just the six of us, was to help out those that stayed on their lands. That was maybe three months ago. Right when things started heatin' up."

They fairly fell into a broad opening where the vines had grown up the trunks of a stand of oaks and covered them over, killing the trees with their smothering, and pulling some down. The two could at last stand up straight as they passed through, giving their backs some momentary relief before having to crouch once more.

"Looks like it's getting cloudy again," Robby said, pointing at a gap of sky just above them. "We're sure to lose our direction."

"Yeah. But maybe we'll get lucky."

They continued on, the day growing darker and the gloomy light beneath the stifling canopy murkier by the moment.

"Anyway, me and my mates got into fights right away, with the promise of silver and gold for our swords. Ha! The only metal we ever saw was sharp, slung at us by Wickermen."

"Wickermen?"

"Yeah. That's what those Wokan soldiers are called. On account of their armor, as you've noticed, a dense woven stuff, kind of like baskets and such."

"Yeah," Robby nodded.

"Well, the folks that hired us did at least feed us and such. But the culters, them Wickermen, started coming in greater numbers and more soldier-like, wearing that viny armor of theirs. I tried to talk folks into going to Edgewold where there were some Kingsmen from Duinnor helping out to defend the town. Even the Duinnor general came out into the country and tried to convince them to take shelter in the town. They should've done it! The town's been attacked a bunch of times, but it's got strong walls and determined defenders, not to mention them Kingsmen. Well, the bullheaded farmers wouldn't hear anything of it, and offered us more to stay on. Stubborn, I'll hand 'em that!"

"What Kingsmen? What general?"

"Oh, well, they were here before I came along. Yeah, a regular army of, I don't know, maybe three thousand? Four thousand? Not sure. All set up there in the town, managing its defense. Not enough to take on them culters head-on, even with the Edgewold folk, I guess. But those Kingsmen are sturdy fighters, they are, even if they're a bit uppity.

"The story I got was this: A few months back some important person of Duinnor was waylaid by the Wickermen at Westlawn and held hostage. Word got to Duinnor, and they sent a bunch of soldiers down to ransom the fellow. But by the time the Kingsmen arrived, the poor fellow had been killed, and all his escort, too. There was a big fight, lots of killing, and the Wokan cult's Wickermen people just sort of went berserk. They started raiding Edgewold, stealing cattle, starting fights, and all such until more Kingsmen came, a whole army of them. They got here about a month before I did. The Duinnor general put the town in proper order, built defenses and handily pushed back the raiders from around the town. That's when the Wickermen started raiding the more outlying areas, right when I happened along. At first everything was easy, them Wickermen being not much more than chanting bullies. And kind of dumb, too, since they always put up a sign ahead of time where there was going to be a raid. I reckon they thought it would scare folks into giving in to them. Ha!"

"I think I saw some of those," Robby commented. "A kind of stick-figure. Made of twisted vines and twigs and such."

"That's right. And sometimes they'd set the dang thing on fire at night. The next day or night, they'd come back, all robed up, with their pointy hats, sometimes on horseback, carrying torches and all that. And they'd set to making speeches as to why they were doing what they were doing, all sorts of guff about the will of Wokan, and how all should join and be a believer or else suffer. Anybody that came out to stand up to them would be beaten and hauled off or killed. Me and my boys sure were a surprise to them! Some fine fights we had, too! We'd come up behind them whilst they were all speechifying. But, like I said, they just got to be too many. And they finally got the best of us last night."

"I'm sorry about your friends."

"Yeah. Me, too. But for every one of us that fell last night, six or eight Wickermen paid the same," Tyrin shook his head. "It was a mean fight, though. Nasty."

They pushed on, every tangle of vines looking like the last and the next. By now, both were weary, thirsty, hungry, and no closer, it seemed, to breaking through into open ground.

"What are they doing with the prisoners they take?" Robby asked, pulling off a tangle that had snapped back from Tyrin's passing and wrapped itself around his own arm.

"Heck, if I know. Probably had something special planned for me. I figure the rest will be slaves or the like. Something's up, though, judging by the jibbering of those culters. Something about a certain number they had to have. Whoa!"

A low shape shot out of nowhere right in front of them, snorting and grunting and squealing, then another much larger shape came crashing toward them with two white tusks jutting up from its snout. The little animal squealed and shot around the other way, and, as soon as it disappeared, the large boar stopped on all fours and stood with its head up and its dark copper eyes glaring, heaving out great grunts and low guttural pants at the two men. Without speaking, they backed away very carefully. The animal stamped with both front legs, bouncing its body up and down in a threatening, springing motion.

"Don't run," Tyrin whispered.

"I really think we should," Robby said.

"No. Just back away. Easy. Easy."

Robby carefully stepped back, glancing down to make sure of his footing. It was hard enough going front-ways, and fear of tripping over some vine now terrified the two. The boar continued to stamp and protest their presence.

"Easy."

They felt it coming and braced for the attack. The beast charged, with snorting and squealing. It made only a few feet, though, when a tiny brown shape shot between the two men's shoulders and struck the boar between the eyes with a mild thump and a high-pitched screech. The boar squealed and snapped at the shape, its momentum twisting it around sideways, veering off from its intended victims as the little attacker circled around its head, striking the infuriated beast about the eyes and ears with its beak and talons.

"Certina!" Robby cried.

"Run!" Tyrin yelled, grabbing Robby and pulling him away as the boar whirled around and around, kicking and bucking at the owl's furious assault. Robby shook himself, understanding Certina's intention, and threw himself wholeheartedly into making good his escape. They crashed through the tangles and around the clumps and under the reaching tendrils, and stretched the distance between them and the sound of the duel behind them. Finally, when the noise of their retreat was greater than that of the screaming boar, they stumbled down together onto their knees, panting and gasping the thick air.

"That was the strangest dang thing I ever saw!" Tyrin managed to get out, still fighting for breath. "Did you see that little bird? I was sure we were goners!"

Robby was nodding, grinning as he outstretched his arm just in time for Certina to land on it. There was blood on her talons, but she seemed otherwise only a little ruffled.

"Hello," Robby said to her, hardly able to contain his delight. She blinked at him with something of an exasperated, put-out kind of look, and Robby actually thought she shook her head and rolled her eyes up. She set to straightening her feathers.

"Well, don't that beat all!"

"Certina, this is Tyrin. Tyrin, this is my friend, Certina."

Tyrin shook his head, bemused. "Your pet?"

Certina stopped preening and gave Tyrin a cold stare which took him aback.

"Certina is no pet," Robby explained. "She is her own person. Certina, where is Ashlord? Is he nearby?"

She blinked but made no gesture or sign that Robby could understand.

"Can you tell me where Ashlord is? Or can you show me? Like you did before?"

"You're not expecting it to talk to you, are you?"

"Certina, please."

She stared at him, and Robby felt his vision narrow upon her eyes until they seemed overlaid with a different set. Her body then transformed into a face, dimly lit, beardless and bald.

"Get to Griferis! Do not delay!"

Robby flinched at the boom of Ashlord's voice in his head, and the odd vision disappeared. Tyrin watched, bewildered.

"We have to get out of here," Robby said to Certina. "Can you show us the quickest way? Whichever way is the fastest way to get out from under these vines?"

Certina shot straight up, punching through the canopy and disappearing for a few moments. She quickly returned and flew past them to alight on a high loop of vine some yards away.

"This way!" Robby cried.

"Whatever you say," Tyrin answered gladly.

They pushed through the tangle, careful to keep Certina in sight. She waited for them to come within a few yards of her, then she darted off, leading the way a short distance before landing on a vine to wait for the pair to catch up. Robby had a feeling that she liked the vines as little as he did, and was just as anxious to get away from the loathsome thickets. It seemed an endless trek, with Certina stopping and going, while Robby and Tyrin rather clumsily fought their way through. The two men said little, watching their way and Certina, until Robby's mind turned back to the morning's events.

"What do the Wickermen need slaves for?" he asked.

"Can't rightly say," Tyrin shrugged, stepping through a curtain of kudzu. "And I don't really want to guess. That sure is some bird! Awhile back some feller escaped and said something was up. The Wickermen make sacrifices, you know."

"Sacrifices? What do you mean? What kind of sacrifices?"

"Blood sacrifices. And not just at their temple. My mates and I were told that it used to be that when they took over somebody's lands, they'd kill any who opposed them outright. About a year or two ago, or so we were told, most of the killing of that kind stopped, and the Wickermen started taking slaves and using them to build their temple. Ever' now and then, they sacrifice some slave or other, or even one of their own folk. Always a big ceremony, overseen by their leader, the grand man himself, along with his so-called priests. But his priests ain't nothing more than his generals and henchmen, so far as I can tell from the ones that've run into the sharp end of my sword. Them in their fine white robes and pointy caps, all well-fed while everybody else lives in squalor."

"How is it done? The sacrifices, I mean," Robby asked cautiously.

"I don't know, exactly. This feller I told you about, the one that escaped, he wasn't too clear in the head, if you know what I mean. But from his babble, it ain't done by fire or knife nor hanging. He kept saying they were squeezed, meaning, I think, that they were killed. But here's another mystery: He said the temple was nearly finished, only a month or so to go, he said. That was about three months ago, I gather. Yet the Wickermen are taking more prisoners than ever."

"Wonder why, if their work is done?"

"Your guess is as good as mine."

"And their leader? What is his name?"

"I don't know that, either."

• • •

Ullin and the remaining company spoke not at all to each other nor to the Duinnor men for a long time, but rode hard and urgently through the lifting fog, the boggy farmlands, and on and on along the road. The company passed empty farmhouses, some burned, others simply open wide, doors ajar and windows broken. Coming around a bend between two copses, they saw their destination.

"Edgewold," said Captain Bartow.

The entire town, no small place, was walled around by upright logs, stockade-style, like Furaman's place only on a vast scale. Along and behind the wall's high, axe-sharpened tops, they could see guards walking back and forth and peering at them. As the riders neared, they saw at the base of these walls were rows of crisscrossed stakes, piles of debris and even bones from recent struggles. Here and there on the sharpened stakes, bits of fabric fluttered, broken lances splintered the ground, along with thickets of smashed arrows, flattened helmets, and other ruined armaments.

"I'm afraid you have ridden right into a little war, fellow Kingsman," said Bartow to Ullin. The gate was opened to them, and, entering, they saw rows and rows of gold and green pavilion tents, the encampment of an army. Farther in was the town, smoky and muddy with the night's rain. Except for the men that rode with Bartow and a few elderly guards and very young watchmen, the town seemed abandoned.

"Have they marched on, then?" Bartow called to a man on the wall.

"Aye, before dawn this morn!"

Bartow nodded with a great sigh, pulling his reins around.

"Right. Well," he said, "let's get to our places, men! About and south!" To Ullin and the others, he said, "You have a longer ride yet. If we push our horses, we should meet with our general some while after dark."

"Is there no way," begged Ullin, "for you to authorize our release? We must find our companion."

"Your companion is most likely done for, Commander. You had best look to your own fate in these parts, least-ways for the next day or so. Until we sort things out with the Wickermen."

"Wickermen?" Billy piped up impatiently. "Who're they?"

As they rode, Captain Bartow told the same tale, roughly, that Robby was getting from Tyrin. Of course, Bartow's view of the mercenaries—Tyrin's band—was none too kind, "though good fighters," he admitted. And Bartow had even less respect or patience with the Edgewolders for resisting Duinnor's leadership for so long.

"If these people had listened to our general earlier on, everything would be over and done by now, and we'd all be back home in Duinnor," Bartow said. "It was only a month ago that the city folk finally gave us leave to lead. Just in time, too. The Wickermen mass for a final attack on the town. We think they mean to come on the morrow evening. They want to wipe out Edgewold once and for all, or so it is reported. But they must go through Soltani Pass, just some five leagues or so from here. And that is where they will meet Duinnor steel!"

"So your general intends to make a stand in open combat?" Ullin asked.

"That's it. Nothing we can't easily handle. Not after our last bout with the Dragonkind not six years ago. We're the Four of the Fourth, after all."

"Four what of what?" Billy asked, screwing his face up.

"Billy!" Ullin hissed, shooting him a stern look. "Have some respect! The Fourth Army of the King is a famed army, indeed, and the First, Second, Third, and Fourth Battalions are the most experienced of all the Fourth Army. The Fifth being a training battalion, for replacements. They are known, and feared, as the Four of the Fourth."

"Then we are in honored company," Ullin said, turning back to Bartow. "I myself saw the Four of the Fourth in action at Darlang Hill."

"Ah, that was before my time with the Fourth."

"I was a youngster, a green Kingsman. And just passing through, as it happened. Attached to the First Army's Engineers as a surveyor."

"Ah." Bartow sniffed with an air of superiority. "I see. Let us pick up the pace, boys! We still have far to go, and we don't want to miss out on the glory, do we?"

• • •

"What's this? A wall?"

Indeed it was, so covered with vines that the stones of its construction were barely visible. Robby crunched through the coarse leaf- and vine-strewn ground to come up next to Tyrin, and felt through the vines to cool stone behind. Neither could see how far it went to their left and right for the thickness of the growth around them, nor could they see to the top.

"Listen," Tyrin held up his hand and tilted his head. It was drums they heard, thudding from the distance beyond the wall and sinking down through the canopy over their heads.

"I don't like the sound of that," said Robby.

"Well, your little bird brought us here," Tyrin replied, laying hold to the vines on the wall. "So we may as well have a look at what's on the other side."

At first, it was easy to climb with the ladder-like vines to grip, but the wall was higher than they expected. Near the top where the leaf-heavy tendrils fell back on themselves it was more difficult to push through. Tyrin, being taller, made it first and then gave Robby a hand up. The wall was only a couple of feet thick at the top, and when they stood from their crouch, they poked their heads and shoulders above the vines and into clear air for the first time since morning. Immediately, they ducked back down. In the moment that they had looked, they saw enough to know that they were at Westlawn.

"We came right where we were trying to get away from!" said Tyrin. "Some guide, that bird of yours!"

Certina landed on a vine nearby, and Robby looked at her, wondering why she had brought them this way. But perhaps the dangers that lay in other directions were just as great, especially in the grasping tangle of vines. He eased his head back through the leaves to look more carefully at the town. Just underneath their perch, the land sloped away, and they could see over the roofs of the many small cottages that were directly below them. It was a broad bowl, about a half-mile across, filled with all of the typical buildings of a town, houses and shops, market places and smithies. It was all that one might expect in any village or town, except everywhere dried vines had been woven onto the walls of all the buildings and around the windows of the huts that crowded the place. To the left, on the south side of the town, there was a large area where it appeared as though all of the people were gathered. And there, rising up was the tall shape of a man, crafted from wicker, that stood nearly a hundred feet high, as Robby judged. It was like a crude doll, two square eyes, a featureless face with no nose or mouth, thick arms against its sides, and standing on two stubby legs. The setting sun, off in the hazy distance, gave the thing a sinister appearance as it cast its long shadow across the town.

"What's that?"

"Don't know," Tyrin shook his head. "Must be their idol or something, judging by how they're all gathered around it."

"Look there," Robby motioned to the right of the giant effigy where a pyramid-like structure stood at the far side of the gathering. Around its sides, standing in tiers, were white-robed men, their heads topped with tall pointed caps which came down over their faces like masks. At the very top of the structure, on a platform above all the rest, stood another man in a black robe holding a kind of staff topped with a shiny golden ball.

"Well, lookee there, if it isn't the Grand Pompous. What I wouldn't give for a longbow right about now. Must be some kind of ceremony in the making."

"How do we get away from here, though? Pretty soon it will be too dark to go back in there," Robby said, thumbing over his shoulder. "And I doubt if we'll get very far along the top of this wall before we're seen."

"That only leaves one direction. Down and through the town. Watch it!"

Two men appeared, dressed in wicker armor and bearing pikes, walking along the path between the wall and the huts. Tyrin and Robby crouched low and listened to their talk as they neared.

"…ain't enough of 'em to make a difference, even for their fancy outfits."

"Yeah, but they know how to fight, and they'll be stubborn."

"Aw, when they see our numbers, I'll warrant they'll turn tail and let the Edgewolders fend for themselves. It'll be a walkover!"

Tyrin stood up, much to Robby's shock, and showed himself to the two.

"What's at?"

"What're you doin'?"

"Hello. Do either of you two gents know the quickest way to Edgewold?" Tyrin asked.

"Get on down from there!"

Tyrin bent to look down.

"It'll be a pretty jump, but I just might be able to crawl down using these vines, here."

"Well, get on with it, and get down!"

Tyrin eased himself down from the wall and dropped to his feet between the two sentries.

"How did you get up there? And what're you doing? Some kind of spy?"

"Just got turned around in all that creepy mess out there on the other side. Sort of lost my way, is all."

"You ain't from around here," said one of the sentries, pointing his pike at Tyrin.

"And you ain't no Edgewolder, neither. Got the looks of one of them mercenaries."

"You've got me pegged. But them Edgewolders reneged a bit. I was on my way here, looking for work, when I got turned around."

"Is that the truth? Or are you just full of talk?"

"Well, the truth is, I'm just full of talk."

Tyrin rushed the one closest, grabbed his pike, and swung him into the other one, crashing the two Wickermen hard against the wall. A moment and several quick blows later, the two sentries were in an unconscious heap.

"Well?" Tyrin said, shaking his hand and flexing his fingers. "Are you coming down from up there?"

Robby scrambled down from the wall and looked around cautiously. Tyrin was already busy removing the soldiers' armor and clothes.

"I figure we'd dress up like them and try to sneak our way out. See if you can strap this on."

Robby took the tightly-woven wicker breastplate and attached backplate and slipped his head through the opening. After some doing and assistance from each other, they had their disguises on, complete with iron helmets and coarse brown surcoats made of a burlap-like material. Tyrin handed Robby a waistbelt with a dagger on it and, after strapping on the other one for himself, he checked the blade of the weapon. They looked at each other. Tyrin's outfit was somewhat small, and Robby's was definitely too large.

"I think we got them mixed up," Robby said.

"Oh, well. It'll have to do, as is."

"What about these two?"

"This way. Grab a foot."

Together they dragged the men one by one to the nearest hut and, making sure no one was home, dumped them inside. By now the sun had set, and they began picking their way between the deserted houses.

"I guess everyone is at the gathering," Robby commented.

"Let's hope they stay there."

• • •

Even in the darkness, Ullin could see signs of a great movement of men that had gone before them. In a hurry, it seemed to him, by the many stragglers and carts full of war-gear that they passed, struggling to catch up with the main body. Bartow led them on, sometimes taking them around columns of Edgewolders, some armed only with makeshift weapons fashioned from farming implements, many without shields, and most having not even helmets. They passed through several checkpoints, manned by Kingsmen or Edgewolders, and their progress slowed as the road became more crowded with traffic. Bartow tried to lead the way around, through fields and across streams rather than over bridges, but it seemed hardly worth the effort. The farther they went, the more impatient Bartow became, and he often shouted orders at those on foot to make way for his party.

"I've never seen so many folk on the move!" said Billy to Ibin. "Must be thousands!"

"Mustbe, yeah, mustbethousands,Billy. Doyouthink, doyouthinkwe'll-findRobby?"

"Don't know, big fella. Don't know."

A line of Kingsmen appeared before them with a challenge, met correctly by Bartow as he dismounted, and he exchanged words with another captain. Ullin waited patiently for as long as he could and then nudged his horse forward.

"What is the delay? I must see your general!"

"You'll see the general when he is ready to see you, Commander," Bartow snapped back. "Do you think he is idle and waits only for guests to entertain?"

"Of course not, but our business is urgent and will only take but a moment or two."

"Still, you must wait. He will be informed about you soon enough." Bartow then turned back to the other Kingsman and asked, "So where is the place?"

"Two miles more and to the west just off the main road."

"Very well, then."

As soon as Bartow regained his saddle, they were off again at a good pace alongside the road to avoid the movements upon it. A thin sheet of clouds hid all but the brightest stars, and the night grew thicker as they went, so they often bumped into one another and other travelers along the way.

"Why don't they light torches or carry lamps!" cried Sheila, a bit exasperated after a near collision with some kind of war machine being towed by many oxen, its wheels nearly as tall as her saddle.

"They do not wish the enemy to fix their numbers, perhaps," said Ullin. "Or to smoke their deployments on the field of battle."

"Kinda like that night-march back in Barley those months ago, eh?" Billy put in. " 'Cept in a vast sort of way."

Ullin nodded, but none saw him do so in the darkness. By now he was beyond impatience and anger was welling in him. "Do you not feel the coming battle?" he said to Billy and Sheila. "Do you not smell it in the scent of the men? Or sense it in the tone of their speech with one another, and in the nervous way they act?"

This time both Sheila and Billy nodded thoughtfully.

"It is the scent of war," Ullin went on, "and my skin tells me that blood will flow very soon."

"Danger, then?"

"Like I have not felt since leaving the deserts."

• • •

Tyrin and Robby moved cautiously along the darkened streets of Westlawn, looking for a way out of the town. The few people who saw them, townspeople not at the great gathering, seemed unconcerned at their presence, and let them pass along the streets unmolested. It was the other wicker-dressed soldiers that worried them more. But the pair made their postures and attitude appear stern and businesslike, stepping quickly, as if marching to some serious duty. They noted how some of the soldiers waved in a peculiar way to others, and they mimicked this gesture successfully as they went along. But just as they came within sight of the northern gate, they were challenged by a soldier who at first saluted them and passed on by, but then he turned back at them.

"Halt!"

Robby and Tyrin glanced at each other and kept going, striding determinedly toward the gate.

"Halt, I say!"

They did so, eyeing the other soldiers who had been guarding the gate but now turned their attention to them. The challenger approached them, looking at their sloppy gear.

"Are you not East Sentries?"

Robby started to shrug, but Tyrin stepped forward to answer.

"Aye, we are!" he said sharply.

"Then why are you not there?"

"Because we were ordered to report to the gate?"

"To the gate? Why? Who gave you such orders?"

"Maybe you could tell us that? He was a big one, never seen him before, but he had a list of men to order to the gate, and we were on the list. Are we to join with others then?"

"There are more than enough," snapped the soldier, obviously of some rank. "I know nothing of any men ordered to the gate."

"Well, where are the rest that we are to meet here?" Tyrin looked around. Robby followed his lead, trying to screw on a quizzical look as he peered around.

"There are no others!"

"I told you we didn't have cause to hurry," Tyrin said to Robby. "Even if the fellow wore them robes."

"What robes? Do you mean he was an Initiate?"

"He was, indeed."

"This is all very odd," said the soldier. He gestured at Robby, "What do you say?"

"Oh, he's a bit, you know, addled," Tyrin said. "Can't talk very well, if you know what I mean."

"Then you come with me, and let's find this fellow. Let him stay and wait. Do not leave this gate!"

"Well, I think we ought to go together, since he got a better look at the fellow than I did," suggested Tyrin. "I'm afraid I was a bit, er, groggy."

"Then you stay. Station yourself at the top of the gate and wait for my return. Come along!"

"But—"

"Do you disobey me?"

"Why, no, sir," Tyrin glanced helplessly at Robby.

"Come, then. You will point out this meddling Initiate!"

Robby strode off behind the soldier, glancing over his shoulder at Tyrin, who was now being escorted to his guard post by other soldiers.

"Sick and tired of these mamby-pamby culters trying to tell real soldiers how to run a war! They never went up against Duinnor steel. They don't know the cunning of the Kingsmen. And now the Initiates ordering around our men like master and ruler."

"Then you do not like the wicker god?" Robby asked.

"Shut your mouth! I said no such thing! All to Wokan!"

They went back through the town, Robby having trouble keeping up with the soldier's quick step since his wicker attire kept shifting off and cluttering his stride.

"Some soldier you are!" the leader complained. "Can't even wear your gear properly!"

They passed into a crowd coming down the street, filtering into homes and shops.

"I guess the evening's meeting is over."

"All to Wokan!" greeted one grinning man as he passed the soldier.

"We'll have our revenge tomorrow, eh?" said another enthusiastic man, nodding to the two.

They pressed on through the streets, the insistent drums growing louder as they neared the far southern side of the town, and Robby could see now and again the dark looming shape of the Wickermen's giant effigy. They entered a large open area at the east side of the place, and Robby looked up at the pyramid nearby that rose up half the figure's height. They passed through two rows of huts, built entirely of wicker. Striding past the open door of one, Robby glimpsed several white-robed figures within.

"What color was the robe of the one who gave you those orders?"

"White," Robby replied immediately.

"White? Are you sure? Not brown?"

"White."

The soldier stopped, and he frowned.

"Well, one of them, eh?"

Just then a group of white-robed men strode out from around a corner, and as the soldier turned to address them, Robby shot off the other way, running as fast as he could between the huts. Heedless of the cries behind him, he darted this way and that, ducking through huts and shoving between confused people until he suddenly came upon the drummers. There were dozens of them, stripped to their loincloths, their skin glistening with sweat in the torchlight, heaving thick mallets against their large pot-like drums. He dashed between them and into the shadows beyond, to the base of the temple as the steady rumbling cadence drowned out all other sounds. He quickly removed the wicker armor and other accoutrements, took Swyncraff from around his waist, and edged along the wall, looking for any sign of his pursuer. But, miraculously, he saw the man go the other way through the drummers, leading a small band of other soldiers.

"Great!" he exclaimed, barely able to hear himself over the din. "Farther away from where I need to go, and just where I don't want to be!"

As he glanced up and down the wall, wondering which way to go was best, he saw coming from ahead of him a line of white-robed figures approaching, and he quickly squeezed into a shadowed crevice between two masonry stones at the foot of the structure. Nervously, he watched them pass only inches away, each figure with his hands clasped, fingers through fingers, prayer like, softly chanting words he could not make out. They seemed in a kind of trance, their glassy eyes fixed before them, their shaved heads and faces pale in the yellow light of the torches that burned around the drummers across the yard. At last, the end of the line came and went, and Robby edged out from his hiding place and turned the opposite way only to see the soldier now rounding the corner.

"How did he get around me?" he muttered, turning to follow the robed ones. Desperate and realizing he had to take a mighty chance, he ran up behind the last one in line. Using Swyncraff as a noose, Robby pulled him violently and quickly aside, dashing his head on the stone wall. He quickly removed the robe from the senseless man and threw it over himself, dragging the man into the shadows at the base of the wall and scrambling to catch up with the line.

"At least they seem to be going in the right direction," thought Robby, until he noticed another line just above him on top of the wall going the opposite way and saw those directly ahead making a left turn up some steps and then left again. As his turn came, he kept going straight for several steps until he saw a group of soldiers idly standing just ahead.

"Good grief!" He grimaced, making an about-face and trotting back and up the stairs to resume his place at the end of the line. Conspicuous because of his unshaven head, he wondered how long it would be before he was noticed. He saw the men in front of him pull their hoods up over their heads, and he did the same just as his pursuers passed by, clueless as to how near their quarry was. The line turned again, entering a kind of open corridor between two structures. Seeing an open door to the left, Robby slipped through it. Glancing around he found himself within a kind of courtyard.

At the far end, about twenty yards away, was a wooden wall, in contrast to the other three of stone, and it was covered over with a thick layer of vine, woven like a basket might be done, from one side to the other and as high as he could see. There was an opening, a small archway, just wide and tall enough for a single person to pass through. Hearing the clink of weapon-metal from behind, he ran through the opening, hoping for a way out. It was even darker in the next chamber, entirely made of wooden frames covered with wicker, and yet some of the torchlight from outside reached in through the cracks. Robby quickly realized that he was inside the very base of the idol, the gigantic wicker figure that loomed over the town. Above him, the supporting beams crisscrossed at all angles upward into the darkness. But there was a ladder, and as soon as he saw it, he threw off the robe and began to climb.

"Maybe I can find a place to hide up here," he thought, "at least until I've rested. And maybe they'll wear themselves out and I can slip away later when their ceremony, or whatever they are doing, is over."

He climbed the ladder, and his eyes became more accustomed to the gloom. He could see the odd way the structure was built, with crossbeams and uprights attached to each other with loops of cord wrapped around the ends and twisted tightly between each piece of lumber so that no wood actually touched another piece of wood. Indeed, as he went upward, the whole thing seemed to flex and sway just a little from his weight, slight though he was compared to the massive structure. Even the ladders he climbed were not attached to any landings, but were themselves tied rather loosely above one another. He came to a place where the space around him seemed to open up somewhat. Looking to his right, he saw the top of another ladder close by, jutting up from a wide round opening just like the one he was emerging from. He realized that he had only been climbing through a single leg and was now peering up into the belly of the thing. He had to move sideways and climb onto a crossbeam to hoist himself further, the beam flexing as its spring-like joints creaked. There were no more ladders, but so many support braces and beams, more than seemed necessary, that Robby had no trouble moving from one to another as he continued to ascend. When he came to what he reckoned was the neck, and saw openings to either side of the shoulders into what could only be arms, he easily continued upward and into the head. Inside that place was quite dark, but stars showed through two square openings, about three feet wide and apart from each other, like windows but without glass.

"Those must be the eyes," he said to himself, making his way to the nearest one to see what he could see. Settling comfortably onto a support, he put his face into the opening, and he gripped more tightly as he saw how high he was. Below and in front of him was the temple, itself well over six stories high, but at least as far as it was high from where he sat. He could see the torches all around the temple grounds and more lights along the northern wall of the town. Beyond the wall were hundreds of yellow lights, the fires of a vast encampment. It was clear that even if he and Tyrin had made it through and out of the town, they would have had to manage their way past what could only be a huge army.

"That must be where most of the people are," he thought. "I wonder why they are out there instead of inside the town? Too many of them, maybe. Or maybe they are getting ready to march away."

Making sure of his grip, he drew himself back in and looked down past his dangling feet into the dark interior. For the first time, he realized that if he fell, he would strike beam after beam on the way down, perhaps being killed well before he hit the bottom.

"I wonder if Tyrin is in as bad a fix as I am? At least I may be able to watch for a likely time to escape. Maybe if they are up all night, they will sleep by day. What am I thinking? Night-time would certainly be the best time to sneak off."

Looking back through the opening before him, he saw more white-robed figures lining their way through the temple yard and past the drummers. Like those he had followed, they too, climbed the stairs and chanted as they took their places alongside the others, standing in tiers along the sloping stair-like side of the temple facing him.

"Looks like they're just getting started!"

• • •

Billy pushed aside the tent flap and peered out. The two sentries standing nearby looked at him blankly. Billy frowned at them, then dropped the flap and turned back to his friends who had been waiting as impatiently as he.

"Will he never come!" he exclaimed. "It's been hours!"

Ullin shrugged and shook his head. "It is war they are about, Billy. Little else is of importance to them but the battle to come. Certainly not a few errant travelers."

"Still," complained Sheila, "how long would it take just to speak to us?"

"I suggest you get some rest," said a voice at the tent opening. He was another Kingsman, a captain. "I am Paghelm, aide to General Teracue who is presently some miles away. I come to tell you that he will not return until morning."

Billy threw up his hands in exasperation.

"General Teracue has been given the news of your arrival and of the capture of your companion. He regrets there is little that can be done at the moment. And probably not at all," Paghelm stated. "I am instructed to tell you that you face great danger by staying here. General Teracue begs you to retreat to Edgewold and await the outcome of tomorrow's battle."

"We cannot abandon our friend," Ullin said. "Will you not grant permission for us to continue on?"

"That is impossible. Word has been spread far and wide that any person not in the company of one of our own, and not situated in or at Edgewold or with this army, is to be considered hostile. And anyone found in that manner is to be captured or killed. If captured, then taken to Edgewold. There is not time to notify all of the units you might encounter nor to give you a pass through our forward lines that would be acceptable to our skirmishers. An escort to assist you southward is also out of the question, for all of our men are needed. I am sorry, but you should return to Edgewold. I am sending a courier to Edgewold in just a moment. He waits outside. Go with him, and he can vouch for you as far north as Edgewold."

"Maybe we can change the general's mind," Sheila said to Ullin, uncharacteristically tugging his sleeve for attention. Billy nodded, while Ibin looked blankly from Ullin to Paghelm and back.

"We will stay and wait and hope for some chance to speak with your general," Ullin said flatly.

"It will be several hours, yet, before he returns," Paghelm said. " I beg you depart with the courier. General Teracue will have little time for you."

"I urge you, please, make some way for us to see him, however brief that meeting may be. I ask only to put my request directly to him."

Paghelm saw the sincerity on their faces and was not unmoved.

"Very well," he said. "I will do what I can. I suggest that you get some rest. I'll have food brought just before dawn. In the meantime, your horses will be minded by the sentries, who will rouse you if there is any alarm. Good night!"

After Paghelm departed, a gloomy mood settled. Billy argued that they should strike out on their own, but Ullin quickly made it understood that they would not get far. "And we would have to overpower too many guards and sentries. Would you raise a hand against men of Duinnor when it is their aid we seek for the Eastlands?"

So they were stuck, and they waited as patiently as they could while the noise of preparation continued about them. Ullin was most restless of all, pacing, often peering outside. It was apparent that old loyalties were urging him to join with the other Kingsmen, in whatever fight they faced. The sound of orders given, the commotion of various units about them moving off, and the creak of war-engines as they were pulled through the night all filled Ullin with a sense of uselessness and frustration. Hour after hour passed. Ibin and Billy slept, and Sheila nodded off, sitting crosslegged on the ground beside them. Ullin continued to pace.

Suddenly, two Kingsmen pulled the flap aside and a stocky middle-aged man quickly entered. He wore fine armor and carried his helmet under his arm. His hair was close-cropped and iron-gray, and his weathered face showed the experience of many campaigns. In the lamplight, his piercing blue eyes sized up the group for only a moment before he spoke.

"I am Artais Teracue, Commanding General of the Fourth," he said as Ullin stiffened to attention. "As you were, Kingsman. Your name and unit?"

"Ullin Saheed, House of Tallin and Fairoak, Captain of the King's Ranks, First Army, Third Engineer Battalion, detached to the King's Post as Special Courier, lately of the Eastlands."

"Orders?"

"Yes, General," Ullin was already reaching into his tunic, and pulled out a small leather wallet. He removed a parchment, unfolded it, and handed it to Teracue. Teracue quickly read it, holding it to a lamp to see the watermark, and handed it back.

"Very well. I know of you, Lord Tallin."

"The title remains that of my grandfather, sir."

"Ah, then he still abides?"

"Aye, sir. In Tallinvale, preparing for the worst because Tracian rebels have marched against the Eastlands."

"What's that?"

"Sir, Tracia sends its might westward and north, gathering strength to join with the Dragonkind armies that we expect will soon march out in great strength from the desert lands. Probably in the spring. It is their plan to destroy the two southernmost realms between their pincers. We surmise they will then march northward together against Duinnor. Thus, the Redvests have invaded the Eastlands in order to capture slaves and supplies that will be needed for their offensive."

Teracue looked sternly at Ullin, and, glancing at Paghelm, he said, "So that is what this is all about." He turned back to Ullin. "Then what brings you west?"

"I am charged with escorting a company from the Eastlands westward to Vanara and Duinnor for their own business, sir, as well as to seek aid against the Redvests and to warn Duinnor of their treachery. One of our company was captured and taken away by those you call Wickermen. We seek to rescue him as quickly as possible and to be on our way."

"Yes, so I was told. Your route is somewhat south, is it not?"

"Aye, General, we have been waylaid and forced this way by the warlords of the Thunder Mountains. The Damar, they call themselves."

Teracue nodded. By now Billy and Ibin had awakened and, along with Sheila, were standing close by and anxiously attending to the exchange.

"Do you have proof of what you say?"

"None, sir, except our own scars of battle, and our own eyes which have seen the Dragonkind upon the plain, scouting their routes. Pardon me, General. Allow me to present Sheila Pradkin, Billy Bosk, and Ibin Brinnin, all of County Barley, in the Eastlands. All good friends of our missing companion, whose name is Robby Ribbon."

Teracue shook hands with Ibin and Billy, and bowed smartly to Sheila.

"I am pleased to make your acquaintance," he said. "I will certainly send riders north with your information as soon as I can. And it is my wish to speak with you further about your news. But, as you are aware, we prepare for battle. We believe we will be attacked in the morning. It is my duty to intercept and thwart the opposing force which is determined to lay waste to Edgewold. They mean to capture these lands for their own master and in defiance of Duinnor. I cannot, therefore, give you leave to depart. If you were captured, information that you might provide could be of service to our enemy. Anyway, I hardly think you will find your companion. I urge you to give him up for dead and move on with your journey."

"We can't do that!" Billy blurted out. "We can't just leave him without tryin'!"

"Sir," Ullin said, "we are determined to go to the aid of our companion, who is our friend and, anyway, who is vital to our journey. I have been charged with his safe conveyance westward, and I must fulfill my duty."

"I see. The decision is yours. You can either stay until the battle is won or lost and then seek your friend, or else I can spare a rider with papers to see you through our western lines and away from here. But you must wait until dawn. I will hear your answer then."

• • •

Soltani Pass was a broad, relatively flat grassland that ran for a mile between two lines of hills to the east and west. To the south, the pass widened, and at the opposite end to the north it narrowed and constricted to less than a furlong where there was a mild rise before it opened to the northern lands, thus forming a gentle but well-defined corridor. At both ends of the pass, armies gathered. To the south, a vast encampment had formed, consisting of many warriors and clans of warriors variously dressed and equipped, with every manner of crude weapons and long two-handed swords. All told, they numbered around twelve or thirteen thousand. Their camps were as untidy and disheveled as their dress, with only the odd wicker armor in common among them. Rags of many colors flew alongside pelts from various animals as their standards, and their campfires lit the sky over the plain with a garish glow that could be seen for miles. Throughout the night, they chanted and drank strong spirits provided to them, making themselves ready by drink and boastful cheers to march north at morning light, to gain the lands of those who defied Wokan, and to destroy their enemies. So confident of victory were they that they posted few guards, and the scouts of Duinnor easily counted their numbers and reported their disposition.

At the north end of the pass, Teracue arranged his forces and was pleased at the reports. Nothing contradicted his carefully laid plan or required any adjustment to his orders. His men continued to methodically form their lines, from experience and training tried by battle, stretching across the northern narrows, from hill to hill. General Teracue rode continually along, calmly giving encouragement and praise to his men. Arriving back at his tent, he received the last reports from the forward scouts before giving the go-ahead to four hundred horsemen. These struck the Wickermen's camp two hours before dawn, coming unexpectedly from different directions, penetrating deep into the enemy's sleepy ranks, killing many, setting fires, and making violent havoc before riding away. It was only a bee sting to such a horde, doing little to diminish their numbers, but it served to create turmoil within the enemy camp and to provoke a great fury in the undisciplined Wickermen forces, just as Teracue intended. By dawn, the sleepless Wickermen, groggy from drink, were laughing at the taunt, swearing vengeance upon the Kingsmen of Duinnor for their audacity. So, when the sun was full up and the morning mists were still lifting into an overcast sky, they began their march northward, cheering and chanting as they went, their white-robed priests riding in front of them, conjuring them to greater and greater fury as they advanced.

Before them, at the distant far side of Soltani Pass, quietly stood five thousand of the combined forces of Duinnor and Edgewold, all that Teracue could muster and still leave the town garrisoned. Among them were old men and young boys and, here and there, a hearty and determined girl. The Edgewolders formed two lines north and south along the base of either ridge, arrayed behind sharp-pointed palisades. Above them on the slopes stood as many archers as could be equipped, about three hundred on either side of the pass. The lines at the base of the ridges curved inward toward the north end of the pass, where a thousand more Edgewold fighters gathered. Before them, facing south, were ranked three thousand Kingsmen of Duinnor. In their green surcoats trimmed with yellow, they stood behind their shields, shoulder-to-shoulder, and prepared to take the brunt of the coming attack.

The commanding pavilion was at the top of the eastward hill, overlooking the pass below, and, just after dawn, Robby's companions were taken there so that General Teracue could hear their answer. It was apparent that Teracue had received little sleep and was simultaneously marking maps, jotting quick notes that he handed to his aides to deliver, and nibbling a piece of bread as they were brought in.

"So?" Teracue asked.

"Sir, we are determined not to continue west without our companion," Ullin said frankly. "Will you not give your leave so that we may mount a rescue?"

"It would be futile. You would have to tear your way through ten thousand raving maniacs who are now on the march. Even if they have spared your friend, they've surely taken him to Westlawn to the south in the Wickerlands. Until the pass is cleared, you cannot reach there."

"Sir, if that is the way of it, then I will do my part to clear the pass. Where would you have me stand?" Ullin replied. "I speak only for myself and not for my companions."

"This is not your fight, Commander, but a blow against this rabble would be a blow against those who took your kinsman."

"We stand together," Sheila said. "And we will do what damage we may to those who took our friend."

"Well, then, I thank you!" Teracue said, gripping Ullin's hand. "I am in need of an experienced commander to manage our right flank at the forward palisades. The position is well-placed, but it is manned with inexperienced fighters from Edgewold. They are good and obedient, but they do not understand the strength of their position and may break when the fearsome tide comes. The flanks must hold and direct the enemy flood into our teeth."

"I understand, sir. If someone could show me the way, sir, I will do my duty."

"I am a master of the arrow," Sheila enjoined, "and I will not be put off from this fight if it is the only way to get to Robby!"

"Same, here!" Billy cried.

"Me, too!" joined Ibin.

Pressed for time, Teracue did not argue. "Then take to the heights above your Kingsman. Mark those on horseback and any who may break through. Our archers have their own orders."

Billy put Ibin in charge of the horses, and the four went quickly to the place Ullin was to defend, the leading edge of the right line at the base of a low but steep hill, some two hundred yards south of the wall of Kingsman shields. It was densely crowded behind the palisades, and as Ullin was led to his post, the aide that guided him explained Teracue's plan and quickly introduced Ullin to the various group leaders along the way. Ibin took the horses to the top of the hill about twenty yards above and behind Ullin, and situated them between two trebuchets that were being set up. Ahead of him, overlooking Ullin's position, Sheila and Billy took their stance, readying their bows and quivers. Billy looked to Sheila and followed her example of standing her quivers upright beside her for quick retrieval. Remembering how she had trained him, he checked his bowstring, gave each hand a wring, flexing his fingers, and notched an arrow.

"Breathe easy," Sheila said as she smoothed the fletchings of a few arrows in her quiver. "Pick your target, draw steady, aim ahead, slightly up, and let go the string. Don't hold the arrow back on the string very long. Don't think too much."

Billy nodded. "Right. I'll try."

Sheila notched her arrow and waited, watching the growing cloud of brown dust to the south. It reminded her somewhat of the approaching stampede out on the plains. In spite of her calm words to Billy, she swallowed hard, understanding the waste that was about to occur, that she would soon be part of. For a moment, she was paralyzed, remembering the fight on the road from Tulith Attis, in Passdale and along the road to Janhaven. The men she had killed there, and later at Redwater Gorge and Tulith Morgair. Her stomach twisted, and she gulped. Then she heard Ullin's loud voice. It shook her from her thoughts, and she looked down the slope in front of her.

Below, Ullin passed around the barricades and palisades and onto the battlefield. Sheila could see him inspecting the rather flimsy-looking defenses as he shouted out orders for quick changes here and there, along with words of encouragement.

"Our task is simple!" he cried out as he went. "Let no Wickerman get behind us. They must be held in front of the palisades so that the men of Duinnor may do their work! The gaps between the posts are for your swords and spears, to keep the enemy from pulling away the posts or climbing over them, and to force them to move on and into the Kingsmen's steel. On this field, a leg wound or a cut to the arm of your enemy is as good as a thrust through the heart. Make your mark in blood and let the next one come to you. The press of battle will finish them! Keep low, and use your shields against their high blows. Spearmen, firm, hard jabs! Do not let them pull down the palisades! Swordsmen, stay low and cut upwards. Here, son, hold it like this."

Even as he spoke, the dust of the approaching horde was rising behind a muddled line that stretched across the southern vale. Soon the noise of their approach reached the ears of the defenders, a low tramp, the rumble of drums, and the blare of ram's horns. Those Wickermen that had shields beat them as they came, closer and louder, and their advance made the earth shudder.

"Lo! What a lot of 'em!" Billy said as the Wickermen came to a halt just a hundred yards south. "Never seen so many people at once! I wonder what's made 'em so mad?"

The attackers halted briefly, and they formed a thick line, over a hundred men deep. White-clad riders galloped back and forth in front of them, and the horde began stamping their feet and clanging their swords and chanting, "Wicker! Wicker! Wicker!"

Then their leaders drew their swords, and a great and noisy charge began, straight at the center of the defenses. Yelling and shouting, they came running. Those in front who tripped or fell were trampled by the mass that followed. Like a tide filling a trough, they flowed into the pass, pressing at the sides, screaming and tossing their spears over the pikes and palisades, and receiving them back in turn. As they neared, the Kingsmen lifted their green and gold shields and began their own advance in slow march, keeping their formation tight, shield to shield.

To Billy, it looked hopeless, such a thin line against so many thousands. As he let fly arrow after arrow at the attackers, his stomach churned and his heart pounded in his chest. In spite of the noise, he heard Sheila's string twang beside his ear and saw her arrow take one of the white-robed riders from his horse. A cheer went up around her as the attackers reached the palisades. Most passed by, their matted hair flying and their long swords waving as they charged the slowly advancing line of Duinnor shields. Billy continued to shoot his arrows and did not understand why the other archers held back, why they simply waited in their tight-massed ranks a little way to his right.

On the frenzied army came, filling the gap between the hills from one side to the other. When they were but fifty yards from the Duinnor line, Teracue gave his order, his drummers beat a different cadence, and the

Kingsmen quickly shifted in to a zig-zag shape, like the teeth of a saw. When the onslaught struck the Duinnor formation, a heart-sinking crunch went up from the field, and the jagged Kingsmen line staggered. As the dust raised by the attackers enveloped and obscured the field, the Wickermen continued to press in, thicker and thicker, being pushed from behind by the others who still came, with little room to move or to swing their swords or raise their spears. For a few long moments, only the continuous shouting and the ring and thud of steel gave signal to the great struggle taking place within the cloud of dust. Then, to Billy's great astonishment, the Duinnor line emerged, advancing within the storm. The sharp teeth of the Duinnor line cut into the horde so that the attackers were forced between each small salient by the weight of those behind only to be systematically cut down on either side by the short thrusting-swords of the Kingsmen. As Billy made good his last arrow, the ground below and before him was so filled with the Wickermen that they now turned right and left, pressing into the flanks of the defenders, the only enemy they could get to for the pushing and shoving of their own comrades. Now, with a whoosh of air, hundreds of arrows took flight from both sides of the vale and hardly a point failed to find blood. A loud, hard thud from behind Billy made him flinch as the trebuchets flung flaming baskets full of oil jars over his head, arcing down into orange explosions of flame in the midst of the Wickermen.

Teracue's trap was sprung, and the slaughter began in earnest. His victims struggled to get out of their flaming wicker armor, and many were set afire by their own mates who fell against them. Yet the gaping holes that all these missiles produced were quickly filled by the continued push of those attackers in the rear who could see nothing of the carnage that they, in part, created ahead of them. And the Duinnor line continued its grim and methodical advance.

Behind the jaws of the Kingsmen followed the Edgewolders, making sure of the fallen. Behind them the mire and gore and bodies of the slain were so thick that Billy could see hardly a blade of grass or fleck of stone. When the Duinnor line neared, Ullin raised his bloody sword high and cried, "Advance!"

Billy threw down his useless bow and ran downhill to Ullin's side, drawing his sword as he went. All of the flanks moved out from behind their palisades and hacked their way along the sides of the opposing warriors, driving them inward and into the grinding teeth of the Kingsmen. Amid the screaming and clanking, Billy nimbly parried and thrust at bigger men, as often using his hilt as his blade to knock his opponents back. No sooner had one man fallen than another faced him. Nearby, Ullin plied, expressionless, with cool disciplined precision. Billy, his heart pounding with madness and fear, caught a glimpse of Sheila, savagely wielding a buckler and mace she had picked up. How long this went on, he could never say, but on and on it went, until his arms were weary with what seemed an endless struggle, felling man after man. The stink of sweat and blood and the choke of dust filled his nostrils and fouled his lips, and still he fought on. Men and boys fighting beside him fell, some crying out the names of those who killed them. Only once did Billy hesitate, when a lad too young to be mixed up in this slung an axe at him. But Billy had no choice, now, it was fight or die, and he groaned with anger as he stepped over the dead lad's body to parry the next opponent who faced him. With animal desperation, he grunted and cried out with every swing and stroke and dodge. Though most of the enemy appeared larger and stronger than Billy, they seemed to be growing just as weak and weary as he.

Abruptly, there was a lull. No one stepped up to take the place of the man Billy had just dispatched, and the ranks of the Wickermen grew suddenly thin as they backed away. Many threw down their weapons and fled. Others, trapped between the enclosing jaws, had nowhere to run. Some of them found mercy, but others did not. Still others, surrounded in various pockets, fought on until they, too, were overwhelmed. The bang and crunch of armor, the ring and clank of iron and steel, gave way to softer sounds of pain and agony, the moan of the dying and injured, crying for comfort and for mercy. Of those last things, there was little to be had as the Edgewolders vengefully advanced upon the wounded.

• • •

As soon as he saw that the battle was won, Ullin began looking for his comrades. He found Billy nearby, leaning against his sword, panting, as Edgewolders pushed past him. Billy, breathless, nodded at Ullin and managed to take his hand.

"I'm alright," Billy said to Ullin's look of concern. "Just need a bath, is all. How are ye?"

"I'm unharmed. You should have stayed on the hill, my friend. Where's Sheila?"

"Over yonder."

Many yards away, she stood, her arms hanging at her sides, still clutching her dripping weapons. Indeed, so horrific had been her fighting that she was drenched to the shoulders with gore, her hair matted and her face and clothes splattered. Ibin was with her, having brought up the horses, and was daubing her face with a cloth that he moistened from a waterskin. When Ullin approached, she looked at him with the wide-eyed stare of shock, her body trembling uncontrollably. Though she looked at him straight, she was muttering—or trying to mutter through her shivers—a song from her blighted childhood. It was difficult for Ullin to understand the words, so shattered was her birdlike voice.

"Pluck a posy red and b-blue, with ivy ribbon tie. A thimble fill...a thimble fill with..with ivory spoon La...Lady Luna's dew. Purple wine in golden cup give to the noonday s-sun. Se..v-ven suitors s-soon will come, your hand and heart to woo."

"Here," Ullin said, loosening her grip on the buckler. "Let go of these things."

He pried her fingers from it and from the mace and threw them aside as he guided her a few yards away and gently pushed her down to sit on a patch of earth miraculously unblemished by battle. Ibin's face was pale, his eyes wide and teary as he followed.

She looked at Ullin, almost as if she did not recognize him.

"What was it all f-for?" she asked. "What have I done? Why have we done this?"

"Just sit. Sh-h," Ullin said to her. "You should have stayed on the hill. Ibin, come. Let me have that rag and the water."

Ibin handed the things over as Ullin knelt beside Sheila.

"Thank you. Why don't you go see to Billy?"

Ullin ministered to Sheila tenderly, her straining heart quite nearly cracking his own. Though his hands were caked with gore, bruised and bloody, though his heart still pounded with the afterglow of battle, but with the terrible thrill of survival, he calmly bathed Sheila, saying to her, "Shh. Shh, there. Shh. It's over."

He washed her face and neck. Then, taking her arms, he poured water over them and wiped them as gently as he could, tinging the grass with watery-red drippings. He looked for wounds, but he found none except in her eyes. Slowly her gaze came back from somewhere far away, back to Ullin, and her look changed from one of shock to one of questioning. She did not understand his kindness, his gentle touch, and she seemed confused but amenable to his efforts. For long moments, she closed her eyes, losing herself in the sudden relief of his soothing hands and the cool, cleansing water, forgetting for a time the terrible sounds around her of so many others more in need of ministering than she. When she opened her eyes, his face was close to hers, dirty and worn, his eyes were sad but kind when she caught them, and she moved her head to keep them in her gaze and to keep hers in his.

"I love you, Ullin."

"No. You love Robby."

"I do love Robby. But I love you, too."

"You only desire me. But I have given myself to another."

"I do desire you. And I fear you. But I do love you. And, though I am given to Robby, I will always love you more, though nothing may ever come of it."

"It is for Robby that we must not speak of such things," Ullin said gently, wiping her brow one last time. "And this field is not a fit place to speak of love or desire, anyway, where so many have lost theirs this day. Come! The army marches on to the south. That is the way we must go. Our fight is not over. To find Robby is our task, and to make him safe is our hope. Is it not?"

"Yes. That is so."

. . .

"Form for pursuit!" General Teracue ordered at the top of his lungs.

"Let us march on Westlawn and free our kin!" rejoined the Edgewolders, and a loud cheer of agreement went up from the town fighters.

"Sowego, sowegofindRobby?"

"Indeed, we do!" replied Billy, reaching up to put his arm around Ibin's shoulder.

"Let us move swiftly!" Teracue continued, not fifteen yards away where his captains gathered around him, all on horseback. "Dispatch our riders to make as much havoc before us as possible. Let us press our advantage before the town may strengthen its defenses. Have the Edgewolders move the light trebuchets and ballistas with all haste to join those we have already sent ahead. We mount our attack before nightfall. May victory be ours by sunset!"

"It is clear," said Ullin as they mounted and followed along behind Teracue's contingent, "that much planning has gone into this day."

Indeed, as he later learned, Teracue was so confident in victory that he had on the previous night sent a large contingent of troops along with many siege engines on toward Westlawn by the long way around to lay in wait for further instructions. Now he sent fast riders to order them to advance so that they could take positions as soon as the main force arrived.

The Kingsmen ranks divided, many taking to the saddle while the rest formed marching phalanxes, and the Edgewolders organized themselves, too. In less than an hour, the horsemen were gone well ahead of the ranks of footmen, all moving southward to the beat of their drums and the call of pipe and horn. They left behind the smoky field of battle, with its wreck of dead and dying, and before them the shallow valley opened onto the plain that would lead them to Westlawn, the Wickertown, as some now called it. Their way was strewn with the litter of the fleeing, swords and lances cast aside, wicker armor hastily removed. Here and there, they came upon groups of the weak and wounded, unable to outpace the pursuing army. These gathered in motley clumps in the crushed grass, begging for mercy and warding off the vultures that patiently stood nearby.

"None who surrender are to be slain!" Teracue ordered. "It is the law of Duinnor. Any who defy it will pay a like price as they exact!"

Some of the Edgewolders, venting a long-held desire for vengeance, ignored the orders. The leaders of Edgewold, themselves among the worst aggrieved by years of Wickerman assaults, saw the wisdom of stopping unneeded bloodshed. But they were powerless to keep many of their people from their victims.

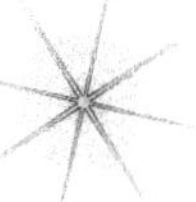

Chapter 11

The Wickerman

Day 132
113 Days Remaining

The chanting and the drumming grew more urgent as dawn approached. Agitated by this, and perhaps too tired to think clearly, Robby carefully climbed down from his perch, looking again for an escape. The densely woven wicker skin was so intertwined that, although it would move when he tugged on it, it would not yield enough for him to pass through. Still, he kept trying as he descended, thinking that if he could squeeze out of the thing, he might be able to climb down the back side of the structure unseen. By the time he reached the bottom without finding a way out, the noise of the chanting and drums was relentless, and sunlight beamed through the tiny cracks in the wicker to light his way. Going to the door, he carefully peered out. Not ten yards away were white-robed men lining up and preparing, it appeared, to enter the structure. Almost as soon as he saw them, they began coming Robby's way, and he scrambled back upward in panic. As he climbed, the men filed into the structure. They moved with steady purpose, and not at all as if they knew he was there. As they ascended, they climbed aside into various places along the crossbeams, some clinging to the interior sides, some even binding themselves into place, while others crawled down into the arms, and still more continued upward toward Robby.

"Trapped again!" he muttered with the same feeling of desperation clutching his chest as he had felt at Tulith Attis when the wolves came. Looking down, he saw the first of the Wickermen reach the neck. Using Swyncraff, Robby began thrusting upward at the ceiling of the head. But the weave was strong and very little space opened. He pushed and pulled, using Swyncraff as a pry bar. Just as the first Wickerman came into the head, Robby was squirming out through the little opening he had made. As he struggled though, using one hand to clutch at the outside wicker and the other still on Swyncraff to pry the opening, he barely had time to notice how high up he was or how far he would plummet if he lost his grip. The structure suddenly shifted and swayed, sending Robby tumbling out. He would have fallen to his death, but Swyncraff instantly coiled itself around a strong place at one end and around Robby's wrist at its other end. He dangled in the air, twisting and kicking, his feet finding no purchase, his free hand scratching at the side of the structure, his heart and lungs pounding. After a moment, it was clear that Swyncraff would hold him fast and would not let him fall.

He tried to force himself to relax a little. Still panting, he looked down and saw a large wave of vines rising up and breaking over the city wall just below, sending several tendrils against the base of the effigy that he hung from. The wave receded, but not the dozen or so tendrils that gripped the structure and shot around it.

"He comes!" someone cried.

Robby saw the vines take hold, and a growing wreath of leaf-covered skin rapidly grew upward toward him. From within, muffled by the beat of the drums and the droning of the chants, he heard the structure creaking, mixed with strange moans of agony and stifled cries of pain and fear. Horrified, Robby struggled up Swyncraff. It flexed for him but did not loosen its grip on his wrist as he gained a foothold on the basket-like covering of the effigy's massive head. Struggling past the hole he had made, he caught a glimpse of a Wickerman within who was being wrapped in snake-like tendrils rising from the innards below, his face bulging as blood streamed from his mouth and nose. Robby focused on his own plight and tried to ignore the terrible gagging sounds coming from the poor fellow being squeezed. Getting another foothold, he scrambled up and found a flat space on top of the head. As soon as he tumbled onto the platform, now swinging with the whole structure, leafy tentacles curled up around the crown and made to grasp at Robby's ankles. He kicked at the vines, then swung Swyncraff at them, the gift of Thurdun hissing cleanly through the living vines like a hot brand, the tendrils breaking and withering away. After a few neat swings, they stopped in their attempts to reach him and instead curled up and back down around the head like a mane. Just then, Certina darted past him, looped back around and landed on his hand. Before he could regain his wits enough to speak, the structure lurched, sending him sprawling on all fours, clutching at the viny top as Certina hovered in alarm. The structure continued to move. Robby peered carefully over the rim, and he saw that the thing beneath him was walking.

• • •

On three sides, Westlawn was surrounded by a sea of kudzu. The fourth side, protected by log walls, faced the northern plain which was formerly farming land, but it was now filled with the combined armies of Duinnor and Edgewold, come to do battle and to take the town. After several probing forays to the wall and to the main gate of the town, the Duinnor Kingsmen reported back to Teracue that the retreating remains of the Wicker army had taken up in the town, but there was little opposition to their forays and very few bowmen defenders.

When General Teracue, with his entourage of aides, captains, and Edgewold leaders, along with Ullin, Sheila, Billy, and Ibin, came over the steep rise that overlooked Westlawn and the plain before it, they could all see the top of the structure that loomed behind the town. Even at that distance, they could hear the incessant drumming and chanting.

"What foul thing do they do?" the mayor of Edgewold muttered.

From their saddles, they could also see strange waves that heaved across the vine-green sea, yet there was no wind to account for the motion. Indeed the sky was once again fully overcast, and the air was heavy, though there was no sign or feeling that it might rain. Duinnor drums beat steadily as the Kingsmen took up their positions.

"Why do you show your strength?" asked one of the Edgewolders.

"To encourage terms," Teracue replied. "We soldiers do not all relish bloodshed, when it comes to it."

"What is your plan?" asked Ullin.

"They have rebuffed our previous entreaties to surrender," Teracue said, turning in his saddle to watch the men on the west flank deploy to their right. "We will make quick work of it, and be done by nightfall. Our ballistas and trebuchets are nearly in position, and the fires are stoked. Their ivy flanks we shall torch, and if they do not surrender to our siege machines, we will knock their gate down and sack the town."

Teracue spurred his horse and galloped down the slope to a position in front of his troops. Turning around to face the Kingsmen, he raised his hand, the Duinnor drummers ceased, and he spoke in a clear, loud voice.

"Hear me! You have fought bravely and well this day. Another battle is now before us. Let us do our duty, but let not our victory this morning be spoiled by the blood of the innocent. Spare all who do not bear arms against us. Let the wounded of the enemy and all those who yield find mercy. To those of you of Edgewold, who have good cause for anger and vengeance upon those who have wronged you, I say this: Let not your wrath soil your honor. It is to free the land of oppression that we come. It is to release this land and these people from the bonds of cruelty and spite. Spare the children. Spoil not the women. Be merciful to those who surrender. Do not create by your anger further feuds to plague this land after the battle is won. But, during battle, let us vanquish all those who oppose us! What say ye?"

Loud cheers went up from all around. By now the crews were ready at their trebuchets and other engines. Teracue nodded to his subordinates, he said, "Let it begin. And may the slain bear fair witness against us!"

The drummers rolled their beat for a short cadence, and when they abruptly ceased, the first trebuchet slung a fiery load into the air. The drummers rolled again and stopped, and a nearby trebuchet groaned. One after the next, the four engines sent flaming balls over the Wickertown ramparts, then started over with the first engine, now ready once again. While they released their missiles in rounds, groups of soldiers with brands dripping with fire touched off blazes to the right and to the left of the town among the vines. Soon, thick white smoke was rising from the flanking sea, and orange flames cracked loudly. From within the town, black smoke began rolling up into the sky from the fires set by the trebuchets. During this prelude, the Kingsmen in the center moved forward and positioned themselves a hundred yards directly before the gate, and Billy saw how they held their shields closely together, and how those within the ranks formed a roof with their shields against the scattering of arrows that came sporadically from the walls. The Duinnor drums ceased their rolling, and the war machines rested as Teracue and a squadron of horsemen galloped toward the gate. They stopped some forty yards out from it. His men kept their mounts close against Teracue's as he called out to the defenders.

"Give up your captives. Lay down your arms. Submit to the rule of Duinnor. Then you will be spared!"

A white-robed figure stood up over the gate and answered, "Fie! Wokan rules here, and he comes to smite thee!"

Then there came a flurry of arrows, but Teracue's men reacted quickly, and the arrows glanced harmlessly from the shields they threw over him. They wheeled around and quickly galloped back, Teracue signaling with his hand. Immediately, the drummers beat a new cadence, the ballistas and trebuchets resumed hurling their missiles, and the lines of Kingsmen advanced.

• • •

Robby saw the flaming missiles arc upward and descend upon the north parts of the town, and he saw smoke billowing up from the east and west. His immediate concern, however, was to maintain his grasp and keep himself from being flung from the swaying crown of the Wickerman. He was desperate enough to consider jumping, perhaps to land on a thatched roof. But he had little confidence that he could jump with any accuracy, and less that he would be cushioned by the thatch roofs. By now, it was apparent that the entire structure was indeed moving forward under some mysterious power. Suddenly, the horror reached his mind that he now rode atop a living thing, some incredible and malevolent giant.

• • •

Trailing behind it a long train of writhing kudzu, the leafy-robed giant reached the platform where its creator awaited. The people on the ground scattered before it, but many became ensnared by the clutching hem of the creature and were pulled into it as the life was squeezed from them. Pulpy red and green ooze trailed behind it.

"Wokan!" cried the priest, raising up his arms to his protégé. "Your enemies are upon us. Go and scatter them from your lands!"

The thing twisted its head northward, then reached with its green-draped arm to the speaker and, before the priest could recoil, curled its fingers about him and held him fast. Appalled and sickened, Robby watched as the terrified man was lifted from the platform, blood spewing from his mouth and nose, and was tucked inside of the monster as one would put a handkerchief into an inner vest pocket. The creature straightened for a moment, and from it came a loud, long, many-voiced moan. Then it lurched forward, striding in its shaggy green skin through the town, spreading its carpet of choking vines over houses and streets as it passed, swallowing those of the panicked crowds who came within its grasp. Robby cried out in horror, clinging desperately on, and he recognized some of those below as his recent fellow prisoners, running for their lives along with everyone else.

• • •

General Teracue's horse reared, spinning around at his command, and he saw the towering figure approaching through the town. So incredible was the sight, the entire army paused in its movement, and even the drummers weakly stopped their beat, gazing upward. In the awe-induced silence that fell upon the plain, they could hear the screams and cries from within the town. Only when the gate burst open and men and women and children poured out did Teracue react.

"Fall back!" he cried at the drummers. "Sound fall back. Fall back!"

The drummers quickly sounded a distinct cadence, and the troops, in spite of their fear, moved back with disciplined order. Looking at the town, Teracue saw Wicker soldiers abandoning the walls, some even jumping over the side, and others threw their weapons down when they emerged running from the gate. And the giant came closer. It approached the fires that now raged on the north side of the town, but it hardly hesitated before turning to pass around them. By now, it was spreading its smothering death before it, too, and the first tentacles of vines began draping over the north wall. In the gateway, a group of town soldiers hacked the grasping vines with their swords until they, too, were surrounded and swallowed into the ceaseless mass.

"Trebuchets!" roared Teracue, and the crewmen shook themselves to action, sending their payloads at the creature. Robby ducked as a flaming ball shot just over his head. Another projectile hit the shoulder of the creature and exploded in liquid fire, making the vile being reel momentarily, wailing and twisting, sloughing off a burning mass of tangled vines only to be quickly replaced by fresh greenery. Onward it came, now passing over the gate and into the open before the ranks of soldiers on the plain. There, it was met by thousands of Kingsmen who hacked away at the advancing form with sword and axe.

"Fire!" Ullin cried to Ibin as he sliced through the vines. Ibin heard Ullin's cry, and he saw a nearby group of men around their trebuchet trying to ward off the kudzu with firebrands. He immediately chopped his way through the vines to reach them. Once there, and without hesitation, Ibin put his shoulder to the heavy machine and with a great shove, he turned it to face the creature. Then he pulled the lever. Nothing happened. A tangle of vines had snared the mechanism. Seeing this, Ibin and the others cut away at the vines. The creature loomed not twenty yards away and surely a hundred and fifty feet over them. When Ibin hacked through the last vine, the machine heaved suddenly, and fire burst all over the midsection of the monster.

By now, there was fire all around, and acrid white smoke clouded the battlefield so densely that it was difficult to see from one side of the creature to the other. The noise of the snapping flames, the yelling of the battle, and the continuous moans of the creature filled the thick air. Amid the confusion, it was Sheila who first noticed that the surrounding smoke was shifting, a light breeze was pushing it back toward the town. The breeze stiffened somewhat as she chopped away with her sword between Billy and Ullin, and the air it brought was cool and fresh. A strange sound reached her ears, distant and odd, like the far clattering of hollow tubes of wood. The breeze continued to grow stronger and fanned the many fires, but as yet the flames seemed reluctant to take hold of the creature as it repeatedly discarded burning sections of its leafy skin and seemingly regrew them before their eyes.

"Sheila, get back!" Billy screamed at her. She found herself nearly surrounded by the clutching stuff, but quickly she cleared a path and ran north into the wind as the green mass advanced behind her. To her amazement, she saw the low clouds clearing rapidly from the north as if being rolled back like one would roll up a rug. And, high up in the blue sky behind, there were hundreds of vee-shaped lines. As a tentacle of vine wrapped around her ankle, she saw a tiny bird dive downward past the leading vee, and the whole formation swooped down behind it, honking loudly as it came. She slashed away the vine and continued to run.

The geese came out of the north, hundreds of flocks, blotting the sky with their dark forms and filling the air with the noise of their honking. They swooped down, line after line, and smashed into the Wickerman with their heavy bodies, tearing away leaf and vine with their beaks before flapping back into the air. As the first ones regained altitude, more and more arrived, diving down against the creature, cracking against it and shredding away its coverings bit by bit. At first the Wickerman seemed as confused and bewildered as the men and soldiers who were scattering away from it. But as it attempted to swat at the geese that tore and pulled at it from every direction, it became what the onlookers could only describe as infuriated.

"Lo!" Billy uttered as he reached the northern rise and looked back, panting and bowing with one hand on his knee and the other still gripping his sword. He could see that the geese were dropping their leafy loads onto the fires before circling back for more.

"Whar's Ibin?" he suddenly straightened up and looked all around. Soldiers were still coming away, and he scanned the scene for a long moment before he caught sight of the big fellow. "What's 'at?"

"Look there! Atop the monster!" someone nearby cried, pointing at the twisting thing as it tried in vain to fend off the geese. On top of the thing's head, amid a cloud of attacking birds, could be seen a figure, the little shape of a man, being tossed back and forth, and now being lifted, somehow, by eight great geese who held onto his sleeves and pant-legs by their beaks. A way through the tumult was made for them by the other birds, now being joined by larks and jays, wrens and sparrows, swifts and even a few herons. Meanwhile, the geese hoisted the man up and away from the monster, and then, with powerful sweeps of their wings, they descended toward Billy. The birds gently landed their cargo some fifty yards away, to the great astonishment of all who watched. Having recognized the hapless passenger, Billy was already running down the slope to him along with Ullin and Sheila, when he heard Sheila cry out.

"Billy! Ibin's over there!"

Billy looked at her but could not tell where she was pointing.

Robby picked himself up and was looking around with a dumbfounded expression when Billy reached him.

"Robby, Robby! I thought ye whar a goner for certain!" Billy cried joyously as he and Sheila pulled Robby away.

"Me, too," Robby managed, looking back over his shoulder with a nervous grin.

"Come away!" Ullin urged, looking over his shoulder, too, as he gently pushed the other three ahead of him.

"Where's Ibin?" Robby asked.

"Back there," Sheila pointed.

They turned midway up the rise and saw Ibin and several Duinnor soldiers who had stayed behind and were frantically working their trebuchet. The vines had receded from around them enough to reveal Ibin cranking hard at the great pawled drum, slowly bringing down the arm of the machine as the others worked to move it around to a new position.

"Sergeant Baygast!" Teracue bellowed at a nearby soldier. "Take your squad and hack your way to those men. Get them out of there!"

"No! General, wait!" Ullin interceded, seeing what they were about. "Give them a chance to do their work."

Large swaths of kudzu were falling from the twisting monster like rags in the wind, revealing the wicker framework beneath. Protruding from gaps all over the hideous body were the arms and legs and heads of all it had swallowed up, groaning in their death pangs as the green cloak of the thing gave way to the red of their oozing blood. Still the creature struggled in sickening staggers, flinging its arms out at the swarms of birds, though now the geese receded into wide circles high overhead, taunting it with their loud and constant honks. A mere thirty yards from its base, Ibin and the other men continued their work, now hoisting bundles of jars into its sling.

"They are overloading it," said a nearby soldier.

"It'll never throw that much weight!" said another.

"Be still and watch," said a third. "Garond is captain of that crew, and he's a master of the machine."

From where they were, Robby's group could not hear the order given, but they saw one of the men lift his hand. Ibin and the other crewmen ran to the side of the engine. With a downward sweep of their captain's arm, the crewmen pulled the release, the arm swung up, and an orange arc of oily fire was flung overhead and onto the Wickerman, splattering up and down its side. Immediately, the oil-drenched creature was engulfed in flames, and black smoke billowed from it as it made its way at the crewmen. Waving its arms around, it staggered, screaming with a hundred voices joined in cruel agony. Ibin and the crew ran away as fast as they could. The giant stumbled to one knee, tried to stagger up, and then, with a crack of twisting timber and a shower of sparks, it fell sideways in a crashing explosion of smoke and fire. A horrid, almost pitiful moan went up from the creature, then it lay still and quiet but for the crackling of the fire that engulfed it.

There was a moment or two of stunned silence across the devastated field as the people regained their wits, then a cheer erupted among them and spread all over the plain. The honking geese rose higher and higher, gathering into their vee-formations as they went. Then they resumed their way southward, beyond the wreck and ruin of Westlawn, and beyond the roaring walls of fire that advanced through the vines behind them. As the sea of kudzu was steadily being reduced by flames to white ash and smolders, the combined armies of Edgewold and Duinnor gathered themselves together for the triumphant march home. While they did so, General Teracue, his chief officers, and the leading men of Edgewold briefly conferred about the fate of their late enemies, many of whom were fervently begging for mercy and for aid to overcome their wounds and misfortunes.

Ibin and the trebuchet crew soon rejoined their comrades. Robby and his company had to wait their turn for Ibin, who was mobbed and greeted and congratulated by Kingsmen and Edgewolders who gave him slaps on the back and earnest handshakes. General Teracue, breaking off from his conference, addressed the men with a sincere speech, commending their bravery, and Ibin especially, for his strength and coolness in battle. Although the victors were joyous, their elation was somewhat offset by fatigue and by concern for their dead and wounded comrades. They were also sobered by their wonder at the creature that had been made here, of the timely arrival of the southbound geese in such numbers as they had never before seen, and how those airy denizens had joined in battle against the monster.

Teracue, thorough in his planning, had explicit orders at the ready, and he quickly commanded that the large detachments already prepared for the occupation of Westlawn do their duty. The Edgewold leaders had already agreed to his plan, and Teracue deployed sufficient men to occupy the town and to ensure order, assuring the Edgewolders that the law of Duinnor would prevail by force, if needed, so that no atrocities would be tolerated. When all this was done, and as detachments of Kingsmen marched into Westlawn, the rest of the armies began the return march to Edgewold.

Among Robby and his company, there was a happy and almost tearful reunion. And when Certina came to light on Robby's shoulder, he wondered aloud if she had somehow been responsible for the arrival of the geese.

"It is possible, I suppose," shrugged Ullin, taking to his saddle. "She is a mysterious creature, with her own ways. Ashlord sometimes called her the 'Little Messenger.' "

At the sound of Ashlord's name, Certina fluttered a little and emitted a soft whistle.

"I miss him, too," Sheila said aloud before she realized it.

"Likewise," Robby said. "But I take hope from her presence that, if Ashlord was in serious trouble, she'd be with him, or she'd find a way to tell us. I'm convinced, after having thought on it a bit, that the fire and smoke we saw on the mountains was Ashlord doing battle with a horrible creature, and that, somehow, he must have triumphed."

They recalled the awful thing that had shot over their heads and the strange lightning bolt that chased after it. They rode together amid the tramp and clink of the marchers around them, their thoughts and feelings running closely along the same lines, until Ullin spoke.

"Then my fears are darker than yours, Robby."

"Mine, too," agreed Billy, softly.

Nearby, a number of soldiers were having their own debate as they marched along, and when the riders passed them by, they heard one say, "Never will I eat goose again."

"Nor I," replied another and another.

• • •

After a while, Robby's group caught up with General Teracue and the mayor of Edgewold.   Ullin struck up a conversation with them, asking about the Wickermen and how the situation had come about. Much was explained by the Mayor, and Robby listened to a rendition similar to what Tyrin had told him, and he suddenly wondered what had become of the rogue. It was too late to turn back and look for him, but he resolved to ask after him at the first opportunity.

"Oh we held our own pretty well," the Mayor said to Ullin. "But them Wickermen kept getting meaner and better armed, too. We were just getting ready to send off to Duinnor for help when they made their big mistake. You see, not all the folk around Westlawn held with the Wickermen, and they weren't trusted too well. Many were killed or made to be slaves. A few made it away one night, and they told us about some prisoners the Wickermen had taken. A caravan of Duinnor folk, and an envoy among them, returning from the coastlands of Altoria. They were held for about two months, we were told, and, one by one, put to death. Well, we sent our messengers off right away with the news, and the General, here, arrived as a result within a month."

"My orders," Teracue picked up, "were to recover the envoy and his party, along with all of their things, and to put down any rebellion, bringing any to whatever justice I deemed fitting."

"I suppose the envoy was bringing news of the happenings in Altoria?" Ullin asked.

"No doubt. I was to make a special effort to recover his diaries and papers, and I have men doing just that as we speak, searching the ruins of the town for any such documents. There are rumors of increasing raids by the Dragonkind in Altoria, and Duinnor is most interested in any reports of such."

"What word have you had of the Eastlands?"

"Little of late, except what you have shared. Duinnor has tolerated the rebellion in Tracia, and has made many proclamations of outrage at the ousting of the Ruling Prince, but has done little to put its opinion to force. Tell me more about the invasion by the Redvests into the Eastlands and its alliance with the Dragonkind."

Ullin repeated what he had told Teracue at their first meeting, but had little else to add. He explained about his appointment in Passdale as a militia captain and of the unexpected Redvest attack. He related their journey from Janhaven to Tallinvale, and through the mountains and across the plains. Robby noted that Ullin did not mention the meeting with Lyrium or the Nowhereans, and he did not say anything about the bounty that the Damar had placed upon them.

"You may not have proof of what you say, but to my mind it explains much." Teracue responded. "For example, it explains why it has been quiet along the south Vanaran mountains this last year or so. And why no tribute has come these last years from Tracia. Surely, the Throne knows more about these things than I, and my hope is that what you tell me is not unknown there. Still, I know less than I would like about the court of Duinnor and its thinking. And, frankly, I am glad to be away from it and all its intrigues."

"Doubtless you will send word? My friends and I go ourselves, but we must first go to Vanara where we have business."

"I am expecting a courier at any time. You can be assured that I will dispatch word back with him."

At that point, and before Robby could ask about Tyrin, a quartermaster's aide rode up and Teracue rode off with him to some pressing duty. The conversation quickly turned to Robby, as Ullin and the others asked about his own adventures. He told them, between yawns, longing the whole while for just a bite to eat and some sleep. The soldiers marching along with them listened in, and one of them offered him a bit of hard bread that was produced from a pocket, which Robby ate voraciously and with much gratitude.

"Just wait 'til this evening," the soldier said. "Then ye'll join us in our celebrations, surely, an' have plenty to eat an' drink, too."

Robby learned about the battle that his companions had participated in. Billy, in an uncharacteristically subdued manner, did most of the explaining, with Ullin filling in some aspects. The battle's ferocity could hardly be imparted, but as Robby listened, he silently looked at his companions' soiled and blood-caked clothing and the sweaty grime that stained their faces, their hands, and their arms. Sheila said nothing, nor did Ibin speak. Their return to Edgewold was by way of a higher path along the southern ridge of Soltani Pass in order to avoid the wreck of bodies and other hazards on the night-darkened battlefield, so Robby had trouble grasping the scale of the battle. Soon the entire company lost interest in speech, and it was an exhausted army that returned to Edgewold that night, though somewhat enlivened by the crowds of women and children who came out and lined the road just outside of town to greet and cheer the returning victors.

• • •

Robby's company was escorted to a bathing place alongside a stream not too far out from the northwest gate. There, by lamplight and torchlight that dotted and glowed up and down both banks, Kingsmen cleansed themselves of the reek of war. Robby and his group were given a private area, and the courteous escorts had erected a blind for Sheila before taking their leave. Though he was not nearly in need of bathing as his friends, Robby stripped as they did and brought out clothes from his saddlebags. Following Ullin's lead, they left their clean clothes at the water's edge and waded into the water next to Sheila's blind. First they washed and rinsed their dirty things, then, using their dripping blouses, proceeded to wash themselves. The air was cool, and the water cooler, so Billy, Ibin, and Robby made quick work of their bath, shivering as they dried off and dressed. But Ullin took his time, and once he had bathed, he came to the bank, picked up his sword, then returned to the water and sat on a rock low in the stream, just as Sheila joined the boys along the bank. They watched Ullin take his sword from its sheath, dip his rag into the water, and wipe the blood from the blade. He dipped the rag again and squeezed it so that the water ran down over his bare shoulders.

"Let this water wash away my transgressions," he said. Dipping the rag again, he squeezed it out across the blade of his sword, saying, "Let not dishonor stain my name."

His companions, unfamiliar with the ritual, watched and listened in silence as Ullin repeatedly dipped and rewashed his body and his weapons. In the light that glowed and flickered up and down the stream, other blades glinted, and other voices also made their offerings, many reciting the same words that Ullin spoke, somberly and deliberately.

> Let this water wash away the hurt I give to others.
> Let no enemy entice me to evil.
> Let this water wash away the blood upon my hands.
> Let no battle blind me to justice.
> Let this water wash away the pain of my heart.
> Let no anger provoke me to discourtesy.
> Let this water cool my wrath.
> Let the just be also merciful.
> Let this water quench my thirst for violence.
> Let the wounded have healing.
> Let the living find solace.
> Let the dead find peace,
> And whisper not to the living for vengeance.
> Let the memory of the fallen
> Be as this water,
> And wash over me as do the tears of my soul.

Ullin sat for a few moments longer, his head bowed. Then he stood, strode ashore to his clothes, and, putting away his sword, he dressed. A new escort approached, a Kingsman who had waited out of respect until Ullin was finished with his ritual, and he invited the group to join General Teracue and others for dinner.

Chapter 12

Repast and Reunion

The celebration was perhaps subdued by exhaustion, but the people of Edgewold did celebrate, with their volunteer soldiers going about joyfully drinking to their survival, to their return to shop and farm, and to their futures and good fortunes. Already they were making boisterous deals, arranging the resumption of trade, planning the rebuilding of houses and shops, and, if only they could bear up to the coming winter, they looked forward to a new year full of the bounty that peace might bring. Some of them, overwhelmed by their losses, of kin and kith, and having not the means, anymore, to make their living, urged the Kingsmen to let them join their ranks, to make their way plying sword instead of plough, or working the bowstring rather than the tailor's thread. Most of these applicants did not interest those of the King's ranks, seasoned veterans all, but the sergeants did take some they had come to know, who had shown themselves stalwart in battle and faithful on patrol.

So, a great hubbub was upon the town, the likes of which had not been seen for a long time. The taverns and streets were full of joyous celebrants, and houses had been opened to the many guests, soldiers and officers of Duinnor, who had fought with and for them, and who had saved their town and families from the fate of so many neighbors. In one such home, that of an elder councilman of Edgewold, General Teracue and his staff were invited, as well as the Kingsman, Ullin Saheed, and his company from the Eastlands who had fought so valiantly. Other dignitaries of the town were there, too, and their wives and blushing daughters, all gaily attired and bringing with them their servants and staff bearing gifts of wine, kegs and bowls of punch and beer, and baskets of all manner of food that could be had befitting a grand gathering, and all for the sharing. There were musicians, some of Edgewold and some from the ranks of Kingsmen who had considerable talent with voice and string and pipe, and they took their turns with lively reels and playful jigs and thrilling aires to set the guests on their feet. The courtyard of the property was set with cloth-covered tables around its perimeter at which those who wished could sup while the younger or less weary could dance about the center, dipping and swaying and twirling with their many partners. There were constant rounds of toasts and salutes from the Mayor to the General, from the General to the townspeople, from the townspeople to the soldiers of Duinnor, and from all to each other.

Ibin did his share of dancing, light on his big feet and more delicate and graceful than one might think, taking time between forays, of course, to increase his happiness with quantities of wine and food. In a far corner, Billy entertained a group of wide-eyed and blinking young ladies, regaling them with the tale of the Wickerman monster. They were fascinated, and they paled and blushed and waved their little fans for air, for no one could relate such things as gruesomely as he. Or perhaps they blinked and shuddered at Billy's massacre of the language. Sheila found herself the center of attention, too, the General's staff having discovered her charm and wit. And none of them were blind to her beauty nor forgetful of her brutal skill upon the battlefield that day.

Tyrin was there, too, feeling awkward, having been left out of the main fighting, and also having somewhat of an unsavory relationship with the townfolk. But he was treated respectfully, nonetheless, and with some courtesy, having saved many prisoners from the Wickermen in a daring escape amid the rampage of the monster. Robby, happy to see him alive, was somewhat surprised at the rather formal and reserved posture Tyrin assumed and at the fine manners he displayed in the most natural way. Having cleaned up considerably, and wearing new clothes he had been given, Tyrin cut a figure as fine and handsome as Ullin, and similar in demeanor, too, though never lacking a mischievous glint in his eye, like Billy. It was not long before Tyrin had attracted some ladies about him, but Robby was further surprised when he overheard him discussing some of the finer points of lace making. Passing by, Robby bowed to him, and Tyrin bowed back and was about to speak when a lady touched his arm with a question upon her lips. Tyrin shrugged, and Robby grinned, allowing the elegant rascal to return to his audience. Robby pressed on through the crowd, retrieved a tankard of beer, and returned to his place beside Ullin, who was conversing with General Teracue.

"This news of Redvest attacks is of great concern," Teracue said as he poured Ullin another goblet. "Though, upon reflection, I cannot say it is surprising. The envoy we were to ransom, the one who was murdered, was to be carrying news of the southern Realms. His papers have not been looked over, yet, although I have word his things were located in Westlawn. I can only guess they may have something to do with the events you describe. Duinnor's mistake was to parley a truce with the red tyrants rather than send force. Now, with their new allies, the situation is grave."

"Aye, sir. It could not be worse," Ullin nodded. "You will send word, as you said, very soon?"

"Yes, as soon as the courier from Duinnor arrives. He is due any time. I'll not send word until then since new orders may come that I must deal with. Anyway, I must report the actions of this day. I fear, however, as I said earlier, that Duinnor will be slow to move. The King is silent and seldom goes forth." Teracue glanced around, eyeing the room in a manner of one accustomed to caution, and leaned ever-so-slightly toward Ullin to continue in a lowered voice.

"Meanwhile, within and around the city has sprung up corruption, and the courts of every palace are choked with intrigue, with webs reaching far from the city. Perhaps news of Dragonkind on the plains will stir some action. But tell me, is there any intelligence you may provide on the Redvest battle strength?"

"I am afraid I have little to offer other than what I have already told you. It may be useful to establish some communication with Tallinvale, perhaps a representative to Tallinvale from you. It is a certainty that my grandfather has well reconnoitered the enemy approaching his gates."

"Yes, I'm sure." An aide appeared, saluted, and then spoke softly into Teracue's ear. Nodding, Teracue placed his goblet on the table, then turned back to Ullin. "Please pardon me, Commander."

Bowing, Teracue turned and accompanied the aide to the far entrance of the place where Robby saw him meet a dust-covered soldier who handed over a leather-wrapped packet. Teracue, dismissing the soldier and the aide, broke the seal on the parcel and, examining the letters within, broke another seal on one of them. For several minutes, while the festivities flowed around him, Teracue studied the parchment. Bowing to a passing lady, he motioned with a glance to Ullin, who rose and met him under a balcony. Robby was about to follow when he felt a tap on his shoulder.

"I must congratulate you on your miraculous escape," Tyrin said to him, offering his hand. Robby clutched it enthusiastically.

"And I yours!"

"I managed to see some of your antics atop that dang creature they made. I caught sight of you just as it was passing through the middle of the town. Looked like quite a ride!"

"I may laugh now," Robby chuckled, "but I was screaming like a girl the whole time!"

"I doubt that very much! But I'm sorry I couldn't do much for you. Sorta had my hands full."

"So I heard! I overheard one of the townsfolk say how you rescued him and dozens of others from the monster."

"Well, I was just lookin' out for myself. They just tagged along with me."

"And I doubt that very much! At least, that's not what I heard. They didn't cut their bonds by themselves, nor did they have wit enough to run the right way away from the thing. They would have all been killed, so they say."

"They exaggerate, I'm sure. I must return to those young beauties over there and continue with my grandmother's lace making stories—you have no idea what stock girls place in lace making—but I wanted to say what a fine escape partner you are. And to thank you. I suspect it wasn't the first scrape you've been in."

"That makes two of us!"

"Ah, well, be that as it may, I'm grateful to you and your little birdie friend. Do you continue your journey soon?"

"We'll be on our way in the morning, I expect. And you? What will you do now that the fighting is over?"

"I was thinking of going back up to Duinnor City. Just to pay a call, so to speak. Especially since my services aren't needed 'round here."

"Well, I left behind in the Eastlands family and friends who could use your services. Though they've nothing to offer in return but their thanks."

"You don't say? Back east? Hm, did you say somewhere around Lake Halgaeth? What kind of fighting is going on there?"

Robby gave Tyrin the short version, and Tyrin quickly grasped the situation, nodding as Robby completed the tale.

"So," he summarized to Robby, "apart from a few Boskmen and some bandits, there are few trained fighters to help out your folk."

"That's the size of it. But I wouldn't exactly call the Hill Town folk bandits. Not anymore, anyway."

"Maybe I ought to take my sojourn back that way. Hmm. Maybe I'll do just that!"

• • •

Ullin and Teracue conferred with each other, often interrupted by well-wishers.

"The courier that I was expecting just arrived," Teracue said so that only Ullin, standing close by, could hear. "Among the dispatches are special orders. They are coded, and, though my scribe does not know it, I can read the cipher. I will give him the orders in the morning to decode for me."

Ullin listened patiently, wondering why Teracue was going at length to speak of such things to him.

"These same orders, I must tell you, go out to all commanders of Duinnor, and all her allies," Teracue emphasized. "Essentially, it is a summons, to be delivered upon one Robigor Ribbon, son of Robigor, of Passdale in Barley, who is thought to be traveling westward. It demands also that any who accompany him from the Eastlands be summoned. He and any in his company are to be delivered under escort to Duinnor with all haste to bear witness before Lord Banis."

"Lord Banis?"

"Yes."

"Is no one else mentioned by name?"

"No, only Ribbon."

"Then we are to be arrested."

"Not by me. At least not until the morrow," Teracue stated. He tucked the folded parchment into his tunic and gave a slight shrug. "It will be late tonight before I realize that I have not given the dispatches to my scribe. And, since he is a busy man with all manner of reports to complete, it will be noon, at least, before he may even begin his deciphering work. Possibly even later, since, as I see, he is well plied with wine and song. Once deciphered, the orders will require my authorization, but I am also a busy man. My attention has too long been directed upon the south and the threat of Westlawn, and I feel the need to ride out and better familiarize myself with the eastern and northeastern flanks of this territory. It will be a long ride, so I doubt if I will be available to review and authorize the orders until late tomorrow evening. Yes. And by then I will certainly be tired, so it may even be the following morning before I get around to passing the orders along to my commanders, who will themselves be busy. That is as much time as I may guarantee. One night's rest and one day of sunlight. After that, I must do my duty, however reluctantly."

Ullin glanced around, making a quick survey of where each one of his company was in the room, holding out his hand to Teracue.

"Then I thank you, sir," he said, shaking Teracue's hand and giving him a smart, sharp bow and salute. "And I beg your indulgence for the use of some barrack or beds so that my companions might get some rest before dawn."

Teracue made a gesture, and an aide quickly appeared at his side.

"Please make some sleeping arrangements for four men and a lady as nearby to my own quarters as you can," he told the aide. "They should be kept together and provided with food, and whatever provisions they need for an early departure. Be sure that their horses are prepared for them at dawn. When they are settled, see to it that they have complete privacy and are not disturbed in any way by the noise of the celebrations, nor the comings or goings of our soldiers. Do you think you might find a suitable place?"

"Yes, sir!" replied the aide.

Turning back to Ullin, Teracue shook hands with him again. "Once more, I thank you for your leadership in today's battle, and for the part you and your companions played in turning the tide against our enemies. I also am in your debt for your news from the east and south. This debt I now seek to repay, at least in part, by delaying my duty to arrest you and your companions. Take care, and may we meet again in happier times!"

• • •

None were anxious to be parted from the celebrations, but saw the intense urgency in Ullin's eyes as he gathered each in turn. He only told them that they must stay together and be prepared to leave with Teracue's aide as soon as he came to fetch them to their quarters. He explained that he could not say more until they were alone. So they sat together, pensively smiling and being as polite as possible, drinking wine and conversing with the townfolk, until the aide appeared, and they all rose at once to depart.

"To the Eastlanders!" someone shouted from across the room. At the door, Robby turned to see many of those within the hall stand or turn to lift their tankards and goblets to them.

"The Eastlanders!"

"The Eastlanders! May your blades remain bright and your eyes sharp!"

The rooms found for them were not far away, in a house owned by the mayor of the town and next door to the one that General Teracue and his staff occupied. Upstairs was a large room made into a kind of dormitory for the lower ranking officers, and since many of them were presently at Westlawn or in that area, it was willingly given over to Robby's company for the night. They were assured they would not be disturbed and that their mounts and provisions would be ready by dawn. The aide and the housekeeper left them alone, and after he made sure the outside hall was empty, Ullin told his friends about the orders received by General Teracue.

"He is a man of his word, I do believe," Ullin concluded, "and we should take advantage of this night for sleep's sake. In the morning, we should make haste westward out of the range of their riders."

Billy shook his head.

"So how can they know about us in Duinnor already?"

"I cannot say."

"Can this be some ploy of Ashlord's friend in Duinnor to give us safe passage?" Robby conjectured. "I mean, Certina is still about. Perhaps she has taken a message from Ashlord to the fellow he mentioned in Duinnor. To Raynor."

"If that were so, I doubt if the summons would have mentioned Lord Banis. Banis is the First Lord of the High Chamber. Only the King holds more power than he," Ullin said. "I do not know him, personally, but he is a powerful Elifaen, of Vanaran stock, and has vast holdings and interests throughout that and many other realms. It is Banis who presses for Vanara to relinquish its lands to Duinnor. I do not think Ashlord would trust him. Oh, I wish Ashlord was with us still! Perhaps he could advise us as to how cautious we should be. Ashlord's friend, Raynor, is out of favor with the High Court, so I doubt if this is of his making. And, for what it's worth, Ashlord told us that Esildre is the daughter of Lord Banis."

"Could she have gotten word to him?" asked Sheila.

"Ashlord said that she and her father were estranged," Ullin said, shrugging. He shook his head, glancing at Robby as if to ask, "Could she have used me?" Robby shook his head back at Ullin.

"At any rate," Robby said, "whether for good or for evil, I cannot go to Duinnor yet. I must find my way to Griferis first. So I must obviously avoid being arrested and taken away."

Ullin nodded thoughtfully.

"Mebbe we oughta split up, Robby," Billy suggested. "I mean, someone must go an' warn Duinnor 'bout them Redvests an' the Dragonkind. Tell 'em 'bout the invasion of the Eastlands, an' get 'em to send help."

"Teracue is sending word by courier," Ullin stated. "His information is as complete as I dare make it, but hopefully his report will carry some weight, coming from the Commanding General of the Fourth Army."

"No, we should stay together," concluded Sheila, "for as long as we possibly can. We should see Robby to Griferis and, if need be, through that place, too. There are all manner of worthy causes that may take us from that goal, the cause of our own homeland but one of them. But all are doomed, if Ashlord is right, unless a great change is made in Duinnor. And we all know what change is needed."

Stated so bluntly, they nodded and looked at Robby.

"Right," he said. "Let's do as Teracue says. Rest and make our way onward tomorrow."

• • •

Ullin stepped out shortly afterwards to find the housekeeper and to make arrangements for their early departure, asking him to send someone to rouse them shortly before dawn. The housekeeper, willingly agreed and also offered to have a light breakfast ready for them if they desired. Ullin thanked him and offered a few coins in token, but they were kindly refused.

"You have helped free us from the blight of the Wickermen," the housekeeper explained. "And so it is the service of this house that is owed to you and your company."

• • •

In fact, they all had a good night's rest. Even Robby, eager as he was to get back to Micerea, was too tired of mind to make the effort (for it was an effort, he realized). And so he instead enjoyed some mild natural dreams that were so insignificant that he soon forgot them upon waking. In spite of the ordeal they had all been through, they awoke refreshed and eager to be on their way and in better spirits than they had been for weeks. The housekeeper was as good as his word, and after providing basins for their wash, he showed them to a table of eggs and bacon, muffins, and bowls of a kind of steaming gruel made of boiled oats and honey that was popular in the region. They were just finishing the meal when there was a noise at the front door. Hearing heavy footsteps and clanking of metal, they all rose suddenly as Teracue and several soldiers entered the dining room.

"Please," he said, "do not be alarmed. Has Commander Tallin apprised you of the situation? Good. I am about to ride out for the day, but I have other news that I must give you."

Teracue dismissed his aides, and waited for them to depart.

"A man, an old acquaintance of mine from my days in Vanara," he told them, "appeared in Edgewold late last night, long after you were settled and sleeping. He is something of a scholar, and he strongly desired to see and examine any of those things that might be found at the Wokan temple in Westlawn. I granted him permission, though I have not yet had a chance to look over those spoils. I arranged an immediate escort for him to go there, in spite of the late hour. I told him about you, and he was greatly interested in meeting with you. He requested that I direct you to meet him at Westlawn as soon as you had risen from your needed rest. He instructed me not to reveal his name but to tell you that he had some news that may interest you."

"Is he to be trusted?" Ullin asked.

"I trust him," Teracue replied without hesitation. "And, though I do not know his connection with you, he seemed to already know much of what I told him about you last night. I cannot say how. He is a mysterious fellow, that is certain, and I have no notion of his business with you."

"Is he alone? Or did he arrive with some others from the west?" Robby asked.

"He is alone. I know not from what direction he came, but my feeling is that he arrived from the east, along the same way, perhaps, that you came."

Teracue began putting on his gloves and made ready to depart.

"I know little of your purpose, why you travel, but I have dispatched riders to the north with word of the Redvest treachery and of the sighting of the Dragonkind upon the plain. I give you this delay in reward for your service to our cause," he said, looking at Sheila, Ullin, Ibin, and Billy. "You could have waited for the outcome of the battle, standing aside without shame, for it was not your fight. But you participated, nonetheless, and probably saved many a Kingsman and Edgewolder by your valor." Turning to Robby, he said, "The loyalty of your friends is beyond price. They risked wounds and death in battle to come to you. It is a quality to be admired. And appreciated."

"I do, sir," replied Robby. "And I hope that I may be worthy of it."

"Hm," the general nodded, looking closely at Robby, as if sizing him up. "Very well. Your horses are ready. I beg you to go with haste to Westlawn. Then you must ride as far and as fast as you can away from these lands. My debt to you is thus paid. Upon the morrow, I must do my duty. Farewell."

"We thank you, sir," said Ullin, saluting Teracue and accepting his handshake.

• • •

A Kingsman of rank was assigned to ride with them in order to convey Teracue's permission for them to pass, and so they departed Edgewold just as Sir Sun began his walk from the eastern edge of the world, still obscured by the low-lying mists. On the previous evening, when they had made their way back to Edgewold after the victory at Westlawn, they could not see much of the battlefield at Soltani Pass, though they could well see the red glare of the still-burning fires and could smell death upon the dark field. Now, as they came into the north opening of the pass, they saw that hardly anything had been done to cleanse the long valley before them. Here and there, fires still smoldered, and mist-mingled bluish-gray smoke layered the still air upon the valley. A few small groups, some with carts, moved among the sea of dead, gathering weapons and armor, boots and shirts, taking from the fallen anything still of use to the living. This was done while a few dour-faced Kingsmen looked on, some with writing tools, some pointing with their fingers as they counted the dead, some as they counted the items tossed into the carts or stacked into piles. Robby's company made their way as quickly as they could, tacking back and forth through the horrid jumble of bodies, some terribly contorted, others peacefully reclined in their unending slumber. Robby's friends spoke not at all, but their guide called out, seeing a fellow Kingsman with a tally book.

"Bream! What number have ye?" he cried, not stopping but turning in his saddle as he rode by.

"Ah, Jan! Two hundred and thirty-eight Kingsmen, so far. About four times that for the Edgers."

"And the others, the Wicker mob?"

"We make six thousand and some. But our captain orders a recount. Can you believe that? A recount!"

"Six thousand?"

"Aye."

"So there!" said the guide, riding on before the company.

"Aye. So there!" replied the soldier, turning back to his duty.

They kept grimly on, Sheila with her eyes closed for long stretches while Ibin stared straight ahead at the hazy distance. Billy rode with one hand on the reins and his other across his nose and mouth, his eyes brimming with water. Robby was aghast. The horror of the place and the scale of it overwhelmed him. It made his chest pound, and it clutched at his throat as he stifled any sob that might break his composure. Ullin rode without expression, from the discipline of his long and unfortunate experience in warfare. But it was Ullin, who outwardly seemed the least moved at the waste, who began singing to himself an ancient lament once sung by the ladies of Glareth, his voice soft and tender, though with a slight quaver. Robby was close enough to hear the words, and perhaps the guide was, too.

> *See the torch-fires in the hills.*
> *See our sweet lads march away.*
> *Hear the songs from 'round the fields.*
> *Our loved-ones go to war this day.*
> *Mind the furrow and the row,*
> *Cut the barley and the hay,*

Bring the cow and chase the crow,
Our husbands go to war this day.

Break the limb and hew the tree
To feed the hearth-flame orange bright.
Sew the blanket on your knee
To keep you warm into the night.
Will your cottage again be host
To your lover's shadow dear?
And the boyish son you love the most
Return with scar and beard?

Spend the evening on the hill,
And weep toward the west.
Fill with tears your lonesome grail,
This ache within your breast.
See the torch-fires in the hills.
See our sweet lads march away.
Hear the songs from 'round the fields.
Our loved-ones go to war this day.

And so they rode on, eventually leaving the pass and coming upon a long line of Kingsmen, holding back many of the Westlawn folk who were desiring to enter the field to search for their kin, their sons and husbands, and their fathers. The Kingsmen kept them in check in spite of their tearful petitions while Robby and his party were allowed to pass.

"Why won't they let them through?" Robby asked.

"It is the way of Duinnor," said Ullin. "The battlefield must, whenever possible, be scoured of weapons and other such things before people are allowed upon it to search for their kin. Sometimes the press of war does not permit such traditional thoroughness."

Robby looked at Ullin with dismay.

"It is not only to keep the enemy from rearming with the weapons of the fallen, Robby," Ullin explained, "but also to keep the fallen from being robbed. There are heavy penalties for robbing the dead. A Kingsman may be publicly flogged and discharged from service for doing so or for permitting it. We are honor-bound to respect the fallen and their kin. If there is some item of meaning to the survivors, to the kin of the fallen, they may ask for it. If no claim is made, the material is disposed of as the commanding general sees fit. Usually, it is ordered that unclaimed things of a personal nature be buried with the dead."

Robby thought again of the locket that Eldwin had told him about, the one the little man hoped to return someday to the descendants of the locket's owner. And he thought, too, that it might be possible that a victorious army may also find among the dead of its enemy papers or maps or other material that might prove useful. He glanced back at the crowd, now a long distance behind him, still held back by the Kingsmen. It was a cruel necessity, he concluded, that established such practices. He was still thinking on such when they topped the rise before Westlawn and saw that the fires within the town had been reduced to smoky flickers, though the kudzu still burned far southward. Surrounding the town was a sea of white ash, looking like dirty snow, and where the Wickerman monster had fallen, a huge black heap still boiled and crackled. Fortunately, as they passed nearby to that spot on their way to the gate, a gentle breeze stirred, pushing the awful smell away from them.

"I don't relish going back in there," said Robby as they neared the smashed gate. After receiving and passing the challenge of the Kingsmen posts, they continued on, being led by their guide through the town. It was surprising that the entire town had not burned to the ground, but it might have if most of the houses and structures had not been built of stone with tile roofs from the time before the Wickermen. There were fewer people about than one would imagine there should be, and Robby asked their guide.

"Many are out upon the battlefield to look for fallen kin," the Kingsman explained. "Others have joined with the Edgewolders and are out hacking and burning away the vines that have been a plague upon them."

But there were many Kingsmen and Edgewolders standing guard, dozens at every corner, it seemed, and more patrolling up and down every street and alley. Ullin knew they were here to prevent reprisals and looting and to establish the King's Law upon the conquered. But he explained nothing to his companions who seemed reassured by the presence of Teracue's soldiers, even though, on the morrow, he and his friends might have a different view of the Duinnor men.

They came to the base of the Wokan temple, crowded with sentries, and after tying off their horses, they began making their way through the gates, then upward along its sloping walls and steep stairs. Coming to a landing and a stone doorway, they were challenged.

"Here to see Teracue's visitor!" their guide responded, handing the guards a slip of paper.

"Very well. He is down the corridor, there, in the chamber at the far end."

"If you'll not be needing me," their guide said, turning to Ullin, "then I'll be back to Edgewold."

"Certainly. Thank you, Kingsman, for conveying us here."

"Then, farewell, Kingsman."

The passageway was dimly lit by unenthusiastic torches, and as they cautiously went along it toward a far door, they crunched on dead vines and leaves. By the torchlight, they saw that the entryway, the floor, the walls, and the ceiling, had once been covered with clinging vines, but were now all dried and brittle, parched as if they had been cut and left out for a long while under a summer sun. When they noisily reached the end of the corridor and stepped into the room at the end of the hall, the vines abruptly ceased as a carpet might come to an end, and they walked instead upon a tiled floor. They stopped to look about. The large room was cluttered with bookcases and tables, with books and scrolls strewn everywhere, some rolled out and hanging off the tables onto the floor, others draped across the backs of book-piled chairs. On the far side of the room was a wide open doorway leading out to a sort of platform, allowing the brilliant morning light to stream in. And there a man stood, his back to them, silhouetted against the light, leaning over a table and apparently studying some document of intense interest.

There was something very odd about this man, something, even with his back turned, that was so striking that it commanded silence. In appearance he was tall and thin, somewhat narrow-shouldered, and was dressed in a light brown travel cloak that reached down to his ankles, his feet in short buckskin boots. As he was turned away from them, they could see only the back of his head, which was nearly bald except for the short stubble of orange hair that sprouted from it like peach fuzz. But the hair was not so thick or long to obscure the red skin underneath, or his red neck and ears. He was sunburned all over, as if reddened by recent and long hours under a full sun, but the red skin and thin orange hair, wavering in the odd light, made him appear to actually be on fire. Leaning against the table was a walking stick, nearly the same as the one Ashlord once carried, but of a dark copper color and topped with a large green crystal that glowed brightly in the light.

"That looks very much like the one Ashlord carried," Sheila whispered to Robby.

"But Ashlord's had a blue stone," Robby replied.

"Perhaps this man is a Melnari, like Ashlord."

"Indeed. I am. And the staff is very much like the old staff of Collandoth," the man said, turning around toward them. His face, like his crown, was wind- and sunburned-red, and his sharp chin and narrow cheeks were covered, too, with the same orange-red stubble of a growing beard. Oddly, his whiskers, like the hair of his head, seemed combed back away, as if some fierce gale had pressed the whiskers back and now that was the way new hair would grow. He had no eyebrows to speak of; at least, they, too, were only marked by stubble.

"In fact, it is the one and the same staff, tried and transformed, as it were, just as I have been."

It was only then, as he smiled, and when they saw the glint in his black eyes, that they recognized him. As if to confirm his identity, Certina flew in from the window and landed on his shoulder.

"Ashlord!" Robby cried, jumping forward and giving him a hearty hug. The rest did the same as soon as they could, amid exclamations of surprise and joy and expressions of astonishment.

"What happened to you?"

"You look so different!"

"How on earth did ye get here?"

"I am overjoyed to see you all again," he said as soon as he could. "In spite of my appearance, I am safe and unharmed! But there is little time for my story, since we must flee away from this place as quickly as we can."

"Then you know about the orders from Duinnor to arrest us?"

"Yes. Teracue told me last night when I arrived. He also told me something of your adventures these last few days."

His friends immediately began scolding him for not coming to them right away.

"You have no idea how worried we've been!"

"You came to town and didn't come to find us?"

"How come ye didn't come to us last night?"

"I know, I know!" Ashlord answered. "And I apologize. But I knew from Teracue that you were safe, and I thought it best to let you have your rest. Meanwhile, Teracue was only too happy to delay any action against you. He also permitted me to come here, and I have spent the night exploring this so-called temple for clues."

"Clues?" Ullin asked for them all.

"Yes, clues to the power of Wokan and his conjurer."

"Was it Secundur, then, behind all this?" Robby asked.

"I fear so, although there is very little here to support that opinion. Perhaps there was a struggle within the enemy's ranks, among Secundur's own lieutenants, perhaps. The one who established himself here, this nameless magician with the power to conjure vines, sought to make his own realm. We may never know. But he lacked Secundur's subtlety to carry it off. Still, it did serve Secundur's ultimate purpose, sowing discord and making havoc. There may be others, too, openly fomenting discord among Men and between the realms. It is somewhat in keeping with what happened in Tracia. From this place, I have learned much of the happenings of the southlands of Masurthia and Altoria, more than I expected to learn. Apparently, these people intercepted virtually every dispatch sent north and south. And they are stored here, in this room."

"What have you learned from them?"

Ashlord took up his shoulder bag and stick, then made for the door when Ullin stopped him. "And where is your sword?"

"It was destroyed," Ashlord said, looking around. "Yes, I may need one."

Seeing a pile of various gear on the floor in the far corner, he strode to it.

"I have learned that the Dragonkind make forays through the Hinderlands into Altoria, small scouting parties, mainly. And the Redvest continue to mass their forces east of Masurthia," Ashlord said as he rummaged through the saddlebags and other things. "These things were obviously taken from the envoy and his entourage. I know I saw one a while ago when I search through...ah!"

He pulled out a long scabbard and drew the sword just a little to look at the blade. It was narrow with a slight curve, its handguard of brass but well made.

"An old blade, from the last age. Probably belonged to the envoy himself or one of his guards. It will do very well, and be an honor to wield, if need be. Let us be away from here and exchange tales when we have the leisure to do so!"

Entr'acte

Entr'acte

So One Dream Ends

On the day that Robby and his company set out from Tallinvale, the forest that lay at the western border of the great plain was alive and at peace, just as it had been since Lady Moon revealed her face fully over the eastern horizon the evening before. Along the leas and glades, in the uppermost branches of the tallest trees, and in the deep, forested vales where brooks and streams flowed over mossy stones, every kind of forest creature stirred. In one clearing, a rabbit nudged aside the paw of a panther to pull up a few delectable shoots. The great cat moved its paw, then rolled over on its back and squirmed upside down to give itself a good scratch and rub of the back. Overhead, a line of wrens sat on a branch, chattering and chirping. Higher up within a nearby chestnut, a snake coiled along the top of a broad limb as an owl hopped out of its way. The owl flapped off to another section of the forest to watch several swans navigate a broad shady pool. Along the edge of the pool, turtles basked in spots of sharply angled sunlight that managed to reach through the thick canopy. The notes of a lyre did not disturb them, as one of the Faerekind floated upward and out of the pool. Stroking watery chords, he stretched out his wings and twirled up and up, through the branches, higher and higher, until at last he was several hundred feet high and near the topmost boughs of the tree. Others of his kind flew around him, coming and going through the air to the glassy-domed city farther off. There, supported by the arms of massive and ancient trees, their dwellings ever-so-slightly and pleasantly swayed as the trees imperceptibly shifted in the late afternoon breeze. Birds with long trailing plumes flew inside one of these airy lofts, and their plumage was barely distinguishable from that of some of the Faerekind who accompanied them. Together the birds and the Faerekind played catch with the nearly weightless seed of a dandelion, blowing it back and forth with gentle waves of their wings.

In other structures, the Faerekind assembled to tell stories, often in song, with words that drifted through the air and teased the thin brooks that gurgled up over the ground and wound their voluble way around trunks and through the branches. The brooks flowed and turned steadily skyward, and they joined with many others like a vast silvery web, converging and climbing from all over the forest. In the middle of the watery web all these sun-glistened streams came together and gushed up like a geyser and then outward like a gigantic fountain, showering gently down through rainbows into a forest lake. The lake drained away in every direction through the forest, sending its children off as streams to dance across rocky courses, and as talkative brooks jumping around massive roots, and as solemn creeks murmuring through the vast forest, each winding out and down, diving through waterfalls, wading gently through mossy-banked pools, and sliding down shoals throughout the forest. Then, as they neared the forest's borders, the brooks and streams turned around to run playfully back uphill and then upward around tree trunks and through high limbs to be joined once more at the wondrous fountain only to start all over again.

A furlong or so from this wondrous waterfall, a high narrow shaft rose up from the forest. It was in form like a slender reed, standing much higher than the waterfall, higher than all of the highest trees, so high that the lone figure standing at its very top could raise her hand and touch the gentle clouds that ambled by. Her name was Islindia, and this was her land. She stood alone, as she always did when the time was come. She smiled at all her surroundings, looking at her people and her forest below. It was a wistful smile she wore, and as she watched her domain she also watched the sky. Time was almost gone. How quickly the day had passed, for Sir Sun was already standing on the opposite horizon from where, but a moment ago, he had arisen to bring the day. It seemed to Islindia that, as his yellow-white light dimmed to a darker golden glow, he hesitated.

Islindia looked at him, and he turned his head over his shoulder to look at her, only briefly, then shot his gaze beyond her. The two had never spoken, nor had they ever met. Yet Islindia knew his hesitation was not for her sake, but for his wife whom he would not see until morning, when Lady Moon was near that part of the sky where he now stood, and when he was, in turn, walking the eastern stairs of heaven. Islindia, atop her reed-like tower, understood Sir Sun's longing. She also understood the bindings of his fate, to move on, ever on, just as her own fate was to remain, ever remain.

She turned to look where he gazed, far across the world to its eastern rim where Lady Moon would soon enough make her appearance. It would be but an hour from now, but Sir Sun would not wait. He could not wait. Alas, for Islindia, neither could Lady Moon, and with her appearance, it would all be over. The day would be done.

Sir Sun went his way and pulled the purple-pink hem of his garment with him. The first bright stars soon after appeared in the deepening sky. Islindia's people still flew and floated, the mighty trees still stretched upward, and the marvelous waters still flowed up and back down. But as more stars appeared and the eastern sky began to glow, the forest seemed to grow sleepy. The laughter rising up to Islindia's ears faded, the flowing waters moved more slowly, and all the evening birds and crickets grew quiet.

Islindia spread her gossamer wings and stepped from her perch. Descending, she circled her tower twice, then floated down and down, through the dense boughs and into the darkened forest, landing softly with her bare feet on a mossy path. Draping her wings about her like a robe, she walked through the hushing wood. As she passed, majestic trees bent and fell gently and silently to the ground like giants going to sleep, and the magnificent structures within them settled into the earth and disappeared under blankets of vine and lichen, and the streams all ran dry and vanished.

She continued eastward as green leaves decayed to brown, as her people turned into mist, and as the dripping brooks transformed into beards of gray moss hanging from stunted and gnarled oaks. Islindia, walking with her head down, did not look about her at the decaying forest; she well knew its time was gone. When she reached a high ridge, she raised her eyes to the east to look beyond the barrier of thorns that encircled her lands, and beyond the plains to the horizon. Her eyes watered, and her heart was full of grief as she watched Lady Moon appear with a portion of her fan across her cold white face. Someday, Islindia thought, perhaps Lady Moon would forget her fan somewhere, would put it aside and never have need of it again. Someday, perhaps Lady Moon would always be at her boldest and brightest, as she had been only the night before when Islindia's domain came to life once again.

Islindia turned. Her father was there, and he looked at her with dewy eyes of yellow berries. His leafy beard and ivy hair drooped in sadness for his daughter, and he gripped his great staff of holly with both of his bark-encrusted hands, leaning upon it heavily.

"No, Father," Islindia said to his silent apology. "I do not blame you, as I have always said to you. I am sorry that you see my sadness, for I know it stirs you to anger against the outside world. It is not the world's fault. Our dream is over yet again. But only for a time. Only until Lady Moon fully regains her courage once more, as she does each month."

Her father's eyes shifted northward, then back at Islindia. She nodded.

"Yes. The carriage that you lent to Lyrium has returned in time. It is no longer at risk. But it returned without Lyrium or her daughters. Perhaps her Sight will show her the way of things beyond our forest. Perhaps the one she goes to meet will indeed be the Hidden One."

The King of the Wood shifted slightly and stood straighter.

"No," Islindia answered. "As you say, his concerns will be for the world outside of our realm. I know that he cannot help us. So you need not worry that I have hopes which will only be dashed. I have none. I live only for the one night and one day given to us each month."

Again, Islindia's father moved, drawing near to her as she touched his mistletoe crown and ran her hand across his leafy face.

"Indeed," she said to him, "Lady Moon's courage is all that sustains me, though it grows and then fades away. My heart sinks as her courage fades, night by night. And the anticipation of my heart grows as her courage increases, until that one night when she is at her bravest. So my fear, if you must know it, is that she will one day grow as fainthearted as I, that she will never put away her fan after that, and that her courage will be forever gone. But if she does come again, as bold as before, I shall not immediately conjure my memories. I shall wait as long as I am strong enough to wait. For it is possible that the Hidden One may need my dream, should he come this way, and I will conjure it for him. Though his affairs do not concern us, by giving him rest and sanctuary, we may strike back at the one who blighted our lands. A small blow, perhaps. But it is all that we have to offer. And I will use the last of my determination to do so, should that be the way of things."

Islindia bowed to her father, then walked back into her devastated realm. The King of the Wood turned to watch her recede into the darkness. The evening dew settled upon him, and his form sagged as moisture gathered around his leafy face into droplets and streamed down from his yellow-berry eyes. In but a moment, his form was drooped and bent, covered with rolling drops that pattered down his body and pooled about the hem of his ivy robe, as if it was raining.

Part II

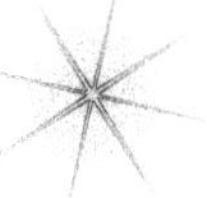

Chapter 13

Valkose the Demon

Day 133
112 Days Remaining

It was very difficult to resist pummeling Ashlord with questions or relating to him their own adventures on the plain with the Dragonkind, the stampede, and all the wonders they had seen. Robby, especially, longed to take him aside and privately share the things that troubled his heart and seemed to weigh him down. But he was nervous about how to tell him of Ullin's behavior. And, besides that, how would he explain Micerea and his own ability to dreamwalk? And there was the matter of the coins that Mirabella wanted Robby to share with the Melnari. Ashlord, sensing the unease within the group, deftly and firmly insisted that they wait until they were far enough away to have some breathing room and no fear of being interrupted or overheard.

"I promise," he told them, "that within the next few days we shall have our chance for storytelling. I am as anxious to hear what you have to tell me as you are to tell me, but let us be patient for a better time and place."

So they left Westlawn, Ashlord on a new mount and the others in their familiar saddles, and they rode out of the smitten place. All around the town, where but a day before was a sea of besieging kudzu, was now a landscape of ash. Looking southward, they could see orange tongues of flame pushing up billowing white smoke where the victorious Edgewolders still stoked the vine-clearing fires. Fortunately for the company, the new breeze was out of the northwest, and after a mile or so the ash no longer blew into their faces or stung their eyes. By mid-afternoon they had left the north-leading road and were making their way once again across a broad rolling plain, the green grass a relief to their eyes and its aroma a welcomed change.

"Uh, oh," exclaimed Ibin.

The others turned in their saddles and saw a company of Kingsmen riding smartly for them, lances upright in their cups.

"We can't outrun them," said Billy.

"And we can't fight them," said Robby.

"Are we just going to let ourselves be taken, then?" asked Sheila, her hand on her bow.

"It is too soon for them to have Teracue's orders," Ashlord suggested, as puzzled as they by the oncoming force. "Let us see what may happen."

As the Duinnor men reined to a halt before them, Robby could immediately see an uncomfortable expression on the captain's face.

"I bid you good day, travelers!" he greeted, "and I must inconvenience you to come with me back to Edgewold."

"May we ask why?" Ullin answered.

"We have standing orders that all be gathered to Edgewold."

"Are not the hostilities between Edgewold and the Wickermen concluded?" asked Ashlord.

"For the most part, yes."

"Then are not your orders, issued for the protection of the people, now unnecessary?" followed Ullin.

"Perhaps. But they still stand and are not rescinded."

"You have not received new orders?"

The captain fairly squirmed in his saddle, saying, "No, we have not. We follow standing orders that all are to be brought to Edgewold, and any horses found are to be appropriated for its defense."

"What?"

"But we need them!" Billy exclaimed.

"You may take that up with my commander when you arrive back in Edgewold. I am as uncomfortable as any at this turn of things, as I, myself, and all my men here saw your valor on the field yesterday. But our orders stand, and we must obey them."

"Your general has no authority to hinder our passage," Ashlord calmly stated, reaching into his shoulder bag and removing a small scroll. He nudged his horse to the captain and handed the scroll over. The captain, eyeing Ashlord, warily took it, and, removing a glove to more easily unroll it, he read its contents to himself, cocking an eyebrow as he did so, but otherwise retaining his stern expression. As much for his men's sake as for his own understanding, he reread the message aloud.

"This writ gives the bearer free passage through all realms as well as the same for all persons in the bearer's company, so that they may pass without hindrance or inspection of their persons or their belongings, regardless of contrary laws, customs, or orders not issued by the undersigned and sealed. Further to this writ, all accommodations, assistance, and protection is to be given to the bearer as requested by the bearer or as deemed fitting to those encountered by the bearer of this writ. By order of the Council of Duinnor." The captain rolled it back up and handed it back to Ashlord. "It is all properly done, signed, and sealed."

"I believe your orders do not apply to our party," Ashlord said.

"That is for my superiors to decide," replied the captain with some suspicion. "Why have you not shown this writ before, if you had it? At any rate, your horses will come with me, whether you are upon them or not."

"Do you seek to provoke an incident, Kingsman?" Ullin angrily pushed through alongside Ashlord. "And with the Council of Duinnor that issued this writ? We need our horses for our journey, and we have Duinnor's guarantee of passage!"

"Guard your tongue, lest I forget you are a fellow Kingsman!" the captain shot back. "This writ applies to persons only. Horses are not persons."

"Says you!" stated Sheila.

"I do say! You may come to Edgewold with your mounts and your writ and speak to my general. Or you may continue along your way without them. The orders pertaining to the horses clearly state there is to be no exception except that given by the quartermaster."

"General Teracue will be furious!" Robby said. "He himself gave us leave and bade us good journey this very morning."

"This is thievery!" cried Billy.

"I will not bear your insults!" shouted the captain, his hand going to his hilt and the lances of his men brought to the ready. "You must yield to my orders, just as I must carry them out!"

There was a moment of raw, heated silence. Then Ullin sprang from his saddle and, without a word, angrily began untying his gear. Reluctantly, the others did, too, with many grumbles, until their mounts were bare of all but their bridles.

"Will you not reconsider and come to Edgewold?" asked the captain one last time as his men gathered and tethered the horses. "Suit yourself then!"

A moment later, the company stood over the heaps of their belongings, watching the Kingsmen recede with their horses, their anger turning to frustration while a somber mood overcame them.

"Well," Ashlord said at last. "At least Ullin had the foresight back in Janhaven to load much of our gear into backpacks. But lightly we should travel, with no more weight than we can run with! Leave the pots and pans, except for the small one for making hot water. Bring each of your water flasks, and one of the waterskins."

"But leave all of the food that must be cooked," Ullin added. "Bring blankets, one each, your cloaks, and a single change of warm clothes. It will be cold before we reach Vanara."

He may have been right, but by now the early afternoon sun was very warm, and, with little wind to speak of, they could already feel the humid air rising from the tall grass. Soon enough, though, they had the contents of their packs reorganized, and had made a pile of the things they were leaving behind. Ibin insisted on bringing his mandolin, Sheila secreted her little book from Broadweed into her pocket, and they began their westward march. Ullin and Ashlord set a fast pace, and before a mile was behind them, they were strung out in a long line across the plain.

"I believe you once said something about preferring your own two feet over riding horses," Sheila said to Billy after several more miles.

"Yeah, yeah. Well, thar're some eggsepshuns," Billy replied. Sheila nodded and smiled, knowing that was as much of an admission of error than she could ever hope for.

The day wore on, and they marched into a breeze, and although it felt cool, it seemed to make going forward more of an effort than was needed. In fact, they were all very tired. The exertions of the past days were hardly erased by the night's sleep, and weariness overtook all except Ashlord. The breeze became unsteady and prone to long lulls, making the air unseasonably muggy. Before mid-afternoon, when they had put many miles behind them, the air hung without movement, and they were soaked with sweat and happy to collapse along the banks of a shallow stream where a lone willow offered a bit of shade.

"Doesn't even seem like autumn anymore," Robby gasped, tumbling down beside Ullin.

"In fact, it is nearly winter," Ullin replied, handing Robby a water flask.

"We must keep moving," Ashlord said. "When tomorrow's sun rises, this land will be scoured for us. And our trail through the grass is easily followed."

"So ye think the gen'ral'll have us taken?" asked Billy.

"He is a Kingsman," Ullin stated. "He'll obey his orders, even if he does not like them."

Ashlord leaned on his stick, eyeing the group. Robby stood, slipped off his pack, and approached.

"Do you suppose we may have a talk?" Robby asked softly. "Just the two of us?"

"Well, would you like to walk ahead with me," Ashlord suggested, "and look upon the way we must go?"

"Yes, that would be good."

"Then get your pack back on." Turning to the others, Ashlord said, "Robby and I shall go ahead to that rise just yonder. Come along when you've had a bit of a rest."

"Very well," Ullin said, somewhat concerned. He and Robby exchanged glances as Robby lifted his pack. "We'll fill the flasks, too."

"Very good."

Ashlord and Robby waded through the shallow stream and walked on up the low ridge that stretched from north to south about a furlong away.

"I must tell you," Ashlord said to Robby, "that, with all that has happened, I never had a chance to put your request to Certina. She was kept quite busy as it was."

"I'm sure," Robby laughed, "and I'm glad of it. If it had not been for her, I don't think I could have made it. Or any of us. I'm certain she fetched the geese that attacked the monster and saved my life."

"Yes, she did do that."

"And, before then, she guided me out of the wicker vines. So I am not one bit upset! Anyway, much else has happened."

"Then tell me."

"Right. Well, I hardly know where to begin."

"Why don't you start where we left each other. I take it you made it to Tulith Morgair?"

"Why, yes. We did. But not without some trouble."

"Ah. And did you learn what it was you went there to learn?"

"Yes. Sort of. But much more has happened since then. There are three different things that I need to tell you about. I don't think they have anything to do with each other, but they all seem important, somehow, to what we are doing."

"Then start with the one and move to the next and the next."

"Well, alright then. I'll try. Much of what I have to tell you will sound, well, you may think me a bit balmy, but here goes: I've been having strange dreams these past months. Since I was at Tulith Attis, actually. And they got stranger and stranger until, well, until I found out they weren't dreams. Not in the ordinary, proper sense."

"What do you mean?"

"Well," Robby said as they continued walking. "I wasn't supposed to tell anyone about this. I may have already said too much to the others, and they may have guessed at what is happening to me."

"What are you trying to tell me, Robby?"

Robby stopped and looked squarely at Ashlord, summoning his determination.

"I am a dreamwalker. At least, I believe I must be. And I have met another dreamwalker who is teaching me how to do it. Or to do it better. The journey to Tulith Morgair was so that I could obtain a sign, to confirm that it is all real. You see, I doubted it myself. I don't blame you if you don't believe me."

"I know little about dreams," Ashlord said, "except that others have them while sleeping, and sometimes while wide awake, I am told."

"Oh, yes, that's right. You never sleep, so you never dream, do you?"

"I do not. Not in the manner you mean, anyway. But I have been around long enough to know of dreams from those who have told me about them. And I have always thought that there must be more to them than most believe. That is, I do not think that visions should be so casually dismissed. And I have heard of dreamwalkers, those who may travel into the waking world from their slumber, and go anywhere they please. Is that how it is with you?"

"In a way," Robby nodded. "But it's all new to me. I am just beginning to learn."

They continued on up the hill, reached the top, and Robby began telling Ashlord about his encounters with Micerea. Robby described how Micerea had shared so much about life and history in the Dragonlands.

He tried to explain about his ability to slip into the dreams of other people and even participate in those dreams if he wanted.

Ashlord did not interrupt, but let Robby talk.

"And that's how I learned some of the speech of the Dragonkind and how I've seen their cities and somewhat of their deserts. She's shown me many, many things, and has explained to me why their lives are so difficult. She is the daughter of Gurasa! Of all people! That's how she found me, sort of. But I already told you that she thought Ullin would be the one to become King."

Ashlord nodded. "She was not alone in that mistake."

Robby suddenly hesitated, shaking his head, then he looked at Ashlord who was obviously deeply concerned by this revelation.

"I'm sorry. Maybe I haven't told it just right. I don't know what to do, though. I know it taxes my strength, that since I've gotten accustomed to this ability, I haven't had much real sleep. Micerea warned me. And each night, well, nearly every night, we visit. She insists that I cut my visits short with her, that I must be aware of the needs of my body, to give it the rest it needs. She has taught me so much! And now I'm beginning to see how I can do other things, things that she knows little about. How I can find out so much by using this ability to move around. And there's another thing, something very strange. There are different levels of this dreamwalking, like different landscapes, in a way. At least three of them. And I can pass from one to another just as easily as we climbed this hill. One is where I can walk about, without being seen, and go as far as I wish. Another is a place where I may enter the dreamworld of others, or join my dream with theirs. This is how Micerea and I have been able to be together. And there's another place, another level, I suppose. It is very strange. But when I go there, it is as if I can see different worlds. I can't explain. I don't understand what it is that I see. Still, the whole thing is a bit, well, a bit awkward. I mean, I don't want the others to know. Not if I can help it. Not yet, anyway. And, there are creatures who abide in the dream world. Some of them are not very pleasant."

Robby shrugged, somewhat exhausted from the long explanation as well as a bit out of breath at the climb, during which he did not stop talking for a second. But he managed to get all said that he thought he should.

"I needed to tell you. I don't know what I should do."

"If I understand what you are saying," Ashlord began carefully, "and if we are to believe what the Dragonkind woman has told you, then I fear you may be delving into something very dangerous. Useful, I grant you that. I beg you to be careful. You need rest, just as the others do. And if you do not get it, you will endanger not only yourself, but your friends, too."

"I know. I'm grappling with that. But I need to use the ability while I can. There's so much I must learn if I am to become a king. Oh, here they come."

From their high vantage, they could see the rest of their company rise up from their rest and put on their packs.

"Yes, so they are. I agree that it would not be wise to tell the others about your ability. I sense that you have more to tell me?"

"Yes. It's about Ullin. And Esildre. And Sheila, too."

He quickly told Ashlord about Ullin's delusions, of his mistaking Sheila for Esildre, and how Ullin had treated Sheila so harshly, but without intending to. How Ullin had threatened to take his own life, so crazed and disturbed he had become at one point in their journey. Ashlord's concern increased. He furrowed his brow, and he absently tugged his ear as he listened to Robby.

"You did right in telling me," Ashlord said when Robby concluded. "He was fortunate to have you as a friend, stopping him from doing himself harm as you did. Yet, I do not believe it is Esildre, ultimately, who is behind such visions that he may suffer. This, too, let us keep between us. At least until I have had some time to turn it over in my mind."

"Very well, but I fear it is harming our fellowship."

"I do not doubt it. Give me time to mull it over. There was something else you wanted to impart to me? You said you had three things to tell me about."

"Yes, something that my mother wanted me to share with you, but I neglected to tell you before we parted company in the Thunder Mountains. Do you remember the old coins that I told you about? The ones that my father got from Mrs. Starhart, the ones that the stranger gave over for the cost of posting parcels to Duinnor?"

"Yes, I certainly do."

"Well, they are here in my vest, making it heavier than I would wish, in more ways than one. But I dare not shed the vest because that is where my mother put them, having sewn them inside for me to keep with me."

"So you brought them along with you."

"Yes. Mother said they were of great value and begged me not to part with them," Robby said as he unbuttoned his vest and carefully loosened a thread on the inside of it. "She said to show them to no one but you. To get your opinion, I suppose."

He took out one of the coins and handed it to Ashlord.

"Here's one."

Ashlord took the coin and stiffened when he looked at it, his mouth open, a dumbfounded expression on his face as he stared at the coin. Then he looked at Robby, his expression unchanged, before staring again at the coin, carefully turning it over as he did so. He made a little gesture with his hand, as if to wave off the approaching company, and, just at that moment, Billy cried out.

"Oh, blast! We left the flasks soakin' in the stream!"

"Oh, good grief!" Sheila chided. "Well, let's go back and get them!"

As they dropped their packs and turned back to recover the water, Ashlord continued, barely noticing them.

"Great stars! You've had this all along?" he said finally, tucking his stick under his arm so that he could turn the coin over in both hands, looking at the intricate patterns cast into it and the bright red stone at its center. "Do you know what this is?"

"Mrs. Starhart called it blood money. There are six others, here, in my vest. My mother sewed them all in for safekeeping."

"You mean to say that you have, here on your person, *seven*?"

"Yes. Seven, all told."

"Seven? Like this one?"

"Yes, seven. Each has a different stone, but are the same in every other way."

"Nimbus Illuminas," Ashlord muttered. "When you told me about Mrs. Starhart and the coins, I had no idea this is what you meant. This changes much! Perhaps everything. I beg you, put it back," he shoved the coin back into Robby's hand, "and do not mislay them! Oh, the thought of all you have done and been through! And all the while having these upon your person!"

"What do you mean? What do you know about them?"

"Entire kingdoms have been lost over such as these, great Houses ruined, battles fought and treacherous acts committed. They are sometimes called Bloodcoins. Mrs. Starhart mistook these for ordinary Elifaen coins from the First Age, which common lore says are bad luck. Lore has mixed and confused things, as Elifaen coins are sometimes called blood money coins. What you have are true Bloodcoins, from which so many legends have sprung."

"Bloodcoins?"

"Yes. Seven sets of seven Bloodcoins there once were, one set for each of the Seven Great High Houses of the Elifaen. Ruby red, topaz pink, emerald green, sapphire blue, amber yellow, amethyst purple, and diamond white. Of each stone, seven Bloodcoins were made. Do you not know the tales of the High Houses? Or of Silmain and the Lament of the Broken Circle?"

"Was not Silmain the first King of the Elves?"

"The title he took for himself was King of the Faere, one which angered many of the Fallen Ones, those Elifaen who wished to reassert their allegiance to Aperion, though condemned with all the rest for their revolt."

"I'm sorry. I do not know those stories."

Ashlord shook his head.

"That these should have fallen into your hands!" he muttered. "So guarded are these, and the secrets they hold, that even few of the Elifaen outside of Vanara know of their existence beyond legend and rumor, much less of their significance."

"But Mrs. Starhart recognized them as Elifaen coins, and my mother and my dad did, too."

"Your mother must have suspected otherwise. No. In appearance, these do resemble some coins of the First Age, and no doubt regular coins of that time were fashioned with the symbolism of these in mind. But the regular coins would never be mistaken for one of these if you held the two together. They are smaller than these, of stamped gold, silver, or copper, not of heavily cast red gold as these are. And the regular coins have smaller stones set into them, often of quartz or polished ore. Do you remember the old coins that I took from Bailorg's purse? In the troll cave?"

"Yes."

"Those were the kind of old coins that I speak of. Though many thousands of those were made, they are now rare, too. But, remembering those old coins of Bailorg, you see the difference. And there are only forty-nine objects like these in all the world."

"So these are not coins at all? Then what are they?"

"They are pieces of the Nimbus Illuminas, sometimes called the Rainbow of Aperion."

"I don't know what that is," Robby said, shaking his head.

"It was Aperion's covenant with the Elifaen that, should the Elifaen ever seek reconciliation, wishing to forsake the earth and join his heavenly host, then they need only to call upon him with a united voice and the way would be made open to them. They would be healed of their scars and forgiven of their misdeeds. As a token of this, it is said that he made a staff fashioned of light and held up to the sky by seven chains of seven links each. He took those links and gave seven to each of the Seven High Houses to hold in readiness. The Bloodcoins, such as those you have upon you, were those links taken from the Nimbus Illuminas. Only by bringing them all together can the way of departing be opened to the Elifaen, so the legend goes."

"Well, that sounds simple enough. Why haven't they done that?"

"Aperion knew that it was not in their hearts to abandon their obsession for dominion over the Dragonkind. Faere blood had been spilled and Dragon blood taken, and the cycle of revenge is hard to break. He knew, too, that the place of birth of all Faerekind, this earth, would hold them fast, and they would not willingly forsake the wind and water, the wood and stone of their essence as the others, loyal to Aperion, had done. And he knew other things, besides, that the Elifaen would need to overcome. So even though each Elifaen House took the Bloodcoins, they paid little heed to his message, prizing them instead for their beauty and as icons of their Houses. Strife soon arose among them and discord spread over which House should have dominance over the others. Silmain, first King of the Elifaen, was not one of those who received the Bloodcoins. But he called upon the Seven High Houses to bring the coins together and to agree to use them so that the Elifaen could fulfill Aperion's challenge and depart the world. But Cupeldain and others opposed him, and Silmain's efforts failed. After Silmain was killed in battle against the Dragonkind, Cupeldain eventually became King of Vanara. Cupeldain managed to fend off the Dragonkind's attacks, and he did much to help his own kind to survive and prosper in the world. Eventually, Cupeldain, too, tired of war and of this world, and, like Silmain before him, he sought to bring together all of the High Houses and their Bloodcoins so that the way could be made for them to rejoin Aperion and depart the strife of this world."

"So Cupeldain called together all of the Seven High Houses once more, and they met in Vanara to hear his argument for using the Bloodcoins and for departing the earth. But a rumor was spread that any one of the Seven High Houses might return without the others, using their Bloodcoins alone and closing the way to the others, leaving them behind upon the earth. It was a false rumor, and some say Secundur had a hand in it. At last, Ormace of the House of Fairbirch threatened to destroy those Bloodcoins belonging to him unless all were redivided. So that was done. Each House received into its safekeeping one Bloodcoin from each of the other Houses and gave up six of those they had received from Aperion. Thus the Forty-Nine Bloodcoins were divided, and Cupeldain's effort was defeated. When the council ended their meeting, and the representatives went their separate ways, the Elifaen's troubles began in earnest. Discord among the Seven Houses continued. Disputes led to war, and feuds were common and bloody. Eventually, Cupeldain was murdered, sparking more bloodshed and strife."

"One by one, the High Houses possessing Bloodcoins failed or were destroyed by some catastrophe or another. The Bloodcoins became scattered and lost. First were the Bloodcoins of Fairbirch, then those of Fairmyrtle and Faircedar and Fairmaple, and at last those of Fairwillow and Fairfir. It is known that the King of Duinnor somehow came into the possession, through his predecessors, of fourteen of the Bloodcoins. But only Queen Serith Ellyn's House of Fairlinden, of all the High Houses, still retains its Seven. To the Elifaen, it is a long story of catastrophe and tragedy. And, you should know that legend has it that the Bloodcoins of Lyrium of the House of Fairfir were lost when Tulith Attis fell, and were likely taken as booty by those few Dragonkind who made it back to the deserts. In fact, that may even be why Tulith Attis was attacked, so far east and north of the Dragon strongholds, to capture the Bloodcoins."

Ashlord's voice trailed off as he fell into deep thought, staring at the coin still in Robby's hand. Robby tried to absorb Ashlord's dense tale, but he had a feeling that there was much more to the story that Ashlord did not explain, or perhaps that Ashlord himself did not know. Regardless, as he, too, looked at the coin in his hand, Robby felt an odd chill cross his neck, as if the spirits of the past breathed down his spine.

Suddenly, Ashlord looked at Robby and said, "Why do you think Queen Serith Ellyn went to Glareth by the Sea? Not for her own safety, but for the fate of her race. It was to take the Bloodcoins of Fairlinden to safety. The Unknown King strives to have her give them over to him for surety in exchange for Duinnor's continued support against the Dragonkind. If what Duinnor does may be called support. Serith Ellyn fears that the King will grow impatient and will try to take them by force or by intrigue. That is why Ullin's mission was so urgent, making the way for them. And it is why Serith Ellyn had to go herself, with the elite of her personal guard, leaving Vanara in the hands of her most trusted lords. Only five people, including the Queen herself, were to know this secret. With you, it is now six. Not even Ullin was told why they went to Glareth. If Duinnor had discovered their mission, the King would have sought to stop them and to take the Bloodcoins by force. And Thurdun told me that on the night the Great Bell rang, his party came close to being attacked. He said the Bell saved them, as I know he told you. Now you know why. Their pursuers were after Serith Ellyn's Seven. As I said, the King already possesses at least two sets, since the Third Unknown King is said to have fourteen of the Forty-Nine, though it was never revealed how he obtained them. The present King covets those of the Queen."

"What good would only a few of them do if you need all forty-nine of them to open the Nimbus Illuminas?" Robby asked. "Why would the King want Serith Ellyn's Bloodcoins if so many others have been lost?"

"Besides their actual purpose, they have become symbols of power, of the legitimacy of Elifaen rule. Only in Vanara, of all the Seven Realms, does one of the Seven Houses remain in power, the Queen's House of Fairlinden. It is said that Serith Ellyn sways the princes and lords of Vanara by showing the Bloodcoins to them every twenty-four years, as is her tradition to do. The last time she showed them was last year. So now she has but twenty-three years to recover them."

"She must trust Glareth very much, then."

"Prince Carbane is a distant relative, and he married an Elifaen, which makes his son, Prince Danoss, Elifaen. Glareth and Vanara have long supported each other against Duinnor's imperial ways, though those lands are far removed from each other."

"It all sounds so complicated, Ashlord," Robby shook his head. "So these Bloodcoins are parts of some device, some apparatus?"

"Not merely some apparatus!" Ashlord said sharply. "They are keys. To bring them all together at the same time and in the proper manner would open the heavens. Doing so would permit the Elifaen to withdraw from the sufferings of the earth and go to the Faere Kingdom of Aperion. And some say that, after a time, Aperion would then return to the earth with his reunited host."

Ashlord paused, allowing that to sink into Robby. But Robby was shaking his head at yet another question.

"I thought that we concluded that Sheila's Uncle Steggan was the one who went to the Starharts and paid Mr. Starhart. If that is so, how did Steggan get them? Did Bailorg give them to him? I mean, since Steggan worked for Bailorg, right?"

"Indeed, those are questions. But now a new light shines upon things, things I before thought were insignificant. I don't think Bailorg ever had them. And I doubt if he knew they were in Steggan's possession. Steggan obviously had no idea what he had. And, from what I've heard, I doubt if Steggan would have waited long to spend or barter them. So if he had them in his possession for very long, what kept him from using them before? One hardly expects a drunkard and a lout to put aside money that could be easily spent. Especially when he is already indebted to so many of his neighbors. It is as if they were locked away, or somehow difficult for Steggan to get at. Or else he had just found them. To use them to pay for post letters! Does ignorance know any bounds?" Ashlord shook his head. "Questions, indeed. Questions, questions!"

Ashlord looked up and nodded toward their approaching friends.

"Put it away," he said. "And do keep them all safe!"

Just then Sheila came close enough to say, "Well? Have you had your chat? Or would you like more time?"

"We'll talk more later," Ashlord said to Robby. "Now we should save our breath for the sake of our feet, don't you think?"

• • •

Before them the land was hilly, but no less grassy, and from their hill, it seemed nearly as endless as ever, stretching away westward to a dark thin line where met the earth and sky.

"West by north, we go," Ashlord announced, and hurried off down hill, the others following quickly. "We will camp only after it is fully dark, and we will rise before the sun does. The miles we have taken all day to cover will be crossed in but a few hours, I fear, by the Duinnor riders that will come. We must be as far away as possible."

"I don't get what chance we've got if they come at us," Billy grumbled. "So what's the hurry?"

"Our hope is that they may underestimate our speed," Ullin commented, "and pull back their search before they go far enough to find us. Remember the Damar who pursued us from Tulith Morgair? They made that mistake and turned around too soon."

"Yes, but these are Kingsmen," Sheila said. "Surely they will be more likely to keep chasing us?"

"That is my fear, yes," Ullin nodded.

"So we must hurry indeed!" Robby said, increasing his stride to nearly a jog.

"Hurryindeed!" Ibin said, grinning and nearly jumping to keep up with Robby and Ashlord. Ullin and Sheila stepped up their pace and finally, with a groan, Billy followed.

For the rest of the day, they jogged and walked, walked and jogged, their backpacks jostling and their shoulders soon sore from the straps. On they persisted, making their way up and down hills, through small ditches and dry, rocky shoals, and around odd stones, tall, gray, and narrow, standing upright atop broad hills, or leaning precariously in odd patterns on the flatlands. Though Robby was as curious as any about them, he did not waste his breath to ask and neither did the others, though all of the company eyed them closely, and Billy somewhat suspiciously. Each furlong, each mile they went in their haste, seemed more difficult than the last. Moments seemed like hours as their labor stretched out monotonously, one hour into the next, each person to their own thoughts, their eyes downward to watch every step. They hardly noticed the dimming of the sky as the sun descended or the long shadows that reached across the shallow vales. Still, up and down they went, going slower and slower with their fatigue until, long after the sun had set and the red sky had turned to purple, Ashlord drew them to a halt and bade them stop.

"This place is as good as any," he said. "It will be chilly tonight, but I think a fire will be safe, if any have the strength to gather wood from yonder copse. Let us see what food we have."

As Robby plunged onto the ground with the others, he was amazed that Ashlord seemed unaffected by their day's journey. True, he was as sweaty and dusty as any of them, but the source of his stamina was a mystery. Groaning, Robby turned over and undid the flap of his pack, rummaged out some hard cheese and some harder biscuits.

"I've got some coffee, here," said Sheila, her head bent over her pack. "But no pot."

"Ihavealittle, alittlepot," said Ibin, producing it and handing it to Ashlord.

"An' here're some carrots," Billy added.

"I believe there are a few links of hard sausage that you may share," Ashlord contributed. "I'll just have a carrot or two. I don't care for any meat."

"And I still have a bag of nuts and dried fruit. From Nowhere," Ullin said.

"Well. I might have some of that. We can make something of a meal, anyway. Though it will be a light one," Ashlord said. He began gathering rocks for the fire ring while Robby and Billy went off with Ibin to gather wood. Sheila and Ullin, following Ashlord's directions, redistributed the contents of the packs so that none was too heavy nor too light compared to the others.

• • •

Later that night, after they had eaten, they eased under their blankets and against their packs, very tired from their exertions, weary but glad to be all together again. Ashlord and Ullin lit their pipes across the low fire from Sheila, who gazed at Ashlord.

"Do I look very different?" Ashlord asked.

"I'll say," said Billy.

"You do," agreed Sheila. "Did you change your appearance on purpose, or—?"

"Oh, no. I have little choice in how I look. I hope I am not too disturbing to look upon?"

"There is a redness about you," Ullin said, drawing a puff as he tilted his head to observe Ashlord's features. "The firelight makes you glow, almost."

"We saw a frightening disturbance," Robby said. "The day after we left you. By then we were out on the plain, looking back at the mountains."

"Yes. It was, itwasvery, itmademeveryscared," nodded Ibin.

"It was like a great and fiery conflagration between the mountainsides," Ullin said. "With dense smoke, black as pitch."

"An' we saw other things, too," added Billy.

"Won't you tell us what happened?" asked Sheila. "Did you find the witch's lair?"

"Yes. I did."

"The bar led ye to it?" asked Billy.

"Yes. She did."

Ashlord drew and blew a couple of times.

"Certina will not enter into a cave," he said. "So she waited for me."

He took another puff, then began his tale.

• • •

"The lair of Paltera was a putrid place, full of witchworms in their cocoons hanging from the wet ceiling. By the light of my staff, I could see them writhe and squirm within their shells, pained by the glow of day that I brought with me. The noise of brittle bones cracked beneath my feet wherever I stepped. For an age or more the lair was kept, a stewing-place for the incubation of vile progeny. Many of the cask-like cocoons were broken open, dripping and oozing into steamy pools, the evidence of Paltera's appetite, for she devoured many of her offspring before they could be suckled. It was my good fortune that her hunger was so great that not a single living hatched bogle did I find. Into every cocoon, I thrust my staff of witchbane, and each little shell boiled and burst, screaming and spewing gore as the cocoon died.

"Deeper and deeper into the cavern I went, spreading destruction, until I came at last to the conjugal chamber. For the first time since the world was made, the Light of Beras, borne within upon my walking staff, fell upon the slabs of Paltera's altar-bed. I saw, too, a great door of immense proportions, gaping into darkness, the door through which her master would come.

"There I waited, with sword and staff. And I appealed to my Creator for strength, my words drifting away through the Black Door, and going far and deep along the fire-carved passageways within the bowels of the earth. Many, many leagues, through the never-lit tunnels, my words bravely floated with the faith of their meaning, until at last they reached the great demon. Valkose was his name, given to him by Morgasir, his ancient sire. Since the Time Before Time, Valkose has existed, coaxed into servitude by Morgasir's protégé, Secundur. The little words I spake at last landed upon the ears of this demon, and he stirred with pain and anger that they should come from the lair of one of his mistresses. Like a tiny thread of spider silk, my words spoke to him of how his whore was slain and all his progeny destroyed, and he was filled with fire and wrath.

"And so he came. League upon league through the darkness he came with growing anger, the silky thread of my soft words entangled about him. Even in the noise and crash of his advance, they stung his ears as they drew him forth to me.

"But just as my words reached deep through the caverns and hidden places of the earth, so, too, did they fly to the uppermost heavens to Beras, and He heard my words. And as I waited, and prayed, He prepared me for the trial, assuring me of my faith and confiding to me that if I could but withstand the onslaught, He and all His agents would become my allies against the loathsome creature.

"Through the giant doorway and into the thick darkness beyond, I watched until I heard the sound of the approaching demon, his growl and the thud of his iron-shod hooves, until I saw at last the fire-glow of his red eyes approaching. Far above, in the free air of the world, day turned to night and the stars wheeled, rising and sinking, and the world moved from day through night's passage and toward another day. But my place was without day and without night, and yet longer than all of the days and nights that ever were or would be. During that time-out-of-time, Valkose came furiously onward. The closer he came, the brighter his eyes glared, the louder the noise of his coming grew with the tromp of his feet and the rage-filled fire-breath of his panting. But even so, the greater became my resolve. When he crossed the last leagues of his advance, and I could see his form and smell his stench, I was ready.

"He, too, was ready, forewarned by my words, and when he burst with blowing heat and brimstone smoke into the chamber, he hesitated before the bright-burning light of my staff, his form filling the doorway with his loathsome mass. There, with every panting grunt, he spewed curses that crumbled rock and split the ear. He stepped forward into the chamber, towering before me, and he smote me with the screaming fire of his mouth. Though my clothes were blasted away, and my hair and my skin were torn from my bones, I held fast my Given Staff before him, and that which I am was preserved by its shield.

"Then he struck at me with inviting words, entreating me to join him as one of his minions and be spared his wrath. I was tempted. My now-hideous form, my innards bared of their coverings, was a sight unnatural to the world, a form that would provoke revulsion and abhorrence in all who beheld me, and would turn them against me in their hatred and fear. Yes, I was tempted by his offer. Almost, in that moment of pain, did I release my staff and yield to him. Almost did my knee buckle in fear and awe, and in agony and desolation. In my grief, I almost gave myself over to him. But I had yet within me some strength to resist, and I answered with a thrust of my sword into his side. As he roared in pain, Beras gave me back my flesh with new strength. Thus, our duel began.

"What can one say of any fight? Far less can I tell you of my travail against the beast, to destroy him utterly, or to be destroyed. He crushed my bones, and I with my sword thrust hilt-deep into him. He flailed away my flesh, and I with my staff put out his eyes. But what creature who lives in darkness has need of them? So he came onto me time and again, and Beras reconstituted my strength and restored my body, so that I came back at Valkose. With his fire-breath he scalded me, and with the cold light of my staff I sent icy bolts of lightning cracking through his fist-thick hide. With every death-stroke I gave, he sloughed off his exterior and burst through the skins of his existence in an ever more hideous form to assault me anew.

"Thus we strove. The demon Valkose, from form to more terrible form, drove me back through the caves, and I realized that we battled not one another alone, but also against those who made us and whose servants we were. More terrible did his voice become, and more subtle the fears he gave me as he cursed and gibed at me in the First Tongue. In spite of my resolve, my strength faltered, and again he pushed me back, even unto the entrance of the lair. There, as I sought to stand my ground, I grew angry. With the light of day flooding through the entrance, I summoned my will.

"You shall not leave this place!' I cried, and I smote him hard and fast, driving him with both staff and sword, stroke after blast, back into the darkness. Yet he sloughed off form after form, until the essence of his will was revealed to me. He came back at me with stinging missiles of flaming, laughing words. I could feel the pent-up resentment of his master, seething forth from all the days of his existence, from the Time Before Time. Resentment that was nurtured and grown and amassed throughout all of the years of all of the ages of this world until that very moment. Forming his hatred into fury, he released it against me with such power that the mountains shook, and I was ripped apart and blasted from the mouth of the cave like the spray of fiery spit from curse-formed lips. As I disintegrated, I felt the voice of Beras say to me, 'Let it be.' And so I did not resist my fate. As the remains of my being spewed forth upon the mountainsides, I perceived Valkose emerging from the cave, rising up to his full height and stature to stride out into the broad, good world. And, in the last moments of my awareness, as the smoke of my dust blew softly away, I saw Aperion, clothed in the White Light of Beras, waiting for him."

Ashlord hesitated, shaking his head, and looked at Sheila with a wry smile.

"It was not my place, you see, nor in my power to vanquish the demon. My trial, my test, was to lure the creature out of the lair. Yet I, in my pride and anger, strove to prevent his exit and so Beras withdrew from me. But Beras did not abandon me to oblivion. During the short battle between Valkose and winged Aperion, Beras remade me, as he has remade the world over and again, out of some essence that remained and had not been obliterated. And so, then I slept. For the first time in my long existence, I slept within an eternal-seeming moment.

"At last, I awoke, lying upon the ash-covered remains of the mountainside opposite of the collapsed mountain wherein the lair had been. Where but a day before was forest, now stood only the charred and blackened trunks of broken trees, many blasted limbless and many upturned and pointing away in every direction. But the forest surrounding was spared, and from it came animals who ministered to my body as I slowly gained shape and strength. Wood-hares came to me and licked and groomed my face and bare scalp. Deer came, bearing dew-filled cups of honeysuckle blossoms for my lips to taste, and the bear came to me with honey given by the bees of the forest. Chipmunks brought the nuts of their storehouse for me to eat, and raccoon came to brush my body with boughs of anise and salvia. Birds brought straw and soft down to weave for me a bed to lie upon. All this was a wonder to me, yet I wondered, too, why I had been brought back from oblivion.

"While I rested and regained my strength, I pondered on the meaning of the ordeal. Why, in my pride, did I not sense the will of Beras? How did I come to think it in my own power to vanquish the demon? I thought, too, on the humiliating curses Valkose heaved upon me, and they weighed upon my soul as a millstone, and they shadowed my wits, and stung my eyes with tears of shame.

" 'Valkose has no power over you,' whispered the hare as she licked my ear, 'and his curses mean nothing.'

"She continued to groom me with tender attention, and the stubble of my hair began to grow, and she said nothing else for a long time. But her words comforted me, and my soul gained some rest. For many, many days I lay upon the bed they made for me, and I often closed my eyes to the comfort they gave me. In silence, I ate the nuts brought to me and drank the nectar fetched for me. Weakness began to pass from my body.

"Then I wondered why I was brought back into life. For, though my body still burned and ached, I was gaining strength. But what could this be for? What am I to do? I reached out and took up a handful of ash from the ground nearby to my bed. As it blew from my palm, I stared at it, all that was left of this little forest vale.

" 'Surely, now you deserve the name that Men gave you,' whispered the hare.

"Then a mighty stag appeared before me and said unto me, 'Your purpose has only just begun. Rise up, and do what it is that you must!'

"At his words, I sat up. Certina came to me, and I wept with happiness as she landed upon my shoulder. And I remembered."

• • •

Ashlord smiled, looking at the faces around him.

"What did ye remember?" asked Billy.

"I remembered my friends," Ashlord said, his eyes pools of glistening joy. "I remembered our good company together, our quest, and the hope that we share, we six, and Certina."

As he said this, looking from Billy to each of the others, all were smiling back at him and nodding. After a long moment, Ullin asked, "Then what happened?"

"The stag came to me and said, 'These lands must do without Collandoth for a while. Get thee upon my back. I will carry thee swiftly to the Open Place. From there, my cousins will take thee to where there is need of thee.'

"So I arose, and he knelt so that I could sit upon his back. He took me, sure-footed and swift, away from that place, out through the mountains and on across the River Missenflo, not far from Tulith Morgair. There, upon the western banks of that river, antelope waited for me. One took me upon his back, and as a herd we raced westward. Like the wind they carried me, resting not day nor at night, passing me from one to another without breaking stride. Sir Sun and Lady Moon walked the skies in turn, one after the other, until, reaching the outskirts of these lands, the antelope left me and departed back to their own places."

"That was last night, just after sunset, and, by what I gathered, just after your return from Westlawn. I obtained some clothing from a friendly but frightened Edgewolder who at first mistook me for a demonic madman. So I entered the town, and heard the most amazing tales of Wickermen, a great battle, and a monster rising up from the enemy's town. And I heard of the monster's destruction by the work of a few brave men at a trebuchet and, of all things, geese flying down from the north. Alas, I arrived too late to offer help. Assured of your safety by asking the right questions, I nonetheless did not reveal my identity to any until I met with Teracue. He is acquainted with me from some years back, and he told me more about you and about Westlawn and the cult of the Wickermen that arose there. From what Teracue and others said to me, I think you should be proud of your endurance, your determination, and your courage. Just as I am proud of you."

"I cannot say how good it is to have you back in our company!" said Ullin. "And to have all of our members restored to us," he said, smiling at Robby.

Ashlord nodded. "Yes, it is good. I know you are all very tired," he said, "but I long to hear more about your travels. As much as you feel up to telling me tonight. About the Dragonkind and their wells, the adventure with the stampede and the carrion bees, and, before that, how you outwitted your Damar pursuers."

So, instead of sleeping as they should have, they were all too eager to tell their tales. They talked, sometimes many voices at once, describing to Ashlord the events of their travels so excitedly that he often had to interrupt to ask a question or to have someone repeat something that was said while someone else was speaking. This went on for many hours under the turning stars until all was told and retold. At last, the talk became sparse and, one by one, the chill air tucked each into slumber until only Ashlord remained awake, drawing on his pipe.

Having not yet recovered from the past days of struggle and strife, Robby slept, too. But it was not long before he woke to dreamwalk. Having little desire to see Micerea, and no heart to join the dreams of his companions, he turned his attention to their camp. Ashlord, as he had always done before, sat beside the fire, his reddened face glowing as he stared at the low flames. Comforted by his presence, Robby was about to turn his attention elsewhere when the swoosh of large wings passed directly over his head. He ducked, flinching instinctively, sensing a shadow cutting through the starlight. It was very large, as big as a person, with broad feathered wings twenty or so feet from tip to tip. They held aloft the body of a young woman and it—she—swooped low, right past Ashlord—giving him a playful flick of the wingtip at his ear—and filling Robby with alarm. Yet the being seemed not to be malicious. She gracefully ascended and then floated down onto her bare feet, standing just behind the oblivious Ashlord. Folding her wings across her back, she put a hand on Ashlord's shoulder, looking at Robby with extraordinarily large golden-fire eyes. She bent to Ashlord's ear and whispered something indiscernible. Ashlord nodded, absently reaching up to pat her hand. At first, Robby thought the transformed Ashlord was visited by one of the fabled Faerekind, descended perhaps from heaven, one of Aperion's host come to fulfill an errand of her king. She looked at Robby, coldly but without malice, proudly but without conceit, her expression completely open yet full of enigma. Robby recognized Certina.

He blinked at the realization, and the vision immediately vanished. The little bird on Ashlord's shoulder continued to stare at him with her golden eyes. And if beaks could smile, hers did.

Robby smiled, too, and gradually turned his attention to other wonders of the dreamscape.

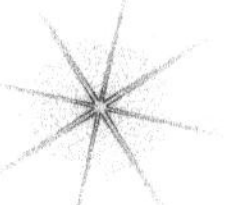

Chapter 14

Forest Islindia

Day 135
110 Days Remaining

The sun was not yet up when Ashlord woke them to a modest breakfast. They ate quickly and prepared their things for the day's march while, somewhere behind the eastern mists, the rim of the world grew lighter in hue. It was a moist hike, the tall grass soaking their leggings with chilly dew, and they were many miles along before the cold air left by the night relented to early morning haze. Up a gentle rise they marched for a long while, as if bearing imperceptibly toward the blue heavens, winding sometimes back and forth to avoid rough places, until they reached a kind of plateau where once again they could see far in all directions. They paused for a brief moment, to catch their breath as much as to look around. To the west and north the brownish-green grass faded away to a distant edge, hardly distinguishable from the sky except by a dark line that marked some ambiguous feature on the horizon. Away southward, the plateau sank out of sight a mile or so away, and behind them the glare of the low autumn sun revealed nothing but the rolling grasslands. And, very far away, perhaps beyond the horizon, a blotchy brown haze hung over what must have been distant Westlawn or the still-burning sea of vines. An urging breeze brought an end to their observations, and they started off again.

"Wait! Look there!" Sheila cried, pointing due east. A glint flashed from the top of a soft knoll about a mile away.

"They come!" uttered Ashlord.

"Let's go!" called out Ullin as he hurried on.

Quickly they followed, resuming the jog of the day before, crunching through the drying grass and trying not to stumble with their awkward packs. The rhythmic thud and click and clink of their gear was accompaniment to their thudding footsteps and pumping lungs, and none bothered to look back for a long while. Every few minutes, Ullin slowed to an easy walk, and, as soon as he was assured that all were somewhat recovered, he took off again. It reminded Robby of the day that Ullin had taken charge of the Passdale Militia, and any who would qualify had to follow him up and down and back and forth across Barley until, of so many who started the hike, very few remained with Ullin at the end. Now Robby understood better that Ullin was only doing in practice and as a test something from his own experience, likely often required of fighting men. Lost to these thoughts, of Barley and Passdale, of the folks back in Janhaven, Robby gave up all notion of passing time. But soon even those thoughts required too much effort, circling back on themselves in a tiring spiral. This moment, like the previous one, was consumed with putting one foot before the other without stumbling. That became his only purpose, and his whole mind and body was bent to that end with no room for any other nagging thought.

All day they ran, stopping with hope each time that they had run far enough. But each time, some distant sign of horsemen pushed them onward.

"They are riding a search pattern," Ullin observed, shaking his head. "How they have missed picking up our trail in this grass is a wonder!"

"Perhaps, crediting some ploy to throw them off, Teracue has ordered such maneuvers," Ashlord suggested.

Ullin laughed. "That must be it! And in the strictest terms, too, those orders. Barring any wavering from them. I'd wager that captain is furious, right now! Ha! And hurrah for Teracue! Let's not waste his gesture!"

Off again they jogged. And ran, and stumbled, and jogged again. When the endless day finally passed into night, and they could no longer see well enough to run without mishap, the company slackened their pace but continued moving nonetheless. Ashlord slowed, and handed out bread and encouraging words to each as they passed him. For his part, Robby was grateful, but he was too tired to eat, so he put the biscuit in his pocket. Nodding his thanks to Ashlord, he picked up his stride to close the gap between himself and Ibin just ahead. Finally, Ullin called a halt, and no sooner than they had their blankets out than fatigue overwhelmed them into sleep. Even Robby fell into a dreamless stupor, too tired even to speak good-nights to Sheila who spooned against him. The stars winked through the cold and dewy air that settled as they slept, and though the night was long, it seemed only an instant before Ashlord's gentle but insistent nudge came, stirring them back onto their feet, once more to be pushed by the chasing dawn. Their night's rest brought little increase in speed. Indeed, they stumbled along more slowly and clumsily than ever. At last, exasperated and near the end of his endurance, Billy could stand no more.

"Rest!" cried Billy. "A moment of rest, I beg ye!"

Without waiting for a reply, he tossed down his pack and fell upon it, panting. Robby stumbled onto the ground beside him, and soon Ashlord and Ullin were forced to turn back for them.

"We must keep moving!" Ullin urged. "We'll not be safe in the open once the sun is up!"

The morning haze was by now rapidly vanishing, revealing the shape of the land, low grassy hills behind as far as they could see, reaching into a muddy pink dawn. To the north and south, the horizon fanned out into the mists, and to the west a murky line of black bordered the far rim of the plain.

"Just a breather!" Sheila argued, lowering her pack, kneeling, and taking her waterskin out to have a gulp.

Ashlord looked at them with dismay.

"We cannot risk being caught in the open," he said to them. "We must reach the forest as soon as possible!"

"The forest? So that's what that black line is!" uttered Billy.

"No, no-no!" Ullin said to Ashlord, taking him by the arm and pulling him aside. "We must not go into Islindia. We must turn north, and around."

"We would never make it," Ashlord argued. "We would be taken before we made two leagues."

"Islindia is bewitched, Collandoth. A curse lies upon it," Ullin persisted.

"That is Forest Islindia?" Sheila asked, looking westward. "Then better to take our chances in the open! At least we have our weapons to fight with and our legs to run with. What good will they be against shadow?"

"What're they talkin' 'bout?" Billy asked Robby. Robby only stared at the ground between his sprawled out legs.

"It does not matter," Billy thought he heard him mumble.

"We must go through," Ashlord insisted. "And we haven't time to argue!"

"But none who have entered that place have ever been seen again," Ullin continued.

"Oh?" Ashlord retorted impatiently. "Then I suppose I am not here, and you cannot see me. For, indeed, I have passed safely through Forest Islindia many times."

Ullin and Sheila looked at Ashlord suspiciously. Robby and Billy listened and looked on, too exhausted to take part in the debate. Ibin was still on his feet, leaning over with his hands on his knees, and with his mandolin dangling sideways off the pack it was tied to. He looked back and forth between Ashlord, Billy, and Ullin.

"It don't matter to me," Billy said. "I'm too tired to put up much of a fight either way we go."

"That's what I meant," Robby nodded.

"If we go into Islindia, and if we keep our wits about us, there will be no fighting and perhaps some rest," Ashlord said to them. "I urge you to trust me and to follow me within, but I will not leave you. If you decide to go around the forest, and to end our quest as captors of Duinnor, I will go with you, and my end will be joined to yours."

Ullin and Sheila looked at each other and at the others in the group. Each saw how ragged and tired they all were, cut and bruised by stumbles and falls, and at their last bit of strength. Now, even big Ibin slumped on the ground, his face worn and full of concern, understanding little about the conversation.

"You are right. We haven't a chance in the open," Ullin finally said. "I dread the wood, but I will follow you there."

"You have not yet led me astray," added Sheila, nodding. "If you have come and gone from the place, then you have more courage than I, and you give us hope of escape. Let's go."

Billy got up and girded his pack. He then reached a hand to Robby, who was still sitting with a distant look on his face.

"Come along," said Billy, pulling Robby to his feet. "We can't stay."

"Aye," said Robby, pulling up his pack.

Having just settled comfortably on the ground, Ibin got back up.

"Ooof!" he said.

They made their way toward the forest as the first rays of the sun cut narrowly over the eastern horizon, beaming warm, yellow light across the silent plain. Mists rose from wild grass and flowed slowly down the slopes and pooled in the dips and hollows that they trudged through. Ahead, the black wall turned a dark greenish-gray as they drew slowly closer. But they could discern little detail other than what appeared to be tangled trunks and gnarled limbs twisted in every direction, thick with the darkest of green leaves that occasionally glinted menacingly in the sunlight. As they neared, Robby could see that they were not trees at all, but the thick trunks of massive thorns, the size of trees, their thick stalks coiling upward like huge limbs and then twisting downward again. Enmeshed with one another, they formed a nearly solid canopy. Only at the edge of the forest did any light seem to penetrate at all, and then only because the late autumn sunlight slanted so low, as if the sunbeams had to duck cautiously through. Billy felt the urge to ask a hundred questions, but as they approached the eaves of the looming forest, he remained silent. There was something solemn about the place, he thought, or a kind of sullenness, or anger.

About fifty yards away from the forest, Ashlord turned and led them north, apparently looking for a suitable place to enter. The day warmed, and the dew evaporated, but no birds sang, no crickets buzzed, and even the air seemed to hold its breath. Only the crush of the travelers' feet in the grass and the occasional clink of metal on their packs broke the air. After almost an hour, Ashlord stopped and leaned on his staff. The rest caught up with him and looked at the two stone markers that lay broken in the grass, about thirty yards apart. Robby could see dim carvings on the stones, ancient writing and strange symbols.

"This is all that remains of the great gates of Halethiris, an ancient realm of the Faerekind, which had long passed away before even the coming of Men. From here, one of the ancient roads passed into the forest, now but a seldom used path. It will take us through the safest part of Islindia, though it will be a walk of many days."

Ashlord then looked at each member in the group as he spoke.
"I do not say it is without peril, but it is a strange place. Yet, as is ofttimes the case, the peril that one may find may be that which one takes with him. Be alert and be silent! There are many strange creatures within, and some do not care for intruders. And there are other things within, things no longer of this world, nor yet fully part of the next. Fair warned is fair armed, so do not be ruled by fear, and above all do not be rash or careless! Watch your step, your tongue, and your heart. Heed what I say, and we may well pass through alive, and perhaps even unmolested. Ibin, have your rope ready. Let's go."

With that, Ashlord turned, and, one by one, they entered, Ashlord first, then Ullin who drew his sword. Ibin and Billy followed Ullin, then came Robby, and last of all came Sheila with arrow notched. The gloom of the forest quickly closed over them as they passed under the first huge vines. Above and before them, the greenish-black thorns clustered on their mighty stalks like thousands of wizened hands raised at them, each poised as if reaching for them with their long arthritic fingers tipped with razor-like nails.

"Ugh!" said Sheila, suppressing a shiver.

After only a few yards, they came to what seemed a solid barrier of these thorns, so thick that they could not see through it. Yet the path clearly led straight into them.

"Well, that's that!" said Billy. "Thar's no gettin' by this!"

"Don't let a few thorns dismay you," Ashlord reproached him.

"Well, good grief!" Billy jabbed a finger at the barrier.

"Look!" Ibin cried, pointing back the way they had come.

They all turned and saw riders appearing over a distant rise, their lance-tips flashing as they came. More and more of them appeared—perhaps sixty horsemen, Ullin guessed just as the muffled thunder of hooves reached his ears.

"Hurry! With luck they will pass by, but we cannot count on that," Ashlord commanded. "Ibin, where is that rope? Quickly!"

Ibin fumbled with his pack and pulled out the long length of thin rope he carried. Ashlord snatched it from him and tied one end around his own waist. Measuring out the length, he wrapped a coil of it tightly around the left wrist of each and lined them up so that there was about eight feet between them.

"Do not let go of this rope!" he commanded sternly. "Come!"

With that, he strode straight into the barrier. The others were amazed that he brushed aside the thick thorns and completely disappeared within, the rope that he held trailing in mid-air. Ullin, shocked at the sight, felt the rope grow taut around his wrist, drawing him forward, and he, too, disappeared, the claw-like hands yielding to him. Next it was Ibin and then Billy's turn to go and to disappear, and soon Robby felt the line tugging insistently at his wrist. Gripping the rope hard in his fist and closing his eyes, he put his right arm over his face and held his breath as he strode forward, remembering his ordeal with the thorns at Tulith Attis through which he had escaped the wolves. He could feel Sheila's resistance behind him, but soon she, too, followed.

Robby was confounded that the thorns did not cut him or even catch on his clothing. It was as if they grew in such a way that their points moved with the direction he moved. He opened his eyes, and could only see the rope disappearing into the thicket just in front of him, but he could hear the swish of the others ahead, amid exclamations of amazement, particularly from Billy. After what seemed a long and slow walk, but was actually less than a furlong, Robby suddenly broke into the open and bumped into Billy. Hearing Sheila coming up from behind, he turned to see her stumble and fall just short of the opening.

"Drat!" she said. Robby instinctively rushed back to her.

"No!" Ashlord cried. But Robby, in his haste to reach her, was already being stabbed and torn by the thorns that he had just safely passed through. Backing out ahead of Sheila, who had picked herself up, the two rejoined the others in the clearing.

"Well, that's a trick!" Robby said. "The thorns let us go through one way but not the other."

"Just the thing to keep us in," Ullin muttered.

"And, hopefully, by their appearance, to keep the riders out," Ashlord concluded, handing the rope back to Ibin.

"Who'd wanna come in here, anyways?" Billy commented, looking around. Above, the huge black trunks shot upward, their massive branches of thorns curling and drooping back down into one another, more like vines than branches, and barely a patch of sky was visible, creating a cave-like feeling below. The leaves were glassy black-green and had barbs all around them, more cruel than holly leaves, but the dead ones on the ground were wilted and soft. Stringy moss like curly gray hag's hair hung down from the forlorn canopy, and beneath these ghostly forms a few other plants grew, sickly and malformed. An earthy and moldy aroma pervaded.

"This is far worse than the sea of vines Tyrin and I went through. But where's the path?" Robby asked, mopping a minor cut on his brow with his sleeve.

"Here," Ashlord replied, indicating an opening through the trees, if they could be so called. "It runs northwest for a ways then takes a westward turn, through the middle of Islindia."

"How can you tell which way is which in here?" Sheila said looking up.

"Or night from day?" Billy added.

Ashlord snorted. "You may find your senses a little finer after spending a few days here. Let us go."

Again, Ashlord led them on. Ullin tired of having his sword in hand and sheathed it. Sheila took longer, though, before she put her arrow back in its quiver and threw her bow over her shoulder. But Robby felt less at ease, often resting his hand on the hilt of his dagger, or upon Swyncraff's knot about his waist.

And so they hiked, carefully picking their way over the thorny trunks that curled across the paths, their long dagger-like spikes jabbing out in every direction. More than once they were forced to crawl under these obstacles, and once while doing so, one of the barbs barely missed slicing into Billy's shoulder, but instead cut through the shoulder strap of his backpack, neat as scissors. Only when the pack flopped down on the other strap did he realize his close call. They stopped so that he could make a repair. The canopy was too low for any of them to stand, so they knelt and stooped close together while Billy worked.

"This overgrowth will not last much longer," Ashlord said, peering into the gloom ahead, "and we'll be able to straighten our backs and travel more easily."

Ibin made to take up his mandolin, but Ashlord put his hand on it and shook his head. "Not now, Ibin."

"Is it just me, or is there a chill in the air?" Ullin asked, rubbing down the hairs on his arm.

"Definitely could use some sunshine," Billy piped up, giving his newly repaired strap a good tug. Putting away his sewing kit, he squinted upward. "But if ye ask me, it's turned cloudy somewhar up yonder."

"I believe you are right, Master Bosk," Ashlord nodded. "And, if I am not far off, snow may be on the ground before we leave Islindia."

"Well, this warm weather's been unnatural-like," Billy commented as he pulled his pack over his shoulders and cinched up the straps. "I mean, for the time of year. Though, who knows? Mebbe it's natural enough in these parts."

"No," Ullin said as they resumed their trek, picking their way onward. "The frost is late coming this year, no doubt about it. But snow?"

"Snow it will be!" Ashlord said from on up the path. "Just a matter of when."

"Not that any would make it through this roof!" Billy grunted to Ibin, who nodded back at him.

"I, for one, will be glad to be away from here," Sheila said to Robby, bringing up the rear. He barely heard her, so lost in thought he was. He was aware of his distraction, thinking that his fatigue was truly catching up with him, for it was an effort to keep going even though the pace was much easier than before they entered Islindia. His muscles ached to the bone, his knees throbbed, and his backpack felt as though it was full of rocks. There was a ringing in his ears, too, but he realized that it was the heavy silence of the place rather than any dizzy-spell or illness.

As true as his word, in less than an hour Ashlord led them through a broad opening where the briary thicket thinned enough to allow them to walk upright, and the path grew more defined, rising gently uphill.

Stepping over and between shoots, runners, and stalks that fell across the path, the hand-like thorns flexed and clutched eerily as passing boots brushed the barbs. At last, they topped the rise and stood in a small clearing where the sky opened above them. In contrast to the bright morning of only a little while ago, the sky was now brooding and gray, and as sullen as the wood before them. Ashlord let them all gather, and gestured ahead.

"Forest Islindia," he said. "What we have just passed through is known as the Ring of Blades, in the Common Speech, part of an ancient barrier placed there to shield the inner forest. The ancient realm of Halethiris once centered upon this forest and stretched far across the mountains and beyond the plain."

"Lo!" Billy exclaimed. "What happened?"

Beneath them, pines shot up from a floor riddled with the fallen timbers of gigantic trees, some nearly as thick as houses. The fallen giants were black, grown over with sparse brush, and partially covered with brown pine needles and dark green moss. In the landscape below, there were a few stands of blasted oak and twisted poplars and stooped elms. Stunted and crouched, they seemed, and the coarseness of their bark and their thick drooping limbs gave testament that the sick trees were old beyond reckoning.

"What kind of place have you brought us to, Collandoth?" Ullin uttered. Although spoken softly, his words seemed quite loud in the pressing silence.

"Sadness," said Robby, standing aside from the rest. "It is a place of sadness."

Ashlord approached and put his hand on Robby's shoulder.

"Yes, that is so," he said. "Much strife did these great trees witness before the day they fell. Many catastrophes came to pass when they died. Behold, the handiwork of Secundur! Done with spite and vengeance ages ago. But the tale of this place is not yet over, some say. For those that the Dark One wished to destroy still abide in this wood. His mind is ever upon this place, so the legends have it, and it irks him that he has no more power here and cannot finish his work. For, though this place is filled with shades and shadow, Secundur, who is the Lord of Shadows, cannot enter."

In the valley before them, restless mists slowly moved about, momentarily settling in low areas, then floating on, sometimes swirling upward in graceful drafts only to curve downward again to snake through brush and over the fallen trunks. They appeared to be ever-seeking, evaporating almost to nothing at times, only to thicken and flow onward again. Here and there, Sir Sun momentarily squinted through the gray sky, blotting the landscape with cheery patches where the mists gave way to his gaze. As one furtive beam faded, with another struggling to penetrate elsewhere, the landscape returned to dark browns and murky greens. There was no sound. No bird called, no cricket chirped, no squirrels chattered. Even Sir Wind seemed to hold his breath. Deep and profound the stillness was, desolate yet pensive, somehow compelling the travelers to lower their voices as they spoke.

"Looks to me like he did a pretty good job," whispered Robby. "What else would he do?"

"You have not seen the White Desert as I have," Ullin put forward in a hushed tone. "Dust of ash, sun that blinds, heat of day that boils away your skin and cold of night that freezes your blood."

"Did he do that?"

"The White Desert was once a paradise of lakes and island gardens," Ashlord sighed.

"What keeps him from it?" Sheila asked. "I mean, why doesn't he finish the destruction that he started?"

"He surely would but for the ones who guard this place," Ashlord told her.

"Who's that?" Billy asked.

"She whose forest this is, no doubt," Ullin said, "and by whose name we call this place."

"Islindia?" Sheila asked.

Ullin nodded. "A Faere enchantress, they say, who can call upon the creatures of the wood to do her bidding. Who ensnares intruders with her shadows, only to drive them mad with melancholia."

"I thought all that was just an old legend," Sheila said.

"Wunnerful!" Billy rolled his eyes. "The Dark One after us on one side, an' on the other, a mad fairy witch."

"Do not compare those two," Ashlord scolded Billy. "They are nothing alike. And the power each holds is as different from one another as they who hold those powers are different. We are not being played with as a cat with a mouse. If the enemy could have, he would have destroyed us by now. And if the keeper of this forest wanted to harm us, she would have already done so. The one wishes but cannot. The other can, but wishes not."

"Are ye sayin' she knows we're here?" Billy asked.

"I imagine she knew we were coming before we did," Ashlord answered.

Robby said, "I heard she was a Faere Queen who lost her lover in these woods and would have no other person enter thereafter. Any who come and who are unlucky enough to meet her are never heard of again."

"Aye, well, she is all of those things, perhaps," Ashlord said, heaving a sigh and leaning heavily on his stick. Not for the first time, Robby wondered how old Ashlord was, and he looked at that moment older than the stones. "And, yet," Ashlord went on, "she may be none of those things. I cannot say who is lucky or unlucky to meet her. I say only this:

speak not of what you do not know! We will need our wits, now, and for the next days ahead. In this place, listen not to your head, but to your heart. Forget the stories and legends that you are mindful of and keep to the calling of your hope. There, you will find strength when all else fails you, no more here than anywhere, but verily no less! If we move quickly, and with luck, we may pass through in less than a week to the borderlands of Vanara on the other side. Come!"

Ashlord set off and strode downward into the somber valley, and the others quickly girded themselves and hurried after him. Here, at last Sir Wind exhaled fresh air, though the forest echoed the whisper of its passing with continued silence. They soon found themselves winding through a wider path, marked here and there by stone remnants, perhaps of structures, but they could not be sure; perhaps they were only colossal markers. Everything here seemed big. Big and dead, or dying. Brown leaves blanketed everything, and blew about in the sudden puffs that sometimes gusted through. The sky settled, overcast and gray, and the air cooled decidedly. On they marched through the forest ruin, seldom speaking, their line thinning out along the trail. Noon passed unnoticed and without rest, and, sooner than they would have thought, it was becoming noticeably darker as the somber day settled into cheerless afternoon. Ashlord hurried them on, and he seemed to know where he was going.

"Ashlord, we should look for a place to make camp," Ullin said.

"Soon, soon," was all Ashlord said as he kept on. Ullin turned to look behind him and was dismayed by the length of their line. He stepped aside to let Billy and Ibin pass and called out to Robby at the rear.

"We must stay close together."

"He's tired," Sheila said to Ullin as she went by.

"So are we all."

A moment later, Robby came up, and Ullin fell in behind him.

"It will soon be dark, and we will make camp," he said.

"I don't know why I'm so tired," Robby said. "Today's been no worse on me than any of the others."

"It's the forest," Ullin said, looking around. "We all feel it."

"Yes. I suppose it is. As if it wants us to linger. Yet, so full of resentment toward us."

"Or maybe it is just our sore feet that make us feel so!" Ullin managed to jest. Robby smiled back.

"That's it!"

Together the cousins picked up their pace until they were urging Sheila to move on closer to Billy and Ibin. Ashlord slowed a bit, allowing everyone to catch up, and soon they were a tightly lined group once more. Continuing, Ashlord was careful not to go too quickly, and Ullin, at the rear, was careful not to go too slowly. The path descended onto the valley floor as it passed under the fallen crisscrossed trunks of two trees.

The tunnel-like passage underneath the natural archway was dusty and smelled of pine needles and moss. Once they gained the other side, the path bore off to the right, and they passed around another long-dead trunk, its thickness more like a great wall over forty feet high, and its underside was sunken deep into the ground.

"Now I know what a chipmunk feels like," Sheila muttered.

Thus they continued, first this way and then that, passing around or over the great fallen trunks, or underneath them, as they ventured deeper and deeper into the forest and as the light became dimmer and dimmer. At a switchback in the path, where Ullin and Ashlord passed nearby in opposite ways, Ullin pondered to Ashlord, "I wonder why the forest hasn't reclaimed these trunks, if it has been as long as you say since they fell."

Ashlord shook his head, shrugging. "I can only guess that Islindia slows their passing away."

"What's that?" Billy whispered urgently, pointing to a movement some fifty yards out to their right. Everyone immediately turned to look, and they saw, passing between the narrow trunks of distant pines, a light brown shape. In a wink, Sheila had her bow out, ripped an arrow from her quiver to the string, and took aim, her bow creaking at the pull. Ashlord hurried to her and put his hand on the arrow, pushing it down.

"Do not harm any creature here," he said, shaking his head, "unless it absolutely cannot be avoided."

"Itisgone, itisgoneaway," Ibin whispered.

"What was it?" Ullin asked. "I only had a glimpse."

"I don't know," Robby said.

"It just sort of floated off," Billy stated.

"Let's move on," Ashlord said. "If you see it again, ignore it. If it means us harm, we will find out soon enough. And if it does not, we will be no worse off for not knowing what it is. Let's go."

Sheila reluctantly quivered her arrow, but kept her bow ready as they moved on. Several times over the next couple of hours, they saw the shape again, moving soundlessly apace with them off in the trees. At one point or another, each in the group had a clear view of it, and all kept silent about what they saw, saying nothing about the hair standing on their necks or the queer feeling the apparition gave them. Silent it went, covered with a long tan robe and hood. No one saw the figure's face, but Robby glimpsed a hand, feminine and fair, briefly grasping a sapling, then pulling the folds of her flowing garment back close to her breast as she turned away and disappeared into a mist. Just before Robby lost sight of her, she looked over her shoulder at him. But there was no face beneath the veil of the hood, only darkness, which filled his belly with moths, and he saw a bright glint of odd blue light flash briefly from the darkness of the hood. She turned her head and was gone. He quickly looked to Ullin, close behind him, who nodded.

"I saw her, too," he whispered, pushing Robby gently onward. "Let's just keep moving."

The air grew cooler as the light diminished, making the browns and greens of the forest darker and even more sullen. The mists that floated through the trunks and across their path thickened before them and behind them, hovering briefly and passing on. For a long time, Robby thought it would be fully dark at any moment, but as the day gradually faded, his vision was hardly any worse off. Suddenly Ashlord led them into the center of a clearing.

"Collandoth!" Ullin called from the rear, trying to keep his voice down. Ashlord stopped and the group gathered around. "Perhaps we should stay here for the night," Ullin said. "It is open, and there is space for a fire."

"We should keep moving for a little while longer," Ashlord said. Ullin came up close to Ashlord and spoke softly to him.

"We are tired," he said, "and we are being watched. Better to have some rest than to stumble into something we haven't the strength to deal with."

"I know we are being watched," Ashlord replied. "But this is a Faere Circle."

"A Faere Circle?" Billy interrupted. "I don't see no mushrooms."

"Yes, a Circle," Ashlord nodded. "Look more carefully!"

Billy turned around, looking left and right, back and forward, as they all did. The clearing was about forty feet in diameter. Around it were small lumps of brush, each about two feet high and about three feet wide, flat on the top. Sheila went to one and pulled off the vines and pine straw atop it.

"It's a stone. Some kind of table or stool?" she said.

"Look closer," Ashlord said.

Sheila pulled away more of the brush until a pale white sculpture was revealed. It was in the shape of a toadstool.

"There is your mushroom, Master Bosk," Ashlord said. "And if you look carefully, you'll see this entire clearing is ringed by them. This is indeed a Faere Circle, a typical gathering place for council and society in the ancient days before the First Age."

"Surely, you do not believe the tales about falling asleep in such rings, do you?" Robby asked.

Ashlord shrugged.

"I only think it wiser to keep moving while we can. And I would prefer the cover of the wood than the open." Ashlord's voice trailed off. Seeing his companions' expressions, he realized he was the only one who thought they should keep going.

"Not many could have come so far in two days without rest or much food," he admitted, "and I will not urge you much farther today. But I would prefer that rest, when it comes, should be as far along our road as possible."

They all looked at Ashlord, and he at them, and they heard, or sensed, a rising sound, soft, like the coming of a distant wind, gathering its power before breaking upon them.

"You can go no farther tonight," a soft voice stated with finality.

Everyone turned and saw her at the far side of the clearing, the mysterious figure who had just spoken to them, the same creature that had paced them these many miles. There she stood, both arms downward, her hands each resting atop stone mushrooms on either side. Yet no feature could be discerned beyond the pale brown robe she wore, for her hood was still pulled low, and there was only shadow underneath. Her hood, like the inscrutable material that swathed her figure, moved gently, as if being pulled by an unfelt breeze, and it was difficult to focus one's gaze upon it, seeming now tan, now laced with sheens of green and blue, and now with gold, and now a dull tan again.

Immediately, they felt their hearts pound up into their throats, and the hairs on their necks and arms stood on end. None had the will to move, yet all felt the urge to take flight. Their arms and hands froze where they were, unable to reach for hilt or shaft. As for her voice, the band of travelers felt it from within, as a rushing of water, though their ears heard it as only a whisper. Ullin, expressionless, felt a terrible dread overtake him, and Ashlord's face was covered with surprise, his mouth open. Sheila looked confused, her eyes filled with panic, as if she would bolt and run a mile, if she could only move an inch. Billy suddenly fell to one knee, struck by astonishment and inexplicable terror, while Ibin stood still as a statue, barely breathing, his whole body trembling. Robby looked as if he might burst in to tears at any moment, so overcome with sadness and grief he was, dizziness swirling through his chest and head. So suddenly blasted by the feeling, the awful yearning to be home mixed with bitter remorse, his heart reeled. His befuddled mind tried to grasp at the source of the wellspring. Then he realized that it came from the very figure before them, from the trees and mists surrounding them, down out of the twilight sky, and up out of the ground beneath his feet. And yet her voice was distant and haunting, akin to the song sung by Elmira and Belmira when he was a child.

"You can go no farther tonight."

The words echoed again and again in their minds.

For what seemed to them an eternity, they stared at her, unable to react, the wash of her voice rolling through them, the mystery of the sound, and the power of it, filling them with awe. Just as the ocean breaker which crashes upon the sands eventually recedes, so did this power. In the churning retreat, they felt the wave as it turned over myriads of little things, memories, feelings, long-forgotten kindnesses, the faces of missed mothers and fathers, lovers and friends, countless bits of life sifted, one and all, like seashells dancing and tumbling in the swirling eddies of the seashore. And so their panic eased, and their terror subsided. Dread abated, regret and longing diminished, leaving them uneasy and a little embarrassed, as if all had been exposed.

Swallowing hard, Ashlord took a step forward and spoke, bowing.

"Queen of the Wood," he said in the Ancient Tongue, "we travelers seek only a way through and beyond your forest and into the realm that lies to the west. We mean no disrespect by our trespass, and we intend no harm to this place nor to any in it."

"I know why it is you have come into my wood," she said in a language that all could understand. She pulled back her hood, revealing a face fair and pale, with hair long and black, streaked with white and red. Her lips were pale rose and her eyes were blue-white, colder than silver in the snows of Mount Vendril. Upon her head was a circlet of yellow gold, and from it against her brow hung a teardrop-shaped diamond which glowed and glittered in every color.

"I know your names, too, Collandoth, called Ashlord by Men. I know where you have come from. And I know where you mean to go, and why you mean to go there. I have seen your sorrow and your toil just as I see you now. I think your quest is of little consequence to my wood, and I am not concerned."

Robby felt as if she caught sight of him, at the back of the group, and was looking right at him. His heart pounded, then skipped a beat before resuming its cadence.

"Yet, if you are determined to pass beyond this wood and out from my realm, you must obey my bidding and have me as your guide. I, alone, may lead you unharmed from this place, and," she went on, still looking at Robby, "I will see that you have more rest than you have had in many days, and in peace and safety."

"That is most gracious of you, Good Queen," Ashlord said, bowing again.

"I bid two things of you in return," she continued. "First, that you lay aside all weapons before proceeding from this Circle."

"Pardon?"

"I will not share my company nor my protection with those who are not of my own kind and who are armed. I offer in exchange of your weapons that which they cannot bring: rest and safe passage through this wood."

"But our path beyond remains perilous, and we would have our weapons returned to us," Ashlord replied.

"Will you return to me the rest I shall give to you?" Her voice bit Ashlord with such cold that he winced. She softened her tone, saying, "Is it in your power to trade from the past a moment of peace from the woes of the present? And what worth are things clung to, but never used? For with these things not one of you shall pass from this place in your mortal coil, and none that you have known before shall ever see your faces again."

"My lady, I have journeyed through your wood several times past," Ashlord said. "Never have any conditions been made upon me, nor any toll asked of me."

"Your past crossings through this wood were allowed," Islindia said, "because it suited us to allow it. You were alone and posed no danger. But now you bring strangers with you into our lands, armed, and with the mark of violence upon their hearts."

"We cannot give up our weapons," Ullin whispered to Ashlord, "and be defenseless." Sheila nodded as the others drew nearer.

"I'm afraid we have no choice," Ashlord slowly said to the group. "Only by her leave have I passed through before, though never has she spoken to me until now. I believe that only by her leave may we escape this place."

"We have seen nothing to be afraid of," Ullin persisted. "Not even a wild beast has crossed our path, not so much as a squirrel or a mouse. What harm would she alone protect us from? What power does she have to keep us here, or to make us stray from our way?"

"Foolish man!" Ashlord scolded in a tense whisper. "Have I taught you nothing? Do you think she fears any harm of us? Look about you! And tell me, how alone do you think this Queen can be within her own domain?"

Ullin turned his head and scanned the forest around them, as did they all. Looking between the gaps in the trees, he at first saw nothing. Then he perceived a movement, as if the darkness shuddered through the trunks. The wood had shifted, moved somehow, silently and without being noticed until now, so that Ullin could not tell where the path into the Faere Circle came or went. The limbs looming over their heads sagged low, the gray moss swayed, though there was no movement of air, and the bushes and green things were thicker and closer than before. The mists that swirled around the clearing played with Ullin's eyes as he strained to see. Thin saplings transformed into tall thick spears, held in the hands of dark moss-bearded giants. The fireflies that wandered through the far shadows seemed now to be the blink of polished steel in moonlight, filling the forest all around with restless glints. Alarmed by these shifting apparitions, Ullin's hand went instinctively to his hilt, his attention returning to one clump of greenery in particular, exactly where he would have thought the path should be. It was inexplicable, but obviously the thick shrub, gnarled and covered with leaves and vines, had been there for decades. Ullin's vision cleared. It was not a bush at all, but a man, a green man, with vines for hair and leaves for a beard and mustache and yellow berries for eyes. Upon the Green Man's head was a crown of white-berried mistletoe, and in his hand he held a great leafy staff of holly. Behind the King of the Wood stood rank upon rank of soldiers, giants all, armored in green and gold, with gray mossy plumes on their helmets and rage in their eyes. Only the Green Man, silent and daunting, his yellow eyes afire, held back those legions. Ullin glanced at Ashlord and then back, but the Green Man was now merely a bush, and the army was only a passing mist.

"What?" Ullin was astonished, as if he had drifted into a dream and was suddenly thumped back into reality.

"The Queen's father is still King in this wood," Ashlord said to him, "as he once was in every wood of the world. Do you think that they have remained here by being powerless?"

More resolutely, Ashlord addressed his friends as he unfastened his scabbard. "I urge you, let us obey Queen Islindia in all matters while we are here."

"I am sworn not to relinquish my sword, save to my sovereign or in death!" Ullin insisted, but with less determination than before.

"I and my father are sovereign here," Islindia sharply stated. "Your king rules only for a short while compared to the age of these trees, and only by the thinnest strand, soon to be cut, as you well know. This place rules you tonight, by your consent or without it. This place will choose to let you go, or will keep you forever! Would you not have me as your advocate? For this wood is in no mood to be kind."

"O-ow!," Billy muttered to Ibin. "I don't like the sound of that!"

Robby silently moved forward. After a brief but deep look into the Queen's cold eyes, he unbuckled his sword and placed it and his dagger on the ground before her. He slid Swyncraff from his waist. As he put it down, it curled and twisted in unusual protest, then lay still. Islindia bent her head with apparent surprise, as if something was only now revealed that was not known to her before. The ardor of her eyes when she looked from Swyncraff to Robby made him think she was about to ask a question. Her gaze narrowed, almost into a smile, and her expression softened. She remained silent and he moved aside, feeling her eyes following him.

Sheila then came forward, pulling off her quiver. Laying it down, she then dropped her dagger and gently laid down her bow. She had made that bow with her own hands, and she dearly hated to give it up, for it had never cracked or broken even though she used it hard.

"Your hands are better suited for other things, I think," Islindia said so that only Sheila could hear. In fact, Sheila did not notice Islindia's lips move at all. "Though anything they touch would be the better, so long as your heart is their guide."

Billy went next.

"Less to carry, anyways," he said, placing his weapons beside Robby's.

"Yeah," Ibin said, putting his sword on the little pile. Remembering the incident at Redwater Gorge, Ibin turned back, unslung his mandolin, and laid it down, too.

"Wait," Islindia commanded. Ibin shook with fear as she picked up the instrument. "Surely this is no weapon?"

"Ye wouldn't say so if ye ever heard him play it!" Billy joked. When he saw Ibin's pained look, Billy's face reddened into immediate regret.

"I-I-I," Ibin trembled as teardrops burst from his eyes and rolled down his face.

"Ikilledamanwithit!" he blurted.

Just as he choked on a sob, he met Islindia's eye and she smiled. He was suddenly at peace within as he had not been since before the bridge at Redwater Gorge.

"Then a mighty player you are!" she said as she laid it back down. Ibin sniffed and smiled back at her, backing into Billy and almost knocking him down.

"Watch out, big fella," Billy said, giving Ibin a pat on the back.

Seeing how the others were affected by Islindia, and not untouched himself, Ullin nonetheless remained hesitant. Robby stepped before Ullin and, facing him, held out his hand.

"To your sovereign, you said?"

Ullin appeared momentarily cowed by Robby's question, and by the outstretched hand awaiting his sword. Then he understood, seeing the terrible fatigue in Robby's eyes and, behind that, Robby's stern determination.

"Aye," Ullin said, nodding to Robby. "Aye."

He undid his buckles, slid off his harness, winding it around the scabbard, and offered his sword. Robby took away his hand, gesturing toward the other weapons on the ground. Ullin dipped his head, and he stepped past Robby and put all of his weapons onto the pile, his sword and bow, quiver, dagger, and dirk. Bowing to Islindia, he moved aside so that Ashlord could lay down his sword and his staff.

"This is not easy for you, I see," she said looking at the group, her eyes coming to rest on Ullin. "Surely trust, these days, is a difficult thing to have. But be at your ease, and let your hearts rest. Gather deadwood for your fire, if you wish. Eat what you have brought. More will be provided to you in the morn. Sleep. And fear not; as long as you are in my care, no harm will find you. When it is time to go, I will come again, or I will send for you."

As she turned, Ullin stepped forward cautiously.

"Pardon, my lady," he spoke, bowing with his hand on his breast as she turned back to them. "You mentioned that you would bid two things of us. One we have agreed to, and there is our compliance." Ullin gestured to the pile of arms. "Pray tell us, what of your other bidding?"

Islindia turned away again, saying as she departed, "That will come." She faded into the mists, and was quickly gone from sight.

For a few moments, they remained silent, gazing after her, none knowing what to say or do.

"Hello?" Billy piped up, scratching his head and looking at the place where they had laid their weapons. Soon they had all gathered around with equal astonishment, for the pile of metal and wood that had been their arms was now a small mound covered with thorny vines with blue and yellow and red blossoms. Billy moved to reach into the pretty tangle when Ullin gripped his arm.

"I think we had best keep our bargain," he said. Sheila, about to follow Billy's lead to retrieve her bow, stopped, too. Seeing Ullin's serious expression, Billy nodded and turned away as Ullin released him. Ibin was already stretching out on the mossy ground, and Robby sat with his back against a stone toadstool, his head just under the cap. Sheila retreated and sat beside him, while Ashlord lit his pipe and approached Ullin, now staring again after the Queen of the Wood.

"Is she truly a queen?" Ullin asked.

"She is now. But in the old days, she was Princess of this realm."

"And is she so old? She seems young to me, and fair. Not like the tales have it."

"Aye," Ashlord nodded. "She is older than these woods, a Firstborn, who remembers the first grass upon the world, the first stars in the sky."

"Why does she remain here, in this dying place?"

"This is her home, the home of her family and her people," Ashlord said. "She stays because she must. She stays until the last blade of grass withers and the last song goes out of the birds. She stays because that is her fate, and that is the curse that has been laid upon her, her punishment and her doom for spurning the Dark One. Have you never heard of the Princess of Sorrows?"

"Yes," Ullin said. "There is Faere blood in my veins, too, you know. My grandmother's people have told of the Sad Girl of the Wood, that her lover betrayed her and her people, and he gave her over to the Dark One in exchange for a crown in a distant land."

"Ah," Ashlord said, sitting on one of the toadstools. "You remember wrong, or was told another tale, perhaps. Islindia was never betrayed by her lover. He was murdered by Secundur, and blame was put on Islindia's brother. By his cunning, Secundur captured Islindia and promised to save her brother from execution if only she would become his consort, thereby making himself ruler of her people by right. But she would not give herself to him. At last, she was set free by her father's craft, but Secundur was enraged. Through dark arts and treachery, he laid waste this land and scattered or destroyed all the folk that lived here, save two, the two you have seen this evening. By the curse laid upon her, she cannot leave, for if she does her power would leave with her, and all here would wither in an eye blink. Only by her will does this land still have some shallow breath of life in it, yet I do not understand how. Thus, Secundur cannot finish his work, nor can he return here, and it is said that it rankles him that Islindia and her forest still abide, stricken though they are."

Ashlord's voice, soft and low, was still the loudest sound in the forest, and, thirty feet away, Robby could hear every word. All listened, and Ibin seemed especially enrapt by the tale.

"What say you to all this, Ibin?" Ashlord asked.

"Idon'tknow," Ibin said. "Maybe, maybe, maybeshe'sstillsad. Maybesheneedssomehelp."

"Help?" Billy asked. "What kind of help would that be?"

"Idon't, Idon'tknow," Ibin shrugged. "Maybe, maybesheneeds, maybesheneedshelpwithherchores."

Sheila giggled while Billy nodded seriously to humor the big fellow.

"Likein, likeinthebirdsong," Ibin went on. He began singing in his soft tenor, as quietly as he could:

> *The bird in the morn gathers grass in the dew*
> *Singing her song, but none come along,*
> *None come along, none come along,*
> *The bird in the grass in the dew.*
>
> *The bird on the limb weaving her nest*
> *Singing her song, but none come along,*
> *None come along, none come along,*
> *The bird on the limb with her nest.*
>
> *The bird in the noon-sun gathering seed*
> *Singing her song, but none come along,*
> *None come along, none come along,*
> *The bird in the sun with her seed.*
>
> *The bird in the pool bathing her down*
> *Singing her song, but none come along,*
> *None come along, none come along,*
> *The bird in the pool with her down.*
>
> *The bird in the night greeting the moon*
> *Singing her song, but none come along,*
> *None come along, none come along,*
> *The bird in the night and the moon.*
>
> *The bird in the morn greeting the dawn*
> *Singing her song, but none come along,*
> *Singing her song, singing her song,*
> *The bird in the morn at the dawn.*

Ibin completed the tune and stretched back out on the ground. Billy shook his head and closed his eyes. Sheila felt very sad, indeed, and sleepy. Robby had his eyes closed, his head down, having apparently already dozed off.

"I think I know what Ibin was trying to say," said Ullin to Ashlord. Ashlord nodded as he stood, tapping out his pipe.

"Yes," he said. "There's more going on inside that head than we credit, I think. He takes things for granted that we barely notice, and he sees through many of the clouds that obscure our eyes. In an odd sort of way."

Ullin nodded.

"I think we should rest," Ashlord said. "We can eat later when we're not so tired and have the strength to build a fire."

"I'll keep watch for awhile," Ullin said as Ashlord spread his robe about him and pulled his hood over his head, settling down on a mossy mound.

"Suit yourself," Ashlord said. "I doubt if there is anything to be watchful for. And you need rest, too, you know."

• • •

In truth, Ullin did need rest, but he could not find it. As the others settled into sleep, and Ashlord sat statue-like in his trance, Ullin paced around the edge of the melancholy circle. His mind wandered over the events of his life and of the past many days as his eyes tried to penetrate the surrounding darkness. No night birds sang, no crickets chirped, and except for the fireflies that continued to float about, the forest seemed dead, indeed. Somehow, it suited his mood.

"Why do you not rest as the others do?"

Ullin turned and saw Islindia sitting on a stone bench that he had not noticed before. Her hood was over her head, but her face was exposed, her hair hung partly over her brow, and, perhaps by the light of the stone there, a faint light seemed to be on her face. She looked at him with curiosity, and there was no hint of threat or menace in her voice.

He shook his head and held up his hands.

"There is so much," he said, then stopped.

"So much?"

"So much, my lady," he continued, "that I do not understand about these days we live in. How things have come to pass, and why. Do not misunderstand me, I do know a great deal more than most of my companions. I know the threats we face better than most, and the dangers we must meet. I know that our goal, that our quest, anyway, is necessary, whether we fail or succeed. And I know there are none else but we here to do it. I do not resent my part, yet..."

"Yet?"

"I do not know how to express my heart. I wish I were young again. Without concern for the world. I despise the pact my people have been forced to serve, and that I, too, serve, as duty and honor would have me do. And though I accepted this task, to serve as I do, there is no joy in it. I have longed for some meaning to my life, some act that would take me into my own life, that would try me, shape and forge me. And surely this quest is it, but I feel no zeal for it. I see only what I have ever seen in strife, the great cost of life and livelihood, the destruction of the land, and the bitterness of treachery. I would endure all and without complaint, but my friends here, why must they be caught up in all this? They are not responsible for the evil ways of this world. They are not soldiers, trained and hardened to pain. Why should they suffer? And there is much else, besides, that wearies me. Pardon my complaints."

"You cannot fight evil alone, Ullin Saheed Tallin of the House of Fairoak," she replied. "Your quest is every bit theirs as well. Do you think they would be here otherwise? It is for them to decide, not you, their own way."

"But they could not turn back now if they wanted," Ullin insisted. "They are too far from home, and their pride would not let them turn away from each other."

"Worry not for them, at least for one night," she coaxed. "Sit here. Rest your legs."

Ullin reluctantly sat beside her. He could smell her scent, that of a woman mixed with sweet fragrances. Conscious of his own grubbiness, he wondered how badly he looked and smelled. He fought an urge to run his grimy fingers through his tangled hair, yet he could not help but wipe his soiled hands on his leggings. Aware of his discomfort, she smiled, but said nothing. Reaching to him, she ran her fingers through his hair for him and away from his face. At her touch, Ullin closed his eyes for a moment, drinking in the softness that fell like a warm blanket upon his heart, and then he felt a little shame at her clean hands touching him.

"Why do you stay here?" he asked suddenly, seeking to distract her from him.

"My hold over this realm is the hold it has over me," she said, putting her hands into her lap. "We have become one, the forest and I. The devastation you see is my devastation and my melancholy. The threat you feel here is my anger and my sorrow. The visions that you walk among are my memories, and the forms they take are echoes of loss."

"And yet," she went on, looking at Ullin's slumbering companions, "even the hopeless may look for hope, if the heart is strong enough. Nothing that happens in the world goes without touching this place, and nothing that happens in this place goes without touching the world. My eyes roam far, and my ears hear much. The world turns 'round, and tides that sweep things aside also bring new things to light and to life. Such a tide now gathers. Another age ends, and so with it perhaps ends my reign, or perhaps my sorrow."

"You have hope, then," Ullin asked. "For this place? For yourself?"

"More for the world, I think," she answered, "than for myself. As for my wood, I cannot say, but only that it will never again be as it once was. Most of my people are gone from the world, dead or scattered, married into mortal stock, as your grandmother did. With them has gone much of the power of this wood and places like this. Men rule the earth, now, not the Faere, and their thoughts are of other things than leaf and twig."

"Yet the world of Men and the world of Faere are joined," Ullin said. "Might they ever be reconciled?"

"The fates of all people are joined, it is true," she replied, following Ullin's glance at Robby. She nodded and then shook her head. "But I cannot see where those fates may lead. The seed of mistrust has rooted deep between the Mortal and the Fallen of the Faere. The tree of discord is strong, and its fruit has spread wide. It is in our bones, now."

"And in our hearts," Ullin nodded.

They remained silent for a while, watching the others settle deeper into sleep as the fireflies danced in the shadows.

"Many of the race of Men have come into this wood. A few have found their way out again, and the bones of others remain. Each according to his heart. You are like other Men," she said, turning her face to him, "and yet you are not like any man I have ever met. Your heart has a weight upon it that would crush even the strongest that I have known. A darkness, even. It does not rule you, though, while the merest shadow on the hearts of other Men have been their madness and ruin." Her look was puzzled, searching. "You have a sadness about you, behind your grins and laughter, that runs deeper than your days and wider than your experience. An old soul, I think you are. So serious, yet kind. I have seen you with the others. They have weight upon them, too, from before this quest and now increased by it. You do not know their burdens, and they do not know yours. But you are gentle with them, and they look to you for strength. Hand in hand you strive with them, but you are apart, somehow. I think you have always been apart from the world."

"Perhaps you see better than I. And you are unlike any creature, Mortal or Elifaen, that I have ever met," returned Ullin. "I feel in you the long agelessness of my own heart and the deep yearning, too, for something, something nearly forgotten. Something from a dream, yet not a dream. I feel," Ullin hesitated, sternly putting himself in check, but her look melted his resolve. "I feel I could become lost here, and still be very much at home."

Ullin smiled weakly, and a sensation swept into Islindia's cheeks that she had not felt for a thousand years, a sudden warmth of heart that was somehow kindled by Ullin's smile. A delightful madness overtook her spirit, of a kind that had been forgotten in those woods. She grinned and, taking Ullin's hand, rose suddenly from the bench.

"Come," she said with an energetic cheer, "and I will show you something to make you marvel."

He stood, glancing at his slumbering companions, but his concern was allayed by Islindia's bright eyes and the tug on his hand. He followed the Queen's light footsteps out from the circle and into the dark wood, and after only a few steps, his fatigue left him. Her hand was soft and warm, small in his, but she held firmly, pulling him forward. Her steps were light, so light that Ullin could not hear any sound from them as he did his own, crunching through dried leaves and snapping twigs as he went. So loud did he think his sound was that he feared to wake the others, at first. But quickly they went. She seemed to float ahead of him, and perhaps some of her lightness of foot came into his own steps and into his heart, and a broad childish grin broke across his bruised and dirty face.

On and on, through the dark wood they went, turning this way and that, moving more quickly than Ullin thought possible with ordinary steps. Fireflies danced before them, increasing in numbers until they were an enormous cloud of winking light. And whether it was the light of the fireflies, or the mysterious glow of the jewel on Islindia's brow—Ullin could not tell which—the darkness was not so deep as before. They entered into a kind of half-light, as before dawn or just after sunset. Although he could see the forest well, the canopy above remained dark, and he could see stars shining through boughs. And, yet, an odd mist surrounded them, without color, that seemed to blur his perceptions. Several times, Ullin rubbed his eyes with his free hand. He perceived massive upright trees where before were rocky walls. And the huge hanging branches that they bowed to pass under he now saw were enormous roots curving out from the massive trunks. At first he thought that he had been shrunk to the size of a mouse, but the fireflies and the leaves, the night flowers and the ferns, all remained the same as before.

Still she pulled him onward, and ahead he could see a light, a golden glow that fanned out in beams between the trees and upward into the sky. Rounding another turn, they suddenly came to the source, emanating from out of the earth in the center of a clearing surrounded by stone columns supporting huge caps, like tall toadstools. They passed under these and into the strange circle. At the center were flat stones embedded into the earth outlining an arched-shaped opening in the ground, and from that opening poured the strange golden light. Smiling, Islindia slowly led Ullin to it. There, he saw a stone staircase of marble leading downward and out of sight into the bright depths. Ullin held his hand over his eyes, trying to shade them from the glare as he peered into the depths of the passageway.

"*Halillan,*" she said to him. "*Turinoth glinith te glinori.*"

"Let me show you my home," is what Ullin understood her to say, but he did not know how he understood the language he had never before heard. Still gripping his hand, she entered the light and stepped down to the first stair. Ullin hesitated. He could feel his hand shaking in hers, but it was not from fear, but out of some great thrill, mixed with awe. For a brief moment, he wondered if he was being lured to his doom as some of the stories told, but hardly had the thought passed his mind than he took the first step.

"If this is a dream," he said to her, "then let me stay."

"*Celand doe ne limiris?*" she asked, smiling. "And if it is not a dream?"

"Then let it be my doom, for all I care," he said, taking another step.

So together they went down the mysterious golden staircase that was so bright that Ullin could barely see the steps before him or distinguish the walls or the ceiling. Down they went, straight and true, and Ullin's ears were filled with a strange humming, like soft voices, and he thought he caught bits of music and song. Each time he looked up from his feet at his guide, she was looking at him, smiling and gently urging him on. At last, the light dimmed as they descended onto a landing. He could feel warm air surround him, blowing gently into the stairway. When they came through an arched doorway, he could at first see nothing but sky, deep, blue, and clean, as on a warm spring day. She led him out into the open, stopping some distance from the stairs. As he realized what he was seeing, his knees buckled, and he shook with panic.

They were at the very edge of a precipice. Only a low wall stood between them and a sheer drop of thousands of feet. But the most fearsome thing of all was that they were not in some deep cavern far below the earth, but at the summit of a great mountain overlooking a sheer cliff. Below was a vast forest. Dotted throughout were vineyards and farmyards, and in the distance was a golden city shining with spires and great curved buildings of glass, suspended within the boughs of gigantic trees. Turning around, he saw the staircase behind him, rising up into an archway and out of view. Yet nothing appeared to be behind the archway except sky, no wall, no building.

"*Doe glinori,*" she said. "My home."

He stared at her, and, weakened by the shock, sunk down on one knee against the low wall, breaking her grip and clinging to the stone with both hands, his heart pounding and his mind reeling.

"Why do you fear so?" she said.

"How can any of this be?" Ullin stuttered. He could not help but notice, among so many things, that her robes in this light were sheer, and every detail of her lovely body was clearly visible. Yet, while this muddled Ullin even more, she seemed to have no shame about it at all. He looked away from her. "I, I understand your speech, yet I do not know how."

"When I am here, I speak the First Tongue, the language of my people and of all creatures upon a time."

"It is much like what we call the Ancient Speech," Ullin nodded. "But it is different, purer."

"Yes, it is the forebear of that language," she said. "The First Tongue was once known to all creatures, though it has been forgotten, except in this place. You may speak it, if you try."

"I do not know if I can. And this," Ullin waved his arm around. "The stairs. Are we under the ground or on top? I do not see the sun, yet it is daytime. But there are no shadows. Surely I have been enchanted!"

"No," she said, taking a seat on the wall beside him. "Unless all are who come here. We are neither above nor atop. You may say we are *beside*. Or perhaps *before*, would be better. What you see was the last refuge of my people, a ray of the past brought forward to you. For it is in my power, and it is my doom, to remember my land as it once was. Between one full moon and the next, that is, one day each month, I am allowed this, to remind me of that which is no more. I choose this day. And I choose to share it with you and your companions, for it has healing powers in its vision. And, to you, it is no dream. Let us go there. Your bearer awaits."

She stood, taking his hands, and tugged him gently back to his feet, nodding to where a handsome red horse now stood, stamping the ground. Along its sides were odd bundles, carefully folded but not held into place by any straps.

"Can you ride bareback?" she asked rising.

"Of course, but—"

"Good. Go to him," she instructed. "His name is Ayreltide, and he knows the way."

"But what of you?"

"In this place, I need no mount," she said. She held her arms out and her airy robes unraveled, fanning out into a pair of gossamer wings, each more than twice as long as she was tall, shaped something like those of a moth. They shimmered and flexed, and immediately she floated up and hovered in the air, her face close to Ullin's.

"Soon you will rest," she said, taking his face in her hands and kissing his lips. It was a long kiss, her mouth soft and moist, her lips full and red, his dry and cracked, worn and painful. He closed his eyes and was carried off into a brief bliss. She hovered, feeling the pain come out from him, and she felt the torment of Mortals, the anguish and the sweet bitterness of brevity. A tear trickled down her cheek onto their joined lips. Ullin tasted something sweet, like nectar. She floated up and backward away from him and over the precipice. Ullin watched her fly on her back, facing him as she descended, then she rolled over and soared downward and away, her body golden in the light and her wings flashing like glass. Rising to greet her, he saw many others of her kind. Some were gossamer-winged, as was Islindia, the wings of others were as those of mighty eagles, some were like those of the dragonfly, and still others were as the hummingbird's. Their hair was golden, black, red, or brown, long to their waists, and their bodies were creamy white, nutmeg brown, coffee black, and rosy pink. He thought he heard girlish laughter and music rise up to greet her, too. Hearing a stamp, he turned to the mount she had left for him.

"Ayreltide, you are called," Ullin said, rubbing the horse's neck and looking the steed in the eye. "I am Ullin."

"Pleased to meet you," the horse said. "Now, please, will you get on? We are going to be late, and I have other matters to attend."

Ullin stumbled backward away from the horse. Ayreltide looked at him, tossed his red mane, and stamped.

"Come along!" he said.

Ullin made no move.

"Look," said Ayreltide, "I am normally a very patient fellow. Not a bit like my cousin, Shartide. Why, he's the worse! No, I have a reputation for gentleness and patience. That's why I, and not my cousin, wait on the Lady and do her bidding whenever she comes. Mind, she doesn't come that often, anymore. But when she does, I am always at the ready. Just in case, you know?"

"No, I—"

"Because she hasn't any *real* need of a horse. Just a symbolic thing, I think, being waited upon by a horse, I mean. Don't know why. Do you?"

"Well, maybe she's—"

"Tradition, probably. Anyway, so what was I saying? Oh, yes! Patience! That's me. But here, we need to be off, do you mind?"

Quickly exasperated, Ullin nervously leapt onto Ayreltide's back.

"Hang onto my mane!"

"Yes, sir."

Ayreltide took four great strides and then bounded over the precipice.

Ullin screamed.

"What!" Ayreltide cried. "What's the matter? What's wrong?"

Ullin opened one eye and saw that huge, broad, red feathery wings had unfolded, and they were soaring smoothly along.

"O-o-o-o-o-o-o-o-o," was all Ullin could utter, closing his eye shut and opening the other as wide as a saucer.

"Aw, I get it!" Ayreltide said. "Not a flyer, are you? Oh well, you'll get used to it after a bit, and you'll wonder how you ever got along before. There's nothing to it. I do all the work. Not that it's work, that is."

Ullin was glad he had not eaten.

"I still remember the first time I was pushed from the stall," Ayreltide continued on, heedless of Ullin's discomfort. "Why, I thought I was gone for good! But then, out of panic, I just put out my wings and POOF! I was floating along as light as a rainbow! Do you mind not pulling my mane quite so tightly? I won't drop you!"

In fact, Ullin had no control over his grip, and even bent over to put his head low against the horse's neck between his fist-tight holds, hardly hearing, anymore, Ayreltide's casual chat, and he was, for all intents, in a faint. Yet, so smooth was the flight that if it were not for the pleasant breeze, he would have had no sense of motion at all as they soared in a broad turn and then glided downward. Once, catching the scent of balsam, he dared to open both his eyes and saw the tops of trees flashing just underneath the hooves of the beast. With three powerful sweeps of his wings, crimson in the bright light, they flew upward over a pine-topped ridge and then banked down into a deep cleft in the forest where a tall waterfall fell straight and misty into a blue pool. Now Ullin could not close his eyes if he wanted to, so filled with wonder was he, in spite of his terror. Ayreltide flapped hard into a hover, and, continuing to flap, he smoothly descended almost straight down into a gap in the trees, landing softly on a flat moss-covered rock protruding from the grass-carpeted shore of the pool.

"There you are!" Ayreltide said.

Ullin, shaking, slipped from his back and immediately fell to his knees.

"I thank you," he managed to whisper, "for a safe descent."

"My pleasure! My pleasure, indeed. If you have further need of me, just whistle. No one here whistles, so I'll know it to be you. I'll be off, now. Enjoy!"

The magical horse sprinted to the end of the rock and leapt outward, his hooves barely touching the water before his wings lifted him skyward. Still kneeling with both hands on the ground, Ullin watched Ayreltide recede beyond the treetops, and he did not notice the four figures walking toward him down a path until they were nearly upon him. He rose, somewhat unsteadily, and bowed as they approached. They were two males and two females, all robed loosely in the same gossamer fabric of their wings as Islindia, and they carried folded bundles and small baskets.

"We have been told of Men and that they sometimes desire to bathe."

"A need we here know nothing of, except as a pleasure."

"Our Queen bids you wash, if you wish to do so. Here are cloths for that purpose, and soaps, and other things."

"And, if you wish, you may leave your clothing here, and wear instead these things we brought."

They placed the items before him, robes and slippers, an empty pitcher, vials of fragrant soap, and downy-soft cloths for washing and drying. A hair brush and a comb were also left for him.

"You will have all the privacy you desire. Rest assured, no one will look upon you until you wish it. This path leads to a garden where you will find refreshments, if you desire them, and company, too."

"I thank you," Ullin bowed. "But pray, what of my companions?"

"They rest, too. Fret not for them. They shall be as refreshed as you when next you see them."

Ullin watched the foursome glide back up the path and away. Now alone, Ullin took off all his things and peered over the edge. Wondering how cold it must be, he took a few deep breaths and plunged in, being pleasantly surprised that the water was actually warm. Filled with unexplained delight, he swam back and forth across the pool several times. Then, finding a shallower place where there was a ledge just under the surface jutting out from the rock near his things, he took up the soap and a cloth and began a good scrubbing. Though he had bathed only two nights ago, it had not been a joyful cleansing. There was still plenty of dried blood under his nails, and splattered gore in his hair and scalp, plus two days of sweat and dust.

So, taking special care to scrub beneath his nails, he thought of Sheila and wondered what may have gone through her mind when she bathed in the River Bentwide those years ago after he tossed her in, having planted the basket of wash-things ahead of time. Did she delight in that as much as he now did in this? He had never asked. He tried to remember how long ago that was. Eleven? No, closer to twelve years ago? As he washed and rinsed, it was not for any ritual, but of pure joy. Surely a simple bath, when one has done without for so long, is the highest of luxuries. His mind returned to Sheila again, wondering what she might think of the splendid baths in the Free City of Kajarahn, surrounded by its fragrant gardens of anise and myrrh, their boughs free for the picking to be rubbed as balmy fragrances on travel-sore muscles. Perhaps the soaps and combs he had given Sheila had been the first she had ever had as her own. Perhaps she even had greater pleasure in that simple river bath than anyone in any palace or grand city ever had. But she was very young at the time, and that was long ago.

Living and working in Barley had been an enviable assignment, far away from conflicts, and in the company of Mirabella's family and friends. And though it was a tedious task, the map revisions he made proved his mapmaking abilities. In a roundabout way, his success in Barley was what eventually led him to meet Ashlord. His senior commander saw Ullin's mapping talent and sent him south with a detachment of engineers to renew their maps of the northern Dragonlands. There, his skill at survival and at finding his way in and out of enemy lines brought him more special missions of a covert nature. It had been the last of these, he mused as he picked up his locket and hung it again about his neck, that landed him in a hospital in Vanara where he first met Ashlord.

His thoughts went back to Kajarahn and not only to the baths, but to the one he had left in that city. He sat, fingering the locket, staring at the reflection of sky in the rippling water, thinking about that assignment as the water dripped from his hair. Even without looking into the secret fold of the locket, he could envision Micerea's likeness. He closed his eyes, seeing her all the clearer in his mind. In spite of all, her spirit remained with him after they parted from each other. And, during the years away from her, since throwing in with Ashlord, he continued to feel her presence, though the leagues between them were countless. Sometimes, he dreamt that she was with him, sharing his campfire or riding beside him conversing for what seemed hours and hours, baring their hearts and worries, their longings and their hopes, happy to do so, as if they had never parted company. The dreams were so vivid and tangible that his heart ached terribly upon waking. But Ullin suspected, silly though it was, that it had been those dreams that had carried him through the days of loneliness and toil, and had given him the strength to go on.

Until Esildre.

Now, in spite of his efforts, the one he longed for the most in all the world seemed truly parted from him, as if their connection had been severed by his licentious act.

"Well, I deserve it. As it turns out, I am unworthy of Micerea, indeed," he said aloud as he dressed in the robes provided to him. Leaving the slippers behind with the other things, he walked barefooted across the mossy path upward into the forest, following the gentle sound of a strumming harp. Ascending stone steps, he entered a garden, all a-bloom with orchids and lilies and every manner of lovely flower, even those that only bloom at night, all spread full and vibrant. And their scents came to him one by one, as if they were individuals, never muddling together with each other, each proud to offer its own unique bouquet for his enjoyment. He came to a courtyard, of sorts, overhung with thick branches from the surrounding ancient trees. There were benches and stone stools, and a marvelous fountain in the shape of a willow tree, from which water streamed gently down every branch in a hypnotic shower. Many people sat, stood, or reclined on the soft grass, and as he entered their company, they stood and bowed to him, smiling, and he returned the gestures, continuing until he came before Islindia.

She was seated at the edge of the pool that the fountain made, with her feet in the water and a harp propped against her. Her wings floated smoke-like as she played, her beauty visible to all without shame or guile. Nor did Ullin feel any shame or any base urgings when he looked upon her. She was, in his eyes, like a lovely animal, one that could be feared, but one that could be admired, too, for its beauty. And surely one that could be loved. But he did not, and he had no longing for anything but her company. For here, there was peace.

She played a light tune, unhurried and sweet with a touch of melancholy in the melody. On the grass nearby sat two ladies who motioned for Ullin to sit with them. When he did so, they poured sweet nectar from a gourd into a large buttercup and handed it to him. They offered him fruit and hearty nuts to eat, and he enjoyed every morsel. More nectar he was given. Whether it was the drink, the food, or his deep fatigue that affected him, he became increasingly sleepy. No one spoke, and several of those in attendance had their eyes closed to the music. He leaned back on one elbow, taking another sip, and closed his eyes, too. He had no cares and was content just to listen.

• • •

When he woke, his head was cradled in the lap of Islindia, and he looked up into her face, smiling down upon him.

"I once cradled my lover's head in just this way," she said, stroking his head, "and he unburdened his heart to me. You have worries, too. But you need not speak them, for I now sense them. You fear that your company will not accomplish its quest. You think there is some division among you that will thwart your efforts. You fear that you are that division. You have had a curse laid upon you by the Dark One. But you have not succumbed because you are strong. Still, he taunts you with unkind visions. You think, therefore, that you will betray your company, that you are the weak link in the chain of loyalty among you. But that is not so. I cannot lift from you the distractions of your heart, but I do see that you will remain loyal to your cousin, even if it costs you your life."

Ullin sat up. They were alone, her lyre leaning against a bench, and the gentle rain-like sounds of the fountain were now the only notes to be heard.

"Yet I have betrayed one who is dear to me."

"No, you have not. You were used. I know Secundur. It was after this place was destroyed that he gained his clutch upon Esildre. He was determined to have one of the Firstborn as his consort, and to thus increase his power over the Elifaen. I did not give in to his entreaties, though my refusal resulted in the destruction of this place. But Esildre did surrender to him. At least for a time. Who knows what threats or coercion he used upon her? Who knows what words of sweet doubt and coaxing he spake to her. I do not know what happened when she broke from him, but it must have been a terrible struggle. As she was about to wrest her freedom from him, he, in his wrath and jealousy, lay a double curse upon her. In the end, he could not keep her or destroy her. Her spirit was too strong. But he made her to suffer the licentious desires of her body a thousand times stronger, making her longings insatiable. Added to that, whosoever she gave herself to would be stricken with madness, unto their own destruction. So, through her, Secundur made yet another way to spread madness and despair into the world, hoping that his shadow would spread through her, and his schemes would be more easily advanced. Knowing these things, she secluded herself in her castle for centuries. That she has left her place and is now roaming about in the world is a great risk, but her only hope is to find the one who may love her truly, and by that love lift the curse from her. Only her true love will not be victim of the curse upon her, nor will he feel it at all. That person was not you. But you have survived the encounter with Secundur's insidious spirit, his curse upon Esildre. You have not been destroyed by madness, only wounded by Secundur's curse, and if there is any mark left upon you, I think it will not be fatal to your heart."

"I understand little of what you say," Ullin muttered, shaking his head. "But I have made my friends suffer because of my weakness."

"All friends suffer the weaknesses of each other. That is the strength and the beauty of friendship. And its test. For friendship's love does not confine itself to family or kin alone, to the near over the far, nor to one sex, or even to one and the same kind of creature. The strength of friendship's love may overcome the throes of hardship, the barriers of race, and may even be shared from one kind of creature to another. Each according to the ability of the heart. As with any ability, love's ability increases with the practice of it."

They looked deeply at one another, and Ullin took comfort from her words. Not the kind of comfort that rids the heart of troubles, but the kind that whispers hope. It was then that he saw, though her words of hope were strong and powerful, that she herself had none, and he marveled at the paradox that she might give that which she did not possess to him.

Looking up at the sky, he nodded, and smiled wistfully, not knowing whether to laugh or cry. They sat for a long while, saying nothing, as the azure deepened gradually, until Ullin noticed the change.

"Is it getting dark?"

"Yes. You slept for a long while. Now this dream draws to an end, and you must return to your companions, rested and ready to lead them on. They, too, will be rested. You will find them on the other side of the city. Ayreltide will take you to them, and I will join you shortly."

She rose, spread her wings, and effortlessly floated upward. She smiled, and, with a graceful flap, she disappeared over the trees and beyond sight.

Ullin watched her disappear, then saw his own clothes spread out on the grass, cleaned and mended. He changed into them and laid his borrowed robes aside. Then, looking up, he gave a little whistle. In only a moment, Ayreltide came gliding over the clearing and landed before him.

"Well," Ullin said as he mounted Ayreltide, "I'll try not to be so frightened this time."

"There, there," came the jovial reply. "And I'll be as gentle as ever!"

Up they went, over the trees and higher and higher, until Ullin could see again the vast forest and, far off, the glittering domes and spires of a marvelous city.

"Would you like a closer look?"

"Certainly, if that is allowed."

"Oh, yes. As long as we do not alight, for my Queen has ordered that none but her own memories may walk there."

Ayreltide banked and sloped downward until they were just a few hundred feet above the trees and then over the city. They passed a fantastic river, one that seemed to be flowing uphill. There were no streets, but instead avenues of Faerekind passed this way and that through the air. And Ullin saw that the crystal and silver buildings were held aloft in the arms of enormous trees. Through many of the clear crystalline domes he could see gatherings of the Faerekind, some engaged in floating dances and others playing intriguing games of tag with long-feathered birds of brilliant colors. Music drifted upward to his ears, and laughter, too. He saw in one place row upon row of scrolls, and desks, floating in the air, upon which some of the Faerekind busied themselves with writing and drawing. Looking ahead, there loomed a tall thin tower, made as if from a single reed, but it was of prodigious proportions, reaching far above them. At its top was a loft, of sorts, with narrow open windows all around.

"That is our Queen's abode when she is in the city," Ayreltide explained as they shot past it.

On they went, with Ullin seeing more than his mind could take in or explain. Fantastic structures that defied gravity, and brilliant hues of every season from spring to autumn in the trees that grew up from the gardens. Everywhere the Faerekind flew and danced in the air, their wings so wispy and powerful, their bodies graceful and strong.

• • •

When Sheila woke, she immediately saw that the forest around them had changed, and she realized they were no longer where they had fallen asleep. She rose, feeling more rested than she had a right to, and the others also began stirring, as filled with wonder as she. Ashlord stood to one side of the clearing, contemplating a poppy that he held. Behind him was a waterfall, streaming through root-crusted rocks, and above them towered grand old trees, full of leaves.

"Did you rest well?" he asked, seeing their confusion.

"Why, yes."

"Where are we?"

"An' how'd we get here?"

"Don't you remember?"

• • •

It was like remembering a clear and vivid dream. A memory of being escorted through the forest by fair maidens, cloaked as Islindia had been, until they came to a large clearing where there was a table set with food and wine. They eagerly dined while one of the Faerekind played a lute. Such was the beauty of the music that none wanted to disturb the peaceful spell by asking where Ullin was. Sensing the question, one of the maidens said, "Ullin Saheed is with our Queen, and he will rejoin you soon," and this satisfied their curiosity about his absence.

After they had eaten their fill, riders arrived on winged steeds, and they took up each of the guests upon a mount, and together they flew into the air. They passed over the forest and over a fantastic city filled with flying beings that they knew were Faerekind. After a thrilling ride, they arrived at this grove and were let down from their mounts. Before they could discuss anything, an urgent drowsiness overcame them, and they fell asleep on the soft grass.

• • •

"Was it real?" Sheila was the first to ask.

"Are you rested? Are you well-fed?" Ashlord smiled.

"Did we truly fly on winged horses?" Robby asked.

"A gift from Islindia," Ashlord nodded. "And we have been taken in one night what would have been a walk of four or five days. And so here we are, on the other side of her forest, near the western border of her realm."

"Where's, where'sUllin?" Ibin asked.

"That will be him, surely," Ashlord said, hearing what sounded like the wings of a very large bird.

"So it was real," Robby said as Ayreltide and his rider appeared over the treetops and spiraled downward to land among them, "and not just a dream. In fact," he added to himself, "I did not dream at all, I don't think."

Ullin was grinning and shaking his head as he dismounted, happy to have his feet back on the ground.

"Thank you," he said to Ayreltide. "Won't you thank your Queen for me?"

"You may do so yourself, good sir! Fare thee well!"

No sooner than Ayreltide was lost among the treetops than another form appeared, her lithe body carried gracefully by her wings between the branches until she alit to stand before them. They bowed as her wings wrapped around her. There was a look of peaceful weariness about her, and she smiled and bade them good morning.

"I have given you a glimpse and a taste of what once was," she said. "But I now know it will never be again. Truly all the days of my waiting have been in vain, for it was never in my power to restore what was lost, nor is it in the power of my father to restore to the world that which was taken away. Therefore, never again shall mortal eyes see what yours have beheld. The world changes, and the world forgets. Now you must leave this wood. I warn you: do not return, for I cannot always restrain my father's wrath from those who enter here."

Then she turned to Robby and said, "Upon you is the burden that I no longer carry. Yet you shall not be as I, waiting for change to come. It is your quest to bring change to the world and to alter the river of events from where they now flow. For that is the only way that you may fulfill your quest and, as you know, survive it. Your survival is wrapped up in the survival of those things you care most for. So they depend upon you. It is my fate to see only the past; I cannot look into the future as some of my kind may do. Yet I may tell you that the place you seek first, the hidden place you call Griferis, once existed at the Great Cleft far to the west. Ask for that place and you may yet find Griferis. The other thing that you must do, the Name that you must name, will cost much. Perhaps more than you have to give. I will give you this paradox to riddle out: The name you seek may only be found in the place where no one living may go and from where no one living may return. Yet you must find a way there and back. I see that you understand what I say."

"Yes," Robby said, ashen-faced and solemn. "Lyrium has already hinted at it to me. And I have come to understand what I must do. Though I do not understand how you came by this knowledge."

"No creature that still has wildness in it may resist the will of my father, who tells me all."

Islindia smiled as Certina landed on Ashlord's shoulder.

"It was also prophesied to me by Lyrium, who was a guest of this forest for many years, that you and I would meet. Her visions showed her that we might converse again in another realm. But her gift of Sight fails her, I fear, for I shall never travel elsewhere. So I tell you this, Hidden One, do not trust overly much in what people say is ordained to happen. Lyrium believes her Sight flows from the future, but mine is ever upon the past, and it tells me that what has been lost can never be recovered. If you are to attain your quest, you must not try to regain what is lost. Rather, you must bring about that which has never been. And none, not Lyrium nor anyone, can see what that may be. If that is your hope, it is a thin one, as thin as the line that divides each moment, where past and future mingle."

"Very well, then," she nodded and turned to the others. "When last I met with you as a company, I said I would bid another thing of you. It is this: I command that you are not to ask this one anything concerning what he must do to obtain the Name," she gestured at Robby. "Let the decision be wholly his own, to tell you or not to tell you. But I think he will not, for he would not unnecessarily fill your hearts with anxiety. It may seem but a little thing now, but of little things may come great calamity. Do not ask, do not delve! Can you bear the mystery of it? I wonder."

"Islindia, Queen," Ashlord put forward, glancing across the faces of his companions. "We will indeed strive to honor your demand. And we thank you for the rest you have given us, and for your protection." He bowed, and they all nodded in agreement, Billy with his own quizzical look, and then they all bowed, too.

Islindia turned and gestured.

"This path will take you safely from my realm and into a land where good people dwell. They will help you, and you have no need of fear in their lands where my kin still hold sway, though in different aspect. Be cautious once you pass beyond that land, for the Men and Elifaen in those parts are stern and without allegiance to Duinnor or Vanara. Go now. It is time for this dream to fade, though may it never pass from your memory! Farewell!"

Each in turn bowed and made their separate thanks and farewells to the Queen of the Wood, and she smiled peacefully at them. Ullin went last of all.

"Thank you for your company, good sir," she said to him. "It was a moment I shall fondly remember."

Ullin kissed her hand, then put his hand to his chest and bowed. "Thank you, Queen," he said, "for your gentle kindness."

"Farewell."

• • •

Ullin followed behind the others, glancing back often until she was out of sight. As they moved off along the easy way, upward and out of the forest valley, their hearts were full of the wonders they had seen, and their spirits were lifted by the peace and beauty of those visions. With much to ponder, they proceeded without discussion. The path was covered with brown pine needles so that their footfalls made not a sound, and the singing of the birds and the tittering of their activities receded behind them until even those noises were no more than memory. Soon it was as if they walked through a kind of tunnel under boughs thick with short green needles and crowded with small delicate cones. To either side of them was the shiny green of sharp holly with thick clusters of bright red berries. All morning they went, hardly speaking, needing neither rest nor conversation, slowly climbing upward. The air moved not at all, and the gray light that filtered through the canopy became cooler and crisp with the scent of hemlock and balsam. By mid-afternoon, they reached a broad flat ridge, and the trees rapidly thinned as they traveled northward. The lush fir gave way to tall pine, yet the light remained subdued by a gray blanket of clouds. They felt, too, a cold breeze, and Robby remembered Ashlord's prediction of snow.

When the path turned westward, they paused to throw on their cloaks. Looking back on the way they had come, they saw only green treetops, unbroken as a carpet as far as they could see. By now, their mood was more somber as the sadness of what had been lost to the world came into their hearts, and more than one of the company heaved a great sigh as they turned to continue on through the forest, which seemed as melancholy as their hearts. But a mile farther, the path dipped through many fallen trunks of enormous size and brought them before a thick wall of the same vines with the razor-sharp thorns as they had encountered upon first entering Forest Islindia.

"The Ring of Blades, again," Ashlord said. "Look there."

Where the path entered the barrier, the vines had lifted and spread apart, making for them an easy corridor to pass through.

"Lo!" said Billy.

"Made just for us?" asked Sheila.

"I imagine so," nodded Ashlord as he led them into the dim and imposing tunnel. So thick was the canopy that arched over them that it seemed like night-time within, but they could feel cold air puffing strongly into their faces, and, after going only a little way ahead, they could see a bright opening. As they passed through the uncanny tunnel, the vines noiselessly closed behind them, barring any return. Almost before they knew it, they came to the opening at the far side and stepped out of the viny tunnel into several inches of fresh snow and into a pine forest through which large flakes drifted steadily down. They stopped and gazed at the barrier behind and at the wood before them.

"Look, lookhere, look!" Ibin cried, pointing excitedly to a shape on the ground. Neatly laid out as if just put there, with hardly a flake yet upon them, were their weapons. Each of the swords had been cleaned and sharpened, as well as the other blades, and the scabbards repaired and conditioned. Sheila and Ullin's bows, and Ibin's mandolin, were newly strung, and their quivers full of fine, strong, long arrows with new steel tips and fletched with white feathers. There were also pouches of medicinal herbs and a sack of nuts and dried berries and fruit. As they took up their things and strapped on their gear, they continued to look about with a mix of caution and wonder.

"Well," said Billy, tugging on his pack. "Snow. Like ye foretold, Ashlord."

"Which way do we go?" asked Robby.

"This way," nodded Ashlord, pulling his hood over his head and drawing up his straps. He stepped off, leading them west.

Ullin lingered as the others followed, and he continued to look back at the Ring of Blades. His face was blank, and when Robby passed by he wondered if it was only the sharp cold air making his cousin's eyes water. Robby tapped Ullin's arm, and the Kingsman smiled and nodded, bringing up the rear as they padded through the soft snow.

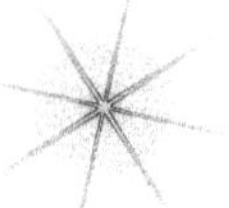

Chapter 15

The Feast of Solstice

Day 136
109 Days Remaining

It was relatively flat terrain, with a few leafless oaks but mostly stands of pine, their stark gray-brown trunks with boughs sagging with snow. The breeze died, yet the air was full of movement as clumpy flakes fell steadily and landed softly, and soon the snow was well above their ankles. There was little sense of time, no shadows to make a judgment of the hour.

Ashlord led them at a good pace through the forest, picking the way easily through the trees and mounting snow, and they moved quickly enough to stay fairly warm. As always when the mystic led the way, his movements were highly deliberate, yet flowed naturally. His head was constantly and smoothly turning, looking and listening. Indeed, though he did not miss a step or even brush a single low branch, he seemed not to look so much at where he was going, but rather in other directions and at other things of interest only to him.

"Do ye hear that?" Billy suddenly asked. He spoke at a normal tone, yet in the silent forest his words were easily heard by all, even though they were spread out over many yards. They paused, looking at Billy, and they listened. He held his finger up then flicked it to their right.

"Thar!" he whispered.

A sound, distant and delicate. It faded, like the soft ringing of a silvery-voiced bird. Just as they started to resume their walk, shrugging their shoulders at what it might be, they heard it again, softly and rhythmically wafting through the flaky air and around the unwavering trees. Again, it faded away.

"I'm not sure," said Ashlord as they looked at him questioningly. "Perhaps there is a farm or village nearby."

"Then maybe we'll find shelter before nightfall," suggested Sheila as she shook snow from her hood.

They continued on and had not gone far when they came to a snow-covered road that intersected their path. The group entered the road and looked one way then the other. To the right it rose gently in a straight line through the pines, then curved away as it topped a low hill in the distance. To the left it continued on straight for a furlong before bending out of sight.

"This should make our going a bit easier," said Ullin.

They turned left—to go southwest, Ullin reckoned—and had advanced only a few yards when they heard the strange sound again. This time it came from behind them and was clearer, its bright rhythmic jangle ringing without echo. No sooner had they stopped and turned around toward the sound than they saw, topping the hill far behind them, a team of eight mighty stags bristling with antlers pulling a large sleigh. Their harnesses and reins were all hung with tiny silver bells, and their thorny heads were bedecked with mistletoe as might be found in the high branches of oaks. On the front seat was a large figure shaking the reins and calling out to his team, "Whoosher! Hee! Haa! Onward my fleet-hooved friends! Yee-haa! There we go a-flying along, light as a bird, quick as an arrow!"

At first, the driver did not seem to notice the confused company spreading out to either side to let the swift apparatus pass. At the last moment, he pulled on the reins and cried, "Whoa there, Thunder! Slow there, Lightning! Easy there, Wonder, nicely there, Prideling! Follow there, Starshine! Likewise, Moonbeam! You, too, Wayfind! Pull up, Iceking!"

The sleigh miraculously slowed and came to a halt in the middle of the way between the astonished onlookers, the buckmarls puffing great clouds. The vehicle was bright red with silver skids and silver footrails, and it was draped with ropes of leafy ivy and sprigs of red-berried holly. Large enough for many passengers, it was instead crammed full of colorful bulging sacks and chests and with boxes of marvelous woods and intricate hardware. On the dashboard was a brass lamp holder and in it was a conical torch afire with smokeless flames of gold and silver, emitting an uncanny and mesmerizing glow. The driver, a very large figure both in height and girth, was attired in a green velvet coat, lined about the collars and cuffs with white fur, with matching velvet gloves and hat. Below his somewhat bulging middle was a broad shiny black belt, buckled with silver and of the same finely polished leather as his boots. A full beard of snow-white surrounded his lips, nearly equaled in color by the rosy blush of his snub nose and exposed cheeks. As he settled the reins, he looked over the roadside gathering, his slightly squinting eyes, the most brilliant blue, glimmering and twinkling at each of the company in the briefest of turns.

"Good travelers!" he addressed them with a powerful voice. "Good day!"

"Good day, sir," said Ashlord.

"G'day," said Billy, grinning at the fantastic sight. "I ain't never seen the likes of such a rig!"

"No? Ha! Yes, a beautiful apparatus, and a powerful team! Ha!" the driver fairly beamed with pride. "Just the thing. And none else would do this day! You make for the west, I gather?"

"Aye," said Ullin, smiling, looking askance at the driver and his vehicle.

"A long tramp, and bound to be a cold one," the driver said. "You'll need shelter this night, for the snow will not abate before a foot more is down."

"We were hoping to find some shelter along the way," Robby told him. "A village with an inn, perhaps. Or maybe a farmer willing to spare space in his barn for our company."

"We'd be willing to pay, of course," added Sheila.

"Ah, well! Willing you may be, but any and all would be made available to you by farmer or innkeeper, for only the asking, I daresay. And I do say! For all the people shall know of your coming, as I will shortly report it, and the honor of your company would be most gratifying. For this is the night we all gather at the Town Hall for our Winter's Feast, and so that is where I bid you go. If my sleigh were less laden, I would gladly take all of you at once. But two and only two may I take, and I needs be on my way quickly to deliver and make ready the feast. Do not fear! Forthwith upon arrival, I shall send others to fetch the rest along. So which two shall join me?"

The company looked at each other, not quite knowing what to make of the offer. Even Ashlord seemed bemused and somewhat baffled.

"Good sir," Ullin said at last, "we hesitate to be parted from one another, and we wonder at your ready trust of our company, being strangers to your land."

"Oh? Ho! Ha! Do you not come just this day from Islindia's forest? For that is the only means to these lands from the way you come! Any granted passage through that place has been blessed, for the King of the Wood brooks no threat, and his hand of protection extends to these parts, too. And the Fair Lady who dwells there would give her company to none unworthy of it. Haha! Ho, then! Come along. Who shall ride with me?"

"Let it be Robby and Sheila," said Ashlord, "and we others will follow on foot."

"Very well! Climb beside me there. That's it, young lady. There. Now, fine gentleman. Good! Slip this blanket over your knees!" He took up his reins, and the bells on the harnesses jingled as the stags softly stamped in anticipation.

"Prepare, my comrades!" he called to his team. Then, as Robby and Sheila settled in, he turned to those still standing alongside. "You'll not need tramp very far. You'll have rides, too, before very long! Just keep to this way!"

Robby and Sheila grinned at each other and at their friends as the driver tossed the reins.

"Fo'ard, ye handsomes!"

As quick as a wink the stags reacted, and the sleigh gently moved forward. The team fell into an easy and proud prance, and the company watched it recede from them, re-entering the center of the road to stare after it.

"Oh, my!" said Sheila, gripping Robby's hand.

"Goodness!" said Robby, turning his head to laugh back at the waving Ibin.

"Lo!" muttered Billy at the smooth grace of the vehicle as it went around the bend.

"Amazing!" exclaimed Ibin loudly, his face shining with an almost meal-like anticipation and glee. "Whowas, whowas, whowasthatman?"

Ashlord, unable to keep a stern face himself, shook his head. "I'm not sure. But if tales I've heard have anything to them, he's a relation to Lady Islindia, perhaps."

"Then one of the Faerekind?" Ullin asked.

"Maybe so."

"Well, we'd best be along," put in Billy, cinching up his pack. "Snow's comin' down good an' steady, now. An' it appears we'll have a warm place to look fo'ard to."

The sound of the harness-bells faded away as the four nodded and resumed their march. Walking through the building snow was less toilsome, and even their packs seemed lighter. Mysteriously, too, the sharp air seemed to bite not so much as before, even though their breath sent huge clouds around their heads and trailing behind.

• • •

After passing around the bend and far out of sight from those left following behind, the driver turned to his passengers.

"Are you good and settled in? Warm enough under the blanket there?"

"Yes, sir."

"I believe so."

"Good! And is the ride not too bumpy?"

"Bumpy?" Sheila laughed.

"Why, it's as smooth as glass!" cried Robby.

"Haha! Ho! Good, good! Then let us make a better pace, for I am awaited, and I am always on time!"

The driver laughed and shook the reins, crying, "Now Thunder! Now Lightning! Lead away there! On Wonder! On Prideling. Follow on fair! Push Starshine! Pull Moonbeam! Heads up and hie! Push Wayfind! Push Iceking! Now let us fly!"

And with that, the ride began in earnest as the sleigh shot forward and the bells chimmy-chimed fervently. The wind of their passage became so great that it tugged away at Robby and Sheila's hoods so that each had to hold a hand atop their heads. The trees flashed by in a blur, and the snow flakes turned to sideways streaks. All the while, the driver laughed and laughed, calling out words of praise and encouragement to the mighty team as faster and faster they went, so fast that the hearts of the two giddy passengers fairly pounded with the thrill of it. Yet so smooth was their ride that it seemed they moved not at all; instead, the whole world was turning underneath them, the landscape racing at them and flying past. They barely saw a farmhouse before it shot by, a waving farmer and his wife almost statue-like in their grinning pose. A turn appeared before them and was taken in such a manner that it was hardly noticed, both the team and the sleigh tilting with all defiance of reason into the curve so that not a nudge was felt, and not a single sack or carefully packed box shifted out of place in the least. When they came to a broad dip in the way, the two passengers gasped as they went straight over it as if an invisible bridge leveled the terrain. Robby, to his everlasting wonder, had already perceived that hardly a hoof-thump could be heard, and he wondered if the team of buckmarls or the sleigh even touched the ground.

More farms came and went, with everyone they passed waving as they flew by, and the driver waved back, crying, "Come all!" or "Joyful day!"

The farther along they went, the nearer they came to a little town spread across the end of a small valley and rising up the far hills. Just as Robby and Sheila saw the town, they were upon it, and the driver slowed his team before entering the gates. To their amazement, all of the houses and shops were decorated with red ribbons and green boughs. The streetlamps, too, wore wreaths of holly hung over the ladder posts and were wrapped in red and green and gold ribbons. Everywhere people went from shop to shop, back and forth across the streets, or they lingered at stands where the aromas of hot cider and roasted nuts swirled. The people laughed and waved at them, crying, "Joyful day!" and "Good Eve!" Musicians played lively music at one corner. At the next, children busily rolled snow into crude figures of men and beasts, while others careened precariously close to mishap on sleds.

"Is it some festival time here?" Robby asked.

"Why, indeed it is!" laughed the driver. "Don't you know what day it is? It is Midwinter's Day! And this night is the night of our Winter Feast. All year long these good people toil and work and have their joys and trials. It is on this night, the longest night of them all, that they gather to celebrate the year and, on the morrow, the lengthening of the days. While the days get colder, the lengthening of the days tells us there is hope. And why do you think we make haste? So that the Feast may begin, that's why! For they never start without me, since I am the Guest of Honor, hee-hee, as I am always. And whoa! Whoa! Ha! Ho-ho! Here we are!"

"So it's already Midwinter's Day," Robby muttered as memories of past Midwinter celebrations flooded to mind. Gatherings with friends, decorating the shop with holly and mistletoe and ribbons on the windows. And, somehow, Robby had managed to see Sheila on each of the previous three Midwinters. The first time was not long after he and Sheila began meeting at the pond. He was visiting Bosk Hall to give his well-wishes and a crate of preserves and spices from Mr. and Mrs. Ribbon. Sheila appeared, having just delivered a turkey to the kitchens, and Frizella had insisted that she remain and help prepare and enjoy the bounty of her hunt. He remembered how Billy's sister, Raenelle, had acted in a somewhat haughty manner toward Sheila, and was a bit too flirtatious with Robby, and that Sheila was reluctant to stay. As he would later learn, Sheila only did so because Robby asked her to remain. He learned, too, that she would not have come at all but she had overhead, a week before, that Robby would be visiting Bosk Hall on Midwinter's Day. It turned out to be a fine afternoon, though it saddened him when it came time to say goodbye and go back to Passdale. That evening, when she walked with him part of the way home, she made Robby renew his vow not to tell anyone about their feelings for each other. He argued, but he already loved her too much not to do as she asked. It would be a vow that would rankle and worry him over the next years, but he would keep it. For each of the following Midwinter's Days, he would invite her to dine with his own family, but she was never willing to accept. Doing so, she argued, would let their secret out. Sheila feared that her uncle would use it against them, and that Robby's family would keep him from her.

And now it was Midwinter's Day once more. Had things been very different, Robby thought, he and Sheila might be, at this very moment, sitting at the table with his parents, laughing and talking, and enjoying a wonderful dinner.

Robby felt a pang of regret, disappointed in himself that he had failed Sheila. He wished he had been man enough to stand up to Steggan, and to his own parents, if necessary. To at least run away with Sheila, to have a bit of life together on their own. Now it was too late. Besides his own failures, the whole world seemed bent on wedging its way between them, on destroying everything he cared for, everything he had ever hoped for. It was a train of thought that he was all too familiar with, and, as always, it left him deflated and in a melancholy mood. He glanced at Sheila again, and she returned and held his gaze, smiling enigmatically and squeezing his hand. Her gesture seemed to say, perhaps in the spirit of the day, "Everything will be alright."

• • •

They came to a smooth stop in front of a very large hall. The steps leading up to the open doors were lined on either side with white-gloved boys and girls wearing green velvet coats, just like the driver, but trimmed with red fur. Atop their heads they sported pointed caps of red with thin white brims upturned to each side. Their shiny black shoes had curled-up toes, and their stockings were banded in red and white. They all stood like soldiers, looking straight ahead, expressionless. Then there appeared at the top of the stairs a taller figure, similarly dressed as the others, but with a red pointed beard curled up at its sharp end, just like his shoes. He strode down the stairs and bowed. The driver got out, and he extended his hand to Sheila to help her descend beside him.

"Ho, Raskin!" said the driver, greeting the waiting man.

"Joyous day, sir!" said Raskin bowing again. "You bring guests this year?"

"Most certainly I do! And four more along the way. Would you be a good fellow and make arrangements to fetch them along as quickly as may be?"

"Right away, sir!" Raskin snapped his fingers, and immediately the other attendants sprang forward, climbing as only children can onto the sleigh and pushing and pulling and heaving out the boxes and sacks and bags and handing them from one to another up the stairs and through the doorway. After calling out a few instructions to the gaily-garbed attendants, Raskin turned back to the driver. "If you'll excuse me, sir, I shall see to the other guests." After a businesslike bow, he crunched away through the snow and disappeared around a corner.

"Let me just get this," the driver said, reaching into the sleigh and pulling from the bracket the long cone-shaped torch. It was banded in gold and rimmed with silver in the form of holly leaves and berries. When he picked it up, the flame on its head brightened and broadened in response to his touch.

"Come! Come along!" he said, grinning to Robby and Sheila, who had been busy dodging the comings and goings of the little workers. Though each went away burdened beyond what one might think they could carry, they had hardly even begun the task of emptying the sleigh. In fact, when Sheila glanced back, it seemed as full as it was before they began. The two followed the driver up the stairs and through the doors and into a vast and somewhat gloomy hall. But as the driver strode through the length of it, the light of his mysterious torch bathed the place with a golden glow. There were long tables being set with pewter plates and tankards, goblets and cutlery, and an additional army of attendants was busy carrying chairs and benches and stools from a side door and lining them up along the tables.

"Oh, Ibin!" Sheila uttered, knowing her own delight was a small measure to that which her friend would have when he arrived. She had to dodge out of the way of a keg rumbling across the floor, and, as it passed, she saw several tiny boys behind it exerting a great effort to push it along.

As Robby and Sheila followed the driver between and among the busy workers, it was as if the candles that were set out on the tables and the lamps that hung from the ivy-twirled columns gained some inspiration from the driver's torch and blazed brighter as he passed. Tall windows, frosted with snow, were draped with green boughs, and from the high ceiling hung long ribbons of purple and green, edged with gold and silver, the ends of which were bow-tied just a few feet over their heads into wreaths made of mistletoe-adorned fir boughs and woven balls of red- and purple-berried ivy.

Most amazing was a tall tree on the far end of the room, nearly as tall as the high ceiling. It was not made of wood and greenbough, but seemed fashioned of clear glass, even to its most delicately shaped needles. It gleamed and sparkled with the light of the hall, glittering red and green and blue and gold as it caught glints from the room and scattered back each one with ten-fold brilliance. So magnificent it was that as each candle was lit, the room seemed to brighten twice as much as one would expect. And with each taper, each votive, every crackling fireplace burning warm, and all the lamps, too, the fantastic hall was as bright and as warm as noontime on a spring day.

Sheila and Robby were fairly hypnotized at the sight and hardly noticed the tall-backed chair to one side of the tree. To this chair, almost a throne, the driver went, and he placed his torch into a stand beside it. Seeing his guests lingering agape at the tree, he laughed and called to them.

"Come! Sit at the table just yonder," he directed them. "There is plenty of room, and your companions will arrive in just a while to join us."

"Thank you, sir," Robby said. He was about to ask his name and make introductions for himself and Sheila, but Raskin distracted the happy fellow with a question. Robby shrugged at Sheila as they moved to the nearest table.

"I was going to ask his name and tell him ours," Robby said.

"He must be someone very important," Sheila observed as Robby pulled a chair out for her. "Thank you," she said. But she remained standing, too fascinated by the bustle and work and wonders about them.

All around within the great hall, the business of preparations continued at a frantic pace, though all of the workers seemed happy, almost giddy, at their toils. Noise of plates and silverware, the popping out of bung corks from kegs, chairs being dragged this way and that across the room, orders being asked for and given by various squads of children. From kitchens close by, the aroma of cake and bread wafted through, along with nutmeg and cinnamon, and sometimes the jangling of pots and pans rang through the din. All the while, legions of children, dressed in their festive attire, marched in and out, bringing loads of packages, sacks, and boxes to place under the marvelous tree. Before it, beside his chair, the sleigh driver stood with one hand upon the back of the chair, and the other grasping the buckle about his coat. He smiled and grinned, nodding to the little workers as they passed, calling each by name and saying "Joy to you, Jimmy-John!," or "Happy Midwinter's, Miss Megan!"

Robby and Sheila watched with fascination, the happy mood infecting them so that they could not help grinning, too. And, as the day grew dim outside, the hall remained bright and cheerful, as if, when each thing was put in its place, the ardor of the candles and lamps grew ever brighter, and the fantastic tree glittered all the more.

At last, after an hour or more of this activity, their driver turned to his aide.

"Ah, Raskin! How are we doing?"

"All is ready, sir."

The two guests noticed, as Raskin answered, that all of the commotion had ceased. Looking around, Robby and Sheila saw that the companies of attendants were lining up to either side of the hall, just as they had stood before along the steps. Some elbowed their neighbors for room, some pulled their coats straight, and one or two were quickly adjusting their caps. They all stood motionless, eyes straight ahead, though a precocious giggle was heard coming from somewhere farther down the hall.

"Indeed! Indeed! Ha-ha! Just as the sun sets! Well! By all means, let the bells ring out! Let the musicians play! And let all our guests, company, families, and friends come, one and all!"

Rankin smiled and bowed low. He turned to two nearby attendants and clapped his gloved hands twice.

"Let it begin!" Raskin called out, gesturing to a boy and girl nearby. Immediately, they walked to the other side of the hall, and, while one tugged a rope that dangled from the ceiling, ringing a glad bell somewhere high above them, the other pushed wide the doors. First came the musicians, playing a merry tune. Behind them came acrobatic dancers leaping and tumbling and joyously whirling into the hall. Next entered the people, throngs of children skipping with anticipation and tugging at their laughing parents' hands. The old and the young, farmers and shopkeepers, clerks and charwomen, men with fine ladies at their arms, both the high and the humble, all came streaming in, chatting and joking and laughing. The young men of the town came, too, some eyeing the room in anticipation of their sweethearts, others with their clutches of schoolmates. All found their way to tables, many bowing and curtseying to Robby and Sheila as they passed. Robby looked eagerly at the crowds, watching for his friends, as the room filled with people and with the noise of good cheer that they brought with them. Then he saw Ibin within the press entering the door, his eyes wide with anticipation, a broad grin across his beaming face. Ullin's face appeared near to Ibin's, and Billy's between, bobbing up and down as he hopped on his tiptoes, craning to see over the two taller shoulders. At last Ashlord, too, came in, and he was the first to see Robby and Sheila across the room. After a time, they were all reunited at the table, talking about their sleigh rides and the fantastic speed with which they were fetched to town.

"No," said Ullin, "I cannot say we ever left the ground, but it was an uncommonly *smooth* ride."

"Yesyes. Stagspulledusalltheway!" Ibin said to Sheila.

"Please be seated," said a passing attendant as he pulled the chair out a bit more for Sheila. She thanked him, and her friends sat beside her and across the table from her.

"Never seen a table as long as this!" said Billy, "Much less a dozen or more in one room!"

"Must be a thousand people here," nodded Robby.

"And what a bewildering tree!" mused Ashlord, looking at its shimmering branches. "Can it possibly be made of glass? Or is it ice?"

"From one feast to another! What d'ye say to that, eh, Ibin?" Billy proclaimed across the table at his big companion. Already, Ibin had his napkin tucked under his chin and a look of surpassing joy on his face.

"Yeah, Billy, yeah, thisis, yeah, this, is, *wonderful!*"

"But I think this fare," Robby said to Ullin who sat next to him, "may be somehow heartier than what we had in the forest, more suiting to plain folk such as me."

"Plain folk?" Ullin smiled thoughtfully. "Do you still think of yourself as plain folk?"

Robby did not know what to say, somewhat taken aback by the question.

"I cannot escape my upbringing," he said at last. "And I don't wish to."

Ullin smiled and nodded, turning his attention to their host who was lightly tapping on his goblet with a fork. The musicians brought their tune to an end and silence came over the hall.

"Good people! Once again the year draws to its close, and once again we enjoy the bounty of our labors, the joys of fellowship, and the goodwill of good neighbors. Nowhere, I expect, can there be found such a land as this, plentiful of nature, at peace, and inhabited by a people so full of goodness and virtue. While no life may be without some strife or struggle, its burden has been less heavy here than upon your neighbors in the surrounding realms. For all these things and more, I know you to be thankful. For as long as memory, you have gathered at this time of year, on this night, in this hall, with your families and in the company of friends, to share joy and bounty with each other. Others likewise gather in their homes and shops throughout the land. And in this way all give thanks to the King of the Wood for his protection over these lands as tribute to his Sad Daughter. This night, above all other nights, we celebrate the renewed hope that she has expressed to us, that her hope might be kindled in the new year as the old one passes away, just as the world may from age to age be remade. So, as tokens of this blessed hope, let those who have need accept these boons, placed before you, and now revealed."

With a gesture of his hand, a sparkling thread of silver light curled from his palm and flew up and down the rows of tables. It passed between those seated, and a delicate chime could be heard coming from it. Tiny filaments of light fell from it to each place that was set as it streamed by, delivering to each person a small gaily-wrapped package. Some of these were in the form of tiny scrolls tied with golden thread, some were little pouches of fine velvet, and others were miniature boxes crafted with exquisite care of exotic woods with delicate little hinges. Soft exclamations of wonder went up from the people as their eyes sparkled with delight and anticipation. No less was the reaction of Robby's party as the gifts appeared before each of them, too, including Ashlord, whose wide-eyed look of surprise and pleasant astonishment was most uncharacteristic.

Then the silver thread, its trail fading as its head grew ever brighter, passed back to the dais and touched the topmost leader of the marvelous tree, where, all at once, a fantastic star burned white and blue. And the entire tree, from icy top to bottom, shivered with a grand tingling and glowed brilliantly in ever-changing hues of bright green and red and gold and blue, warming the great hall with its exuberant light.

"Joyous New Year!" the host proclaimed happily and was answered by cries of the same from all the people while, at that very moment, the attendants marched out carrying trays of dainty treats, candies and fruit, cakes and cookies, and nuts glazed with honey. Quivering dishes of flaming pudding were brought, kettles of steaming punch, and newly tapped kegs of beer. The musicians resumed a happy jig as the guests opened their gifts.

Robby watched as a gentleman nearby carefully undid the ribbon on a tiny scroll, and, with his elderly eyes nearly tearful with anticipation, he put his spectacles on.

"Let's see. It says here 'Great honor shall come to my name.' Now, whatever can that mean?"

"I'm sure I don't know, my dear," said his white-haired wife next to him as she tugged his elbow. "Listen to this: 'My lace will this year adorn a child of a child.' Why I haven't done lace in years. And we have no grandchild." A look of light came across her face, and she beamed as she turned and looked down the table at her daughter, presently holding the hand of a handsome young man. "Oh, my. I'd better get to work!"

Behind where Robby sat, he heard a child ask, "What does mine say, Mommy?"

"Why it says 'I will learn to read and to write.' "

"Oh! Then I am to go to school after all!"

" 'There will come peace into my household,' " read a swarthy man just down the way.

"What might this mean? 'A mighty lord shall give to me his oath, and it shall be kept.' "

All around, the people read wonderful and hopeful predictions, and by the looks and attitudes of all who did so, there was no indication that this year was any different from any other year before. It was apparent from their excitement that they had every confidence that these things would come true, as they always had before.

" 'My hands shall make my idle fiddle sing once again.' "

" 'A promise to me will be kept, though long forgotten.' "

" 'This year,' oh my, I dare not hope this can be! 'This year, my love shall return to me!' "

Such was the mystery and joy all around Robby and his company that they grinned and smiled as children, though they understood nothing of how all of this came to be.

"Will you not open your presents?" asked the lady next to Sheila. Sheila looked awkwardly at the little box before her and then at Ashlord. He shrugged, obviously as reluctant as she.

"I hardly think these can be for us," Sheila replied.

"How can they be?" Billy interjected. "We only just got here. Passin' through, like."

"And surely, we sit in the place of others whose right it is to be here," Robby added.

"Pish-posh and ridiculous!" the lady laughed, jabbing her stout companion next to her who laughed with her. "None sit at these tables nor enter these halls except those whose places are made ready for them."

"How can that be?"

"How can any of this be, if you put it that way?" said the elderly gentleman next to Robby with one of the kindest smiles he had ever seen. "But such is the goodness of our host, and the power of goodwill, that even the unexpected is taken in easy stride, and all fits as fitting should. Now, go ahead. Open your blessings, for they are given whether you read or not."

Robby reached for the little pouch before him.

"Very well."

Robby drew out a small tablet of stone on which was carved these words: "From over the White River you shall return."

"What does it mean?" he asked the gentleman next to him, showing him the tablet.

"Honestly, I cannot say! Where is the White River?"

"I haven't the foggiest notion. Perhaps it is on ahead in our travels? Ashlord, have you ever heard of the White River?"

"No-o. I can't say that I have ever heard of a river by that name."

"And what might this mean?" Sheila looked up from the little scroll that she unraveled with her fingers. " 'A familiar face shall be strange to thee, as a stranger's face shall familiar be."

"Or what about this?" Billy cleared his throat and read from his. " 'You shall speak before the mighty, and they shall heed.' "

"More riddles than blessings, if you ask me," Ullin commented without divulging what was on the scroll that he was in the process of rolling back up.

"Well, I know, I know what mine means!" said Ibin enthusiastically. He leaned across the table toward Robby. "Listen, listen: 'The great, the great-knot of, of your life shall be untied.' "

Robby blinked, expectantly, as Ibin grinned and looked around proudly at his companions. Seeing their confusion, he shook his head, but kept smiling.

"Ican't, Ican'texplainit," he said. "Butit'sagoodthing, Iknowitis!"

"What of yours, Ashlord?" Sheila asked.

Ashlord, smiling, looked up from a metal disc on which words were cast in an odd script.

"Oh, it is a nice sentiment," he said, slipping the disc into his vest pocket. "Probably intended for someone else. But a pleasant thought, nonetheless."

Before anyone could press Ashlord further, the gentleman next to Robby leaned over.

"Might I inquire whether you have made arrangements for your evening? That is, would you care to be guests in my house for the night?"

"Oh, well, we haven't decided where to stay," Robby replied. "I mean, surely there is an inn?"

"No. No inn. We don't get enough travelers for that. But my house is large, and I have many rooms with beds that would otherwise be empty tonight."

"Well, I don't know—"

"Oh, come now!" said the smiling woman next to the gentleman, leaning around to be heard. "Stay the night with us, and we'll see to it ye get a nice breakfast, too! It'd be a great honor to us."

"Let us not press them too much, sweetie," the man said quietly to the woman, "for they may be wary of offers from strangers such as us."

"Oh, pardon my hesitation," Robby put in. "It's just that we will likely be on our way very early."

"I doubt that," the gentleman said. "Unless the snowfall eases, it'll be halfway to my knee by morning, and that'll make travel difficult. My name is Stavin. Garnor Stavin, and this lady here is my wife, Dorcilla. I have been a cobbler by trade for many years, but my shoes do not wear out fast enough for a good living, so I also make belts and hats and gloves and harnesses and whatever needs making of leather or thick cloth. I've done rather well, altogether, haven't I, Dory? And so I have a great big house over the shops and workrooms."

"Mr. Stavin, Mrs. Stavin, how do you do? My name is Robby Ribbon, and I am a store clerk by trade. I am please to make your acquaintance."

Stavin and Robby shook hands and bowed heads to one another just as the musicians struck up a loud and rousing tune. Everyone rose and pushed back the tables, opening a broad floor that was quickly filled with dancers.

"I will pass along your generous offer to my companions," Robby nearly had to shout to be heard over the raucous stamping of feet and calling and clapping. "And you will have our answer soon. Thank you very much!"

"Very well!" Stavin called back to Robby as his wife merrily dragged him by the arm out to the dance floor where they were soon lost among the other jumping, hopping, and jigging couples. While all who wished to do so danced, others sat or stood to lean against the tables, and many clapped their hands to the music as they watched the dancers. When Robby turned back to his company, he saw that Ullin was bowing to a young lady and gracefully taking her arm to the floor. Ibin was nowhere to be seen, until his head appeared on the far side of the room bobbing up and down and with a grin that beamed down upon a partner too short to be seen in the crowd. Sheila was shaking her head at a young man who offered his hand, and likewise Ashlord to a lady. But they both gave in and joined the others on the floor. Only Robby and Billy remained, looking at each other and at the others who cheered on the dancers. They each saw unaccompanied girls, on opposite sides of the room, and, nodding to each other, Billy and Robby parted to ask their hands. With only a minimum of coaxing, each had a pretty partner, whirling into the joyful crowd.

There was no reason Robby and his company should have felt so gay and carefree. Yet, even though their thoughts were never too far from the trials of their quest, they were happy enough for now to dance and clap to the music, to laugh with each other and with the many other guests of the banquet. Strangely, they felt accepted, and there was something so genuine about the way the people greeted and joked and chatted and talked that none of the travelers had any doubt that this was how they always were with each other. It was as if these people had some bond of survival, some ordeal they had all shared in, one that had made them ever thankful and appreciative of their friends and families and of their modest but fortunate land. Sheila wondered that none of the men she danced with, young and old, made any forward remark or gesture, nor did they treat her with anything but respect and courtesy without pretension. She first thought that it was because she arrived with Robby on the sleigh of the host, and that the mysterious patron's canopy of influence gave her and her friends some kind of status with these folk. But she gave up that notion upon further observation of their behavior, and after listening to and partaking in many conversations. Instead, she came to realize that these people wanted nothing of them, needed nothing from them, were not afraid, and had no qualms with sharing their goodwill and habitual courtesy with strangers, just as they did with each other. They were, in short, a happy people, in spite of the melancholy smile that sometimes crept across their lips. Her conclusion, unspoken, was the same that each of her travel companions came to, each in his own way from his own interactions and observations. And it took none of them very long to arrive at the same end, as some of the joy and peace of these people came into their own hearts and served to lift their spirits and increase their wonder.

After a while of dancing and carrying on, the six companions found themselves back together at the table for another round of treats and meats, beer and cake. Mr. Stavin and his plump wife stumbled giddily out of the dancing circle and sat nearby to Robby, panting and laughing so hard that their cheeks were red with their happy exertions. When they had caught their breath somewhat, Robby leaned nearer.

"Tell me, who is he?" he asked Mr. Stavin.

"He? He who?"

"Him. Our host."

"Oh! Have you never met him before, or had the pleasure of his company?"

"No. I can't say that I have."

"Do you not have joyful celebrations where you are from? To well-wish the passing year, perhaps, and to greet the new?"

"Why, yes. Indeed, we do! But he has never, as far as I know, graced our festivals with his presence."

"Oh, ho! Well, I doubt that somewhat. It is said that whenever there is goodwill and good cheer, he is there, too."

"I don't see how we could have missed seeing him. And, anyway, it is hardly possible to be at all of the celebrations that happen this time of year."

"You don't think so, eh? Perhaps he is not looked for in other places, as he is here, and therefore is not seen. But that is no reason to suppose he is not there!"

"Perhaps," Robby nodded. "But what is he called?"

"We know him as Uncle Solstice. That is because he is as a good uncle to us and comes this time each winter to feast with us and again with the coming of each Midsummer, though his spirit is with us all the year long."

"I see." Robby watched as various ladies and men approached Uncle Solstice, some with children, speaking with him briefly. Then, with bows and curtseys, they made way for the next in line. "He has the appearance of a king or lord, I must say."

"Well, he is, in a manner of saying. But there is little need for him to judge or to rule or do most things that the kings of other lands must do. We get along most admirably, if I may say so, and there are few disputes that goodwill cannot resolve. And his kin do not permit troublemakers to enter our lands, though good-hearted travelers, such as yourselves, are never turned away."

"But you and your people may come and go as you please from these lands?"

"Oh, yes, we may. I, myself, have been to Vanara and even to Duinnor. That was long ago, when I was young and adventurous. Many have left Greenfar, and it is a source of some sadness to see someone go, for many never return, some that are ever after missed."

"And Uncle Solstice is your protector? He guards these lands?"

"We view him so, yes, but his brother and his niece do as much or more than he, for their forest surrounds us almost entirely."

"The Lady Islindia, you mean?"

"That is her name. She is called Queen of that wood, though she is more as a princess, for her father holds sway there. And he," Stavin gestured at Uncle Solstice, "is his brother."

• • •

Ashlord, who had danced with uncharacteristic abandon with partner after partner, sat nearby. He turned his chair around with its back against the table, as many others had done, so he could watch the festivities more easily. And, as Robby looked over, he saw that Ashlord had at some point acquired a toddler whom he bounced on his knees, spreading them apart as if to make the little boy fall but catching him each time, sending the child into hysterics of laughter with each drop.

"So you travel westward," asked the gentleman standing next to Ashlord and to whom the grandchild belonged. He had already made his introductions to Ashlord, Byrn Tallock, tradesman and town clerk. He had also owned up that the precocious little ones who pulled on every pant-leg as they crawled back and forth under the table, as well as the one who unabashedly climbed upon Ashlord's knee, were his granddaughters and grandson.

"Yes, we make our way west as best as we may," Ashlord answered over the shrill screams of the red-faced child. He pulled a handkerchief out of the ear of one child with his left hand, while causing another little girl's eyes to bulge as a walnut disappeared from his right hand. He revealed the walnut within the folds of the handkerchief and handed it to the child in his lap. This was too much, and the little one simply collapsed in uncontrollable fits of laughter, holding up the walnut like a prize and nearly tumbling off Ashlord's knee onto the floor.

"Your slight of hand is most impressive," said Byrn.

"Just a little something I picked up."

"Very entertaining. Now, now, children! Give the gent'man a rest! Here, here, run off yonder for a moment and show your Nana your walnut. I suppose you'd like to continue when the snow lifts, but surely you'd want a place to stay until then."

"Yes, we mean to move on as soon as possible. But I believe arrangements have already been made for us."

"You'd be mighty welcome at our place, too," said a rotund woman who leaned over from behind Byrn. "An' I set a fine breakfast!"

"Well, I think the Stavins have already spoken for us."

"Oh, have they?" Mrs. Byrn turned in her chair, looking around. "Where is she? Oh, there! Yoohoo! Dory! Dorcilla Stavin! Do you mean to put up all these guests at your place?"

While the two ladies negotiated their roles in regard to the visitors, Sheila, at the far end of the group, had been introduced to another lady sitting next to her, somewhat shy, who wore a red bonnet tied underneath her chin with a green ribbon, and who was looking at Sheila over a pair of square spectacles. She had a round, simple face, but not without a touch of loveliness, and though she smiled and grinned, she was quite reserved, with a perpetual look of embarrassment about her.

"You have come far from your home, then," Miss Applewait was saying to Sheila. "Surely it has been a difficult thing for you, being such a lady and the only one among your companions?"

"No more difficult for me than for any of us," Sheila replied.

"But it must get lonesome. So far from the company of other ladies, I mean."

"Well, I'm not sure I am what you should call a lady," Sheila explained. "And I've never had much in the way of friends, other than those here, and maybe just a few others."

She felt a little pang when she remembered, and missed, how Mirabella had treated her when she stayed in Passdale, how Frizella had taken care of her, and how Mr. Ribbon was so gentle with her when he gave her the proceeds from her uncle's estate. Her hand went absently to the little book in her pocket which had not left her possession—not even in battle—ever since Mr. Broadweed had given it to her, and she thought of him now with inexplicable tenderness. All these thoughts and emotions touched her so deeply and with such sweetness that her eyes misted suddenly. She looked away from Miss Applewait, smiling at the dancers who passed close by.

"Forgive my silly questions," Miss Applewait apologized, her cheeks red with a new blush of embarrassment. "I am very awkward in my ways, I know."

"Oh, no, do not trouble yourself. There is nothing to be sorry about. I suppose I do rather miss my home. I never imagined I'd say that. But I do. And I wish we could all be back there, safe and together with our families and our friends. Why I had to come all this way to realize that, well! But I have seen wondrous things, met wonderful and interesting people. And, I'm sure, there is more yet to see, and more to meet. Just like you!"

"Oh, bless me!" Miss Applewait put her hand to her collar and giggled sweetly. "You are too kind!"

An attendant offered a refill of their punch glasses, which they both accepted as it was exceedingly delicious. They sipped, and Miss Applewait giggled even more and was about to say something when a pair of young men appeared before them.

"Joy to you, Miss Applewait!" said one, a somewhat swarthy fellow, with curly brown hair that fell across his shoulders. He bowed as he greeted her.

"Joy, sister," said the other young gentleman who seemed no older than Sheila and was wearing the same awkward expression as Miss Applewait.

"Joy, brother. And joy to you, Mr. Bywaters," Miss Applewait replied, so positively crimson with shyness that her entire countenance screamed of her thrill to be addressed by this particular gentleman. Regaining her composure, she slowly took back her hand and shook herself.

"Oh, my word, I forget myself. Let me introduce you to Miss Sheila, of the Eastlands Realm. This is Mr. Bywaters. Oh, and that is my brother, Harrald."

"I am delighted to make your acquaintance, ma'am." Mr. Bywaters bowed, as did Harrald, saying, "Pleased to meet you."

"A fantastic party, wouldn't you say? Why I think it almost beats all before!" Mr. Bywaters declared, nodding. "However, if I may be so bold, only one thing is lacking to make it the best ever of all."

"Why, what could that be?" Miss Applewait asked with a sudden look of desperate confusion at the thought of anything amiss. She looked around quickly, distressed to think that she had missed something that was perfectly obvious to everyone else. "I am quite sure it could not possibly be any grander, any finer, any more delightful than it already is!"

"Well, one thing only is needed. And that is for you to take my hand and permit me the honor of this reel!"

Miss Applewait, after a brief fit of shaking, and nearly spilling her punch, shot to her feet, shoved her cup at Sheila, and then demurely offered her hand to Mr. Bywater. As Mr. Bywater led her away, she glanced back at Sheila with a giggle.

Sheila put Miss Applewait's cup on the table, and drank her own punch while Harrald nervously hovered nearby. They watched the expert and graceful steps of Mr. Bywaters and Miss Applewait, who was now transformed by the dance, her veil of nervous shyness having fallen away to reveal a dazzling, spirited, and exuberant partner for the handsome and strong young man. They were, as was obvious to all, a natural and beautiful match. Sheila took a gulp, glancing over the rim of her cup at Robby.

• • •

Ashlord, now relieved of his audience of toddlers, and taking advantage of a lull in his conversation with Byrn, stood up and made his way to Uncle Solstice, smiling and bowing to those he passed. The enigmatic figure was just concluding a chat with a young girl, who curtseyed and moved away, and he smiled at Ashlord.

"I hope the festivities are to your liking."

"Indeed, sir," Ashlord bowed. "I and my companions have not been so well entertained and dined in a very long time, if ever so well at all. I thank you!"

"You and your companions are most welcome, and may the joy of this evening carry forward within each of you!"

"That is kind of you."

"You have questions, I imagine?"

"I do. But it is hardly fitting for a guest so warmly treated as I to burden his host with them."

"Yet that is what I do. I take the burden, such as I may, from all who join me here. I spread it out, so that the many may carry the weight of it with the fellowship of their hearts. Some come to me with their concerns and to express their wishes, as you have seen them come. Most others keep their worries to themselves. But don't you think that good company, in and of itself, often lifts the spirit? And that a joining of joy and thankfulness, one with another, from person to person, gives to all a strength made of hope?"

"I do! I certainly do!"

"And so it is that I am here. What more do you need to know of me?"

"Nothing, in need. But I am curious. It is in my nature to be so. For example, I am given to understand that you come here twice each year, in winter and again in springtime. But where do you abide for all of the rest of the year?"

"Where? Why, wherever there is goodwill and kindness among people. I seek it out, and I never have to look for very long! Indeed, I never fail to find it. Wherever I go I find love and joy and charity and hope and gladness, in great or small amounts. Some in these parts say that I bring such things when I come, but that is not so. Ho! Ha! Ha! No, that is not so at all, for those things are already here in abundance!"

"Then you travel widely?"

"I do! No place is barred to me where there is love."

"Are you then one of the Faerekind?"

"Faerekind? Oh, well, yes I am, or once was, that is. Indeed, I was amongst the Fallen Ones who were first in the world. Ah! I see by your look that you wonder at my attitude; why is it that I, of all my brothers and sisters who had wings, do not act sullen and forlorn? Do I not remember, you may wonder, the marvels of the Time Before Time, when my kind rode the air like the effortless cloud? When all things spoke one tongue, one kind to another, and we heard the whispers of the grass and trees and the grumble of stone and the laughter of the stream? Yes, I do remember, and remember well. But I am blessed with those memories, not cursed by them as many of my fellows. And I do not resent the taking of my wings or the scars upon my back because I elected to stay, I and my brother of the forest. It was a gift to me, for I love the creatures of the earth and all that abide in it. Yes, all! And I still rejoice in the greatness of Beras and his many manifestations. I do not war against the plight of the world, nor do I strive to change it. That is not my place. If I do anything, it is simply to help people see in each other what I see in them. So I am allowed to remain, and I was given over to this form, likened unto Men who grow whiskers and beards, to mark me different from my fellows."

Ashlord smiled and nodded, but obviously wanted more.

"My answer does not satisfy you?" Solstice chuckled. "I speak in riddles, eh? But I ask you: Did you not just come from seeing the marvels of Forest Islindia? Am I any more a wonder than what you beheld there? You, a Melnari, should be accustomed to such. Is not your companion, the little Familiar who now darts about the hall, such a wonder? The fabric of this world is such that these things may be. And other marvels, besides. Compared to those, I am but a mundane thing."

"But you have the gift of Sight, do you not? The ability to reveal things to others about the future?"

"That is because I pay attention, just as you do. However, my attention is given to other things than those that fill your concerns. Some of my kind are overburdened with memory, but memory is not a burden to me. Others of my kind fear the future and disdain the fellowship of Men. But not I!" He waved his hand in a sweeping motion to indicate the happy gathering. "I rejoice in hope, and I take joy of the goodwill that any person shares with any other. Though I am one of the Fallen, I have been blessed with a marvelous change. So much blessed, that when my kind are once again called away, it is my faith that I, or something of my spirit, shall remain in the world."

Solstice tilted his head and smiled, sensing that Ashlord was still not entirely satisfied.

"Do you know why your kind are called Melnari?"

Ashlord's eyebrows shot up. He had actually never thought about it, and he shook his head.

"In the Time Before Time, when the spirits that sprang from Beras came forth into the world, some lingered on the edge of this existence, not wholly in the world, but not remaining fully in that which was before. When the Sundering came, and the great Scathing, and Aperion's host left the earth, those that were not fully come into this world were stranded in their half-formed existence. But then came others, a few others, who helped them and so were called Helpers, or Melnar by those who spoke the First Tongue. Like midwives, the Melnar were, and are. And your name, Collandoth, means "out of the ashes." Surely you have become that name, have you not? A Watcher, you have been, but now you are truly a helper, a midwife, and you are to aid the birth of something new from the ruin of something old."

● ● ●

Solstice eyed Ashlord serenely as his mind floated off in thought. The secrets and mysteries of the Melnari, Ashlord knew, were many, and no one knew them all, not even Ashlord. Yet Solstice seemed to have some knowledge that was beyond Ashlord's comprehension. However, the mystery of how Ashlord's rare kind come into the world, fully grown and ready to take part in it, was not something he, Ashlord, pondered very much. Each is given his own instructions, such as they may be, from Beras himself, just as they are given their own time in history to carry out those instructions. Yet, each must find his own way, just as anyone and everyone, and so each is given his own peculiar abilities, to be used, developed, and refined according to his own personality. Over time a Melnari might encounter others of his own kind, and might even form alliances and collaborations, though some Melnari are more reclusive than others. Ashlord had only met two others of his own kind, Raynor, who still lived, and Istorgus, who had taught Ashlord so much but was lost at sea long ago. Ashlord knew that there had been at least three others, but he really had no idea how many Melnari had come into the world. Surely only a very few.

In but a brief moment, Ashlord's mind reviewed all of this, along with his memory and his suppositions. In light of what Solstice had just said, it all made a new kind of sense. For the first time since his ordeal with the demon, Valkose, Ashlord felt some confirmation, some satisfaction, that he really did have a role to play in things. He shook himself, realizing that he had been staring at the hypnotic tree.

"And you have someone in your company," Solstice said with a smile and looking past Ashlord, "whom you have guided and counseled, one whose destiny may very well bring about the fulfillment of your own, and much else besides."

Ashlord turned his head and saw Sheila and Robby moving together to the dance floor. Certina landed on Ashlord's shoulder.

"And you may also find," Solstice continued, nodding to Certina, "that being a helpmate and soulmate is a way of passing along those qualities to another, giving birth, as it were, to more than you may imagine."

Solstice's smile broadened, and his eyes glittered with an almost mischievous happiness. Ashlord, somewhat overwhelmed at the confirmation of his purpose, his faith, was stirred to the core with profound happiness. He wanted to give thanks, but his voice cracked and his eyes misted over with emotion. He nodded and bowed, backing away as he would only do to a true sovereign, and took again his seat among his friends.

• • •

"The last time we danced, we were interrupted," Sheila said to Robby as they circled the floor, just one pair within a pinwheel of partners.

"That seems so long ago," Robby replied, guiding Sheila away from collision with another couple. The dancers, boisterous all, and all fairly aglow with wine and punch and beer, cared less for the form of the dance than for the fun of the dancing itself, and so there were many jolts, jabs, stumbles and bumps. But all were in good and high spirits, and none took the jostling without appropriate bows and pardons and a fair amount of laughter. Already, since the reel began, several giddy couples had been so overtaken with fits of laughing that they could do nothing but stumble out of the way until their mirth subsided.

"You still wear the neck-piece I gave you." Robby nodded to Sheila's throat as she turned around him, first to one side, then, as they changed hands, to the other.

"I have only removed it once since you put it there. Back in Edgewold to rinse the blood from it."

Robby wondered at this. He knew her dreams—some of them, anyway—and knew that he was not the only man in her heart. Glancing over at Ullin, who sat alone a few chairs away, he nodded again. It struck Robby as incongruous, how this neckband that Sheila wore came to be about her neck, possibly touched by Bailorg's own hand, and how she wore it all the while since, through chase and battle, from Passdale to here. Was she afraid that if she took it off he would think less of her? That he would have some clue about her feelings for Ullin? He wished he could tell her that he knew more from her dreams than she could ever tell. Yes, he knew she dreamed of Ullin, even longed for him in the most private ways. But Robby also knew that when she dreamed of homey places and warm hearths and deep happiness, which she sometimes did, it was in the company of a store clerk and not a Kingsman.

"You don't have to wear it all the time," he said. "Aren't you afraid it might break?"

"It has held up pretty well, so far," she replied, taking his hand. "Don't you think?"

"Better than one would expect, I'd say," he answered, squeezing her hand gently.

Just then, Billy and his dance partner—a very large girl of a size perhaps more befitting Ibin than the spindly Boskman—stomped past Robby and Sheila, Billy's knees kicking high in exaggerated steps, looking more like a spider than anything else—that is to say, in his normal way of dancing. But he grinned from ear to ear while his looming dance partner laughed shrilly with her head tossed back as they careened by.

"Goodness!" cried Sheila, barely able to contain herself.

"What was that?" laughed Robby.

Ibin was not lacking in partners, either. At the moment, in fact, he had two, for while he made delicate steps with a very young girl who stood with her toes on his big feet, her even smaller brother clung to his back, dangling with his arms around Ibin's thick neck. Ibin held both of the girl's hands in one of his while his other hand was occupied behind his back holding up the bottom of her little brother who shrieked deafening laughter directly into Ibin's ear.

As for Ullin, who had danced once or twice most elegantly, he now declined any further hints of availability. Instead, he watched, his eyes going from person to person as if looking for something, or perhaps just observing both the festivities at large and also all the little pockets of celebration that crowded the hall. He sat by himself, comfortably leaning with his back against the table and with one arm and elbow upon it, holding in one hand a tankard from which he seldom drank. His foot tapped to the music and his other hand, still holding the tiny scroll—which was no bigger than his little finger—tapped his knee. By holding the scroll just so against his knee, he could unroll it with only that hand to look once again at the writing there.

" 'Out of unfounded grief, a longed-for reunion shall come,' " he read again, as he had done seven times already. He turned his eyes once again to the dancers, letting the scroll curl back up in his hand.

• • •

They slept well. Even Ashlord seemed to find peace and restful meditation, as comfortable in the old stuffed chair by the fireplace as the others were in their snug blanket-layered and pillow-piled beds. The party had ended some while after midnight, when Uncle Solstice drew his weight up from the chair and stood. Being the first to leave, he took his time, bidding adieu and joyous year to all and to each, shaking hands, giving hugs, and patting shoulders as he moved through the hall. At last, having had at least a word or two for each person present, he made his way onto his waiting sleigh. Laughing and calling out to his proud team, each member by name, he fairly flew away, jingling into the snowy silence of the winter night. Robby and his companions lingered a bit longer, until Mr. Stavin came to lead them to his house. There, he gave them hot sweet drinks to sip before the roaring fire of his great room. And while they did that, his wife and he, along with a few others of the town who insisted on coming along to help, made ready the rooms. They stoked up the hearths in each one, laid out fresh linens and blankets, filled basins of hot water, and put new candles in every candlestick in every room.

Downstairs in the great room, none were too anxious for sleep, and they talked excitedly about the evening, the wondrous Uncle Solstice, the splendid music, the mysterious gifts, and, as Ibin pointed out again and again, the very good food. But the hot drinks and the warm fire settled them down, and they were all taken upstairs to their rooms, all except Ashlord, of course, who desired only a chair and his pipe, much to the bafflement of his hosts. So while he abided the night in his own way, his companions and all those of the house, and indeed of the entire town and countryside, slept well and peacefully, with smiles as their last expressions before slumber reached them and even somewhat afterwards. Even Robby, who remained solitary in his dreams, felt inexplicably contented.

Ullin also smiled as he slumbered. His dream was filled with happy anticipation as he rode Anerath across a sparkling stream on his way to see someone who would—in this dream at least—be equally happy to see him. And, as he reached midway through the sun-glistened waters, there she stood, on the far bank, smiling. Somehow, he knew that it was only a dream, and no matter how far into the stream Anerath took him, it seemed just as far as ever to the far bank where she stood. The dream dissipated. He woke briefly, then fell peacefully asleep once more. It was only a dream. But that did not seem to matter to Ullin. She was there, somewhere, on the other side, waiting for him.

• • •

When morning came, they roused themselves early to a big breakfast, laid out by their hosts, while through the window at the end of the dining room, they could see that it was no longer snowing, though still overcast. They talked cordially with each other and their hosts, who ate with them, about crops and farming, good places to fish, about shopkeeping, and about the customs of this land of Greenfar. Already, Mrs. Stavin told them, folks were looking forward to the winter games that would be held in a month and, after that, to all the parties that would come with springtime. At this, the guests became somewhat quiet, except for Ibin who was most interested in the parties. None of the hosts had asked what serious business took them so far from home, and none of the guests volunteered any news of the terrible and dark days that had come upon the world. But their hosts, kind as ever, sensed a cloud over them, or the occasional moment of worry that briefly distracted them from conversation.

"I have it from one of the old men of our town," said Mr. Stavin, "that it will be a damp next few weeks. And likely, he says, that there will be sleet before snow comes again. He knows such things and is rarely in error. Would any of you be interested in outfitting yourselves with new cloaks or shoes, more fit for traveling in such weather?"

The company looked at each other, shrugging.

"We could all do with better boots," said Ashlord.

"And I could do with a less tattered cloak," Robby nodded. "But we are somewhat limited in coin."

"Well, money is no object," said Stavin. "In fact, I have it from Mr. Shannon, the clothier whose shop is just down the way, and from others, too, that there is a desire to contribute to your quest, er, travels. I share in that sentiment completely, and so my shoe shop is open to you without price."

"Well, the offer's mighty kind," Billy responded. "But why don't we have a look at things, first. Could be, we've enough silver for what we might need."

"We'll see. At any rate, take your time, and get good and ready before departing. You've got rooms here for as long as you'd care to grace us with your company."

Ullin wiped his mouth with a napkin and looked around at the others. "I believe we'll be on our way as soon as we can. Later this morning, perhaps. Or early afternoon."

"It was a marvelous evening," Sheila said, rising and turning to the hosts and giving a bow and curtsey. "A comfortable night and a splendid breakfast. We are all very thankful to you."

This was seconded by the others as they stood, too, and bowed.

"Oh, not at all, my dear!" Mrs. Stavin rose and gave Sheila a hug. "You are very welcome, indeed!"

Mr. Stavin then led them down the hall, through a door, and down a few steps into his shop. It was lined with racks and racks of shoes, some labeled with the names of particular customers. Off to the side of the shop and behind a counter was another area of workbenches, shoe saddles, stacks of leather, and all of the tools of a cobbler's trade.

"The shop is idle today and all my apprentices are away for the holiday. But please look around and see what you'd like. Take your time. Here, Mr. Bosk, these look about your size. They are very sturdy and warm, I assure you."

After but a little longer, they all, in fact, had new boots with good soles and lined with warm shearling. And with every pair, each of them received four pairs of stockings, two of soft cotton and two of thick wool.

"Good boots deserve good stockings," Mr. Stavin said. "I have these from Mr. Shannon's store by special arrangement. And that is who we should go see now, since I believe he is expecting us."

So, Mr. Stavin led the way, and they trudged through the high snow and down the street to the clothier's place. There, after Mr. Shannon briefly sized them up, they soon found coats and cloaks and fur-lined caps. And, like Mr. Stavin, the clothier staunchly refused any talk of payment.

"It is a tradition with us," he said. "Perhaps you do not know? But any who pass through our town during this time of year are given whatever is required for their journey. Food, clothing, whatever we have that is needed. Few come this way, and fewer still in winter, so it is not a burden to us. Indeed, it is our proud pleasure!"

"You were guided here by those who extend their protection around our lands," Mr. Stavin continued. "And besides, local legend has it that, generations ago, a beggar who was sick, cold, and weak with hunger, passed this way. He was taken in and treated kindly by our ancestors, healed of his illness and fatigue, and clothed for his continued journey. He never spoke a word while he was here until the day he made his departure. Then, as the story goes, he said, 'Other strangers will come and pass through your lands. Treat them with the same kindness and charity as you have treated me, and your lands shall prosper, your people shall thus be happy in their goodness, and the shelter the forest gives you shall be preserved. Verily, one shall someday come, and though he shall not be known to you, he shall become your King, and he shall remember you.' "

Had Mr. Shannon dropped one of the pins from his sleeve, his customers would have heard it strike the floor. Fortunately, before the company's gobsmacked reaction could be discerned, two large sleighs pulled up outside. Rankin hopped down from the lead one and came into the shop.

"Happy New Year to all!" he declared, doffing his cap and bowing.

"And joy to you, Rankin!" Stavin returned.

"I and others come in our sleighs to offer conveyance to your company to the edge of Greenfar lands, if you would accept the offer," he said to Robby and the others.

"That would be most welcome, I'm sure," Robby replied. "But we left our bags at Mr. Stavin's place."

"Then, whenever you are ready, so are we!"

By the time they returned to the cobbler's home, his wife and her neighbors had prepared a second breakfast on the sideboard as well as a bag of lunch, "Suitable for travel," she said, "in keepin' with the situation."

• • •

It was not long before they were gliding away from town on the smooth rails of two sleighs, with two of Rankin's colleagues up front in one, and Rankin and a driver guiding the other. Though still overcast, it was a beautiful and peaceful ride, the jingle of the sleigh bells, the light whoosh of the rails underneath, and the rhythmic and easy stride of the buckmarls giving the passengers under their blankets a sense of calm. They passed through forest and field and over stone bridges and even a frozen pond, and never was a word spoken between any of the group. After what seemed like only minutes, but was more than three hours, they passed through a dense forest, and then abruptly entered a rather flat open plain, sparse of trees, about a mile wide and several long. In a while, they could discern hills rising before them, and the sleighs slowed as they neared the foot of them. The snow here was thinner, and the ride sometimes bumpy until they came to a narrow wooden footbridge that crossed a stream, where they stopped. Rankin hopped down, and they understood that this was the end of their ride. The drivers helped them unload and don their packs, and Rankin turned to them.

"This is as far as we may take you," he said. "Those hills beyond the stream mark the bounds of Greenfar and the outlands of Vanara. Beyond the hills is a wood and then a lake. If you keep to this path, you will come to a ferryman who will take you across the lake and into the domain of Hemlock. There is a village on the other side of the lake. My master begs you to be cautious of all you may encounter. They are a sullen people and do not trust strangers, but they should not hinder your passage if you treat them with care. They have little to do with the world and are sundered from the rest of Vanara, so do not expect much of them. Safe journey to you!"

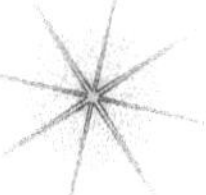

Chapter 16

Across the Haunted Lake

Day 137
108 Days Remaining

Rankin and the other sleighmen made sure the company crossed the ice-crusted footbridge safely, then made their goodbyes by waving before sliding away on their sleighs and out of sight. Across the stream, the path moved upward, cutting back and forth across and between a ridge of hills, then up and across a higher ridge. The land was rocky and sparsely treed, and snow drifted in some places across the nearly indiscernible path. From the ridge, they could see ahead of them a dense forest of pine spreading westward into mist and cloud. When they descended into the trees, the sky darkened even more, and before long a light drizzle mixed with sleet was falling through the needles overhead. But the path was not too muddy and was easy to follow, with only gradual climbs and descents. Moving farther away from Greenfar and deeper into the forest, they all felt as if they were waking up from a long and marvelous dream, and they struggled to settle their minds into the humdrum routine of travel. But the spirit of what they had seen and done over the past few days was still in their hearts, and perhaps would never leave. So it was with a sense of comfort, not melancholia, that they marched on toward the unknown end of their journey.

If only the weather was as comforting to them as their thoughts. As the day progressed, the drizzle changed completely to sleet with pellets clicking steady and hypnotic. Late in the afternoon, just when the icy path was becoming crunchy under their feet, it began to rain once again. At first it was a very hard and very cold rain, with gusts of wind that shook the pines loose of their rime. Pulling up their hoods, they bore on with many sighs, but they spoke little until they topped a rise and saw through the trunks the silver sheen of water some distance ahead, just as the rain eased to a light sprinkle.

"Well, thar's the lake," Billy said. "So we can't be too far off from the village."

They continued on, but it seemed that the path took them no closer to the lake. And soon, with the sun lowering behind the dense clouds, and with patches of fog and mist rising through the forest, it was far too gloomy to catch any sight of the lake or any village. When night came black and cold, it was still raining, but in fits, and they could not tell whether they were any closer to the lake than before, or any closer to the ferryman's place that Rankin had mentioned. They moved along very carefully, all their eyes keen to stay on the path. By now they were soaked and miserable, and their fondest thoughts could not distract them from the cold they felt or the wet shivers that ran up their arms.

"Look there," Ullin's voice came from ahead. "I think I see a glimmer of light."

He pointed downhill, and as they huddled around him they could see the lake below, not fifty yards away. Through the trees was the clear sign of a cottage with dim yellow light cracking through closed shutters.

"Finally!" Billy exclaimed.

"I don't think I've ever longed so much for a warm and dry place," added Sheila.

"Well, let's hope we get across the lake quickly, and on into town to find our lodging for the night," Robby put in as they made their way down the slope to the landing. Soon enough they splashed through the muddy yard, and Ullin banged on the door.

"Hullo! Ferryman?" he called.

"Aye? What d'ye want?"

"Are you the ferryman?"

The door opened, almost blinding them in the process as the light from within poured out, and a grizzled old man stood with one hand on his door and the other holding a cudgel.

"Aye, I'm the ferryman," he said gruffly. "I take it ye seek passage across? The lot of ye?"

"We do."

"Well, it's dark. Ye must wait 'til mornin'," he stated flatly, then made to close the door, but Ullin put his foot in to prevent it. The man instantly raised his weapon, but Ullin held his hands up in supplication.

"Can you at least give us shelter, some lodging that is dry?"

"No!"

"Then we must cross to find some place to stay the night."

"Where ye stay the night is no concern of mine. I do not cross the lake at night, as any from these parts will tell ye."

"We will pay you well," Robby said.

"With what?"

"Silver. Gold!"

"An' where d'ye expect I'd spend it? Eh? I have no use for coin."

"What, then, is your usual fee?"

"I have no fee. I am bound to give passage to any an' all that ask. But it is for me and me alone to say when to cross. An' I don't cross at night!"

"Then may we pull ourselves across?"

"Ye may not! That would be thievery, for who would pull the barge back? That is, if ye even made it halfway. Kindly remove yer foot from me threshold, sir, or have yer brains join it there!"

Ullin complied, but Ashlord leaned in and spoke, removing his hood so that the man's angry glare at Ullin would be attracted to his own eyes.

"Sir," Ashlord then said, calmly and deliberately, "we are visitors to this land, and we are weary and cold. We seek shelter across yon lake in the town there. Will you not take us across? Take us to find lodgings for the night?"

"I..." the man blinked, "perhaps I.... No,...I cannot. Dark. It is dark, no! An' no more of yer tricks! Begone!"

He slammed the door.

"Can't you try again?" Robby asked. "He seemed to hesitate before he refused."

"No, Robby. He seems determined to resist. I can but encourage him toward what he is already inclined to do. And, apparently, laboring at night is not the thing for him."

"Well, I hope he's got a dang good reason for not venturin' out!" said Billy. "I say we take the barge anyhow, without his say so!"

"No, that would not be right, and you know it," said Ullin as they walked away, looking for any kind of shelter, for now it was raining hard again, with bits of sleet mixed in. Through the rain, they could make out a few dim lights of the village across and some distance beyond the far lakeshore.

"Anyway," Ashlord added, "we do not want to antagonize the inhabitants of these parts. Remember what Rankin said to us."

"Have you ever had any dealings with these people?" Robby asked, pointing at a shed near the shoreline.

"No, though I am somewhat acquainted with someone from near here, I believe. But he lives in Glareth, now."

The shed was an open three-sided affair, made of stone with a plank roof that had seen better days. But it was empty except for a few rotting oars, old bits of harness, and lengths of rope hanging here and there within. They quickly tried to squeeze themselves under its cover.

"This ain't gonna work," Billy commented as they backed into one another.

"Well, I'll take the first watch," said Ullin, putting his pack against the wall and pulling his hood over his head. Before anyone could argue, he stepped out into the blowing rain. His absence made only a little more room.

"I suggest the four of you try to sleep," Ashlord said. "I'll keep Ullin company."

"Don't this just beat all for inhospitable treatment!" Billy complained, slumping down between Ibin and Sheila, who had already made themselves a place against the driest wall. Robby remained standing, looking at the ferryman's house, dimly visible in the rain. He abruptly turned and made himself a place beside Sheila, saying, "I must go to sleep!"

She thought his tone of voice odd. She pondered on the many other odd things Robby had said and done over the past few weeks as she put her head on his shoulder. The rain came down all the harder, and the sound of it served to lull her and her huddled companions to the place that Robby sought. Outside, Ullin and Ashlord leaned against the tallest wall of the shed, somewhat protected from the brunt of the rain, and they spoke in low tones.

"You never speak much about your last trip into the badlands and beyond," Ashlord commented. Ullin shrugged mildly and shook his head.

"That was a long time ago. And it seems to have little to do with anything," he replied. "Why do you ask of it now? If that is what you are doing."

Certina pushed her way around Ashlord's neck and edged out from under his hood as if to listen without getting too wet.

"You have seen Robby's ring," Ashlord stated.

"Yes."

"He showed it to me. It is of a most unusual sort. One of a kind, I do believe. He said you might know something of its origin."

The rain now became fitful with gusts of wind, as if the night did not know whether to rain, or whether to blow, so doing a bit of each.

"I know its history," Ullin said.

"And you know, too, the giver of the ring?"

"Aye."

"Is it her likeness that you wear about your neck? In the locket that your mother gave to you?"

Instinctively, Ullin's hand touched his cloak where, underneath all his shirts, he confirmed it was still against his chest.
"How did you—"

"I do not sleep, Ullin. And even while I seem not to be doing so, I keep watch. I do not see everything. But I see enough."

For many moments they were silent, and the rain fell as if there would be no end to it, the cold puddles at their feet rising over the insteps of their boots.

"Although Esildre is free to come and go in the world as she pleases," Ashlord suddenly said, "she is not yet free of Secundur, her former lover. He spites her defiance of him by his long poisonous touch, and he uses her whenever he may to spread madness and discord. It is like a kind of sickness he has given her, so that her desires cannot be quenched. It is his revenge upon her for leaving his bed, and for throwing off his domination over her. That he has allowed her to live is a wonder, except that now he may torture her for all eternity with his curse. She knows this, and though I think she resists with admirable determination, she must, from time to time, be overwhelmed by it and give in to its affliction."

"As I gave in to mine."

"Hmm. If that is what you think. But you were made to pay for it by the madness that came upon you. It is Secundur's way. To act through others."

They listened to the downpour, standing as close under the overhanging eaves as they could.

"Islindia told me much the same as what you say. But why does my madness take the guise of Sheila? Why not the one I truly love and long for, as it did when I..., I mean, back in Nowhere?"

"Because Secundur's curse upon Esildre failed to destroy you then and there. The curse learned. It learned that for you to be with the one you most desire, even for a moment or two, would be a sweet blessing to you, and such a moment would strengthen you and fill you with greater resolve to live with honor and hope. Yes, the curse which landed through Esildre upon you is an insidious one, and it learned from your survival. And it came back at you. To use Sheila as a thorn in your heart is dark genius. She is torn in many directions, as you are. Her love of Robby, her desire and her fear to see him fulfill his destiny, her growing fondness of you—these are but a few of the many matters that weigh upon her heart. Sheila is close by, ever-present on this journey. She is someone whom you feel a great fondness for. Her resemblance to Esildre is remarkable, too. Who's form better to use than hers? And Secundur's curse did so, pursuing you. Who knows? By surviving, you may have inadvertently quenched a portion of it from Esildre, somewhat like a poultice may draw poison from a wound."

"But I have punished Sheila by my conduct. I have longed to tell her what is happening, but Robby swore me to silence about it. How could she ever understand, anyway?"

"I doubt if even Esildre knows or understands, though she cannot be ignorant of her curse. Tell me, when was the last time the dark vision came to you?"

"After Edgewold. The night before we entered Forest Islindia. I saw Esildre's form sitting across from me in Sheila's place."

"Ah," Ashlord said. "As I suspected. The spirit of the curse could not enter Islindia's realm, for no part of Secundur may go there and survive. And surely, the feast of Solstice also provided some relief to the wound inflicted upon your heart."

Ullin nodded.

"But I fear the damage has been done," Ullin said. "Islindia and Solstice both took some portion of my pain away. But I do not feel the same as before. It is hard, it seems harder, to keep going. I don't know what to do about that."

"It may not be entirely up to you, my friend. But you are strong, else you would have already succumbed to the very worst temptations of your malaise. Remain strong! Be kind to Sheila, as you have struggled to be. Healing, I am sure, will come. With time and with patience."

Ullin looked through the darkness at Ashlord and reached out to grip the mystic by the shoulder. "You do not know what it means to me to hear your words. I cannot imagine how you have come to see into my heart as you have. But well do you deserve to be called a Watcher."

The rain tapered off to a sprinkle, and the drips from the roof of the shed and the limbs of the forest were now the only sound in the cold air. The two stood listening, each in his thoughts, when a loud cry came from the cottage along with the sound of something being knocked about.

"What is that?" Ullin exclaimed, tossing his cloak aside from his hilt.

Behind him inside the shed, Robby opened his eyes, sat up, and grabbed his pack.

"Time to go, I think!" he said, shaking Sheila awake. "Time to go. Sheila, get your things. Billy. Ibin. Wake up. Let's go!"

As Robby stirred his companions, the door of the house was flung open and the ferryman, holding a lantern high, came rushing out.

"Are ye still abouts?" he shouted, peering around as he made his way to the landing and struggled to get his other arm through the folds of a hastily donned coat. "I say! Are ye—"

"We are here!" Ashlord called out.

"What is the alarm?" demanded Ullin, stepping toward the ferryman, looking about cautiously.

"Alarm? No. No alarm," the ferryman responded as he stopped to shine his lantern at the group. "That is to say—"

"Will you now take us across?" Robby called to him.

"Why, yes. That is to say, yes! Indeed, I shall! Ye still want to go, d'ye not?"

"Certainly."

"Then let us be off," he gestured to the barge at the landing.

"An interesting change of heart," observed Ashlord, pulling up his pack.

"I'll say."

"Let's go! Step on, step on!"

The ferryman's voice calmed to an urgent whisper as he showed them the way onto the barge and lit more lanterns at each corner of the craft, forward and aft. The flat boat was large enough for a wagon and team, and the company wondered as they boarded if the ferryman would need help pulling the vessel across. But when Ullin asked, the ferryman declined.

"No, me lord. Not at all," he said as he grasped the pull line that stretched out into darkness. He glanced across the black water. "Just all of ye be as quiet as can be. Speak only in low whispers, if ye must speak at all."

Billy let his pack drop onto the deck and the ferryman turned on him. "An' no thumpin' about! Be still, I beg ye!"

His manner of pulling, eyes ever darting out to the surrounding black surface, along with his words of caution, put all of his passengers on guard and ill at ease. Soon, though, the barge creaked away from shore so that nothing but a glassy undulating surface could be seen all around them, with rings from stray raindrops scattered here and there.

"Why did you change your mind and decide to take us across?" Sheila asked quietly and cautiously as the ferryman came to the bow to grip for his next pull.

"I was given a sign, missy. In a dream," he said, looking over his shoulder first at the other passengers then out over the water. Reaching for his grip, he put his head so close to hers that she could smell the liquor on his breath. "An' ye don't ignore such signs as I was given. That's all I'll say. Now let me pull."

The rain stopped altogether, and not a whisper of air disturbed the surface of the water. Overhead, the sky lightened, and everyone glanced up at the stars that suddenly showed through a break in the black sky. Except for the gentle creak of the barge under the ferryman's steady pull, and the soft lap of their passage, there was not another sound to be heard. Lady Moon then showed half of her face through a veil of gauzy clouds and revealed to the passengers columns of foggy vapor rising from the lake. Robby was reminded of the tale his mother told of her own night passage across Lake Halgaeth, seeing similar sights. The ferryman's pull was so gentle that it was difficult to tell if the columns of mist moved past them of their own power, or if their barge moved through them in its progress to the other side.

"A trick of the light!" Billy whispered, gazing at one just a few feet away. Turning toward it, the others saw, too, wreathed within the rising mist, the faint shape of a man taking form, as if standing waist-high from the water, attired in strange armor, and with pale ghostly wings drooping from his back.

"Do not look upon them!" hissed the ferryman.

"Beras preserve us!" Ashlord muttered. Hearing Ullin slowly draw his sword, he said to him, "Earthly weapons are of no use here."

It was not the cold air that made them shiver as they passed among dozens of these eerie beings. Kneeling beside her pack on the front corner of the barge, Sheila saw the head and shoulders of a woman rising from the surface nearby, her gray-blue face dim but beautiful, her hair spread about on the waters around her. The creature rose higher from the waters, her form comely and yet terrifying as she turned her baleful eyes upon Sheila, filling her with such horror that she was unable to move or to take her gaze from the apparition. Nearer it came, floating alongside the barge, reaching her arms out toward Sheila in a tender gesture, her lovely face tilted in a silent plea. At that moment, a distant splash was heard, the apparition recoiled from Sheila and turned its head to gaze over its shoulder to the direction of the sound as did all of the other ghostly figures. Then the mist they were made of dissipated as the figures sank back into the watery depths.

"What was that?" Robby muttered, gripping Swyncraff, ready to pull it from about his waist, his other hand on his dagger.

"A fish, maybe?" Billy offered tentatively.

"There ain't no fish in this lake," said the ferryman. "An' no livin' thing in these waters, 'cept, if one may call it livin', the creature what feeds on the former bodies of those who died here, ages past. It's their curse. None may be released from this place. That is, 'til their bodies are fully consumed by the creature what keeps 'em here."

"What kind of creature?" wondered Ullin.

"The kind that takes its time. Now ye know why I do not cross at night, nor on gloomy days, for the spirits trapped in these waters care little for the bright light of day, walkin' deep an' far below 'til the passin' of the sun."

Ashlord leaned on his stick in thought, listening with the others to a long gurgle that came over the water out of the blackness, and the moon and stars were again swallowed by the low sky.

"We'll see no more spirits tonight, I think," concluded the ferryman, resuming his toil.

They were by now more than halfway across. Above, Lady Moon, a few stars with her, once again showed her face, but she was inconstant this night, hiding halfway behind her fan, and gliding in and out from behind clouds. Still, the passengers on the barge could make out the dark shoreline ahead, rising steeply, thick with bare trees. Lights could be sometimes seen through the branches, dimly blinking high up the hill before them. It was not much longer before the barge bumped into the far landing, and the ferryman tied off the line and waved them to step off.

"It's a fair climb up the way there to the outskirts of town," he said. "Likely to be muddy an' slippery so take a care. Ye'll find lodgin' at the Golden Hearth, if the keeper'll take ye."

"Won't you at least accept a piece of silver for your trouble?" Robby asked.

"No," he said firmly. "But I ask, if ye ever pass this way again, that ye take some other way 'round, an' trouble me barge no more."

With some hesitation, and still a bit unnerved by what they had just witnessed, the group moved on up the hill, and the ferryman, wasting no time, pulled away and back toward the other side. It was apparent that the town lay at the top of the ridge overlooking the lake, and they passed only a few cottages along the slow climb, all quiet and dark, without even a wisp of smoke from the chimneys. As they moved along, Robby and Ashlord trailed some distance behind.

"A change of weather along with the ferryman's change of heart," said Ashlord. Robby, as grateful as any that it was no longer raining, glanced up at the sky.

"Indeed!"

"It is almost as if the ferryman had a bad dream," Ashlord added, "for the suddenness of it. Very convenient for us, though. Especially since, as we saw, he had good reason for not wishing to venture out."

"Yes. I suppose so. I'll be glad to be away from the lake."

"Robby. Did he have a dream?"

"He may have."

"Answer me straight, I beg you," Ashlord pressed. "Did you influence his change of heart?"

"Yes, Ashlord. I did."

"I thought as much. Do you not consider that to be meddling and manipulative?"

Ashlord's words, though spoken with gentleness, caused Robby a pang of guilt and embarrassment.

"Perhaps. Well, certainly. I suppose it was. But that's why I did it. To get him to deliver us across more quickly so that we could get on into town and to a dry and warm place." Robby heard the tone of defensiveness in his own voice and tried to check it, but with little success. "I did him no harm. Only shook him up a little. Gave him a nudge, you might say." In spite of himself, he could not help but smile at his prank. "There is so little I can do. Why not use those abilities that I have to accomplish some little bit of good now and then?"

"Some little bit of good? Yes, I suppose. No doubt your abilities may someday enable you to do a great bit of good. But what if the spirits of that lake had not been so passive toward us? What if the creature had seen us as a threat to its domain? You caused a man to go against his experience and his better judgment, and it could have resulted in our destruction."

"But—"

"I beg you to better consider the use of your power before the use of it comes too easily, leading you to do such things with little thought or consideration. The result may be different, next time."

Robby was silenced by the rebuke, and, with some anger at himself, he realized how he had, indeed, put his entire company at risk.

"I am sorry," he said at last. "I guess I didn't think things through quite enough."

Ashlord paused in his stride, and Robby stopped with him. They were nearly at the top of the hill, and the others waited for them a little distance ahead.

"Perhaps I scold too much," Ashlord said. "Much weighs on you, and more will as time goes by. You are young and still lacking in experience. But you are not like the others, here. One day, you will become one of the Elifaen and, if our quest is fruitful, much more. Who knows what powers you may yet gain or lose? What abilities may wax and wane in you? Recall the gifts that Lyrium offered you, that you refused. Think deeply on why you refused them. The Ring of Hearing, especially. You are gaining, through your own natural ability, something akin to that ring, so that in some manner you may see the innermost workings of others, and travel freely into their most private places where they think no one may intrude. Kindly, with earnestness and love, I say to you: Beware of power!"

"But how am I to learn unless I use my abilities? Learn how they may make some difference in the world?"

"You are right in that, I do admit. It is not for me to say 'do this' or 'do not do that,' for I cannot know except by my imaginings what limits or possibilities are before you, nor what may confront you in the future. You have confided in me by telling me about your ability to dreamwalk. And, indeed, it seems fitting that the one who is to become King should have extraordinary powers. But keep in mind the old saying, that the gods demand much of those they curse, and more of those they bless. Surely such a gift, a blessing, must come with great responsibility."

The others, though out of earshot of their low voices, understood that Robby and Ashlord were having a serious conversation. Though they were anxious to find lodging, they were patient, concerned at the apparent ardor of the discussion.

"Our friends await us," said Ashlord. "I'm sure they would be grateful to you, if they knew what you have done for them." Ashlord smiled oddly. "In fact, there is one in our company that may well benefit from something that only you can bring about."

"Oh?"

"Yes. And the more I think about it…. But we should not keep our friends waiting. I will think more on it and tell you later."

They caught up with the others and made their way up the hill along what became the muddy main street of the little town, ill-lit with smoky streetlamps. The meager shops and houses they passed had all seen better days, their windows dusty and dark, except for one or two dim candles that showed through upstairs shutters. There was little sign of activity, no one on the streets at all, until there rounded the corner two men, one with a lantern hanging from a pole he carried over his shoulder.

"Who goes?" the other challenged as they approached.

"Who asks?" Ullin replied.

"Sheriff's men, that's who," the man shot back. When the two came closer, the man with the lantern held it out so that he could better see the faces of the company.

"We are travelers," Ullin stated. "And we seek lodging for the night."

"Travelers, eh? An' what way brings ye to Lochton?"

"We come from the east," Ashlord stated while the two examined him closely, his red face glowing in the lantern light. He reached up and pulled back his hood so they could have a better look at his complexion and at the stubble of red hair that was sprouting across his head and face.

"Lor!" said the one with the lamp, recoiling a bit. The other did not flinch and moved from Ashlord to Ullin, then to Sheila.

"From the east, eh? An' how might ye have done that, I ask?"

"Theferryman, ferryman, theferrymanbroughtus," stammered Ibin, grinning down at the man.

"What's 'at? Ye say ye crossed the lake?"

"That's right," Robby replied as he, in turn, was examined.

"Well, 'at's a tale," said the one with the lantern. "Ol' Ferryman ain't never out on his barge at night."

"Well, he was this night!" Billy retorted, attracting the man's attention.

"He was, was he?"

"You can ask him yourself when you may please," Ashlord stated. "He told us of an inn here in town, called the Golden Hearth."

The men squinted at Ashlord, then hesitantly nodded.

"Aye, it's up yonder just a ways. What's yer business in these parts?"

"We are only passing through," Robby said. "On our way to Vanara."

"Yer in Vanara, if ye didn't know," said the lantern holder. "Leastways, the very edge of it."

"We mean to bear on in the morning."

"Is 'at so? Well, afore ye may proceed, ye must put down yer names, an' pay the toll."

"What toll?" Ullin pulled back his cloak so that they could see his Kingsman's tunic. "The Queen forbade all tolls in Vanara."

The two men swapped looks with each other. And the challenging one scratched his dirty beard. "Kingsman, yer far from home," he said.

"My home is my business. Now what about the toll?"

"It is by order of Lord Threshmere, laird of these parts."

"In defiance of the Queen?"

"Well, not exactly," he explained. "It is, after all, completely voluntary."

"Oh, I get it!" said Billy. "Some game yer runnin'. I bet if we asked yer laird, he might say he knows nuthin' 'bout no toll. Whar's his house?"

"Oh, he's miles away, an' cares not for our town business one way er other. An' he takes no visitors, neither."

"Then I suggest you show us to the inn and leave us to our business," Ullin stated. "Which way?"

"Right up yonder, then."

The two watchmen stepped aside.

Ullin gestured for the others to move along while he held back, eyeing the watchmen with a blank expression on his face.

"We'll of course, be reportin' ye to the Sheriff."

"Whatever your duty requires of you," Ullin replied, turning his back on them and following the others.

"Rankin was right about these people," Sheila commented.

"I'll say," nodded Billy.

"Here's, here's, thisistheplace."

Ibin pointed at a weather-worn sign dangling outside a two-story building. In faded yellow, there was depicted a fireplace along with the name of the establishment, the Golden Hearth, written in the Vanaran style of lettering.

"I'll have to see it to believe it," muttered Billy, shaking a coat of mist from his cloak as he stepped up onto the porch of the place. He opened the door, "Shall we?"

As soon as the doorbell rattled, there was a stir inside, and a stocky man in a thick sweater and tight-fitting cap approached the entering group.

"What is it? What's the meaning of this?"

"We seek lodgin'," said Billy.

"What's 'at? Rooms ye want? Oh, well, come in, come in! Ye've come far, eh?"

"Far enough for one night."

"Travelers. Not enough all month an' then six all at once, an' late, late!" the keeper muttered, raising the bar gate and moving behind it to the counter. "Very well, rooms. Let's see, six of ye. That'd be the upstairs side room, I think. Common bed, there. What's this, a female? Travelin' with all these men? Related, I hope."

"How impertinent!" Sheila responded.

"She is my ward," Ashlord said before Sheila could say anything more.

"Eh?" the keeper said, gaping at Ashlord suspiciously, then making a rude smile. "O' course. Yer ward. A separate room, then, for yerself an' yer ward?"

"No, we will stay together. One large room will do, as she is in our protection," Ullin stated, pulling aside and removing his cloak.

"Oh?" the innkeeper gazed at them with increased seriousness, now. "Well," he said, taking out his register, quill, and inkwell. "Put down yer names, then, and whether Elifaen, Mortal, or Mixed Blood."

"Why?" said Robby. "What business is it of yours?"

"It is our law. An' I must abide by it so that Lord Threshmere may know of any guests who stay here."

"We would prefer," Ashlord said, "some private arrangement, if that is possible."

"Arrangement?"

"Aye," picked up Billy, taking out his purse and giving it a jingle.

"*Private* arrangement?"

"That's right. For one night only."

"I dunno," the innkeeper said thoughtfully. He slowly closed his book. "Private arrangements can be costly. Aye, they can be. As it is, lodgin' is a might dicey, these days, even if I do say so. What with few guests to offset expenses of keepin' in readiness all the time. There's not only the lodgin', but the food, I'm sure. An' the cook's fee, an' the help's keep. Then, too, there's the taxes an' tolls."

"We will leave all of that to you," Ullin said. "To manage in your own way."

"Duinnor coin? Or Vanaran silver?"

"We have both, and some Glareth sovereigns."

"Let's see. Thirty-weight, Duinnor scale of silver, would about take care of a room."

"A room," said Ullin, "a full dinner. And ten-weight is more than ample."

"Twenty."

"Let's go," Billy said, tugging at Ibin. "I'm sure we can find a barn or empty shed somewhar nearby for just a coin er two. An' we still got our own victuals, anyhow."

The others all nodded and turned to the door.

"Fifteen!" said the keeper.

"Twelve," said Ullin. "And a hot breakfast, too. No skimping."

"Aye, aye, aye!" The keep threw up his arms and rolled his eyes. "Twelve-weight, then. One big room, dinner, an' breakfast."

"Indeed." Billy slapped down six coins on the bar. "Six now, six when we leave. If we're mighty satisfied, that is!"

"Yes, yes." The keeper scooped the coins off into his hand. "The usual supper crowd is long gone, an' the stove's cold, an' the cook won't be none too happy startin' all over." He shuffled away, pointing at the great room. "Help yerselves to the hearth, an' stoke up the fire if it pleases ye, an' I'll see to things."

They moved on into the large room, dropping their packs, and removing their wet cloaks and pulling a couple of rough-hewn benches near to the stone fireplace. Ullin stirred the coals with a poker and tossed on a few logs. As they settled down, they could hear pots and pans banging about somewhere not too far away. A boy hurried through and ran upstairs with arms full of blankets while another lad emerged rubbing a freshly cuffed ear to pour a couple of pitchers of beer from the keg at the bar. The innkeeper returned, followed by a woman who was tying on an apron. She came over while the innkeeper sat on his stool behind the bar and took out his pipe.

"So it'll be six of ye? I kin spit a couple of birds to warm, but there's little bread afore morn. Ample taters, though, an' gravy…oh, my!"

These last words were exclaimed upon seeing Ashlord's scarlet face. He smiled at her, and his eyebrows, what there was of them, went up in amusement.

"Whatever you bring will be appreciated," he said.

"Pardon me!" She made a slight curtsey. "Right away, then."

The boy brought the beer and set out tankards on a table behind Robby. But as he poured, his stare became so fixed upon Ashlord that he missed a tankard entirely, and only when Robby tapped the pitcher did he recover.

"Oh, excuse me, sir! Oh, I am sorry!"

"Now look what ye've done!" cried the keeper, rushing over.

"Clumsy waif!" the cook scolded, mopping the table with her apron.

"Do not blame the lad," Ashlord said, halting the keeper. To the boy, he said, "One cannot always help one's appearance."

"Yes, sir. I'm sorry, sir. Was ye in some kind of accident?"

"Get along with ye!" The cook pushed the boy away, taking the pitcher and finishing the job. "To the kitchen with yer impertinence! There ye go," she then said to Robby and nodded to the others. "Enjoy."

Smiling, they moved to sit at the table, and Sheila actually giggled.

"What?" Ashlord asked, taking a tankard held out to him by Ibin. "What is it?"

"Well," replied Robby, "you are quite striking."

"Especially by firelight," added Sheila.

"A certain glow," added Ullin. "Wouldn't you say, Billy?"

"Positively," Billy nodded, finishing his gulp of beer and wiping his mouth with his sleeve.

"Hrumph!"

The front door opened, and a stocky figure stomped in. His muddy travel cloak hung heavy and wet over his clothes, but the helmet he wore was clearly of Duinnor. Ullin touched Ashlord and nodded at the newcomer as the innkeeper made his greetings.

"May I help ye?"

"Food would be a great help, sir!" said the soldier. "Ah! And a warm hearth most welcome. Something to drink. Later, a room. Might I have my horse seen to?"

As he spoke, he cast off his cloak, and Ullin saw by his tunic that he was not part of Teracue's army.

"He's a Post Rider," he whispered.

"Then he's unlikely to know what's inside the letters he might carry," Billy commented hopefully, giving voice to their fear that some in these parts may know of the orders for their arrest.

"I'll tell the cook there's one more," they heard the innkeeper say. "Pitchers of beer on the table there by the fire."

"So here he comes," said Billy as the man came their way. The Post Rider nodded at the group.

"Pardon me," he said as he hung his cloak over a chair nearby to the hearth. "Just want to warm up a bit."

He rubbed his hands and looked at the group in a friendly way.

"A somewhat raw night, eh?" he said, smiling. He was fit, in his mid-thirties, perhaps, and a beard of many days was showing below his sideburns. After taking a long but not too obvious look at Ashlord, he turned to face the fire, glancing across his shoulder at Ullin several times.

"Pardon me, sir. But don't I know you? A Kingsman?"

"Yes. Assigned to Special Post," Ullin replied.

"Ah. I thought so. You probably don't remember me, and, I daresay, I don't recall your name. But I do believe we rode together for a day and a half or so. Back up from Airemoor to Duinnor. Oh, a year ago at least, I'd say. Maybe two, now. You were with a company returning from the Dragonlands, and I joined you at Airemoor and kept with you. Me and another Post Rider. You may remember him, big swarthy fellow, talked all the time."

"Yes. I believe I do remember," Ullin stood and offered his hand. "Commander Ullin Saheed Tallin of Fairoak. Ullin, I am called. I don't believe we ever actually exchanged names."

"Maybe not. I'm Leander Fascomb. Call me Lee, if you want. Glad to meet you. Or meet again, as it were. Assigned to Special Post, eh?"

"That's right."

"I was in the Regulars before I re-enlisted as Post Rider. Was in the south parts for over a year. Didn't see any action, though. Mostly guard duty. But, if I recall, the company you were with saw plenty."

"That is so."

The innkeeper brought another tankard as well as another full pitcher, pouring and giving the tankard to Leander.

"Thank you."

He took a long drink, closed his eyes for a moment, then nodding, took another. "That's what I've been longing for all night!"

He stood quietly sipping his beer and enjoying the fire. The room began to warm nicely, and they were all grateful to be indoors.

"Well, I don't mean to intrude upon you. Just waiting for a bite and a room."

"Not at all. So are we. I hope we'll be dining soon. Perhaps you would join our table?"

Leander looked at the others who nodded back at him kindly.

"That's very good of you. Thank you."

"Allow me to introduce everyone."

Ullin did so, and Leander shook hands with each in turn, giving Sheila a courteous bow, as well.

"Please have a seat," Ullin then said. "And here comes our supper!"

"Thank you!"

Leander pulled out a chair at the end of the table, saying, "Barley. Barley. Is that in the Eastlands?"

"Indeed, it is. We travel to Vanara and then to Duinnor."

"Oh? Taking the long way around?"

"It was the only way left open to us," Ashlord stated as the cook put down a half-loaf of bread and a crock of butter on the table. The boy followed with a tureen of boiled potatoes and carrots while the keeper laid out pewter plates and utensils. Back and forth the cook came and soon the table was well-laid with meats, thick mushroom stew, and steamed beans.

"The northward passes are closed by snow, I reckon," Leander went on once their plates were laden and eating commenced. "Still, if I recollect, you are south of the usual track."

"We have had some detours and unexpected turns," explained Robby. By now they were all confident that the rider knew nothing of the orders issued against them, and his open demeanor and friendly way of chatting put them at ease.

"Well, then. What news of the Eastlands? Still as peaceful as ever?"

"I wish I could say so," Robby told him. "But I'm afraid war has come to our homeland."

"What's that? War? Between who?"

Robby and the rest shared somewhat of their adventures—to Leander's continued astonishment—but they said nothing of their actual mission. They explained their odd course from the east was due to warlords and bandits (meaning the Nowhereans, though they elaborated none at all), and a chance encounter with Dragonkind, not to mention (but they did) the battle with the Wickermen.

"And so," Ashlord concluded, "we worked our way around and about until we wound up here."

"Well! I'm bound to say that you've had more than your share of adventures and trials! No wonder you're so far off from your track. So you must have come through the forest? And across the lake?"

"Yes."

"Judging by your wet things, you must have only just arrived. Don't tell me you came across at night? I didn't think that old ferryman would go at night. Last I was here some folk told me that he and others say that the lake is haunted. Lucky, they told me, that my business didn't take me that way."

"Well, he brought us across easily enough," said Ullin.

"I reckon so. Tell me, do you mean to press on soon?"

"In the morning."

"And do you think you'll be taking the westward road?"

"If that's the best way toward Linlally."

"It is, though it is a fortnight, at the least, by foot."

"A fortnight?" Billy shook his head. "So far away as that?"

"I'm afraid so," Leander paused, fork halfway to his mouth. Putting the fork down, he asked, "I say, would you mind a great favor to help out a fellow Post Rider?"

"If I can," Ullin nodded.

"Well, as it happens, I'm to ride out to Lord Threshmere's place. I have the rather unpleasant duty to deliver a King's Summons on his eldest."

"Oh!" Ullin put down his tankard. "I don't envy you that."

"You were never served with one, I'll wager. Few actually are."

"I joined before I was called."

"Most do. And that is as it should be! Well, anyway, I've got one to serve. And folk in these parts don't have much to do with Duinnor, these days. They even hold themselves apart from the rest of Vanara, too. Oh, I don't mean to say they are a bad lot. It's just that, well, I don't expect any trouble, no reason there should be any. But this sort of thing can be awkward, that is, when it gets all the way to the point of having a Summons served."

"You mean to say you don't fancy going there alone."

"That's the size of it. But if there was a Kingsman along, and others. Well, maybe then Lord Threshmere might not be too bold to make trouble for the messenger."

Ullin looked at Leander thoughtfully while the others listened and watched with concern.

"It is my duty," Ullin said to Robby and Ashlord, "and my sworn charge to render assistance to the King's agents. Though I can hardly refuse without good reason, I cannot speak for the rest of you. And since we have no contrary orders—"

"No, no," Leander interrupted. "This is only a favor, I ask, no more. I do not wish to impede your travel or impose upon your own business. It is truly my duty alone, not yours."

"I do not know Threshmere," Ashlord said. "And I have little enough knowledge of these parts, though I have passed through unmolested several times. We are in a land considered under the rule of Vanara, are we not?"

"Oh, yes. These lands reach to the shoulders of Cormund Valley, some fifteen leagues west. But I know what you are thinking. You are thinking that a contingent of Duinnor must be nearby, or at least a post of the Fellfaere. Well, the Fellfaere posted out of Vanara seldom patrol these lands because their ranks are so thin. And Duinnor sends its troops to Vanara across the Cormund. So the folks in these parts must see to themselves. Oh, there are sheriffs and rangers and so forth, but all loyal to each other, if any loyalty they have at all. They mostly keep good order. But Realm Law is let to slide somewhat, and these folk don't care for meddling by outsiders. Most of the estates nearby were wiped out ages ago, with only Threshmere's House of Hemlock barely hanging on."

"Who are the Fellfaere you speak of?" asked Sheila.

"The fell warriors of the Elifaen," Ashlord said. "So called by folk in the westlands."

"Aye," nodded Leander. "And as stern as they come, I reckon, from the ones I've run into."

"If my companions will agree to come along, and if it is on our way," Ullin told Leander, "then I will certainly accompany you."

"I don't see why we shouldn't," Robby offered.

"Might as well," shrugged Billy, yawning. "So long as it ain't too early!"

They talked more about the happenings in the world, as far as they knew or surmised. The innkeeper came to tell them that their rooms were ready, and the dishes were taken away, too. Leander was the first to excuse himself for bed, with Billy, Ibin and Sheila following his lead. Ullin finished his pipe and excused himself also.

"Robby, may I have a few moments more with you?" Ashlord asked.

"Certainly," Robby sat back down across from Ashlord.

"This ability that you have to dreamwalk. I cannot say that I understand it. But I am concerned."

"As you said earlier."

"Yes, as I said, a powerful thing it is. More powerful than the gifts you refused from Lyrium."

"It has its price, you know. It wears on me. I'm learning how to control it, though. Micerea says it will get easier, and she also tells me that I will soon surpass her abilities."

"Hm. How far may you go with it, I wonder?"

"What do you mean? I'm sorry about what I did with the ferryman."

"That is not what I mean," Ashlord leaned back and looked at the fire. "Tell me about Micerea again. You have a strong connection to her."

"So it seems. In a way. I don't know how to explain it. Her light is strong in my eyes. My dream eyes. She says mine is, too, in hers, because I am a dreamwalker. She says she thinks all dreamwalkers perceive each other in that manner. I can't tell you whether it pulls me, or whether I follow it to find my way to her. The landscape of dreams is not like any other. There are layers, hills and dales, sort of. From the hilltops, I can see people as they are, awake or asleep. And if they be sleeping, I can see their dreams. It is like standing on the hill across the river from Passdale. At night you can see the lights of the town shining out of the houses. Some are near and others are far. I can get to the light, the person, by moving toward it, downhill, sort of. The nearby ones are easy. The distant ones are a bit harder. The landscape is confusing. And above there is yet another landscape. If I go there, it is much easier to move great distances, but...I can't describe it...there is even yet another layer of landscape above that one, too. It is like standing under a starlit sky, but with such stars as you can't imagine, like pinwheels, some. Others like torches. Some are like long trails of glowing fur. Some are shaped like dishes, round and swirling with dots of light. Micerea says that her master, the one who taught her, could travel any distance, to any place, and observe any event happening in the world."

"What is Micerea like?"

"She doesn't look like other Dragonkind," Robby said. "She is more like us. Very beautiful, though. Tough, I believe. Trained in combat, too, I think. But she hides those abilities, and all her abilities, from the world. She is seen by her kind as lazy and spoiled, seeking only pleasure and whim. She strives to be seen that way. She, like others of her station, partake in a substance, a medicine, I believe, that prevents the worst effects of the desert from harming her. She says that it also protects her mind, somewhat. Ashlord, I do believe that the sands of the desert are poisoned.

That is why her people suffer. At least, partly why. But they are like us. They have families, friends, cares and concerns. They work, and they laugh, and they die, just as we do. Except they die sooner, very young, for the most part."

"I know, Robby," Ashlord nodded sympathetically. "I did not spend my time in those lands without learning a thing or two. But I think Micerea has not told you everything about herself. I have pieced together in my head something remarkable to tell you about her. And about Ullin."

"Ullin?"

"Yes. I've suspected something of the sort for a long time, but you confirmed it for me when you told me about Tulith Morgair and showed me the ring you found."

"What is it?"

"It boils down to this. I think you can help Ullin in a way that none of the rest of us may."

"Oh? Whatever I can do for him, you know I will."

"As you know, there has been a hex placed upon Ullin's mind. It eats away at his heart."

"You speak of the witch, Esildre!"

"She is no witch, Robby. You do not understand. She was only the unwitting messenger. She herself is cursed to be so. She cannot help it, and I believe she moves in the world in an effort to find a way to break her curse."

"She is cursed?"

"By Secundur."

"Well perhaps it is deserved," Robby stated bluntly. "Say what you will. But she did curse the Nowhereans, remember. It was not only Bailorg and Navis that brought hardship upon those people. And now she's brought this torment upon Ullin."

"Robby!" Ashlord shook his head. "These things do not work in so simple a manner. But that you do not blame Ullin for his condition is a start. And you may be able to help him."

"How so?"

"When next you go to Micerea, demand of her all she knows concerning Ullin."

"What may she know that might help him?"

"I believe she knows, in her heart, what it is that Ullin longs for and needs the very most. And, I believe, if she told you honestly and truthfully, you would understand what you could do to bring about his healing. And, I believe, it will also help Sheila, in the long run."

"What do you mean?"

"I mean you, too, will be released, somewhat, by Micerea's truth."

"I don't understand what you are talking about."

"Sheila knows very little about Micerea, except what you have told her," Ashlord went on relentlessly.

"I have said very little about her to anyone but you."

"She senses that you are drifting away from her. That your affections for her have changed."

"They have not! What do you mean?"

"She is no fool, Robby. You may be withdrawing from Sheila because of your feelings for Micerea. In fact, perhaps that is the right thing to do, even if you mistake the reason."

"What are you saying?"

"Only that if you and Sheila are to be parted, as you will be when you enter Griferis, then perhaps you should resolve things with her before that takes place. While you still can."

"Do you mean I should cast her off? Set her free of me and my quest?"

"I mean you should let her choose her own way."

"I have not obligated her. She came of her own free will."

"You wanted her to come. That desire on your part obligated her. And she will remain loyal to you regardless, Robby."

"What would you have me do? Change my feelings for her? Stop loving her?"

"If you love her, if you care for her, then help her prepare for parting from you. She can cope. Perhaps better than you may wish to think. But do not betray her by some misguided infatuation with Micerea."

"*What?*"

"Search yourself carefully. What are you willing to do for Sheila, after all she has done for you? If you fail to become King, and thus fail to make the needed changes come, what kind of world do you think she'll have? If you have any hope for her happiness, then spare her your selfishness."

"How dare you!"

"Listen to me, Robby." Ashlord stood up when Robby did. "Look at me! And, now tell me: who do you care most for? Who would you make cry? You know already what is coming. You have formed in your mind a plan. I see the calmness of that decision upon you. It came to you out on the grassy plains, did it not? You know what you must do. But you know that Sheila will stop you if she can. And that would not only doom her, but all the world, too. Do this thing for Ullin. Ask Micerea. It will help you understand what it is that you should do."

Robby stared at Ashlord, unable to break away from his earnest gaze.

"I don't understand."

"Ask Micerea to tell you all. Promise me that."

Robby, his heart pounding with dread, nodded.

"I promise. I will."

• • •

He meant it. And, that very night, he went to Micerea, not only to fulfill his promise to Ashlord, but also to put into play the first part of his own plan.

His visit to her was not unexpected, but she was surprised by his first question.

"Are you pleased with my skills at dreamwalking?"

"You are far more skilled at dreamwalking than I will ever be," Micerea told him. "After but a few weeks, you have mastered moving around and seeing into the dreams of others, things that took me years to learn, and still I am awkward. I think you are naturally suited to this, while I am not. And your skills continue to grow so that I wonder if I will be of any use to you much longer."

"Do you?"

"I thought, perhaps wrongly, that I could use this way of being together to teach you about my people. But you learn faster than I can teach. I confess, I thought I could be a good teacher, but you often ask questions to which I have no answer. It may be time for you to teach me."

"There is much more, yet, that I wish to learn from you," Robby smiled, "even though, indeed, I do think I could show you a few things. But, as you often remind me, I need my strength. Dreamwalking may be easier for me than for you, but it is taxing just the same. Give me time. Do not try to find me any more. I will come back to you when need be, or when the time is right."

"I don't understand."

"It is for your own safety. Do not try to find me. There are things I must do, places I must go, and I cannot foresee the dangers of what I must do. I do not want you to have the same fate as the friend you told me about, the one lost to the dream-dogs."

"Will you tell me what you seek? What you plan to do?"

"I dare not. Only that I do have something of a plan. I must explore the plan."

"What shall I do in the meantime?"

"Be watchful. Patient. Above all else, be safe. I will need you when things are ready. But, right now, there is something very important that you can do for me."

"What is that? I'll do whatever I may."

"Tell me everything about you and Ullin."

Micerea's face reddened, and she slowly shook her head and shrugged.

"Please, tell me everything."

A hint of pain crossed her face, but she nodded.

"It was before I learned to dreamwalk. About five years ago. And it was fate, I believe."

She told him everything. How she met Ullin in the desert. She described to Robby how Ullin saved her life, and how they took refuge at the dead city, and how the little rabbit showed them to the hidden spring. She recounted how Ullin made a basket, of sorts, of the flower stalks, and how he filled his bag full of more stalks and flowers, and, when they departed the place, how Ullin carried the rabbit with them out into the desert, giving it more care and attention than she had ever seen given to any creature.

"I had already fallen in love with him, and I think he with me," she said to Robby. "But seeing him act as he did with the little one touched my heart and made me love him all the more. When we reached the Free City, we had our plan worked out. We told the authorities that my caravan was attacked and all were killed but me. That I bribed the renegade Ullin to be my bodyguard and to help me escape his comrades and reach the city where I would pay him handsomely. Such things are not uncommon in those parts, so they believed me. Ullin and I stayed in the city for a month. Ullin kept rooms with the gold I gave him, for his service to me, and we secretly visited each other as often as we could. We dined and luxuriated in the cool baths, and as we grew to know each other better, our love deepened. He was asked by many to join this or that band of mercenaries, or to serve in other capacities, and he strung them out, saying he was waiting for the best offer. But, in fact, he was preparing his means to leave the city, though I think he was reluctant to go."

She sighed and shrugged.

"He had his duty. And I could hardly face my father with honor if I was the reason that his important dispatches did not reach the north. So, one day, we said goodbye. A week later, I began my return to my own home, thinking I'd never see or hear from him again. And I didn't. Not until I learned to dreamwalk. I told everything to my father, even though I did not intend to do so. And because he knew that I was becoming a dreamwalker, he arranged a tutor for me. When I was accomplished enough, I used my abilities to spy for my father. Last year, seeing how I pined ever more deeply with each passing moon, and remembering my feelings for Ullin, he told me more about Ullin and the Tallins. Knowing that I might attempt it anyway, my father said that I should seek Ullin out, to keep an eye on him, that he might one day become King. I was to report back to my father all that I learned. And I have done so. Except now my father grows weaker by the month, and I fear he is not long in this world. The strain of his life, his sadness, and the exertions he has made in the last years to counter the power of our King Belsalza speeds him to his grave. So it was due to my father that I met Ullin in the first place, and due to my father that, seeking to cool my eyes by looking once again upon Ullin, I sought him out and kept company with his dreams. And that's how, ultimately, I found you."

Robby nodded.

"I understand. There is another thing that I must ask. Do you still love him?"

"Yes. And, yes, I know of his infidelity. But I have no hold on him. Although he offered his word to me, I refused his promise. How can there be love such as ours between his kind and mine? The world would not permit it!"

"Have you not seen his dreams? Have you not felt through them his heart, his anguish, his longing to be with you?"

"Yes! Yes!" she said, and tears rolled down her face both in the form Robby looked at, and upon her sleeping cheeks, leagues away. "Truly I have seen his dreams! And I have felt his longings. They match my own, yet they are a torment to me! How can you ever understand? What can I do? He is there, and I am here!"

"First, do not give him up to the visions and taunts of that black spirit that comes to him in the guise of Esildre!"

"What do you mean?"

"I will tell you how it is between them, and how her curse is one shared in spite of her. But I ask you to make me this promise: If you still love him, be ready! Watch over him, but give him no torment. Do not enter his dreams or make yourself seen by him. In due time, I will come back to you. And you will tell me then if you still believe that love is impossible between the two of you! Until then, do not seek for me in the dreamworld. Do you agree?"

"Yes!" she sobbed. "I do!"

"Very well," Robby said. "Thank you. And now I shall tell you what has been told to me this very night concerning Esildre and Ullin."

Chapter 17

The House of Hemlock

Day 138
107 Days Remaining

As far as Named Houses go, if the structure was any indication of the name, then Hemlock was one in need of repair. Like the lands that surrounded it, there was still evidence of the grandeur it once had, but also of a generation, at least, of neglect. Few of the fields they passed showed any sign of past crops. Instead, they were overgrown and dotted with saplings among the patches of snow and clumps of briar. Outbuildings and barns were missing large portions of thatch or tile, and flocks of swallows puffed out through the bare rafters or gaping doors. Even the road, once it entered the region of the estate, was overgrown to a mere path, with a long-fallen tree obstructing the way in one place, and in other places small bridges of stone and wood that creaked and shifted nervously as the company crossed. So when they came onto the proper grounds of the old place, entering through an opening in a low red-brick wall which encircled it, they were not so surprised at the dilapidated condition of the mansion. Broomstraw waved where perhaps smooth lawns had once been and even sprang up between the stones of the paved landing that spread out from the portico. The stones of the tall mansion seemed to cling to the ivy and moss that covered its walls instead of the other way around, and all of the windows above the lower level were closed with weather-worn shutters, some dangling precariously by a single stubborn hinge.

"This is a gloomy place," commented Sheila.

"I'll say," Billy agreed.

Nowhere could any tenant be seen, though a trail of smoke weakly rose from one of the high chimneys above.

"Where are all the people?" Robby asked Leander. "I thought you expected trouble."

"It is very odd, I must say," Leander replied. He led his horse along the way so that they could all walk together, and now he handed his reins to Ibin. "Do you mind?"

Ullin and Ashlord were cautiously looking around, and the others, taking their cues, loosened their cloaks to clear the hilts of their swords.

"Let's get this thing done," said Ullin.

Leander took his summons in one hand, walked up the steps to the great double door, and pounded on it with his fist.

"Open and present yourself!" he cried, "The King has business with ye this day!"

To everyone's surprise, there immediately came a rattling of bolts being thrown and lifted away and then, as Leander stepped back, both doors groaned open, pushed by an old man with long salt and pepper hair, many weeks unshaven, dressed in old clothes and a long, fur-collared house robe. But he stood unbent by age, and firm defiance shot from his blue eyes.

"I can guess that you bring yet another Summons!" he said in a deep voice.

"If you are Lord Threshmere of the House of Hemlock, that is the case," answered Leander. "And it is my duty to make this summons heard by you before all witnesses present."

"I am Threshmere. Get on with your duty, and then get off my land!"

"Very well."

Leander unrolled and held up the Summons, showing to all the royal seal that was on it, then he read:

"By order of the King, Laird True of All Domains and Realms, and as required by the Laws of the Seven Realms, the eldest son of the House of Hemlock is called to duty, to forthwith travel to the King's city in the Realm of Duinnor, there to enter by his own hand his own name into the Musters of the King's Own Men, to give his allegiance forever to the One Sovereign above and before all others, and to yield his own life for the term of service required or until released.

"Be it known, that any who fail answer this call to duty shall be forfeit of his own life, the pennant of his House struck down from the Hall of Banners, the property and lands of his House given over to Duinnor, and the heirs of his House forever without honor. So sayeth the King. So be it done!"

While Leander read the Summons, Threshmere simply stood, his arms crossed and his whole form passive, save the blazing hatred in his eyes.

Leander rolled up the parchment, and further addressed Threshmere.

"What say you? Do you now surrender to the King the one named Theoditus, recorded in the King's Census as your son?"

"I do not!"

Leander looked from Threshmere to Ullin who, his head down, was nonetheless keeping a close watch upon the proceedings.

"Are you resolved in that, sir?" Leander went on.

"That is so, and how it must be."

"Very well. Much is my regret, then, to deliver to the rightful Sheriff of this shire a writ of forfeiture, being this the third and final Summons given."

"Be that as it may. Deliver your writ, and may the King himself come with *all* his men," Threshmere shot back, glaring at Ullin, "and it will thus be settled."

"Sir," said Ullin, stepping forward, "what say your son to this? Can you not at least produce him so that he may speak upon this matter? For it is his inheritance and his name that will be lost, and his freedom as well."

"Thus is the crux, Kingsman. That you are sent here by Duinnor, like all before, in ignorance of the matter, and make demands that Duinnor knows full well cannot be met."

"I am not sent, but come along only by chance and at the request of this Post Rider, being one myself, to see the King's Law carried out."

"King's Law! But where is the King's reason?" Threshmere suddenly stormed down the steps and past them. "You wish to speak to my son? To hear his own words? Follow me, and I will take you to him! Hear for yourself, if you may, his own reply!"

Belying his age, the old man sped through the tall weeds, and they could do nothing but follow. Threshmere charged through the side yard, down an overgrown walk, and to a small arched gateway in the crumbling outer wall. The company followed briskly into a broad grove of trees, their frosty limbs reaching over the soggy remains of an ornamental garden, where the thorny branches of dormant rose bushes and the hardy pale limbs of myrtles sagged and draped over the bulging remains of tombs.

"Here!" Threshmere cried, his voice now shaking and his finger pointing. "Here is my son, if you care to speak to him. By all means, ask your questions. And tell me what he says to you, I beg!"

The visitors stood at the tomb and glanced back and forth at each other, none knowing quite what to say.

"It appears by the condition of this tomb that he has been dead for a long time," Ullin said softly to Leander.

"Aye. Twenty years, taken from me when he was not yet five years of age," Threshmere stated.

Leander, as much as the others, was embarrassed, and looked at the papers he still held.

"Why did you not report his death on the census?" he asked.

"How many reports must Duinnor have?" Threshmere asked, clearly trying to get a grip on himself. "I did report it. And after the first Summons came, I myself traveled to Duinnor. It was my aim to locate the census records and show the report of my son's death. But the recent census tallies from these parts were misplaced, and they continue to be misplaced, year after year. After my return, I dispatched to the Court papers of testimony, giving full account of my son's death. When I traveled a second time to Duinnor, I learned that those papers never reached the Court. For two weeks, I waited for an audience with General Kecker who himself issues all the Summons. But he would not see me.

Indeed, even when I sought him out by going to his home, I was set upon as a vagrant and arrested, jailed for five months! I was then given a hearing, and was released, but only after signing liens of forfeiture, giving all my lands over to Duinnor's holding until my case was resolved. But it was trickery! Beware, Kingsman! This is how even you may be treated, for I, too, was once a Kingsman, and I served faithfully and bear the scars of my honorable service. But once the forfeiture hung over my name, I could not even claim the right of hearing that all Kingsmen are to have. When I returned home, I found all the tenants fled, as well as most of my other workers. See for yourself what stigma will do! It is bad enough that my mother was not Elifaen, though my father was, so I will be the last of that lineage, anyway. So more's my despair, since when my banner is taken down upon my death, Hemlock will be no more. All act as if it has already happened, and sometimes I think it may as well have. Look upon this place! I can entice none to trade with me, nor any to come and work the land, for it is now a House of shame. I am prohibited from selling the least acre, for none would have a lien of forfeiture passed to them."

"But the forfeiture has not yet been carried out," said Leander, "and you do remain on your lands. And a new Summons was issued, here."

"My lord, it is as if," Ashlord observed, "as far as Duinnor is concerned, nothing has changed for all your efforts."

"That is the sum of it."

Leander shook his head, "Just doesn't sound right. Sir, do you have any proof of your claims? Can you show me anything, any reason that would take my duty away from me so that I may forego the writ?"

"What would you have me show you?" Threshmere gestured at the tomb. "What would release the forfeiture and clear the name of this House? I have no other sons to send."

"Perhaps I may go instead."

Turning, they saw a slight figure standing in the archway of the graveyard. He was a young man, bent over crutches, wearing an old house coat over his simple clothes, with a close-fitting cap pulled down over his thin blond hair. His face, pale and unshaven, had a sickly look, but his blue eyes, as intense as Threshmere's, blazed earnestly.

"What are you doing out here?" cried Threshmere. "Go back into the house, I beg you!"

"Wait," ordered Leander. "Who is this?"

"One of the few household servants left to me, that is all. Pay him no heed. I keep him out of pity's sake, for no one else will have him."

"I have heard," said the fellow, ignoring Threshmere and addressing himself to Ullin, "that, on special occasions, another may be sent to serve instead of the one called. Is that not so?"

Ullin hesitantly stepped nearer to the young man, who also moved forward to stand before the Kingsman.

"What is your name?" Ullin asked.

"I am called Borwain."

"Borwain. That means 'bold son' in the old speech."

"I did not know that."

"And you are in service to this House?"

"I am, sir. And I have been all of my life."

"And how old are you?"

"I do not know my age, but I am told that I was brought here to be in service many years ago."

"I see. And why would you wish to serve as Kingsman?"

"Why would I not wish to? Why, in the first place, would any man not wish to serve in that honored league? And why, in the second, would I not wish to do honor to the only House that has been home to me? And to the man who has been most like a father to me?"

"Borwain! Borwain!" said Threshmere, shaking his head and coming over to him. "You do me too much honor. And it is not your place to go. Return to the house before the damp and cold cause you to suffer."

Threshmere put his hand on Borwain's shoulder to guide him back to the gate, but it was gently shrugged off.

"My lord, let me be heard at least! Let me have my own say just this once, and have my own hope, brief though it may be, before any answer comes to strike it from my heart."

Looking at the others, then back to Ullin, he drew himself up as tall as he could, shifting both crutches into one hand, and with only a hint of unsteadiness, he stood proudly.

"Sir," he said to Ullin, "I can read, and I can write. I can do numbers and measure and draw the angles of geometry. I can render likenesses of what I see with ink and pen, and draw things accurately from memory alone. I know the care and preparation of weapons, sword, shield, dagger, and bow. And I can parry and slash. I can use a bow and strike far targets with ease. And I have often been upon horseback."

"How did you come to know such things?" Ullin asked gently.

"Lord Threshmere himself instructed me in all these things. And more."

"The writing and the numbers are things all should know," Threshmere explained, shaking his head and waving his hand dismissively. "The other things were merely for amusement."

"Hm. I see," Ullin nodded. "Borwain, you do your master honor for your offer, and clearly you are sincere. But, without meaning to offend you, I tell you that a Kingsman must be able to march and to stand firm and to advance with shield and sword. He must move swiftly to shelter from the enemy's missiles, and he must carry away the wounded of his brethren. A Kingsman must ride without tire for days, and must do without food and without comfort when that is the way of his mission. He must run with speed and courage over a litter-strewn battlefield, leaping over the slain to climb the walls of the enemy's stronghold. And, of course, a Kingsman must fight with strong arms, determination, and great endurance."

Borwain pulled in his chin, trying to form a reply, his eyes stinging at Ullin's words.

"Is there no other way to serve as Kingsman? Do the Kingsmen not use scribes? Do they not have someone to write orders or to draw plans, to keep accounts, or to record the annals of battle?"

"Yes, surely all those things are indeed done by Kingsmen," Ullin said patiently. "But, in the field, one who does such things must also be ready at a moment's warning to throw aside the pen and take up the sword, dashing to where it is needed."

"Come, good fellow," Lord Threshmere said, putting his hand again on Borwain's arm. "Return to the house and await me there. It is too raw for you to be out."

Borwain took up his crutches and turned to go.

"You have an honorable heart, sir," said Ullin after him. "No doubt someday you will serve your King with as much honor as you have served your lord."

"Thank you," Borwain said over his shoulder. "But I don't see how that may ever be. If you wish to see for yourself copies of the testaments that Lord Threshmere spoke of, I will show them to you. I keep all of the letters and documents of the House of Hemlock."

The company hesitated, Leander shaking his head.

"Oh, how sad," Sheila said quietly to Robby. Ibin, his face pained by what they had seen and heard, looked at Billy. Billy sighed softly and patted Ibin on the back, but said nothing. Ashlord did the same to Ullin's shoulder.

"Come along," he said to him. "Let us make our way from here."

As the group walked back to the house, Ullin suddenly spoke to Leander.

"Perhaps I may help in this matter," he said, watching Borwain and Threshmere move slowly on. "Would you be willing to deliver a letter to Duinnor for me?"

"Don't see why not. Of course, I would."

"And would you be willing to deliver it in person, and before you make your report or deliver your other dispatches when you get to Duinnor? First off, as soon as you arrive, before any other business?"

Leander scratched a sideburn.

"What are you up to? It would be highly irregular. But I could probably manage arriving late at night. Too late for other matters."

"Good." Ullin moved quickly ahead and caught up with Threshmere. "Lord, if you have pen and parchment, I may be able to intercede on your behalf."

"I don't see what you may do that has not already been tried. But I will gladly accept any assistance you may offer."

The rest of Ullin's company remained respectfully silent. Robby felt, as perhaps the others did, some sense of shame mixed with their general embarrassment. Ashlord, leaning on his stick, eyed Ullin with interest and glanced at Robby. Now, as they made their way along, Ashlord ventured a question.

"Forgive my asking, Lord Threshmere, but what was the manner of your son's death?"

"It was a marauding wolf that came through these parts," Threshmere said. "Most cunning and foul. It killed two villagers and maimed one of my tenants. My son, unfortunately, wandered away one morning and went missing. We found what was left of him ten days later."

"How awful!" said Sheila.

"I am sorry," Ashlord said. "And he was your only child?"

"He was."

"Does your wife still abide here?"

"No. She died shortly after giving birth to my son. It is her grave that is beside his."

They approached the front doors, and Lord Threshmere hesitated, saying, "I'm afraid the place is in disrepair, and I have no footmen."

"We needn't all go in," Ashlord interrupted, seeking to avoid further embarrassment, since the gentleman obviously lacked the means to host the group.

"Well. Suit yourself. There's little worth seeing, anyway. But there is a stable just around the corner, that way, where you'll find some shelter from the wind and oats for the Post Rider's horse."

"Thank you. We will go there and await our companion."

Ullin, Leander, Threshmere, and Borwain went into the gloomy hall and closed the doors behind them. Ashlord turned and led the way to the stable.

"I take it Ullin has it in mind to write a letter to someone he knows in Duinnor," Billy stated, taking the reins from Ibin.

"That is my guess," agreed Ashlord.

"But won't that give us away?" asked Sheila.

"Ullin's too wise for that," Robby said. "I'm sure he'll be cautious."

"Besides," Ashlord added, "unless we mean to waylay Leander, the authorities in Duinnor will no doubt hear of our whereabouts from Leander's report."

"And it will be some time before he even gets back to Duinnor."

"An' about how far is that? Is Duinnor?"

"Hm. From here, for a good rider and horse, at a good pace, stopping for nothing but sleep, at the very least a fortnight. But more probably the better part of a month, with good weather. Ah, here is the stable."

As they turned past an overgrown hedge at the side of the decrepit mansion, they saw the stone stablehouse, large and befitting the estate, but in somewhat better condition, overall, it seemed, than the other buildings they had encountered. There was a workman, the first they had seen, emerging with a wheelbarrow of manure, who saw them and stopped, lowering his load and eyeing them suspiciously.

"Who might ye be, then? An' what are ye doin'?"

"Visitors," said Robby. "We've come to stable the horse and get out of the cold wind while Lord Threshmere does business with our companions."

"I see. So ye won't be stayin'? Course not," the workman pushed open the doors for them, "nobody comes, hardly ever. An' none stay. Trough is just there. Feed bags yonder. Close up the doors when ye leave!"

"What happens to Named Houses, such as Hemlock," Sheila asked as they entered the barn, "when the last of the lineage dies? Can't Lord Threshmere leave his estate to some relative or even to Borwain?"

"If he has title he may do so," answered Ashlord. "But if none carry the Threshmere name, the House will be dissolved. Its banner will be taken down from the Hall of Banners in Duinnor. If Threshmere leaves the estate to another person, it is up to Duinnor whether to declare it a Named House or not. Few new Houses are Named, these days, unless they are wealthy, influential, or powerful in some way. In other words, if they could possibly be strong enough to pose any sort of threat. Then the rules would require a Kingsman from the new House. Even if Threshmere was able to bequeath his property, he cannot bequeath his title, and so there will never be a House of Hemlock again. The newly Named House, if there is one, would require a new name."

"Oh."

• • •

"You have no servants at all, besides Borwain?" Ullin asked.

He and Leander were led through a foyer that had, at one time, been as grand as that of Tallin Hall, perhaps even grander, but it was now a dark and unpleasant ruin, filled with dust, its marble floors hardly discernable under layers of dirt. Many statues stood about the place, mantled with moth-eaten and web-covered sheets, and even the coat of arms, hanging over the balcony above, was subdued by grime. Down a dark hallway, Threshmere picked up a smoky lamp and held it high to somewhat illuminate their way. The lamplight did little to dispel the gloom of the place, draped with cobwebs that hung like moss, and there was also the evidence of gnawing rats on the moldings and furniture.

"None for the house," Threshmere said. "I manage to employ a few laborers for the stables. And we still manage one or two fields, but it is only a paltry crop of vegetables they yield. Few can be enticed to work here, only those old hangers-on who have been most loyal to this House."

He pushed open a door, and they went into a spacious study where Borwain was tossing a few faggots onto the grate. He turned with a look of surprise and hobbled awkwardly to his crutches leaning on a nearby chair.

"Borwain, will you find some ink and quills and suitable things for this gentleman to write with?"

"Certainly, my lord."

"Borwain knows this room best, for it is where he occupies himself much of the day."

There were bookcases noticeably free of dust, crammed with bound manuscripts and scrolls, and there were drawings and sketches layered on tables and chairs and some hanging over shelves with books as weights to hold them in place. It was immediately apparent to Ullin that Borwain was the one who rendered the sketches and, moreover, that he was of prodigious talent, far beyond the skill of any he had ever seen. Not only were the animals in the sketches life-like, they were so finely detailed in form and in expression and posture that something of the character of each individual creature was apparent. As Ullin and Leander looked around, Borwain and his master cleared away a chair and the top of a writing table near a window.

"Please," Borwain motioned to the chair. Ullin sat, and Borwain continued to clear space by sliding away some drawings and stacking others. Ullin brushed his hand across one of the sketches, to wave away what he thought to be a moth fluttering there. But when it did not move, he looked again and saw that it was part of an unfinished drawing, and what he took to be a moth was the depiction of a small bird taking flight from a bramble in a forest scene.

"How odd," he muttered as Borwain swept the drawing away along with others, revealing the finely finished wood of the desk.

"There's a space at last," Borwain said. "Here, then."

He placed an inkwell and a cup of quills before Ullin, then a stack of writing paper.

"I'll fetch the sealing wax."

"Thank you. These drawings are quite impressive."

"That is kind of you to say."

"Borwain has talent, to be sure," Threshmere commented from where he stood stoking the fireplace with a poker.

"Uncanny!" Leander said, rubbing his eyes with one hand as he put down a sketch he had been admiring.

"Yes, they will play tricks on your senses if you look too long," Threshmere continued, "or perhaps if you do not look long enough. So, Kingsman, will those do?"

"Yes." Ullin dipped a quill and prepared a sheet, saying, "I have in mind to write a letter to an acquaintance in Duinnor who may have some influence. A fellow Kingsman from my Academy days, a Captain Thrubold. Do you know him?"

"Can't say that I know the name," said Threshmere.

"He may be in a position to look into things," Ullin said as he began to write, "particularly any writs and testimonies from you that were mislaid or undelivered."

The others watched Ullin write and listened to the soft scratch of his quill. After a few lines, Ullin paused.

"I would like to relate somewhat about the articles of forfeiture that are held. Would you tell me the agent that holds the liens? And the Duinnor address of that firm?"

"Why, yes," Threshmere nodded. "It has been years since—"

"I'm sure it is in one of the letters," Borwain said. He moved to a cabinet at the far wall and, taking out a set of keys, opened a door and began rummaging through packets and scrolls within.

"I don't understand," said Leander. "Wouldn't the articles be held by the King's ministers?"

"No," answered Ullin. "Liens on leases are given on the articles just as if they are deeds. Whoever paid the lien holds the articles, but they can only take possession of property when the court acts on forfeiture. It is a kind of speculation."

"I still don't understand. If the property is forfeit to the King—"

"It is a way of making money for the Crown," Ullin went on. "The agent must renew the lien on the articles each year until the forfeiture is acted upon. Usually, forfeiture deeds are made only when the lands no longer produce taxes. When the agent receives the forfeiture deeds, he may dispose of the property however he sees fit, usually generating more taxes for the Crown. Hence the delay. That is why Lord Threshmere is able to remain on these lands. It is being held up."

"Aye. I've managed to pay out my taxes until very recently," said the lord. "I am not sure how much longer I may be able to do so."

"Here it is. The agent," Borwain stood up and brought to Ullin a small parchment, unfolded.

"Misters Norogus and Harmalway, Number 10 Farbrick Court, West Noringtown, Duinnor," Ullin said as he copied. "Do I know that place? The names Norogus, Harmalway, they seem familiar, somehow."

Ullin shook his head as he continued to write. "Rings a bell, for some reason."

After a few more lines, he carefully folded and addressed the outside and sealed it.

"Now," Ullin said, rummaging through his shoulder pack. He took out a small metal seal, daubed it with ink from the well, and pressed it onto the outside of the packet. He handed it and two silver coins to Leander. "Will that do?"

"Yes, indeed. And I will do my utmost to deliver it firsthand and first off."

"Thank you." Ullin shook Leander's hand. Turning to Borwain and Threshmere, he said, "I can make no promise of any relief for your situation, but perhaps my acquaintance may look into things. There is little else I can do. But, as you know, if the Court finds that your son is indeed dead, and that you have no more heirs, your banner will be taken down upon your own death."

"That is only fitting," Threshmere shrugged, "since the House of Hemlock will be no more." Reaching for Ullin's hand, he continued, "It is most generous of you to do this. And we are indebted to you for the effort. I truly regret I cannot offer better hospitality to you and your companions, but, as you can see...." Threshmere held out his hands in a shrug.

"Well, I hope," Ullin replied, "by whatever means that is just, the condition of the House of Hemlock may improve."

Ullin's eye was drawn to a sketch that hung near the window, a drawing of a workman, his face turned to the artist. Ullin was certain, or at least he thought, that but a moment before it depicted a man laboring to empty a huge basket of apples into a cart. But now the basket was empty upon the ground, and the man was leaning against the loaded cart, grinning. Another sketch nearby, one that Ullin had earlier thought to be a rendering of a winter forest with stark bare limbs shrouded by mist, was actually, upon closer look, a springtime woodland scene, dark with lush foliage filled with birds above and cavorting rabbits beneath the healthy branches.

"Most remarkable drawings!"

• • •

When the company had long parted from the estate, and Leander had turned back northward, they continued to talk as they plied their own way westward. The mysterious lake and its eerie ghosts, and the down-on-its-luck estate they had just left behind, were all discussed and pondered. The acquaintance in Duinnor, Ullin explained to them, was a former Kingsman commander that Ullin knew from his time serving in the Dragonlands. But he had been recently put in charge of the King's Constabulary in Duinnor, those Kingsmen who enforced law within the city. He was an honest man, with high standards of conduct, and he would have the connections to look into Threshmere's problem. After explaining all of that, Ullin described the terrible condition of the hall, and he told them about the uncanny drawings of Borwain.

"It is said, as you may or may not know," pointed out Ashlord, "that the House of Hemlock is descended from Alonair."

"No! That I had not heard," Ullin responded. "That may explain much!"

"Alonair?" Billy asked. "An' who's 'at?"

"One of the Firstborn," said Ashlord.

"He had the gift of carving stone," said Ullin.

"Statues," said Sheila.

"So wondrous in their appearance," Robby told Billy, "that even the Dragon King, Kalzar, desired to possess one of his works."

"Yeah," said Ibin. "Don'tyou, don'tyouremember, rememberthestory-Ashlordtoldus?"

"Well, pardon me for a mere lapse of memory!" Billy responded.

"In a way, it was Alonair who started this whole mess," said Robby.

"Many believe that he was allied to Secundur," added Ullin.

"I do not," put in Ashlord. "In spite of the common tales."

"But was it not he who baited Kalzar," Sheila asked, "by promising a fantastic sculpture if only Kalzar would move a stone big enough for the carving from the mountains to his great city? Wasn't that in the story you told us?"

"I don't doubt that part," said Ashlord, "and it may be that Alonair was influenced by Secundur. But that is a far cry from being an ally."

"I thought Alonair disappeared from the world," said Sheila.

"You remember your lessons well, my dear!" Ashlord replied. "Yes, after the Fall, he was not heard of again, although there are many tales and legends concerning him. One tale has it that, before he disappeared, he had children and that it is through that line that the House of Hemlock emerged. Another says that he ventured eastward for a time."

"Another legend says that it was not because of the strife with Kalzar that he went away, but because of the troll people," Robby added. "And that he sought to give life to the stones he carved and thus created the trolls. But, so the legend goes, they were crude and a disappointment to him, lacking in grace or in graceful spirit."

From Ashlord's amazed expression, Robby realized that he should not have said anything about that.

"Did Mr. Broadweed teach you that?" Ashlord asked mildly.

"I sure don't remember that lesson!" said Billy.

"Me, meneither," added Ibin.

"But, then," added Billy, his eyes glinting, "I warn't always payin' 'xact attention to ol' Broadweed."

"Just picked it up somewhere," Robby shrugged, returning Ashlord's smile.

"A dry tale?" Ashlord winked.

"Most certainly," Robby nodded.

"What does that mean?" asked Sheila.

"Just an expression," Ashlord said.

• • •

The day continued overcast and cold, but with little rain, and the wind thankfully eased up quite a bit. The way was easy, and they put many miles behind them, encountering no other travelers, passing through forest and field. The road went gently up and down, and sometimes ran alongside ice-banked streams or over mossy-stoned bridges. By the end of the day, when the gray clouds were growing darker with the coming night, they realized that they would not find lodging and looked for a place to make a sheltered campsite. It was not long before Ibin was pointing out a tall structure on a nearby hill. Making their way to it, they found the graceful ruins of an ancient temple. It was the first they had encountered during their journeys, besides that of the Wickermen. This one was made entirely of stone, cracked and crumbled here and there, and it was round, like a broad turret, some four stories high, with a flat top. There were graceful arched buttresses, several still intact, that fanned out like the fletching of an arrow. As the group spread their blankets and made their fire, they talked much about the practices of the Faerekind, and how such places came to be built or abandoned. Ashlord was asked many questions, his explanations sometimes quite long, but Robby, from his own source of knowledge, surprised all of them by the questions and the answers that he contributed.

While walking around the place gathering firewood as he went, Billy eyed the structure very carefully. When he returned, he pronounced an observation.

"It's very odd," he said to the group, dumping his armful of sticks. "That is, if ye look at the place all 'round, as I've done. I mean, see them arches that fly upwards with all the curves an' runes? An' along the walls, tumbled though they be. Well, this is the thing: thar ain't no doors. Not a single one, so far as I can see. Nope. Nary a door, nor winder, neither, 'cept way up yonder. Odd kinda place to build, seein' as ye can't get in."

"I see what you mean," Sheila nodded, looking up from where she was stacking the fuel Billy had just dropped.

"The builders of this place had no need for doors, Billy," Ashlord said, smiling. "And those that worshipped here had no trouble getting to their altar, up at the top of the structure."

"But thar ain't no stairs, er ladders, er such, neither," Billy pointed out.

"They had wings," Ullin stated.

Billy looked at Ullin blankly, then he craned his neck back around and, squinting one eye, gazed up at the structure.

"Oh," he said.

• • •

Cold air settled around the ruins as they unpacked their gear and cleared a place to camp under the shelter of one of the high walls. The spot provided some protection from the breeze, and the paved ground around the structure was relatively dry. Before long, Ullin had a fire going, and Robby and Ibin brought more wood for the night while Ashlord unpacked their victuals. Sheila and Billy made places to spread the company's blankets between the fire and the wall, and they even found boughs of fir to give them some cushion against the hard floor. Those buttresses that still stood loomed on either side of their camp, their curves a reminder of the places they had seen in Forest Islindia. Although anything but sad in its design, the tumbled-down condition and the forlorn nature of the place had its inevitable influence on the company, and they spoke little.

Robby saw that Ullin continued to keep his distance from Sheila, as he had done for the past weeks, although he had not told Robby about any further visions or disturbances. He also noticed that Ullin was careful not to respond to Sheila during conversation, allowing others to respond first whenever possible.

Ashlord did his part, too, by staying close to Ullin. He sought to deflect Sheila's attention away from Ullin to himself, often answering her about some little question that she directed to Ullin. Ashlord could see that it irritated her for him to jump in so and answer for Ullin. And he could see something in her new sadness that confirmed to him that Ullin was having an entirely different influence than his actions out on the plains might have been expected to produce. He saw the way Sheila glanced to Ullin, the way she paid attention to each word he said and everything he did. And it was not wariness that Ashlord saw in her eyes. Even now, as he stirred water into a pot and mixed in ground oats and bits of dried fruit, he watched her as she, in turn, watched Ullin tend the fire and prepare a tripod for the cooking pot.

Indeed, Ashlord, keener now than ever, could not help but notice the change in the company. During his absence, much had happened to them and among them, and these things had taken their toll. He was sure that even Ibin, stalwart and optimistic, was more subdued and thoughtful, even if he was as inscrutable as ever. Billy was less jovial; certainly, his jokes and jests were not as frequent as before, and he went for long spells without lecture, even with the ever-receptive Ibin. Billy was a kind of weatherglass, sensitive to the mood of the others, his mirthful character moderated by long, silent periods of contemplation. Ullin, Robby, and Sheila were more obviously preoccupied, each with their own concerns. Certainly, the violence of the battle at Soltani Pass affected the company deeply, though they spoke little of it. Sheila's spirit had been especially wounded by the horror and waste. Ullin was now more reserved than ever, some might say cowed. Ullin's reticent demeanor was strained, bordering on despondence. Yet Ashlord's faith in Ullin's character, in his sense of duty and honor, dispelled his darkest fears about the Kingsman. And, Ashlord still believed that Ullin, of all the group, was the one most capable of seeing Robby's quest through. Things might have turned another way had it not been for their passage through Forest Islindia and their visit with the good people of Greenfar. Both of those places, and the people they had encountered, seemed to have provided a bit of badly needed healing and reassurance for each one of them, but especially for Ullin.

Like Ullin, Robby, too, was withdrawing. Although Ashlord understood it to be necessary, he wished there was a way to help Sheila understand the changes taking place in Robby. The boy from Barley was rapidly growing up, the responsibilities unfairly heaped upon him heavier than his friends could imagine. They did not yet comprehend the difficulties that confronted Robby, or that Robby's concerns spread wider and farther than their own, in keeping with his quest and magnified by his newly acquired powers. It was sad, the mystic felt, and his heart especially broke for Sheila.

And they were edgy, nervous, cautious at every step. Who could blame them after all they had been through? What new challenge might await at the next turn of the path? What additional test might confront them? What fatal threat might be just over the hill, or lurking yonder in the trees? What new trap might any one of them step into, the ground opening beneath them as it did when Robby fell into the Dragonkind's well?

Ashlord saw all these changes, considered all of the causes, and pondered the possible consequences. Even he did not know how Robby could hope to make it to Griferis, or, if he did find the place, what it might do to him. It was a mystery to Ashlord how Robby might take the throne, or what Robby might do should he succeed in ousting the present King of Duinnor. And, Ashlord continued to wonder, if all these things came to pass, would Robby do any better than he who ruled Duinnor now, or any who did before? No, Ashlord admitted inwardly. Yet he had every reason to think that Robby could do no worse. And he had every hope that the well-meaning shopkeeper's son had a goodness in him that would somehow prevail. One way or the other, Robby would tip the balance, and Ashlord's faith sustained him in that opinion.

Ashlord mused on while he did his chores for the company, and he concluded that it was still a strong company, none coming for themselves or for their own gain. Ibin came for Billy, Ullin came for Robby. Robby came for his people, as did Billy. And Sheila would not be parted from Robby.

And why did Ashlord come?

He smiled when this question came to mind once more. He felt Certina's light grip on his shoulder. He glanced over at Sheila, helping Billy with the firewood, and then he looked at Robby, Ibin, and Ullin who were kneeling close together, busily looking for food in their packs. An apple was handed from Ullin to Robby to hold, then from Robby to Ibin, then back to Ullin who took it, looking confused. Their laughter made the air less cold, made the night less dark, and took a stone's weight from everyone's heart. Ashlord's smile broadened.

• • •

By the time the sun was fully set and night had taken reign over all the sky, they had eaten and were settling into their blankets, with Sheila taking the first watch with Ashlord.

"I don't think there is much to watch for, tonight," Ashlord said. "And I will certainly remain awake, as always."

She shrugged, standing on the other side of the fire from Ashlord, and pulled her hood over her head.

"May as well keep up with our prudent habits," she said. "It will at least keep Ullin happy."

"You need not concern yourself with that, I think."

"He has as much right to happiness as any, does he not?"

"Surely. But you need your rest as much as any, too. If you wish, make your watch a short one. Let us make all of the watches short ones tonight. I will fill in the gaps, if any. And Ullin will have the pleasure of the last watch before we break our fast."

"I don't understand, even after all this time of being with you, how you can go without sleep. You eat very little, work without tire, and seldom close your eyes."

"It is the way I am made," Ashlord shrugged. "I was given much rest back when we lived together at Tulith Attis. You have seen me meditate. That is my rest. My body is not like yours and needs very little sustenance. But I do take pleasure in eating, in the flavor of things, and even in heady spirits, as you know."

"Still, you are a mystery to me, and ever shall be."

"Are we not all mysteries, each of us our own world? Is that not why we make so much of our friendships, even our enemies? We sense the abiding mystery of each other, even when we do not think about it. Because therein we find some way of understanding. It is not perfect, but can be adequate. Weak and tenuous those understandings are, sometimes too weak for words. But, however dimly, they do light our way."

"Perhaps. But they can also make one very muddled."

"True."

"I don't think I have ever thanked you for what you did for me. The way you took me in. The way you taught me how to read, how to speak, how to strive to have a right mind and heart. I was in a terrible state when I came to you. I could have given up. I wanted to give up. You don't know how many times I stood on the walls of Tulith Attis and thought, 'If I only step off, it will all be over.' "

"What stopped you?"

"Little things. The thought of you looking for me when I did not return. The thought that you, at least, would be disappointed in me or hurt. The thought of never seeing...."

Sheila glanced over at Robby, sleeping nearby.

"My dear. Never have I had children, and never shall I. But if one can be a daughter to a man in his heart only, and not of his blood, then you surely are as my own daughter would be. For in my heart you have made a place, in spite of my reluctance to take you in. Little Certina understood long before I did. And it was she who watched over you as you stood on those walls, and it was she who showed me your temptations. And while I paced for your return to our cottage, my eyes were not always dry. This was a fright to me, but it informed me of my heart. For in all my long years, I have cried only three times. And when you returned to me, I was filled with joy, and I gave my thanks to He who made me and put me here. For it was He who sent you to me. You needed me, perhaps that is so. But, as it turned out, I needed you, too. So do not thank me for anything I may have done. For I do not have the words to thank you."

By now, golden flame-lit tears rolled down Sheila's face, and, as she came around the fire, Ashlord stood and received her embrace. She wept quietly against his shoulder, saying, "There is so much I have not told you!"

"You need tell me nothing, sweet child! Only what you wish, when you wish, should ever you wish to."

● ● ●

Later, after Sheila had walked around their camp a few times, Ashlord talked her into going back to her blankets and to her sleep. He then woke Billy to take his watch, handing a cup of hot coffee to the yawning Boskman.

"Make your watch a short one," Ashlord said. "And then wake Robby for his. There's no point in being out in the cold when there is nothing amiss in the night."

"Sure?"

"Quite sure."

"Well, I'll take a turn 'round the ol' place, just the same," Billy said, swallowing the last of the coffee and turning away. "Just a circle er two."

● ● ●

The clouds, as they love to do, played swift chase with Lady Moon, though little movement of air was felt near the ground below. The surrounding forest and fields were still, with only the snap of the fire and the crunch of Billy's steps to be heard. He picked his way carefully around the ruins, trying to be as quiet as he could. Several times he stopped to gaze upward, and he thought of the night they all spent at Tulith Attis looking at the sky, and how Ashlord pointed out stars and gave their names.

"That's whar it all started, I reckon," he said to himself. "Leastways, some of it. But who could count on them Redvests comin'? Pretty well messed up things, that did!"

He gripped a broken column for balance as he moved around some blocks of stone and, feeling a pattern through his mittens, he looked at the runes carved there just as the moon emerged. The Lady's blue-gray light made the letters glisten with frosty dew, and he studied them for a long while.

"What are we doin'?" he shook his head. "Don't get why we ain't makin' for Duinnor in a beeline. Raisin' all kind of fuss to get help back to Barley."

Stepping around the column, he thought of all that had happened since the Redvests had come to Barley. The fights, the folks left behind at Janhaven, Hill Town, and Tallinvale. The strange Faere folk who had come to Tallinvale to see Robby.

"An' then thar's them little folk of Nowhar, an' thar treasure an' all that stuff 'bout curses an' such."

He remembered the witch and poor Ibin's narrow escape, and, if it had not been for Robby's Swyncraff, how Ibin might have become her meal that night.

"Oh, an' 'bout then, er shortly after, no, it whar out on the plain, after he got that ring from that watchtower, that's when ol' Robby started actin' so strange. Like he'd lost his strength, in a way. Like he lost his mind, in another way. It's too much for the poor boy! To be King! Crazy talk!"

Circling his thoughts as he did the ruins, Billy remembered the Wickerman, all aflame, and how the geese lifted Robby and flew him to safety. And he recalled Forest Islindia and the wonders they saw there.

"That makes two queens Robby's met," he mused. "That's a sign, surely!"

He paused again, smiling at the memory of the fabulous party at Greenfar, putting his hands together in appreciation of his mitts and the other gifts from those kind people, gifts that were now keeping him and his friends warmer than they would otherwise be.

"To be King," he muttered. "Might not be crazy talk. Not crazy, just, just more than a mind can take in all at once! I reckon if I was ol' Robby, I'd be all swallered up, as I nearly am, bein' only me."

He continued to struggle with his feelings and his thoughts, not having Ibin to bounce them off of, and hardly daring to voice them even to himself.

"Yep, I must take care not to worry the big fella," he said at last. "I owe him as much at least. Not to mention the others. Likely we've all got our worries, an' none of us wantin' to add to 'em by complainin'. An' good ol' Robby's got as much to worry on as anybody, an' so much more, I reckon. I ought not be such a lout. Just need to bear up! Just keep an' eye on things, an' do what I can do. Which is about all I can do, I reckon."

His course brought him back around to the campfire, where Ashlord still sat, judiciously adding faggots so that the fuel would last until morning.

"All's quiet," Billy said to him.

"Good. Good. Why don't you rouse Robby and take his place for sleep's sake while he takes yours?"

"Sure. Certainly. But, I was wonderin' somethin'."

Ashlord sighed inwardly, and took out his pipe and pouch.

"Yes?"

"Well, it's about Certina."

From her perch on Ashlord's shoulder, Certina turned her head to Billy and looked at him. Billy suddenly had the feeling that if an owl could frown, she was doing it.

"Oh?"

"Yes, sir. I mean, I was wonderin' how far she can fly."

"She could fly back to Barley, if that's what you are wondering. It would take her many days each way, perhaps a fortnight, depending on the weather between here and there."

"Oh."

"You wish for news, is that it?"

Billy nodded. "If I could only know if things whar alright. If our folks whar holdin' out. If, if… "

Ashlord had never before heard Billy's voice crack, but now it did, although Billy was trying desperately to be nonchalant by making shrugs and by nodding his head to his own thoughts.

"See, I never said goodbye to me ol' man. That night. He was s'posed to come on to the festival the next night an' was gonna see me. I was gonna let 'em get a good look at me in me uniform an' all. Show him, that is, make him proud, was me hope. But…but, if I could only know. For sure, I mean. Pop always wore this here band 'round his left wrist, ye see. A wee thing, ye might've seen it? Me mum gave it to him back when they whar courtin', an' he never took it off. It had a little heart made into it. Silver an' gold. If Certina could just peck around in the ashes thar. I'd know, ye see. If she found it, I'd know. I should've gone back thar. I should've gone back when I had the chance. I mean—"

"Billy, Billy," Ashlord interrupted the distraught boy. "I was there, on the hill overlooking the Manor. No one could have survived the inferno when the house collapsed. Anyone who did not get out died quickly. And I myself was commanded by your father to leave. It was he, as astute as any could be, who ordered the evacuation of Boskland. And it was he, by his fighting on to the end, who ensured the escape of your mother and so many others of your kin and friends. Many Redvests, attacking from within the house, also died. Your father's leadership, prowess at arms, and sacrifice held the invaders at bay and surely upset their plans. I am sorry that you must hear this again. If by some miracle your father survived, and if he survived unscathed by fire and falling timbers and flying arrows and swords slung at him, well, it would be a miracle, truly."

"I should've been thar."

"It is our good fortune that you were not. Now, you are the hope of your mother and your family and friends."

"But what've I done? What good've I been to 'em? I've always been a no-account!"

"By your sword, by your defense of your friends, by your loyalty, wit, and determination, you have protected hope. You may not think much of it, but, bit by bit, you have added hope to hope. Because of you, those in the Eastlands may have a powerful new ally, for it was you who instructed the Nowhere people on how to lay the timbers and build the platforms they needed for their swine in an effort to break their curse. Because of your quick reaction, Ibin was saved from a terrible fate at the hands of the mountain witch. Because of you and your companions, a dark power was defeated at Soltani Pass and at Westlawn before it could gather strength to add its threat to the many others that face our world. You have done much, as each in your company has, and your father would be proud of you. And, as sure as your name is Bosk, you will do much more, for you have only just begun your journey. As much as any, you must keep to hope and do what it is that you may."

Billy nodded. He brushed his eyes and nodded again.

"Yer a kind feller," he said. "Yep. An' I thank ye."

"You should know, Billy, that Robby also asked me to send Certina back to Barley. He, too, bears the weight of doubt and uncertainty and longs to know the fate of those left behind."

"Yeah. We've talked about it some. I'm sorry for askin' about Certina. I know ye need her."

"Do not apologize for that. I will tell you what I told Robby, and that is that I will put it to her. Whether she goes or not will be up to her, but when I asked her on Robby's behalf, she refused."

"Do ye know why?"

"It is much to ask of her. When I sent her to Duinnor some weeks ago, she nearly did not make it back. It frightened her terribly. When I did battle with the demon, she was parted from me again, and did not care for that, either. I do not think she will go."

• • •

Ashlord watched Billy return to his blankets. Certina dug deeper behind his collar and snuggled against his neck.

"It is turning out to be a restless night, after all," he said to her, looking up at the buttresses and the remains of the once-fabulous temple. "Perhaps this was not such a wise place to camp." Certina clucked a soft response. "Yes," Ashlord said, "on the other hand, perhaps the best place of all."

• • •

By this stage in his journey, Robby knew enough to be careful, in words and in action. And the more he considered what he had done to the poor ferryman—coaxing a nightmare upon him, and pointing the way to it for the creatures who feed on such—the more ashamed of his actions he became. Ashlord was right. It was foolish to be so brazen, and it was a mean thing to do. He was lucky, just plain lucky, that no one had been hurt. He was still trying to shake the images of those forlorn lake spirits, and their gloomy nature certainly lingered in his thoughts. Providence alone could be thanked, but the fact that he and his friends had passed through the apparitions unmolested, and unchallenged by the mysterious lake creature that guarded them, was of little consolation to him now as he chided himself. By coercing the ferryman, Robby knew he had endangered his friends.

"Thank goodness Micerea wasn't watching," he said to himself.

Her scolding surely would have put Ashlord's reprimand to shame. At least, he did not *think* she had witnessed the stunt. But she might have. She could have been in disguise, just as Robby had disguised himself in the ferryman's dream. The thought that she might have seen it all was unsettling because, since Micerea had not stopped him or taken him to task about it, perhaps she was ashamed of him.

"No, I doubt that," he mused, hopefully. "She would have said something had she seen what I did. And now that I've asked her to keep away from me, I suppose I won't know."

Normally, as soon as his watch was over, Robby made every effort to go to sleep and to resume his dreamwalking explorations. Tonight, he was in no hurry.

"Just plain old sleep is what I need." But he knew that as soon as sleep came, he would feel compelled to dreamwalk, to keep learning, to keep practicing his skill.

He made another round about the camp, the slumbering figures of his companions huddled closely together near the protective wall, and Ashlord, as usual, tended the fire nearby. The clouds were broken, and a clear breeze swirled them eastward. Through the westward trees, Lady Moon, her face half-covered by her fan, sank like a large orange bowl through the bare limbs. Robby picked his way west around the temple, away from the glow of the fire, and stood in a clear open space, watching the sky. Far away, somewhere beyond the moon, perhaps, was the end of his journey.

"Perhaps the end of everything," he frowned. "At least, for me."

In the shadow of lost beauty, now crumbling to dust and tumbled stones, here, under the enduring ardor of steadfast stars, Robby finally reconciled himself to the truth of Ashlord's warnings about his new-found power of dreamwalking. With a sigh, the weight upon him seemed to shift, as did his thoughts. Micerea's tale concerning herself and Ullin still affected him, as Ashlord surely suspected it would. When she wept, he had to fight back his own tears, for he had felt the love she had for Ullin, and the sadness of their separation. But it was done. And now the plan he had in mind was set. Suddenly, Robby's determination was renewed. There were yet many pieces to puzzle out. But each in turn.

"I know the things I must do," he thought, "even if I do not know how I am to do them. Or how I shall endure the doing of them." He nodded. "Dread of such will not serve. I must bear up. I may not survive the effort, but clearly I would not survive the avoidance. And it is better, I think, to be trapped by fate, and find some solace within it, some freedom of action within the walls of that prison, than to run from it and be forever condemned in my heart as a coward. If I can only keep from doing anything stupid, I might have a chance. And if I don't accidentally stumble into any more situations like with the Wickerman!"

Then the words of Belmira and Elmira came back to him:

"What one does accidentally..."
"...another calls fate."
"And what some call fate..."
"...others call destiny."

Sighing, he turned back the way he had come, nodding resolutely.

Ashlord appeared to have hardly moved, so still he sat by the fire, its flickering glow giving his complexion the color of reddish gold. His pipe was propped into his mouth by his hand and his glittering eyes were fixed upon the flames. A tiny wisp of smoke puffed inaudibly from his lips, telling Robby that he had not been meditating—if that's what it was called—for very long. Taking one of the hewn stones nearby and shoving it nearer to the fire, Robby sat beside Ashlord and pulled his cloak about his legs. There was a steaming pot dangling from a spit, and Ashlord gestured to it with his pipe.

"You should have some soup, then get some needed sleep."

"I'm not too hungry, and Ullin will be grateful for it when his watch comes."

"I will watch for the rest of the night. And there's plenty where that came from. Besides, I need the pot emptied so that I can make a breakfast with it when the time comes. It will do you good."

Robby took the pot and hugged its warm sides, the relieving warmth coming right through his mittens as Ashlord removed the lid so that Robby could sip.

"Mm. Warm."

After only a couple of sips he could feel the brothy heat spread through him, the steam from it driving the chill away from his cheeks as he tilted his face over it.

"Thank you."

Ashlord nodded and gently puffed. Certina poked her head from under his hood and gave a low cooing whistle.

"Certina is glad to be in the west, again," Ashlord said. "She is from a place not too far from here, to the south and east, and she looks forward to visiting it soon. It is a mere pocket of forest where axe has never hewn, not in all the long ages of the world."

"Is it a hidden place?"

"No. Not hidden, except from memory. A forgotten place, one might say. Not even the size of Barley, but vast in its beauty and deep in its enchantment."

Certina cooed again. The fire crackled. Robby slurped. Ashlord puffed. Ibin gave a little snort and huddled closer to Sheila. Ullin turned over under his blankets. Billy snored continuously and perhaps even contentedly.

"Is that where you met Certina?"

"Yes, it is where she and I were bonded."

"Bonded?"

Robby remembered the vision—or was it a dream?—that he had of Certina some nights ago, before they entered Forest Islindia. How Certina revealed her form to him as she came to Ashlord by the campfire.

"Are you two...married?"

"Married? Hmm. Not in the usual sense of the word. But like many mated ones, we share a way of knowing that is unbroken even when we are parted. And we share our lives with each other. She is my helpmate. And I am her reminder."

"Reminder?"

"By being my companion, she learns to be what she was intended to be. Not an owl, but another kind of creature altogether. That I have some role to play in her saga is in keeping with my race."

"The Melnari?"

"Yes. It is for each one of my kind, each Melnari, to have such a companion. It is part of the reason we were brought into the world. But only a part."

"She is a person, is she not?"

"Certainly. As each creature was meant to be, but few have become. But Certina is not a creature who became a person. She is a person who, because she had little choice, took the guise of this creature you see and, taking the guise, had to also take much else of the creature's nature. Over the long and lonely time of her existence, she has forgotten much. But now, after so many ages of the world have passed, her person begins to assert itself, and she begins to remember. As do the others of her kind."

"Her kind? I'm not sure I follow."

"Shall I tell you about them?"

"Please, do."

"Then, while you eat, I will tell you what I have learned, and have recently had confirmed to me, though I still know so little about them and they are a mystery to me in many ways. The unfinished story of Certina, and others of her kind, goes back to the very beginning of things, back to when the world was fresh and new and still being formed, before Sir Sun and his Lady Moon were parted from each other's company and began their wanderings, and before the seasons of the world were known. All was as one glorious day and glorious night when Sir Sun and his Lady Moon held hands in the sky, and with the stars they all shone together their light upon the earth. It was when the spirit of the earth was young and growing, bringing forth in its seas and upon the land and in the air all the myriad expressions of life. The forests grew and the grass of the plains. Creatures of the deep swam, and birds of the air soared high. Of every place came life."

Ashlord tamped out his pipe, and refilled it as he continued.

"Later, in that splendid Time Before Time, and out of the heart of those places and from the spirit of the creatures therein came forth new spirits, and they, mute and misty, gathered strength and moved about the world. These spirits rejoiced in fellowship with all of the things of the earth, rock and river, the feathered, the foliaged, and the furry, and those with scales of the sea and land. These new spirits that moved about the world gave and were given something of all they touched until, in the afternoon of that First Day, they gained bodies of their own, soaring upward into the air upon their wings, and thus were born the Faerekind, one by one.

"So at the end of that long, timeless span, while the First Ones of the Faere still came forth from the spirits of the earth, and before the Sundering of the Sun from Moon, those things which made history began to happen. The First Ones, exerting their strength, brought forth new creatures and the Dragonkind. And when Beras made the night and the day, causing Sir Sun and Lady Moon to part from each other, and while the Firstborn and all other creatures were given ways to make offspring, and when Time began to be noted by the passing of Day and Night—all during this time new First Ones were still being formed of the spirit of the earth and of the creatures and plants and places therein."

He paused to fetch a twig from the fire to his pipe and, after a few igniting puffs, continued, the new coal in his bowl glowing ominously.

"But when came the Fall, when Aperion called forth all of the Faere to choose and be judged by Beras, when he took with him the True and Faithful and stripped the wings from those who remained, when all this happened, many of the unformed longed to go, too. But they had no means to join, having yet no bodies, and they remained in the earth, unfulfilled. These spirits continued to roam without hope of awakening. But, it is said, after a time Beras took pity on them and made a way for them to gain somewhat of their intended expression. And so, mysteriously, Certina was born, and likewise others of her kind, some of fur, some of feather, some of scale, some of foliage. Some of rock and some of river, and some of other things. They are seen by most of this world in the form of those familiar things and have the spirit and nature of those things, too, along with their own nature. And so they are something of what they are seen as, and yet they are something else, too. That is why their kind are called The Familiars.

"As I said before, there is still very much I do not know about them. Yet, through Certina, I do feel their urge to come fully into the world. For the past many years, I have felt their urge grow, and their impatience. They do not have it in their power to transform. The Melnari, my kind, were to have some role in that. There have been six of us, but only two Melnari still remain in the world. Raynor and myself. We two have struggled to understand these things about The Familiars, and what it is that we should do for them. What that role may be, I cannot yet say. But the growing urge of The Familiars is, I believe, one of the signs that a great change is coming."

"Great change," Robby repeated. "Just as you and others have said. I, too, can now sense it. Our encounter with the Wickermen, the mountain witch, your battle and recovery, the mood of Islindia—so many things—signs that the world is, indeed, being stirred."

"Yes, history is playing out. And everyone, all things, will have a role."

"The changes that are happening, and those to come, they are not set in stone, are they?"

"No, they are not. True, there are forces, like currents of a river, that we may ride upon, guiding our boat as best we may. We cannot change the frothy waters underneath our hull into the gentle mirrors of a pond. Great acts may, if great enough, turn the current this way or that. But stopping one current merely channels others along different paths. Like the waters of the Lake Halgaeth. Heneil dammed the Saerdulin, and waters that would have flowed there turned instead to the Bentwide. And, even then, the waters of Halgaeth rose, ever exerting its force against Heneil's Wall, longing, as it were, to return to its natural way. Until at last the dam fell, putting things back the way they were. Such is the world we live in, for good or for ill."

"Was it the Bell that made the dam fall? Or was it the great storm?" Robby asked.

"They came together. If it had not been for the storm, you would not have rung the Bell. And perhaps, without the storm, the Bell by itself could not have pushed aside Heneil's Wall. I cannot say."

"Like the leaf that fell upon the forest pond, and with its ripple destroyed an entire kingdom."

Ashlord smiled. "Just so."

"I try to pay attention and bear in mind all that you say," Robby went on. "And I do apologize for doing what I did, back there at the ferry. I am sorry for being upset at you. You were right, though. It was too risky. And, even without the risk, it was wrong of me to do what I did. The ferryman did nothing to deserve the fright I gave him. I am sorry for causing you such distress. I am sorry for disappointing you. I promise that I will refrain from ill-considered meddling, and I shall not meddle again unless I truly think it is needed. But, even then, I will strive to think it through. I promise you that."

"I am glad to hear you say so." Ashlord smiled again. "You need not apologize to me. Concerned, yes. But I was not angry. Nor am I disappointed in you. Perhaps I spoke too quickly and sounded too harsh. I did not mean to."

"Not at all," Robby put the pot down and looked at Ullin, sleeping somewhat apart from the others. "About the other thing," he lowered his voice further. "I have begun what you have asked. Micerea has told me about Ullin. Indeed, they know each other, and they are deeply in love. It is a fantastic story, Ashlord, how they met, how they fell in love. They suffer terribly by their separation. I plan to arrange a reunion, if I can bring it about."

"I see. Good. Thank you. Ullin is a good man, and he would be grateful for your efforts, if he ever knew them."

"Yes, he is a good man, and she a fine lady. There are other pressing things I should do first. Before I see Micerea again. Forgive me if I do not share everything, even with you of all people. The time is not right."

Robby stood. "And I suppose some sleep would do me good."

He hesitated, looking at his companions as he spoke.

"You have known all along, haven't you? I mean, about the Name of the King. How it must be obtained. From the beginning, all the way back to Janhaven when you first told us about Griferis. You knew even then."

"Yes."

"But you needed for me to figure it out on my own. You needed to see if I held to the quest."

"Yes, Robby. Telling you would have served no good purpose and would have caused your friends to revolt from our quest. If they come to fully understand what is required of you, I have no doubt they will try to stop you."

"That's what I thought."

"Only, my greater concern was for you. How you bear up to the problem. If you arrived at the solution on your own, discovered in your own mind what it is that you must do, you would more likely be apt to take it on. If I had told you, on the other hand, I may have filled you with unnecessary fear and dread. It is a fearful and dreadful enough task, as it is. And it is why Islindia bid us all not to ask you about your plans."

"Bear up? It has been many weeks and many miles since what I must do first dawned on me. At first, I was terribly frightened. Well, I still am. But I am determined, now, to see it through. If I shrink from the task when the time comes...." Robby shrugged. "Only that moment will tell."

Ashlord nodded in understanding.

"Tell me, though," Robby asked. "Is there a good apothecary in Vanara?"

"Among the best in all the world. Why do you ask?"

"That is good to know. I do have something of a plan. Please let me keep it to myself."

"I will not press you on it."

"Good. Thank you. Then good night! I shan't wake Ullin. I leave that to you, if you see fit. But he'll be upset if you let him sleep too long. Duty, and all that."

Chapter 18

A Kiss To Be Remembered

Day 139
106 Days Remaining

Indeed, Ullin was a bit perturbed, though Ashlord woke him well before the others.

"You need your rest as much as any," Ashlord replied to Ullin's protest. "Perhaps you'll lend a hand with the breakfast fire. Before we wake our friends, we could have a little chat."

They worked together and prepared the makings of a hot meal, and Ashlord told Ullin about Billy's request.

"Robby made a similar request back in the mountains, on the morning just before we parted ways," Ashlord explained. "I did put it to Certina, and she refused, and Robby hasn't asked again since we've been back together. I think he has resolved his mind on the subject." Ashlord did not say, but thought, "Unless he now has another means of acquiring the news that he desired."

"It would be a difficult journey for her to make, surely," Ullin observed, putting a sachet of ground coffee into a steaming pot. "One that I would not ask of her."

"I know you would not. You well know how useful she is to me. And you understand, better than most, having had much experience being far away from those you care for."

Ullin glanced at Ashlord, wondering if the mystic knew how true that was.

"Not to mention," he said to Ashlord after a moment, "that you'd fret day and night until she returned."

"Perhaps." Ashlord smiled as he stirred the bowl of oats and added a lump of sugar that Mrs. Stavin had given him.

"You would not be telling me this unless you were seriously considering asking her to go."

"That is so. If I do, I would certainly ask her to look in on Tallinvale."

"What would be the point?" Ullin asked. "What good news might she bring that may not change by the time she returned? And what bad news could give us heart to continue?"

"I have considered the same questions. Almost certainly Tallinvale is by now engaged against her enemies. There is no reason to think that your grandfather would not hold to his plan. By the time Certina arrived, she would doubtless find your home under siege. Robby's father should have made it to Glareth by now, if he has escaped his pursuers. But who knows how long it would take Prince Carbane to send relief? If he is able to do so at all. I see little that could be of hope to Billy, as far as his father is concerned. No one could have survived that inferno."

Ashlord paused to taste the meal he was preparing. After a moment of consideration, he added just a dribble of Fetch and tasted again, nodding.

"After all that, do you still think she should go?" Ullin asked, helping himself to a cup of coffee.

"You are a Kingsman. Think of the importance, one way or the other, of the news she could bring. The military intelligence she could gather could be useful, besides the other news. Especially if some great event, some surprising turn, has taken place, a dramatic change in the forces deployed around Tallinvale, for instance. If we succeed in rousing Duinnor and Vanara, they will debate whether or not to send their forces to the east or to the south. You see my line of thinking."

"I do. It is from the south that the merged armies of the enemy would come."

"And Certina knows it. She has hinted that she feels the urge to fly that way."

"Perhaps to warmer places," Ullin winked at Certina. She only stared at him coldly.

Nearby, the aroma of brewing coffee was tickling the nostrils of their sleepy companions. Ibin, ever keen to hints of mealtime, was already sitting up and blinking at the cooks.

• • •

Within the hour, they had broken their fast and packed their blankets and bags, with the cold air speeding their efforts, and they were on their way once again. The road was not too muddy, and in some places the puddles of water from the previous days of rain were iced, especially in the shady hollows. And the road was not too hard in its track, rising and falling easily. The company made good progress, and by noontime their exertions had warmed them considerably, and the sunlight brightened their spirits as much as it did the land around them. They were at last in Vanara, and that also bolstered their moods, for they all looked forward to seeing Linlally, the home of so many famous Faerekind. It was a relief to see the many signs of habitation, fields carved in to the forest here and there, and cottages tucked away into the trees with well-used paths that led off from the main way.

Conversation came and went, with a few long silences between, disturbed only by the sounds of their march. They talked about the lake crossing and the spectres they saw. They speculated about Uncle Solstice and melancholy Islindia. Ashlord and Ullin tried to answer their questions about Vanara and Duinnor, about how the King would soon make his annual journey to the Oracle of Beras, and what the new

Royal Year—which would begin on the first day of spring—might then be named. Sheila asked why the King kept a different calendar than everyone else, and Ashlord answered that it was just tradition. Then the question of the King's Avatar arose once more. They wondered what new form it might assume, and Billy offered a few bawdy "idears on the subject," and suggested a few other items of cookware besides "fryin' pans."

"Have you seen the Avatar many times?" Sheila asked Ashlord.

He nodded. "And each time is as uncanny as the last."

"Has every King of Duinnor had one?"

"Yes, since the First Unknown King."

"How many have thar been?" asked Billy. "Av'tars, that is."

"There have been six Unknown Kings with Avatars since the two hundred and thirty-first year of the common calendar," Ashlord said. "So that makes six hundred and thirty-nine Avatars. The present King has ruled for five hundred and thirty-eight years, almost five times longer than all the previous kings combined. He is the Sixth. That is why, on the emblems and crests of Duinnor, there appears that number, in actuality or in symbols."

"See here," Ullin pulled out his shoulder bag, the one he kept his papers in, and showed them the flap. "My Post bag."

The leather flap was embossed with the emblem of the King's Post, a horse rampant. Below the horse were five other much smaller horses depicted in like pose. Each horse wore a crown upon its head.

"It is very worn, but you can see the six horses and crowns. Here, almost rubbed away, above the middle crown, is the number six, in the old script of Duinnor."

The group examined it, nodding.

"The pommel of my gladius," he put away the bag and pulled out his Kingsman sword, "bears the insignia of the King's Men."

"Butit, butitonlyhasfive, fivecrowns."

"That's right, Ibin. It was forged during the time of the last King. It is very old."

"Why do you carry it and not a newer one?" Robby asked.

Ullin held it up, looking at the sword, shrugging, and gave it a couple of slight dips. "It feels better to my hand than the new ones. A better heft and balance. And the steel is just as good."

"Do you prefer it to your long sword?"

"Depends. This one draws quickly, and is good for close-in combat. Good to use with a shield because it is shorter. But my other sword is best for two-handed work. Longer. At Soltani Pass I used the long sword because I had no shield. But I carried the gladius at my belt in case I needed it. A good thing, too, since I wound up using both against the Wickermen, one sword in each hand."

Putting the gladius away, he said, "There were just so many of them."

Billy and Sheila knew what Ullin meant, nodding at the unpleasant memories of that day, the horde of Wickermen, and the terrible fight. They moved on, the entire company remaining quiet for a long while. Billy's thoughts eventually turned back to the previous line of conversation.

"Back to this here Av'tar," Billy continued, addressing Ullin. "Ye've seen it, too?"

"Oh, yes. Many times. Once it passed very close to me. Like Ashlord said, uncanny. Maybe it is some kind of shapeshifter."

"Shapeshifter?"

"That is as good of a theory as any," Ashlord replied. "But it must be an unusual kind."

"Aren't shapeshifters just myths?"

"They are mysterious," Ashlord stated. "And they are rare. But they are real. And they are dangerous. Unpredictable. Solitary, I think. I have only encountered one. That was years ago. It was in the form of a black panther. I was with a party of Vanarans escorting prisoners from the south."

"Dragonkind?"

"Yes. We captured them and held them as spies. We were ordered to take them to Duinnor for questioning. We only learned later that we were being stalked. As we neared the border of Duinnor, the panther attacked us, killing two of our prisoners and wounding one of our own men. Two nights later, it attacked again and killed the last of our prisoners."

"How do you know it was a shapeshifter?" Robby asked.

"It left footprints. Footprints that turned from those of a cat into those of a person."

"And you never saw it again?" asked Sheila.

"No. Never again."

"Why did it kill the prisoners? Because they were unarmed?" Ullin asked.

"Perhaps. It was definitely not from hunger that it attacked. Or else it would have made some effort to drag its victims away to devour. I think it was after the prisoners all along. Perhaps it knew why Duinnor wanted to question them, and its aim was to prevent that."

"So it was in league with the Dragonkind," Sheila concluded. "And they couldn't allow prisoners to answer any questions."

"It would seem so. But I have my doubts. It had ample opportunity to attack the rest of us. But it did not. Surely one in league with the Dragonkind would not hesitate. We were a small party, far from any shelter we could reach. After the last attack, we moved quickly. But it did not reappear. I later heard that attempts were made to catch the creature, and that many traps and snares were set. It evaded capture, though, and as far as I know it has not been seen since."

"Very strange," Ullin stated.

"Very strange," Robby repeated.

"Look there," Sheila said, pointing ahead.

They had just topped a hill, and through the sparse trees that lined the road they could see a village in the dale below. There were many cottages clustered together, and a few other buildings, too. As they came to a stop, they could hear the ring of a blacksmith's anvil, and they could see people coming and going, some driving carts, others on foot with field tools over their shoulders.

"Maybe, maybeit's, maybeit'sagoodplaceforlunch!" Ibin declared.

• • •

It was. There was a modest tavern located just beyond the blacksmith, and the keeper welcomed the travelers warmly. After settling on the price of a hot meal, they were soon served with a good stew, fresh bread, and a pitcher of beer.

"On our way to the city," Ullin said in reply to the keeper's mild questions. "Any news from there?"

"No, well, not much lately. The Queen is still away, last I heard, but things have been mostly quiet, thank goodness. From the eastern realms, eh? Well, ye've come a long way. But not much farther to go. The main road turns away south just a mile out from here, so ye'll want to take the west way as soon as ye come onto it. Near a little bridge. Goes mostly cross country, an' it ain't as well used this time of year. No good for wagons an' the like. But seein' as yer on foot, it'll be a week's less walking than the main road."

• • •

They found the path with ease, and by late afternoon had gone several leagues, passing through broad stretches of grassland as the way gently descended into a wide valley. They could just make out a mountain range, low on the far horizon, almost invisible against the blue sky. Ashlord was about to comment on the sight when Certina flew excitedly to his shoulder, then tittered away to rapidly circle him.

"What is it?" he asked as the others gathered around.

Ashlord offered his arm, and Certina landed on his sleeve. She whistled and hopped and clucked, and Ashlord nodded seriously.

"I see," he said.

She flew off, making widening circles around them until she was out of sight.

"Well, we must split up," Ashlord stated.

"What?"

"A large force from Duinnor is coming, and we're bound to run into them if we keep going this way."

"What kind of force?" Ullin asked.

"An army. At least two thousand, according to Certina. They are Duinnor Regulars, making easy march southward across our path."

"They are sure to have outriders on all their flanks," Ullin stated.

"Yes. You and Robby should keep on. The two of you should be able to pass through their lines undetected. The rest of us will turn north to Duinnor."

"What? An' leave Robby an' Ullin to fend for themselves?" Billy protested.

"What? But what if they are captured?" Sheila demanded.

"I trust in Ullin's skill to see to it they are not. Meanwhile, I still have the papers that should give the rest of us free passage. And, if they carry warrants for our arrest, they'll be looking for a party of six, not four. So we may be able to fool them on that point. If we stay together, they are bound to detain us all. Ullin and Robby, just the two of them together, can more easily evade the army, hiding and darting according to Ullin's vast experience at such things."

"No!" Sheila cried. "We should stay together!"

"I think Ashlord's right," Billy said. "It'd be hard for 'em to miss seein' the crowd of us. An' we prob'ly can't back up fast enough the way we come to outrun thar riders. 'Sides, if we can get on to Duinnor, we'll have a chance of raisin' the alarm about them Redvests sooner than if we all went on to Linlally first."

"How close to us is the army?" Ullin asked with a tone of growing impatience.

"Certina says their vanguard is within four miles of us."

"Oh, great stars! It's a wonder we haven't already been spotted."

"Can't we let them pass? Wait them out?" Sheila suggested.

"We'd better decide, and be quick about it," put in Robby, looking around. "We've got a ways to go to find some cover to hide in."

"Then let's be on our way, Robby," Ullin said.

"When you get to Linlally," Ashlord said to Robby, "go to the Library at the Hall of Ministers and seek out the scrolls of the First Age. Find the Chronicles of Nimwill. He was a scribe who served the court of Parthais. Nimwill. Read his last accounts, called the Last Book of Nimwill. He describes the discovery of Griferis."

"Nimwill."

"Yes, and ponder his writings very carefully."

"I will do so. What else?"

"You will know what else when you read that account, but," Ashlord shrugged, "there is much I have not told you or the others. The less they know, the less they can tell, freely or by force. This is the crux of the matter: I have had a gathering worry—which began before we had even departed Janhaven—that we may be too late to help the Eastlands. Too late, even, to prevent the greatest of catastrophes. It is imperative that you get to Griferis as swiftly as you can."

"What are you saying?"

"Ye mean all has been for nuthin'?" Billy cut in.

"We should make haste," Ullin stated.

"Not all things may be done in haste," Ashlord retorted.

"Why are you telling us this? Now, after we've come so far?" Sheila pleaded.

"You take away our hope?" Robby puzzled.

"No! That I do not do! Listen to me for a moment. Remember the witch? Why did she stir to confront us? Was it mere coincidence? And the Wickerman? What power do you think raised that monster? I fear that all is taking place too quickly, and that it is not the sleep of Duinnor that is most fearsome, not even the growing alliance between Redvests and Dragonkind. No, it is Secundur who quietly puts out his hand into the world. He is not the ally of good flesh and blood, nor of frankness and truth. He is the master of subtle poison and deceit. He cares not for the Dragonkind. He hates the Elifaen and despises Men. But any and all he will use to his own end, bending to his will any who may serve. And most do so willingly, not knowing that they serve the lord of Shatuum, that they work toward their own destruction."

"What're ye sayin'?"

"There is more to save than the Eastlands, or even all the Realms. For all these ages, Secundur has held back. He uses shadow and intrigue only to bring about the conditions of his own desire, to set the pieces of his game into place. And when all are weakened by the coming war, he will then make his move."

"An' do what, 'xactly? Bring in his own army, er somethin' like 'at?"

Ashlord bent his head, as if listening to Certina, but she was high above them by now.

"Yes. In a manner of speaking, that is what I fear."

"So? Great!" Billy exclaimed. "One more enemy, more er less." He threw up his hands, "Why didn't ye just say so?"

"Billy! Don't you understand?" Robby said as it was just dawning on him. "Secundur's been holding back. But even he can't control everything. Evil leaks out from him, even when he would not have it revealed."

" 'Oldin' what in check?"

"The witch!" Sheila gasped.

"The Wickerman," Ullin said, almost to himself.

"The demon," Ashlord nodded.

"Will somebody talk plain?"

"I think what Ashlord is saying," Robby explained, "is that the witch, the Wickermen, and the demon were all a taste of what may come. Can you imagine an army made up of the likes of those? A whole army? Ashlord, do you really think they were in his service? That they broke loose, somehow, before he intended?"

"Yes, I do. Can you imagine what the outcome may have been if Teracue's army had not been in Edgewold to counter the Wickermen? What would have happened if that blight had been allowed to grow unchecked?"

Billy scratched his head, nodding, "I reckon it would've gotten bad, and purty quick."

"Read the Last Book of Nimwill," Ashlord repeated to Robby. Certina dove down and landed on his shoulder, calling loudly and fluttering with great agitation, then hopping onto his head, then to his other shoulder, pushing aside his hood to get to his ear.

"Yes! Yes, I know, Certina! One moment. Robby, when you enter Griferis, do not leave that place until you are ready to be King, no matter how long you must stay. If you leave before you are ready, all will be in vain."

"But how? How will I know?"

"You will know. This is not about becoming King. It is about what you must do once you become King. You will know. And, then, do what you must without hesitation or delay!"

"But without you—"

"We must part company immediately!"

"Then let us go," Ullin urged. "One way or the other!"

"Get Robby to Vanara. See him to Griferis, if you can," Ashlord hurriedly shook Ullin's hand, and they gave each other a quick hug. Then Ashlord turned back to Robby, and they hugged.

"All rests upon you," Ashlord said, nodding and smiling. "Now, go!"

Quickly, Billy grabbed Robby's hand.

"I reckon this is the way of it, then," he said. "I hope the next time we meet, ye'll be merciful to a commoner such as meself!"

"You are anything but common, my friend," Robby said, hugging him tightly.

"An' don't worry 'bout us! Do what it is ye gotta do! An' we'll do the same! Take care of him, Ullin!"

"Goodbye, Billy!"

"Idon't, Billy,Idon'tunderstand. Whycan'twegowithyou,Robby?" Ibin pleaded.

"Ibin, big man that you are," Robby took Ibin by the biceps and turned him to look face to face. "I need to go on with just Ullin. We have things to do, and so do you. Take care of Sheila and Billy. Will you?"

"Yes, Robby, Robby, I'll, I'lltry."

"Farewell," Sheila said to Ullin with a hug and a kiss on the cheek. She turned to Robby and looked deeply into his watery eyes, seeing his fear, a bit of panic, a bit of sorrow, a great deal of tenderness. She thought, in that brief instant, that perhaps he saw in her eyes the same feelings. She did not sob, and fought hard against it when Robby pulled her into his arms.

"I'm so proud of you, my love," he told her. "Thank you for your strength and for your love."

"I will always love you, Robby Ribbon."

Her voice cracked, she held him tightly, unable to speak further. She took his face into her hands and kissed him long and sweetly on the lips, long enough and sweetly enough to be remembered for a lifetime. She abruptly turned away and, without looking back, followed after Ashlord, who was already some distance away.

"This way," Ullin called. Robby shook himself, girded up his pack, and gave his friends one last glance before jogging off to catch up with the Kingsman.

• • •

"I foresaw that our company would split up," Ashlord said to Sheila as they hurried northwestward across fallow fields and through hilly woods. "But I thought we would all make it to Linlally before we parted ways with Robby."

"Will we ever see him again?"

"I cannot say, but I certainly hope so."

"Ithinkwe, Ithinkwe, we'llseeRobbyandUllinagain," Ibin said brightly. "Juststandstoreason."

Billy gave Ibin a sidelong glance, as did Sheila. Ibin reached out and put his arm around Sheila and gave her a squeeze. "Robby'svery, he'sverysmart. Andbrave, he'sverybrave,too."

"Yes, I know he is, Ibin."

Certina swooped by and shot out ahead of them, flying upward over the treetops. Circling back around, she whistled at Ashlord before shooting away once again.

"We'll be seeing soldiers before sunset," Ashlord said. "Listen to me, this is what we'll tell them...."

• • •

It worked, and seemed too easy. When the soldiers came over the hill toward them, they stopped and waited. Ashlord presented his papers, and, putting on a gruff air, insisted that the soldiers not only let them pass, but also that they provide horses and an escort to Ashlord and his party.

"Our business is to the south," said the lead soldier. "And I have no authority to delay you. I cannot provide an escort or horses without permission of my commanders. You can ask them if you like."

The soldier gestured at a line of trees some few hundred yards away. Turning, they saw about twenty armed men, mounted on buckmarls, moving in a line northward.

"Fellfaere," Ashlord said.

"Who?" Billy asked, marveling at their beasts and the light greenish armor and helmets of the riders.

"Soldiers of Vanara," the captain said. "They've been following our movements since we entered Vanaran lands."

"Why? Are you not allies with them?"

"Allies? Indeed, we are supposed to be." The captain gave a little laugh. "But they trust no one. Not even those come to give them aid against the Dragonkind."

"Perhaps they are just being cautious," Ashlord said. "After all, Duinnor Regulars have a reputation for seeking spoils."

"Not all," the captain shoved Ashlord's papers back to him. "Some of us can serve in no other way."

"Forgive me. I meant no offense."

"None taken. But I would watch my tongue if I were you. Others may not be so easygoing as I am. Here, take this."

The captain reached into a pouch and pulled out a small tin square and gave it to Ashlord.

"This is a token for you to present to my comrades. You will encounter them soon. It has my personal insignia on it. You will be directed to my commander, and you can present your request for mounts and for escort to him. But do not get your hopes up. We are ill-equipped as it is."

"Thank you."

"Good journey to you then," the captain said, mounting his horse and waving his men onward. Glancing back at the trees, Billy saw that all but two of the Fellfaere had disappeared.

"Apparently we'll have an escort, after all," Ashlord said. "Let us move on, then."

"Will they challenge us, too?" Sheila asked.

"I doubt it. Most likely they'll just keep an eye on us. I think they are more concerned with the Regulars."

That they did, moving along some distance away, keeping easy pace with the four travelers. Several times over the next two hours, other soldiers were encountered and, each time, Ashlord showed them his papers and the token he was given. Each time, they were directed to move on, until at last they came over a rise and saw below them the long train of the army passing slowly along a roadway about a half-mile ahead. Here, they were challenged again. This time, the soldier looked at Ashlord's token and gave a shout down the hill. A finely uniformed soldier looked up from his saddle and rode to them.

"These travelers have a token from Preston. They say he told them to speak with you."

"I am Commander Telday," the soldier took the token and pocketed it. "What is your business?"

"We travel on important business to Duinnor," Ashlord said, showing him the transit papers. "Our horses were taken from us several days ago. Therefore I ask that you provide mounts and an escort to us to speed our way."

"Your names?"

Ashlord told them, as Telday took a paper from his saddle pouch and looked over it.

"From the Eastlands?"

"I did not say that," Ashlord said. "In fact, I am a citizen of Duinnor."

"Do you have any proof of your identities?"

"None is required, if you'll examine the writ of passage I have given you."

"Yes, yes. I can read. My apologies. We were told to be on the watch for a certain party. Can you at least vouch for me that these two men," he eyed Billy and Ibin, "are who they say they are?"

"Certainly. Who else would they be? Who is it that you watch for?"

"An Easterner. That is all I may say."

"Well, then," Ashlord took back the writ of passage. "What about our horses and escort?"

Telday shook his head. "That I cannot do. We have few enough mounts for our own needs and no men to spare. You'll have no difficulty along the way on your own. These lands are free of highwaymen. Here, take this." He handed Ashlord a blue colored tin square, much like the previous one. "This token will grant you passage through our lines without question or delay. Just show it at any challenge and you'll be waved through. Good journeys!"

Telday reined around and rode off.

"Well, I reckon we'll keep to our feet then," Billy said.

"I did not expect them to provide horses for us, Billy," Ashlord explained. "But it adds to our legitimacy with these types if we take a demanding attitude. The ranks of Duinnor Regulars are not known for care or caution, and often have little respect for the rules. So they are less likely to be diligent in their work. Fortunately, for us, they either do not have a list of names in their orders or else they are too lazy to check. Either way, it appears as if we may pass through easily."

"But it seems like they have some kind of description of Robby," Sheila said.

"Yes," Ashlord nodded. "How they got that, I cannot guess. Let us hope, then, that Ullin's skill will see them through safely. Meanwhile, I trust these men as little as the Fellfaere do. So let us hurry to get ourselves well beyond them. Sheila, it may do us well for you to pull your hood and cloak about you."

• • •

The pinkish purple sunset came quickly and the four skirted along the road, picking their way carefully until it was blocked by the beginnings of campfires. Realizing that the army was making bivouac for the night, Ashlord took them into the center of their numbers, where the road cut through.

"At least this way will be easier to trod," he said. As a group of soldiers looked up from their fire, Ashlord unexpectedly waved at one, and called out, "You, sir, come here."

A young man pointed at himself questioningly.

"Yes, you."

"Aye, sir, what is it?"

"I have here a pass from Commander Telday. Would you be so kind as to escort us to the rear of your camp?"

"Well, I was just about to get some supper."

"Your meal can wait. Pick up your arms and do as commanded."

"Well, I'll have to check with my sergeant—"

"Do you answer to your sergeant ahead of your commander?"

"Well, yes, er, I mean, no. I mean, it don't seem right to run off."

"Come along, then. Make haste with your arms, and let us go. I have no time to waste."

"Yes, sir! Right away, sir!"

Soon they were moving along rather quickly, the enlisted soldier waving away checkpoint guards, while to either side of the road a vast encampment spread out, dotting the hills with tents and fires. Behind them, unmolested by any of the soldiers, but eyed warily nonetheless, came the two Fellfaere riders, keeping their distance.

"Are they with ye?" their escort asked.

"They watch us as they do all travelers and passers-through."

"I'll say. They've been all around us since we first came into these lands. On either side of our march."

"It would be my guess that you are not welcome," Ashlord stated.

"I reckon not, though it beats me why. We go to defend their homeland, don't we?"

"Is there a new battle with the Dragonkind brewing?"

"There's always one brewing. If there ain't one, we mean to brew one up, don't we? I mean, we didn't come all this way just to see the sights, as it were."

"I see. Enough talk."

• • •

They were relieved when, after less than an hour more, they reached the rearguard. Ashlord dismissed the soldier, with a coin for his good conduct, and the four continued on, keeping their pace as quick as they could along the road between the camps of such followers that trailed every army.

"Wives, some," Ashlord explained, hurrying his companions along. "Whores, others. Speculators, usurers, and other criminals seeking opportunity for theft or spoil. You saw how unkempt the soldiers were. Duinnor Regulars are hardly selective about those who serve in their ranks, and they lack real discipline and training. If these had been Kingsmen, we would not have passed through so easily, though. Kingsmen and Regulars fairly despise each other, by the way. But these," Ashlord made a gesture to a group of men coming to fisticuffs over some matter, knocking over a rack of wares being hawked by a third. "These are likely kin and kith of those wearing uniforms. And they would think nothing of taking advantage of four unescorted travelers, so let us march quickly away from here!"

"I wouldn't exactly say unescorted," Sheila commented, nodding her head to the outskirts of the encampments. There, two of the Fellfaere riders still kept easy pace with them.

"Yes," Ashlord said. "They will most likely turn back when we reach the edge of this mob. I'm sure they are more interested in reporting the strength and nature of these who come into their lands."

"Theyare, theyarekindaspookylooking," said Ibin.

"A stern lot, indeed, Ibin."

"So, how far is it to Duinnor, ye reckon?" Billy asked.

"About two weeks to the border. Nearly another two to Duinnor City."

"Oh, good grief! Will thar be no end to our travels?"

Ashlord stopped and faced Billy.

"Now who was it that insisted on coming along? Who said someone must warn Duinnor and seek aid for the Eastlands?" he asked. Before Billy could answer, he went on, "As I recall, it was a certain Boskman, was it not?"

"Why, yeah. Just askin'—"

"We make our best way, at our best speed," Ashlord said. "Rather than bemoan the time this takes, perhaps you should begin considering what it is you will say in the Court of Houses."

"What I'll say?"

"Yes. You are now master and laird of Boskland. Though yours is not a Named House, it is an Honored One, and your pennant hangs in the Hall of Banners, giving you the right of hearing. That distinction has been held by your family for generations. Any whose banner hangs in the Great Hall of Duinnor, within its Hall of Banners, has the right to address the full Court of Houses, which I presume you know."

"Why, no. I had no idear."

"Then you discredit not only your name, but also the lessons that I am sure that Mr. Broadweed gave you."

"Ashlord," Sheila intervened, "do not be so hard on Billy."

"I do not mean to be," Ashlord stated. "And I regret I have not had you under my own tutelage concerning such matters. And perhaps it is my fault for not spending time upon this subject before now. I am sorry for my harsh words, Billy. But much responsibility has fallen upon your shoulders."

Ashlord started off again, followed by Ibin, then by Billy and Sheila.

"Billy—," Sheila began.

"No, no, it's alright, Sheila," Billy said. "I got tougher skin than that, I hope. 'Bout time somebody said somethin', though, don't ye think?"

"I suppose."

"Ashlord," Billy hurried to catch up, "Ashlord, how come ours ain't one of the Named Houses? I mean, we Bosks go way back to the first ones what settled after comin' over the sea. An' if ours is an Honored

House, well, what's the difference? Why ain't we a Named One?"

"That is often a touchy question," Ashlord replied, satisfied that Billy was ready to begin his lessons. "The Bosk pennant was hung in the Hall of Banners in honor of your namesake, Bilaylin the Hammer, who gave his life in the defense of Tulith Attis. That makes yours an Honored House. Some houses are not Named because they are too modest of estate or power to warrant the control of the King, or to draw his attention. Remember, all Named Houses must submit their eldest son for service. Any that fail in that duty, well, you saw for yourself the trouble that has befallen the House of Hemlock. If a Named House is unable to honor its duty to the King, it must pay heavy fines. Many are dissolved, their banners ceremoniously taken down and burned. But Named Houses have the right to keep a representative in Duinnor to decide important matters along with the other Houses. Usually these are Kingsmen who must serve in Duinnor anyway. But few Houses see any advantage in allowing another House to become Named, which would further dilute their own power and influence."

Billy nodded. "I think I foller ye. But—"

"As for the Bosk estate," Ashlord went on, "I was given to understand by your father that he was not wealthy or powerful enough to be a threat, and yet wealthy and powerful enough to bribe certain officials in Glareth to exclude certain deeds from the tally books, a practice established by your forebears. It makes Boskland appear smaller than it is to the King's tax men. And it has kept the sons of Bosk from being drafted into the King's service."

"What? Ye say me ol' man *cheated?*"

"Your father merely followed a longstanding tradition practiced by the Lairds of Boskland before him. But he chuckled when he told me about it, many years ago. And I'm sure he would have told you, too, if only you had shown more interest."

"I know, I know," Billy admitted. "Don't think I ain't kicked meself back an' forth an' up an' down for bein' the lazy rascal me ol' man always said I was. An' I ain't got no excuse, neither. But on about this here Court o' Houses. Is thar a great number o' folk in it? An' what all should I say 'bout things?"

"At my last reckoning, which was some years ago, there were sixty-three Honored Houses, thirty Named Houses of the Elifaen, and one hundred and seventy-nine Named Houses of Men, and two Joined Houses. Most of the Named Houses of Men are located in and around Duinnor, but there are quite a few in the other Realms. Fifteen of the Named Houses of the Elifaen are in Glareth, one is in Masurthia, and two are in Altoria. The rest are in Vanara. The Honored Houses are mostly in Duinnor, Vanara, and Glareth."

"So Ullin is of one of the Joined Houses," Sheila asked. "Where is the other?"

"It is the House of Beech, of Glareth by the Sea, Prince Carbane's house."

"Man!" Billy shook his head. "I got some catchin' up to do, eh?"

Ashlord smiled to himself and picked up the pace, leading them on nearly at a trot as the evening descended. Still, Ashlord pressed on, seeking to avoid any camp followers, stragglers, or others who trailed the army of Duinnor. Only when they had walked well beyond the last campfire, and when it became too dark to safely see their way, Ashlord slowed and whispered something to Certina, who then flew off into the night. After another hour of fast walking, Ashlord paused again and Certina landed on his shoulder. He nodded to her message.

"We are miles from any other travelers along this road," he announced as he started off again. "So we'll go a bit farther to a place Certina has found for us to camp."

A little while later, Ashlord guided them off the road and through a wooded copse, then down a short distance to a clearing beside a stream.

"This will be our campsite for the night," he pronounced. "Since it is getting cold, let's make a small fire for some warm broth, and have a bite to eat."

This they gladly did. After they had eaten their supper, they sat in a circle around the fire, wrapped in their blankets. It had been a long day, they were tired, and they did not talk very much. Ashlord smoked his pipe, Billy absently fed the fire, sometimes holding a stick for a long time before placing it in the flames, and Ibin did not even pick up his mandolin.

For her part, Sheila felt as gloomy as the night itself. She doubted if the others felt as lonely as she. It seemed strange not to have Robby and Ullin nearby, even though feelings between her and those two men had been strained and confused. Until now, she had thought that she would resolve her feelings for the two, and find her role in their quest. She supposed, until earlier when they parted, that she would be with Robby at least until he reached Griferis. By then, she had imagined, she would know what to do.

Now, separated from them, she felt as if some protection was gone. It was as if Robby, or Ullin, or both of the men, had shielded her from something, something she could not put her finger on. At least Ashlord was back. While he was away, things were very tense. And upon his return, she seemed to regain her waning self-control. She came to guard her words as carefully as she guarded her feelings. The worst of it was that, after the battle, and after she regained her composure, she felt she had betrayed Robby. She knew that Ullin would say nothing of her declaration. That worried her not at all. But she realized that her love for Robby had only increased during this journey. The way he refused the powerful gifts that Lyrium offered him, how he handled the Nowhere people, and made his edict concerning the Treasure. Those were reminders of the void between her and Robby. The same chasm that she felt before all this began, back in Barley, when she knew she was not good enough for him. Robby was a different man, now, from the one that she had fallen in love with back in Barley.

The thought jolted her. She realized that she now saw Robby as a man. And that she admired the man she saw and only wanted to be with him. Even though he was becoming that which she feared he would become, that which she always saw in him from the very beginning. A man of greatness, with an extraordinary future. That was why she had gone to Ashlord. It was her chance to make herself worthy of such a man.

Ullin had confused her. And she felt a fool. There were many great men in the world, she now understood. And when they were good men, their attraction was powerful. At least to her. Now, glancing at Ashlord, and remembering his patience and kindness, the memory of all the good men she had ever known flooded her heart. The quiet old man who taught her how to fish. Mr. Broadweed, gentle soul, who made such efforts for her only to be insulted and disappointed. Mr. Ribbon, upright and plain-spoken, who took it upon himself to look after the property she had inherited, and who kindly took her into his home. Ullin, kind soldier, who gifted her with those soaps and brushes, the first person to hint that she might be a pretty little girl. And Robby, with his good heart and his tender affection, who honored her by keeping his word to her, who loved her when no one else would even befriend her, and who was proud of her, ever longing to be open about their romance so that he could openly demonstrate his love for her to others.

Oh, Robby!

Ashlord, without moving his head, glanced at Sheila and saw how her eyes glistened more brightly by the firelight than did Billy and Ibin's. She caught his glance and looked down. She knew that he saw and understood so much more than she ever could tell him. And she knew that he understood her heartache. He knew that she would never have the chance to tell Robby all those things that weighed upon her. Knowing where Robby was going, and why—it was as if he had died.

Ashlord saw this, and he understood the shock of the sudden separation was only beginning to settle. Grieving, as Ashlord understood, took many forms and came into one's heart through many open doorways. He sighed audibly, just as Billy finally spoke.

"Do ye think Robby'll make a good king?" Billy asked softly.

"Who can say if he will ever become a king?" Ashlord replied, somewhat surprised that Billy would ask. "But what do you suppose a good king is like?"

"Oh, as to that, well, I don't rightly know," Billy said, tossing another twig onto the fire. "I reckon one who'd look after the regular folk, for one thing. One what's strong to make men obey an' yet one what has a sense of right an' wrong. Who ain't afraid of talkin' plain to folks an' don't hide away in palaces an' all so as nobody can get to know him. I reckon a good king would have fair judges, wise an' good couns'lors, an' a pow'rful army, too."

Ashlord nodded.

"Is that a fair accountin' of a King of Duinnor?"

"It most assuredly is not," Ashlord said firmly. "But maybe it will be one day."

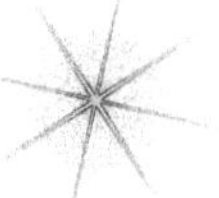

Chapter 19

Moon's Henge

It had been nearly a fortnight since the Ring of Fire around Nasakeeria blazed forth and killed the Dragonkind who had inadvertently crashed into the hapless cadets from Duinnor. The Dragonkind's bones were flung back across the border as violently as their unscathed belongings were thrown into Nasakeeria. They were soon gathered by Prince Nightar and brought to his town of Nuvodarini. There, they were placed in the council room of the Great House from which Nightar governed his people. Nightar would say nothing concerning what was found until he had completed his examination and study.

At first, the principal chiefs of each village and town—a great many of whom had come to Nuvodarini—were anxious to learn what was discovered, and many of these chiefs stayed in Nuvodarini, hoping for some word from their prince. But Nightar invoked the law and tradition of their land which made any thing which entered Nasakeeria the property of the Ruling Prince, to dispose of or use in any manner he deemed fitting. Nightar reminded the chiefs of the law, and he isolated himself within the confines of the Great House for several days and nights to examine the things. When he was informed that several of the chiefs still remained in the town, and that the people were likewise anxious to have some news from the Prince, he stepped out to address them, and saw Seleesa and Aremon in the crowd that gathered to hear his words.

"I have studied those things recently cast into our land by the Fire of Aperion," he said to the gathering. "Although we cannot be sure of what may have transpired that night, it seems to me that the intruders were bandits from a far-off place, and knew not their way or the danger that lay in their path. There are such things as may be expected for traveling bandits to have, weapons, cloaks, bridles from their horses, shoes, and other such items. I shall continue to study them, but I have seen nothing to make me think that there is any immediate threat to our land or to our people. Let praise and thanks be given unto Beras that Aperion's Fire still protects us. I bid you go in peace back to your towns and villages, and return to your homes and families. Tell your people what I have said. Tell them that I shall speak further on this matter, and shall send messages to all, once I have concluded my studies. Go in peace!"

This served to break up the crowd. After speaking personally to several of the chieftains to further relieve their concerns and to thank them for staying on to hear him, Prince Nightar went back to the guarded door of the Great House, calling upon one of his men as he did so.

"Ask Aremon and Seleesa to stay. When the others have departed, bring them to me," he said.

When Seleesa and Aremon were escorted to the room where Nightar was, they saw on the long council table not only the many items that he examined, but also a number of books and scrolls laid out. He waved them in, and the doors were closed behind them.

"We shall speak only in the dialect and language of Duinnor," Nightar commanded. "It is so that I may judge your preparedness."

"Yes, my lord," said Aremon.

"You both heard me speak before the others?"

"Yes, Prince."

"I will tell you something more than what I said outside. Come. Look."

Nightar first picked up a sword and showed them the markings on its blade, then showed them the little book and the writing within it.

"The writing in the book is remarkably similar to our own way of writing, my lord," said Seleesa.

"It is. You are trained by Traveshia in the language and writing of the Northmen of Duinnor," Nightar said, "so you know it is not their script. It is also not of Vanara, since I have compared it to the old scrolls, here, that were found generations ago and that have been kept by our forefathers. But look here at this passage in the book that I found amongst the things cast into our lands the other night. Do you not see the symbols here?"

"Yes," Seleesa looked at the flowing script. "They are as ours are, but they do not make words."

"That is because they are intentionally written out of order to conceal their meaning. But these other symbols along the top, here, are clearly numbers."

"What do they mean, this writing?" Aremon asked.

"I cannot say. But since each entry into the book is preceded with numbers, I think it is a record of travels, with each passage being some description of the day and observations made along the way."

"Along the way from where, my lord?" Seleesa asked.

Nightar picked up the sword again, and showed them again the symbols stamped into the metal. He put the blade of the sword against a page of the book and showed them a very similar set of symbols.

Seleesa's mouth dropped open as she looked back and forth from the book to the blade.

"You see, do you not?" Nightar asked.

"See what, my lord?" Aremon shook his head as he looked over Seleesa's shoulder. "I see only little symbols that look like—"

Aremon suddenly pulled his chin in.

"It is the Dragon Crest of Kalzar the Despised," Nightar stated. "And this symbol, as you know, means 'son.' It says, roughly, Son of Kalzar."

"They were Dragonkind who crossed the border?" Aremon asked.

"Yes. Not only that, all of their arms are of the same type and make, and they bear the same stamp, such as those that might be issued to soldiers. I think they were soldiers of someone who claims to be a descendant of Kalzar, and who now rules the desert lands."

Seleesa grasped the implication immediately. Aremon took a moment longer before he remembered the stories, just recently repeated during the Midwinter's festival, that recounted how and why their people came to Nasakeeria, driven out of the Dragonlands by Kalzar in the ancient days.

"Then Kalzar's blood has risen to power," Seleesa said. "It is as foretold by Aperion, as a sign that our days here are numbered."

"It is confirmation, of a sort, of what the little owl revealed. And so your mission will be all the more urgent," Nightar said, putting down the items. "Aremon, do you follow our speech?"

"Yes, my lord. It is not much unlike our own talk."

"Good. Continue your lessons with Seleesa, over the next two days, and redouble your efforts. After your departure, I will summon a great council to inform the chiefs of my findings here and of my decision to give you my totem. But it is best that you are away before then. I will set to them the task of preparing our people for departure. I imagine it will be a debate of some fire, but I intend to prevail."

"And our destination, my lord?" Aremon asked.

"I am still undecided. Meanwhile, I shall see the both of you at sunset in two days at Moon's Henge. It is close to the western border, so it should be a good place for the transformations. Now go, and continue your preparations."

• • •

Two days later, Nightar and Aremon rode together with one of Nightar's serving men to the broad hilltop known as Moon's Henge. It was crowned by a circle of standing stones, and when the three riders came out of the forest some half-mile away, they saw smoke rising from the fire that already burned within the place. All along the way, Aremon and Nightar talked in the language and manner of Duinnor, even though they rode hard, speaking of a great many mundane subjects. Nightar asked Aremon about the weather, about horses and hunting, and about clothing and directions. It was, as Aremon knew, Nightar's way of being sure of him, and he hoped that he held his own with the Prince.

They dismounted at the base of the hill, tied their horses to a sapling, and proceeded on foot up the steep path to the top.

"You have done well in the short time given you, and your speech should suffice," Prince Nightar told Aremon as they walked toward the standing stones. "But let Seleesa do most of the talking, since she has had years to practice the speech of Duinnor."

"Yes, Prince Nightar," replied Aremon. "Although their tongue is not that different from our own."

"As you have said before. Nonetheless, let her be the one who speaks. Ah, there she is."

Outside of the circle of tall, coarse stones, Seleesa awaited. She was barefooted, had a blanket wrapped around her, and had removed all of her jewelry. She bowed as the Prince and Aremon approached, then took Aremon's hand.

"My lady," Aremon said, bowing to her.

"All is prepared, my lord," she said to Nightar. "Traveshia will assist, to make Aremon's transformation easier, if you are still determined that he should go."

"I am," Nightar answered. "And so, before we begin, I will tell you what your mission is to be. Go to Duinnor City. Seek out the one called Raynor, just as the owl did. Strive to meet with him privately. You are to ask Raynor about the ringing of the Great Bell, about the Liberator, and about Griferis. Try to assess from Raynor the state of things with the present King of Duinnor. If possible, ask if Raynor has any news about the desert lands. Learn what you can as to how the various lands of the world are disposed toward each other, if there be alliances or strife between them. But you are not to reveal to Raynor or to anyone else where you come from. He may surmise that you are desert people, but let it be a mystery to him concerning us. Do you understand?"

"Yes, Prince Nightar."

"Learn from him as much as you can. Ask as much as you dare. As much as you think he is disposed to answer," Nightar said. "But be wary of Raynor. It is too dangerous there for you to take many chances, and it is daring enough simply to go there. At the slightest hint of danger, you must flee the city."

"We shall do as you say, my Prince," said Aremon.

"Good. Now I will tell you secrets. Shortly after the first members of the Order learned to transform and to go out from our land, it was decided to make a way so that those who followed in later years would have an easier time of things. With great care, and over time, with many failures and setbacks, a place was at last made for us within the city. It is kept available at all times, in exchange for a great sum of coin. I will not go into how it was done or how the gold used to pay for it was obtained. Suffice it to say that a house within the city awaits you. However, getting into the city and to the house will be your challenge. As you know, you may transform back and forth as often as you wish, but if you are seen to do it, you will be in great danger. Also, since there is a great hatred for desert people, you cannot be seen outside your animal form without great risk."

"How may we see Raynor, then?"

"First, locate the house."

Nightar explained in detail the information that was secretly passed down to him by his father and Traveshia. Although the sun was rapidly setting, he went over the directions several times until he was sure that they understood. He also told them how to find the cache of gold that was secreted for them within the place.

"Traveshia says that she left ample the last time she was there, but it was some thirty years ago. Hopefully it is still there. I will tell you that some of the coin was given over to a business firm that is in charge of looking after the house, its upkeep and such, for a term of fifty years. You may use what is needed of the coin to secure all that you may need during your short stay, food and such. But be prudent and frugal and vigilant. Do all that you can do by note and messenger. Even that will be full of risk, so strive not to leave the house unless you absolutely must, until it is time for you to return. And take no visitors except Raynor, if he will come to you."

Nightar looked over his shoulder at the setting sun.

"After the transformation, I will not be able to repeat these instructions. You must depart immediately, and you will not be able to assume your human form until you are across the border, so you will not be able to ask any questions. Do you have any now?"

Seleesa and Aremon looked at each other, then shook their heads.

"You are to return as soon as you can. I remind you, the power to transform into your totem animal will expire when the next full moon rises as it does now."

Aremon looked over his shoulder at the orange ball low on the eastern horizon.

"If things go badly, and you are delayed beyond a month, go to the Temple of Beras that overlooks the city. You may be able to find refuge there. When it is safe to do so, you may attempt to come to our border and signal us. Use drumtalking or a shiny bit of metal to flash the talk. But you will not be able to re-enter these lands if you are late returning. Not ever. So do not be late! Return before the rising of the next full moon."

Nightar looked at them seriously.

"If all goes well, I may send you back out," he concluded. "Traveshia awaits. I'll go first, and we shall transfer my totem to Aremon. That will be taxing, not only for Traveshia, but for me as well. Your transformation, Seleesa, should be easier since you know the ritual and are trained at it. Are you both ready?"

They nodded, then followed Nightar into the torchlit circle of stones. Traveshia was there, hobbling around the brazier in the center of the circle, throwing handfuls of herbs into the fire whilst mumbling to herself and waving her walking stick around in the air. She did not seem to notice the three who joined her, but kept going around and around the brazier. Nightar undressed, and knelt down. Aremon flinched as Traveshia suddenly cried out loudly and rushed at Nightar with a knife and cut off a lock of his hair. Slicing her hand, she kneaded the hair with her blood before coming to Aremon. He closed his eyes as she smeared the blood and hair on his face. When the old woman hopped up and down, waving her arms like a wounded bird, Seleesa touched Aremon's arm.

"Get undressed," she said. "And kneel down. It makes it easier."

Aremon nodded, and took off his garments and knelt, watching Traveshia as he did so. To his great consternation and wonder, she was now chanting unintelligibly and hopping about in a frenzy, shooing away invisible creatures with her stick, and rushing from one side of the stone circle to the next, tossing more aromatic herbs into the brazier each time she passed it. After watching her odd behavior for a few moments, Aremon glanced over at Nightar and was surprised to see that the Prince was not there. Just as he craned his neck around to see where Nightar may have gone, a large black bird flew past Aremon's head, making him flinch. The creature swooped past Traveshia, who waved her stick at it, then it came around at Aremon again. The third time this happened, Aremon suddenly felt dizzy and lightheaded. The raven landed on the ground a few feet away, then walked straight up to Aremon, staring at him with its gleaming eyes. The hunter heard himself panting as a hand seemed to grip him in the pit of his stomach and tug on his insides. His vision narrowed as the bird stepped closer, and, for an instant, he thought he saw a man kneeling before him instead of the bird, and he vaguely recognized himself.

• • •

"They go! They go!"

Nightar rolled over and then stiffly got to his knees. The sky was growing light with the coming dawn, it was cold, and Traveshia was standing over him waving her walking stick in the air, her long gray hair a mess of feathers and twigs.

"They go!" she cried, pointing with her stick in one hand while with the other she pulled out the debris from her tangled hair.

Nightar jolted, staggered to his feet, and stumbled out of the henge, not stopping to don the robe that his servant held out for him. He ran westward, down the hill, through a cold stream, and then to the top of the next high hill. Panting and shivering, he stopped and gazed through the mist at the fields below that spread out to the border only a few hundred yards away. Then he saw them, Seleesa bounding through the frost-laden bracken, and Aremon just behind her. He watched until they were across the border, but lost them in the distant mists beyond the stone marker. Prince Nightar's servant finally caught up with him, and offered a heavy robe.

"Thank you."

"So they are off and on their way."

"Yes. Yes, they are. And may Beras protect them."

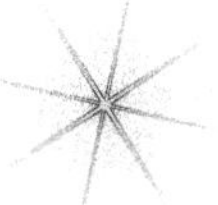

Chapter 20

Linlally

Day 156
89 Days Remaining

The city of Linlally cannot be described without telling of the mountain valley that it occupied. Perhaps the most inspiring feature was mighty Mount Cassos, the tallest of all the Megrinor Mountains. Its massive girth loomed wide and blue across the western sky, and the upper third of the mountain, often shrouded by clouds, was covered year-round by snow. Its middle third was grayish tan with rocky crags and clefts, and only on its lowest shoulders were there any trees. There, a portion of the eastern mountain spread two arms stretched out league after league. Between these two arms flowed a river that was frozen year-round, until a few leagues west of Linlally, where it fell into a steep ravine. From there, it seasonally melted and moved downhill in a frigid gush. This in turn followed along between the two arms of Cassos, which gradually widened their reach, and then the river tumbled into a high, round lake. In the center of this lake was the White Palace, home of the Kings and Queens of Vanara. The lake, not quite a half-mile at its longest and shaped somewhat like a teardrop, pooled atop a sheer cliff some thousand feet above the valley floor below. Through clefts in its broad eastern rim spouted five waterfalls—the Falls of Tiandari—which fell long and thin into a somewhat smaller lake below, forming the headwaters of the River Iridelin.

Beneath the waterfalls, along the banks of the river, was the city of Linlally, with its streets and avenues, its neighborhoods and places of commerce, descending in steps with the river. At each step, the Iridelin gushed over additional falls, some quite high but narrow, others broad and low, all dwarfed by the great falls above and behind them. Thus the Iridelin first flowed eastward, through narrows spanned by marvelous bridges of stone, and more peacefully though swift across broad shoals along wide avenues. Some five miles from the five high waterfalls, and some thousand feet lower still, the river bent toward the south to begin its relentless journey along the feet of the long range of the Tulivana Mountains. From that range, the Iridelin gathered into itself many other small rivers and streams until, some six hundred leagues away, it fanned into the briny marshes of the Hinderlands before slowly undulating into the ever-heaving sea.

. . .

For miles along the banks of the Iridelin southwards of Linlally, there were roads that ran close to the riverbank so that teams of horses could draw barges upstream. These ways, the beaten, the paved, and the watery, were always busy with the comings and goings of commerce and travel. Barges and wagons filled with grain and crops, trade goods and materials, and travelers, too, moved northward and southward whenever the weather and season permitted, to and from other parts of Vanara and from as far south as Altoria. As those who plied upstream passed many villages and towns on each bank, and the closer to Linlally they came, the more densely packed these hamlets were until they merged to form the Lower City. This portion of the city, on both sides of the wide bend in the river, was separated from the Upper City by the first of many shoals. There, a bridge crossed the river, and as it was now midmorning in Vanara, the bridge was crowded with people and wagons and carriages, all moving noisily across it. Some people rode tall stag-like creatures—buckmarls they were called—in the same way that horses were ridden, sometimes with fine saddles, but just as often bareback and with bitless bridles. There were numerous soldiers of Vanara in their tan and gray tunics and cloaks, and many of Duinnor in green, and others, too, some with the insignia of faraway Glareth Realm. And there were quite a few newcomers to Vanara, easily identified by their wide eyes, gazing at the splendid sights, and by their trouble negotiating the crowded streets owing to their distraction, sometimes bumping into fellow travelers.

Across the bridge, the roadway, now smoothly paved, broadened and ramped upward between stone steps and curved sharply back around to continue upstream through busy markets and toward the next step-like waterfall.

This main thoroughfare, following alongside the river, joined with other smaller avenues and passed through wide intersections. It was lined with tall buildings, some of which were apartments and others that were places of commerce and industry. And though the sky was clear, the air fresh and breezy and the streets were dry of ice, the roofs and lampposts wore caps of snow as did the heads of the marvelous statues along the way, rising up from splendid fountains or leaning out from high facades. This avenue, called Navia, turned over another graceful bridge and took the arriving pedestrians to the North Bank and through another district of shops and taverns before bearing westward again to a wide paved square. There, many of the pedestrians climbed onto horse-drawn trolleys in order to more comfortably continue their way through the city.

Among those who gave the driver a coin and squeezed onto the benches were two men dressed in travel-stained cloaks who appeared as tired and weary as any could as they sat and put their traveling bags on the floor at their feet. The taller of the two leaned against the outside rail of the trolley and closed his eyes in an effort to nap, while his travel companion, somewhat younger in appearance, sat erect and sought to take in everything within his gaze. As the trolley bumped noisily along, he watched the crowds and his fellow passengers, and studied the buildings and parkways and statues they passed. But his eyes always turned back to the tremendous Cassos, filling the sky with its bulk, and to the wonderful high Falls of Tiandari, visible from miles away, that fell from its cliff. After a few minutes the trolley stopped, letting passengers off and on, and the sleepy one stirred, looking about.

"We will keep to this trolley for an hour or so," Ullin said, shifting his weight against his shoulder and closing his eyes again.

The driver tossed his reins, and they jostled off again toward the river. Passing other trolleys traveling the opposite way, they continued up hill, going between magnificent structures. Some of these had glass-domed roofs through which could be seen the spring-like greens of gardens untouched by winter. One of these buildings spread over the avenue and river alike, and the trolley went right into it, revealing to Robby shops and other places of commerce protected from the elements by a high glassed dome whilst the rush of the river and the clop of the horses happily echoed within. When they emerged, Robby had to crane his neck harder to see the tops of the brilliant cascades that fed the river. He thought he saw a structure at the crown of the high falls, sometimes shrouded by mist, and other times blocked by the mansions that lined the avenue.

"Fairwillow!" the driver called out as he pulled the trolley to a stop. Nearly all of the other passengers got off, leaving only the two travelers, three or four workmen, and an old gentleman in a neat overcoat with its high collar upturned around his white hair. He sat serenely on the bench just behind the driver with his hands atop a silver-balled walking stick.

The driver flicked his reins, and the trolley rolled on. After crossing a bridge, the avenue curved and rimmed a portion of the Lower Lake that caught the now-audible cascades. Through gaps between buildings, Robby glimpsed the far side of the great pool where the falls were received by a tumultuous spray that billowed into rolling mists, split with rainbows. Twisting around, he could see much of the city below to either side of the silver river, stepping down into the distance like so many terraces until, far to the east, the wide and hilly valley opened into a colorful patchwork of fields and woodlands that stretched to the horizon.

Turning back, and stifling a yawn, Robby looked up through the open roof at the enveloping mountains. As the trolley turned to pass between two rows of colonnades, he caught a glimpse of a very large bird high above, nearly as high as the top of the falls. It was the strangest bird he had ever seen, having no tail and hardly any body at all. Its wide motionless wings were swept back sharply, as a hawk preparing to dive; but it did not dive, only floated along gracefully. The creature banked slightly, flashing a silver glint, and just before a column momentarily blocked his view, Robby thought the bird carried something dangling beneath. As the column passed by, he saw it again, now nearly overhead, and he stared at it as it soared away eastward.

"You are new to Vanara?"

The elderly gentleman had turned on his bench, his hands still upon the ball of his stick, and was smiling.

"Pardon me?"

"You gaze up at the Shrike as if you had never seen one."

"Oh, indeed I have not! A very strange-looking bird, like no shrike I have ever seen."

The man chuckled mildly.

"And, yes, I am new to Vanara. I suppose the bird is but one of many wonders within this Realm."

"Indeed."

"Are there many such creatures?"

"A number. That one is a Shrike. But there are others, too. Falcons, Sparrowhawks, and Eagles, all named for the smaller cousins who bear like names."

"Oh! And are they hunters, too? They would have mighty appetites, I'm sure."

"Hunters? Some are. But they generally eat the same as we do, and in the same proportions, as they go about their business."

"Business?"

"Why, yes. They are all servants of Vanara. The Shrike you just saw most likely carries important dispatches to the Lower City from the Palace."

"Oh, I see."

"Well, I hope you find our city pleasant," the man said as the trolley came to a halt. He rose and stepped off and walked toward a line of shops as the trolley moved on. Ullin opened his eyes and looked around.

"We get off just ahead," he said as he sat up.

"I just saw the most fantastic bird."

"Oh?"

"Yes. It was huge. And very high up."

"Oh. Probably a Shrike."

"It looked quite strange."

"I suppose it would seem so if you had never seen one before. Here we are."

The two stood up before the trolley stopped and made their way to the exit. As they stepped off, several people who had been waiting climbed aboard.

"We go this way." Ullin motioned to a narrow lane between two walls. They trudged along the lane and rose up to the next level where they entered a park of sorts. Walkways crisscrossed between squares of snow and trees, the undersides of their huge bare limbs glistening with icicles that dripped shady patterns of holes in the snow around them. There were many statues, most of normal size and so life-like, even with their icy coats, that more than once Robby thought he saw a change in expression as they passed by, or a slight shift in their pose. Some of them were carved to look like animals, deer, rabbits, foxes, and buckmarls. One, fairly close to the paved walk, was a particularly striking figure of a wolf in the pose of lying on its side, its head up and watchful. It was somewhat disconcerting to Robby, as the stone eyes seem to follow their progress as he and Ullin hurried by. So distracted by the wolf, Robby nearly bumped into a figure coming toward them.

"Pardon me," he said before realizing that it, too, was a statue, planted in the middle of the walkway, and carved in the aspect of a brisk stride. It was a tall man depicted, carrying a stout staff in one hand and bearing a bundle of scrolls under his other arm. On his head, somewhat obscured by snow, was a gold metal band and, showing from his breeze-tossed robe, was the hilt of a sword.

"That is a likeness of Lord Heneil," said Ullin, amused. "It was carved by Alonair himself, as were these other statues along this way. These are said to be the last of his works, made before Heneil disappeared from the world, before Tulith Attis. After these were carved, Alonair was seen no more."

"Alonair. He who made the statues for Cupeldain's city? Who challenged the Dragon People with the Great Stone?"

"I am amazed by your knowledge, and the gaps in it," said Ullin as they climbed a broad stair to another level. "How you know about the Great Stone, but not more about Cupeldain's city. Yes. It was Alonair who provoked the Dragonkind by the challenge of the Great Stone, and it was Alonair who carved the statues for Cupeldain's city. This, in fact, *is* Cupeldain's city, and these are those statues. Some of them, anyway. We might see more of them, perhaps, depending on where we go."

Now they turned through another snow-covered green, this one set next to the lake on one side and the sheer cliffs of Cassos on the other. There were fountains that shot water from the mouths of sea nymphs, and basins that passed tumbling streams over large upturned hands that reached from the ground. Now the roar of the great falls, barely a furlong away, was very loud, and from time to time light mists from their spray rolled over the scene.

"This promenade is often covered with ice during this time of year, formed by Tiandari's moisture. But it has been a warm season thus far, or so it seems."

"Tiandari?"

"The Falls of Tiandari," Ullin gestured upward.

The top of the falls was too high overhead to be comfortably looked at, and the sky too bright, but Robby looked, anyway, squinting and bending his head backwards to do so as they hurried toward a large building on the shore of the lake that the falls poured into. The building seemed an imposing structure to Robby, some six or seven stories high, at least, and many times longer than it was tall. It had hundreds of windows, the top-most curved gracefully to a point, and many of the lower ones opened onto balconies carved to appear as if they were supported by the limbs of a mighty tree. People could be seen going along these balconies, and now and then a glass door flashed as it opened and closed. The green-coppered roof glistened with the drizzled mist of the colossal falls looming behind the structure, dwarfing it to toy-like proportions against the mists and spray that billowed up. And along the eaves were fashioned many spouts in the manner of birds and drooping flowers from which water sprinkled into catchments.

"Does it snow very much here?"

"Yes. Usually a good bit. The last time I was here—that would have been in the Year of the Battle Lance—all was covered with snow up to my knees."

"The Year of the Battle Lance. I don't know if I'll ever get used to the Duinnor way of naming years."

"Well, it was about three years ago. This way."

"You've been here many times."

"Yes. I was garrisoned here for a while."

He led Robby on toward the building then up the main stairs in front. There was more coming and going of people dressed in fine long overcoats, many wearing fur-lined caps and velvet gloves. And there were many soldiers of different forces and Realms, their uniforms and styles of dress as varied in style and color and decoration as the civilians.

"This is the Hall of Ministers, from where Vanara is ruled."

"So this is where the Mayor works?"

"No. The city halls are down the hill. We passed them on the way up. No, these are the ministers of the realm, who oversee Vanara. This is also where Duinnor's ambassadors and military liaisons have their chambers, since Duinnor has permanent garrisons in Vanara."

"Oh."

At the landing before the multiple glass and copper doors, Ullin stopped. He pushed back his cloak to show his Duinnor tunic, resituated his Post Rider's shoulder bag, and he attempted to brush off some of the mud from his leggings and clothes. Turning to Robby, he did likewise to him in an attempt to make them both more presentable, and then he turned Robby around for inspection.

"We go first to the cloakroom in the foyer, where we must leave our weapons and obtain our passes to enter. Once that is done, I am required to report to the Liaison of Kingsmen. Until you are given leave, and a pass to go with it, you must stay with me. After I've made my report, I'm sure I'll be asked to report to various others, too. That's to be expected. The library is located here, so there's no avoiding following protocol. But we must gain admittance to the library. It may take a while."

Ullin made a last attempt to straighten Robby's clothes and to fix his own.

"I'm afraid we are somewhat lacking in polish," he said. "We should have gone to the baths, first, I suppose. But here we are, and there's no helping it, now."

They entered, and Robby was surprised to see that the vast foyer stretched the width of the building. On the far side was a wall of windows reaching up several stories, and a constant cascade of water ran down the outside of them. In the center of the wall of windows was one of stained glass, depicting a massive tree, coiled with ivy and topped with a constellation of stars. The dappled sunlight shining through the flowing water on the other side of the glass made the green leaves of the tree appear to sway and rustle as if pushed by a gentle breeze. The roaring falls behind the glass hummed throughout the room, somewhat muffling the clicking steps of the scores of people constantly going this way and that across the polished floor. Many chandeliers hung from the ceiling—one was being lowered so that the oil in its lamps could be refilled—and to either side of the room were doors and staircases leading up right and left to the next balconied levels. Nearby was a long stone-topped counter, behind which were several people dressed in walnut-brown uniforms, and Robby followed Ullin through a little gate in a banister to a portion of the counter where there hung a "Visitors" sign.

"May I help you?" asked a smartly uniformed young clerk from behind the counter. She wore a brown tunic with a white feather pinned to her left shoulder, and her blond hair was cropped to her ears.

"Yes," Ullin replied, unbuckling his sword belts. "Kingsman to report, and a guest to accompany."

As Ullin laid his weapons on the counter, Robby did likewise.
"As Kingsman, you are not required to relinquish your issued sword. But all other weapons must be held here," the clerk stated.

"I understand," Ullin nodded. "You may have all but my Duinnor issue."

"Very well. Please sign here." She turned a book toward him and pushed over an inkwell and a cup of quills. "As a Kingsman, you need only put your assigned Kingsman rank and name. When you've signed that, please sign this ticket." She put a card of paper beside the book.

Ullin signed the ledger, then the ticket, saying, "We'd like to put all of our things on the same ticket, please."

"Certainly. That would be fine."

"You'll need to sign here," Ullin directed Robby. Robby took the quill carefully—because he was more accustomed to using his pencil—and he dipped it into the inkwell, and wrote his name in the places Ullin indicated, and then wrote the town, county, and realm from which he came.

The clerk turned the ledger around and tapped lightly on a glass chime. Another clerk came from the door behind her and took the basket and a ticket stub that she placed on top of the things and disappeared with it back into the room from which he came.

"Your first time here?" she asked Robby as he craned his neck to see through the door. "Don't worry, your things will be safe. You'll need to step over there to have your bags inspected and then you may proceed."

"I remember you from the last time you were here," she added to Ullin. "That was about three years ago."

Ullin did not look surprised. "I am not Elifaen," he said, "but I think I remember you, too."

"Very well, then. Keep this stub for your things," she said. Glancing down at the ledger, she cocked her head back, looking again at the ledger, then at Robby.

"Wait. You did not write your true name," she stated.

Robby looked at her, not understanding.

"Pardon me?"

"This is True Ink," Ullin said, shaking his head. "I forgot all about it."

"You must write your true name or you cannot enter."

"True Ink?" Robby gazed at the page and saw the ink of his name fading away until it had entirely disappeared.

"What is this? What happened to my name?" asked Robby, looking to Ullin. "I wrote my name right here."

"True Ink fades if what is written is not so," Ullin said.

"Oh? But I wrote what I have always been called."

By now, other clerks, along with an armed guard, had gathered behind the counter to look at the ledger. Two more guards approached and stood behind the visitors.

"I know of no other name," Robby explained to the girl.

"That is the name he was given by his parents," Ullin stated.

"Unless you sign your true name, you cannot proceed from here," said the guard standing behind the clerks.

"But I wrote my name."

"He speaks the truth," Ullin added, looking both embarrassed and frustrated. "Can I not vouch for him?"

"The ink does not lie," stated one of the guards, putting a hand on Robby's shoulder. "I think you should come with us."

"Now, just wait," Ullin protested. Using his thumb and index finger, he gently lifted the guard's hand away from Robby's shoulder, then held his hand before the guard's eyes, saying, "Would you harass agents of the Queen?"

They stared at the ring on Ullin's finger, then took a step back, giving an embarrassed shake of their heads. But the guard behind the counter, though clearly impressed, kept his place.

"Her Highness and Her Highness's brother, Thurdun, also gave my companion a token of even greater esteem." Ullin gestured to Swyncraff, still around Robby's waist. Robby shook himself, then quickly undid it so that it flowed snake-like through his hands then stiffened into a straight rod, and he offered it to the guard behind the counter for inspection. The guard took it, somewhat suspiciously, and looked up and down the length of it while the girl gazed at it, too.

"It is so, Barmon," she said to the guard. "I, myself, have seen this very wood coiled about Thurdun's shoulder."

The guard nodded. "Is it a weapon?" he asked. "Or is it…an article of clothing?"

"It is what I will it to be," answered Robby, holding out his hand. Swyncraff sprang from the guard's hands across the counter into his grasp.

"The branch of Shadowbane obeys only he to whom it is willingly given, so there is our proof of what they say. They are truly honored by the Queen," the girl stated, "and should be treated as she would have us treat them."

"But what of the name?" asked the guard. "Has this ever happened before? That someone has signed who did not know his own true name?"

"Not in my time here," replied the girl. "But I have only been in service at this desk for a short while, not even forty years. Perhaps Nerron would know."

"If you can wake him."

"Be kind. He is elderly."

"He must write in this book," said a voice behind them.

In the doorway behind the guard and the clerk stood a very frail white-haired man, stooped with age. He was wearing the same type of brown uniform as the other clerks, but with a shawl over his shoulders. There was a pince-nez perched on the tip of his nose, over which beamed bright blue eyes. He stood leaning on a cane with one hand and held a leather volume tucked in his other arm. The guard and the clerk parted so he could approach the counter where he placed the heavy book.

"I am Nerron, Chamberlain of this Foyer," he said. He put his hand on the book.

"High or low," he said to Robby in a patient tone, "all must sign truly before entering this hall. Now, young man. You say that you do not know your right name. Are you an orphan or a foundling?"

"No, sir. That is, I don't think so."

"Very well, then. It is unusual. But we will sort it through," replied Nerron, opening the book and turning pages as he spoke. "We have not had a nameless one in many years. It took me a few moments to find this, the Book of Vouchings. Here we are. Yes, not since the Year of the Blue Flower, by the Duinnor way of reckoning."

He turned another page to one that was blank, and he lifted the quill, dipping it carefully and tapping the nib on the inkwell, and he slowly scratched a few lines across the top of the leaf. When done, he looked over what he had written, and blotted it carefully, and turned the book around to face Robby. He moved the inkwell and quill toward Robby.

"You must write, here, what I tell you to write."

Robby took up the quill. On the page, the man had written, "I, Nerron of Vanara, Servant of Queen Serith Ellyn, Steward of Her Ministers, on this the Tenth Day of Firstmonth, of this the Eight Hundred and Seventy-first year of our Queen's Rule by the reckoning of Vanara, being by the King of Duinnor the Year of the Red Door, do attest that the following was written in my presence."

Then Nerron instructed Robby on what to do.

"Write 'My name is,' and write your name just as you did before."

Robby did so, as carefully as before, but with a more nervous hand, then paused, watching his name disappear as before.

"Now write, 'My true name is unknown to me. I am called by those who know me what I have written above, being, as I have said,' and write your name again."

Robby did so, following Nerron's dictation, and re-wrote his name. All of this remained visible.

"Very good," said Nerron. Ullin nodded with relief, and the girl smiled. "Are your parents known to you?"

"Yes."

"Then write, 'My parents are...' "

Each time Nerron bade him write, Robby carefully did so, trying to make his script clean and clear, while the others looked on. After each line, they all waited and watched for a moment, but the ink remained as black as when it flowed off the nib of the quill.

"Now, as to the purpose of your visit to the Hall of Ministers. Is your reason for coming such that you may say what it is? Or is it a matter of privacy?"

Robby looked at Ullin, who nodded.

"Well, a friend, who is something of a teacher, said that I should come here to the library so that I could read some of the chronicles and tales of the ancient times in order to further my knowledge of such things."

"I see. Then write that."

When Robby had written what Nerron instructed, the gentleman took the book and turned it around to examine all that was now written.

"Very well, then. I should tell you, however, that admittance to the Hall does not grant permission to go just anywhere you please. And only the Librarian may grant permission to use the Library, by order of the Queen."

"Where might I find him? To ask for his permission?"

"His chambers adjoin the Library, on the third floor. But I do not think he has yet arrived for the day."

"That is right," said the girl. "He has not."

"You may go to his chambers and wait for him. Any of the pages can show you the way. I do not think you will have trouble convincing him."

Nerron took from beneath the counter two blue feathers and handed one to Robby and the other to Ullin.

"Pin these to your left shoulders, and you will be given every courtesy as guests of our Queen. Since you are accompanied by the Kingsman, you may be allowed into those places that he has rights to go. That is his advice to give, and his superiors' decision."

By now there was a line of people waiting behind them, and at first Robby thought they had been attracted by his situation. Another clerk appeared farther down along the counter, the line shifted to him, and the waiting people began signing in and receiving their shoulder-feathers of various colors, hurrying past Robby and Ullin.

"I apologize for the inconvenience," Nerron was saying. "But I will delay you no longer. Good day, gentlemen."

He smiled and bowed slightly and turned away, carrying the Book of Vouchings. The clerk lifted up a portion of the countertop on hinges and pushed through a swinging gate to help Robby attach his feather.

"Allow me," she said, taking the feather and the silver badge it was affixed to. "Don't mind him. Nerron has been at this post longer than any of us and should have retired to an easier job long ago. But he always has things done in the proper manner. There!"

She patted the feather, which now sat smartly on Robby's shoulder like an epaulet.

"We call these 'flashes.' Those with red flashes are guards, and those with green ones are pages. For the most part, they are all very helpful and will strive to guide you if you lose your way. White flashes are for clerks and the like, mostly those who work here, like me, see? And black flashes are worn only by the highest ranking officials, members of the court, military, and so forth. Yours is a blue flash. It means that you are here on the Queen's business. You will see very few blue feathers here, and it will be sure to make eyes turn."

"Thank you. What is your name?"

"I am called Aphona. Perhaps I will see you again when you return your flash and pick up your things."

"I hope so."

Ullin nodded to her and walked with Robby to a nearby table, where they placed their bags to be checked by the guards stationed there.

"All these precautions," Robby commented after their bags were handed back to them.

"You'll get used to it," Ullin replied. "This way."

They passed through the gate and entered the great foyer which was humming with the flow of water outside and with the talk and chatter and buzz of people moving from passage to hall, from step to step on the stairs, and from room to room. A few appeared to be ordinary folk, just like Robby, with the same expression of wonder in their eyes. Most, though, were finely dressed, many with caps and canes, some with long flowing hair, often in braids over their shoulders just as Lord Tallin wore his. And there were many kinds of tunics and uniforms and surcoats, with every kind of insignia, from the livery of the pages of the Hall, to that of Duinnor or Vanara, even some of Glareth, and very many styles of dress that Robby had never seen before. Most of the people seemed to know where they were going, but a few were being directed by pages who pointed one way or another. Other pages carried scrolls or packets of papers, sometimes in large trays, and many of the others of the hall likewise held papers, rolled or folded, and some had books with them. There was even an old woman being carried in a sedan chair, her long robes flowed comfortably, draped over her chair, and almost swept the floor as they went across the wide room. She was fair and finely dressed, indeed, and her white hair was bound by a circlet of gold that glittered with brilliant diamonds. Ullin and Robby stood aside as she passed, and she tilted her head at them, smiling as she went by. Ullin returned a little bow, then nudged Robby to follow him onward.

"Who was that?"

"I have no idea."

Up more stairs they went and into a wide doorway over which was a large blue shield with Vanaran Stars emblazoned on its field. They entered a long hallway, its rich dark panelling covered with portraits, shields, banners, and what appeared to be important military objects and prizes, helmets, weapons, and even a chunk of greenish rock, polished along one side, displayed on a pedestal with a placard that read, "Taken from the Green Citadel, 843 S.A."

There were many doors to either side of the busy hallway that they marched along, the gray marble floor loud with the clicking of so many boots. The hall was made even busier by staff who were sweeping and polishing and cleaning. Robby noticed how some of the soldiers saluted as they passed each other, putting their hands up to their heads.

"Do you not have to salute?" he asked Ullin as they avoided a page pushing a hand-trolley full of large scrolls and manuscripts.

"I am not in proper uniform," Ullin explained. "So my rank cannot be seen nor acknowledged. I have seen no one who outranks me, and I do not salute others of courtesy. Unless I wear my rank flashes openly, none are obliged to salute me. I'll soon obtain an armband showing my rank."

"I see. You kept your Duinnor sword, though. Does that not show rank?"

"Hardly. And, as you see, there are others besides Kingsmen who are allowed their swords within here."

They approached a foyer connecting two crossing hallways where a woman in dark-gray armor stood. She had a sword on her back, and she was speaking with a man richly dressed in a dark blue velvet coat and was holding a bundle of scrolls under his arm. His long black hair draped over his shoulders where a black feather was pinned. He turned to glance their way, showing a pale fair face and dark green eyes. Robby immediately saw a resemblance between the two, the same eyes and hair, though hers was closely shorn on the sides with a thick band sweeping back from the top of her head in a long plume-like tail. They were of equal height, taller by an inch than Ullin. The man turned back to the woman, but then he immediately turned back around as Robby and Ullin continued to approach. He grinned broadly and came toward them, shifting his scrolls to one arm so that he could stretch out a hand to Ullin.

"Faslor!" Ullin was already reaching out and smiling. They shook hands in the lingering way that old friends do.

"Ullin Saheed! It has been a long time! Too long. What a wonderful surprise to see you!"

"You, too! I thought you were in Duinnor."

"I was, I was," Faslor said. "But I've been back here for the past month or so. You were headed off to the Eastlands the last we spoke. Does your post route bring you here? Or are you still running errands for Collandoth?"

"Both, in a long roundabout way. A long story."

"And how is the old mystic? Did you manage to catch up with him?"

"Yes. He is as well as ever, I suppose. How are your wife and boys?"

"Lydia is well, thank you. And the twins remained in Duinnor, taking their studies, supposedly. But if I know them, they are making mischief with their tutor. Someday you must meet them. Not that they'd say much to you. They so rarely talk that I sometimes wonder if they can speak at all."

Faslor took Ullin's shoulder and turned him, inspecting the Kingsman.

"But look at you! Except for the Queen's flashes you wear, which I'll ask you about momentarily, you look a mess! Pardon me for saying so. A long road, eh? Of course, I *have* seen you worse! Excuse me, you have a companion?"

"Yes. Let me introduce you. Robby, this is Faslor, to whom I have the pleasure of owing my life. Faslor, this is my cousin, Robby Ribbon of Passdale in the Eastlands."

"My pleasure, sir," Robby bowed and shook Faslor's hand.

"All mine. And Ullin exaggerates his debt to me. Yes, you do! And this is my sister, Coreth, who, as you can see, is of the Palace Gray Guard."

Robby and Ullin bowed again.

"So you are Ullin," she said. "Faslor has told me about you. But I think this is the first time we have met."

"Faslor has told me about you, too." Ullin bowed. "And I would certainly remember if we had met before."

"You two have traveled from the Eastlands together, then? A long journey. We have had disturbing rumors from those parts."

"Yes," interrupted Faslor. "Do you bring news?"

"I am afraid so. And I must make my report. I will tell you this much: War has come to the Eastlands and, I fear, to all the realms."

"What? War?"

"What do you mean? The Queen!"

"She is safely in Glareth, and she was there when Redvests attacked and invaded the Eastlands."

"Oh, my," Faslor shook his head.

"Is that where the Duinnor attaché is these days?" Ullin pointed to the end of the hall where several Kingsmen stood.

"Yes. Ah, you must make your report. Perhaps we could accompany you to hear it?"

"That would be good."

Together, and in a more serious mood, they marched on, Faslor and Ullin, followed by Coreth and Robby.

"When did you depart the Eastlands?" Coreth asked Robby.

"About ten weeks ago, depending on how you count."

"And do you know the Queen? An agent on her behalf, perhaps?"

She gestured to Robby's blue flash.

"I have met Serith Ellyn, and she did me a great honor. But I am not in her service."

"Did you see her in Glareth?"

"No. We met near my home. That was on Autumn's Day."

"And it was her brother who passed Swyncraff to you?"

"You recognize it? Yes, Thurdun and his sister, that is, the Queen, presented it to me."

"Thurdun was never without it. He showed me how it could do many things. You must be a man of great deeds to have deserved such a gift."

"No. I am only a store clerk."

"A clerk?"

"Yes."

"Then it must be a remarkable store."

They both had the sense that the other was saying less than they knew, and though they smiled, it was not without strain. They had reached an alcove and were entering a doorway over which draped the colors of Duinnor. Inside were several desks and lines of people; some were soldiers and others were not, all waiting to conduct some business with the uniformed aides.

"Dispatches from the Sixth Battalion," Robby heard one person say, while at another desk, an aide put a wax seal on a packet, and said, "Here are your transfer orders and your new commission."

They squeezed through the crowded room to another set of doors before which was a small table. Standing behind it was an older soldier of Duinnor speaking to an even older civilian.

"I am sorry," the soldier was saying, "but we cannot spare any troops to sit idle on your lands."

"But you know as well as any that when the lull is over, they will come again up the Garthorn Slopes."

"Until they do, you are responsible for the defense of those lands. The General is clear on this: No new troops are to be deployed in that region. My advice to you, if you are so worried, is to give over the lease and go eastward with your kin as the Queen has done."

"The lease! Bah! Our Queen shall return, and we mean to still have our lands when she does!"

"Then you are full of nerve to ask Duinnor to protect you without giving Duinnor the lease."

"We know all about leases. I alone, among all in my shire, still live upon my lands. Duinnor holds lease to all my neighbors' lands while they are robbed of the means to pay the reserve. It is a black practice. But don't you see? We haven't the men to properly man Darlang Hill and to protect Garthorn Pass, too. It is, for all practical purposes, wide open to the enemy. If they come in force, we cannot hope to repel them all by ourselves."

"Yet you have done so up to now."

"But only small parties have come against us. And, come spring, we will need our men for the planting."

"That cannot be helped, I suppose."

"If they take Darlang Hill, it cannot be retaken without a great battle! Surely you remember the last time that happened? Don't you care? It is because of Duinnor that we are in this fix."

"Sir, I was at Darlang Hill when it was retaken. I suggest you speak with Captain Corvis of the Home Guard."

"Where do you think I just came from? Do you think I would first ask Duinnor? Our boys are spread thin enough. Corvis sent me here!"

"I am sorry. But there's nothing to be done at the moment."

"Just let me speak with the General myself."

"No, I'm sorry, but his orders are clear. This is your fourth visit in as many weeks, and you have nothing new to say. Why don't you wait until spring approaches? We shall see how things stand at that time."

The man, obviously frustrated, turned hesitantly, then saw Faslor and Coreth.

"I've been as patient as a man can be," he said to them. "But I'm all out! Another foray like we had last summer, and my lands will belong to the Lizard!"

Coreth looked at him sympathetically and said, "Your lands are north of our main frontiers. But if it will make you feel any better, perhaps a patrol can be arranged. To take a look around."

"They won't find a thing," he replied. "What we need is a permanent watch. Some relief to my boys out there in the hills. But the Home Guard says the same as this fellow, that none can be spared."

"We'll see."

Meanwhile, the soldier, relieved that Coreth was leading the disgruntled Vanaran away, turned to the others.

"Faslor? Here to see the General? Not another one of your schemes, eh?"

"No schemes this time," Faslor stated. "My sister and I only wish to keep company with my old friend, here, and his cousin. He is a Kingsman, as you can see, and is just arrived from the Eastlands with dire news, I'm afraid. He wishes to report directly."

"Oh?"

"Ullin Saheed Tallin, First Kingsman, First Army, Third Engineer Battalion, detached by orders to King's Post as Special Courier."

Ullin handed his orders over, and the two Kingsmen saluted.

"I am Tavus Beerman, Aide to General Portius. What is the nature of your news that you do not report in the usual way?"

"War, sir. Treasonous war."

"What war? In the Eastlands?"

"Yes, sir. Tracian Redvests are on the move and have seized lands in the Eastlands, near to Glareth even, and in the southward parts near Tallinvale."

A hush fell on the room as the people within clearly overheard Ullin and turned their attention his way.

"Perhaps we should discuss your news within," Beerman said, opening the door behind him and leading them into an anteroom. As soon as he closed the door, the others remaining in the room broke out into loud speculation.

"Wait here for just a moment."

Beerman stepped through an open door and almost immediately returned to usher them into a large office. There were maps hung on all the walls and, in between, were pennants and lances captured in desert campaigns. Otherwise, the room had a sparse look to it, in spite of the sofa and upholstered chairs. Behind a large desk stood the general. He had short-cropped gray hair, was once very physically powerful but now was edging toward corpulence. Although he was immaculately dressed, he had a haggard look about him, and he had not shaved for a day or two.

"Commander Tallin," Portius stepped from behind his desk and, after saluting, offered Ullin his hand. "Faslor. Captain Coreth," they exchanged nods. "And this is?"

"May I present my cousin from the Eastlands Realm, Robby Ribbon, who has accompanied me these past many weeks."

Robby and Portius shook hands.

"Now. What is this all about? The Triumvirate on the move at last? We wondered how long it might be. We've even sent envoys to get some sense of their intentions, but we have had no news from them."

"Yes, General." In a efficient manner, Ullin related details of the attack on Barley, of the situation in Janhaven, and how Robby's father was attempting to make his way to Glareth.

"It was decided that six of us would come west, but we traveled first to Tallinvale."

Ullin then told how his grandfather was preparing his people for siege, and of the Redvest armies massing to the south of Tallinvale. He said very little about Robby or the other members of the company, and nothing to hint at their true mission. He addressed the situation in Tallinvale and was beginning to tell of their journey west when Portius interrupted.

"Please," he said, "why don't we all be seated?" He went back to his seat behind the desk. Ullin took the plainest chair and Faslor and Robby sat on the sofa while Coreth remained standing by the door, her arms crossed.

"Let's get the senior staff together, Beerman," Portius said to his aide. "And notify our ambassador that I would like to see him at his earliest convenience."

"Yes, sir. What shall I say to those outside who may have heard the news?"

Portius frowned. "Tell them that we are still learning the situation and that we'll know more later on. Tell them, unofficially, they should stay near their units and await orders. Notify me immediately when Twenty-Second Corps arrives."

"Yes, sir."

They saluted and Beerman departed.

"Now, pray continue. You said you had further bad news."

"Yes, General Portius," Ullin resumed. "From Tallinvale we went west through Damar territory. Somehow, we think through spies, they heard of us, and we barely escaped capture. We learned also, through the villages we passed, that all able-bodied men and boys are being impressed for service. The Damar warlord is also summoning mercenaries. I believe the Damar are in league with the Redvests of Tracia, and that they mean to strike together against Tallinvale. Once we made the plains our journey was fairly swift. On the fourth week, we saw a party of Dragon soldiers. We managed to avoid detection, of course. We saw they were lightly armed, more than a company. When we came upon them they were just completing work on a hidden well."

"Dragonkind? On the plains? Digging wells?"

"Yes. They salted it with desert herbs, then hid it and moved northward."

"That can mean only one thing."

"Yes, sir. They prepare an assault and think they may reach as far as the plains."

Portius stood and went to one of the maps on the wall. Ullin stood, too.

"Where would you say you saw them?"

"This map does not show territory east of Forest Islindia," Ullin said. "But I would put it about two weeks march east of the town of Edgewold. And, speaking of Edgewold, we came on more bad news there."

"Oh? Edgewold? I know that place. And I know the Fourth was sent to put down an uprising in those parts. We had word of some cultish league of bandits or whatnot. Hostages taken and so forth."

"Yes. And much more. I'm afraid the hostages had been murdered by the time we arrived. The cult there was called Wokan, and they worshipped a sort of wicker effigy, made of vine-stalks . They raised a large army in defiance of Duinnor and had been attacking nearby settlements and towns. My company of travelers were present when General Teracue put down their army in battle, defeating it utterly, but not before their priests unleashed a monster."

Ullin described how Robby had been captured and how the rest of the party joined with Teracue's army as they moved against Westlawn, the Wickerman stronghold. Robby then related how he was taken to the Wickerman town and how he managed to elude capture, only to find himself on the very top of the monster, a huge object made of wicker and living flesh in the crude shape of a man. When Robby concluded the tale of its destruction and his own narrow escape, Portius sat again.

"Incredible! Who can have such dark powers but a minion of Secundur himself?"

"That is our thinking, sir. Yet, whoever it was, he was killed by his own creature, as Robby said. And, afterwards, we found nothing to indicate Secundur's direct involvement. Perhaps the sorcerer broke away from Secundur. We do not know."

"And when you left Edgewold? What was General Teracue's reaction to your news? I assume he was alarmed at the prospect of Dragonkind on his flank."

"Indeed, sir, he was. On the morning we left Edgewold, he himself rode out with a patrol to reconnoiter the plains."

"Hm."

"I believe the Dragonkind were more concerned with stealth than confrontation. And it was only a little more than a company."

"There are bound to be others," Portius added. "And what of Teracue's opinion about Tracia?"

"He was very concerned, naturally. I believe he dispatched news of our reports to Duinnor."

"Hm. All this news answers many questions. And changes everything. You have served in the desert frontier?"

"Yes, General. I have."

"Then you know the lay. But the Dragonkind have been quiet this past year and a half. Only probing forays. No attacks of consequence, and we have reopened the roads to the Free City of Kajarahn. Though our caravans are harried by renegade marauders in the badlands, there has been little effort on the part of the Dragonkind to stop our movements. Scouts and spies continue to report that their lines remain in strength, and though we watch for a buildup that would indicate an impending attack, we have seen no such signs. Indeed, they seem uninterested in fighting and resist tempting feints on our part to come to open battle. Now we know why. Tell me, did Teracue suspect any connection between his assignment and events farther east or south?"

"If he did, he did not share any such opinions," Ullin said. "As far as I could gather, neither the Tracians nor the Dragonkind had anything to do with the Wickermen or events there."

Portius stood again and pondered the large map on the wall.

"And he has suffered few losses, you say?"

"Yes, sir. The Wickermen were vast in numbers but poorly organized. As far as I could tell, they had little in the way of planning or battlefield discipline. The Four of the Fourth easily defeated them with only a few casualties of their own."

"Well, I know what I would do if I were the High Council," Portius stated. "Teracue has the Fourth, with all four battalions. I'd send two to the south, to establish base camps to make the way for supporting troops that would be sent to support Altoria. I'd also have him leave a battalion in Westlawn and send the last to the east against the Damar and to relieve the flanks of Tallinvale. What do you say to that?"

"Well, sir," Ullin replied, shrugging, "I'd say that any aid sent east would be better than none. But I doubt if so few men could do much more than harry the Damar. I'd send them to Janhaven instead, to join with the local militias being raised there. Perhaps, with forces that may come from Glareth, they may strike from the north against the Redvests who lay siege on Tallinvale. If Tallinvale falls, Tracia's northern flank becomes secure, and the Triumvirate can commit all of their might against the south realms. But if Tallinvale prevails, a way south can then be made, cutting off the Redvests from their supplies. They will have to turn away from their western objectives. That may even break any alliance between them and the Dragonkind."

"Hm. Very good points. Perhaps."

"And, if you pardon me, sir, I'd send all of Teracue's force, not just a portion. There are no defensible positions on the southern plains for such a small army against the united might of Tracia and the Dragonkind. Not between Westlawn and Masurthia. Duinnor would not be able to move sufficient troops fast enough to counter such a force, and Teracue could not hold out. It would be better to strike a decisive blow in the east, to prevent the Redvests from becoming an effective ally to the Dragonkind, and possibly taking them out of the game entirely."

"Maybe. Maybe. But, in fact, I doubt if our leaders will do anything very quickly. And, even if the King ordered any such action, our armies are, quite frankly, in shambles. Generals and officers are appointed by the merits of favor rather than those of experience or training. The forces that they send to Vanara are little better than rabble, more interested in looting lands and taking prizes than protecting the Realms. For three months, we've awaited replacements, and now we hear that two thousand Regulars approach under a general determined to launch an offensive against the Dragonkind! One year ago, that same general was no more than a courtier of Duinnor, and has probably never even seen flowing blood. In fact, so inept of a leader that his little army got lost on the way south and had to ask Post Riders to show them the way. They camped for an entire month waiting for directions, eating up supplies badly needed here, and turning their misbehavior against the homes and towns of the district they were in. The locals of that area began raising their own militia to drive them out when they finally left. That is the kind of help Duinnor gives us!"

"You speak like a Vanaran," Faslor commented mildly, a slight smile at the corner of his lips.

Portius shook his head. "I am a career Kingsman, sir, and I do not shirk my duty. But this land cannot bear much more abuse from my realm, and those supplies were promised to the Vanaran defense."

"Are things so bad that Vanara can no longer equip herself?" Ullin asked.

"You have been away for a while. The lands are fertile enough, and the Vanarans resourceful. But Duinnor leases the best farmlands and lets them go idle. So much so that the other remaining farms cannot supply enough for all. And it is not just farms. Many foundries, shops, and crafthouses have been bought out to also lay idle, with furnaces and wheels gathering dust. Yet, all the while, the smithies, plantations, and moneylenders of our own realm grow all the more prosperous, year by year. Oh!" Portius stopped himself and looked at Robby and Ullin. "Pardon me. I mean Duinnor, of course. And perhaps I am too critical of my own homeland. But that is how things are."

"If Vanara is to guard the southern flanks against the Dragonkind," Robby ventured, "how is it that Duinnor continues to weaken the very defense that it depends upon?"

"Why, indeed! But who can say? The King exerts little influence to change matters, so the people of my land, the high and the low, look to their own advantage without thought to the future. Generation has passed down this attitude to generation for a very long time. And, with your news, I fear that the children must someday pay for the ways of their fathers. Perhaps those days are upon us? You, sir, do you confirm all that your companion has told?"

"Yes," Robby nodded. "I do. And I beg, if you have any influence, to use it to send relief to Janhaven and to Tallinvale."

"I'm afraid I can do little directly, on my own authority." Portius sat back down behind his desk. "But I will do what I can. Commander Tallin, I shall want your report in writing as soon as possible. Please see to it right away."

"Yes, General Portius."

"And what of your present orders?"

"Sir. Robby, here, is the son of the mayor of Passdale. The agents of Tracia are keenly interested in him, probably to make an example of him. I am to escort him as his bodyguard on his business here, and then should events bear out, on to Duinnor. I believe he means to add his voice to those of his companions, who are already on their way northward."

"I see. But while there are Tracians here in Vanara, I doubt if they would be too interested in him with all else that is happening. And I doubt if the Redvest general in Barley has much communication with his counterparts here. As tempted as I may be, I am reluctant to countermand your disposition or to interfere with your present assignment."

"Since I am At Large, perhaps I may do both my service to Robby and to you?"

"Perhaps. Will you be in Vanara long?"

"I cannot say." Ullin looked at Robby.

"I am not sure how long it will take for me to conclude my business here," Robby offered. "And, being a stranger, I'd rather not be parted with Ull...Commander Tallin."

"I understand. I see by your flashes that you have high status. Might I be of help to you, then?"

"Thank you, but I don't think so. Whatever you can do for the Eastlands would count as help to me, General."

"Yes, I'll see what I can do. I do not mean to pry, but does your business have to do with things other than the Redvest attack on the Eastlands?"

"I was advised to leave my homeland so as to avoid capture," Robby explained. "It seemed inevitable that I would be taken if I remained. I was also instructed to come here to continue my studies for a short while and to relate what news I could bring with Commander Tallin."

Robby prepared himself for the battery of questions that he was sure Portius would ask. Instead, the general tapped on his desk with a small dagger-like letter opener, and blankly looked at Robby, his eyes going from Robby to his shoulder flash, to Faslor. None but Portius could see, among the papers and dispatches piled on his desk, the one he tapped. Portius picked up the dispatch and moved it aside.

"Very well, then," he said, rising. Ullin stood as did the others. "Please keep yourself available, Commander Tallin," he said, exchanging salutes with Ullin. "And let us have your report immediately."

"Yes, sir. Thank you, sir."

As Robby and Ullin passed through the anteroom, Ullin was assailed with questions by the crowd that had gathered. He managed to refuse to answer them and was quickly ushered into a side room where there was a small table and writing paraphernalia.

"This will occupy me for a while," Ullin said to Robby. "Would you mind being on your own? Perhaps you can see the library and ask about the chronicles that Ashlord mentioned."

Faslor stood aside, talking to one of the office aides, and Robby, taking advantage of the moment with Ullin, spoke softly.

"General Portius asked too few questions," he said. "He must be curious, at least, about our friends. And he must have had a summons delivered to him, just like General Teracue."

"Yes," Ullin lowered his voice to a whisper, "if Teracue received it, Portius must soon have it, if he does not already. But then why doesn't he act on it? I think, though, that we must have somehow beaten the summons here, just as we hoped to do."

● ● ●

Just a couple of rooms away, Beerman questioned Portius on the very same point.

"I have my reasons, Beerman," Portius said, dropping the summons onto the desk, which he had just deciphered an hour before the appearance of his visitors. "Either they do not know of the summons or they do not fear it, else they would not have come here so boldly. And now that they have the blue flashes of the Queen, they are somewhat protected from arrest while they are here. Our relations with Vanara are tense enough, as you know. We should not provoke further trouble unless it becomes necessary."

Beerman frowned and shifted the papers that he held.

"Look at it this way," Portius went on, putting his hand on Beerman's shoulder to guide him back to the door. "Commander Tallin went to a great deal of trouble to bring along his companion. It may be to our advantage to find out why before we pack them off to Duinnor. Lord Banis can wait. And, if the news they brought is true, I'm afraid we'll have our hands full. Commander Tallin will give his report, and we'll see how things fall. Meanwhile, let's keep an eye on our visitors, shall we?"

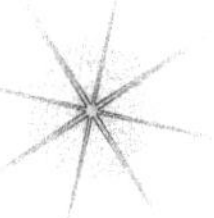

Chapter 21

The Library and the Palace

"Ullin," Faslor interrupted the discussion, "do you and Master Robby have some place to stay while you are here?"

"Well, we haven't gotten as far as that."

"Then leave it to me. Meanwhile, would you prefer to wait for Ullin to complete his report? Or would you like to have a look around?"

"I don't know," Robby shrugged.

"I would rather we stay together, as Robby is under my protection, and he is a newcomer to Vanara," Ullin put forward. "But he's probably safe here within the Ministry, and this report could take a couple of hours, at least. I'm sure to be asked to report again, in person, possibly with the General's staff, to answer their questions directly."

"Most likely," Faslor nodded. "And I should report as well to the Home Guard. But my sister is off duty. I am sure she would agree to be Robby's unofficial escort."

"I would like to get to the Library as soon as I can," Robby said. "Surely that would be safe enough."

"Certainly. Why don't I walk you over there and have Coreth meet you there after a while?"

Ullin thought for a moment, then nodded.

"Very well," he said. "I will try to find you at the Library as soon as I can get away. I would enjoy visiting the Library again, anyway. It has been too long. Meanwhile, if anything happens so that you need to find me, come back here or see if there is a message for you at the entrance desk where we left our gear."

"Alright. I'll do that, if need be. Good luck here," Robby said, turning to follow Faslor.

"And Robby," Ullin said with concern.

"Yes?"

"Let us not linger any longer than we must, but be on our way as soon as possible, whatever your plan may be, and wherever it should lead us. We should stay only long enough to do our business and make our preparations for travel."

Robby nodded. "I understand. And I agree. Until later, then."

• • •

The anteroom and the hall outside were a-buzz with activity and anxious faces. Kingsmen came and went, and high-ranking soldiers gathered outside a meeting room farther down the hall. Faslor hurried Robby through the crowd, declining to answer the questions posed to him by those they passed by. The two pressed on through the staffers and Kingsmen until they came to the balconies overhanging the great central foyer. Instead of going downstairs, Faslor motioned for Robby to follow him to the right.

"Your business has some urgency, I take it?" he asked Robby as they walked across the high balcony that ran along the huge windows and overlooked the foyer. The mist on the other side of the glass was so dense that Robby could not see the falls, but their presence just outside could not be ignored due to the powerful throbbing that made the glass hum. Robby wondered how in the world the glass did not shatter. Looking the other way, over the bannister, he could see the entrance desk below where a line of uniformed figures were now passing through, depositing their weapons and signing the book just as he and Ullin had done.

"Urgent enough," he replied to Faslor.

His guide glanced down at the entering stream of soldiers. "Well, whatever it may be, you and Ullin Saheed have caused quite a stir. The likes of which I have not seen in a long while."

"I, for one, am glad to see some stir," Robby stated. "It gives me some hope, at least, that action may be taken by Duinnor."

"Hm. Naturally. I must say, though, that Vanara is not Duinnor. We have long been at the front of things, so to speak, much to the purpose of Duinnor and much to our own inclination. Duinnor's attitude, however, is not the same as Vanara's. We are more apt to take meaningful action if for no other reason than we are more accustomed to doing so. Even when it goes unrewarded. Duinnor, even when it acts, does not always act so predictably, nor so wisely. In fact, some might describe Duinnor's actions as meddling rather than support. And Duinnor has a habit of embarking on useless and costly military campaigns against the Dragonlands, and dragging us along even when it is not in our interests to participate."

"I have been in Vanara but a short while," Robby responded, "and I already begin to understand your bitterness. I also now understand somewhat better the mood of the Queen when I met her some while back. That is, her sadness. Or at least her worry."

"I would like to hear more about your meeting with the Queen, should we have the opportunity."

"Gladly. It was a chance encounter, you might say. And brief. But I wonder, who rules while she is away?"

"This way," Faslor directed Robby to the left along a hallway, then he pulled open a doorway, and they ascended a winding staircase to the next level. "Serith Ellyn rules here through the Star Council. And Lord Seafar, who is Chancellor, rules as Regent in the Queen's absence. Though she may be far away, they receive messages from one another regularly."

"Through Post Riders?"

Faslor smiled. "Hardly. Through our own messengers. And the Queen has other means of communicating with Lord Seafar. Here we are."

They walked through another foyer, pushed aside a glass door, then entered yet another foyer within. Immediately in front of them was a tall desk with a young boy behind it perched on a stool. He was dressed in the same brown attire as the other clerks and pages that Robby had seen. But this one was reading a book as they entered. On either side of the desk sat two guards, in tall-backed chairs, and they, too, were reading books. One of the guards wore spectacles and glanced up as Robby and Faslor entered. He and Faslor nodded to each other, then the guard resumed his reading. Behind the desk was a large room with orderly rows of shelves, some designed to hold scrolls and others were lined with books. On the far side of the room were windowed alcoves within which were tables and chairs.

"May I help you?" asked the clerk, closing his book and giving them his attention.

"My friend here is a visitor and would like to use the Library."

"May I see your pass?"

"I do not have one," Robby replied. "I was hoping to gain permission to read a few things."

"Oh. Well, the Librarian is not here right now. But I expect he will not be long. He had some business in town that has delayed his arrival today. Would you care to wait?"

"Does not the Queen's Flash give permission?" Faslor asked.

"I'm afraid not, sir. By Her Majesty's recent order, all must have a pass from the Librarian."

"I see."

"Well, I'll not keep you," Robby said to Faslor, offering his hand. "Thank you for showing me the way. I'll just wait for the Librarian as long as I can."

"Are you sure? Very well, then. I'll send Coreth to you soon. And I hope to see you later."

Faslor bowed and departed, nearly bumping into a clerkish-looking man who was entering. He was stooped over and carried a bundle of papers held close to his jacket, and, glancing up, he nodded to Robby.

"Good morning," Robby greeted him hopefully. But the man only smiled awkwardly, his head down, avoiding any but the briefest glance at the smiling Robby. The man then mumbled an indiscernible reply, nodded once more, hurried on around the desk, and pushed through a side door.

"That's only Cuffdare, one of the staff," said the clerk, seeing Robby's obvious confusion. "Don't mind him. He's just exceedingly shy."

"Oh."

"Yes, but don't let that fool you. I don't think we could manage without him. He keeps our shelves in order and manages the addition of new books and such. Always scurrying about from place to place, sorting, stacking, making lists, checking lists, writing summaries of lists, and all such work. Is this your first time at our library?"

"Yes. I am just arrived in Vanara, so all is new to me."

"My guess is that you are not from Duinnor. Are you from Glareth?"

"No. Just a small town in the old Eastlands Realm."

"Oh. Have you come all this way to see our collection? We do get many travelers from far-off places. Sometimes, anyway. Or are you just curious? Have you ever used a library before?"

"Well," Robby shrugged, "in a way the answers to all those questions are yes and no. That is to say, I have used only very small libraries before, more like large collections, actually. I am curious about this one, true. However, my business brings me through Vanara, and part of it, in a manner of speaking, requires that I do some reading. It's complicated."

"Well, I don't mean to pry, but if the Librarian grants you a pass, perhaps I may help you find what you need. Or, if I am not available, Cuffdare would certainly be glad to help."

"I would be most grateful. Do you think he will be long? The Librarian, that is."

"No. He is usually here by this time of morning. But, if I know him, he'll be here as soon as he can." The clerk pointed to a nearby bench. "Perhaps you would like to sit?"

"Thank you."

Robby stepped back toward the entrance and settled onto a leather-cushioned bench, nodding at one of the guards who nodded back as he turned a page. Robby saw Cuffdare moving up or down the aisles between shelves, sometimes rolling a little cart, sometimes holding an armful of scrolls or bound volumes. Robby watched as he carefully placed the materials on the shelves, shifting items already there as he did so, or straightening the stacks. The door beside Robby opened and a woman entered, showing a pass in the form of a square green card of thick paper. Without speaking, the attendant nodded, and she entered the Library and disappeared off to the right. Others came in, and each time Robby hoped it was the Librarian, but an hour passed and he had not arrived. Robby grew increasingly worried and unsure of what to do. Since Coreth had not yet appeared, he considered whether he should leave to find Ullin, and perhaps come back later.

Just when he had decided to wait a little longer, the doors opened, and the guards stood as a man entered. The clerk descended from his stool and stood beside the desk. Robby also stood. The man, cloaked in a fine overcoat, shifted his silver-balled walking stick from one hand to the other as he turned and closed the door. When Robby saw the stick and the man's silver hair, he instantly recognized him as the man on the trolley with whom he had chatted about the fantastic birds.

"Good morning, Librarian," said the clerk.

"Good morning, good morning!" he replied smiling. Seeing Robby, his smile broadened even more and his blue eyes twinkled. "Ah! We meet again! Had I known you came to use the library, I would have lingered to chat with you more. How do you do? I am Marcus Greendale, Librarian to Queen Serith Ellyn."

Robby took his hand and bowed. "I am pleased to make your acquaintance. I am Robby Ribbon, of the Eastlands. Yes, among other reasons, I have come to look at some of the books here. However, I do not have permission to do so."

"I see," Greendale glanced at the clerk, who shrugged.

"I know, sir. He wears the Queen's Feather, but still. I was only following the rules."

"And rightly so, Hempel. Rules are rules. Mr.…Ribbon, did you say?"

"Yes, sir. Robby Ribbon."

"Did you receive your feather flash as you entered? Or was it given to you later?"

"The man in charge of the entrance gave it to me to wear. Along with my companion who is elsewhere on business here."

"I see. Well, my Uncle Nerron gives no blue feather without good reason. And his reasons are always the best. Therefore, I would be happy to grant you permission. Just step into my chamber here, and I'll make it official."

Greendale gestured to a door, which a guard promptly opened, and the two entered a room that was modest in size but richly appointed with tapestries, fine seating, and a large desk of dark wood, highly polished. On the floor was a thick rug of red with green and blue figures woven into it depicting various trees and birds. Greendale dropped his stick into an ornate holder and hung up his overcoat, revealing a suit of dark blue velvet. He went around his desk and, dipping a quill, wrote out a few words on a slip of paper and applied an inked seal to it.

"There," he said, coming back around the desk to hand it to Robby. "Show this pass to the desk clerk, and he will admit you."

"Thank you very much!"

"You are most welcome. And do not hesitate to ask for assistance, should you desire any whatsoever."

"You are most kind. Thank you."

Robby went back to the clerk, who had already inked a pen and was preparing to write Robby's name.

"It was Robby Ribbon, correct? Of the old Eastlands Realm?"

"That is right."

"And your pass?"

"Here it is."

"Good. Very well, then. Your pass allows you full use of our library until we close this evening. We ring a bell a short while before we close to warn everyone. You may go on in. Just let one of us know should you like help finding anything."

"Thank you. For now, perhaps I could just look around for a bit?"

"Certainly."

Relieved to be within the library at last, and remembering that Ullin knew where to find him, Robby relaxed as he walked through the next set of doors and looked right and left. As far as he could see, there were rows and rows of shelving filled with books and scrolls. Proceeding along the aisle between the shelves immediately in front of him, he looked at the spines as he went. Many were in writing familiar to him, the Common Script, but most were in scripts or languages that he did not know. Some of the volumes seemed new, with bright gold lettering, and others were worn and had faded inscriptions. Some of the books had no inscriptions at all, and others were very loosely bound, the stitching that held the pages together showing through their frayed spines. The scrolls, he saw as he pulled one out and then another, had ribbons around them that were written with the title of the work or some description of the contents. Judging from the titles, this row of shelving contained works of poetry and song. At the end of the aisle, he entered an alcove, running his hand over the marble-topped table there, and looked through the window. Several stories below, he could see the park with its lifelike statues that he and Ullin had walked through earlier.

Resuming his exploration, he walked along the alcoves, looking down each aisle as he went, then realized that the end of each row of shelving was marked with signs, written in several languages, describing the contents of the section. As he passed one, he saw Cuffdare emerge farther on down and pass around to disappear behind another row. Turning into a section marked "Second Age: Court," he again studied the titles, sometimes taking down a volume to look at. But he could find nothing about or by Nimwill. Nearly an hour later, and having gone nearly to the end of that side of the room, Robby was no closer to finding what he wanted than when he began, and he was once more growing nervous about taking so long. But the temptation to browse and sample was too great.

And there were plenty of works written in the Common Tongue to distract him. He found a book of folktales from Glareth, filled with sea stories and colorful illustrations of sea serpents, ships, and exciting maelstroms. Farther along, there was a small book of history pertaining to the Eastlands and the coming of Men. He found a dense volume, one of a large set of twenty, filled with very realistic illustrations of plants, along with written descriptions. Flowers and vines, trees, shrubs, and grasses were all described and illustrated in beautiful watercolor. Turning a page, he saw, illustrated in frightening detail, the thorny plant he had encountered not too long ago that ringed Forest Islindia.

"What did Ashlord call this? Ring of Blades?" he asked himself. He read the description, "Retagator Simplus Habilis. Hardy vine known only to grow on the outskirts of the former lands of Halethiris. Known as the Ring of Blades, and also known as Hand-of-Thorn. The peculiar pattern of growth of these plants enables passage by men or animals in only one direction. Some attempt was made to harvest the thorns for use as needles and other tools, but are only cut from the vine with great difficulty, and, once cut, they soon decay. The leaves of this vine are evergreen..."

A short while later, Robby had retraced his way and had passed over to the far side of the hall. His dilemma was now clear to him. If he did not ask for help, he might never find the manuscript that Ashlord wanted him to read. But if he did ask, revealing what it was he was interested in, he might divulge more than was wise about his quest and why he was actually here.

"If only I had some ally, one that knew this place and could be trusted," he thought. "Or if only I had time to learn how this place works. And time to read and read!"

Then he saw Cuffdare again, far down the aisle, pushing a ladder along a track and climbing up to put away scrolls. When he descended, he turned, head bowed as usual, and glanced at Robby who stared back blankly, still wondering what to do. After a moment of first stepping one way and then another, nodding and shaking his head as if grappling with his own problems, Cuffdare hesitantly approached. Robby watched, stepping out of the way as the hunched figure came down the aisle and then abruptly stopped, giving Robby several jerky bows.

"Excuse me," Cuffdare said. "That is, pardon me. I mean to say, may I help you find anything?"

The clerk fidgeted and flinched as if at his own words, and stepped back away from Robby, seemingly in pain as he asked his question. Nervous though his manner was, there was something odd about him that contradicted the sheepish way his glances bounced from Robby to the floor, then to the nearby books, and back at Robby, as if the man's thoughts screamed loud interruptions within his head, forcing him to regain, moment by moment, his agonized nerve to speak. It was clear to Robby that it had taken him an excruciating effort to even approach, and so, without hesitation, Robby smiled and answered, as Cuffdare shot out his arm past Robby's head to straighten some books, causing Robby to jump.

"I'm afraid that I am somewhat overwhelmed," Robby told him. "And I would indeed be thankful for some guidance."

"Then perhaps," Cuffdare stepped back then forward again, turning sideways, "that is, are you looking for something in particular?"

"Well, yes. I'm looking for—"

Robby caught himself, and hesitated. To say what he needed might reveal too much about why he was here. Realizing he had little choice, he went on.

"I'd like to read about the Queen, Serith Ellyn. And particularly about her early years. Before she was Queen."

"The Queen. Yes. You are in the right section," Cuffdare made as if to run away but instead pushed past Robby and zig-zagged quickly down the aisle. "This way."

Robby followed, and they went to the end of the shelves, rounded to the other side, and went back the other way. He nearly bumped into Cuffdare as the man suddenly stopped and, standing straight, looked at the higher shelves with his hand up, ready to grasp and pull the volume he was looking for as soon as he saw it. Cuffdare's hand passed slowly along the spines, then suddenly dropped. He whirled around and shot out his arm. Robby flinched as Cuffdare plucked a book from just behind Robby's head. As soon as he had it in hand, Cuffdare resumed his hunched and shy posture.

"This," he said, patting the cover of the book, "this book tells of the Queen and her brother Thurdun, and of their birth and early days."

Turning the book around, he offered it to Robby with both hands.

"It has stories, too," Cuffdare went on as Robby took it and opened it. It was copied in an oddly fluid script, but Robby could make out that it was in the Ancient Speech. As he examined it, Cuffdare shifted back and forth, as if not knowing whether to stay or leave, but intently watching as Robby turned a few pages.

"Will it do?" he asked, touching the book with a finger and quickly withdrawing his hand as if he had touched a hot stove.

"Well. I'm afraid I'm lacking in the ability to read this script. I can't make out the meaning of the lettering, or the words."

"Oh!" Cuffdare retreated sideways, then came back. "It is in the old language, some call it the Ancient Speech."

"I can read only some of it. I know the Common Speech quite well, though I've only seen these runes in a few places before and, well—"

"We do have reading rooms."

"Pardon me? Reading rooms? I'm sorry. I am new here. How would a room help if I cannot read what I take there?"

"Oh, you need not read to yourself," Cuffdare shook his head, but smiled, his head tilted so far down and his body bent over so much that he was almost looking up at Robby. "Our reading rooms have readers. They can read all of the languages and scripts and runes of the library. Nearly all, that is."

"Oh, I see. People employed to read to users of the library?"

"Just so, just so. Shall I take you to one?"

"Perhaps. Do you read the old language?"

"Oh, yes. Of course. My duties require the skill."

Robby decided to take a chance and just ask for what he was looking for. After all, it was probably something that everyone around here was familiar with, and none would think twice as to why someone would want it.

"Then could you tell me if any of the tales in this book are written by Nimwill?" he asked.

"Nimwill?"

Robby handed the book back to Cuffdare who, for once, was standing still and gazing back quizzically.

"Yes. Nimwill."

"Nimwill. No," Cuffdare paged through. "No. I do not think so."

"He was Court Chronicler, I believe."

"Ah. Well. No, no. The Queen's scribe is Orinus. Yes, Orinus has been the Court Chronicler under Queen Serith Ellyn. Nimwill, yes I remember. Nimwill was chronicler of Parthais during his reign. You mix the two. You need Orinus for the Queen's history."

"No. That is to say, I misunderstood. Never mind Orinus. I need to see the Chronicles of Nimwill."

Cuffdare slowly placed the book back in its place, adjusting it carefully, then wagged his finger at it.

"Court chronicles are another matter," he said to himself. To Robby, he said "Court chronicles. Nimwill. I don't think they have been copied yet. No, not yet. You must see the Librarian about that. He would know, I'm sure."

"Perhaps I could just look at them?"

"Well, just so. Of course you would. I understand that. But, that is, they are not here."

• • •

When Robby and Cuffdare re-entered the Librarian's chamber, they found he was with Faslor's sister, Coreth.

"Ah, Master Ribbon," Greendale greeted them. "We were just about to look for you."

"I've come to be your guide for a bit," Coreth said, taking the pass Greendale was holding out to her. "My brother asked that I do so until you rejoin Ullin Saheed."

"Thank you," Robby said. He could not tell if her smile was one of annoyance or amusement, but he decided it was at least somewhat friendly and smiled back at her. The last thing he wanted was another person knowing just what it was he was looking for, but it seemed inevitable that more people would become involved. "That is very kind of you. I hope I do not take you away from your duties, though."

"I happen to be off my watch until tomorrow evening. And I'm honored to be your escort."

"What do you think of our Library?" Greendale asked.

"Oh, it is quite wonderful! I wish I had the time and the skill to read all that you have here!"

"That would take a great deal of both, I think. But we do have readers who can translate for you."

"Yes. Mr. Cuffdare told me about them. Only, he says that the books I want to read are not here."

"Yes…Nimwill," Cuffdare said. He fidgeted from one foot to the other. "Court Chronicles."

"Oh, that's right," Greendale nodded. "We only have a few copies of the more recent chronicles. You need the older ones, I take it?"

"Yes. I would like to read some of the writings of Nimwill."

"Ah, the Chronicles of Parthais. We have not yet copied that far back. You see, all of the court documents, including the chronicles, are kept in the Royal Archives at the Queen's Palace. Our scribes must go there to do their copy work because those accounts are not permitted to leave the Royal Archives. And even I lack the authority to give you permission to see them. Lord Seafar must grant that privilege. He is Regent in the Queen's absence, you see, and has authority over the White Palace."

"Oh."

"And I cannot give you permission even to go there. "

"Well, that is no problem, if he must go there," interjected Coreth. "I have free admittance there, and, since you wear the Queen's Feather, I believe you might obtain access to the Royal Archives."

"I don't mean to be troublesome."

"Not at all!"

"Well, do you think it will take long? Is the White Palace far away?"

"No," Greendale said with a grinning glance at Coreth. "It is not all that far. Here," he scribbled a note, "take this. Just a little note of referral, confirming your need. I address this directly to Lord Seafar, if you are allowed to see him. He is a very busy man, so whether you will gain an audience, who can say?" Greendale shrugged, handing Robby the note.

"Do you wish to see Ullin first? To tell him where you must go?" Coreth asked.

"Yes, if at all possible. And perhaps he may accompany us. He has a great love of books."

• • •

It was not to be. By the time they found Ullin, he was on his way to deliver yet another report, this time to a hastily called meeting of commanders and other necessary parties keenly interested in his news. Coreth led Robby and Ullin aside, to a small alcove in the hallway, and stood some few yards away to give them privacy.

"Yes, to the Palace," Robby explained. "It is what Ashlord asked me to do."

"You are my envy today," Ullin sighed, a smile forcing its way across his face. "You will enjoy seeing the Palace. But look at this."

Ullin pulled up his sleeve, and Robby saw how every hair on his arm stood on end.

"Your feeling?"

"Yes. Ever since we met with Portius."

"What do you think it means?"

Ullin shook his head, pushing his sleeve back down. "I cannot be certain. I fear that we tarry too long. That perhaps coming here was a mistake. Now I am ordered, more or less, to appear at the meeting Portius has called. It may take hours. So you may as well make the most of your time. Just be careful."

"When and where should we meet?"

"In the Great Foyer. I'll make my way there at sunset. But do not wait long for me. I'll check the desk for a message from you. And you do the same for one from me. If we have not found each other by the second hour of night, make your way as best as you can to the village of Resa...."

Coreth stood with her back to them, intercepting a stray soldier or two who wanted a word with Ullin before the meeting. Robby and Ullin shook hands and said goodbye, and Ullin was whisked away by fellow Kingsmen. Coreth led Robby the other way and, after a few turns, briskly down a long flight of stairs. Thoroughly lost, Robby followed her long strides into a wide marble-tiled foyer. To the left, behind a line of stern Elifaen statues, all warriors, hung many war pennants, some with the flowing script of the Dragonkind. The opposite wall was lined with windows of stained glass depicting the Firstborn, still with wings, some wielding swords and flying downward at a Dragonkind army. The background of sky was done in pale blues, and the rolling mists of the waterfalls outside made the glass shift in color and in light. The whole room buzzed and hummed at the steady rumble of the nearby falls, and Robby thought he caught a whiff of moist air. There was but one portal at the opposite end, a large and ornately carved set of double doors shod in steel, and guarding it were a dozen soldiers, all in shining green and gold breastplates and helmets, leg guards and wrist bands of similar hue and design, and long gray robes. All had sword hilts protruding over their shoulders, and half of them held upright ornate but deadly pikes. Seeing Coreth and Robby, they stiffened, and one of the guards saluted her as she handed him her pass. He looked at it and quickly saluted again, handing it back. At his sign, two other guards pulled open the doors.

Immediately, the noise of the falls filled the room. Amazed, Robby followed Coreth into a long hall, of sorts, covered over with glass walls and a curved ceiling of glass through which Robby could see water cascading down on both sides. Coreth said nothing—indeed, they would have had to shout to be heard—but she winked at him as he gazed and grinned back. They were in a kind of passageway outside of the building, and it seemed to Robby that he was being led to the very base of the falls, such was the increase in sound of the violent water nearby. He could not help but stare up at the sun-rippled water dancing over the glass. They continued along for a few minutes as the way curved along and then rose gently. The glass now gave way to stone and the sound abruptly lessened.

"We are now within the mountain," Coreth said.

"The mountain? And this is the way to the Palace?"

"It is the shortest way."

The tunnel inclined gently, well lit with many lamps, and they passed several other openings and passages leading away to the right, and little gutters running with water were along the base of the walls. Each time they passed a junction with another tunnel, the dull roar increased, and cool wet air blew into the main passage where they walked. Every once in a while, he also heard a thud, accompanied by a metallic groan and creak that echoed throughout the tunnel.

"We'll take this one," Coreth gestured to the side where a passage opened. A short distance away there was bright misty light, and the way continued to a paved ledge. There was a brass bannister in front of them with a gate situated at the edge of a platform that jutted away out into empty space. Just beyond, some thirty feet more, water fell past them in a broad white torrent.

"Are we behind the falls?" Robby shouted to Coreth, who leaned closer to hear him.

"Somewhat. We must wait here for a bit."

Just then, a large object, several yards wide and long, descended slowly through the down-gush, the water striking the top of the object and spraying in every direction and splashing on the outer ledge. They quickly took a couple of steps back to avoid getting drenched. A figure cloaked in oilskins and a rain hat appeared and moved along the outer ledge toward the thing, gripping handrails as he went. Robby was baffled at the purpose of the apparatus, and Coreth did not explain.

It was large and boat-like, made of wood and iron and hanging in a sort of cradle. But the cascade of water came even closer as it continued its descent, obscuring Robby's view by its spray. Coreth touched him on the shoulder and leaned close so that she could be heard.

"Perhaps we should move back just a little more," she suggested. They stepped back just in time as the gush washed over where they had been standing. The splashing and the spray ceased altogether, along with the noise of the cataract, and Robby could more clearly see the object. Water drained out of its bottom through many holes as it continued to slowly descend beyond his view. But now he could see that it was itself suspended below another smaller object, a cage with a curved glass roof within which several people stood. The attending man, by pushing and pulling on several levers, guided the contraption until the cage came to rest on stone supports, then he pulled on a rope and a gangway swung out from his landing.

A man stepped out from the cage and adjusted the end of the gangway, then made a signal. The passengers emerged and crossed over the gangway and onto the landing. The attendant promptly opened the gate and let them through, a well-dressed group, somewhat elderly but spry and chatting away as they passed by. One, seeing the Queen's Feather on Robby's shoulder, nodded respectfully.

"All aboard!" cried the attendant.

"Oh?" Robby said.

Coreth led him across the landing and onto the gangway, and he saw that the waterfall had somehow moved and was now some thirty yards away to his left. Looking to his right, he understood that they were in a kind of cove, and he could see across a broad expanse of water to the Hall of Ministers from which they had just come, shrouded by rolling mists from other waterfalls that were beyond his view.

"Watch your step," said the attendant, holding a gate open for them. Entering, Robby was further amazed to see that it was decked within, like a boat might be, and large enough for a dozen people. It had open sides with hand rails and iron columns supporting a curved glass roof. The whole thing was suspended by a system of thick cables and spars affixed to iron rings that hung from a boom which was itself hanging by two other cables that receded skyward. The attendant came aboard, made a few adjustments to some levers, pulled a chain wrapped over a block, and did other things that puzzled Robby. At his signal, the other attendant at the landing moved to a place on the cliff wall and pulled up a long lever attached to another thin cable that rose upward and out of sight.

"This apparatus is operated from above," Coreth explained. "He signals that we are ready."

"Ready?"

"Yes. Take hold of that railing."

Robby immediately did so just as the whole thing lurched, and they began to rise, swinging ever-so-slightly from side to side.

"Oh," Robby said. "Oh-oh, oh!"

They rose slowly but steadily over the pool. The waterfall fell past them a few yards away to one side while, on the other side, a view of the city came into sight. They continued upward, and the roar of the falls receded. Looking up through the glass roof, Robby saw only clouds. Coreth grinned at how tightly Robby held to the railing.

"You are in no danger of falling," she told him. "But many who take this way keep their eyes closed."

"I don't dare close my eyes!" he said, grinning nervously. "Lo! What a sight!"

The valley stretched out, opening to the far hazy horizon, the orderly city below giving way in steps to forests and farmlands. He surmised that they ascended the high cliff adjacent to the great falls. And, though the rock face blocked much from view, what he could see was spectacular. His eyes always went back to the city and the view beyond, although he was intensely curious about the vehicle that bore them up and how it worked. In some places on the wall of the nearby cliff—so near he could almost reach out and touch it—the rock seemed to have been carved away, perhaps to make room for the lift.

Effortlessly they rose up, the air growing cooler by the foot, and the lift was so steady that Robby loosened his grip somewhat. The attendant stood nearby, not holding onto anything, with his legs apart and his arms crossed, and Coreth leaned easily against one of the columns that supported the glass roof.

"How does this thing work? It must be a mighty team of horses that draws us up!"

"Not at all," said Coreth. They were high enough now that they could easily talk, for the cascade of water nearby made little sound as it plunged by.

"You will see in a few moments."

They continued to rise, and Robby saw above, in the middle of the stream of water, another platform such as their own, slowly descending. The waterfall splashed over its curved roof, and as the lifts passed each other, the attendants on each waved to one another.

"The water flows off of the roof and into the large basket below the gondola," Coreth explained. "The driver controls how much is retained by opening and closing outlets. When the water makes it heavy enough, and is just right, it descends, pulling us upward. At the top, as you may now see if you look, is a gateway that releases the water into a sluice, first to one side and then to the other. That way, when one gondola is all the way down, the other at the top can serve as a counterweight in its turn."

"How clever! Is this the only way up the mountain?"

"There are other ways to the Palace, but they are long and arduous."

"And all this is done by the waterfalls I saw from below!"

"No, the Falls of Tiandari are to the other side of the cliff, just around yonder, out of sight from us. But the same water that feeds them also powers our gondolas by being channeled and redirected this way."

Robby shook his head in wonder. "I suppose, then, that the Palace must be a very safe place."

"Safe from attack, we hope. If that is what you mean," Coreth said, her smile vanishing. "But not necessarily from other threats."

Robby was distracted from further questions by a movement of the operator, and he looked up. They were not more than three feet from the smooth face of the cliff, and the operator moved to that side of the gondola and placed his hand on the gate. Their ascent slackened suddenly, then continued very slowly a few feet more until they came in line with a landing, much like the one below. As they drew to a halt, an attendant on the landing lowered a narrow drawbridge with handrails onto the step of the gondola. Their operator opened the gate, secured it, and stood aside.

"Have a good day," he said with a slight bow.

"Thank you!" replied Robby, grinning as he followed Coreth across to the landing.

"This way," Coreth said. She led him through a short tunnel, then up steep stairs, and they emerged onto a tall wall laid with white stone and smoothly paved like a street. On one side, Robby looked down from the dizzying height at the rainbow-lensed city below, its streets and buildings tiny, dropping away in steps toward the far forest and fields. To his left was a teardrop-shaped lake, rimmed on this its broad side by the wall they walked along. On the far opposite side, the lake tapered into the mountains, and, nestled between flanking cliffs, there rose a magnificent white castle as if floating upon the water's surface, with many tall spires and towers roofed in glass and gold, some higher than the nearby cliffs. Beyond the castle, a misty river tumbled over steep shoals and into the lake, and the colossal snow-capped peak of Mount Cassos was reflected in the lake's surface. The lake itself was perhaps a half-mile at its broadest, and Robby could see a long narrow causeway leading from a place some distance ahead to the High Palace.

"Oh, my! How beautiful!" he exclaimed.

Coreth smiled, and gestured for him to walk with her along the top of the broad wall. It curved gently between water and sky, at the very edge of the precipice. They walked on, with Robby enthralled by the vistas, and crossed through a towered keep and onto an arched bridge. Underneath its span, the blue water of the lake flowed, turning white as it poured over the rim to begin its long cascade downward. Some distance further along, they passed over another bridge like the first one, spanning the top of another waterfall. From there, Robby had a better view of where the long causeway from the Palace joined the wall ahead at a large flat structure that gracefully reached out from the wall, under which the next waterfall poured. The platform atop the structure protruded many yards out, directly over the precipitous waterfall, and was held in the air by supports that curved out in the shape of wings. Robby stopped in his tracks, seeing a man hoist what he took to be a set of sails and jog straight toward the edge.

"What's he doing?" Robby exclaimed, catching his breath in sudden fear, for the man leapt right off the edge and, for a moment, plummeted.

"Oh! Oh!" Robby cried.

Coreth put her hand on Robby's shoulder to steady him.

The man soared away, the sail-like wings now carrying him smoothly and swiftly over the city. Robby's terror quickly transformed into wonder and amazement as another flyer confidently took off just behind the first.

"People are flying! Those aren't birds at all! They are people!"

"Just so. These are the messengers of the Palace, going about their business."

"Oh, my gosh!"

Coreth grinned at Robby's astonishment, his expression full of delight and awe and a little fear. They stopped to watch two more men take flight before proceeding on. After a few moments, Robby shook his head in wonder. In any direction he looked, there was something fascinating and intriguing. The colorful flyers who gracefully defied all reason, the shimmering lake, blue and serene and gently textured by the breeze, the grand vista of the city, fanning out far and below, and the white Faere castle, seemingly afloat on the water. All bounded by the overwhelming mass of the mountains, some of their peaks reaching into the blueness of the sky. One of these had a lavender top so sharp that it looked as if it scratched the heavens.

He felt, as all first-time visitors must, that he had entered into a completely different world than any he could have imagined, one rivaling the marvels of Islindia, even. No wonder his mother said, as she had done only a few months back, that Linlally was the most beautiful city in the world. He glanced at Coreth. Though she was very stern in her appearance, he caught her smiling at his reaction.

"We are very lucky to call such a place home," she said humbly. "It is beautiful in all seasons of the year."

"It is spectacular!"

"Yes."

She stopped and looked out over the precipice and shrugged. "Of course, the city has grown, and did not always stretch out so far. Do you see there? That bridge, just there?"

From this height, the valley appeared to be a staircase, with the river cutting through the middle, its foaming shoals and waterfalls looking like snowy puffs.

"Yes," he said, putting his hand up to shade his eyes. "That one?"

"Yes. It was once the edge of the city, in the days of Cupeldain. Roads were made later, after the Fall. But from there to the river's bend where it turns southward, yon, was forest. And, on the other side, as far as you could see, was forest, too. So green and thick it was that from here you could not see the river beyond the bend, except in the wintertime, such as now, when the sun was low in the morning sky and it glistened through the forest branches. Only a line, the gap in the trees, showed where the river ran. King Parthais continued Cupeldain's road-building. And it was he who made the bridges. When Men came into the world from the far sea, some of them established a village right at the bend. Over time, it grew and so did the High Town, as they called Old Linlally. Eventually the two settlements merged into one. That place, where the Men were, is still called Landings by some. During the reign of our present Queen, our city has grown and prospered with trade, though times are not as good these days as they once were."

Robby considered what she said as he examined the city below, trying to imagine what she described, and how it must have been before there were roads.

"Do you remember those days? The time of Cupeldain?"

"I was born the year Cupeldain died. Mathos was my father and Atlana was my mother."

"Atlana, did you say?"

"You have heard of her?"

"Yes. I met her sister, Esildre, and she mentioned Atlana and their brother, Navis."

Coreth stiffened visibly and gave Robby a very odd look.

"My family does not speak my aunt's name," she said bluntly. Before Robby could ask why, Coreth's tone changed slightly, and her shoulders slumped as she asked, "Where, may I ask, did you meet her?"

"In the Thunder Mountain borderlands, east of the plains. As my party made its way west."

"Hm. So she has emerged from her seclusion and has entered the world once again."

"Seclusion?"

"Ah. I see that you do not know her tale."

"Only some parts of it," Robby shrugged. He knew that he must be careful about what he said. "She didn't say that much about herself. She was on her way eastward, but did not say where she was going, exactly."

"Well, if you are from the Eastlands, you must know of Tulith Attis. And the battle there. It was after she returned from Tulith Attis that her troubles began. I don't know what she saw there, but it must have been horrible. I do know that she searched for days for her cousin's body, whom she loved very much and who served Lyrium's household. When she returned from the Eastlands, she was deeply troubled and somehow became entangled with the vile one."

"Secundur, you mean?"

"Yes. We do not like to speak his name, either. For many years she was his…courtesan. By all accounts, that is putting it kindly. They had a violent parting, it is said, and his curse has been upon her ever since. For centuries, she isolated herself in her castle, in an inhospitable, mountainous place between here and Duinnor. They say that those who go unbidden to her castle never return. And she bids no one to come."

Coreth turned and led Robby onward.

"It is rumored, though," she continued, "that she was seen recently in Duinnor."

"Yes. She mentioned that she came from there. I thought her father was there."

"My grandfather, Lord Banis, has become a Lord and High Minister to the King. But I have never met him. He is powerful, and no one can tell if his influence aids or hinders his homeland. To many, he is our foe. Some say he is to blame for Esildre's woes. Her brother, Navis, traveled to Shatuum in an effort to gain his sister's release from Secundur's hold. But he never returned. Years later, my aunt came to Vanara to see me. She said she did not know the fate of Uncle Navis and was unaware of his mission to free her until I told her of it. It was a difficult encounter, and she bore the mark of Secundur upon her, keeping her face veiled to hide it. We quarreled horribly. Faslor tried to intervene, to soothe my temper, but it was too late. She went away, and I have not seen her since. And I do not wish to."

"What of your mother and your grandmother?"

"My grandmother, whose name was Tiryna, went away with Aperion because she refused to fight the Dragonkind. My mother and father were both killed in the borderlands, at a place now called Gory Gulch."

Robby nodded. So many lives were affected by the violence that took place there, he thought to himself as he remembered that Ullin's father had died there, too.

"I hope no misfortune befell you because of my aunt," Coreth went on, breaking into his thoughts.

"Oh, no. I do not think so," Robby replied, recalling how Ashlord said that it was Secundur, not Esildre, who was ultimately to blame for Ullin's recent woes. "Why do you say that?"

"Rumors abound," Coreth shrugged. "About the curse that the Dark One put upon her. Some say she is a sorceress, even, and revels in the dark arts."

"Oh?"

"And I have been told that she uses her charms to fill men and women alike with salacious desires and with madness."

"Hm. Well, she is very beautiful," was all that Robby had to say, growing more uncomfortable with the conversation. They were approaching a fork in the way, one way going straight ahead into a tunnel which, Robby could see, emerged on the other side of the large platform, and curving left upward steeply then twisting back around to the top of the keep. The other way curved to the left to the causeway that led to the palace. As they approached, a gust of wind blew one of the flyers just over their heads, causing Robby to duck reflexively.

"Whoa!" he cried. But the airman was in control, and he steered his delicate-looking apparatus out over the falls to slope away gracefully. In that brief moment, Robby saw that the wings were made of cloth stretched over a frame, held taut with cords and lines, and below it hung the airman in a harness something like what a draft horse might wear. They watched the flyer recede before moving on.

"Are there many accidents?"

"I have not heard of any recently. It has not been long since we learned to do such things, perhaps only fifty or sixty years ago. It was Lord Seafar himself who perfected the design of our wings, being an expert flyer from his youth. It was he, too, who established our Flying Corps, before he became Chancellor and Regent. I do not know much about the art. Frankly, the idea terrifies me. I force my eyes to stay open each time I see one go over the edge."

"You do?" Robby gave her a bemused look.

"I know. Ironic, is it not? That one such as I, with the scars of wings on my back, should be afraid of that which my kind most longs for. I am not one of the First Ones, so I never flew as they did, but most of my kind, even the First Ones, feel as I do."

"Well, not all, obviously," Robby gestured at another one preparing to launch. Coreth glanced that way.

"But he is a Newcomer," she said, "one of the race of Men. As are all those who perform that service to the Realm."

"What? None of them are Elifaen?"

"As far as I know. To risk death in such a way, when their lives are so short, anyway, is a mystery to my people," Coreth went on. "As are so many things about the race of Men."

Coreth directed Robby to a staircase and they ascended upward to the platform. Passing a landing halfway up, Robby saw several sheltered enclosures just below the platform, with separate steps going from those places up to the top. There were hoists so that workers could move the flying devices up and down, presumably to make repairs or to prepare the gear for use. Some men were sewing, others were working on the harnesses or the long struts and poles that served as frames to the sail-like wings. Others were helping unfurl the wings while those preparing for flight adjusted the straps and harnesses that they wore. Once at the top steps, Coreth touched him to halt, pointing upward. Above them, a flyer circled, then smoothly descended onto the platform as several men grabbed the wings to hold him in case a gust of wind came along. Robby watched as the man undid himself, and then he removed a small pack strapped to his back. Another man took it away and marched off toward the causeway.

"The messengers that land here come from the mountains overhead," Coreth nodded upward, "where there are many outposts and keeps that watch over us. Otherwise, those that fly down to the city must come back the same way we did. I thought you might like to see all this. But we must go back down to get to the causeway."

She turned to go back the way they came, and Robby followed. Below, they went beneath the structure to a covered intersection where the causeway met the wall. They were soon back out into the open, moving toward the Palace on the causeway. Robby glanced back over his shoulder at the fliers.

"I should dearly like to know more about how it all works," he said.

"Or perhaps go for a little flight yourself?"

"I don't know about that! Well, maybe. That might be fun."

The low paved causeway ran atop scores of stone arches, and the White Palace loomed larger and higher as they approached. Coreth told him how the lake was natural, but was bounded by the outer walls to help protect the Palace and to make channels for the small waterfalls needed to power the lifts.

"In the winter, the lake freezes over. Sometimes there are parties out on the ice, celebrations, banquets, and skating. We have games, too, in the winter time, and skaters race around the lake to win the Queen's award. Do you notice anything odd about the Palace?"

By now they were over half way across, and the air that blew over the water was gentle but very cold.

"To my eye, everything in Linlally is odd. And amazing."

Coreth drew Robby's attention to the entrance, still some distance away, then pointed above, to the ornate columns that surrounded the walls of the castle.

"Well," Robby observed, "the stonework is different. The lower part seems to be made of a slightly darker stone, creamy, rather than the snow-white stones of the upper portion."

"Yes, the lower parts were modified and added on. Behind the surrounding walls and above it is the original palace built by Cupeldain. But after the Fall, the Palace could not be used as before. In fact it was abandoned, as was much of the city, for a very long time. My people were confused and scattered, striving to learn how to survive without wings and how to fashion the things they needed. This causeway and the entrance ahead were added so that we could come and go on our feet. That portico, up there..."

Robby looked up. Some six or seven stories high, there was indeed a part of the structure that did look for all the world like a huge ornate porch of sorts, carved of stone and covered by its own roof. But there were no stairs or steps of any kind that Robby could discern that led up to it from the outside.

"...that was the original gate of the White Palace. The interior as well as the exterior had to be rebuilt. Doors, such as you might call them, did not exist before, nor were there floors to walk upon. The rooms were high and open, and near the top of each room was a window leading to the next room. Our people flew, you see, coming and going without much use of their feet."

"Oh, of course. During the journey here, we passed by an ancient temple. It had no doors on the ground, either."

Coreth nodded. "There are still a few such places left from the Time Before Time. When Cupeldain finally reunited our people, he set them to work remaking most such places. Like this one. And some of the past glory of that lost era has been regained. At least in part. Now the Palace is a busy place, constantly being changed to suit the occupation of both Men and Elifaen, and to accommodate the Queen and her ministers and advisers."

• • •

Vanara, though still ruled by the ancient houses of the Faerekind, was populated equally by Men, and they, too, shared high ranks both in society and in government. Indeed, the Lord Chancellor and Regent of Vanara was a Man, and though neither of his parents was Elifaen, he had many Elifaen relatives. The House of Seafar was proud of its ancient lineage, going back to those Men who first came to the shores of the world. It was the namesake of this honored house, Tritian Seafar, who, as a lad, formed an alliance with the Elifaen in those early days. He joined his village with the people of the House of Fairmyrtle, the Elifaen who once occupied the coastal regions within present-day Tracia. It was Seafar folk who fought with the Elifaen, side by side, in the Great Dragon War of that era, winning honors and forming loyalties that reached across time and spanned the divisions that plagued the relations between other Men and the Elifaen. Eventually, the alliance led the descendants of that great friendship to Vanara, where the House of Seafar cemented its place of loyalty within the court of Queen Serith Ellyn. Although the House of Fairmyrtle had long ago passed away, the Seafars lived on, and they served Vanara, distinguishing themselves in battle, commerce, diplomacy, and in court.

Lord Seafar held, like his father before him, the highest appointment in the land, and was in power second only to the Queen herself. He was a thin, broad-shouldered man of average height, forty-one years old, with gray-streaked black hair, black eyes, and a neatly trimmed beard. He waited patiently at his desk for his guest to arrive, looking over various letters. Before him were two communiqués, each received some weeks ago. One was from the Queen, still in far away Glareth, and the other was from a scholar in Duinnor.

The Queen's message was brief, and Seafar's eyes wandered again to a few of the sentences written by her own hand.

> *So I am convinced that he will eventually come to Vanara, perhaps in the company of others. If so, he will seek to go northwest. It will not be Shatuum that he aims for, but rather the particular place that the Land of Shadow has guarded since the time of my father. You will know him by two signs. First, he will bear Swyncraff, which my brother gave over to serve him. Second, he will have the blood of Tallin and of Fairoak, but neither of those names shall he have....*

Seafar's eyes jumped to the end of the message:

> *Gaiyelneth sends her love. I think she longs for our return
> even more than I.*

He smiled, which was in his disposition to do naturally, and turned his attention to the other letter, written in a fine but more masculine hand.

> ...and so I write to you, on behalf of our mutual friend, to beg you to give whatever assistance you may to this person who might wish to read the Chronicles of Nimwill, and to permit him to do so himself, if he may, and also to give this person any other aid that may please your lordship."

So here were two items, sent weeks apart from one another, from vastly different people and places, and received some while back, pointing, he was convinced, to the same person. Who else, outside a few academics, would be interested in those records? Shuffling those notes aside, he fingered another one, just received this morning, from old Nerron, who watched the comings and goings at the Hall of Ministers. It was in response to a request Seafar privately made to him weeks before, shortly after he realized the import of the Queen's letter. Written on the note was a single phrase, "The one you are interested in has arrived."

There was a tap at the door, and the lord's secretary put his head in.

"There is a gentleman to see you," he said.

"Yes?"

"Yes, my lord. He seeks your lordship's permission to view the archives. He has a referral from the Librarian."

"Is he alone?"

"Coreth of the Gray Guard escorts him."

"Ask Coreth to be so kind as to wait, and show the gentleman in, please."

"Yes, Lord."

Seafar rose from his chair and came around his desk just as Robby was shown in.

"Your Lordship," said the secretary. "May I introduce Robby Ribbon of Passdale? Mr. Ribbon, I present you to Lord Chancellor Seafar, Regent Royal of Vanara. "

Seafar acknowledged Robby's bow with a pleasant but puzzled look.

"Thank you, Henders. That will be all."

The secretary bowed and retreated, gently closing the door behind him as Seafar continued to gaze at Robby. Robby thought perhaps someone else was expected, so he went right to his business.

"Lord Chancellor," Robby said, holding out the note from the Librarian, "I seek permission to view the Royal Archives."

"So I have been informed." Seafar took the note but did not look at it. "Pardon me, won't you have a seat?" He gestured to a chair, and sat in another nearby.

Robby sat, somewhat nervously, sensing Seafar's note of the Queen's flash and of Swyncraff over his other shoulder.

"You are the one, are you not, who came in the company of Commander Tallin? Bringing disturbing news?"

"I am, Lord Chancellor."

"Lord Seafar is sufficient. Or Brandis, if you prefer. I've just received a preliminary report of your claims. But your business here is otherwise from Tallin's. To view the archives."

"Yes, Lord Seafar. I am given to understand that the manuscript I am interested in has not yet been copied for the Library at the Hall of Ministers, and that it remains here at the Palace."

"And you have traveled all this way to see them?"

"My travels are timely, given the events of the world, and not entirely just to see the manuscripts."

"And what is it that you wish to see?"

"Those Chronicles of Nimwill that pertain to the last years of Parthais."

"I see."

Seafar studied Robby, wrinkling his brow for a moment, but his expression remained pleasant, with a hint of amusement.

"Pardon me," he said, "but you are younger than I expected you to be."

"My lord?"

"Your coming was foretold to me. Do you mean to strike out for Griferis soon?"

Robby's stomach fluttered as he stiffened.

"Foretold?"

"I apologize. But I believe I have the advantage of you. Are you not related to the man who came with you to Vanara?"

"Yes, Lord. He is my cousin on my mother's side."

"And is that not the gift of Thurdun over your shoulder?"

"Yes. It is," said Robby.

"My Queen suggested in a recent letter that you might come this way."

"Oh?"

"Do you know of one called Raynor?"

"I have heard of him."

"He is a friend of a friend, so to speak. And perhaps Raynor's friend and my friend may also be a friend of yours?"

"Do you mean Ashlord?" Robby asked.

"Here he is known as Collandoth. I believe he and Raynor are colleagues. But at any rate, Raynor has written to me from Duinnor asking that I give whatever assistance that I deem fit to anyone who may wish to view the Chronicles of Nimwill. I believe, unbeknownst to each other, Raynor and Queen Serith Ellyn refer to the same person. But, I had no idea he would be so young."

Seafar spoke very casually, still smiling, as if taking great pleasure in speaking with Robby. But Robby forced himself to keep a blank face and to remain still, in spite of a powerful need to squirm.

"I quite understand why you may not trust me," Seafar continued. "But I will do whatever is in my power to alleviate you of fear and to gain your trust. It is Nimwill's last book that you need to see, and you most certainly may use the Royal Archives where his records are held. Indeed, I place the entire resources of Vanara, all of its might and power, at your disposal, according to the desire of my Queen. I do not require you to answer to me, nor shall I ask anything of you in return. You need not confide to me anything that you do not wish to share. But should you leave Vanara and strike off for Griferis, I beg you to allow me to assign an escort to serve and to guide you. Those are dangerous lands, and in winter the dangers of the season make it a perilous trek. Please, when you have read the Chronicles, perhaps you may consult with me about your route and confide in me your needs, should you have any. I desire only to make your way as easy and as safe as possible."

Before Robby could reply, Seafar rose and offered his hand. "I will have arrangements made for your stay here in the Palace."

Robby stood, somewhat stunned by Seafar's statements, and he hesitantly took his hand.

"You are very generous, Lord Seafar," he managed to say, bowing. "But I would prefer to stay in the city with my companion. And, if possible, to visit some shops there for sundry needs. Perhaps an apothecary, too. And I left all my things down below at the Hall of Ministers."

"We have a fine apothecary here within the Palace. The best, actually, in all of Vanara. I'm sure you will find what you need there. And we shall certainly send for your things, and for Commander Tallin. Any other needs that you may have will likewise be provided here or sent for. There is no lacking for room, I assure you, and you will be much more comfortable here and, frankly, you will be safer. Everywhere below are agents of Duinnor, as you know."

Seafar's voice softened even more. "Should Duinnor learn of your visit to the Palace, and why you come, then your purpose may be guessed by those who might seek to stop you. And they would surely use any means in their power to do so."

Robby immediately realized that Seafar was an ally. And one more powerful than he could have ever hoped for.

"Then you should know," Robby said, "that already a summons has been made for me by Duinnor. I and my companions have only narrowly avoided having it served upon us. So I guess you may say I am already sought for."

"A summons? Do you know the nature of it?"

"Only that I and any found with me are to be escorted under guard to Duinnor to face Lord Banis. I first learned of it three weeks ago."

"Hm. I am surprised that word of it has not reached me. And I am doubly surprised that you made it this far."

"I have been fortunate, yes."

"But so long as you are in Vanara, you are under the Queen's protection. You are certainly safe from molestation here in the Palace. But, you must not leave here or wander the city below without an escort. Duinnor is not above using underhanded means to get what it wants. You came here with an escort, Coreth."

"Yes."

"Does she know about the summons? Or of your quest?"

"No. I do not think so."

"Very well, then. I shall speak to her momentarily, telling her as little as possible. She is most capable, has served and survived many dangerous assignments, and she knows how to carry out orders. And, with your permission, I shall send for Commander Tallin and your things. Meanwhile, I imagine you are anxious to see the Archives. My secretary's assistant will see you there."

Seafar moved to the door, and Robby followed.

"I hope to see you later today," Seafar said, putting his hand on the latch. He hesitated and said, "There are other things, besides the Archives, that you ought to know about."

"I am woefully ignorant of much," Robby nodded. "My education has been good, but very provincial. Other things I have picked up along the way. As best as I could."

"That is not what I mean, though you seem fairer of speech than I would normally expect someone from the Eastlands to be. What I mean is that here at the Palace are things I may show you that may be useful to you."

Seafar looked away for a moment in thought, saying, "Yes. There is much to be done." Suddenly he looked back at Robby and smiled broadly. "But first to the Royal Archives! Allow me to speak to Henders."

• • •

Outside, Robby and Seafar chatted with Coreth for a moment, before Henders, Seafar's secretary, returned with a woman of about sixty.

"Mr. Ribbon, this is Sonya, my assistant," Henders introduced the two. "Sonya, Lord Seafar would like for you to show our guest to the Archives and give him access to whatever he requires there."

"Yes, sir," Sonya replied. "Pleased to meet you Mr. Ribbon. Right this way, if you please."

Robby bowed again to Seafar and Henders, and nodded to Coreth as he followed Sonya down the hall. They went up a broad spiral staircase that wound around the inside walls of a wide tower. Coming to the top, they entered a very large room, circular in shape, domed over with copper and glass. Within it were rows of shelves filled with books and scrolls, and many tables scattered about. It was not long before Sonya, having been told what Robby needed, had him seated at a table while she fetched the material he requested. When she returned, she placed a large tome in front of him.

"These are the final accounts given by Nimwill," she said. "They are written in the speech and writing of that day. Can you read it?"

Robby opened it and looked through a few pages, illustrated and adorned beautifully in red and yellow gold, with blue and green vines drawn around the borders of each page. Some letters of the script he recognized, but not enough to make out the words they spelled. Crestfallen, he shook his head.

"No. I cannot."

"Then shall I call a reader for you?"

"If there is one available. I would appreciate it."

"Then I'll bring one to you. There is usually one on duty at all times."

Robby continued to page through the book. Since he could not read it, his eyes were naturally attracted to the illustrations. There was one of a hunter stalking a ram. Several others depicted a marvelous bridge, of sorts, leading to a castle in the air. He turned a few pages and came to a particularly gloomy illustration showing a kingly person speaking with a smoke-like figure. A chill crawled up Robby's spine.

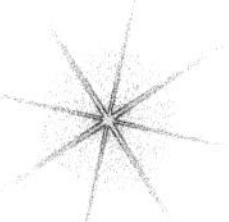

Chapter 22

The Last Book of Nimwill

"This is Ean," Sonya said.

Robby shook himself, looking up to see an elderly man standing beside Sonya. He wore the same type of gray uniform that Coreth wore, and he bowed to Robby, smiling, and held out his hand.

"I am Robby Ribbon."

"How do you do? What shall I read for you?"

"I am well, thank you. I would like for you to read this, if you please."

Robby handed Ean the book, and as the old soldier looked over it, Sonya retreated, saying, "I will wait just outside, there."

"Thank you, Sonya."

"Not at all."

"Since you speak in the Common Tongue, shall I translate it into that manner of speaking?" Ean asked.

"Yes, please do."

"Very well."

"Won't you sit at the table?" Robby suggested.

"It is not our custom, though you should make yourself as comfortable as you can. There are decanters of wine just there, if you wish."

"No, but thank you. I'll just sit here. And I would be more comfortable if you sat, too."

"Then I shall do so. Thank you, sir. Now. Nimwill, I see. It has been a long while since I last read his accounts. I shall first tell you just a bit about Nimwill. Nimwill the Scribe, son of Lissin of the House of Spruce, was appointed by Parthais to be his Chief Scribe, and to record the happenings of the court in the New Writing of that age. He served in that capacity until the King's rule ended. At the end of Parthais's rule, Nimwill served Serith Ellyn for a very short time, then retired. Now I shall read to you...."

• • •

The Last Book of Nimwill

I.

The Tale of Elrasil

This, then, is the Tale of Elrasil the Hunter, as told by him to Parthais, King of Vanara, son of Cupeldain, in the year 1,149 from the First Day of Reckoning of the First Age, and set down by his

430

scribe, Nimwill, in the New Writing, as heard in the company of the King's Court, including the Prince Thurdun and his sister the Princess Serith Ellyn, son and daughter of Parthais:

I am called Elrasil. I hunt the wild game for my people who live in a far valley, for our lands yield little from the rocky ground and so we eat flesh and make from the wild creatures warm clothes that we need to cover ourselves against the bitterness of wind and snow. I have come hither, sent by the elders of my people, to tell thee of what I have seen, and to ask what omen it may contain.

It was on the day after the first moon, two months ago, that I and several of my kinsmen departed into the mountains to hunt. Westward we went, up the slopes, and we took stag and many fowl for three days until there was ample to carry home. Then, on the morning of the fourth day, as we prepared for our return, there came upon a hill overlooking our camp a mighty ram. Its fleece was the color of bright steel and its great curled horns as polished copper, and we were amazed by its size and hue and at the majesty of its proud form.

"I will have that fleece," I vowed, taking up my bow and lance, "and of its horns I shall make a mighty trumpet!"

"But we are burdened enough," said my kinsmen, "and have no need of more."

"Go, then, and I will take it alone," I said, aiming my arrow. But as I drew my aim upon it, the ram kicked and leapt from view, and my arrow went far from it.

"Come, let us depart," urged my kinsmen. But I left them immediately and took up the chase of the ram, leaving my kinsmen to the bounty of our hunt and to return without me.

For ten days, I chased the ram, stalking it through the mountains and into places I had never been, westward and upward through passes filled with ice and along the terrible faces of sheer cliffs. Each day I neared close enough to him to let fly an arrow, but each time he stepped away unharmed, until on the tenth day I spent my last arrow. Yet I continued on, climbing after him, seeking to take him with my lance. But he was ever just out of reach of me. Deftly, and with great ease, the beast stepped from rock to rock and vaulted from ledge to ledge, while I climbed after him slowly and with great effort, hunger and weakness overtaking me as I went. Often he seemed to wait for me to catch up somewhat before climbing on, and sometimes he would let out a powerful bray which echoed loudly from wall to wall and from slope to slope, taunting me and encouraging renewed strength in my arms and legs.

Then, on the morning of the full moon, he stood over me as I awoke. But I was too weak to lift my lance. He brayed at me and tossed his head and stamped upon all four hooves. Turning away, he climbed a rock nearby and stepped out of sight. Mustering all my remaining strength, I climbed after him onto a broad shelf below the western peak of the mountain, and I was filled with wonder at what I saw.

How may I tell of it? For I overlooked the Crack of the World, that which few have ever seen except those who remember their wings. There it was, running north to south, straight and true, a deep, smooth-walled canyon filled with mist, and out of it from far below came a low rumbling. Beyond was nothing but air into faraway peaks, their tops bound with snow and towering over the place where I stood. Yet before me, at the very edge of the precipice, stood a gateway, fashioned of two columns of white marble, each standing eight cubits high, and the width of its opening between these was eight cubits. An untarnished silver arch spanned the two columns and at its apex was set a black disk three cubits in diameter. Upon the ring which held the black disk was inscribed figures which are likened unto those used by the Dragonkind for conveying messages. And as I gazed upon these figures, I understood their meaning, though I have no knowledge of writing, and they said to me the name of the thing I looked upon, "The Bridge of Rulers, Gateway of Worthy Sovereigns."

Then, lo, out of the sky came a stormy cloud, full of fire and drums. And the storm surrounded the gate and smote it with its blinding fire so that I was full of fear and cast myself down into the rocks and into a crevice to hide my eyes and to cover my ears against the terrible crack and rumble of skyward-drums. But soon there came a lull in the storm, and I looked up and beheld the black disk was afire with blue light, as a star in the heavens, and the silver arch in which it was set rang with a chime that did not fade from hearing. And then I perceived between the columns, stretching out into the air, a narrow causeway into the storm-cloud beyond. And in the cloud itself I saw a mighty castle floating. As I beheld the marvelous castle, the gates thereof opened, and from it came the sounds of many trumpets, and onto the bridge from the castle came two figures. As the trumpets blared out and the clouds swirled around the causeway, the figures crossed over toward the gate and unto the mountain where I still hid myself. But I saw that it was a very young boy, still in swaddling clothes, walking beside and a little behind the magnificent ram that led me to the place. I watched as the boy guided the ram by tapping it lightly on its flank with a golden stalk of wheat.

When they stopped on the threshold of the gate, the trumpets ceased their blare and the boy held up his other hand in which was a sandglass. He held out the sandglass and turned it so that the sand ran from top to bottom, and all while the sand flowed, no sound but the ringing of the arch could be heard, though the clouds that blew around the castle and darkened the sky over the bridge were split by white fire all the while. From my hiding place, I looked on as they stood there. The sand of the glass fell, and so eerie was the sight that the hairs of my skin stood on end from the back of my neck to the back of my arms. I sensed a movement some small distance from me, and I shrank back as another figure emerged from nearby to where I hid. This figure was a person dressed in strange garb and fabric like those that the Newcomers weave and wear. Whether male or female, I could not discern, but the person approached the gate and strode resolutely through and stood before the ram and the child who waited there. Then the ram and the child turned, and together they led the person across the bridge and into the castle. When they had all disappeared within, there came a deafening clap of thunder as the gate shut behind them and once more the noise of the storm raged, and the castle faded from sight as did the causeway that led to it. Into nothing they faded, as the storm lifted and dissipated, and no sight of the castle or the bridge remained, but only the gate and the clear cold air and the distant snow-capped mountains beyond the Crack of the World.

All this I swear to thee, my King, that I did see with mine own eyes, and upon my life I assure that what I hath told is a true reckoning of what I saw and heard.

II.
Griferis

The King and his court were curious and asked many questions of Elrasil about his adventure.

"Tell us," asked Parthais, "couldst thou find the way back to the place thou hath told us of?"

"If the need was dire, my King, or the reward great, I believe so," answered Elrasil. "But it would be a mighty effort."

"I desire to look upon the place and to see with mine own eyes the Crack of the World and the gate thereupon it and to delve into this mystery."

Parthais declared to his treasurer to give precious jewels to Elrasil as a reward for his tale. The King then made preparations to go out from the city with many of his court to find the place Elrasil described. And so, on the very next day, Parthais departed with Elrasil and traveled into the mountains and unto the village of the hunter. This was in the springtime and the rivers and streams gushed with melting snow, and the way was difficult and slow. When they came upon the village of Elrasil, they were received with much honor and gladness, and they were made welcome by Elrasil's people. And Parthais lavished gifts upon the people there, and while they waited for the streams and rivers to subside, he built there a temple to honor Beras.

When the summer was full and Elrasil judged the conditions best, he led King Parthais and those who accompanied him into the mountains. And those that accompanied him, besides those of Elrasil's people who served as bearers and guides, were many of his court, the Prince and the Princess, his children, and I, his scribe, to faithfully witness and record these events.

It was a difficult task, full of deadly hazards. On the second day, some of the party were killed by an avalanche of rock, and others turned back, departing with the King's permission. For three weeks, we climbed. More were killed in falls and other mishaps, and many more were injured. On two occasions only the quick hand of Elrasil saved Parthais from plummeting to his death. But at last we made the summit and beheld the gate. I, Nimwill, his scribe, Elrasil, the hunter, the King's daughter and son, Serith Ellyn and Thurdun, my assistant, and several porters of Elrasil's village were all that remained of our party among all who had departed from below.

Parthais ordered a camp to be made upon the summit, and, as he had done many times before, he bade Elrasil to repeat his tale. Then Parthais, King, said, "I shall abide here and await a sign and see for myself if the mysterious bridge may appear. And, should Beras will it, I shall cross over and inspect the castle in the air."

"Sire," said Thurdun, "we have not the means to remain very long."

"Majesty," said Elrasil, "who knows if the bridge shall ever again appear?"

"The gate remains, does it not? Why should it remain for nothing? And, look ye all at the fashioning of it. The threshold and the columns are of one piece of marble. And, see, there is no grime or weather upon it, but rather it appears to be new-made. And behold the arch that spans it, what manner of writing is that so that we may all know its meaning? Like the First Tongue, it is. And look ye at the stone made into it, look at its sheen! Surely this is a work of Beras himself, or at least of some agent of Aperion!"

And so camp was made upon the windy place, and we spent our days in awe of the view around us. Often the clouds completely covered the scene so that we had to be careful of our steps. But it was more often clear, and we could look out from the gate and gaze downward a league or more into a straight cleft cut into the world. Wide, it was, and it was walled on the far side by straight, smooth cliffs, clean, as if cut with a knife. And farther away, blue in the distance was another mountain, higher even than the one we were upon, jutting up to a jagged point and covered on all its high flanks by snow and gleaming ice. On some days that far mountain was the only feature we could see, rising up from a blanket of clouds that spread out below us like an endless sea, stretching in all directions.

For many weeks we remained. When our food ran short, Elrasil and his kinsmen, the porters, made their way off the mountain, and after a fortnight they returned with new supplies for us. All during this time, Serith and Thurdun pleaded with their father, King Parthais, to abandon the place. But he was unmoved by their words and was determined to remain.

Then, on the evening of a new moon, a storm brewed far in the west. We watched it approach for all of the night until, when the first ray of the eastern sunrise met our promontory, the sky grew violent with wind, and the light of morning was dimmed to darkness as the storm came upon us. Firebolts split the sky, and hail pelted us, and the wind and rain blew away our tents and scattered us into the rocks and crevices for protection. We covered our ears against the terrible sound and kept our eyes shut fast against the blinding light, just as Elrasil told us he had done. After some while, just as Elrasil had told before, a lull came, and we looked up and beheld the black disk now shining as a brilliant blue-white star, and we perceived a steady ringing as if a giant rubbed his wet finger upon the rim of a mighty crystal goblet. And there appeared to us, far out over the abyss of sky, and floating in the swirling storm, a grand and mighty mansion, like a fortress. And a mysterious narrow bridge stretched out from the gateway to it, suspended, like the castle, by nothing that we could perceive. As soon as these things were revealed to us, a mighty blare of trumpets sounded forth, as mighty as the storm itself, and louder. At that moment, the far gates of the castle opened up, and from it emerged a small figure, alone, who walked slowly across the causeway. It was the same figure that Elrasil had described to us, a child, still in swaddling clothes. In one hand, he carried a wand of wheat and in the other was a sandglass, and it was many long moments for the child to walk the distance between the faraway castle to the gateway upon our summit. As he came upon the threshold of the gate before us, we stood in wonder at the sight of him. Our sovereign, Parthais, though restrained by his children, stepped forward to face the child.

"What manner of place is this?" he cried out. But his words were lost in the maelstrom of noise and carried away on the powerful wind. Yet the child appeared not to see or hear Parthais and stood aside on the threshold and raised the wand of wheat and smote the threshold with it three times. And on the third time that he smote the threshold, a great mist bellowed forth from the open gates of the fortress and from it came galloping a terrible warrior. His robes and the livery of his horse were the color of crimson blood, edged in gold. His armor was black, and around his helmet curled the horns of a mighty ram, and upon his face-plate was the likeness of a skull. Upon his back was a great sword and in his saddle cup and in his black-gloved hand was a tall lance of black, banded in red. Such was the dreadful aspect of the warrior, thundering forth on his cinder-hoovéd beast, that we were all filled with terror, and those of us with weapons drew them in readiness. But then we saw the rider pull forth his lance and draw it down upon the child who stood without motion and who showed no knowledge of the doom crashing down upon him. All of us that beheld this cried out in horror, yet our feet were unable to step forth to the child's defense in time to avert his murder. But as the lance tip came upon the child, he raised his stem of grain and smote aside the lance so that it shattered and split apart. Without care or concern, the tiny one then tapped the passing beast on its flank with his wand, and under this insignificant blow, the horse stumbled and fell along with its rider over the edge of the bridge, and the two terrible creatures plummeted down into the cloudy abyss. As if nothing had occurred of any significance, the child turned again toward us and raised his sandglass and turned it over so that its sand trickled from the top to the bottom of the glass.

All became silent, save the ringing of the archway. Even the flashes of lightning about the far castle held their bright and jagged place so that no sound came of them. No breath of air stirred, and there was no motion within the clouds or anywhere about the summit but the steady fall of grains in the glass.

But Parthais approached the child, stepping upon the threshold of the gate, and he knelt before the child, placing down before him his sword.

"Wondrous and terrible child," he said, "tell us what manner of place is this, that it appears so mysteriously. And what manner of child art thou to wield such power upon a grim warrior?"

The child turned his eyes upon Parthais, and with many voices, those of the young and of the old, of both male and female, he spoke.

"This is the entrance to the place of judgment, called Griferis."

"Is this wherein the dead come to be judged of their life?"

"No, it is the living we judge of their worthiness to rule others. And it is revealed only to those desiring fitness to rule."

"Who, then, would come, except those who wish to overthrow their sovereign?"

"Any may come hither, regardless of station or intent, both the wise and the foolish may be judged."

"Why shouldst any come who may take the throne otherwise?"

"The giving of thrones and kingdoms is not our concern or affair. Our task is merely to make ready the ruler-to-be."

"Tell us of the warrior which was smote before us and destroyed. How was it that we saw what we saw? How be it that a terrible warrior is so easily vanquished by a child?"

"The warrior was Ambition, and he rode upon Power. His lance was Cruelty, and his sword is called Wealth. He wore the red and gold trappings of Conspiracy, and the headgear of Force. Yet I wield the wand of Justice, made heavy with the fruit of True Prosperity, holding within its chaff the grains of Wisdom and Truth and Humility."

"Why, then, dost thou comest forth from yonder castle?"

"Only in my company, and as the grains of this glass still fall, may a person enter the place of Trial."

At these words, the child turned away and walked back to the mysterious castle. The doors of that place took him in and shut upon him with a great clap of thunder, and the storm once again beat upon those of us gathered, and the black clouds, split with lightning, engulfed the scene. After only a few moments, all noise dissipated, and the rain ceased to beat, and the clouds faded away unto the bright morning sun. Gone was the bridge, vanished was the fabulous castle, and dim black was the stone above the gate. And all who witnessed it were filled with wonder and amazement, and we stood for many hours pondering what we had seen and heard.

III.

Parthais

But Parthais the King grew agitated and was much concerned about the words of the child and entered into deep thought, turning dark of aspect. He ordered all to make ready to depart immediately, and so we did, leaving in haste to his sudden mood. It took as long to come down from the mountain as it took to go up it, and a week more as well owing to an avalanche that blocked our way. But when we reached the village of Elrasil we did not tarry, even though it was evening and the night was cold, but at the insistence of Parthais we parted from Elrasil and his kinsmen and traveled onward and back to Vanara and unto his court. All during these travels, Parthais kept his own counsel and spoke little, seeming vexed and short of temper. When we returned once more to the court of Vanara, and to the White Palace, all worried over their King's mood, none more than his son Thurdun and his daughter Serith Ellyn who feared for their father's condition. Yet, he shut himself away from all company for many days and weeks, even unto winter, desiring to see no one, not even his own family. And often, so the servants told his children, mutterings could be heard from within his chambers, as if some other was within there with Parthais, and together they spoke and sometimes argued. Then, one day, he emerged with a fearsome aspect, pale and wild-eyed. He ordered his builders to come to him, and he summoned, too, his fell generals and his chief counselors.

"This I command," he told them. "Get ye to the far mountains and unto the place called Griferis and into the lands thereabout that peak. Make ye there an impossible way for anyone to ascend. Lay the paths with terrible pits, and at every turn place snares of great cunning. Destroy roadways ye may find, and cause the canyons that may be crossed to be filled with subtle traps. Destroy also the village of Elrasil and all those who dwell there. Bring the hunter's head unto me that I might see that he lives no more. Leave none of his kin or kith alive who may tell of Griferis or show the way unto the summit."

Thurdun and his sister Serith Ellyn who attended their father heard these orders and were filled with dismay and fear.

"Sire?" Thurdun asked. "Thy commands trouble my heart! What madness overtakes thee that thou wouldst slay the innocent? What fear hast thee of the mountain and the mysterious gate that thou should make of the land a deathtrap for the unwary and blameless?"

"Not for the blameless, nay!" cried out Parthais. "But it is come to my understanding that Griferis is an evil place, vying to usurp my throne and to cast down my house and make waste of our realm. Madness it would be for me not to act. What wouldst ye have me do, son and daughter? Not forever will the desert children rest, and in days that may come again we may needs to war with them. And I must then take up the sword in battle as is my place. Yet if some rebel passes Griferis, and comes to hold the power of that place, what would he not do to take the throne from me whilst we are away to defend the lands? Would ye have me be idle? Would ye have me do nothing that is within my sight to do? At least if I fall in battle, the throne would be preserved. Which between ye should then sit here?"

"It would be my sister," said Thurdun. "For I do not have the wisdom to rule, nor the place, being the younger."

"Oh, my brother, speak not of such! What state would our people be in should I rule them? Where should wisdom be then? But Father, why be not fair and content with destroying only the gate of Griferis? And why should not builders and soldiers be cunning with their deceptions and pits, so that none may dare intrude there, and be it at that alone, with warning to all not to trespass there? Why then, with that burden of cruelty, also take upon thy head the blood of Elrasil and his people? What have they done to deserve this of their King, except to show him safety and good fare and be as guides to their Sovereign, even to their suffering?"

"I do what I must do, for any else would be folly!"

"What is the greater folly?" cried Thurdun. "To poison thy children with thine obsession? To preserve a house with a dishonored name?"

"Speak not, nor any more!" Parthais bellowed back, laying his hand upon his sword and stepping toward Thurdun as if to draw it.

"Get thee away, and be never again in my presence to gainsay me so! Go! Let not thy shadow fall again upon my doorstep!"

"Oh, Father!" cried Serith. "He is thine own son!"

"No more! And speak with a mind to care, daughter, if thou wish to remain so!"

Sobbing, Serith left Parthais and went to Thurdun her brother.

"Oh how I wish Mother were still among the living!" she said. "She would dissuade his madness and cool his temper!"

"I am thankful, sister, that she cannot see the fearsome aspect of his countenance, nor hear the terrible voice of his words. Nay, it is better that she has died upon the sword of our enemies to the south than to have this shame upon her. But do not fret. I will tell thee what we must do."

Then Thurdun told his sister that they should go together to Griferis, before the builders and soldiers of Parthais could arrive. "Elrasil and his people we shall warn," he told her, "and give them the means to flee to far parts, northward and east, to escape this threat. I shall defend their retreat. I, with any who may follow me. But thou, my sister, must climb Griferis and truly delve the secret of that place. Mayhaps our father is not long to rule, for I am sure that such madness cannot be quelled by these acts, but must forever pace back and forth in his heart, seeing new threats in every shadow of thought. At last, it shall lead him and our land to ruin. Make thyself ready. Yes, listen, yes! This thou must do! Go and be tried by Griferis for worthiness to be Queen of our people."

After some weeks, Parthais stirred and asked where his daughter was. It was then that he was told that she had departed with Thurdun. Enraged, Parthais then sent out his warriors to find them, knowing that his children would defy his will.

By this time, the others Parthais had already sent had climbed the summit and found the gate thereupon. Taking their tools, they tried to destroy the gate. With their hammers and their chains they tried to crack the rock and pull it down, but it would not be moved or even scratched. So instead, as they descended, they made mischief with the paths and ways, and they worked and reworked the mountains and the passes. With chisel and pick, they made smooth ways rough and perilous, and they made easy ways to lead into dead-end walls looming high, or into sudden lance-bottomed pits. Delicate traps they laid all along the ways, even unto the precipice, sprung by the smallest movement to rain avalanche and to flood rocks upon any who might intrude, or to make the paths collapse into deep crevasses.

When at last they finished their work, they returned to Vanara and reported their work saying, "O, King! We have done as commanded and made a terrible place for any who may tread there. So dreadful and cunning are the obstacles we made, and so deadly are they, that even we who made them dare not disturb again those paths for fear of being crushed, or cut through by sharp spears, or dashed down into the deepest defiles."

"And what of Elrasil and his village?" Parthais asked of them. "Where is the sign I bid thee bring me?"

"King, we builders know not what became of them, for their place was abandoned and not even a mouse stirred there or anywhere in the hills and dales surrounding. The general that was sent and all his men even now seek them out, having vowed never to return to Vanara without completing thy command."

"And was there no sign of my children?"

"No, sire. None that we could read or discern."

Having news from messengers that Elrasil had escaped and all his village, too, Parthais grew in his rage, certain that it was the doings of his children, thwarting his will not only as their father, but doubly as their King. But he was also greatly disturbed by this news, and he went from his court and unto his high chambers and brooded there for many weeks while his kingdom fell into gloom and dread.

There was in those days a conjurer by the name of Tythos who practiced dark arts in the woods nearby to the southern mountains of Vanara. Tythos was one of the First Ones, as Parthais himself, and, it was said that he had even been a minion of Morgasir but had escaped Morgasir's doom when Beras destroyed his thralldoms. And, it was said, Tythos had since allied himself with Secundur, to be his servant. It was Tythos that King Parthais now called to his chambers.

"Summon thy master," Parthais ordered him. "For I wish to bestow a gift upon him."

Then Tythos went to the candle burning at the window of the chamber and with his hand he snuffed out the flame, saying, "As ye will it, my lord."

"I am here," said Secundur, wafting outward from the deep shadows of the chamber to stand, vague of shape, before Parthais. "I am here, as I have ever been. What have ye to say to me?"

"Take thee the lands of the north and west unto the place called Griferis," said Parthais. "Make therein thine own lands and spread there thine arts dark and foul, so that none living may pass through. Keep unto thyself any who venture there, and make it a place to be thine own."

Secundur laughed softly in Parthais's ear with grave-breath, cold and final, saying, "What would I have to do with that place? I, who may roam the earth wherever there be shadow or darkness? What more value to me would be the place ye speak of than any other?"

"None, save to defy Beras, whose gate is upon the high mountain there. And this gate was set forth to make his kings and his queens upon the earth and among the newcomers, Men, who now populate our eastern lands. Is spite's sake not enough for thee? I also give thee this: Go there and make a place of thine own desire, and I will send unto thee slaves from the desert, prisoners of my conquests. And I will provide to thee captives from amongst the Men to serve thee. Foul beast and lowly form thou canst fashion of them without reprisal, and, once upon every tenth winter of my rule, I shall send unto thee a prince and a princess of the high houses of my lands, fair and strong, to please and serve thee. Whilst ever I am upon the throne of Vanara, this pact I shall keep, so that none may be sent against thee, nor tread of my permission upon those lands."

To this Secundur agreed, and thus made a black pact with Parthais. And Secundur went immediately to those lands and set about his purpose. And there he yet abides, it is said, west and north of the lands of Vanara and west and south of the lands of Duinnor, in the unknown and forbidden places near the end of the earth.

But, unbeknownst to Parthais or any other in his court, Serith Ellyn did not go with Thurdun unto Elrasil's village, nor did she see or speak with any but her brother while they traveled. For when they left Vanara and fled to warn Elrasil, Serith Ellyn parted company before they came upon the village. With kiss and embrace, Thurdun bade farewell to his sister, and she to him, trusting in Beras to make their separate ways, Thurdun to rouse the people of Elrasil to flight, as Serith Ellyn climbed the heights to Griferis, to enter into the place of mystery.

Many, many years passed, and the rule of Parthais became ever more wicked and cruel. At the same time, his country was weakened by his severity and his mistrust of all around him. Oft it was that even those of high rank who met the displeasure of Parthais were never seen again. Thus high princes and princesses were taken away and given over to Secundur. Likewise, many prisoners, Men and Dragonkind and even Elifaen, were taken secretly away to that place.

And in the lands surrounding Griferis, a cruel and black kingdom arose, ruled by foul creatures, witches and goblins, and patrolled by vile warriors who lined the borders of those lands with the impaled bodies of their victims. That land came to be called Shatuum, and the little kingdom of Duinnor, which lost many of its settlements to the place, sent an army against it, but few returned to tell of the horrors they encountered. In spite of Duinnor's entreaties, Parthais refused to join in the attack, heedless of the growing power that threatened from there. Pressed by the Dragonkind from the south and cut off from the northwest by Shatuum, Vanara suffered defeat after defeat, and many of the Firstborn who still lived were killed in useless battle. At last, when three hundred and thirty-one summers of the world had passed since Parthais ascended the throne of Cupeldain his father, and when Vanara teetered on the edge of collapse and complete ruin, a stranger appeared in his court. She was tall and beautiful and garbed in the dress of a powerful queen. When she was ushered before Parthais, and did not bow before him, his counselors were filled with fear and dismay, and the King was sorely offended.

"Why dost thou not bow before the sovereign?" one of the courtiers demanded.

"I bow before no sovereign but Aperion, true King of all Faere, whom Beras himself appointed, until the day that the King of Kings may come, whom also shall be appointed by Beras to rule over the earth as Aperion now does in the heavens."

Her words filled all who heard them with fear, all but Parthais, and he rose from his throne in a rage and took from his sword bearer his iron lance, and made to run it through the stranger. But she smote it away with a rod of wood which shattered the steel blade utterly and sent a bolt of bright lightning up his arm and into his heart. Parthais then fell to his knees, mortally wounded but not yielding. He took from his belt his dagger, but as he raised it against her, she struck him again about the wrist so that the wooden rod transformed, likened unto a serpent, and it twisted about his wrist and held it fast. Then were the eyes of Parthais opened, and he saw that it was his own daughter, Serith Ellyn, who had returned and who smote him.

"Daughter!" he groaned, struggling to free his hand from the wooden rod about his wrist that Serith Ellyn held.

"Call me not daughter," she cried. "Call me Retribution! My house thou hast made into a shameful place. My legacy thou hast poisoned by thy lust. My people thou hast misused, cheated, and murdered. Thou hast squandered their goodwill. Thou hast turned their goodly hearts dark with thy deeds of avarice, and thou hast weakened the realm by thine injustice and by foul deceits. It was their woe that called me forth, they who yearn for relief, who have cried out for deliverance from thy cruelty. And it was they who, in union with the Newcomers of the east and with the Kingdom of Duinnor, and that of Glareth, have banded together to oppose thee. This night, thy kingdom is overthrown, the throne of Vanara I claim for its people and in the name of Beras!"

Serith Ellyn then released Parthais from her grip, and with her sword she struck his head from his body. At that moment, the windows of the Palace blew outward, and every shadow fled the place, and all the candles and lamp-flames leapt upward and burned once again with clear bright light which filled the halls and every room and every tower. Those with her, fell warriors of Thurdun and many of the race of Men, and many, too, of the people of Elrasil, laid hands on the supporters of Parthais and slew them. Then Serith Ellyn ordered the body of Parthais her father and the bodies of his chief generals and counselors to be burned. Their bones and ashes she made to be cast with mortar into hard stone, and these stones were laid on the walks of the White Palace so that all who came and went would trod upon them. She met with all the people and begged their consent to continue the rule of Fairlinden over Vanara, and they rejoiced at her return and gladly confirmed her as Queen. Without delay, she set about to right the many wrongs of Parthais, to make compensation to those he made to suffer, and to punish those who Parthais made lords of terror and earls of fraud. Yet so deep was the hurt and evil that Parthais fell into, that even she, with all her power and grace, could not repair the deep wounds that he made in the world, nor could she confront Shatuum, the ultimate expression of her father's folly.

And that was how Griferis was found and then lost to the world, and how the place named Shatuum came to be a land of shadow. And all the powers of Serith Ellyn could not lift from that place the darkness and terror that had settled upon it. To this day, it is a forbidden land from which no wanderer has ever emerged. And from that place come loathsome beings, demons and witches, worms and warlocks, corrupted creatures that once were wolves or lions, and many others, some on four legs and some on two. Some of these once wore the aspect of living things but now are no longer living, yet neither are they dead. And it is said that Secundur abides patiently there, growing his dark thralldom, and sending his spies and provocateurs out from Shatuum into the bright world to test it, to measure it, or to prepare his sullen design.

This, then, concludes the last book of Nimwill, Scribe to King Parthais, a witness to these things, faithfully recording all that was, as it was.

• • •

Ean closed the book and looked at Robby, who was lost in thought. After a moment, Ean stirred.

"Is there more that you desire for me to read? Or shall I read this to you once again?"

"Oh. No. No, thank you," Robby said. "I don't believe I shall require your services any longer."

"Then I will go to my other duties." Ean stood and bowed. "I hope you enjoy our collection and will not hesitate if any of us can be of service to you."

"Thank you very much," Robby said, rising and offering his hand. Ean smiled and took it.

"Have a good day, my lord."

"Good day to you, too," Robby said quietly. He sat back down, and as he fingered through the book, he thought carefully about what he had just learned. It was clear why Ashlord wanted him to know this tale. And now he understood better than before where it was he had to go. Northward, it seemed, into the frigid mountains and onward into Shatuum. He sensed a movement and turned to see Sonya gesturing toward him as she spoke to Coreth. They smiled and chatted like old friends might do, then they parted, and Coreth approached Robby.

"Did you find what you needed?"

"Yes, and it was read to me. This is it."

"Ah, Nimwill. I have read this."

She looked at Robby, obviously bursting to ask questions, but she was too tactful and too mindful of her duty to ever do so without his leave. He understood, but was himself reluctant, still, to share too much. She could make whatever assumptions she wanted to, he thought, and he may as well ask his own questions.

"Would you sit for a moment?" Robby stood and gestured to a chair. "I would like to ask a favor of you."

"Certainly." Coreth slowly sat, her curiosity about him growing stronger.

"I do not wish to answer too many questions about why I am here," Robby said. "Nor why I am ignorant of so many things that seem common knowledge to others. But I wonder if you could tell me whatever you can about something?"

"If I can, I shall."

"Shatuum."

Coreth glanced at the door, then back at Robby.

"What do you want to know about that place?"

"It is still the land of Secundur, is it not?"

"Yes."

"Do you know what manner of land it is?"

"Somewhat."

She stiffened, and Robby saw that she was uncomfortable with his questions.

"You told me earlier that your aunt was there for a long time," Robby plowed on. "And that her brother Navis was lost there in an attempt to rescue her."

Coreth nodded.

"I just thought you might know something more of the place."

"I will not ask why you want to know," she told him, "but it is an unpleasant topic. And I am sworn to secrecy about certain aspects of the place."

"I see," Robby nodded. "Then I will tell you why I want to know, after all. I must go there. I do not wish to. But it is my duty to do so. I would like to avoid Secundur and his lot, if that is possible."

Coreth glanced at the book on the table, then at Robby, then at the

Queen's flash on his shoulder.

"You mean to find Griferis, don't you?" After a brief look of astonishment, she instantly regained her composure, eyeing him with a searching look.

Robby nodded and smiled.

"You just said you were not going to ask why. But, yes, that is what I mean to do."

"I am sorry." She shook her head in disbelief. "I cannot help you. There is nothing that I can tell you that will prevent your death if you go there."

"I'm sure there is much here, in this room and elsewhere, that is recorded about Shatuum," Robby went on, ignoring her morbid statement. "If you only told me those things that I might read for myself, if I had time. I do not ask you to break any vow, nor would I have you betray any confidence."

She thought about this proposal for many moments, studying Robby carefully. His firm gaze did not falter. Seeing that he was serious and determined, her expression changed from disbelief to pity and then, slowly, to understanding as it dawned upon her why he sought Griferis.

"You are so young."

"I'm getting tired of people saying that. Yes. I am young. But even the young sometimes have things pressed upon them. Things not of their choosing but things they must nevertheless do."

"Yes. Well. So be it. I shall tell you what is open knowledge about the place, if not commonly known. Such that I can, anyway. How shall I begin?"

"Begin with Elrasil the Hunter. Did he or any of his people go back to their homes when Parthais was dead?"

"Yes, I believe so. But I'm not sure what happened to them. Their lands were on the eastern borders of Shatuum, in the foothills. That place is now known as Mosslorn and has become a place of mist and fog and dark woods. No one goes there willingly. Nor do any natural creatures live there anymore."

"As far as is told in these writings or in tales, has anyone seen the interior of Shatuum since the days of Parthais? Besides your aunt and uncle, that is?"

"None that I may speak of."

"Has any one been there lately?"

"None that I may speak of. I beg you not to press me on this."

"I see. Then I will ask other questions, if you will bear with me."

"Very well."

"Shatuum is sometimes called the Land of Shadow. Is it because Secundur takes that form?"

"Perhaps. But it is so often covered with cloud that there is little difference between night and day, like the land of Mosslorn, only darker."

"In my country, tales are told of terrible beings who come from there.

Goblins and trolls, witches, wraiths, and sorcerers. And galafronks."

"Galafronks? I have never heard of those creatures."

"It is a kind of demon, I think, perhaps just made up to frighten children."

"Hm. There are accounts given by travelers who say they have seen strange creatures in those parts. Wolf-like creatures that ride black horses. And there is a rather famous legend about a group of Dragonkind who sought to go around Vanara and attack from the Shatuum side. The legend says they were eaten by witches."

"Oh."

"But it may only be a tale made up to frighten children, as you said of the other creature."

"I see. What more are you allowed to tell?"

"There is much I wish I could tell you. But only Seafar may do so. Perhaps you should ask him."

"Perhaps I shall."

"There are maps here," she offered, gesturing around the room. "They are old and out of date. But the mountains and rivers have not moved all that much, I imagine, since they were made. Would you like to see them?"

"Certainly!"

He followed her to the other side of the room where there were large shelves full of rolled up charts and maps. She looked through a few and then pulled down one and spread it out on a nearby table, weighing down its corners with small felted stones that were there for that purpose. Up and down the left side of the map was depicted a long mountain range, and there was marked the border between Vanara and Duinnor, running roughly east and west along a river. This border split and went around an area taking up about one-third of the left side of the map. The characters that indicated Shatuum were strangely made and had the very look of foreboding. While most of the map had fair details of rivers and streams, forests and settlements, the area of Shatuum was sparsely drawn, showing only a few peaks and some canyons.

"What is this, along the side of the map here?" Robby ran his finger along a line near the border of the map, to the west of all the lands. It ran nearly straight along, cutting through mountains from north to south.

"That is the Great Chasm," Coreth said. "It is too deep and too wide to be crossed. No one knows what lies on the other side of it."

"But it is so straight."

"Yes, it is a mystery. It is the edge of the world. Some early accounts of it say that it runs with flowing ice and constantly rumbles with the noise of a powerful cataract. No one living that I have ever known or heard of has seen it, and the old accounts are few and strange."

"So it borders Vanara, Shatuum, and Duinnor on the western extremes."

"Yes, and continues southward to also border the Dragon Lands. I have heard that, in their tales, the salt sea on the far end of the earth is churned by a great outrush of water from the Chasm. The currents created by the flow are violent and powerful, and it fills the sea with rocky places, so that the Dragonkind have never been able to venture very far from their coast in boats."

"Hm. Well, there isn't very much here that helps me as far as Shatuum goes. Where is Mosslorn, the land of Elrasil?"

"It is not shown but is here," Coreth swirled her finger around a portion of the map, "surrounding the area where the borders of Duinnor and Vanara come into Shatuum."

"Are there other maps? Ones that show any routes? The mountains that are shown seem very rough."

"Those mountains are treacherous, especially in late winter and early spring. There are many avalanches of rock and snow," she said while searching for another map. "Steep and lifeless expanses of ice. In the spring, floods of meltwater crash through gorges. I imagine it is the same within Shatuum. Ah, here is another."

But it was not much better than the first. There was more detail shown within the area of Shatuum, but only more mountains and gorges. There were no routes marked and nothing that gave Robby any clue about the best way to get there.

"I am surprised," he said, "that there aren't at least a few outposts on the border. Places to keep an eye on Shatuum. Seems rather trusting to me."

Coreth frowned, uncomfortable at the mild accusation.

"My people are watchful," she said simply.

Robby looked at her and smiled.

"Then there are outposts," he said. "And that is what you cannot tell me about."

"Perhaps Lord Seafar may tell you more than I," she replied. "But I cannot say yes or no to you."

"Your oath."

"Yes."

"You speak of me?"

Turning, the two saw Seafar approaching.

"Lord Seafar," Coreth said. "I was just suggesting that Mr. Ribbon put his questions to you for better answers than I may give."

"Ah. Oh? About," Seafar looked at the map, "Shatuum?"

"Yes, sir," Robby said.

"I see. You must forgive Coreth. If she has been hesitant to answer you, she is only being faithful to her duty."

"Yes, I understand that. It is just that I need help understanding what is ahead of me."

"Yes, you do. And I release you, Coreth, from any restrictions on your speech. You may tell him anything that you and I might discuss."

"Yes, Lord. Thank you."

"But I myself will strive to answer some of your questions, Robby," Seafar gestured for them to come with him. "And I will provide you with better maps and other information, too. If you will come along, we'll get started. Coreth, I have sent for Commander Tallin, and I'd like for you to go to the lifts and escort him to me, if you will. I hope he will arrive within the next hour or two. It is important that he come with you alone. No one else, save your brother, if he accompanies Tallin. But I think Faslor will remain below. Given the general situation, I believe he will be fairly busy."

Chapter 23

The Scribblers

"Just a point or two, Commander Tallin, to be sure I have this right. You first parted company with Collandoth in the Thunder Mountains."

"Yes, sir."

"And, somehow, he caught up with you at Edgewold, the day after the battle took place there."

"Yes, sir."

"And his business, in the Thunder Mountains. You have reported that he was going to track down the lair of a witch? With the intention of destroying it?"

Ullin, surely as accustomed to reports and briefings as any military man could be, was by now impatient with the way the meeting had meandered along. He had written his report, given it to the commanding Kingsman, General Portius, then delivered it verbally to his lieutenants. For the past hour, Ullin had been giving a verbal report to another group, made up of four lesser generals, three Duinnor envoys, four Vanaran commanders of high rank, and one or two other men in fine attire and of high authority, it seemed, but who said very little. If only the others had been as taciturn. But it was difficult enough to get through his entire report, having to stop and answer questions as he went. Now, just when he thought all was understood, General Capstor of the Duinnor Sixteenth Regulars, seemed to want to start all over.

"The lair of the so-called mountain witch that Collandoth had killed the night before."

Ullin took some little heart in the fact that others were displaying courteous impatience, too, sitting back in their chairs and sighing.

"Yes, General, that is correct."

"And then, later on, after you encountered the Dragonkind out on the plain, you fought against some sort of vine-monster?"

"Sir, I am sure you will receive dispatches from Teracue about all that."

"Well! Let us hope so!"

"General Capstor, what is the point of questioning Commander Tallin over and over? He has told us all that he can, surely." General Portius spoke with practiced control. He was as impatient as any at the table, but he well understood the value of due respect to fellow officers.

"Well! Witches! Monsters! Cultish rebellions. Bands of wandering Dragonkind! I mean, I beg your pardon, but all this is a bit preposterous, don't you think? Until some proof arrives that any of these events happened, that witches and monsters exist, I hardly see how the rest of the Commander's tale can be credible."

"General Capstor!"

"Frankly," Capstor went on, oblivious to the scowl that shot across the table from Portius, "I must wonder why anyone would spin such a yarn!"

"Sir!" Ullin challenged the accusation, standing suddenly from his seat at the end of the table. Portius gestured to Ullin and halted the Kingsman from calling out Capstor then and there.

"I will not have an officer of the King insulted in my presence!" Portius fumed at Capstor.

Faslor, who had been leaning casually against the back wall for the entire meeting, his arms crossed and a look of complete disinterest on his face, now stirred.

"I am surprised," he said as he unbuttoned his tunic, "at the General's lack of experience. But surely even he knows that the bodies of my people heal all scars of battle, eventually. That is, those wounds that are not mortal."

Faslor approached the table and pulled aside his blouse and showed a long red line that ran around his side and up across his chest.

"It was a mountain witch called Mariglia who put that mark on me," he stated. "You do not know the name? You should. It was a young Kingsman who saved my life that day by cleaving her head from her body with a blade made of witchbane just when she was about to give me her stroke of death. Yes, and such was the pain that shot through him when he did so that he lost the use of his arm for the rest of his life. Does that begin to ring a bell? It should, for it was your own great grandfather."

Capstor went pale, then turned red-faced, so flabbergasted he was. It was apparent that others at the table knew the tale better than he. Properly chastised, he leaned back in his chair and said no more.

"All of this is beside the point," said a wiry man dressed in black sitting near Ullin. "The Dragonkind are our chief concern, and the Commander's report of their presence out on the open plain is cause for worry."

"Agreed, Count Dialmor," Portius nodded. "We must decide the disposition of our garrisons, and coordinate ourselves with the Vanaran Fellfaere. Meanwhile, we should send our own patrols out to Teracue to receive further word from him, and send warning to Duinnor and to the southern realms. I shall also order patrols into the desert lands. If the Dragon King is massing his armies, we must know where and when they plan to strike. Meanwhile, all leave is canceled, and all units are recalled to be put at battle readiness. We have questioned Commander Tallin enough. I am sure he is weary from all this and from his arduous journey. We have his written report, and I give him my gratitude for it and all that he has recounted. I have sent a copy of the report to Lord Seafar, and doubtless there will be a Council of War convened very soon."

Rising, Portius turned to Ullin. "Commander, I will not countermand your present orders. No doubt Lord Seafar will want to see you in person, so make yourself available to him. Meanwhile, or when you can, get some rest. I will have additional orders for you within the next day or so. You are dismissed for the time being."

"Yes, sir. Thank you, sir."

Ullin saluted, bowed slightly to the others, and walked out, with Faslor following just behind him into the hallway.

When Portius had seated himself again, the wiry man turned to him.

"I trust Commander Tallin and his companion will be remaining in Vanara, should we need to consult with him again."

"My understanding is that they will be here for at least a few days. One of my aides told me earlier that Mr. Ribbon, Commander Tallin's charge, will be staying at the Palace. I imagine Tallin will join him there to make his report to Seafar."

"Hm. They are honored to be given such accommodations."

"Apparently, the boy is considered a person of some importance in the East." Portius did not mention the summons pertaining to him, assuming that the man he spoke with already knew. And probably knew before he himself did. "Now. To business."

• • •

When the door was closed, Faslor made a little whistle. "Never have I seen such a grilling! You must be exhausted. If you were not already, that is."

"How did I do in there?"

An aide hurried up to them and handed Faslor a note.

"Splendidly! You filled the room with fear!"

"Well, that was not my aim."

"Wasn't it? Anyway, Portius was right," Faslor waved the note. "Seafar wants to see you immediately."

"Oh, good grief! Do you suppose I could at least clean up a bit somewhere? And maybe find a nibble before I go up there?"

"Right this way." Faslor grinned, leading Ullin down the corridor. "You won't find better soap or finer nibbles anywhere than in my chambers over in the next wing. Why, I practically live here these days!"

• • •

Count Dialmor emerged from the meeting room. He watched Ullin and Faslor disappear around a far corner before turning to walk the other way. Several downward flights of stairs later, and through a labyrinth of narrow passages in the basement of the building, he reached his own modest but official chambers. When he entered, his aide stood behind his desk.

"Has Captain Faradan arrived?" Dialmor asked as he hurried through the anteroom to his own chamber.

"He awaits within, sir."

"Good. Cancel all appointments and be at the ready."

Dialmor strode on through the next door and closed it. The soldier in question was slouched on a divan, reading some dispatches and eating an apple. Seeing the Count, he stood and wiped his mouth casually. He was a tall swarthy man, in his early forties, and must have once been handsome, but too much fighting and drinking had taken its toll, and his blue eyes were now constantly bloodshot. Though he was shaven—Dialmor insisted on some semblance of discipline—it was a coarse stubble, dotted with gray, over a face hardened by the desert. And yet it was a cold visage, barren of expression. Dialmor did not need to hide his distaste for Faradan, for the soldier hardly cared what anybody thought of him. And that, in part, was what made Faradan valuable to Dialmor. That, and the fact that he was the cruelest, most efficient man he had ever known when it came to certain skills, skills that included the infliction of pain or death on others. And, though not a Kingsman, he was fanatically loyal to Duinnor and its King. These qualities, combined, made Faradan priceless to Dialmor. Indeed, everything depended upon just such men like Faradan, and those of Faradan's elite company.

"Prepare your men," Dialmor said brusquely, going around to sit at his desk. "Operation Noose will be carried out tomorrow night."

"Noose? Tomorrow? Are you serious?"

Dialmor looked up, scowling at Faradan who was wryly smiling back at him.

"Well, then," Faradan said. "So be it."

"It is to be carried out as planned, but the target has changed. Can you be ready?"

"Certainly. But a new target? In the White Palace?"

"Deploy your men, and put everything in place, then come back here. I'll brief you before you join them."

"If the target has changed, I'd like to know now."

"Be on your way. You will find out as soon as you need to know, and no sooner."

"Very well. I'll be back in about three hours."

Dialmor watched Faradan leave and sat thoughtfully for several moments before getting up and going to the anteroom.

"Send one of the pages for food and drink," he told the aide. "And send word to the stables to have all three of my horses saddled and provisioned. I leave for Duinnor tonight on urgent business. Let our rooms here remain closed tomorrow, and do what you will until my return. Take this purse. It should hold you."

"When shall I expect you back?"

"Not for two months, at least. Perhaps longer."

Dialmor was uncomfortable with lying, and felt himself a poor practitioner. It was better to find some truth to tell, if at all possible, rather than making up something. But sometimes there was no way around a bold-face lie. Because he mistrusted his skill at the art of lying, he had formed a habit of steadily eyeing those he spoke to, feeling that it was in shiftiness that words were suspect. And since he had a reputation for frankness, he hoped his little insignificant lies would be accepted, like the one he had just told. He could not help but smile as he returned to his chamber. By the time he was missed, no one in Vanara would care one way or the other. His absence would be a trivial thing, smothered over by the avalanche of events to come. He sat at his desk and began preparing documents, all forgeries, to show that he was urgently needed in Duinnor. They would be found when his chambers were inevitably searched. In a few hours, after he told the surprised Faradan the new target of their scheme, and after the soldier dutifully went to carry out the orders of his well-paying King, Dialmor would indeed ride away, trailing two spare mounts behind him for speed. But he would go south, not north. And the King of Duinnor, when he learned the news, would be as baffled as any. He meticulously dipped his pen and copied the style and manner of writing used by his superior, Lord Banis. As he did so, Dialmor could not help another smile, this time at the gullible Faradan. And everyone else, for that matter.

● ● ●

"I have two things, at least, that I would like to show you," Seafar said to Robby. "And this is the first and most secret of all. In fact, it is the most secret thing in all of Vanara, and many have lost their lives to safeguard it, though it may seem a mundane thing to you. Understand that I show you this only because I firmly believe my Queen would have me do so. Otherwise, I would not dare."

The guards responded to Seafar's nod and opened the door. The two entered a small room, more like a closet, with a single opposite door. Seafar waited for the guards to close the first door, then took out a key and unlocked the second one and bade Robby enter the next room. It was a large chamber, filled with shelves of scrolls and bound volumes, much like those in the library, but more densely filled and with no tables or chairs available for the use of them. Seafar led the way through the stacks to a small door on the far side, then took another key from his pocket and unlocked it.

"Remember. What I am about to reveal to you must remain a secret."

Robby nodded, and Seafar pushed the door open. They entered and Seafar locked the door behind them as Robby took in the room. There were many tables and desks in the large space. At nearly every table sat at least two people, each busily writing away. Other people moved about, placing stacks of paper on desks beside the writers, carrying away other stacks, or refilling inkwells and cups of silver quills. On the walls hung maps and charts, some quite old by the looks of them, and others so fresh that people were still making marks on them. Bright lamps hung from the ceiling, adding their light to that which streamed in from the many high windows. Here and there were small, iron stoves, keeping the room warm.

"The Dragon King may have his spies, and Duinnor its agents, but we, too, have ours, going about the business of gathering information and news," Seafar explained. "Most of them are in distant places, but a few, some of our very best agents, in fact, sit here day after day, reporting news of distant realms, without ever leaving this room. Each table is devoted to some realm, or some task. Over there is our Altoria Bureau. This is the Duinnor Bureau, and here is the Home Bureau, concerning itself with Vanara."

As Seafar spoke, they walked slowly through the room. Several times, those writing or shuffling papers stood and stiffened to attention.

"Carry on. Carry on," Seafar would say, or "Don't mind us," or "How are you this day?"

At the other side of the room Seafar halted as two young girls rose from behind their desk and bowed.

"Good day, ladies," Seafar addressed them kindly. To Robby, he explained, "These are two of our newest Scribblers, as we call this special group. These two concern themselves with various matters of weather, domestic events, and a few other topics." Turning again to the girls, who wore gray uniforms akin to Coreth's, Seafar said, "Tell me, will it snow tomorrow?"

"No, Lord Seafar," replied one of the pair, "it will not snow again in Vanara until the day after, when it will come thick and windy, but brief."

"And what is the weather like in the Eastlands?"

"Snow mixed with rain was falling this morning over most of the eastern realms, from Glareth to northern Tracia."

"Might you inquire for me as to the weather in the town of Janhaven?"

"Certainly, my lord."

The two girls immediately sat, each pulling some paper in front of them and dipping their pens to write. They often looked at each other's written words, and in but a few moments each had written several lines. They paused and looked over what they had written, consulting quietly with each other, as Seafar smiled benevolently at Robby. The girls nodded to each other and stood from their seats.

"Sir, it is overcast and cold," said one.

"And a light sleet will fall tonight," said the other, handing Seafar the two sheets.

"Thank you. Please resume your work." Seafar motioned for Robby to follow to the corner of the room where there was a plain table with writing supplies at the ready and several empty chairs around it.

"I keep a table here for my own use," Seafar said as he pulled a chair out for Robby and then sat very close by as he spread the girls' writings on the table. "Let us look at this together."

Robby looked at the papers and saw line after line of script.

"You cannot read our script?"

"Not very quickly," Robby replied. "I am not yet accustomed to it, I'm afraid."

"Well, let me tell you what it says here," Seafar pointed to one line. "See these dots going down the page? Beside each dot was written a sentence, it is now invisible to the eye. But see below that the last sentence remains and can be clearly read?"

"Yes."

"This," Seafar pulled over the second sheet, "is a copy of what the first Scribbler wrote, line by line. It reads, 'It is sunny in Janhaven.' But on the other first sheet, that sentence is gone."

"I see. It is written with the same kind of ink used at the entrance of the Hall of Ministers."

"Just so. It is called True Ink."

"And all the other lines of writing, the ones that are gone. They are false statements about the weather?"

"Precisely. Rain, snow, heat. And so forth until a line remains intact and complete. Overcast."

Robby looked across the busy room of Scribblers, all diligently working away, his mind racing at the implications of their work and the scope of their power.

"I think you begin to understand what we do here," observed Seafar.

"It is a way of spying," Robby nodded slowly. "May you learn anything? About anywhere or anybody?"

"Not exactly. We are still new at this. True Ink is very precious and difficult to make. A year of fermenting and several barrels of carefully prepared rare mixtures only yield a thimble of ink. For centuries, alchemists all over the world have struggled to concoct a better way of making it. Last year, our alchemists finally discovered the secret of doing so in large quantities, and now we produce by this new method several gallons each month. But what we produce is of a lesser quality than the traditionally prepared True Ink. It loses its potency within a few days of production, and it fades away within hours of being used. That is why we use copyists, to record in regular ink what is written with the True Ink. Also, our new concoction's ability to see and reveal facts of the world is limited to only seven days past and three days into the future. So there are problems with the use of it, as you can imagine."

Robby looked around again, this time noticing other uniformed men and women going from desk to desk, apparently checking the work of the Scribblers.

"You understand why this operation is one of the most carefully guarded secrets of Vanara," Seafar went on. "And we are very careful how we use the information we glean. There are fewer than a dozen people outside of this room who know about this, including Thurdun and our Queen. If even our allies learned of this, it could spell disaster. And not just for Vanara."

"But surely all who come to the Hall of Ministers and sign to enter must know of True Ink. Do you not supply it to them?"

"No. They use the old traditional kind of True Ink. As far as they know, it is the only kind available, and they have the rights to all supplies of it. But it is expensive and tedious to make, as I mentioned. One inkwell of their stuff costs more than a hundred times its weight in gold, and any containers that were previously used to mix or store True Ink cannot be reused for a new batch or the new ink will be ruined. All True Ink is very finicky stuff. And it does not travel well, except in specially-prepared vials of pure amber, so it cannot be easily transported. Also, several key ingredients are made from wild plants that grow only here in Vanara. The plants cannot be cultivated and must be harvested in the wild at the proper moment. Occasionally, some ink goes missing. But not often enough nor in enough quantity to cause great alarm, certainly not enough to support an effort such as you see here. As long as we are vigilant and careful, we remain safe."

"How long have you been doing this?"

"For less than a year."

"And no one suspects?"

"As far as we can tell, no."

"Why do you show me this? You obviously know why I have come this way. Are you not afraid that, if I succeed, Duinnor will, through me, know about all this?"

"It is to help ensure your success that I show you," Seafar answered firmly. "Much is at stake. Do not misunderstand me. I serve the Queen and share her confidence. And she serves Vanara above the union of the Realms. Our allegiance to the empire is more of an alliance as far as we are concerned. We cannot prevent Duinnor's abuse of us, but we strive to blunt it. While we, here in this room and elsewhere, use our skills to keep watch on the world, we also aim to prepare for the breaking of it."

"What do you mean?"

"We are on the brink of great change. Tracia has openly rebelled. The Dragonkind prepare for a mighty assault, the likes of which the world has not seen for centuries. Duinnor's might wanes, irresolute in all things but its arrogant meddling with Vanara. Our people grow thin, as does their patience. Many other realms suffer as we do from the arrogance of Duinnor. Tracia is not without sympathizers, though what the new rulers of Tracia have done to that land and its people frightens everyone."

"I am aware of some of those things," Robby nodded, "and I intend to do what I may to change things."

"I believe you. And, should you come into a position to do so, I believe you will try. But time runs short. Things are happening that may be beyond any king or queen to remedy. New powers arise from ancient roots. Forces long in slumber rouse to take part in the world. They begin to test, probe, flex their power."

"I think I know what you speak of. Somewhat, at least. Several times on my way here, members of my company happened on mysterious creatures and uncanny beings. Some of them were, well, quite dangerous." Robby lowered his voice. "Monsters. Demons. Witches."

Seafar leaned back in his chair. "You understand, then, some of what I mean," he replied quietly so as not to be overheard. "Perhaps, later, we may speak at greater length about such things, as I have more to share with you along those lines. I want you to know something more of what you face. We face. But!" He leaned forward again. "Back to this. You have already received a great boon from the Queen and her brother," he nodded at Swyncraff, "and I trust it has served you well."

"Indeed. Swyncraff has saved my life several times over!"

"Well, here is another boon. Not so grand, perhaps, but useful."

Seafar pulled out a drawer and removed a small unadorned box, not much larger than his palm. He placed it on the desk and carefully unlatched its lid and opened it. On the inside of the shallow lid were fitted four small pens with intricately-worked silver nibs and shafts of dark carved wood. Set into the box was a small tray containing cut sheets of parchment which he lifted by its felt tabs and put aside. Below, fitted into carefully shaped recesses cushioned with cloth were four small amber vials, sealed with wax stoppers.

"These are small vials of True Ink. The traditional kind, not the stuff we use here. Each bottle holds enough for just a few lines of writing. These are yours to take with you, to use as you wish, if the need arises. You must use a fresh pen for each vial. If any dried ink comes in contact with fresh ink, the fresh ink will be rendered useless. Remember, a fresh pen each time. When a bottle is opened, it must be used within two days. After that, no matter how well it is resealed, it will dry to a powder and cannot be reconstituted. Do you understand?"

"Yes, Lord Seafar. A fresh pen each time. Two days only, after a vial has been opened."

"I need not tell you how dangerous this could be if it fell into the wrong hands."

"I understand." Robby looked around the room again. "But it troubles me that such power may be in such a small thing as ink."

Seafar nodded.

"It is a good thing that it troubles you, as it should all of us who use it. It makes secrets very difficult to conceal. And some things are perhaps better left unknown. The temptation to use it for spurious ends is powerful. Our Queen has established the harshest penalties for the slightest abuse of it, to be carried out without mercy. You, however, may do as you wish, but..."

Seafar's voice trailed off as he shrugged. Robby remembered meeting with Thurdun and Queen Serith Ellyn by the lake, and he also recalled Lyrium's offer of gifts, that he refused to accept, the ring and the sword. His fingers twined around Swyncraff as he considered this offer. Should he refuse it? He longed for news of his family back in the Eastlands, and to know how his companions were faring on the road to Duinnor. He watched Seafar carefully repack the writing kit. As the lid was closed and latched, he made up his mind.

"Perhaps you might like some privacy?"

"Pardon me?" Robby shook himself from his thoughts.

Seafar pulled over to Robby a sheet of clean paper and an amber inkwell, and held out a quill.

"If you wish to make a few inquiries. Or I could guide you?"

"Oh, well if you could just give me a few tips," said Robby as he took up the quill.

"Form your statements carefully," Seafar instructed. "Start with something that you know is not true, to test the ink."

Robby wrote. "The sun rises in the west."

"Ah, a common mistake," Seafar said as the entire sentence faded. "Write: The sun rises in the east."

Robby did so, and the entire sentence faded, too.

"I don't understand."

"To the ink, the sun neither rises nor does it set. Perhaps the ink does not know of day and night as we do. Or else the ink does not trust that Sir Sun or Lady Moon will always follow the same path. The sun is above us. If you wish to know something of the future or past, you must say so. Write: The sun rose this morning in the west."

Robby did so and the sentence faded. He went on to write, "The sun rose this morning in the east," and the ink remained unchanged. "Hm. This will take practice."

"Indeed. So it is best to practice now," Seafar tapped the box, "so you do not waste your ink later on."

Robby wrote, "My mother is alive." It did not fade, and he wrote, "My father is alive." When it did not fade, he sighed.

Seafar nodded and rose. "Please. Don't get up. Do you see that stove, just there? A fire is kept in it at all times. Put your writings into it when you are finished. I must go and attend other matters, but I will not be very long."

Robby stood up, anyway, and bowed. "Thank you very much."

"Until later, then. Oh. If you need any assistance with wording or anything else, don't hesitate to ask anyone here. That man over there, with the red epaulets, is the Duty Officer, but you may ask anyone."

"Thank you."

"Good luck."

Seafar smiled and went over to have a brief word with the Duty Officer who nodded at Robby as Seafar spoke to him. With a quick look over his shoulder, Seafar unlocked the far door and departed. The officer checked the door to be sure it was locked.

• • •

Although each night Robby still sought a way to travel freely in his dreams from place to place, he had not yet succeeded in doing so. He was certain that it was possible, that he did not need to jump from one person's dream to the next as Micerea did. But so far he had met with little progress, managing to go a little farther on each attempt before slipping back into his own dreams, like slipping back down an icy hill. Without the distant light of another dream to guide him, he had only managed to dreamwalk a few miles from his own place of slumber.

But now, with True Ink, perhaps he could find some peace of mind about a few things, and learn about those things that lay ahead.

Turning to the sheet before him, Robby pondered his questions and how to formulate them. He did not know how much time he had, and he tried to relax, thinking that Seafar would not be back for at least a few minutes. He dipped the quill and began. After a few moments, he was satisfied that, according to the ink, Sheila and the others were well and safe, they were not captured, and they were still on their way to Duinnor.

He paused thoughtfully, then began writing furiously, making mistakes in his phrasing, rewriting, sometimes saying, "Aha!" aloud, or "Hmm," as sentences did or did not fade. Through the statements, he gained information about Shatuum, Griferis, the situation in Tallinvale, the Tracians, both those in exile and those who formed the Redvest armies. And he learned much about the Dragonkind. His mind raced from questions to quick efforts to write answers to them, then to the answer itself. He wrote so fast and automatically that he knew that he was not absorbing all of the answers that he gathered. Yet he felt strangely transformed, having now the power of knowledge about so many things so quickly. His head soon ached with the exertion, and he hardly noticed wiping away the beads of sweat from his brow with his sleeve. Soon the large sheet was covered with lines of his writing, and he turned it time and time again to write in the margins and between places he had already written, too absorbed to even turn the sheet over. He muttered as he wrote, leaning closer and closer to the fast flowing ink, lost in a kind of madness, until, suddenly, he had learned what he needed. The ink did not fade.

Robby sat back, satisfied, and sensed a presence behind him. Lord Seafar made a little noise with his throat. Robby turned to see a look of astonishment on his face. Glancing at the mess before him, the paper blotched, and hardly a white space left on it, Robby's face reddened.

"I'm afraid I have used the whole sheet," he said apologetically as he put down the quill, "and a large quantity of ink."

"Hm. Yes," Seafar looked at Robby with an odd expression. "Pardon? Oh, that is of no matter. There is more where that came from. Forgive my surprise. I should not be surprised at all, in fact. But I confess that I am. No, no, it is not the quantity of writing, nor the profusion of ink, but rather the manner of it."

"What do you mean?"

Seafar gestured at the paper.

"You write in the First Tongue. A language that all understand, but few may speak, and fewer still may write."

"What? I do? Oh, my!"

Now Robby's face was full of astonishment. The paper crawled with a vine-like script, from tendril to line, each character and word beautiful. And the entire sheet, taken as a whole, made the most intricate drawing, every scratch and jot contributing to a line or shadow or texture. All lines and letters joined and were formed into a kind of lacework pattern, full of flowers and birds and trees, even a stream running through. There were, here and there, hints of faces, too, those of his friends and family, and there were lettered shapes that moved to form the outlines of far away structures, one of which seem to float in a bed of moving clouds.

"I'm afraid...," Robby nearly stuttered. "I hardly believe it myself. That is, I did not realize what I was doing."

"I should not look upon it," Seafar said, turning away. "Your business is your own, to share or not to share. But I must confess, I could not help but see the part concerning the Dragonkind, that they mass their forces well away from Vanara to the southeast of their own lands. The rest I will not read, but I'll tell you that we have obtained the same information about that as you have. And not only through our ink. Come! You must burn it, beautiful though it is. Then we should go meet Commander Tallin, who is on his way. Oh, yes. You mentioned the need to visit an apothecary?"

"Yes. A few things for the journey."

Robby made his way to the stove, and, taking a last look at the writing, he slipped the paper into the slot as he had seen others do. As the flames took it, he could have sworn he heard the sound of chirping birds and swishing water come out from the stove, and even the echo of very distant thunder.

"In that case, perhaps I'll have Coreth show you to the apothecary and I'll go wait for your cousin myself. She returned with word that Commander Tallin is delayed by his duties below, but that he will come as soon as he can. So, we'll all join up when he arrives, to discuss things and perhaps have some supper, too. I'm sure that you two could use some rest, so rooms are being prepared for you here in the Palace. We'll try to make it a short evening."

Seafar took Robby out the way they had come. After a few confusing turns along different hallways, they came upon Coreth, waiting for them near a staircase.

"Ah, Coreth. Robby has need of our apothecary. Would you mind showing him the way?"

"Certainly, Lord Seafar."

"And, if it is convenient, along the way you may show him around the Palace, too."

"It would be my pleasure, sir."

"I will find you when Commander Tallin has arrived. Does that suit you?"

"Yes, thank you," said Robby. "It does."

"Until later, then."

They parted ways, and Coreth led Robby down several flights of stairs and through doors to a broad hallway of pale blue marble walls and white stone tiles of milky quartz. Along one side were wide arches, windowed in clear glass, overlooking the northern lake and the cliffs that towered against the sky. On the opposing wall hung a myriad of flags and banners, and there were displays of armor and weapons, helmets and swords, shields and breastplates. They passed bows and saddles and horse-armor, too.

"These are trophies taken in battle with the Dragonkind," Coreth explained. She stopped in front of a suit of black armor that attired a faceless mannequin. Its helmet was of gold, banded with black metal, its sides flared out around the neck. The breastplate was of black bands, trimmed in gold, as were the plated skirt and leggings.

"This armor was worn by the Dragonkind King Salkasin at the battle of Tamkal Plain. King Parthais slew Salkasin himself in personal combat while his army scattered the enemy. Our Queen also took part in that battle, as did her brother, Lord Thurdun. As a result of that victory, Vanara knew peace for many years and, under Parthais, grew prosperous and powerful."

"But the Dragonkind were not completely defeated," Robby put forward.

"No. Some say the Dragon People will never know ultimate defeat. They recovered and even grew more powerful than ever. Eventually, they overran the eastern lands, spreading ruin and terror across the green earth. Although they could not hold those realms, they wreaked havoc. They amassed their armies in a last effort to take and to secure their hold on the east. They were victorious at the Battle of Tulith Attis, though at great cost. But a second great battle soon took place, as the forces of Glareth, Duinnor, and Vanara came upon the Dragonkind at a place where the River Lerse meets the Saerdulin, not far from present-day Tallinvale. There, the entire invading army was annihilated. If I understand the reports that you have made, it is somewhat south of there that the Redvest forces now gather for their offensive."

"Hm. Could well be. So much fighting and dying. And what for?" Robby mused, studying the workmanship of the armbands, noting the intricate gold patterns made into the black steel.

"Wealth. Power," Coreth answered. "Pride."

Robby nodded. "And, for some of us, survival."

"Yes."

They looked at the armor for a moment longer, then Coreth said, "Since you have read something of Parthais, you may be interested in seeing a part of the Palace that is just along the way, here."

She led him on down the long hall, and where it ended at the corner, they turned right into another similar hall, lined with elegant statues and fine murals, and approached a large, double door. Four guards were posted there, but, without challenge, they opened the doors and stood aside, bowing to Robby.

"Seafar has spread word to give you access to all, it seems," Coreth said. They entered a very large and wide courtyard, open to the sky and bounded by high walls topped with large urns from which hanging roses grew, their branches running thickly down over the walls, full of pink blooms. The yard itself was tiled in wide stones, checked in white and black, about an acre large, Robby guessed, slightly longer than wide. The two crossed through the middle to a line of high arches that supported the roof of the building at the far side. To his right rose the walls of the Palace, and he could see cliffs looming very nearby ahead and behind him. To his left he could see no mountains, and he realized they were at the front of the Palace, several stories above the lake, probably just above the main gate.

"This was once the main floor of the Palace," Coreth explained, "and the original entrance during the early days of Cupeldain, before the loss of our wings. Things had to be changed, as I pointed out earlier when we were approaching the palace along the causeway. After Cupeldain, it fell to Parthais and Heneil to continue the work of making it a place that could be used by my people, who must now walk as others do."

They reached the other side and went through a broad open arch and into a room equal in size to the courtyard. It was tiled in the same way and surrounded by high arches with clear glass, like much of the Palace. A line of columns ran to either side of the room, supporting balconies and the lofty ceilings above.

"This roof was added, along with the glass, and the supporting columns to hold up the roof. This is the Throne Room of Vanara."

There, on the far side of the room, surrounded by a company of armored soldiers, was the throne, on a carpeted dais. Seeing the two approach, the guards positioned themselves around the throne, but none spoke or challenged them.

"Your feather gains us admittance," Coreth said as they stopped just in front of the line of guards and about twenty feet from the throne. "But no one may step closer without the direct bidding of the Queen. Whether she is here or not."

It was a marvelous chair carved of white stone, lined with elegant green and blue cushions and draped with red silk. Its back was in the form of two feathered wings coming together, and the arms of the chair were banded in gold and studded with rubies and emeralds. Where the wings came together, they held aloft a cup of gold from which a massive amber stone protruded, carved into a likeness of flames.

"It is said to be the most magnificent of all thrones," Coreth told him. "But I have seen no other."

"It is the last one left, is it not? The last throne of all the Seven Realms? Duinnor has gathered all of the others, isn't that so?"

"Yes. Though there are other minor kings and queens, none are permitted a throne, nor do they have true sovereignty in their lands or over their people."

"Why hasn't the King taken this one?"

"He has not yet managed to swindle it from us," Coreth replied frankly. Robby thought he saw a faint smile pass the lips of one of the guards, then vanish as his chin rose with a hint of pride. "And he would not risk war by demanding it. Though unlikely, he would not risk us making a treaty of peace with the Dragonkind, opening his realm to their threat. Conflict between Vanara and the Dragonkind works to his advantage, if held in check properly, and gives him the means to weaken us over time. He does not need the throne in order to control much of what we do."

"I see."

"That then," Coreth gestured to the throne, "is the very place where Parthais sat when Elrasil the Hunter came before him with his tale. Over there was where Nimwill sat, making his accounts."

"Oh!"

Robby remembered the illustrations in the Book of Nimwill, and he imagined the voices of those chronicled, saying here the words that Nimwill recorded.

"Before the time of Parthais, back when the Palace was built by Cupeldain, this was all open," Coreth turned and waved at the windows and roof, "for, of course, everyone had wings."

"And you said earlier that, after the Fall, the city fell into disuse for a time."

"A long time. The Elifaen were scattered and had to learn to walk and run and fight and survive on their feet. Many did not learn and were lost. And the Dragonkind roamed freely over the lands. But Cupeldain, and others, banded together and eventually retook the lands of Vanara and restored and rebuilt the city and the Palace to their new way of existing."

"I'm a little surprised," Robby commented, "that this hall is so plain. I mean, no decorations or anything."

"The Queen ordered all decoration removed during ordinary times. But, several times each year, there are celebrations, and this hall is made most grand, I assure you! Now, let us make our way to the apothecary."

When they turned to leave, Robby noticed odd flecks of white protruding from the square stones that tiled the floor. He paused, looking at the paving stone at his feet which had a large cluster of the white flecks that almost seemed to be in the form of a flattened skull facing up.

"Parthais," Coreth said.

• • •

During the time when Robby was with Lord Seafar and Coreth in the high White Palace, and Ullin was at last on his way to meet Robby, Faradan had given the orders for his men to gather at their usual place, and had gone back to Dialmor to officially receive his assignment. It was what he expected, but the object of the assignment surprised him, though he did not show his pleasure.

Twice before, this quarry had thwarted him. Once, out in the desert, a sandstorm intervened when he and his men attempted to intercept messages from Vanara to the Free City of Kajarahn. The powerful sandstorm struck when he almost had the parcel from the Dragonkind courier. Out of the blowing dust suddenly appeared the Kingsman, joining with the defenders of the caravan and disappearing into the dusty wind with the one who carried the messages. Between the fighting and the storm, only Faradan and five others survived, returning to Vanara and reporting their failure. Somehow, Lord Banis in Duinnor learned that the Kingsman had arrived in Kajarahn with the Dragonkind, who turned out to be a woman. New orders were sent to Faradan. To atone for his previous failure, he was sent back into the desert to wait for the Kingsman, who would inevitably attempt to return with secret dispatches. Those dispatches would reveal traitors, those who conspired with the Dragonkind, and Faradan anxiously desired to be instrumental in their capture, for his success would assure his rise in the ranks and a place among the high commanders of Duinnor.

But it was not to be. They lay in wait for weeks. And, in order to conceal their purpose, Faradan and his men had to kill many Vanarans who stumbled upon them, soldiers and civilians alike. He arranged the bodies to make it seem as if there was a Dragonkind intrusion into the mountains, and they continued their mission.

At last Faradan spotted the Kingsman through a spyglass, alone, moving north through the crumbly rocks of the southern mountains, weak from thirst and hunger. But, just when they were closing on their prey, a contingent of Dragonkind appeared, also tracking the Kingsman.

Thinking that they wanted the dispatches as much as Duinnor did, Faradan ordered half of his men to attack the Dragonkind while the other half remained with him as they maneuvered to take the Kingsman.

It all went strangely wrong.

While the Dragonkind were stealthily killed, one by one, before they could close in on their common prey, the Kingsman somehow slipped away. It was as if the Dragonkind were protecting him by giving their lives. And, just when Faradan had retraced the Kingsman, and had stalked him within easy range of his arrow, a rabbit, of all things, a *rabbit* darted out of the rocks at Faradan, startling him and making his arrow miss by inches. The Kingsman quickly disappeared into a fall of boulders and slipped away, this time for good. Faradan was the laughingstock of his men. Three days later, they ran into a Vanaran patrol of Fellfaere. The Elifaen, thinking that Faradan's party were renegades, since that was how they were dressed, set upon them and quickly dispatched all but Faradan, who barely escaped.

Gone were all his chances for easy advancement. Gone was his credibility. And gone was any hope of an easy life back in Duinnor. He was recalled and demoted. Only when Dialmor came along was he resurrected from shame. Under Count Dialmor, Faradan was given an elite squad of men to command, to train and prepare for a special mission. This mission.

But when the announcement came that the Queen had left Vanara to travel to Glareth by the Sea, it seemed their mission was indefinitely postponed. Dialmor gave orders to continue practicing and training, but he secretly dispatched Faradan with a large squad of horsemen to track down the Queen's party. They almost had her, out on the plains, and by stealth had positioned themselves for a night attack. Even the Queen's elite Gray Guard could not save her, for they had relaxed their vigilance.

As Faradan and his men took their final positions around the camp, a mysterious rumble rolled through the plains, coming up from the ground, it seemed, though the ground did not shake. It was strange and loud, and enough to alarm the Queen's camp. Three times, the rumble came. And the Queen's party quickly drew itself into a defensive posture, almost as if they knew an attack was imminent. Thinking they had been given away, Faradan and his men withdrew into the rain. The next day, they called off the pursuit, and returned to Vanara.

So the Queen was gone, but Faradan and his men continued to prepare for the day she would return.

In the meanwhile, Faradan had learned the name of that elusive Kingsman, and resolved to have his revenge should the chance ever come. And now it had, handed to him by Dialmor on a slip of paper. Even though the Kingsman was not the primary target, he would be in the way and must also be eliminated. It would be Faradan's pleasure to do so at last.

A satisfied smile crossed his once-handsome face as he tossed the orders into the fire and turned to face his men, gathered together in a private dwelling on the southern outskirts of Linlally.

"So there you have it," he said. "Since the Queen took with her so many of her best Gray Guard, it should be an easy task before us. There is little business at the White Palace these days, and only our two visitors."

A few of the men chuckled. Some were sitting on chairs and some on tables, attentive to their captain. A few calmly smoked their pipes, while others ate. One of them, buttering a slice of bread, turned to Faradan.

"We will depart immediately to our positions," he said. "The equipment and all of the other materials were checked and tested just day before yesterday. All is in fine working order, and they remain well hidden."

"Good," Faradan replied. "Then I will see you at the appointed time."

He picked up his cap and put it on as he went to the door. His men respectfully stood. Faradan turned and called out, "Long live the King!"

"Long live the King!" they resounded loudly.

● ● ●

Coreth took Robby to a low level of the Palace, passing by a lakeside landing where swans preened while others of their kind slid silently across the inner lake between the Palace and the low wall that ringed it.

"They are beautiful," Robby uttered. "I've never seen such birds."

"They are swans," Coreth said, amused. She stopped so that Robby could watch them for a moment. "These are the Queen's Swans, so called because they abide here at the Palace year-round. Although they are normally unfriendly, when she is here they often follow her around. And she is quite fond of them in return. On pleasant days, she often holds court here and has her counselors meet with her on a barge out on the water, instead of on her throne. Just yonder you can see the royal barge."

"So those are swans," Robby said. He turned his attention to the way Coreth pointed and followed her onto the landing and out from under the overhanging portico. There, tied to a dock, was a wide boat, its sides of carved wood and its bow reaching high, curving up and back down in imitation of the necks of the swans. On the barge was a small canopy-shaded platform where sat a divan draped in pale blue silk and lined with pillows.

"It is always kept in readiness," Coreth said. "And though she is far away, I suppose the Palace routine goes on. The apothecary is just around the corner, not far."

Back inside, she led him a little farther to a pair of glass doors which she opened. They strode into a brightly lit storeroom, laid out much like a little shop. Like in his father's store, there were all sorts of things stacked and shelved, but much more orderly and less cramped. They walked down an aisle between shelves of towels and linens, and then turned to go to the back of the large room to another door.

"Here we are," Coreth opened the door and entered after Robby. This room was more like home, Robby thought. Every nook and cranny was crammed with boxes of herbs or jars of oil or stacks of bark neatly arranged in small bundles tied with twine. More herbs hung from the ceiling: broad dried leaves like tobacco, clumps of onion-like bulbs in nets, and other nets full of what looked to be dried flowers. The aroma alone, a mix of musty-sweet spice with dusty-grassy scents, was stimulating. As they moved toward a counter on the far side, Robby noted the array of cutting instruments, racks of vials, and a variety of mirrors, small and large.

"May I help you?" asked an old man from behind the counter. He wore dense glass spectacles and had long gray hair that draped across his white smock. His face was clean shaven but very wrinkled, and the spectacles made his green eyes look as large as walnuts. He smiled in a businesslike way.

"I prepare for a journey and there may be hazards," Robby explained. "So I would like to obtain certain things that might be needed."

"This is a guest of the Queen," Coreth said. "Please provide whatever he requires."

"By all means."

"I'll await outside," she said to Robby. "Please take your time."

"Thank you." He watched her go, relieved to be alone with the apothecary who waited patiently for him to continue. When Robby hesitated, he raised his eyebrows.

"A hazardous journey? Do you need salves and such for the treating of wounds?"

"Yes." Robby had mentally rehearsed for this and was ready. "A good, clean wad of hanging moss and grease salve to make a poultice, for starters. I have needle and some thread, but I lack a small pair of scissors."

"I see. Well, we do have some air moss. Would a small pouch do? It is tightly packed."

The apothecary fetched a cloth pouch and showed Robby how the contents could be unpacked.

"Yes. I hope that will do."

"Good. Good. As far as the grease salve, we have one that is good both for gashes and for burns. Here is a little tin of it."

Robby opened the tin and put his nose to it. It was not the least bit rancid and had just the slightest hint of camphor.

"Very good."

"I see you know your salve." The man took the tin and put it beside the pouch of moss on the counter. "We have a variety of scissors and implements for surgery over here. Do you see any that will do?"

"Just some that will make a clean cut on bandages and stitches. Ah, yes, these will do nicely."

"Very well. What else? Tinctures, perhaps?"

"Yes, one that would be good for small wounds and cuts."

"Well, the salve will do for many, but we have this, too," said the apothecary, reaching up to the top of a shelf and bringing down a small wicker wrapped bottle. "It is particularly good for itchy scratches, such as from thorns or whatnot, and good for stings and rashes, too."

"Thank you," Robby took the bottle and saw that it was sealed tightly. This was the moment, he thought. His plan, the one he had formulated weeks ago, back on the plain, hinged on what happened next, and the importance and danger of what he intended made him nervous, so he tried to show no emotion. He could not let anyone have any hint of his actual purpose here at the apothecary. Not even Ullin could know.

"That's great," he managed casually, handing the bottle back to the apothecary to put with his other things. "And do you have foxdire oil?"

"Pardon? What kind of oil?"

"Foxdire. I'm not sure if it is an oil or an extract or a tincture. Some call it Grave's Breath."

"Oh! Sigh Mortabilis, we call it. But it is called Grave's Breath in the east, I believe. Yes, we have a solution for nerves. Let's see. Ah, here we are. And there is another solution, blended with brandy, for more serious needs."

"Do you not have it in the pure form?"

"Why, yes. We have a stock of it that we use for our own solutions. But Sigh Mortabilis is very dangerous. In its pure form it brings on a slumber from which no one may be roused until it wears off. In some cases that we have known, the patient sleeps for weeks, wasting away all the while until starvation takes its toll. The rules of my Order prevent me from giving it out in pure form unless I give the sternest warning."

"I understand. But I have heard that it may be used to give one rest without pain of body so that serious wounds can be treated."

"That is true, but in very small amounts."

"How small?"

"Well, for a full grown man, one small spoonful will cause a sleep of an entire day. Double the dose, double the time, and deeper the sleep likened unto death, hence its name."

"How many doses in a vial?"

"Well, the smallest that I can provide for you would contain two doses."

"That should be more than ample. Would you prepare a vial for me?"

"Are you certain one of the brandy solutions would not serve you in a safer manner?"

"I have need to save weight and space. A small amount, pure and potent, would be easier to pack and protect from the bumps and jostles of a hard road."

"Yes, of course. I understand. Then you insist?"

"I guess I do."

"Very well, if that is what you wish. It will take a few moments, if you don't mind waiting."

The man hesitated, then turned away to the room behind the counter.

"Thank you."

Robby waited impatiently, hoping that Coreth would not return. Not that she would say anything about it to anyone. Just better not to take the chance. Much to his relief, the man soon returned and presented Robby with a small vial of thick-cut glass, banded with leather. The face of the leather was embossed with a skull and crossed bones.

"It is required of me to make an accounting of any essence such as this that we give out," the man said. "Would you sign our book? And I shall first put my name down, the date, and the other particulars."

Robby hesitated as a volume was produced, and the apothecary made an entry. "I write both in the Vanaran way and in the Common Speech," the man said as he finished. He turned the volume around and showed Robby where to sign, handing him the freshly dipped quill. Robby wrote his name and while the man carefully packed all of the things into a sack, he spoke again of the dangers of Grave's Breath.

"I must repeat my warning about this essence," he said. "It will kill if not used properly and carefully. Under no circumstances should an Elifaen take any dose of it. The effects may not be as expected and could be far worse. As for Men, the usual dose for one night's sleep is one small spoonful for a full-grown man of average stature. Far less is required for a child or one who is frail."

"I understand. And I thank you," Robby said as he took the sack from him.

"You are welcome. Good luck on your travels. May it be a safe journey with no need of any of these things."

• • •

Ullin had finally arrived, and Robby was relieved to see him waiting outside with Coreth and Seafar.

"Ah, Robby!" Seafar greeted him. "I hope you found the things you wanted?"

"Yes, thank you," Robby said, turning to Ullin. "I'm glad to see you, cousin."

"I'm sorry to be so late," Ullin said, shaking Robby's hand. "But our news has stirred a great deal of consternation down below at the Hall."

"And here, too," Seafar said. "Perhaps the three of us may chat in my rooms before supper? Robby has told me much, but I have questions aplenty. I know it is the last thing you want to do. Answer more questions, that is. If I know Portius, he subjected you to far too many already."

"I shall willingly answer all that I may, Lord Seafar," Ullin replied. "Especially if it leads to some action."

"Yes, action. That is what we must decide, is it not? Just as those down at the Hall of Ministers are scurrying about trying to decide, too. Coreth, I would ask you to join us, but I know that you have little off-duty time left. Please accept my apologies and my thanks for taking up so much of your time. And thank your brother for me, for looking after Commander Tallin."

"Certainly, my lord. It has been my pleasure."

"I hope we shall see each other again," Robby said, offering his hand. "And I don't know how to thank you for your patience and kindness."

Coreth took his hand and bowed.

"Think nothing of it, my lord. I do hope we shall see each other again."

Coreth departed, and Seafar led them through a maze of hallways, some quite elegantly decorated with plush carpets and murals. Several times along the way, the group was interrupted by aides coming to speak with Seafar. He would step aside for a word or two, once signing some papers and handing them back.

"This way," he gestured down another corridor. "I've just arranged for your escorts. You'll meet them tomorrow morning."

"Escorts, my lord?" Ullin asked.

"Yes. You see, Robby has told me much. And he has confirmed information that I was given before you arrived. We will discuss it privately at some depth when we get to my rooms, but I have decided that your presence is serious enough to warrant special escorts. For your safety. It will be good for you to get to know them before your departure, because they will also be serving as your guides."

"Guides?"

"Here we are. Please come in."

Somehow, they wound up at the suite of rooms where Robby first met with Seafar, and he showed them through to his official chamber, and gestured for them to sit.

"Yes, to escort you to Shatuum," Seafar said, "and, hopefully, on to Griferis."

Ullin looked wide-eyed at Seafar, then at Robby.

"I see you have been sharing quite a lot that I dare not breathe," Ullin said to Robby.

"Lord Seafar guessed, or already knew, much about our quest, Ullin," Robby said. "And I believe we can trust him."

"Oh, please do not misunderstand me," Ullin responded.

"Trust does not come easily to you," Seafar observed, "and that is a good thing. I'm afraid I took Robby by surprise with my foreknowledge of his purpose. But I have been in touch with the Queen, and others, who have some knowledge, and suspicions, about your mission. I have already given Robby my full support, as I know my Queen would have me do. But I also know that others, not so supportive, may also suspect who Robby is, and why he may wish to go to Griferis. These are perilous times, and I wish to take no chances unless I must. So, yes, I have arranged escorts for you, to serve as bodyguards and, later, to guide you along your way. They are trusted by the Queen, and I can vouch for each and every one of them. You will form your own impression of them soon, and, if there is a problem, we will work it out to your satisfaction."

"That all sounds very reasonable and prudent, Lord Seafar," Ullin nodded. "Only I was hoping, perhaps foolishly, that our way to Griferis would not be near such a dangerous place as Shatuum."

"I have only learned since arriving here," Robby said to him, "and since reading those things that Ashlord instructed me to read, that the only way to Griferis is through Shatuum."

"Truly? *Through?*"

"Yes. That is the way I must go."

Ullin looked steadily at Robby, then leaned back, thoughtfully. "The tales told of the place—"

"Do not come close to the actuality, I'm afraid," Seafar interrupted. "I hope to share with you some inkling of what you will face. You see, some of us here in Vanara have been keeping watch on those lands for a very long time. I will tell you more later, but let me assure you that our knowledge of Shatuum, though greater than any outside of that land, is still quite rudimentary and, well, sobering. The sure knowledge that we do have is, frankly, of a horrific place, filled with terrible creatures who are doing awful things under the whip of cruel and demonic masters. All serving the inscrutable will of Secundur, working to fulfill his dark purpose, whatever that may be. But, and this is the important thing: as far as anyone knows, Griferis has not been seen since our Queen Serith Ellyn left that place all those centuries ago. According to her account, already Shatuum was being formed by its new master, and her escape through it was perilous. Since then, she established a watch upon those borders, and we have learned much. Enough to warrant, nay, to require escorts and guides to help you along the way."

Seafar waved his hand in the air. "Of this we shall speak more, tomorrow, and of the arrangements I am making to assist you. But I know you are both weary and probably hungry. I have sent for your things to be taken to the rooms we have prepared for you. Soon we shall retire for the evening. But, though I know you must be very tired of this, Commander Tallin, I dearly wish you could share with me the report you gave to Portius."

Ullin chuckled. "I could probably repeat it in my sleep, so often I have retold our tale today. So I think I can manage another go at it. Robby, here, has probably already shared some or most of what I would tell, anyway. Shall I start with the events in the Eastlands? The coming of the Tracian Redvests?"

"Certainly, if you will. I wish to know as much as you can bear to tell."

"Very well, my lord. I was appointed through my orders to serve as Special Courier of the Post Riders, reporting to Collandoth, one of the Melnari race. It was I who carried the dispatches for the Queen, preparing the way for her. I was selected for that duty, I think, because Vanaran couriers would have been treated with suspicion, especially in Duinnor, and a Kingsman would be less apt to be molested."

"Ah, so you are that Kingsman," Seafar said with pleasure. "I knew that Collandoth had a trusted messenger, but he never told me the name. All of Vanara is indebted to you for your service, especially since you wear Duinnor colors."

"Thank you, sir. Collandoth told me," Ullin said, "that he selected me and asked me to be assigned to him because he knew something of my family, and he knew that he could trust me. He did not say, but implied that he did not want anyone at the Hall of Ministers to be forewarned or to question my activities as a Post Rider. It was made to seem that I was being given a relief assignment, after some difficulties in the desert. And that no one would question a Post Rider who was also a Kingsman. That was a few years ago."

"I see," Seafar nodded. "Do continue."

"After I completed my part of the mission for the Queen, and returned from Glareth by the Sea, I had reason to pass through the Eastlands' county of Barley. That is where Collandoth resided, and where Robby lived. It was Robby, as you know, who rang the Great Bell at Tulith Attis, causing a stir. Collandoth watched over him, not yet knowing the nature of Robby's destiny. As things turned out, I was asked to be the temporary commanding officer for a local militia that the people of Passdale wanted to form. I agreed, and Collandoth, as my superior, permitted me to drop other duties in order to perform that service."

Ullin described how he attempted to train the militia, but how they were overwhelmed by the invading Redvests, and how the people had retreated to Janhaven with many losses. He then went over Ashlord's revelations about Robby and how they were convinced to bring Robby west to Griferis. He related the visit to Tallinvale, and how Lord Tallin prepared against the invaders, and told about the trip through the mountains. But Ullin did not say anything about the Nowhere people, or Esildre, jumping on to describe the encounter with the mountain witch. After another hour, he had related their sighting of the Dragonkind, their encounter with the Wickermen, the great battle that took place and the monster that was defeated, and told of their reunion with Ashlord. He summarized the tale from then on, being brief about Islindia, Greenfar, and the haunted lake, and telling why their company split up. By then Seafar was pacing up and down the room. He interrupted only once or twice, mainly for confirmation that his ears did not deceive him about the incredible events that Ullin related.

As Ullin concluded his tale, it was well past sunset, the room was dark, and the mood was gloomy. A knock came on the door, and Seafar opened it to one of the servants who entered to light the room's lamps, providing bright relief to its occupants.

"I hardly know what to say," Seafar told Ullin and Robby after the servant had left. "And I hardly know what to think, or what to make of all your tidings. Lyrium lives! Dragon soldiers on the plains digging wells. Witches and demons. Wickermen…monsters? Dark arts at play there! Despicable! But then, Islindia? She still lives, too! So the tales about the place are true, in part, anyway. Incredible. All quite incredible. Well! You two and your companions have certainly been through much! Perhaps you have become as trained as any might be to venture where you intend to go."

"I don't know about that," Robby said. "But to be as prepared as we may, I would like to see more maps of the region that you might have."

"That would be a good beginning to our preparations," Ullin nodded. "And if copying is allowed?"

"Yes, you may do so," Seafar agreed. "I shall make available to you all of our latest charts. The best are not in the Archives, but I will have them taken there and a place set aside for you to work and study, if you wish. Tonight, I will be meeting with Commander Strake, who will be in charge of your escorts. Well before this time tomorrow, he will have his men prepared. Is there anything else that you can suggest?"

Robby and Ullin looked at each other and shrugged.

"I can't think of anything at the moment," Robby said.

A soft chime was heard, coming from the hall.

"Well, if you do, please notify any of your escorts, and it will be done. But forgive me! The hour! I truly apologize for keeping you from fare and rest. Come! Let me have you taken at once to your rooms. There you may sup privately and rest and sleep as long as you wish. I shall see you in the morning. If my head has stopped spinning from your news by then, perhaps I shall spin your head a little with news of my own!"

Chapter 24

Menagerie Macabre

Robby and Ullin were escorted to their suite by two members of the Gray Guard and a footman. As the two soldiers stationed themselves outside, the footman took the visitors inside to a common room which adjoined two bedrooms, each with its own washroom and spacious wardrobes. Each room was decorated with fine tapestries, sculptures, and paintings, with windows overlooking the southeastern parts of the mountain lake and the nearby cliffs beyond. Not only did they find their things had been brought up, including all of their weapons and their packs, but there was an elegant supper prepared and ready, complete with servers to wait upon the two guests.

After washing up, they sat to a somewhat lavish meal. Robby took his cues from Ullin, infinitely more accustomed to the way formal courses were served. They made smalltalk in the presence of the waiters, but after a while ate silently until the meal was complete and the servants had taken the dishes away, leaving behind several bottles of various wines for their enjoyment and a tray of bread, cheese, and fruit. Ullin went to the door and, opening it, took a casual glance up and down the hall, nodding at the guards outside, then closed it and latched it securely, turning back to Robby.

"I'll have some of the white, here. Would you care to join me?"

"Certainly, just a touch," Robby said, getting up to stretch and going to the window to have a look.

"So it is to Shatuum we go," Ullin stated as he handed a crystal goblet to Robby and poured until Robby gestured. "Griferis can only be reached by that route?"

"Thank you. Yes. There is no other way. Or if there is, it is hidden to me. According to everything I have learned today, it is in the south-western reaches of Shatuum."

The dusk still gave ample light, enough to make the icy ledges of the nearby cliff glisten. Robby sipped, looking upward at the top of the cliff where he thought he saw some movement. He realized there must be a roadway or path along there. Some four or so stories below his window, a line of white dots were gliding ghost-like across the dark water far below, their vee-shaped wakes barely visible as pale trails. Turning his gaze to them, he was briefly reminded of the haunted lake and the ferryman who took them across it, and the strange apparitions they saw there. Certainly, he had seen many wonders on his journey, some of which were dreadful, indeed, while others made the heart glad and full of hope. Until this morning, Robby had never before seen a swan, except in the storybooks belonging to Mr. Broadweed, or outlined by stars in the night sky. But those fell far short of their true beauty and grace. As he watched them from so far above, he felt a pang of homesickness.

"We have come all this way," Ullin said. "But I would be no friend if I did not ask."

"I know. It still seems incredible and hopeless," Robby conceded. "And I do not feel any more worthy to be a king now than when we left Janhaven. Nor any more prepared. I'll be too late to help our people, regardless. Certainly it will take weeks to reach Griferis, even if we do not run into trouble, which we almost surely will. Yes. It seems impossible. From everything I've learned, the mountains are difficult enough even in summer when the passes are somewhat clear of snow and ice. Now, it can only be bad and growing worse as the winter season deepens. If we somehow manage to get through, and are not waylaid or worse by those who occupy Shatuum, will I be allowed into Griferis? And, if I am allowed in, will I pass the trials the judges there must subject me to? And even then, to become King of Duinnor?"

Robby turned to look at Ullin, strong, determined, world-wise Ullin, and he smiled.

"I am grateful to you for bringing me this far," Robby said. "For protecting me and our friends along the way. I don't see how any of us could have made it as far as we have without you. But I do not see why you should accompany me any farther. Too many are put in danger because of me."

Robby gazed at Ullin in genuine appreciation of the Kingsman who was shaking his head with concern.

"From the very beginning," Robby went on, "you grasped what this quest was about. At your own peril, and the peril of your House, you swore loyalty to me over the present King whom you have served for so long. Perhaps you comprehend more than I do. Out on the plain, you despaired, thinking you would fail me through some madness. But you have not. I forced an oath from you then, and you have fulfilled it. So I release you from it and from all service and from any commitment to me."

Ullin put down his goblet and came to Robby and put his arms around him and hugged him. Putting his hands on Robby's shoulders, he gave him a weary but earnest smile.

"It is my dream," he said, "that someday there will be peace between all peoples, and that justice and law will be above race or position. A time when war does not blight the earth and the threat of it does not cloud the day of the living. I did not know or have hope that such a dream could come true, but now that I have dreamed it and tasted its sweet peace in my heart, how can I not work for it, bending my will to bring it to pass? And, having had that dream, how can I not but be emboldened by the workings of it to have other dreams, dreams of daring hope? No. I would rather drink from the bitter cup of failure than to lose those dreams. Say what you will, but I cannot abandon you now. By making an oath to you, I took an oath to myself to uphold it, and also an oath to something greater than either one of us. If you order me, I shall obey. But if you order me away, I beg you not to do so unless you give me some task worthier than this splendid dream."

Robby nodded, and they grasped wrists firmly, each reaching the understanding of the other.

"Then you shall be my companion and my helpmate," Robby said. "And I shall most probably be your burden. Together we'll see how far we can go, and how much we can do, to bring your dreams to pass."

They chatted a little longer, sitting in comfortable chairs across from each other, until Robby yawned and excused himself to bed. Ullin remained for a while longer, then put down his glass and went to his bedroom. There he checked his bags, taking the time to look over every detail of the straps, flaps, and contents to be sure of them. Loosening his tunic, he went to the window and gazed out at the blackness. He stood thusly for a long time, fingering the locket hanging from his neck. After a while, he paced out of the room and back to the food tray and nibbled a little biscuit and poured another glass, glancing through the open door at Robby, already deep in slumber.

Ullin envied Robby's ability to drop off to sleep practically anytime and anywhere he wished, a skill the Kingsman seemed to have lost these past many weeks. There was a time, back when he rode Anerath to and from all parts on long and lonely errands, that Ullin could sleep in the saddle. Quite often, he would dismount and stretch out on the ground for a nap while Anerath kept watch. Rest time was important, but never predictable, nor wise, when wary of bandits, marauders, or beasts, or when pressing onward against the urgency of the messages he carried. He would dump a few coins into roadside barkeeps' hands so as not to be disturbed as he nodded off in a chair by a fire. Or, in his barracks, he could calmly doze amid the raucous turmoil of his young, off-duty comrades. Before battle, when other men were nervous and restless, keeping vigil during what might be their last hours on earth, Ullin could find sleep leaning against a rampart, or stretched out on the hot sand with only the shade of his hand over his eyes.

But lately, it was a chore to sleep, and a fretful activity when it came. He had known other men who took to drink to calm their nerves. Some of these, over time, lost themselves to those strong spirits, needing more and more as the power of the bottle and jug to soothe grew weaker, along with their own spirits. Knowing his limit, Ullin put down the glass, though his inclination was to drink the bottle dry and fetch another. He looked through the door again at Robby. On the floor just beside the bed was his knapsack and shoulder bag. Ullin smiled at how, during their journey, Robby had gotten into the habit of packing everything and keeping it handy, ready to grab at a moment's notice. And Ullin knew that he had been Robby's example in that behavior. Turning his head, he looked at his own things, ready to go, beside his own bed. Yawning, he shrugged and stripped down to his shirt, went to bed and, in spite of himself, soon drifted off into a good sleep.

• • •

When Robby woke up, and had washed and dressed, he came into the adjoining room of the suite to find Ullin already up and reading. There was a low table beside his comfortable chair by the window and on it was a plate with breakfast crumbs, a cup of tea, and Ullin's pipe. He had the window cracked open and sat facing away from Robby with one book in his lap and another opened on his crossed knee. He was leaning with one elbow on the armrest, his chin cupped in his hand, and with his other he tapped the page as he stared at the mountains, watching gray puffs of mist floating along the cliffs.

"Morning."

"Oh! Good morning, Robby. Did you sleep well?"

"Pretty well. You?"

"Just fine. There's a bit of breakfast on the table over there. A pot of tea by the fireplace. The other pot has coffee."

"Thanks. What are you reading?"

As Robby filled a plate and poured coffee, Ullin related how he had gone out earlier to the Royal Archives to borrow a few volumes to look over.

"I was thinking they might reveal something of what is before us. This one is an account of the hunter, Elrasil, and in it he tells some of what Nimwill recorded. But not much of great use to us, I'm afraid. And this one is a collection of travel tales, detailing certain routes and byways. There are a couple of interesting accounts of strange beasts on the way from Duinnor to Vanara along the old western mountain route. I don't want us to rely too much on Lord Seafar's guides, you understand."

"I feel the same way." Robby buttered a roll and, with his coffee, sat nearby. "I looked over some maps in the Archives while I was there, but they were not very useful. Lord Seafar said he had better ones, so I hope we'll be able to see them today."

Ullin let Robby eat while he continued to flip pages. Robby got up and took the lid from a plate and, seeing it held eggs, sausage, and gravy, pulled his chair to it and began eating in earnest. Ullin was glad to see him do so, noting again how gaunt Robby was beginning to look. He seemed fit enough, Ullin thought, and he eats like a horse, even. Compared to his rather pasty appearance of just a few months ago, Robby was, indeed, now much lighter in weight, and he appeared taller, too, for some reason. But Robby seemed paler than one ought to look after so much time out of doors. And he seemed tired all the time. Well, not exactly tired. Weary was more the word. But why shouldn't he be? Ullin mentally shrugged. He had turned his attention back to the book on his knee when there was a tap on the door.

"Come!" said Robby as he swallowed and wiped his mouth with a napkin. It was Henders, Seafar's secretary, who entered.

"Good morning, gentlemen," he said, bowing. "I hope your breakfast was adequate."

"Oh, yes," Robby replied, rising from his seat. "Thank you very much."

Ullin stood, too, and put the books on the chair.

"You are welcome. I also hope that these rooms suit you?"

"Indeed," Ullin said. "They are very fine."

"Good. Good. When you are quite ready, and no sooner, Lord Seafar would like to see you. An escort awaits in the hall and will show you to him. Until then, if there is anything else that you need or desire, just give the bell rope a tug and a footman or servant will see to it."

"Thank you. We won't keep Lord Seafar waiting very long," Robby said.

"Please take your leisure. That is his wish."

Henders bowed once more and departed.

Ullin went to his room while Robby quickly finished eating. He was just downing the last of his coffee when the Kingsman reappeared, having donned his shoulder harness. After a quick examination, Ullin slid his sword into its scabbard.

"Even here?" Robby asked.

"Seafar would not have had all of our things brought to our rooms if we were restricted from them," Ullin stated, putting a foot up on a stool and drawing his dagger from his boot for a quick examination before returning it. "And, yes. Even here."

Robby nodded, going to his room, and did as Ullin had done, but slipping his dagger into his belt instead. As he turned to leave, he held out his hand. Swyncraff, draped across the back of a chair, straightened so quickly that it bounced itself from the chair and across the room to Robby, who caught it and, with one movement, slung it over his shoulder where it coiled and knotted itself comfortably.

Ullin nodded his approval when Robby emerged, "Very good," and then he opened the door.

In the hall, two armed guards snapped to attention. They wore the same neat gray tunics as had Coreth and some of the others they had seen, but these two also wore black leather wrist guards, gloves, and shin guards. Their breasts were crisscrossed with straps that supported a sword belt and two fighting daggers, one on the hip, one on the shoulder. They also wore black open-faced leather helmets that came across the back of their necks, snugly strapped under the chin.

"Good morning," Robby said to them.

"Sir! Good morning, sir!" one of them answered, stepping forward.

"You are?" Ullin asked. "At your ease, please."

"Yes, sir. I am Tiller, sir. Corporal, Sixth Wing, Second Regiment of the Queen's Gray Guard, sir. This is Trooper Helms."

Helms clicked his heels and saluted, "Sirs!"

"Helms and Tiller?" Ullin asked with a smile.

"Yes, sir! I know, sir," said Tiller.

"Our escort to Lord Seafar?" Robby asked, somewhat bemused by their appearance and formality.

"That is so, Lord Ribbon. This way, if you please."

Tiller and Helms turned and marched in front of them down the corridor. There were two more soldiers standing stiffly to either side of the doorway, and as Robby and Ullin passed through, they filed in behind them. They turned and went down several flights of stairs and then emerged into another hallway where two more troopers joined in at the front of their group. A little farther along they filed down a narrow winding stair to the lowest region of the castle and into another long broad corridor lined with armaments and many doors, opened to reveal armouries within. Lord Seafar was at the end of the hallway, standing beside another soldier who was helmetless, and behind them was an iron door and three other soldiers.

"Form a line, troopers," the soldier beside Seafar ordered as they approached. The soldiers smartly shifted to the left of the hallway and stood in line facing them.

"Good morning!" Seafar greeted them with a bow.

Robby shook his hand, saying, "Good morning. Quite an escort!"

"Hand picked, each and every," Seafar nodded. "Allow me to introduce Commander Strake."

The soldier clicked his heels and bowed. "At your service, my lords."

"How do you do?"

Robby and Ullin shook his hand while Seafar explained.

"Commander Strake will be in charge of this squad. They will be your escorts here at the Palace. He, and they, will also go with you on the next leg of your journey, along with a few others under his command."

"Lord Ribbon. Lord Tallin," Strake bowed again. He appeared to be in his forties, with longish brown hair streaked with gray, lightly greased back from his high brow with two braided strands framing his weather-toughened face. He had piercing amber eyes and thin straight lips over a hard wide chin. As tall as Ullin, he stood somewhat more relaxed than his men as he studied and took measure of the two visitors.

"Strake knows as well as any what is before you," Seafar went on. "And, like his men, here, he is as capable as they come."

"I'm sure," said Robby. "But I think we should not be so formal. I wish to be called Robby, if you please. That goes for your men, too.

I hardly know it is me that you address when you speak so elegantly."

"Forgive our formality, my lord," Strake said. "It is our tradition to address the Elifaen heir to a Named Vanaran House such as Fairoak in such manner."

"Oh," said Robby, a bit embarrassed. "Forgive me."

"Not at all, my lord."

Ullin chuckled to himself as Strake glanced at Seafar, who was himself smiling. Ullin was accustomed and trained to such formality, knowing that it was often a necessity in the ranks to preserve and enforce lines of authority. But while Robby was certainly no soldier, Ullin could not help but wonder how he would be as King.

"I thought it best that we first meet here," Seafar said, "because what I am about to show you will speak more to what you face than any words I may tell. These men, and many others like them, have all served in the region where you go. They are all very familiar with the nature of those lands. Commander Strake, the door, if you please."

Strake motioned to one of his men, who took a set of keys and began unlocking and removing bolts from the iron door. While he did so, Seafar addressed Ullin and Robby.

"Secundur has delved too much and too long in the dark places. It was ever his nature to do so, taking advantage of them to his own will. His immortal body cannot any longer bear the light or any products of light. His sustenance is not food as we know food, and his air is no longer air like we breathe. He therefore does not have power in the world to act as most creatures do, and he can only exert the force of his will in strange and mysterious ways. Through whispering shadows, it is said. That is his power, and he is ever in the exercising of it, in ways too black to fathom.

"Since the time of Parthais, none have seen him. At least none have told of it. Yet, slowly, he established for himself a domain in the land that Parthais granted to him. Shatuum. In the early centuries of the Queen's rule, very few paid attention to those mountains as the shadows there deepened and covered over them. At the time, there were greater concerns of war with the Dragonkind. But the Queen came to understand the threat within that land, and she set a secret watch upon it. Slowly, Secundur has pushed forth its boundaries, swallowing the canyons and hills with dread, and he has filled those places with terrible creatures of mysterious origin. The mountain people who once lived in the region rumored terrible stories, but those people are long gone away, and their towns and villages have all long been abandoned. Our only reports come from our Gray Guard that occupy our keeps and watchtowers along the border and who patrol the area. Recently, that is, over the past half-century or so, some of the old rumors have been confirmed. Slowly, a picture has emerged of the activities within Shatuum. I wish to show you some of our evidence. I beg you to brace yourselves, but I promise, no harm will come to you from what you will see. I would not show you this, and I would not show anyone, unless I felt it to be absolutely necessary. Do you understand?"

Robby and Ullin looked at each other.

"I believe we do," said Robby.

"Lead on," nodded Ullin. Robby glanced at Ullin's arms, but his long sleeves prevented Robby from seeing whether any hairs stood on end.

Seafar nodded to Commander Strake, who stood beside the opened door and who, in turn, nodded to his men. Four of them picked up torches from the brazier and entered the room with Strake.

"Let them light the way for a moment," Seafar said to Robby and Ullin.

Even from the hall, Robby could see that it was a vast room, something like the armoury in Tallin Hall, with vaulted ceilings. Within, the guards went back and forth, lighting lamps and other torches, making the room glow brighter and brighter until Strake returned.

"The lamps have been lit, my lord."

"Thank you. Please recall your men and await us here."

"Yes, Lord."

A few moments later, the guards filed back out into the hallway to wait.

"Very well," said Seafar. "Let us enter."

Seafar led the way, then, a few feet within, stood aside.

"Make of this macabre collection what you will, and I will tell you what I know about the things you see."

Already, Ullin and Robby were shocked, moving slowly past Seafar with looks of dark bewilderment, their mouths open. But Seafar knew that it was good for them to see this place for themselves, for how could he, or any person, describe these things?

Standing like a stuffed bear just to the left was a creature, obviously dead and preserved like one would mount a trophy. But while it was as tall and as big as a bear, its every aspect was hideous. Matted fur covered its arms and legs, its head was short and squat, with no discernable neck connecting it to broad muscular shoulders. Like a bear, yes, but the face was dog-like, with a flat, flared nose that protruded over a wide grimace filled with teeth, long, sharp, and yellow. Its eyes were deep-set—closed, thankfully—and the ears on the sides of its furry head were broad, almost like sideburns, tapering upward and away in cat-like points. And it was clothed. Across its chest a plate of iron hung from chains attached to crudely bent plates of iron that covered its shoulders, and it wore plates of iron hung over its loins, too. Its feet, two hands wide and three times as long, were shod in thick leather boots studded with protruding spikes of sharp metal. On the floor beside the stand that held the thing up was a helmet of black iron, flat on the top, with a long nose guard to fit over the top of the creature's snout, open on the sides for its ears to protrude, and with a single curved horn jutting out from its crown.

"Great stars!" Ullin muttered.

It was but the first exhibit they saw. There were several more creatures in whole or in part, or their skeletons. Heads arranged on shelves, skulls, teeth, and…were those hands? Or claws? There were displays of weapons and clothing, armor and other things. To the opposite of the first creature was another in the likeness of a man, housed inside a glass case, also, like the first one, standing on two legs. The creature was thin and hunched over at the shoulders. The skin of its face was drawn tight over its skull, in obvious decay, but its nose was still long and hooked. It wore a dark-colored tunic, over which hung a shirt made of iron rings, like coarse mail. On its head was a pointed helmet, the sides of which were hung with flaps of leather, and in its hand was a curved sword, crudely wrought.

"This creature killed seventeen men before it could be subdued," Seafar said pointing up at the first large monster. "When it was finally tracked down, just outside of Shatuum, it was in the process of eating three more of the forward scouts of the tracking party. In the ensuing fight, six more men were killed. Including, I might add, my great-uncle who was among the fiercest fighters Vanara has ever produced. Of the remaining thirty-four men, each was wounded before it fell. That was sixty-seven years ago."

Seafar turned to the smaller figure.

"About ten years later, one of our outposts was assaulted at night. It was estimated that there were about twenty raiders, and they were easily beaten back without suffering any casualties. The next morning, this one was found along the line of their retreat, dead of arrow wounds. There was no sign of the rest of the party, and our soldiers dared not follow them too deeply into Shatuum where the attackers had retreated."

"Look upon these other creatures. Some are dog-like, or wolf-like, perhaps. Some, as this one here, resemble a sort of four-legged bird. See the long beak? It eats flesh, too, and hunts somewhat like a lion. Notice those lines along its back and shoulders? And look over here at this."

Robby and Ullin followed Seafar through the hideous displays and looked at the next creature he pointed out. It was cat-like, having a long bare tail with a tuft of fur at the end. But its legs were decidedly not like those of a cat, ending in claws more akin to a hawk. And though there was a fur-like mane around the head, it was odd-looking and mottled. The head itself was every bit that of an eagle.

"It is not fur, but feathers," Seafar said.

"And the two lines?" Ullin asked.

"Those baffled us," Seafar said, turning with a gesture for them to follow. "The remains of the creature were found some twenty years ago, and it was preserved and restored as best as our artists could do. Still, the patterns on its back seem odd, surely."

He stopped before a tall case draped over entirely with a large cloth so that nothing within could be seen. Robby steeled himself for another grim display.

"I'm sorry to have to show you any of this," Seafar said. "Obviously it is not something I enjoy having in the Palace, and I would not burden anyone with the knowledge of such things if I could help it. But I fear that someday, and perhaps someday soon, creatures like these will be widely known. I'll explain in just a moment. I show you these things because you need to know what you face."

He pulled on the cloth that draped the case and had some trouble with it, so Robby stepped up and swung a corner of the cloth upward so that Seafar could pull it over the top and down the other side.

"Thank you. Now, look at this."

Inside the case was another man-like creature, much like the one across the room, but of a gray, almost silver complexion. It was somewhat stooped, but taller than the first, and it was dressed in breeches of dark leather, plated with bits of metal, but was bare-chested. Its eyes were closed, and its face was scarred and pitted, but Robby could not tell if it was from decay or if it was how the creature was in life. Its nose was slightly less disfigured than the other, but it had the same ears, and its entire head looked as if it had been squeezed inward on both sides to make it narrower and longer from chin to crown, which flowed with raven-black hair, shot with streaks of red.

"As I said, the bird-lion's marks were a mystery to us until this creature came along. He led a raid that took place seven years ago. It was many miles outside of Shatuum, and consisted of over a hundred creatures such as himself and others more like the one over there. They were fierce, and sought to steal supplies from an armoury train sent to re-equip our outposts and watchtowers. As luck would have it, our supply train was traveling within horn call of a company of our soldiers that was patrolling the region. Coreth was there, and can tell you more about the battle. It was hard-fought, but the raiders were repelled. This one, riding a creature something like a horse, was felled by one of Coreth's arrows. Now, come look at this."

Robby and Ullin exchanged glances, and walked with Seafar around to the rear of the display, and looked at the back of the creature. Two long lines scored their way down either side, from shoulder to hip.

"He is Elifaen!" Ullin declared.

"*Was* Elifaen," Seafar corrected. "At least at some point in his existence. We think he started out as a prisoner. But we aren't sure. At any rate, he was transformed by some act, by some black art, into this."

"How? And," Robby shuddered, "why?"

"By the will of Secundur, surely it was done. And, just as surely, to serve him."

"And the other creatures? Were they once something else, too?"

Seafar shrugged. "I do not know. They may be demons, somehow preserved from the ancient world, or the offspring of demons. I cannot say for certain. Perhaps your friend, Collandoth, would know."

Seafar allowed them to look a little longer, then said, "There are other creatures, and people, if you can call them that, who occupy those lands. Duinnor knows of these things. We have shared our information with the highest ranks of the King's court. But they do little to guard their own lands against such creatures, and it is our belief that they come and go about Duinnor's frontiers as they please. Except, and this is an interesting thing, they do not seem to trouble Duinnor as much as they do our borders."

"Are you saying that some accord between Shatuum and Duinnor has been reached?" asked Robby.

"Perhaps," shrugged Seafar, "or perhaps Shatuum is not interested in Duinnor. But their probes into our lands increased some fifty years or so ago. Then, about five years ago, all became quiet along Shatuum's borders, with very few encounters compared to past years. The Queen, early in her reign, established the Gray Guard as her personal guard. They serve that duty well. But she uses that to mask the true purpose of the Guard: to watch over Shatuum and to gather information about that place. Besides those who serve in the Gray Guard, only the Queen, myself, and a few others know about the Gray Guard's activities and purpose. As far as Duinnor is concerned, it numbers only around five hundred strong, an adequate force to serve the Palace and the Queen. But its true numbers are six times that. Service on the border of Shatuum is difficult and full of trials. Not only the terrain, which is harsh enough, but the duty itself. You'll soon understand, I dare say."

"Shatuum is a large land, is it not?" Ullin asked.

"In area, I'd say it is perhaps half the size of the old Eastlands Realm," Seafar said. "But it is a mountainous region."

"And it has been Secundur's domain for a thousand years, more or less," said Robby. "That's a lot of time to build up quite a number of these kinds of creatures."

"Yes. It is."

"How many might there be?" asked Ullin.

Seafar looked from Ullin to Robby, then back, almost hesitant to answer.

"A great population, I'd say," he said at last. "We have no real way of judging. But from the smoke and furnaces that we have noted from afar, and from the extent of their walls and battlements, I'd say no less than many tens of thousands. Indeed, that is another mystery. While every observation that we have made over the past thirty years indicates a tremendous population, we do not see how that can be. There is no indication of any agricultural activities—the land is too inhospitable for that. Yet such a large number of these creatures must require a prodigious supply of food. So it is a conundrum."

Seafar led them out of the room, and as troopers went about extinguishing the lights, he addressed Commander Strake.

"I would like for you to secure the Royal Archives for the exclusive use of our visitors," he said. "And please have all of the maps and charts that may pertain to your route delivered there."

"Yes, Lord," Strake nodded. "What shall we tell the staff?"

"Only that I and my guests wish to study. We go there now, and I will speak with our readers to let them know their services will not be required."

The door to the macabre menagerie was closed, bolted, and locked, and the keys returned to Seafar. As he guided Robby and Ullin back upstairs to the archives, accompanied by Tiller and Helms, he explained that he had already taken the charts and maps from his own personal collection to the archives.

"Should the space turn out a suitable one for your studies, I will have my Shatuum journals taken there as well. Meanwhile, Strake's men have already begun their preparations for the journey. I have arranged a luncheon for you and the rest of the men who have been selected to go with you. So that you all can meet each other. Would an hour past noon suit? That's another four hours."

"I think we can last until then, thank you," Robby said.

"Very well. I see you both have good clothes, well-made, too, they appear. But they may not be enough. Winter is bearing down, and you'll be traveling through a very inhospitable land. So, perhaps we can arrange some additional gear for you. More appropriate boots and hats and whatnot. Also, you'll have to carry quite a bit of gear, so you must keep your own things to a very minimum. It is good that you travel light, but anything that you might leave behind would be one less thing to carry."

"I understand," said Robby.

"Robby does not have much to spare," Ullin said. "But I can do without my longsword, I believe. And I suppose we won't need the remainder of our meager provisions?"

"Provisions will be provided. And your sword will be put in my private chambers for safekeeping until you return for it."

When they arrived at the Royal Archives, just as the staff were filing out, Ullin and Robby saw that several men and women of the Gray Guard were on duty, others were stationed outside in the foyer, and two more within.

Inside, several tables had been pushed together, and a stack of maps rested at one corner of them. Seafar explained that there was no order to them, so not to worry about mixing them up.

"Also, as you can see, they are all northern-oriented. But they are of different scales. This one is on a two hundred miles to an inch, not too useful, perhaps, except as an overview. These are fifty miles to an inch, and overlap somewhat. But they do not cover a portion of the region you will travel through."

Seafar stood between Robby and Ullin, quickly going over the charts, pointing out flaws on some, and particular aspects of others. The collection was fairly numerous, over two dozen maps and charts. As they examined the maps,, the doors opened and several soldiers entered, each carrying rolls and stacks and cases, and one even brought in an easel.

"Ah! Some tools!" Seafar reached for a case and took out a pair of dividers and several rulers. "I'm sure you could probably instruct me on the use of these," he said to Ullin, "so I will not insult you with my explanations."

"You are being modest, I'm sure."

"You will notice that there are very few routes marked," Seafar continued. "And none of our outposts are shown. That is deliberate, I'm afraid. The routes and passes that are shown are those that are either old ways, from before Shatuum existed, or ways that run farther east than you will be going, like this one here that runs past Averstone. We make it a point, through our agents, to acquire maps from Duinnor, or to obtain copies. That way, we keep aware of Duinnor's knowledge of roads and routes. And we share maps with Duinnor that are misleading or of little use. But our men know the way, and should snows cover certain passes, they know alternate routes."

Ullin looked at Seafar with a furrowed brow. Seafar shrugged.

"You know the value of charts as well as any," he explained. "We cannot have our numbers and disposition made known, or else Duinnor would insist that we properly account for our forces. If the King knew the number of our outposts, and the routes to them, he could surmise the numbers it takes to support them, with supplies and relief. Besides, as you saw earlier, we do not wish for it to be revealed, through maps or otherwise, how much we know about the region in question."

"So you do believe Duinnor and Shatuum have some sort of accord."

"I do not make any assumptions to the contrary," Seafar stated bluntly. "Besides, even with the best of intentions, Duinnor is sure to be as full of Secundur's agents as any other land. Why take chances?"

"Yes. I understand."

"So, with all those limitations, I'm not sure how useful you'll find these."

"They will at least give us the lay of the land, somewhat," Robby said.

Ullin had picked up the dividers and made a quick estimate of the straight-line distance to the nearest border of Shatuum.

"Hm," he said. "Thirty leagues, at least, if we were crows."

"Yes," nodded Seafar solemnly.

• • •

For the rest of the morning, Robby and Ullin pored over the maps. Ullin, more knowledgeable than Robby about the workings of libraries, used the collection's catalog to locate books that he thought might be useful. Once, as he pulled a book from a shelf, he noticed nearby to it one that Robby might be interested in.

"Look at this when you get a chance, Robby," he said, placing it on the table next to Robby. It was a book of history pertaining to the arrival of Men. Robby thumbed through it, glancing at the chapters about the coming of Men, some containing tales and legends of the sea voyage before they arrived, and one describing the early settlements in the Eastlands Realm.

"Look, Ullin! A list of settlers. It lists a cooper by the name of Couris Ribbon, who settled near Calletshire. It says that he had seven children, two sons and four daughters."

"Let me see that."

Robby handed Ullin the book, and he flipped through several more pages, stopping to read one.

"Oh, there's more," he said. "It says here that another group of settlers also made homes there, amongst them 'Bilaylin Bosk, namesake for he who would in later days be called Bilaylin the Hammer, who fought so valiantly at Tulith Attis.' "

"No! At Calletshire?"

"Yes! I suppose Ribbons and Bosks have known each other for a long time. Look for yourself."

Robby did, grinning and shaking his head. "I know what Billy would say!"

Ullin scrunched up his face, "Who'd a thunk?"

They nearly choked on their laughter, much to the consternation of the stern members of the Gray Guard. After settling back to their studies, they remained silent for a long while. Robby felt as if a bubble of loneliness surrounded Ullin and himself, each separated from the ones they loved, each with so many unspoken concerns and longings. Robby wondered how Ullin had held up to it for so long, if he had but a fraction of the longing for Micerea that Robby felt for Sheila. There was not much he could do for Sheila, now; she was in Ashlord's care. But Robby resolved to find a way to help Ullin and Micerea, though he had never even revealed to Ullin that he knew about them. Somewhere, he knew, Micerea waited. Just as Ullin did. Going about their duties and their days unenthusiastically, every moment overshadowed by hopeless yearning. Sighing, Robby turned back to the maps, blinking away the mist that his own yearning put in his eyes.

"I wonder how our friends are getting along," Ullin said.

"Perhaps someday, you may learn how I know this," Robby replied, "but take my word: Our friends are well, they are safe, and they are nigh upon the borders of Duinnor."

Ullin stared at Robby.

"I promise," Robby stated.

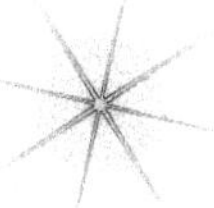

Chapter 25

The Shapeshifters

Day 157
88 Days Remaining

Just as Raynor was putting fresh hay into Beauchamp's box, there was a knock on the door. The rabbit leapt joyously into the pile, pushed it around properly, and began to munch as Raynor went to the door.

"Oh, good morning Miss Tarrier," he said to his landlady.

"A couple of notes just came for you, sir, and I thought I'd bring them up and tell you that there's a fresh pot of tea downstairs."

"Why, thank you," Raynor said, taking the folded wax-sealed notes. "I'll be going for my stroll in a few moments, otherwise I would love to have a cup."

"Very well, sir. Then have a pleasant walk."

"Thank you. I'm sure I shall."

Raynor brushed an errant bit of straw from his robe as he went to his desk and sat down to read the notes.

"Let's see," he said to Beauchamp as he broke the seal on one of them. "Oh. It seems that young Mr. Farby is back in town, and he wonders if we might be interested in a couple of volumes that he picked up while in Glareth. He says he must travel off to Mount Vendril on business, but that he should be back within a couple of weeks and for us to send a note as to when a good time would be for him to drop by. How nice of him to think of us. I wondered what became of him."

He picked up the second note and cracked the wax seal.

"Hm. Interesting writing, done with a brush rather than a quill," he mumbled. "Well, Beau, we are asked if we might be willing to meet with two travelers from out of town late this evening. Oh. Apparently, they are reluctant to come here, and wonder if I might pay them a call at the house where they are staying, over at Number 12 Brawton Street. If so, I am to come alone, as late at night as possible, and need not reply ahead of time."

Raynor looked over the note and across the room to Beauchamp, who was sitting in his box looking back at him with a long stem of hay slowly disappearing into his mouth as he chewed.

"What do you think of that? Mysterious, eh? No, it's too soon to be our friends from the east. Not unless they sprouted wings, that is. I imagine there is some mundane reason behind it. I'll think it over. Meanwhile, I'm late for my stroll!"

Raynor tossed on his overcoat, picked up his hat, and departed into the cold winter air. He had it in mind to go for a long walk today, perhaps all the way to Miller's Pond, although he knew that it was not yet frozen. But it was nearby to Brawton Street and so would afford a chance to reconnoiter the meeting-place mentioned in the note. He remembered the area as a neighborhood of modest little houses, occupied by tradesmen and their families for the most part, and so he thought perhaps someone wished to consult with him on a routine task or job, perhaps as a tutor. He continued speculating about it as he leisurely went through the city, enjoying the crisp winter air under the intense blue sky. It took him all of the morning to reach Miller's Pond, and once there he strolled around the park-like place, nodding at the couples he passed on the walkway that rimmed the small pond. Although there had been a dusting of snow, only a tiny bit of ice crusted the water's edge and floated on the breeze-chopped surface. It might be another week or two, perhaps longer, before it was cold enough for skaters to venture out. He had a particular fondness for watching them glide and spin, and looked forward to bringing a good book and a warm blanket when the time came.

Leaving the park and pond behind, he quickly made his way through the nearby streets, turning down Brawton a few blocks away just when the city towers chimed the noon hour. Going along the grassy path alongside the street, he noted that the small houses were as neat and trim as he remembered them, with each little yard and walk as tidy as could be. He watched the numbers on the gates, and when he came to Number 12, he suddenly stopped, shrugged, and entered into the yard. He went up to the door, and gave it a knock. The patter of an animal's feet came and went on the other side of the door. Perhaps a small dog, Raynor thought, and he caught a glimpse of a small, narrow snout pushing aside the curtain from a nearby window, but the creature disappeared before he could get a good look. He was just about to knock again when he heard soft shuffling footsteps on the other side of the door.

"Who is there?" said a man's voice.

"Raynor."

The door cracked open, and a figure with a hood pulled low over his brow peered out.

"You were at night supposed to come," said the man in a very unusual accent. It was evidently one of the travelers he was to meet.

"I am here now," Raynor said. "But if you wish that I come back tonight, then I shall give it further thought. I may, or I may not return."

The man shifted his weight hesitantly, glancing over his shoulder. Raynor shrugged, turning away.

"Wait. Give us a moment," the man said.

"Very well."

The door closed. Raynor heard again the patter of paws. After a long few moments, he was about to leave when he heard footsteps once again, and the door opened. It was the man, again, covered from head to bare shins in a long brown robe. The hood was still pulled low, but the man nodded and held the door wide.

"Please come in."

Raynor entered, removing his hat, and noted the musty smell, as if the house had been empty for a long time and had not been properly aired out before its present occupants moved in. It was dim, with the curtains all closed, but he did not fail to see a long black feather on the floor.

"How odd," he said, reaching down to pick it up. He held it in the sunlight that was beaming through the open door. "Iridescent. Like that of a crow, or a raven."

The man took the feather from Raynor before he could examine it further and closed the door.

"Pardon the state of our house," the man said. "Would you come into our parlor, just here?"

Raynor followed the man into the side room, which had only two straight-backed wooden chairs, a fireplace which was unlit, and no lamps or rugs or anything that indicated that the place was actually occupied.

"I shall my companion fetch," said the man, gesturing at one of the chairs. "Please you to sit?"

"Thank you. I don't mind if I do."

The man left, but almost immediately returned, holding the door open for a young lady. She, too, was in a long robe with her hood pulled low, her eyes in its shadow. Raynor stood and bowed, observing that both she and the man were barefooted, and seemed not to be wearing any clothing under their robes, in spite of the chilly house.

"I am Raynor," he said, bowing.

"I am Seleesa," the woman replied. "And this is my companion, Aremon."

"I am pleased to make your acquaintance."

"We, too, are pleased," she said. "Although we thought our note stated that we wished to meet you at night."

"My apologies. I was in the neighborhood on my morning stroll and thought I'd take the chance that you might be at home."

"I see. Won't you have a seat?"

"After you, my lady."

Seleesa smiled and went to the other chair to sit. When Raynor was seated, she spoke.

"I am sorry that I cannot offer you a cup of tea," she said. "We are visitors here, staying for only a short while, and we do not keep the proper things in the house for making tea. We hoped to have some refreshment brought to us this evening in preparation for your visit."

"Please, do not apologize. That is quite alright, I assure you."

Aremon crossed his arms and stood beside Seleesa. Raynor eyed him with some wariness.

"I am curious, though," Raynor went on, "as to how I may be of assistance."

"Aremon and I are travelers, and we have been away for many years. In fact, we have been isolated from the happenings of the world for quite some time. However, we recently decided that we should come to Duinnor and try to learn about those things that have come to pass since we have been away."

"And why, may I ask, did you think to get in touch with me?"

"We know that you were, and perhaps still are, a teacher. And also that you read much, and have a great fondness for books. We could think of none better to talk to."

"I see. Well, I am no longer a teacher. But I do try to keep up with events."

As they spoke, Raynor observed what he could of the two strangers. He could see from their exposed feet and hands, and somewhat of their faces, that they were both of very dark complexions. The woman had long coal-black hair, a strand crossed her cheek, and the man had a black beard, short-shaven and pointed at the chin. He suspected that, unless they were Elifaen, which he doubted, they were both in their twenties.

"We were hoping," Seleesa was saying, "that you would be kind enough to review for us those events of the world that might be important to know. And we are willing to pay you for your time."

She gestured to Aremon, who stepped forward and held out several gold coins and then put them into Raynor's hand.

"I would be happy to do so," Raynor shrugged, looking at the heavy coins, turning them over in his palm. "And, I must say, this is a most generous sum. But where should I begin? Do you wish to know about Duinnor only? Or do you also wish to know about other Realms?"

"All, I think, that you would care to tell us."

"All. Hm. Well, tell me, what is the last event of consequence that you are familiar with? That might be a good point to start from."

"Yes," Seleesa said, somewhat hesitantly. "Perhaps, as a start, you might briefly tell us those important events that have transpired in the eastern realms. We are given to understand that there has been unrest between the Eastlands Realm and Tracia Realm, and that the Ruling Prince of Tracia may wish to annex lands that are part of the Eastlands. Certainly the King of the Eastlands would defend his lands."

Raynor cocked an eyebrow, looking from Seleesa to Aremon, and back.

"Indeed you have been away and out of touch for quite a while," he said. "The Eastlands no longer has a king, and it has been under the stewardship of Glareth Realm for many generations. And, more recently, Prince Lewtrah of Tracia was ousted, and a trio of despots have ruled Tracia quite unchecked for nearly twenty years."

"We did not know those things. Do the new rulers of Tracia seek conquest upon its neighbors?"

"It is very strange that you should ask that."

"We have heard rumors. And we are curious."

"Rumors. Hm. Well, I, too, have heard rumors. It is possible that Tracia envies her neighbors, and covets their lands."

"So you have not had any news from the east concerning such matters?"

"Have you? If so, I would dearly like to know."

"Rumors only, as I said," Seleesa answered.

Raynor could see that Seleesa was, all of a sudden, as uncomfortable as he was.

"Then tell us, if you will," she went on, "what you may know concerning the strange sound that Aremon and I heard some months back, during the summertime. It was a peculiar rumble that seemed to come up from the ground. Where we happened to be at the time, it shook all of the bells and gongs, setting them ringing as if struck by invisible mallets, although the ground did not shake. Did you experience anything of the sort here in Duinnor?"

"Why, yes," Raynor nodded. "It was most unsettling. All of the bells and chimes, from the largest to the smallest, rang most violently of their own accord. Three times they all rang. It caused a great deal of panic and alarm, I can assure you."

"Do you know the cause?"

"I cannot say for certain." Raynor remained expressionless. "But there have been rumors."

"I see. What sort of rumors?"

"Oh, the usual talk of spirits and omens, foreboding doom and destruction."

"We have heard that there are legends of a magical bell made so that, if rung, all of the bells of the earth would ring with it. As a call to arms. Have you heard of such?"

"There have been a few such legends in circulation."

"Could it be that one of those legends was true?"

"Anything is possible."

Seleesa sat back in her chair, obviously not pleased with Raynor's elusive answers.

"I think that you trust us not, Raynor," said Aremon. "Your answers are most not helpful."

"I have no reason to trust you," Raynor replied, smiling. "In fact, I have every reason to be suspicious of you."

"Why is that?" Seleesa asked. "Because we are strangers to your city?"

"No."

"Then why?"

"The things that you know seem as strange as the things you are ignorant of. You paid me in three gold coins, all of which were struck well over six hundred years ago. It is strange that you do not know that three or four of these coins would purchase this entire property, yet you have virtually no furniture. Then there is the manner of your dress. You seek to hide your appearance, but your accent is strange. I don't think I have heard anything quite like it, although it is very much like that of the Dragonkind."

Aremon let his arms drop, and he and Seleesa exchanged looks. Slowly, she pulled back her hood, and Aremon did, too, revealing their dark skin, long black hair, and brilliant blue cat-like eyes.

"Ah," said Raynor. "You have every appearance of being from the desert lands."

"Our ancestors were from there," said Aremon. "But we are not."

"And where, may I ask, do you call home?"

"We cannot tell it to you," said Seleesa. "We promised not to say, out of fear for our kin's safety. I can tell you only that we avoid the world, for obvious reasons, and have come out of hiding only to learn what we may concerning late events. You should understand that we must be very careful."

"Oh, I do understand. I am surprised, in fact, that you dared to come to Duinnor at all. It must be very important, or else you would not take such risks."

"It is important to us."

"And, besides the two of you, are there very many of you?" Raynor asked. "In the place wherein you hide?"

"No. Not very many."

"And why do you think that you may trust me?" Raynor asked, looking from Seleesa to Aremon and back.

"We are not certain on that," Aremon said bluntly.

"That is a good answer," Raynor said. "Well, I, too, have my secrets, and so you must forgive me if I cannot answer all that you may ask."

Raynor leaned forward and gave the coins to Seleesa.

"But I will not cheat you," he went on. "I will freely and gladly tell you about any and all that is within my power to speak of, except concerning those things that I must not tell anyone about. Since you do not seem to know much about Duinnor, I should first tell you that I am not very popular amongst the King's servants. I have been jailed, twice, just so that the King's Court could let me know that I am not very much appreciated for my criticism of the King, and to warn others from keeping company with me. So you may be in more danger than you think, for I am often followed by the King's agents, and almost everything that I do is watched."

"Oh!"

"I do not know whether or not I was followed today," Raynor went on, "but, if I was, it is likely that this house will be searched soon after I depart, if not beforehand. Some in Duinnor think that I conspire with others, and have secret meetings and so forth. Therefore, you, sir, should probably keep an eye at the window."

Aremon, with an expression of panic, rushed to the window and carefully parted the curtain to peek out.

"And I would advise that you both depart as quickly as you can," Raynor added, "with as much stealth as you evidently used when you entered the city. Frankly, I don't know how you have not been discovered. But I can assure you that it won't go very well for any Dragonkind caught within Duinnor. I am astounded at your audacity."

"We shall take your advice," Seleesa said. "I thank you for your candor."

"Not at all. Now, what else may I tell you?"

"Is it true that the present King is not very well liked?"

"Oh he is liked well enough, I'd say," Raynor chuckled. "At least by the corrupt, the criminal, and the bigoted of Duinnor's people. And his chief minister, Lord Banis, does all that he can to ensure the continuation of corruption, crime, and prejudice against other realms, not to mention against the Dragonkind. To those ends, Banis is perfectly willing to make victims of his own people, who are Elifaen, and of his adopted people of Duinnor as well."

"I imagine that the black eagles of the King help in that," said Seleesa. "Are they not creatures of the dark lord, Secundur?"

"They are, indeed," said Raynor. "But it was Lord Banis, not the King, who brought them to Duinnor. Somehow, Lord Banis has convinced the King to use them."

"I see. Then the King and Shatuum are not in league."

"Who can say for sure?" Raynor shrugged. "At times, it certainly seems that Duinnor does the work of Shatuum."

"This present King of Duinnor has ruled for a very long time, has he not? Do you know if he may ever be replaced? Or will he rule forever?"

"Oh, let us hope that he is replaced!"

"Do you know when that may happen?"

"I do not."

"May it be soon?"

"I do not know. Why do you ask?"

This time Seleesa shrugged, as Aremon glanced over his shoulder at her.

"These are unsettling times," she said. "When the bells and gongs of our lands rang, some said it was an omen of great change. What greater change may there be than for Duinnor to have a new king?"

"That would be a great change, indeed, after all these centuries," Raynor agreed. "But, here in Duinnor, some view the ringing of the bells to be a sign of an even greater change to come. It is foretold that our next king will be the last King of Duinnor, to rule in the last days before the world is remade."

"Our tales say something of the same. In our legends, it is foretold that the new king will come from the east but will arrive from the west. Is that also how it is foretold in the legends that you know of?"

"Some legends have it that way."

"Do any of your legends mention a place called Griferis?"

"Soldiers!" called Aremon, craning his neck at the window. "Just now entering the street."

Raynor and Seleesa stood.

"They are pointing to this house," Aremon said, pulling the curtain closed and spinning around.

"Is there a back way out?" asked Raynor.

"Yes."

"Then, go! I will delay them, should they come to the door," Raynor said, pushing Seleesa and Aremon into the hallway.

"What of you?"

"I'll be fine unless they find you here. Get out of the city, as quickly as you can," he instructed.

"Here," Seleesa pressed the coins back into Raynor's hands. "Thank you!"

"Go!"

Aremon was pulling off his robe, pushing Seleesa ahead of him down the hall and toward the back door as Raynor turned to the front door. Glancing back, he was surprised to see Aremon's robe floating down to the floor, and Seleesa's trailing out across the back threshold, the two Dragonkind nowhere in sight.

Raynor opened the door just as a soldier was poised to knock.

"Oh, hello!" Raynor said. "What can I do for a member of Duinnor's Regular Army today?"

Surprised, the soldier hesitated then pushed past Raynor. Several more came through after the first.

"May I help you?"

"Is this your house?" the first soldier gruffly asked as the others went from room to room.

"Why, no, it isn't. I believe it is to let, and I thought it quaint, so I thought I'd take a look at it. But it isn't very well furnished, as you can see, so I don't think it would suit me at all."

Raynor saw a soldier go out through the open back door, while another lifted one of the robes, then dropped it to go outside. The two almost immediately returned.

"No one else is here, Captain," one of them reported. "No one out back, either. It's walled all the way around, too, with no gate. Too high to climb over. The front door is the only way out."

"You are looking for someone in particular?" Raynor asked in a good-natured tone of voice.

"We had a report of suspicious activity within the neighborhood," said the soldier. "Just making sure of the place. Criminals, and such."

"Oh? I thought Kingsmen normally patrolled in such a manner," said Raynor. "Or does Lord Banis now seek to enforce laws with his Regulars? That would be strange."

"I don't know what you mean," said the captain gruffly. "We only happened to be in the area, Raynor."

"Oh. What you say is even stranger, since I don't recall giving you my name," Raynor said. "But I am fairly well-known, I suppose."

"Let's go!" said the captain to his men. Eyeing Raynor suspiciously, he gave a curt bow. "Good day, sir."

Raynor watched them go, and he chuckled as he turned back into the house and walked down the hall to the back door that was still open.

"Better luck next time, boys," he said.

Stepping out onto the back stoop, Raynor put his hands on his hips and looked about. It was a tiny back yard, filled with dried weeds, and surrounded all the way around by a high wall.

"Hm. Come out!" he said. "They are quite gone."

Stepping down, he saw no hiding places, and no way that anyone could climb over the wall without ropes or a tall ladder. He saw a gap at the base of the wall where several stones were long missing, but it was too small for any but a very small child to squeeze through.

"How strange."

Going to the hole in the wall, he bent over and plucked a tuft of reddish fur that was caught on the inside edge of the stone. Glancing around once more, he continued to examine the tuft of fur as he went back inside, his brow furrowed in thought. Just inside the doorway, he picked up the robes. He noted again how dusty the floor was, and, in spite of the scuffings of the soldiers, he could clearly see the bare footprints of Seleesa and Aremon, their sets distinct from one another by their size. Stooping over, he looked more closely. Aremon's prints simply vanished a yard from the door, just where his robe fell. And Seleesa's footprints seemed to disappear, too, replaced by that of a little dog such as he had seen earlier.

"But during the entire time that we talked," he muttered, "I did not once see it. What kind of little dog does not like company? Or at least does not like to bark at company?"

He looked at the robes in his hands, then tossed them over the chair in the parlor. Leaving the way he came, he jingled the coins in his hand as he strode off homeward, shaking his head and wondering about the strange encounter.

"I suppose their years away from the deserts is why they appeared so healthy," he mused. A stiff breeze suddenly blew through, sharp and cold, and Raynor quickened his steps, pulling his cloak tighter.

"I certainly hope they have some means of finding warm clothes," he said to himself. "It is getting colder by the moment!"

• • •

Raynor walked southward through the city, suddenly anxious to get back to Beauchamp and his books. While he did so, there was something of a stir along the streets to the north of him as a red fox ran as fast as its legs could carry it toward the northern gate of the city. The people jumped out of its way, amazed that such a creature brazenly ran, as though in a panic, through the busy avenues, dodging carts and wagons, and scurrying around corners. At one point in its course several braying dogs set after it, creating an even greater commotion. People laughed and pointed, but were further amazed when a large raven swooped down upon the pursuing canines, scratching at their snouts and pecking and flapping at them so furiously that the dogs yelped, twisting and turning around in confusion. So intent were they on fending off the cantankerous and determined bird that they entirely gave up on their quarry, which by now was sprinting through the north gate of Duinnor City. The fox made a sharp turn off the road, darted between several warehouses, and bounded off toward the east, still going as fast as it could. It made it to the eastern hills overlooking the rich farmland surrounding Duinnor City, and then it eased its pace until it reached the top of a steep knoll. There the fox scurried under a clump of vines that covered over a stone ruin, and it lay down, panting. The raven joined it there, hopping over to preen the ears of the fox with its beak. After a little while, once it was more rested, the fox pushed deeper into the cover to lie next to the old wall, and the raven hopped after it. A foggy mist rolled over the two creatures, and, after a moment, Aremon was lying naked beside Seleesa, putting his arms around her in an effort to keep her warm.

"That didn't go too well, did it?" she said.

"It might have gone worse."

"Those dogs nearly had me!"

"But they didn't, my love," Aremon said. "I only wish we had learned more. It just didn't seem worthwhile."

"We learned enough."

"Still, we're on the wrong side of the city, and miles from our cache of clothes and coin."

"Then we should keep moving," said Seleesa. "If we don't get back before the full moon, we'll be stuck out here, unable to transform!"

"Seems a bad way to do things, as I've said over and over," Aremon shook his head, pulling Seleesa closer. "It seems as if one of your Order would have figured out a better way to do things."

"I have told you before. It was not those of the Order who came up with this way of doing things, but Aperion. He foresaw the need for us to send out some of our people from time to time. But if we can't transform into our totems, we'll never be able to cross the Ring of Fire safely. That's the way it is, and it isn't likely to change just because we complain about it."

"Has anyone ever failed to return in time?"

"Many. We don't know what happened to most of them. Only that they never returned."

"How many? Are there records of such?"

"Yes. Over the years, seventeen of our Order have failed to return. Traveshia herself almost did not make it back before her time was up. Her totem was a panther, and she got her leg caught in a snare. She gnawed her way through the bindings, but not before her leg was terribly cut. That's why she walks with a limp."

"Hm."

"I was told about one of our kind who returned but did not survive," Seleesa went on. "She was late, and missed her full moon. Three days later, she was seen by our people who watched from the hills. She was being chased by a band of Elifaen on buckmarls. She was swift, but could not outrun them."

"Oh. They caught her, then."

"No. She ran straight in. And, along with her pursuers, was consumed by the fire."

"Oh!"

"Yes. We have everyone to fear, it seems. Even Lady Moon, who will not wait for us."

"Well," said Aremon, getting to his knees, "then, if you are rested, perhaps we should hurry along!"

Chapter 26

Flight From Danger

The luncheon took place in the dining hall of the barracks. When Seafar took Ullin and Robby into the room, two dozen of the Gray Guard stood to either side of the long table, dressed smartly in their uniforms, but without their leather helmets. They stiffened to attention as the trio entered. At Strake's command, they all lifted their hands to the sides of their heads in salute. Seafar saluted Strake and as his hand swept down in return, so did those of all of his men.

"Commander," Seafar shook Strake's hand. "Would you be so kind as to introduce our guests to the men?"

"Certainly, my lord. It would be my pleasure."

Strake led Robby, followed by Ullin, down one line and up the next, introducing each soldier by rank and name. In turn, each flyer, as they called themselves, clicked his heels and bowed. Robby and Ullin shook hands with each of them in turn, recognizing Helms and Tiller, and a few of the others from earlier in the day. Robby was amused at some of their names, all very nautical, it seemed, and he was impressed with their apparent athletic vigor, their comradery, and their friendly nature. At last, returning back around the table after greeting the last guardsman, Seafar addressed Robby.

"These will be your escorts," he said. "They are all experienced and capable. They will see you to our outpost, but they know nothing of your mission, which, for obvious reasons, I wish to remain secret until you are well on your way."

Turning to the men before them, he continued. "Gentlemen. Commander Strake has informed you that you are to serve as bodyguards to Lord Ribbon and Commander Tallin, here. He has also told you that you will escort them northward as soon as they are ready to depart. By now, you have completed your preparations, or have nearly done so. Therefore, hold yourselves in readiness to depart at a moment's notice, as soon as the word is given. Probably first thing in the morning."

Seafar paused, with a brief look of contemplation, then continued.

"It is imperative that Lord Ribbon and Commander Tallin reach their destination safely, and I know that each of you will do your duty to protect and defend them, and to guide them. Henceforth, they are your commanders, equal in authority to my own. Surely you have already noticed that Lord Ribbon carries Swyncraff across his shoulder. As well,

Commander Tallin wears upon his finger the Queen's ring. Indeed, you are to obey and protect Lord Ribbon and Commander Tallin as you would the Queen herself."

The men remained expressionless, but a couple of them glanced at Robby. Seafar turned to him and asked, "Do you wish to address the men before we dine?"

Robby looked up and down the two lines, and he suddenly had the feeling that he was responsible for them and not the other way around. He cleared his throat, and nodded.

"I am from the Eastlands Realm," he said. "I am fairly inexperienced, barely educated, and not as prepared as a person should be for what is ahead of us. I will say this, though: I will listen to your instructions, and I will try not to be too much of a burden. If I could do what is before me all alone, I would. But I know that I cannot. My companion, Commander Tallin, here, is world-wise, battle-hardened, and experienced in the ways of military customs. I am none of those things. If I am green, I am less green for his patient instruction and example. Do not judge him by my shortcomings, I beg you."

"Commander Tallin?" Seafar inquired.

"I only wish to say that some of you may know my name, and somewhat of the House of Fairoak. If you do, you know that my connections with Vanara are deep and ancient, even though I wear the colors of Duinnor. Lord Ribbon is my cousin, my father's sister's son. So, if blood runs true to honor, then his is the truest. I, too, will endeavor to heed your instructions, for I do not know the way or the hazards before us. But I know, by personal experience, that the Gray Guard have no equal in skill or honor, and no peer when it comes to devotion to duty."

"Well said, Commander, thank you," Seafar nodded, then to the men, "So consider your questions, should you have any that can be answered, and enjoy the luncheon. Please be seated!"

Servers rolled out platters and tureens and filled plates and bowls with a hearty fare befitting fighting men. They brought pitchers of ice-chilled wine and frosty beer. Indeed, so lavish was the luncheon that it was more like a feast. Although conversation was at first politely sparse, with Seafar and Strake leading discussions, soon the entire table was noisy with talk. Robby was asked about the Eastlands, and the rumors of war that were circulating, and he told what he knew of it, describing the plight of his people and the preparations at Tallinvale. Meanwhile, Ullin was asked by one of the men if he knew such and such Kingsman, and by another if he was the same Tallin whom Faslor had mentioned on occasion. Ullin answered that, yes, he was that very same Tallin, and briefly explained that Faslor had saved his life a few years ago. Before long, the talk ran the gamut of topics, all but their mission, that is, from wicker armor to shopkeeping, and from Tulith Attis to Dragonkind out on the plains. Robby even allowed himself to be imposed upon to demonstrate his ability with Swyncraff. He tossed it as a limp coil onto the floor beside Tiller's chair. When the trooper reached to pick it up, Swyncraff sprang back into Robby's hand as a stout rod. This brought a round of laughter and cheers, with several comments of satisfaction from those at the table.

"I am very interested in your flying apparatus," Robby said to Tiller, gesturing at the linen-covered wing that hung on the wall. "Does it take much skill to work one?"

"Don't ask him!" called out Helms. "He's the worst flyer there ever was!"

"I beg your pardon!" Tiller responded indignantly. "Who smashed four wings before he ever got a yard above the ground, eh?"

"That wasn't my fault! If old Keel had harnessed me up in the right way, I wouldn't have veered off like that. And that was nine years ago, I'll have you know, and not a mishap since. Which is more than I can say for some, as several of our fellows still have the scars to show."

"Hear, hear!" cried several of the group.

"I can't help it if you don't know enough to get out of the way of a gust!"

"I can only say," said Strake to Ullin, "that it is good to see that not all cousins are as quarrelsome as they! But, in spite of the talk, they are two of the finest flyers in Vanara, and each as good a soldier as any. But tell me, might you have any notion of when we may begin our journey?"

"I imagine no more than a day or two hence," Ullin shrugged, looking at Robby, who also heard the question and nodded.

"I think we should be on our way very soon," he said.

• • •

Afterwards, their spirits lifted by those of the men, Robby and Ullin returned to their studies for the remaining afternoon. By the time evening began to fall, they were not much more enlightened than when they began, but not for lack of trying. They went over maps again and again, and Ullin spent a great deal of time looking for more descriptions of the lands in their travels. When Seafar stepped in to see them at dusk, and asked after their progress, they admitted that they would indeed rely upon the skill of the men that would be their escorts.

"As I expected," Seafar said. "But one never knows what new eyes may glean from old maps. By the way, Lord Ribbon, Strake tells me that his men would be happy to show you their flying wings tomorrow, should you be interested. He has even offered to take you for a flight, if that may interest you."

"Well, yes! I mean, if it would not be too much trouble."

"It would be his pleasure, I am quite sure. What about you, Commander?"

"Oh, no. I'll content myself with more studies, if that is quite alright."

"I do have a question for you, Lord Seafar," Robby asked.

"By all means, ask."

"It is about the Queen. Are there any writings that may describe her stay at Griferis? About what happened to her while she was there, I mean?"

"There are no writings pertaining to it, and she does not speak of it," Seafar said. "I have asked her many times. As have many others, I am sure. She says—I'm sorry to tell you—that the mind cannot comprehend its mystery."

"Hm. Well, I needed to ask."

"I quite understand. I wish I could tell you more."

"In that case, since it is late," Ullin said, "perhaps we should have supper in our rooms and turn in?"

• • •

Faradan pulled around his heavy cloak against the cold draft that raced through the tunnel, took out a red feather and slipped it through his left epaulet. Proceeding on, he smartly turned the corner and marched to the landing.

"The lifts are closed for the night," the operator said as he approached.

"I carry urgent dispatches from Duinnor for Lord Seafar," Faradan answered.

"Your pass?"

Two guards stood close behind the operator, and Faradan smiled amiably and nodded as he reached into his cloak and produced the pass, prepared by Dialmor. The operator read it, holding it up to a nearby lamp.

"Very well." The operator handed the pass back to Faradan and frowned as he reached to pull on a lever built into the wall. "I hope someone up there is still about."

Soon enough an answer was telegraphed back down, the lift was prepared, and Faradan was on his way up. When he arrived at the top, he walked along the outer wall that ringed the lake, eyeing the Palace. The lamps along the causeway gave the White Palace a ghostly glow, reflected by the black surface of the lake. He glanced up at the nearby southern cliffs, confident that his men were prepared and were now watching for his signal. He presented his pass again at the causeway gate and opened his cloak to them so they could see that he carried no weapons.

"Lord Seafar is bound to be asleep by now," said the captain of the watch. "I hope it is urgent, indeed."

"So say my orders," Faradan shrugged. "Urgent enough to keep me from my favorite tavern."

"Right." The captain returned the papers to Faradan. "Probably more bad news."

"I can only imagine."

The captain raised a lantern and lifted a metal cover several times to wink its light toward the far side of the causeway. An acknowledgement came blinking back.

"Very well, then. Let him pass!"

Faradan walked the long stretch toward the Palace not too fast but with a proper air of purpose. Again, he looked at the cliffs, black against the starry sky. He took professional pride in his work and had a sense of satisfaction that his timing was just right. The moon was not yet up, and only starlight or bad luck could give his men away.

"Who goes?" came the challenge as he neared the gate of the Palace's outer walls.

"Faradan! Of the King's Special Service!"

"Approach and state your business."

"I've come to deliver urgent dispatches to Lord Seafar."

Several lamps were uncovered and glared down from the wall. Faradan blinked and put his hand up to shade his eyes. The sally port opened and several sentries stepped through, one bearing a lantern. It was held close to his face for a moment.

"Your pass?"

Faradan knew as well as any that Duinnor men were resented in Vanara, and the sentry's tone betrayed that mistrust. Faradan reacted by smiling, and he confidently produced the pass, remaining silent as it was examined.

"It says here that you are to personally deliver your dispatches."

"That is so."

"Hm. Seafar's secretary will have to be roused to take you through, and he'll be grumpy, I assure you!"

Ignoring the tone of warning in the sentry's voice, Faradan shrugged. "I can't help that. Just following orders."

"I know how that goes. Very well. Starsail!"

"Sir!"

"Escort this gentleman to Henders. Then back here on the double."

"Yes, sir!" One of the men stepped up to Faradan, saying, "This way, sir."

The two passed through the gate and on across the drawbridge and into the Palace.

"I know my way," Faradan told the guard as they passed into the main hall and turned down a passage. "I can conduct myself there."

"All the same, I have my orders, too, sir."

Faradan had to make a decision, and as they went up a case of stairs, he knew he would have to pick the time and place soon. It was true, he did know his way. Though he had only been in the Palace twice, Dialmor had provided good floor plans over a year ago, and he and his men had studied and memorized them as part of their training for this mission. He was satisfied with his familiarity of the place and confident that he knew exactly where he was in the vast building. Dialmor's information was not complete, though, and there were many blank spaces representing areas that even Dialmor could not identify. But they did not matter; Faradan thoroughly understood the important parts.

They emerged from the stair into a long corridor, more dimly lit, and Faradan knew they still had two flights more to go.

"Need to make a quick stop, if you'd pardon me for a moment," the escort said.

Baffled, Faradan shrugged, following the guard down the corridor to a small door.

"Please wait here, sir. Won't be but a moment."

The escort ducked into the door and closed it behind, leaving Faradan alone in the hall, trying to remember the floor plans. But he could not place this room, he did not recall any blank spaces where it was, and he was suddenly nervous. He looked up and down the hall, anticipating sentries at any moment. Hearing a sound from within the room, he smiled, realizing that it was a water closet. This was a lucky break, and he could not pass up the opportunity. Loosening a cord from his cloak, he entered the toilet. His escort was surprised but did not have the chance to speak. Faradan's cord made sure he would never speak again.

A moment later, Faradan was back in the hall, putting his cord back into place. Glancing up and down the way, he went back to the stairs. Taking the steps by twos, he hurried to the next level and peered around the corner. Dialmor was right, and there were no guards posted at the end of this corridor where the double doors were, and he hurried to them. After giving the lock a quick examination, he took from his boot a small tool. The lock opened loudly, he shot a glance over his shoulder, eased the heavy door open, and slipped through to the darkness of the courtyard. Pausing for a moment to let his eyes adjust to the dark, he then skirted along the wall, carefully making a circuit of the courtyard to be sure no one was posted there. Passing the doors to the throne room, he hesitated, fingering his pick. A less disciplined man might have succumbed to the temptation to enter and have a look, but Faradan hesitated only for the briefest moment. After completely rounding the large courtyard, satisfied with the loneliness of the place, he moved to the center of the yard, looking up at the black southern cliffs that shadowed the stars.

Removing one of the fake dispatches, he rolled it up and then, striking a firestick, he lit the end of it, making a little torch. This he held up over his head and moved it left and right slowly. Almost immediately, a light blinked at the top of the cliff and then blinked off. Faradan dropped the flame and stepped on it, then moved back against the wall to wait and to scan the sky. He had to look hard to see them, and it was only when they came very near that he was sure, but, yes, several shadows moved, hardly visible against the dark backdrop of the cliffs. They descended quickly and silently, and began landing, each flyer skipping along on padded shoes as quiet as could be, their harnesses and packs muffled. When the first one was down, Faradan ran out and silently helped unharness the man from the black wings, then the two quickly folded the apparatus and moved it aside to hide it in the shadows of the far wall. As each flyer landed, quickly stowing their wings with the others, they moved to Faradan, who gathered them close, crouching near the inner wall, and counted. Six, ten, twelve, sixteen.

"Alright, then," he said to the group. "Let's get ready."

Without further instruction, one man passed a sword and dagger to Faradan as the others loosened their weapons and made themselves ready. They were all dressed in black, with only their eyes showing from their tight-fitting balaclavas. Faradan took his own headgear out and put it on, then nodded. With practiced stealth, they followed him into the Palace.

The courtyard—large, open, and relatively unwatched—was the only place Faradan's men could land from the southern cliff, and flying in was the only way so many could gain entry to the Palace. But it was on the wrong side of the Palace and four floors below their target. To move so many men without detection was Faradan's first concern, and to thwart any alarm that might prevent their bloody work. Timing was all-important, and he knew that another team, six crack engineers, were preparing to do their bit up on the higher cliffs, assembling their powerful weapons, sighting them, and carefully turning the windlasses that cranked the powerful bows. With any luck, and with good aim, they would take care of all. Between the blow they would deliver, and Faradan's Daggers, as they called themselves, their quarry would have little chance of survival.

There were not only the posted sentries, but also the roaming watches to contend with. Each man was directed by hand signals past open doors and through risky foyers between halls, with Faradan leading. He had favored a different plan, requiring fewer men, but Dialmor insisted they risk all on bold action, since any attempt was practically suicidal, and could not be repeated if it failed. Faradan did not push his own plan, knowing it would do no good, and he was quite resigned, either way. Afterwards, he would try to make his escape. That part of the plan was simple. Once the mission was accomplished, he and his men would fight their way to the Main Landing near the falls, steal as many wings as possible, and smash the rest. He would be well on his way, perhaps even landing on the other side of the city, if he was lucky, and would be miles away toward Duinnor by horseback before any pursuit could be mounted. If any of his men made it, too, then so much the better. If not, at least they would have performed their duty.

• • •

They moved quietly and efficiently through the Palace. All of their weapons and every bit of metal was cloth-bound against any possibility of noise, the soles of their boots suede-covered. By using hand signals and small mirrors to look around corners, they darted like silent shadows in their black garb in relays of one or two men at a time, awaiting the proper signal from those ahead, and dowsing hallway lamps as they went. Faradan carefully avoided the main halls whenever possible, and from his studies he knew just which junctions and passages had standing guards, which were patrolled and when, and which were left free of any inspection during the night-time hours. So, by back ways they came up a winding service stair in the south wing and to the doorway that opened to the main hall leading to the guest apartments. Making sure that his men were huddled close to him, he carefully reached up and turned the latch on the door. There was a gentle click, too loud for Faradan's liking, and he froze, listening, his hand still on the latch. He nodded to the man next to him who, taking out a vial of oil, bathed the hinges. Faradan then eased the door open just a crack and put through it a wooden rod with a mirror attached to the end of it. With this, he scanned the hallway, and by its reflection he saw the two sentries posted at the doors at the far end. Withdrawing the mirror and carefully closing the door, he signaled with two fingers, and his men nodded. This was what they expected.

He took out a small cloth-wrapped box and opened it. Within was one of the new timepieces from Duinnor, a delicate, mechanical affair, and he could hear the ticking of it. He studied it and saw that the hour wheel was just starting to turn over. They were on time, and as he put away the device, the Palace chimes sounded softly. Soon they could hear the noise of the changing of the guards, the tramp of feet at the main staircase, a few indistinguishable words, then after more tramping, silence. It would be another hour before the next watch changed places with this one, as they rotated throughout the Palace. Faradan's men got ready, drew their weapons carefully, and crowded closer to the door.

At the end of the hall, the two fresh sentries relaxed and chatted. They were permitted to sit, and their orders were to speak only in low tones within this wing so as not to disturb any guests. Behind them, the two doors were closed to the interior foyer, adjacent to a dining room and a guest library each on either side of a wide stair leading up to the guest rooms. Faradan knew that there might be other sentries inside the foyer. If so, things could go seriously wrong.

• • •

In the secret room on the west side of the White Palace, where the Scribblers toiled, all of the lamps were extinguished except two that overhung a table in the far corner. At the table sat a young man and a girl, writing furiously but silently. Leaning over them was Duty Officer Harrin and three others of the Gray Guard, all crowded close to read over the shoulders of the Scribblers, and all wearing grim expressions. This was one of the Homeland desks, and these Scribblers were charged with coaxing from the True Ink threats to Vanara. Almost an hour earlier, the pair of writers had an indication of some military threat when they wrote, "An attack will take place within Vanara." It was a standard line, written at every watch, but this time, the ink did not fade. They instantly called out to Harrin and began trying to discern the nature of the attack. It was frustrating and slow work, going through many possibilities, "in northern parts," or "on the southern border," and "from the Dragonkind," and so forth, each time resulting in fading ink.

Harrin knew better than to rush the pair, and he could see the beads of perspiration on the young woman's brow as she glanced up at him whilst dipping her pen into the ink. They were well-trained, experienced, and knew the procedure. But they needed guidance.

"Forget who," Harrin said gently. "Aim to find out where."

They continued, "…in the region of Shilling Hill…," "…in the region of Lake Tallstone…," "in the region of…" and still the ink faded.

Then the writers paused. The ink was not fading and the words remained clear: "An attack will take place in the region of Linlally City."

"Here? In the city?"

"Try, 'within the city.' "

The ink did not fade.

Harrin turned to the man next to him, handed him his set of keys, and in the same soft tone, he said, "Notify Lord Seafar."

The aide took the keys and hurried away.

"Upper city," stated one of the Scribblers.

Harrin sat and pulled over a sheet and dipped a quill. The other officer immediately sat beside him, understanding his role as copyist.

"You two keep working on where the attack is to take place. We'll work on when, and try to get something of the nature of the attack."

In contrast to the fury with which the four wrote, the room was silent but for the scratch of their pens, the occasional rustle of their paper, and the snap and crackle from within the nearby stove. Ten minutes passed, then the young Scribbler looked up.

"Here! At the Palace! The Palace will be attacked!"

Harrin nodded and continued to write. He stopped, staring at the writing in front of him.

"Sound to quarters!"

The officer beside Harrin leapt up, overturning his chair, and raced across the room to a cabinet built into the wall, taking out a key as he went. There, he unlocked and jerked open the door, revealing several long levers that were attached to cables. He reached in and pulled one lever downward, setting off steady chimes, loud, off-key, and dissonant, ringing throughout the Palace.

"What part of the Palace?" Harrin ordered the question as he wrote. "You take the—"

"South Wing! South Wing!"

"How many attackers? Lieutenant, notify the Watch! Converge in force on the guest apartments!"

• • •

At a fast walk, almost a trot, Seafar was still strapping on his sword as he and an aide hurried to the Scribblers Room, fetched by Duty Officer Harrin's messenger. As they came to a turn in the hall, the chimes began ringing harshly. It was the alarm to General Quarters, meaning the Palace itself was under attack.

"To the guest wing!" Seafar cried, breaking into a run back the way they had come. The surprised aide followed, and the two of them ran as fast as they could through the passages and up stairs and along corridors toward the opposite side of the Palace. As they passed other guards taking their positions, Seafar ordered them to follow, and soon two dozen men, swords drawn, were making their way into the south wing.

• • •

Robby slept. Or, rather, he dreamwalked. And he was nervously elated. He had finally discovered how to travel the dreamscape without the need of jumping from dream to dream or even following the distant light of others as Micerea had to do. He quickly learned how to skim along the rim of dreams, as one might follow along the crest of a ridge, picking the way above the tempting slopes where one might slip down into someone's dream. At least, that was how he thought of it. He owed this discovery to the strange and frightening creatures that fed on nightmares. He came to think of them as dreamdogs, ever on the prowl for disturbing dreams, sniffing as they went along the ridges between dreamers, sometimes standing on their hind legs to look around. They had an uncanny ability to sense the presence of cindergnats, and more than once Robby followed the beasts to someone having a nightmare. They moved quickly along the ridge, then dove down to the hapless dreamer to feed with the cindergnats.

So, following their example, he, too, managed to travel in a like manner, and he flew far and wide, even all the way back to Janhaven. He saw nothing threatening. His mother was chatting with Frizella in a tiny hut, the two sitting beside a small glowing hearth. He saw, too, the roadblock at the Narrows, and many patrols going about in the hills surrounding Janhaven. Satisfied that his mother and her people were at the moment safe from the Redvests, he quickly ventured southward. There he saw that Redvest armies had closed in around Tallinvale, and they had laid waste to the forests, cutting timbers for their war machines and their camps. He hurried back westward, and at last found his friends, who were at the moment eating a modest meal around a campfire. He reached out to touch Sheila's shoulder, but his hand only passed through her as if she was made of air. His heart ached to be with her, but he knew that she was safe and in good company. So he left them to their meal and set his mind to puzzle out something Micerea had mentioned.

Simply put, if a dreamwalker had a different aura from everyone else who dreamed, as Micerea had told him, then he should be able to spot them as easily as finding her. And, once he put his attention to the problem, gazing out through the ethereal world that he occupied, he finally understood. Suddenly he realized how to look, and what to look for, and he saw them nearly everywhere he went. Other dreamwalkers. All over the world. Only, to his surprise, they merely wandered around as if not knowing that they were doing more than just dream. One little boy, now living in a van on the far side of Janhaven, roamed the dreamscape as if on a curious stroll, slipping into the dreams of others who slept nearby. Another one he found, this time in the village called Chiselpeck, did not even leave her dreams. But, in spite of the perplexing ignorance the dreamwalkers displayed, Robby knew this was an extremely important discovery, as important as the skill of moving around in the dreamscape.

Now he at last held the keys to answering many questions. He was pleased, for not only was he suddenly confident in his own abilities, but he was filled with many ideas and many possibilities. The two discoveries, both made in a single evening after so many nights of struggle and failure, served to lift a great burden from his heart. It was as if he was finally beginning to understand dreamwalking, and to realize its power and its potential.

Before he returned to his own sleep, he looked in at Janhaven one more time, and he found his mother as she slept. Before he could slip into her dream to say hello, he was astonished to see another dreamwalker do so. At first, Robby was excited at the prospects of making the acquaintance of another who had this ability, but he suddenly became wary, and held back from approaching Mirabella's dream. The stranger, dressed in a black tunic and a black broad-rimmed hat, was asking Mirabella for directions as she swept the front porch of the store.

"And how many miles is it to Janhaven?" he asked.

"Oh, quite a few. I'm not sure, but, at a canter, a day or so," she serenely replied.

"And how many men are at the Narrows?"

"Enough, I hope."

"Enough to hold it against the Redvests?"

"Oh, yes. Are you sure you don't need something from inside? We just received a shipment of sea foam from Glareth, and it would make a nice trim to your coat."

"No. Perhaps another time. Is there a password or some sign to give the men at the Narrows? So I can get through?"

"No, just show them a rainbow's shadow."

"Hm. That might be difficult. I suppose there are many more garrisoned in Janhaven, aren't there?"

At this point, Robby's suspicions reached a boil, and he entered the dream quickly, coming down the stairs and into the shop.

"Mother! Come quickly! The dishes are dancing again," he cried, suddenly remembering a bedtime story. "And the kettle is playing fiddle on the spoons."

"Oh, my! We can't have that. Not again!"

Before the dream went any further, Durlorn, who was downstairs from where Mirabella slept at the stockade, dropped a log intended for the fireplace and upset the poker that leaned nearby to the hearth which then banged into the ashpan. The noise roused Mirabella, and her dream quickly faded. Robby retreated, not wishing to be discovered, but saw the stranger recede quickly, as if being pulled away by some string. Finding a ridge at the edge of dreams, Robby followed. This took him back to Passdale, to the Common House where the Redvest general had made his headquarters. There, in a room to himself, Robby saw the man rouse from his dream, sit up in his cot, and shake his head.

"Drat!" the man uttered. He yawned, fluffed his pillow, and turned over, pulling his blanket up around his shoulders.

Robby stood for a long while and observed the man as he slept. When he began to dream again, he watched, and learned a great deal about this spy. After a while, knowing he needed sleep, too, Robby retreated to his own slumber, his previous pride and elation having completely evaporated.

"At least," he thought, "the man is a novice, and has no idea how to get around outside of other people's dreams. He is like Micerea. Only he works for the other side."

Which, of course, was a great worry for many reasons. And Robby realized, just as he seemed to be waking up, that the man had to be stopped.

"If only I can figure a way."

● ● ●

"Robby! Get up!"

Robby sat bolt upright at Ullin's urgent call, then slung his bedcovers off, Swyncraff flying to his hand as he stood.

"Dress! Get your things!"

Robby could see Ullin standing in the adjoining room, his pack on his back and his sword drawn.

"What's amiss?" Robby asked, flinging his clothes on and quickly making himself ready to fight or flee.

"Something, surely," Ullin said, his face stern in the candlelight. When Robby came to his side, they listened together but heard nothing amiss.

"The hairs on my arms and neck are like bristles," Ullin whispered. "And they tingle like mad!"

"Any notion why?"

"No. What's that?"

The chimes of the palace alarm rang down the hall, and Robby and Ullin faced the door, hearing noise in the corridor. An eerie yellow light quickly bathed the room, coming through the windows behind them, suddenly growing bright and throwing their own distinct shadows against the door. Ullin shoved Robby hard onto the floor as both bedroom windows on either side of them blew inward with flames and flying debris, immediately engulfing both beds and filling the place with boiling burning pitch and rolling black smoke. The door smashed inward, Ullin jumped up and spun around to face the intruder with his sword. It was Seafar with two guards.

"This way! Quickly!" Seafar cried.

Robby and Ullin scrambled after him into the hallway where they were surrounded by guards who, swords drawn, urged them with hands on their backs, pushing them to follow Seafar. Looking through the smoke blowing out from the door, Robby saw and heard fighting taking place just beyond, the ring and thud of weapons only a few yards away. A dart shot past his head and glanced off Seafar's shoulder plate and embedded into a ceiling beam. At this, Robby's guards crowded closer, side by side, acting as shields, and the distinct dink of more bolts rang from their backplates. Ahead, a door was held open to them by Strake, and two nearby soldiers were crouching to notch arrows on their short bows.

"Take them!" Seafar ordered Strake. "You know what to do!"

Seafar turned back to the fighting.

"But, sir!"

"Go! You and you! With me!"

Just before Seafar disappeared into the arrow-laden smoke with two of his soldiers, he turned back to Robby.

"Good luck!" he cried as a bolt splintered into the wall near his head.

"Come!" Strake ordered. They squeezed through the small door and onto a landing below a steep spiral stair. "Up! Go up! Go up!"

With a nod to the man still outside the door, Strake slammed it shut and threw the two heavy iron bars, locking them within and leaving the rest of his comrades to their fight and fate.

"Steady! Not too fast," Strake called out from behind and below as Ullin and Robby took the steps by twos. "It is a very long climb, and we will need our strength at the top."

Of the four men ahead and three behind, Robby could only see the one directly in front and Ullin right behind, so sharp and steep and narrow was the turning of the stairs. It would have been pitch black but for the small lamps that the guards carried. He fought off the same panic he had felt at Tulith Attis when wolves snapped at his heels, his heart pounding again with fear and exertion. On and on they climbed, careless of their noise and panting, their feet stomping dully, their weapons clanking, the alarm bells an insistent echo. All were at the limits of their lungs when they at last reached the top and broke out through a door. Cold air gushed over them as they stumbled onto a wide, flat space, open to the stars, then moved briskly to a large door held open to them by more guards, swords drawn. Within was a large room, well-lit, with many racks and shelves ladened with cloaks, harnesses, and other odd gear. Strake turned to Ullin and Robby.

"Do exactly as you are instructed," he said calmly but firmly. "We mean to get you away as quickly and as safely as we can. You will lessen the danger to yourself and to the rest of us if you obey instructions. Do you understand? This is Lord Seafar's arrangement. We are well-prepared, and experienced, but you have to put your trust in us."

"I understand," said Ullin.

"Lead the way," nodded Robby.

"First, put aside your things. You may carry only the most essential of what you need. All else will be provided. Hurry!"

Robby started piling his things onto a table, but he kept Swyncraff around his waist. "I must keep my shoulder bag."

"That's fine," Strake said. "Off with your cloaks and outer garments," he added as he himself stripped. Elsewhere in the large room, Robby saw men donning suits of shearling-lined leather that were laced up along the sides of their legs, and soon Robby and Ullin, too, were being fitted with these costumes. Robby understood what was happening, and his heart thumped harder as he breathed heavily with nervousness. Ullin was as pale as a ghost, but said nothing as he worked to put on his suit.

"It will be cold. Put this over your head."

Robby was handed a kind of balaclava, but made with leather like the suit that was being strapped onto him, lined with thin shearling. The headgear had narrow slits to see through, and he tried to copy one of the others who was dressing nearby, but could not quite fit it on so that he could see out from it. Someone helped him straighten it, then turned Robby to face him. Now Robby could see, but he did not recognize the man tying his chin straps since the person was dressed just as he was now, covered from head to toe.

"Good, good," someone said. He felt someone else tugging on his leggings and checking his waist straps. "Very well, lift your left leg."

"Take hold of my shoulder," said another voice as Robby's hand was guided to a thick arm to hold to. Soon he was being fitted into a harness of sorts that went around and between his legs, about his waist, then up over and around his shoulders and across his chest. It was tight.

"How are you doing, Ullin?" Robby asked.

"Fine. Feeling a bit like Anerath, I must say. All these bridles and cinches and such." His voice was very nearby and, turning, Robby saw Ullin's eyes, a bit wild, looking out from his own headgear.

"All good?" Strake demanded of his men.

"All good, sir."

"All good, Commander."

"Very well. This way, gentlemen."

Robby and Ullin followed, a bit awkwardly, to a door on the other side of the room. When it opened, a soft red light bathed them from the other side. They entered and saw that the light was from lamps with red-tinted glass lenses, and they were directed to sit on a wooden bench along the wall of the room. Strake went to a ladder and climbed up to a trap door on the ceiling. He opened it and called out, "Ready above?"

"Two minutes!" came the answer.

"Two. Very well," he let the door slam back down and then called to the men huddled in the room. "Ready in two!"

Ullin fidgeted, and Robby nervously tapped his foot on the floor and bit his lip. Neither asked what they were waiting for, but it seemed an eternally long time until the trapdoor in the ceiling was flung open from outside and a man shouted down, "Six ready! Two heavy, four escorts! Eight more preparing!"

"Go!" cried Strake, and two of his men shot up the ladder. "Now you, Lord Ribbon. Now you, Commander Tallin."

Robby and Ullin scrambled up the ladder as best they could, and when they emerged, helping hands pulled them up to their feet as an icy blast bit at them and made them blink. Guided along by a soldier, Robby glanced up at the bright stars, and caught a whiff of acrid smoke.

"Come up behind me and squeeze against me, Lord Ribbon. Commander Tallin is being taken care of." Someone was pushing Robby against Commander Strake's back as he crouched. "Put your arms through my shoulder straps and cross them over your chest, gripping the straps at your shoulders tightly. Yes, I'll carry you piggyback."

Strake crouched a little lower to make it easier for Robby to comply, and as soon as Robby had, someone began clipping the rings on the front of his leggings and his harness to rings on that of Strake.

"Don't worry," Strake said. "I'll take good care of you."

Before he knew it, he was being hoisted up as Strake stood, and a large shadow moved over them, blotting out the stars.

"Let me carry your weight. Bend your knees a bit. Try not to struggle, I've got you."

Robby nodded, too nervous to speak, and sensed that Strake was grasping onto something as he suddenly strode forward with Robby hanging from his back. He could hear Strake's heavy footfalls on the wooden deck, and, just before they stepped over the edge, a breeze caught the great wings that Strake carried, and Strake's footfalls ceased. Suddenly, to Robby's amazement, they were flying. Though his eyes watered and stung with the cold air, Robby could see the faint glimmer of stars reflected from the lake far below. As they banked into the wind, suddenly the Palace came into view. Bright yellow flames licked upward through many windows, and orange spark-filled smoke billowed up into the clear sky. They banked again and Robby felt an upward tug as they climbed. He caught a blurry glimpse of other shapes, broad dark wings, suspended in the air nearby, seemingly motionless. He thought he heard Ullin whimper, and he fought a sick feeling at the top of his stomach.

"Try to relax!" Strake ordered. "This won't take long. We're already halfway there."

• • •

Ullin knew enough to be frightened. Being none too fond of heights did not help, either. And his recent experience on the back of Ayreltide, flying over the enchanted forest city, was of little comfort. But at least that was a horse, of sorts. The apparatus he now hung from, and pressed and tied against the back of its driver, was something entirely different. To his mind, they were flimsy, delicate affairs, and, anyway, who should defy the ground but those creatures made to do it? Who should court disaster with Lord Wind with his shiftiness and caprice? On top of all that, and even more strongly framing his fear, was the memory of seeing a wing such as this, high over the city, suddenly fold like so much paper, then plummeting, careening in a terrible and swift gyration out of sight behind some buildings. His mother, riding in the trolley with him, made an effort, too late, to cover his eyes, but the horror of it gave him nightmares for years. Now, fear and shivers racked his body, and his heart and lungs competed for space within his chest as they pounded blood and air, his panting louder than the wind that whistled past his hooded ears.

"Relax!" commanded the man dangling in front of him. "Say the word 'warm!' "

"Waaarrum!" Ullin stammered.

"Say it again! Warm!"

"Waarum!"

"Breathe in through your nose and out through your mouth as you say it. Warm!"

"Warm…warm!"

"That's it. Keep doing that. Over and over. We're almost there."

• • •

"You are doing fine," Strake said over his shoulder to Robby who, like Ullin, was struggling to control his shivers. Robby opened one eye and saw, ahead and somewhat below to the right, a line of four green lights, small dots against the black mass of the northern cliffs which loomed high and ominous like a wall. He could, now and then as they banked, catch a glimpse of the stars, but his view was limited by the wing that bore them. They were descending, now, toward a ledge of sorts, an opening in the cliff like a wide cave lit from within by yellowish torches. He closed his eye against the tearful cold, and when he looked again a moment later their target had grown significantly larger as they sank downward to it.

"Bend your knees, pull up your legs," ordered Strake. "Let me carry your weight when we land. Might be a wee bit rough!"

It was a huge cave, nearly three stories high within and a bit wider. They shot through the mouth of it, some ten feet off the smooth floor, and men ran alongside as they settled, Strake's feet thumping hard for several steps until they stopped. Robby was amazed that he did not stumble.

"Stand up, now. Please," Strake panted. Immediately, the apparatus was lifted away, and assistants swarmed over the two, unhitching them from each other. Robby could hear the others landing nearby, but was too preoccupied to look, trying to keep his shaky knees from buckling. Strake took his arm.

"This way, lad."

As Strake led him away, Robby looked over his shoulder and saw two men supporting Ullin by his arms as they brought him along a few yards behind.

"We'll get you warmed up in no time," Robby heard one of Ullin's assistants say.

"Just hang in a little longer, sir," said the other. "You'll get your legs back before you know it."

"How p-p-pitiful!" Ullin stammered, his teeth chattering.

"None of that! You did just fine. Better than fine. Not exactly the best conditions for a first-timer."

Several more gliders floated into the cave and landed as the group ushered Robby and Ullin into a large cage that was soon hoisted upward by unseen mechanisms. They were led out and along an iron balcony that ran high up along a wall of the cave. Robby saw workers taking away the gliders and carefully putting them with many others in orderly rows on the far side. His group turned through a stone passageway and into a long room located above the opening of the cave. There was a bank of glass windows, many of them opened to the night air, and several men stood by them with spyglasses to their eyes. Others held writing tablets and copied what the watchers reported. Robby craned to look out as they passed by, and he could clearly see the Palace and the bright yellow flames that now engulfed a large portion of it. One of the men at the window was toggling a lamp's cover open and closed, pointing it at a similar blinking light at one of the Palace towers.

"Report!" Strake bellowed.

"Fighting still taking place, sir," came the immediate reply. "War stations ordered. The fire is still spreading and is just now being fought."

"Great stars! Let's hope they can save the flight decks. See to our guests!"

Robby and Ullin were ushered into a side room where an iron stove glowed. As they were helped out of their flying gear, Ullin looked at Robby and shook his head.

"I didn't think I was going to make it."

"I was scared, too."

"None of us like to fly at night, sir," said Ullin's pilot, himself shaking with cold as he pulled off his gear. "Even though we've done it often enough."

"And winter's the worst time," nodded another flyer, nearly hugging the stove as he stamped his feet.

"We'll be warm enough pretty soon, though," continued another one of the group. "Then up and out again. Quickly, too, if Strake has anything to do with it."

"Not another flight?" Robby exclaimed. Ullin looked aghast.

"No, no! But we hit the trail northward, and it'll be just as cold."

Commander Strake entered and began taking his own flight gear off.

"How's everyone?" he asked. "Starting to recover, I hope."

"We'll make it," Robby said.

"I do apologize for the rough handling," Strake said as he squirmed out of his coveralls. "Pandemonium rules the White Palace, now. It's a good thing that Seafar anticipated the need for haste. Though I hardly think even he could foresee such a brazen attack."

"What has happened?" Ullin asked, moving as close to the stove as he dared.

"Reports are still coming. A bit sketchy. But definitely a well-planned assault aimed against the guest wing. Against you two, obviously. We are not privy to your business, and I have not yet unsealed my further orders, but someone obviously wanted to stop you."

"So the Palace is not still under attack?" Ullin asked.

"Doesn't look like it. From what we can tell from here, you were the only targets of the attack."

"And Lord Seafar? Is he safe?"

"I do not know. Our plan was to fly you here at first light, thereby saving two days from the next closest route, climbing around the city. The attack has now given us even more of a head start, by a few hours. From here, we take a north route through the mountains. It will be cold and difficult, and the days are short. We will travel only during daylight. The way is too difficult to do otherwise, so we have a couple of hours to rest and prepare. Our main enemy will be the cold. It will be relentless. We will provide you with warm clothes and gear, and we will show you how to survive."

An aide entered with cups and a steaming pot of tea and poured for everyone.

"We will move slowly," Strake went on. "The air is thin, the snow deep, and the ice precarious. But we will follow well-established ways, using tried and true methods. There are winter shelters and supplies prepared every ten miles or so, and we will do well if we can cover that much ground in a day."

"You said you had further orders?" Robby asked.

"I am to open them once we get well on our way. Not before."

"I see."

Strake got up and closed the door.

"My current orders are to get you away from here, and move toward Fort Defiance—our largest outpost on the southeastern border of Shatuum—to travel along our westernmost route to that place, and to protect you at all costs. I do not expect you to share any hint of your mission, and, unless my orders require me or my men to know, I would rather you not volunteer anything. Let us speculate as we may. I do not know who you are, really, why you are so important, or what may lay ahead of us. But Lord Seafar instructed us to act as if the Queen herself depended on us, and so we shall, every man of us. This journey will be equally dangerous for all. And Seafar does not risk men needlessly, I can assure you of that."

Robby nodded.

"Then I shall tell you this much," Ullin said to Strake. "It is he who is important, not I. I have given my oath to serve and to protect him. So, you see, if anything happens along the way, and only one may be saved, it must be him."

Strake looked solemnly at Ullin, as did the others in the room. He then turned his gaze to Robby who, though somewhat embarrassed, said nothing and fixed Strake's eyes firmly. Strake could have questioned Ullin's oath, one that obviously had overthrown the Kingsman's previous allegiance. He could have doubted Ullin's sincerity, even his honesty, for Ullin still wore the uniform of Duinnor. But whatever went through Strake's mind did not show or change his expression one way or the other. However he sized up the possibilities, he did so quickly. Still looking at Robby, he said, "So be it." To the others of his company that were present he turned, and he repeated, "So be it."

Strake glanced at Ullin then went to the door. "We move out in two hours. Sergeant Hull!"

"Sir!"

"I'll see you in the Equipment Room in one half an hour with the rest."

"Yes, sir!"

By now all were fairly thawed, and Sergeant Hull said, "Haskin, you and Gullwing stay with our charges. The rest of you with me." Then to Robby and Ullin, he said, "We'll fetch you up in a bit, sirs, when we're near ready. It being warmer here."

"Very well. Thank you. Hull, is it? Thank you, Hull," Robby nodded. The two troopers who stayed moved to the door to watch the goings on in the outer room, where reports were still coming from the observers there. Robby and Ullin moved to the stove for a closer chat, their backs to their escorts.

"Who do you think is behind the attack?" Robby asked Ullin, lowering his voice.

"I am baffled. Whoever it is must know our mission. But how? I assure you, I guarded my words well. If the Duinnor summons has reached here, why were we not taken into custody?"

"Unless Duinnor's aim is to kill us. Not merely arrest us."

Ullin shook his head. "I don't doubt that Duinnor means us no good, but if they wanted us dead, the writ would have said so in no uncertain terms. No. Duinnor wants us alive. At first, anyway. To answer questions. So I don't think the King is behind this attack."

"Then who? Who would want us not to talk? If that is what it is about?" Robby glanced over his shoulder at the door, lowering his voice even more. "Who would want us not to be arrested and taken before the King?"

"I don't know, Robby. Someone with much to lose. And someone who knew that we would be safeguarded by Seafar. Probably even knew we would not pass back through the city. Someone who thought that attacking the Palace was the only way to stop us."

"But who could mount such an attack on such short notice?"

"It must have been well laid before we arrived. Probably with some other target in mind. Seafar. Or even the Queen. The question is: who could know such things about us to spring it?"

Robby frowned, thinking of Micerea and her many warnings.

"There are those who may have some power of seeing," he ventured. "Of spying in ways that we cannot imagine."

But Robby could imagine, all too clearly. His face reddened with anger and chagrin that he, while dreamwalking, might have had company. If the Redvest in Passdale had a dreamwalking spy, there could be others, too. Did not Micerea warn him? His mind raced, feeling that his abilities, though awesome, must still be crude by some standards, like a child blithely playing in some wondrous wood, all the while being stalked by an unseen predator. How could he have missed it? Part of him wanted to go to sleep right then and there, to dreamwalk and search out that realm for interlopers.

"I have been such a fool," he muttered.

"You know something?"

"No. I mean, I have suspicions. But I cannot talk about it. I'm sorry. All I can say is that I may have given away our plan."

"How? To whom?"

"I'm sorry. I cannot say. Not for sure. Ullin, I cannot even breathe what I am thinking, not even to you who, above all others, I wish to share this with. Damn!"

Robby slammed the coveralls he was still holding down onto a bench. The two troopers looked over their shoulders at him. Ullin gave them a glance, and they turned their attention back to the outer room.

"I beg of you," he said to Robby. "Tell me!"

"I cannot," Robby stated bluntly. "But we must get to Griferis before all is lost! If we are in such danger, I only hope that Sheila and our friends are somewhat safer by our separation! I can tell you this, though: I am convinced, more than ever, that the only hope is to get to Griferis. And then—I don't like it, not one bit—but I know what I must do. I've known for some while, now. Only now every other path is truly closed off. I have no choice but to go on."

Ullin nodded. "Well, I will have to accept that you know more than you can tell me. But if we have been betrayed.... I must have let something slip. Someone must have gathered from my report more than I intended."

"We may never know, Ullin. But if that is so, how could they have acted so quickly unless they were already waiting for us?"

"So you suspect some other."

"I'm afraid I do."

"And you will not tell me who it is."

"I dare not. Not until I am sure, one way or the other."

"Then we talk in circles."

Robby could see that Ullin was not pleased to be left in the dark. But there was nothing he could tell Ullin that would make sense unless he told Ullin everything. About dreamwalking. About Micerea. There was no time for that, now. And Ullin would probably not believe him, anyway.

"They are ready for us," one of their escorts said, gesturing to the door. "If you would come this way."

The glow of the burning Palace added a harsh orange tint to the red-lit observation room, and more men and women were now there, watching the blaze as Robby and Ullin were led through and then to a winding stair. After a climb, they entered a long passageway and were shown into a large room, carved like all the rest out of the living rock of the mountain. In this place were rows of shelves and racks full of equipment, weapons, packs, clothing, ropes, and other gear. At long tables, men worked to assemble supplies and gear into large white backpacks.

"Over here," Sergeant Hull called to them. He stood at the end of one of the tables where two packs were opened.

"We'll try to make these as light as we can," he explained, "but each of us must carry certain things. You should know what is in your pack. Extra stockings, itchy but warm. Firesticks. Do you know how to use them? Good. Tinder. Five pounds of coal. These rocks here. They burn and give off light and heat. A flask of brandy. Strong rope. Some lighter cord. Rations. Pick out some gloves that fit you at that table, there. And some overmittens. We'll provide you with cloaks suited for our journey."

Oversized white pants were brought to them, made of stiff, oiled canvas and lined within by thick quilted flannel. They were helped into them and given help adjusting the suspenders that held them up. They were also fitted with overshoes, thick sweaters, and white fluffy-thick outer coats with fur-lined hoods.

"Layers of clothing work best," said one of the attendants. "The outerwear will help you keep dry, too. We'll be sure you're all buttoned up before we step out. Don't want to get too warm beforehand."

While Robby was being turned, his attendant checking him over, he saw the men loading packs onto a hoist at the far side of the room and lift them up where the stuff disappeared through the ceiling.

"This is for your face." Robby's attendant gave him a balaclava of fine, silky material. "And this is for your eyes. You put it on around your head and look through the slits. The sun is very bright, and if you don't wear it, you'll eventually go blind. There, right over the balaclava. That's right. When we go outside, pull it down over your eyes. You'll be given more things upstairs. Here."

Robby was then handed a white flat-topped hat of stiff wool with a bill on the front.

"These flaps on the side can be pulled down over your ears," the attendant said. "Yes, it looks like it fits fine."

"Are we ready?" bellowed Commander Strake as he entered at a brisk walk. He was already dressed in the white clothing, with his hood pushed back and his balaclava rolled up around his head.

"Aye, sir! Just getting there!" reported Hull.

"Very well. Gentlemen! Your attention, please."

"Attention!" barked Hull. Everyone put down whatever they held, turned and stood rigid, and the room fell silent. All eyes were on Strake.

"Stand easy. We have just had signals that Lord Seafar is safe. The fighting in the Palace has ended. At least one attacker has been captured, the others appear to be dead. Several of our comrades were killed in the attack. I do not know which ones. There are many wounded and hurt, and many missing. The Palace is in flames, and fighting the blaze now occupies everyone's attention. There is much that I do not know, but this much is clear: The attack was directed at our two charges, and it almost succeeded. It is fortunate that Seafar ordered our preparations when he did, or many of us would probably be standing atop an inferno. But here we are. Prepared and ready to do our duty. We are to see to it that these two are safely escorted as far as Fort Defiance. Getting there will not be easy, as you know. The trail has its own dangers. Let us hope that is all we will face, for it will be quite enough. But! We must assume that the enemy will learn of his failure to stop us and will try again. There you have it. So it is one hand for yourself, one for your mate, and a sharp eye to the enemy. Are we ready?"

"Sir! Yes, sir!" came a loud chorus.

"Move out!"

The last of the packs were tossed onto the hoist and lifted away while the men filed up an iron staircase through another opening high up.

"Lord Ribbon, Commander Tallin." Strake gestured for them to get in line at the stair as he spoke. "We will move in two companies of eight men each plus you two who will be with the second company. I'll take lead of the first and will try to make the way easier for you. Your group will follow somewhat behind under the charge of Sergeant Hull. I am assigning Trooper Gullwing and Trooper Haskin to look out for you. They are experienced. Do as they direct, I beg you. It's time to go."

It was another trudge up the metal stairs then into another red-lit room with a low ceiling. Here, the men were putting on their hoods, belting up their parkas, and getting their packs settled onto their backs. All this was noisy, though few words were spoken, but added to it was the din of several men pounding away at an iron door that was crusted with ice. When they had freed it, a gust of frigid air rushed into the room. The men who opened the door then grabbed axes and shovels to clear a path through the drift of snow and ice that had piled up on the outside. The packs for Robby and Ullin were brought, now with snowshoes strapped to the outside, and two poles stuck up from sleeves made into each side of the packs. They were being helped on with the packs, while the rest of the Gray Guard assembled into two lines. Ullin and Robby were then shown their places within the ranks of one of these lines.

"Hook up!" ordered Sergeant Hull from ahead and a line was handed from him back, each man passing it through a loop on their belt. When it came to Robby, Gullwing showed him how to pass it properly through his own loop, and then he passed it on to Ullin, who was helped by Haskin.

"This is so that we don't lose each other. As we walk, try to keep some slack between us. Enough so that if one of us falls, he doesn't pull the other down. Mind that it isn't so much that you get it tangled with your feet."

Robby nodded.

"First squad!" Strake cried, and he led the first line of men outside, crunching into the early morning light.

"Take these." Gullwing handed Robby two poles of sturdy wood, each with an iron point sticking from a plate at the base and a looped leather grip at the other end. The trooper showed Robby how to pass each hand through a loop and how to grip the poles.

"You'll need these to keep your balance on the icy stretches. You've got spare ones on your pack if these break. Along with a set of ice axes for the rough spots. And, in the side pocket, here, you have a set of crampons that match your boots."

"Ice axe? Crampons? I don't know what they are."

"You will before very long!"

Satisfied, Gullwing turned and took his place ahead of Robby, and the company waited, facing the glowing doorway, blowing with loose snow. At the head of the line, Sergeant Hull watched the first squad. At last he saw the signal.

"Let's go!"

When they were outside, Robby could see on either side steep snowy peaks bathed in the morning sunrise. Before him was snow and ice-covered rock, and the path made by the first company was a bluish line in the snow. Already, they were a far distance ahead, and Robby saw the last of those in the lead pass over the rise and out of sight. He learned quickly that he had to watch his step and keep up, and it was hard not to gape at the landscape, devoid of trees, blue-white in the shadows of the mountains. It was difficult for him to see with the cap and hood restricting his view. He slipped several times, unaccustomed to the clumsy overshoes, but each time he quickly recovered without falling.

"Take it easy and slow," he heard Gullwing say. "You'll soon get your snow legs."

When at last they topped the rise and began making their way down a long gradual slope, Robby looked ahead, and his heart sank. As far as he could see was only snow, ice, rock, and craggy peaks and ridges in shades of white, gray, and blue. In the distance, barely discernable as white on white, small dots all in a line, was the first squad, pushing their way through knee-deep snow. The enormity of what they faced hit Robby with the weight of a thousand mountains, and he stifled a lump that rose into his throat.

"What have I gotten us into?"

"Keep moving, boys!" came Sergeant Hull's shout from the front of his line, a brusque encouragement made small, swallowed into insignificance by the vast and beautiful desolation.

●　●　●

High and above, a tiny speck hunched against a rocky outcrop. Nearly a mile away and far below, the two lines slowly moved. The speck waited patiently for them to pass, then dropped from the cliff, spread its black wings, and soared unseen to the northwest.

End of Volume Three

87 Days remaining

Afterword

Afterword

Thank you for reading *A Distant Light*! I hope you are enjoying this tale. And I cordially invite you to share your thoughts, questions, and comments at

www.TheYearOfTheRedDoor.com

The Adventure Continues with *The Dreamwalker*

The easy part of Robby's quest nears its end. He must now find a way to stop a dreamwalker from betraying his people in Janhaven. He must also find a way into Griferis to be tested and judged for worthiness to be King.

Robby's friends face their own trials and dangers. The Unknown King is determined to keep his throne, a maniacal Elifaen is bent on destroying Sheila and her friends in Duinnor, and Ullin must grapple with his own demons, as well as those of Shatuum.

In the east, Lord Tallin and his people seek to buy Robby the time he needs as a vast Redvest army prepares to deal Tallinvale a deathblow. And the Redvests in Passdale find a way to outflank Janhaven, putting Mirabella's people in danger of annihilation.

These events push the world closer and closer to the brink, just as the Lord of Shatuum has planned. He awaits the perfect moment to pour forth into the world his hordes of wraiths, demons, and witches.

I hope you will continue the adventure!

Thanks again!

William Timothy Murray

The Door is Open!
www.TheYearOfTheRedDoor.com

Maps, Stories, Chronologies,
and much more.

Leave a comment or ask a question.

The Author would love to hear from you!

Sign up for the newsletter.
Get perks and exclusives delivered right to your inbox!

The Year of the Red Door

Volume 1
The Bellringer

Volume 2
The Nature of a Curse

Volume 3
A Distant Light

Volume 4
The Dreamwalker

Volume 5
To Touch a Dream

www.TheYearOfTheRedDoor.com